A Glance Away

*To Homes
and the people who have made mine*

Prologue

It is afterall a way of beginning. To have never quite enough so hunger grows faster than appetites and satisfaction never comes.

On an April day insouciant after the fashion of spring insouciance the warm secret of life was shared with another. Bawling milk hungry mammal dropped in pain from flanks of a she. Him.

Fine, healthy boy, eight pounds seven ounces.

Mystery repeats itself to boredom. And he shall be called Eugene. In the name of the grandfather who balding, high on dago red, waited news in a cloud of garbage smelling smoke at the foot of steep, ringing marble stairs of Allegheny General Hospital.

—Wonder what they's doin' to my littlebaby. Martha better be all right. Freeda, I got me a grandson. Big 'un he's gonna be. Big and bad like his granddaddy Eugene. A big, bad nigger-Gene, said the tall baldpate man clomping on bunioned feet loudly up the stairs, shrugging off tentative back holding hands and small voice excited of pale receptionist starched white at desk. A bigniggerGene.

—You can't go up there sir.

—My little girl's up there lady. You hear me, my little Martha's there and nobody on God's green earth's gonna keep me from my girl. Off shuffling to tune of *Gimme that wine spudie-udie* he went, dedecorumed in glee of life renewed bearing his name, his flesh and blood redone forever in two bodies precious together under hospital blankets.

That man is crazy. Lord knows how much gut rotting wine he's drunk already today. Freeda's face, handsomely molded, skin lined finely under eyes and across her forehead testifying to three children grown and two dead seemed fixed in an attitude of fear and pride. Broad husband's back and long legs like cords in baggy trousers as they disappeared around a landing were for her so familiar that each time she found herself watching him leave a strange panic danced in her bowels. Girlish flutter of first romance, him insubstantial because he was so closely interwoven with her dreams. More hope than dream, hope that absence assaulted, changed to helplessness before a truth she fought not to conceive. Each time he would never come back. Rakish broad-brimmed hat, flapping trousers, the boy's swagger, his broad back swaying . . .

Up the forbidden stairs. Her Gene, and what did he fear. A curse dropped echoing in the high-walled foyer. He'll go there, and no one will stop him. He'll do it if it kills him.

Unguardedly the forbidden word dropped. Gene gone. It would never happen, could never happen to him, bold swiller of wine whose veins received it like sun. DaddyGene paperhanger, half-dago giant who handled his tools fine Italian handwise like short, dark men he worked beside. Hang that shit like two men. Later slouched in easy chair dangling over armrests, huge feet stretched to middle of livingroom, a king. Like when loaded, stumbling into kitchen, opening iceboxdoor and placing chair close to its exposed innards spoon in hand devouring every edible morsel and some that weren't.

How could he go away after all these years. But certainly I have learned, I am an old woman, children grown and dead, not much time for either of us. But please God, me first. Take me first if we can't go together.

She had spoken to her daughter in the kitchen. Martha, you must be patient. Clarence is young, headstrong. It's hard for him too. He hasn't done so badly up to now. With the way most of these young fellows act today, your Clarence ain't been half bad.

—But Mama, leaving me like this. If I ever needed him, it's now. Now when I'm carrying his baby. Just going off like he did. One minute standing talking to me in the bedroom, asking how I felt, how long the doctor thought it would be, if I needed anything—acting so gentle, so loving, as if he really cared. Talking the way he used to, before . . .

—He's young, Martha. Like you're young. He has to fight for a while, show himself now that he's found out what living with a woman really means that he can still love you. It has to be a different kind of love, cause after a month or a year the old kind gives out. It hurts, it scares them worse than it ever does us. He's young, hotblooded. No patience—everything has to come at once. Quick, easy, black and white with no waiting around. Right now I believe he just don't know how to wait, how to believe, how to hope. So you have to wait. Be there always when he comes back. And he will honey, he will. The man, and he's gonna be a man, loves you.

GENE, GENE THE PIPER'S SON STOLE A PIG AND AWAY HE RUN. Belch innard deep lurched up through chest tasting garlic and stale wine, swaying, perched in throat, a honeyed song that danced smiling unto the old man's features. Of all the damndest things me drunk on these stairs upgoing to little skinny Martha, firstborn of my brood to see firstborn of her still secret brood somewhere hidden in loins of dark boy who came and courted and caught little Martha skinny's fancy, how drunk I am on that first drink neverending after paper is hung on walls with care and we don't care folding ladders, gathering tools cramped in pickup truck how many together we take and then home to Freeda still fine and fair whose skinny daughter lies as she did how many years ago the first time pale and long hair plaited over pillow, afraid, squeezing till blood stopped in my hand laid on her blue flowered shoulder she wept and was afraid as Martha dark eyes damp waits me winding up these white man's stairs and through silent corridors to her side.

OVER THE HILLS AND EVERYWHERE.

Please God let Clarence come. I need him now beside me. The pain, the pain God. For him, this flesh that is his, God, my husband's flesh. Clary, please come. Her eyes fixed on rectangular opening in the wall, dim edges visible around curtain serving as a door where if he would come, he must enter. Through gauzy space of curtain her eyes strained to catch any movement. Invisibly it fretted. Shifting outlines like hands moved behind it, becoming fuzzy, indistinct, absorbed by the whiteness of the walls, disappearing as if the walls melted and grew together under her intense stare. I want him so much. And nothing, no one answered because she was but a woman in pain, lone woman in hospital gown languid on her bed of pain. Clarence please come. The flimsy curtain danced. Only tears came that squinted through made a mist between her eyes and small wound in the white wall. She remembered how she had only a glimpse of the baby's red, wrinkled body, and then he was whisked away. Hygienic, uncontaminated by her closeness and need.

—I'm comin' girl. Little Martha yore Daddy's comin'. Don't let 'em take the little nigger away till I get there. His besotted voice quavering and resonant in echo chamber of marble halls reached her. Things had begun again. The dream of her pain so certain and complete had ended. Soon DaddyGene would fill the room with eagerness and brash, assuming ministrations. Authority of his movements, sour smell of wine as he leaned giddily rough cheek against her flesh to rub and kiss and whisper as he had always done to mend her bruised knees and feelings, treating his girl child as if nothing in the world could not be hugged away or forgotten in gentle rhythm of *Froggy went a courtin'* hummed while she bobbed like a cork on his slowly bouncing knee.

—Daddy—where is he Daddy?

—Ain't they told you where they took the little nigger. It ain't right snatching a woman's son afore she even gets to look at it good. You'd think it belonged to 'em, and you doing all the suffrin'. Just be still li'l Martha, I'll get 'em back in a minute. He's a big red 'un I bet. Bald just like his DaddyGene. I'm gonna see for myself, and bellowing, Nurse git in here with this child's baby, he stood up tall, still cock-hatted, face drawn into a parody of stern command and fierceness.

—That don't do any good, Daddy. It's supposed to be this way. There's germs in here.

—Well they's your germs, and I ain't got none you ain't got. We's all one family, and he might as well start gettin' used to us. Hey—bring that boy back here.

—Please Daddy, they'll come and chase you away. Please be still . . . just sit here next to me.

—Stop your crying li'l Martha. It's all over now girl. You're a woman ain't you. I know it's hard, I been through it many times, sittin' beside your mother, holdin' her hand while she cried and prayed. She even asked the Lord to kill 'er once, begged him just to let it all be over with. But she's a good woman, your mother is, girl, and I know you'll be just like 'er. So hush, it's all over now. You's safe and the young 'un probably sleepin' somewhere, dreamin' about his Mama. Hush li'l Martha, your hands is cold.

Bed dipped, receiving his whole weight as he unstraddled its edge lifting both feet to stretch out atop the blue spread.

—You know somethin', your Daddy don't feel too well. He's kinda sleepy, been workin' since early this morning, and I ain't as young as I used to be. The humming of *Froggy* grew less and less distinct shading off into deep wheezing sound of sudden, heavy sleep, song to snore that rumbled uneven and loud beside her. She looked at huge hand wrapped around, hiding hers, veins blue and intricate were raised thickly, seeming to strain against the skin which had begun to dry and grow thinner, gaining the waxlike quality common to children and old men. She thought of trees, fall, winter trees, branches spreading into delicate fan-shaped designs stark, naked in gray-yellow light. Nights filled with formless fears, with shapes that fed on darkness and grew at an incredible rate into threatening beasts, of her Daddy beside her, her body cached deep in a peaceful valley between warmth and bulk of her parents' sleeping flesh. *Now I lay me down to sleep.* How she had finally parted from Clarence that first night, exhausted, drained, awakening later to feel his naked back against hers and the sudden fear of finding only space in front of her eyes as morning filtered behind her through a thin paper blind into their borrowed room. Quickly, as if pursued she had turned away from the emptiness and drawn closer to his body, encircling him with her arms till he turned drowsy eyed and wrapped her into his.

—Clary, I think we're going to have a baby.

Guarded, unfamiliar words between mother and daughter. Alone together in kitchen; cooking sounds mellow, subdued as food simmered to a precise warmth and consistency just before serving time. Respite when Freeda's voice would come from far off, disembodied, trying to accustom herself to the girl who must suddenly share women's secrets. Uneasiness, even embarrassment as her advice had to take the form of intimacies revealed, experiences related that she was forced to recognize as her own and now her daughter's inheritance. So small and frail. Had she been like that? Barely developed, her little girl's body soon burdened with the weight of another life. Of two lives. Lean, dark stranger who it seemed only yesterday she had seen carting groceries at the big supermarket in a makeshift wagon propelled by baby carriage wheels. Man-boy three times a week sitting on front porch steps, lingering over good-night always until Martha told a second time her father wanted her to come to bed. The Lawson boy. Rather wild, but no worse than the rest, anxious to please, very polite and respectful in face of his elders—nice enough—wants to go to college someday, be a doctor—always hustling to some little job after school or on weekends. Make something of himself. But much too soon for those kind of thoughts. Just a girl. Just a boy.

In kitchen, grease stains on ceiling, on wall in back of stove.

Perpetual. Icons spattered by a subtle hand on the paper Gene
had hung, kaleidoscoping to a thousand shapes as wide girl
eyes concentrated on them, trying to fix something solid in her
mind beyond the one unavoidable truth of her belly, to somehow return order to the baffling landscape of her life over
which her mother's voice floated like an ominous fog.

   —We can't tell him. After you're married and the baby comes
will be time enough. By then, what's done is done. You'll be
Clarence's wife, and your child will have a name. If your Daddy-
Eugene gets mad, then I can talk with him, but now . . . it
just frightens me to think what he might do. And what it
would do to him. Lot of people started with a lot less. Just
pray Honey, you're lucky he wants to marry you and you're
both in love. What you were gonna do anyway, wasn't it.
Everybody said so . . .

   —Just a little harder, Baby, that's all. We got each other. I'll
make good, for you, for our son. He's gonna be a son too,
your looks and my smarts. Hey—what you frowning at . . .
lips poked out a mile, you ain't pretty at all like that. Maybe
he'll have to have my looks too. C'mon now Baby, ain't you
gonna smile no more. Let me kiss those tears away. It's gonna
be all right. We got each other Baby—it ain't like you to mope
around. I like you smilin', laughin'. We're gonna go dancing
soon, at the Roseland Ballroom, stay out all night. Old Daddy-
Gene can't fuss now like he used to. We're almost married.
Gonna be my girl now. Man, was he shocked. Bet your Mama
had a hard time making him believe his little Martha had grown
up enough to have a husband. But she sure has, she's gonna
be my Baby always, aintcha' Hon. C'mon, dry those big, brown
eyes. What are you lookin' so sad about.

   At times in the small room Martha remembered as always
being hers, just after undressing and feeling the cold slide of
sheets over her bare skin, a feeling of finality enveloped her
whole body, nothing so definite as a word or idea, but a wave
of dizzying, impalpable images, succeeding each too quickly for

any to be distinct, a terrifyingly real and unswerving motion that swept her far, far away until some part of her insubstantial as a ghost was removed, and from a distant wind-swept height it could look down pityingly at her body, which, frail and alone, she knew would never stir again.

Little red wagon you ain't got far to go. And there's fifteen cents at the other end. Fifteen pennies closer to them fine clothes and fine house and me and Martha the two biggest shots in town ridin' in our Lincoln.

–It won't hurt. You know I wouldn't do nothing to hurt you Baby. I know, I know your scared, but nobody's comin' in here, Uncle Carl's gone for the whole week, it's ours any time we want it till he gets back. Our first bed, Baby. C'mon, not so stiff, it ain't gonna hurt . . .

Mirror on high, old-fashioned bureau caught Clarence's head and shoulders for a moment. She looked away, fearing the weight that would soon press down on her stomach. Mirror, mirror on the wall—combing long, black hair, gazing at freckles she hated and two teeth too large Martha Beaver cried over when martyred she was in turn by the others, red-eyed as Mama brushed and oiled, telling how beautiful it was, silklike, falling over shoulders, but then braided so tight in strands to be grabbed and teased. How hard it was to be a little ugly girl. She wept inside and wanted DaddyGene to sing her to sleep softly . . . brush and hand so smooth, flashing white in mirror.

Somehow the hem of her skirt lay ruffled inches from her eyes. Funny, she had never noticed how untidy each stitch lay on underside of red-flowered material, how colorless cheap cotton dyed on one side seemed and laced edge of slip peeking over . . .

Teeth closed on rigid tongue, warm liquid spread in mouth, washing over gums, salty like gravy then unfelt as body split in two aching pieces. String hung light began to dance, her eyes fastened on it till they glazed over and began to sting not daring to look down over posy flung redness to where on all fours trembling he crawled into her bowels.

Rain, rain, go away, little Clarence wants to play. Scrawling moon faces on the steamed window, eyes that melted to tears and streamed down pane, face collapsing, spilling down in rivulets like wax man in a fire. Rain washing streets, sitting in quiet beads on fuzzy hair and oilskin coat as he stood framed in doorway. —You'll catch your death coming out in weather like this. Off shrugged he his coat and into warmth careful not to falter or shiver or seem to care about sodden levis pasted to his thighs or shirt damp on shoulders and chest, nor did Martha protest chill of quick coming together there in livingroom beside fireplace crackling, spitting like a hungry whip. Nobody was home.

Rain. Her whole body seemed drenched by a tepid, clinging rain. And it fell still, a puddle of moisture between their naked bodies. Oily, glistening on his chest as he moved away, caught in beads on his body hair, tiny globules like dew clumps she had seen early mornings in the grass. Urge to cover herself, to end her unexplicable first nakedness before a man, but powerful swell of tenderness made her leave sheets where they lay— half on, half off the bed, while with an ease she would have never dreamed possible, one leg was drawn slowly up, its toes caressing her calf and stopping midway on her thigh, fully conscious of Clarence's eyes watching the movement, and his bronze hand dropping slowly to retrace the path of her foot.

—I tell you I don't like it Freeda. Something wrong about this. All the sudden jumpin' up, thinkin' they's grown enough to marry. Martha ain't hardly stopped suckin' her thumb.

Secrets—a woman's secrets. Painful, kicking inside Freeda like all the grown and dead ones had. How much could she take, how much and how long could she hold them inside before they burst out wailing, demanding their due. Was it a sin . . . was she lying to Gene . . . did he know anyway . . .

would he forgive Martha . . . and even more, would he forgive her? She prayed the prayers of the damned, damned because her sin must continue, must go on at the very moment she kneels to ask forgiveness.

BLUE FOR A BOY, PINK FOR A GIRL, but I know, DaddyGene knows.

It shall be a boy, and his name shall be called Eugene.

Spring ended and was forgotten, but soon came again, again and again, repeating itself, forgetting in its own way, each time imperturbable, resigned as if nothing else, no other season happened.

From a height, from a blessed height another fell, wingless, full of grief, sorrowing even as he plunged down through the darkness.

Splat.

I'm goin' home to see my Baby, I'm goin' home, I'm goin' home.

You, goatman! Play for the children. Shyly from undergrowth hobbled the faun on wobbly hind legs. Cloven heels and tiny horns made him appear satanic, vaguely threatening, until his huge, empty eyes, limpid and bovine, turned to stare vacantly at the gruff voice, features slack in an idiot glance caught forever between something he cannot remember, and something he cannot forget.

Sweetly sounds pipe he lifts to lips. Faun plays . . . flute sad and fragile in brilliant afternoon air. At some point Centaur joined piping, his voice inseparable, one with mood, impelled upon spring day and minds that were listening. Sounds first, unintelligible murmurs, subdued, secretive like whispers, then kindling presence of the word, his voice lifted and pipe floating backward, receding to calm and stillness like an audible hush of all nature listening . . .

Whining did the faun complete, all had been said, played, night closed their eyes.

Fa la, fa la, faaa la la, la la, laa la.

Beat the drums softly, pipe the pipes slowly. Full of embalming fluid, waxen and gray, DaddyEugene in a flower draped box received his last and proper obsequies.

The next time I go in that place, they'll be carrying me.

Right you are, blasphemer, pagan, stay-at-home, Sunday-morning infidel.

Alas, we all knew him well. Family . . . community . . . church . . . Christian household . . . while not personally . . . everyone had a good word . . . saw fit in his own way . . .

High above the broken cobblestones of Casino Way, mounted on DaddyGene's shoulder his second grandson Edward swayed and sang with him.

Froggy went a courtin' and he did ride, uh huh, uh huh.

Going to hear the Sanctified, and watch Tiny dance.

We had to sneak, and sharing the secret for a day or a morning was half the fun. Like those wine bottles he hid I always knew where and Grandma Freed searched for, but I wouldn't tell and she knew I knew and told me how bad it was and how much it hurt DaddyGene and someday he might go away and it would be because of those straw-bottomed bottles tucked everywhere she couldn't find and perhaps cry till sometimes I trotted off and brought back one or two but felt sorry afterward and wanted to confess to him but instead only crawled on his knee to listen to him sing or snore till I too slept and forgot my guilt.

Nobody here don't care at all, drifting down Casino Way. Passing a peach tree whose plump fruit one day I would eat, every juicy one when big enough to climb the fence and with a stick chase away the nodding, red-eyed wolf dog.

Go tell it on the mountain, lifted down I was on wall opposite low brick building. *Tioga Street Sanctified in the Name of Jesus Christ Church* said glassed over scroll in homemade gold letters on black cardboard. Two large windows, that on hot days had to be opened faced DaddyGene and me on our perch. Almost like being inside from where we sat, only pulpit invisible, words coming mysterious and faceless from a velvet-voiced throat beyond our view. Plain, yellow-gray plaster walls, cracked in places, decorated with posters, homilies, proverbs, maxims, bits of wisdom edited from every conceivable source. *Over the hill and everywhere.* Like mourners all were dressed in black, white shirts of men crackling in contrast beneath dark heads and necks, women's hair cropped and netted or veiled so each had a black, fat bag atop her head. All strangely lambent, benign, listening to the word and the melodious bursts of music punctuating prayers, scripture and notice reading. Passive nervousness. Crowd on the edge of something—orchestra tuning up, barrage starting, bull rumbling bewildered into a ring. Still point before the entertainment begins, before the blood and voice can participate.

Olay.

With a knock down, drag out, them dirty blues chord it began, quickly hand clapping and tambourines shrill jingle, jangle. Lord I've got good religion.

DaddyGene's big foot started tapping. From his inside pocket a flask was produced—guzzle, guzzle, click of metal on metal, spin and foot tapped faster. His jaws, large and square, moved fluidly in an exaggerated chewing motion. Wad of tobacco puffing out one cheek was reduced methodically, undisturbed by faster rhythm of foot and music. Two streams of thick oxblood spittle were expelled loudly onto cobblestones—splat.

—They's happy today, Eddie. Just started and listen to 'em wail. Love that stuff. These niggers fightin', cussin', and shootin' all week then comin' here like ain't nothing happened since the last time, all purty and clean, there's deacon Washington—Hey you black devil, hey you all you got the devil in there, he was drinkin' wine last night on the corner, yes he was—hey debil Washin'ton, sing your black butt off, go on knock yourself out, but don't put all yore pennies in the plate, we's got to get us some blood tomorrow—or tonight. Can't tell when you're going, and I ain't gettin' caught dry—splat.

–Work out sister Lucy, work out girl. She sure can sing can't she, boy. If I could just sit and listen to her everyday—splat—I'd stay in church. Get me a jug and lay back on a couple of them chairs and dig that fat sister chirp. Work out girl—splat. They's all gettin' heated up—watch 'em Eddie, they's gonna be dancing soon. Hey Tiny, hey you black elephant—splat—don't you feel the spirit yet?

Inside nothing but the shouting and chanting of the voice next to you could be heard. Let the King of Glory come in. And he did in top hat and tie, wearing striped pants and immaculate white, gold-buttoned spats on shining shoes. His teeth glinted brighter than diamond stickpin or rings big as quarters on his fingers, a slender, silver-tipped cane winked as it whirled enchanted in the air. Won't you come home Bill Bailey, won't you come home. Who is the King of Glory. Your host Baby, your toastmaster, and number one promoter of the biggest scene going. And they hallelujahed and wept and laughed with joy, shaking their heads—um um—eyes aglow like when Willie hits a grand slam or makes an impossible catch. Um—um. Let the King come in—tall and sparkling, heady and sweet—a brown eyed handsome man. Didn't it rain children, didn't it rain. And joy showered down, inundating the crude, crowded room and the bouncing hearts, and the tired, dark faces for a moment reflected the soul's smile.

Tiny started to sway. Barely perceptible at first, then his broad back rolled from side to side, first to the left then to the right, off time—a rhythm all his own—warming up—shaking his body's chains, palpitating inside each roll of fat, reviving the dead, hanging flesh so it quivered, so it jumped like so many nervous cats and in a moment on his feet, not lumbering as his tremendous bulk should move, but agile and smoothly coordinated like the lithe body of a shake dancer. Tiny up and feeling good. Arms out at either side, bent at elbows so fingers pointed up trembling with joy, his head rolling from side to side, glazed eyes staring as if possessed by some miracle on the ceiling. He switched down the narrow aisle, wide buttocks wagging more supple than swivel hips of brown girls in tight dresses on the avenues. Twitching, shaking, light on his toes and balls of feet Tiny danced. In his world, in that moment he lived for, when the tremendous weight of his soft, spreading flesh would be cast off, and somewhere like a leaf or a gust of music he would be lifted by the wind, borne off lithesome on a cloud of grace.

Tiny's moment was DaddyGene's moment and in a subtle transformation became eternal in small boy wide eyed, excited beside him. One chubby hand slapped loud and gleeful on faded denim of old man's bibbed overalls, while the other seemed unable to rest in one place, rubbing his pug nose, finger deep in mouth, attempting to imitate loud pops of DaddyGene's fingers, sometimes just waving in the air.

The old man watched as sweat poured down Tiny's black cannonball head. Like a fat, heavy top spinning his motion slowed, gradually dying so the minute, barely touching point could no longer sustain the ponderous weight above it. Down crashing soon, its lightness and grace impossibilities that could never be repeated, that were only dreamed. Slower, slower, flush gone, sweat drying and cool on wrinkled, wet neck.

Old man intent, rubbing stubble of his still jaw. Regarding blood stained pavement between his knees. Tiny sprawled exhausted in a chair. Boy's hand stopped its rhythmic patting on his grandfather's knee. From nowhere an odd tickle made the old man cough, for an instant as if a shadow passed he felt a chill penetrate deeply to his bones though the sun never stopped. A low, concerted mumbling came from the small, crowded room, punctuated from the invisible corner with hollow throat deep exclamations. Wine that is my blood, stale loaf going bad of my flesh—will He answer to my name? Drew he the still glowing boy on his knee, studied smooth skin and undefined features for some trace, some hint . . . of what he wasn't quite sure, even why seemed not to matter, but the child, Little Eddie straining to understand what was being intoned on the other side of the wall, Little Eddie seemed to contain an answer. Not strong and loud like Little Gene or like himself, but something significant and unshakable that reminded the old man of a vast uneasiness, a youthful anxiety he believed he had forgotten. It never had been articulated, but he knew it was a question. A question he had to rise up tall to face, a question elusive and demanding that he felt would best be avoided. Nothing positive ever came of it, only a vague longing regret, and a threatening chiplike obstinacy that he never dared to disturb. Down his black beaver hat came, high crown covering Eddie's head, brim wider than round, soft shoulders it dropped to. Panic like a cat in a box, as small hands struggled to remove hat DaddyGene held lightly down. Blinking, flushed Eddie laughed, and his arms went around his grandfather's neck as hat came away, his tender skin excitedly aware of rough, abrasive feel of stubble chin. Hat in hands, sun glinted off DaddyEugene's bald pate, the waxen skin transparent, delicate in the golden glow. Huge hand circled boy sweeping him in one motion high back to shoulder perch. Down Casino Way lurching in late afternoon they went, a trail of rusty splotches behind them as a fresh wad was mangled violently in Daddy-Gene's jowls.

Splat.

To Freeda's reproaches and Martha's where have you been young man he down came and sadly watched giant suddenly tired disappear into livingroom followed by Freeda's slim, straight figure, His mother quickly took him upstairs for a nap chiding him gently for not telling her he was going off—even so, over her voice, and the stairs that squeaked, and through the door after it was shut, he heard angry voices from the livingroom.

Dearly beloved we have gathered here.

Splat—with a hollow rattle first earth bounced in tight balls on the wooden box.

He came that they might have life. Those three grown and two dead ones pushing up now other sprouts, big-headed brown boys.

Down the muddled tow path flanked by slow going bronze stream they ambled, neophytes unshorn of innocence boldly holding hands, flesh to flesh uncovered, tasted pure as sun on backs, grass damp squelching up between toes ticklish on undersides and backsides when they sat to picnic there beneath shade of spreading tree applehung and fragrant from early dying ones Psmanthe had kissed away they ate in silence as the earth turned languid as a lover in the morning.

—Time was when nothing, boy, nothing here but high weeds and wild grasses, hunted squirrels and whatever else moved right over there where you see them factories. Different then. Not so many niggers, not so many of anything 'cept what lived in them grasses and weeds.

—You be going to school soon. Listen to what they tells you Edward. But don't let 'em scare you, they scared me and all I done was learn to fight 'em and scare 'em back. If they tell you something you ain't sure about, just come right home and ask your DaddyGene.

A triptych of sorrow. Freeda flanked by Martha and her son-in-law, Clarence. In black a compact group, the two younger people obviously supporting pale, veiled woman who stared with precarious dignity outward, eyes fixed, reflecting gray of overcast sky dim like shadow of pride and fear so familiar when for years she had watched Gene go. So close the three yet each frozen in some vague distant posture as if the secret core of each being had moved out from the soul's recesses to circumscribe and isolate the figures, catching a pose, a gesture, an inevitable attitude or expression which made escape or penetration impossible, touching like stone figures twisted into some baroque fantasy, but distinct because the stone is unfeeling, cold, dead. Freeda felt herself sink into the soft earth, each shovel full of dirt landing heavily in the hole seemed to lower her deeper and deeper, sucked down into the vacuum of the earth's bowels. Little Martha skinny, trembling in an invisible wind, a sound of someone crying deep inside her floating up to her throat, pouring out as a sigh or sob each time she relaxed the pressure on her tightly drawn, bloodless lips.

Fall day, day falling to death rattle of dirt clods on wooden box, drum roll Clarence listened to oddly aware of black silk thrust through his arm, Freeda's weight rigid, stone cold like flesh not at all; black silk on a stone mannequin who when he moved would topple into the mud. House that Gene built small now, thought he, doubly awkward in the face of love and death. Returned he had to manless women, to their sorrow, to Daddy-Gene's wine-rotten death in the bathtub and his own slow dying in mirror eyes of woman he loved. To his sons already strangers, already were Eugene and Eddie straight limbed and silent.

For thine is the kingdom.

Words he could never say unless in a group—suddenly aware of Freeda's lips, white, flaking, even behind the veil obviously immobile. Dry eyed too, as if waiting, like swollen gray clouds overhead to pour down on the mound rising from the earth, wash it away levelling, secreting the grave, carrying gaudy flowers to oblivion.

If there be a season fit for planting, for the dead to be laid in rows, and faith to cover them over, and hope to wait for their return, if there be a season surely it is now. Now when rains threaten, earth is soft and the heart has sunk so low only a long winter's sleep will do.

Il pleut dans la ville.

Into rented black limousines they filed, doors slam shut—quickly windows are steamed and rain streaks the glass. Doggedly back and forth wipers sway, final, unswerving as pendulums. And on that great gettin' up morning there will be some who have never fallen asleep.

Back to the city, Allegheny County cemetery, green mound behind them.

Fa la la, fa la la, faa laa laa.

Goats nibbling at the blossoms—wilted, faded, brought by a bronze stream filling soft rutted earth. Bumblebees watch disdainful, no honey there they buzz, damn the scavenging goats, beards waterdipped and brown.

Fa la la, fa la, fa la.

Froggy went a courtin' and he did ride, uh huh, uh huh—

O N E
. . . . .

Of course it was raining. Eddie knew it would rain the day he left. He had a long walk down the hill. Gradually the slope levelled revealing more and more of the countryside to the slim figure in its tardigrade progress down from the gray walls. They were behind now. The gray walls, that gate always open and beckoning. Slowly on his shoulders it fell. Warm, silent rain, the rain some flower had been awaiting, the rain Eddie knew would come.

It was hard to believe he had passed through. Voluntary commitment, he was familiar with the concept, yes, it had appealed strongly to him, yes, it was probably the thing that had finally made up his mind. The gate is always open, and so it was, and so it was today as he walked through it across the gravel driveway and down the wet, green hill, rain on his shoulders. I am going home, again and again repeated somewhere inside his chest, from all of this I am going home.

The bus didn't come to the top of the hill. Grierson told him that just before Eddie left. Dr. Grierson, across the miles of mahogany in sacerdotal tones. —It won't be easy. We all know that. If anything has been gained here, it is simply part of yourself that for some reason or another you grew careless of and lost. We hoped at best to give you back to yourself. Grierson looked briefly over his shoulder through the huge, gray pane of glass, but when he spoke he knew all there was to know of the sky, —I'm sorry it's such a poor day. But then who are we to expect sunshine. For you, I'm afraid the clouds will hang heavy for quite a while. It won't be easy especially at first, we know that, don't we Eddie. We don't teach illusions here, do we; it will certainly be difficult at first, but then who are we . . . ending with a reminder that the bus stopped at the hill's foot.

The grass was wet and slippery, but resilient under his slow-going steps. He could see the sheltered stop deserted beneath him. Corrugated tin siding and overhang loud as in a few moments he stood under it. Grierson had said it wouldn't be a long wait; Eddie shivered and believed. Somehow that huge, gray pile brooding on the hill top seemed dependent on Grierson's simplest utterance. As if it too rested on implicit faith rather than concrete sunk into the earth. It *would* come soon winding up the road, its windshield wipers working inexorably. He must remember to go to the back when it came. Go to the back, slinking in as unobtrusively as possible. And if the bus became crowded he must not sit while a white man stood. Strange that after such an interlude, after being in limbo for over a year he would immediately recall the necessary facts. His whole effort would be to remain unrecognized, appear to belong, not to be a smart northern nigger. More than the hospital the thought of going South had frightened him. He had dreamt night after night of pursuit, torture, horrible death. Mutilated black bodies hanging from trees, smouldering on charred crucifixes, debowelled, blinded, chopped by axes. He had received whispered warnings from old people born in the South, read secondhand stories of horror retailed in Negro magazines. During his trip down he had spoken to no one, met no eyes until arriving at the small island of federal authority to which he had committed himself. In a rush it had all come back. How to be nothing. The months of self-intensity, of self-awareness faded with him as he shrunk inside the bus. If there was an eternity somewhere, even that would not be long enough to forget some things.

He rode alone in a corner listening to the rain. Gradually the bus filled, picking up knots of passengers as it lurched to a stop beside other tin shelters. Luckily it was a suburban express that skirted city traffic and congestion until it dipped off the expressway on a newly built extension directly to the rail and coach terminals. The bus had been too intimate for Eddie. Its steamed, rain streaked windows crowded in upon the occupants trapping the tentativeness and dissatisfaction each rider breathed into the stagnant air. The transparency of cheap plastic raincoats, hats pulled down, peaked rain hoods and scarves, collapsed, pointed umbrellas—all seemed to exclude Eddie, bareheaded, his suit damp and clinging to his shoulders. He knew the white woman in the blue plastic raincoat (probably something she could carry concealed in her purse) had stared over her thick, dark rimmed glasses. Beneath the blue hood her hair, gray-brown, was pressed to her skull and resembled a nest of snakes. A woman, unattractive, even repulsive behind thick round spectacles whose slightest whim, whose pleasure or displeasure was worth his life. He could hear the crackle of each movement she made. Irresistibly he felt glances steal from him, covert, destructive glances feeding on her ugliness. The heavy ankles, the shapeless bulge of thigh and hip under the translucent material. Her feet swelling red from the edges of clogs. How long had it been. A year at least, but certainly not brought to this, not brought as low as this. But thought too must die here. Plastic lisping, the crackling umbrellas lolling, shaking off bright beads of water from their loose fluttering ends were sharp beaked birds of prey responding to his thoughts echoing loud through the bus. If she would cry out, if she would point, he would be dragged out and murdered. Always that thought. That sleeping violence which he feared and courted in her female ugliness. A woman after a year. But even after that not her, not this one with her worm hair. I look because I do not love. Because I want her to know. I wouldn't have her even though she is a white woman. The first one. White Clara naked on his bed. He had been so confused, so tender, and afterwards the pasty, sour smell of her sex wouldn't leave his fingers. A dancer she was, strong limbed whom he had watched many times in the ballet school, sensing a dreadful heat and energy in her mysterious white flesh rippling beneath leotards. I love you I love you not, her cigarette breath and bad teeth, but she didn't care what you were, just men and women in the world, just men and women . . .

Alice, would she be waiting? Could she forgive?

Dear Alice:

I am going away. This is something I must do. I've tried to fight it by myself but now I know I can't. Maybe where I'm going they'll be able to help. I don't know what else to say. I just couldn't come to you the way I am, please try to understand. Why can't we touch without having it hurt? Your eyes Alice. I saw how far I'd fallen when you looked at me the last time. So much has happened to us. Please wait. Sometimes I believe this trip will make a difference. I'm afraid, but I think there is a chance. Do not forget. I love you.

Alice, the most beautiful dancer, would she forgive, would she remember . . . those distant things huddling naked in the frail warmth of his memory.

Another bus, another corner. A Greyhound scenic-cruiser, trembling, wheezing with life beneath him as its pigeon-necked driver gunned the engine. Eddie was early, and he sat alone suddenly chilled and tired. Already the morning had seemed years. If only sleep would come, he thought, if only I could draw it like a coat around my shoulders and close out the day. He huddled on the coarse grained seat, trying to adjust the headrest, twisting his body to take up the least space and still stretch out his long legs. The cheap suit now thoroughly soaked clung to his thighs, back and shoulders. If he moved the wet material away from his bare legs an icy draft curdled between the suit and his flesh. At least as the dampness chilled him, his body heat imperceptibly warmed it in return so he stopped avoiding his wet clothes and pulled them closer round him.

Mostly Negroes boarded the bus. Dusky farmers, big footed, big handed, foreigners emigrating to another country. Awkward signs of what they expected and what they had left behind stamped them. The ill fitting, ill styled suits, florid bow ties and clodhoppers, the elegant fedora and coveralls beneath. Women in little girl dresses with slips hanging and too many colors. Hitching a ride on the freedom train. The strength and animal litheness of their bodies were revealed unexpectedly—a dark stare, a slim brown calf, hips and breasts thrusting against shapeless dime-store cottons, brutal hands. One day, in the city these things would be brought forth, what might have slept forever would be violently realized in the city's heat and passion. They took their places, shopping bags in hand, boxes, bundles, flour sacks, containers of every description piled overhead precariously in racks, flowing out, strapped and roped together in the aisles. Carting away all they owned to the promised land. A peculiar rootlessness visible in their eyes. Eddie knew what they would become. Could tell by the angle of a hat, or the color in a tie who would catch on and who wouldn't make it. Brighteyes would be hooking on the avenue in less than a month. That big, black boy with the bandana around his throat would run numbers, beat somebody up then be found sliced or shot in an alley. An unsolved murder the police would never investigate. Eddie felt he had something to say, something they could understand. He wanted to roll up his wet sleeve, walk up and down the aisle like a preacher testifying. Somehow turn this load back, tell them the best they could expect and show the cost. But the Negroes sat sullen and suspicious, and Eddie shivered in his corner.

When she could walk, when both her sons were away at war, each morning Martha would go down to the gate and wait. She said she knew it would be morning when they returned, a bright, sunny morning, but she went down the bricked path every dawn rain or shine just in case. She would stand, still in her housecoat, either by itself or flapping below her man's old brown overcoat until the postman came. Not until she greeted him and took her letters when there were letters would she leave her post by the gate and return to the house. When she was sick for a week and confined to her bed, she wept even though her daughter Bette went and waited. One came back, Eddie, her youngest son; the postman in an envelope brought all that was left of Eugene, her firstborn.

She was different then. Even after the telegram from the war department she continued those morning vigils. Clarence couldn't stop her, and after her scenes, tears, and a cold, cold anger he feared in himself he stopped trying.

There had been three children who lived, but the man too loved most his eldest son. Eugene had been big like his father. He grew fast and rank, a strong hard-handed boy whose shoes had to be left outside at night. Huge, smelly things Martha would carry dangling like fish from their strings, holding her nose but laughing and loving the ritual when he would forget and she would point and shout, making jokes to the others while Eugene cringed and almost cried. It was just to be forgiven and for her to forgive. The tiffs they had. Him standing still, towering a foot over her head listening to her shrill angry voice and cowing from her threatened blows. But when she hit him, it really did hurt her more, his elephant hide and bones and buckles and she would cry.

—These shoes. From me, from my body came something that fits in these shoes. She loved the others, but it could never be the same. She had found and nourished different things in each, knew Edward or Bette could do things Eugene never could, but then how could she love everything about them, how could every moment, every action of theirs be an original and unrepeatable truth between mother and child. She was a child herself with him, and her man, still almost a boy when the first baby had come. She loved the child closely, intensely. It was something the father could only watch from a distance, sometimes jealously but usually simply in awe. Clarence would come and go, awkward in the face of their deepest magic; no matter how long he would stay away from home, he knew the child would remain an iron chain looped round them. Father and son grew up almost strangers, but loving and being loved by the same woman. After the war, Clarence stayed away and drank even more. Home at the end, his heart went bad and he died.

—Daddy, Daddy, Bette screamed at the dead man. Eddie was out, and her mother who moved very slowly then and always near sleep did not answer. Bette sobbed, deep, heaving sobs, suspending for a moment the hysterical screams she knew must come again as she moved across what seemed an endless space her fingers to stroke the dead man's brow. She shuddered at the touch, and screams burst from her gut shaking her body in wild convulsive heaves.

The two women couldn't lift Clarence. When Eddie came in they had only managed to straighten his body out and clean the floor around him. Eddie got a neighbor to help him place the corpse in the bedroom. After the funeral his mother stopped walking. She cursed her God and forsook him when she was delivered from her stroke.

All their relatives and friends brought food. Chicken, ham, cakes, pies, everything imaginable to fill the house. Then they came again to mourn and eat. During the viewing the house was filled with baking and cooking smells. From the kitchen rattling of pots, pans, and the eager, happy sounds of female activity drifted. Oh, we ate that week. We ate like kings. And all the niggers in the neighborhood greased with us. He was a fine man.

Eddie didn't look like his father; some older people said he looked just like his dead grandfather, but others said not at all. He was tall, but slim and fragile. He had his mother's high forehead with its taut, shiny skin showing his skull beneath and a palpitating vein that in anger thrust itself forward. Prematurely his light brown hair, wavy but thin, crept back from his forehead making its delicately molded surface dominate his face. Cheekbones high and prominent, brown eyes deeply sunken completed the impression of boniness; it was always an eggshell or skull people thought of. But when Brother Small saw him stepping off the bus, Brother thought of a scarecrow, or of a little boy in a borrowed suit. But it was Eddie all right, Eddie again after a year coming home.

—Eddie, Eddie Baby. Brother had his arms around the taller man before he could speak. When they stepped apart both were smiling almost to tears.

—Man, you been gone a long time. Eddie couldn't answer. He just looked at his friend letting his smile become something deeper. A vacant lot, brick throwing, chased down Dumferline Street, high on wine, high on pot, music, Mrs. Pollard's niece and back yard, chased down alleys.

—It's good to see you, Brother. Brother as always had his cap on. He wore his tan hustling jacket and pegged gabardine slacks flapped around his skinny legs. That was just how Eddie left him; it was as if he waited there all the time. But the wing tips were gone, walked out in a year's worth of sidewalk, replaced by a pair of canvas and gum casuals mostly rag.

—Times is been hard, Eddie. Like always. They were arm in arm now, and Eddie quickly looked up from the pavement. He met Brother's pale, red-rimmed albino eyes, disconcerted for a second, till the familiar warmth of the milky stare returned. His friend had probably been at the station all night.

Brother's jaw bulged with a wad of chocolate. He pushed a half-peeled Hershey bar towards his friend. As a bite melted to thick, sweet paste in his mouth, Eddie remembered how Brother used to eat chocolate all the time because he thought it would make him brown. But it only gave him pimples, big, ugly and white.

—You still eating that stuff? Brother grinned back remembering.

—Yeah man, can't you see, I'm gettin' a tan. He doffed his cap, presenting the bright dome of his cue ball head.

—Still going around blinding people you old skinhead. I used to think of that mirror of yours every morning when I shaved.

—Since when are you shaving every day? I knew you'd come back putting on airs. Least you got back outa there without no rope burns. They were quickly out of the terminal and moving towards the trolley stop.

—Shit, Brother, it's a holiday—the buses will be hours apart. Let's catch a cab home this once. I'm tired of buses anyway.

—Damn, you done come home with bread? If they pays you and feeds you down there, I might make that trip myself after-all.

—I got a couple dollars I saved, that's all, but it should get us home.

It was early morning and a cab was easy to hail. They moved steadily along Baxter Boulevard away from the center of town.

—Good thing we're going this way. Just look at the other lane. Bumper to bumper as far as I can see. Eddie didn't answer, and after a brief look, Brother understood. The wheels hummed monotonously, a kind of lulling silence that after a while wasn't heard. Eddie was worn out. Brother, after watching the stalled cavalcade of facelike chrome grills and head lamps, settled back content with his friend's quiet mood. They drove along a shelf cut into the hillside. Below them gradually terraced, clumps of houses, factories and warehouses tapered off and culminated in endless rows of smokestacks lining the river. A haze obscured everything but the broadest outlines. Above them, clearer it seemed, the chiselled stone and raw rock beyond cut off any view of the sky. They were an island whirring along an un-cluttered gray channel, serene except for an occasional impa-tient bleat from the other side of the highway. Wearily the sun made an effort to poke through masses of stagnant gray clouds. Hanging over the river a brief patch of blue would glimmer then be swallowed up. Eddie was home and snoring; Brother slept beside him.

One more class. One more class, Thurley thought, and then perhaps a few welcome days of self and peace. Perhaps a chance to get to the book. This respite from class, the long awaited one when he would make the break, begin to write again. Still a boy, he thought, a dreamer still who chooses to believe. But afterall, those things long in coming often the best. The most complex mammals have the longest gestation periods, and what's more satisfying than the bowels erupting after a week's constipation. The door would open. Words hot, thick and pungent pour out so fast that his arm would grow weary transcribing before the flow from his brain diminished. A boy still. It is enough Sancho to believe, enough that I believe they are giants. And off to get bloody hell knocked out of me again. Thurley stood and went to the window. His office faced the new classroom building; he could see the two windows of lecture room 120. Soon the paths would begin to fill up. Students would file in disorderly spurts through the halls, in and out of the glass doors. Lecture room 120 will become alive. Thurley reflected on the collective mind he must meet, his own gross person and the tenuous threads of learning he must fashion into a screen between himself and the predatory audience. He comes that they may have light. All forty-five of them, forty-six including himself gathered like a pile of leaves into that room by forces too simple and too dizzying to conceive. Intention, motive, need, impulse—each day some odd assortment of causes conspired to throw them together. Or perhaps it was just the inscrutable, causeless principle behind all things that allowed so much disparity, so many cross-purposes, contradictions and antagonisms to settle regularly into intimate juxtaposition. Robert Thurley the preceptor, Thurley at whose feet this flock would gather. He turned his back to the still sparsely peopled walks, refusing any further mental comment to the invisible but powerful forces materializing outside his window.

The lawns seemed so placid, so cool at this afternoon hour. Often Thurley wanted to leave his brown, bookish cubicle and stretch out beneath a tree. Be a lolling undergraduate again, watch girls, read or write poetry, just sit quietly and exude his youth and beauty benignly as a light touching the passerby. But that was another day, another Thurley still firm fleshed and clean before alcohol had hollowed out his stomach. He took down the sleek black volume of French plays he was using for his course in tragedy. He would talk about Oedipus today, Oedipus from Sophocles to Cocteau. Swollen foot. Child abandoned in the forest—the good shepherds who raise him then lose him to the stars. Would they listen, would they understand? It's not something dead, not a fairy tale either, or a dirty joke to be snickered at. *Jocaste*—mother, wife, to the lost father, son, ghost. Ghost of the dead boy long abandoned. Do you see it all? The inimitable circularity, the gruesome beauty *Oedipe* cannot bear to look on. The scream, the scissors a jagged cross in his hands. But even so, we endure, we go on though we lean on the thin arm of our shame made manifest, though we are led by the irretrievable fruit of our sin.

A thousand sailors. The love call of their brutal laughter, the caress of their angry blows. And yet I would go each night, humbly to seek peace, to unhungry the animal that must feed on love. No substitute I've found. Oyster shells, sawdust on the floors. Will they understand?

With unseeing eyes Thurley regarded his watch. It was necessary to repeat this purely instinctual motion to really check the time. He did have a minute, enough time to extricate his concealed half-bottle of Southern Comfort from the bottom drawer and longingly wet his lips. A gulp, then the fiery thread thrilling into his maw. Sometimes it could be so good. It could make the difference between cowering in this cramped space and striking out boldly to meet the denizens of 120. Thurley raised the ungraceful bottle again. He knew, his blood knew it would not be easy today. Many of his students would have left early for the holiday and those who remained would be either helplessly restless or overtly pugnacious. And Thurley would meet them at feeding time. Sometimes the impending struggle made him cold, unfeeling, but often heavy, uncontrollable moisture would slick him beneath his clothes. Even after so many years, he was like a baby, wet like a baby when he met them.

How far was it across the quad? How many steps to the other side, to 120 and the forty-five? Addice, Anderson, Bennett, Bond, Bowie, Boyd, Carr . . . The girls near the front, their dresses unnecessarily high, knees shapely, the calf muscle bulging pleasantly where it crosses and spreads against the thigh. Watson, West, Westbrook, Williams, Windsor. How shall he presume? The first step out of the chair close to impossible. Thurley tilted the bottle again. From the golden-brown triangle it formed in one corner the liquid lapped to meet his tongue. It lay hotly in the space between his lips and teeth, burning as he slowly drew it in swills across his gums and down into his throat. It could be so good. Clearing the space, leveling the phantoms that had gathered outside his window. It would be difficult today, but the show must go on. It was simply a question of the stronger will. His or the forty-five. What he loved most he must protect even to the cost of his own blood. If he gave up, if he submitted to the intimidating, hulking indifference, it would respond like a dog when it knows someone fears it. The coward would rise, curl back its lips and attack.

In a hazy moment he was perched cockily on the corner of a desk. Since the desk sat on a raised platform he could peer owlishly down at the forty-five over the steel rims of his glasses. But the chill was becoming overbearing. In spite of the whiskey, in spite of his resolve he felt the ice, the thickly packed layer after layer that he must walk upon to reach them. He had blithely begun; without trepidation or fear he launched into the glacial atmosphere. Yet even the way they responded to the roll call was cold. The tone of each voice belligerent, almost an afterthought rather than a reply to Thurley's voice tolling names. *April 20.* Many gaps, many little x's in the close columned book. Each absence one x, a tiny scarlet letter Thurley duly had recorded. But for him, for the teacher something etched much deeper. They don't care, don't give a damn about what I'm saying. It's a requirement, an obstacle to be gotten over with least bother. So they come and demonstrate their disdain. They wait for me to play the fool, to live up to the stories that circulate about me. A clown, a showman, who, if they're patient, they may see pull some colossal blunder, involve himself in one of his periodic scandals which they can say they saw enacted live onstage. Thurley teetered, dangerously close to falling from the edge of the desk. He experienced the profound vertigo of absolute solitude in a crowd. The eyes of his students were glazed over, and they saw nothing. Their lips were sealed, they spoke nothing. Their ears were clamped shut, and they heard nothing. Thurley veered away from his carefully planned lesson. Like so many beautiful white birds settled on a lake it had been till a sudden noise shocked them into abrupt confused flight. He saw white forms soar, float up and scatter—gone. No one had read. No one had the slightest interest in what he so desperately wanted to convey. The absurdity of it all, him intoning from his rock to the deaf multitude. His life depended on what he said, on how he defended his cause, but the jury was composed of wood. Mocking images of life diabolically set out to confront him. In their unpreparedness, the class formed a solid block against him. If someone had read, had understood, they would be too aware of the battle lines that had been drawn to cross them. It was their will against the professor. They would combine and by their very weight nullify his accusing effort. The forty-five would smother his just one little candle to plunge 120 into comfortable darkness.

But still Thurley had to speak. Calmly and with the fatal

poise of resignation he was ready to begin his final speech. Of course in its futility and detachment, its introspection and blindness, it had to be a soliloquy. He slid from the desk, nearly losing his balance and evoking a snicker, to stand before them. Without realizing the ridiculousness of the motion he hiked his trousers over the protruding slope of his belly. For him, this slight adjustment and the quick combing motion of his fingers through his sparse hair served to restore whatever dignity had been lost in his awkward dismounting of the perch. A cigarette was the final prop. In a moment one hung suavely, pasted to his lower lip as he fished through his pockets for a light. Those closest to Thurley sensing his helplessness had already begun to smile, and a low murmuring from the classroom's rear was becoming audible. To Thurley it was the sound of ice cracking. It was his unsteady footing giving way to plunge him into the numbing depths. It was the earth moving as gigantic glaciers collided. His hands hung at his sides, and the limp cigarette dropped from his mouth as he spoke again. This time it was word unfettered, the pure, intense content of a moan articulated. Thurley's mind began to cry. It wept for things only the mind that has suffered can penetrate and know. Dry-eyed he tried to hold them in their chairs, tried to make them see what he saw, comprehend the gray annihilating cloud that was settling upon them. He was as usual eloquent in his grief and perfectly incomprehensible to the students. At last he settled for laughter, for their jeers and grins at him and his throes of ineffectuality. He released them and his hold on the truth by transforming their uneasiness and his fretful being into the hollow composure of laughter. He was the prancing butt, he was the grimacing clown they could crucify. In a flash it was over; they growled and bounded after him, their teeth sinking into his rubber flesh, their claws tearing away his limbs that stretched and popped like bubble gum. They destroyed him and in the passing of their wake 120 was quiet.

Thurley thought of the sea. Of a beautiful young sailor

who had robbed and beaten him. It was a beatitude. A scene for Raphael to paint in his reds and blues.

Thurley replaced the forgotten book of plays in his briefcase. Before his eyes swam *Jocaste*'s preternatural scarf. Outside the walks had filled. Thurley found another cigarette and finally discovered his matches on the desk behind him. It took several tries to light it, but when the smoke finally curled through his nostrils and carried its mist into his lungs Thurley sighed a heavy sigh of relief. As his gaze lowered from the ceiling he caught the image of a figure half hiding in the doorway. Before he realized what the impression meant and could turn again to find who had been watching him from the doorway, the sound of running footsteps resounded in the marble hallway shattering the stillness. He could only tell that it was a girl in cleated loafers, and from the soft sound distinguishable before the shoes' staccato echoes, she had been crying.

It was a beautiful piece of jewelry. Green stones set in quincunx on a plain gold frame.

—It was my mother's, he said. It was my mother's, Thurley said to the boy sitting on the edge of the bed.

—She gave it to me many years ago and I want you to have it now. How she would have died again to see the bony, black creature reach out its hand closing its long fingers to make the pin disappear. Like catching an insect they clamped so quickly.

In a moment the boy was gone, clutching his treasure, afraid almost to look at it, to open his hand until it could be dropped in some glass jar to behold. Through the dark streets he ran, his prize hot in his hand. The stars were eyes, but tonight they were laughing.

I really loved the little nigger thought Thurley sitting later alone in his study. It was the den of an epicure, heavy with the possession of things. A Munch, mostly skull, hung over the artificial fireplace, blackened bronze statuettes of classical horses and gods crowded the room, jade figurines, Buddhas with empty laps for receiving incense, a marble topped table, a rococo inlaid and gilded writing desk over which hung El Greco's *Cardinal Guevara,* all contributed to an impression of repleteness but at the same time were isolated in their hard individuality. He smoked, satisfied with the silk against his skin, with fragrant wreaths floating above and around him. Night seemed always full of forget, full of promise, after a satisfying physical interlude, that life would continue to be played out in half-light, in pleasant bodily fatigue to which sleep would bring completion.

From a corner an oboe related a lugubrious theme. Thurley knew the oboe was the sound of death.

We had eaten together. Huge chunks of tenderest steak. The little black boy all eyes and silent but for his chops working furiously. As if it would disappear before he had finished. Music then too, but lighter, violins and candles subliminal, but certainly what he would remember later when hot meat taste had gone. Somehow everything had led into those moments, as everything floundered ungainly into these. My guest: a gamin, urchin, pickaninny, street boy to partake of the fatted beast.

On North Street I found him. Dirty of course, skin of cocoa, sheep hair curling into a thousand dusty beads. Ask of him a question. Traveller in another country you see. I would like a pack of cigarettes. Shy of course. Timorous, ready to run or kick, to cry out if approached too quickly, if affronted or embarrassed by the sudden intrusion of huge mass of my white flesh speaking. He answered from behind a bush, one foot and hand still in the undergrowth anchoring his slowly emerging voice. A dog slinked by. The boy's brown eyes followed pit-pat of the mongrel's feet on the pavement as it skirted them tail between legs. I am not afraid now tone, slight smirk as if to say, my world, he pointed mumbling —Right around that corner mistah.

—I'm looking for a cab, and I'd hate to miss one by moving off the main street, son, if you could please run and get cigarettes for me you can keep the change, producing a half dollar.

The brown hand hesitated then was thrust abruptly forward, unfolding like a dirty flower. Suffer the children to come unto me. Away quickly walking, then trotting towards the corner all long legs and stick arms dangling he diminished trailing one clenched fist.

The oboe receded. Two voices in duet taking up the theme, antagonistically opposed in counterpoint, miles distant, irreconcilable. Male, female.

Thurley unseated himself, trailing scarlet folds of dressing gown through the dining room, then entered his small kitchen the red silk billowing around him as he knelt to remove a pat of butter from the floor. Things were still piled on the sink. Pots, pans, the Dresden china with its thin blue bands, silverware caked with remnants. A plastic tray bent by firm pressure from both his hands expelled with the sound of chicken bones cracking triangular pellets into an ice bucket. He only half-filled the airtight receptacle knowing this would suffice for his final gin and tonics of an evening.

In religion an aesthetic Catholic, in politics a passive Communist, in sex a resigned anarchist. He filled his tall glass. His check was late, spent anyway, but late. There was some satisfaction in possession if only for a moment, in dispensation if only a token, salutary displacement where he pleased. Butcher, Baker, Candlestick Maker and Hermann.

—Ya, sure docktor herr professor Thurley. Ya, ya you buy here things, Hermann has much to choose from you buy all here professor docktor sir, pay later, anytime. You would honor me herr docktor. And he did have it all. Gray grainy bottles of bitter lemon, pâté, smoked salmon, crab meat, lobster and shrimp canned of course but everything from Scandinavia, Germany, France, Russian caviar, Polish vodka and of the Herr Docktor's patronage an irreducible debt.

Traffic swooshed by infrequently on North Street. He stood on the pavement dressed in a wilted lightweight suit, stylishly olive hued doing its best to disguise the weary obesity his body moved irresistibly towards. The pants had slipped below his paunch. If one comes I will hail it and wait till he returns. Somehow I'll get him in it too.

After the meal the boy had been sleepy. His big eyes drooped and the weight of the strange white man's house tired his meagre shoulders. —Mistah Bob, I wanna go now. Thank you very much for the food, but I think I better go now. The room full of objects cowed him. Made him start as gazing from thing to thing each one momentarily seemed to measure him in return. The buddha with the empty belly, the skull death-colored staring from the wall. At times they spoke aloud, but at others moved out of his range of hearing and vision to continue their malevolent life free of him and the man reclining on the couch. When they spoke it was distinctly, but in a language incomprehensible and of things he wished cloaked in silence.

Thurley too heard voices: Crime in the streets: City shocked by vice exposé. Well known university professor arrested soliciting male partners for unnatural acts. Amid furor President Goodfellow announced immediate dismissal of offender promising at the same time masculinity oaths would be administered to all faculty members, women included. The professor was charged today in morals court on sixty-nine counts. The star witness, a vice squad agent who disguised as a twelve year old Negro boy permitted himself to be molested. Pictures on pages five, ten, twelve, thirteen, seventeen, twenty.

I loved the little nigger, Thurley thought drinking alone. If love comes into this cluttered world, it is in the quiet space between orgasm and not orgasm.

The thick blue book was opened. It was a diary, album, commonplace, letter, scrap, miscellany optimistically inscribed on its opening leaf *These fragments I have shored*. Thurley wrote: April 21, Easter Eve: Consummation—the momentary reconciliation of black and white in the heat of coition. I have paid for it with her jewel of great price.

The remark completed a page. He pondered its contents,

dwelling a moment on the last entry, then turned the leaf with his right index finger. The new blankness was oppressive. Two wide, long sheets of heavy paper blandly white. A mirror, a dark, white mirror, refusing his image. Hopelessly confused but somehow ineluctably true the metaphors danced and persisted. Dark-white, transparency-opacity, returning-refusing his image. The strands of experience, the rainy days and nights, mistakes that would go to fill up the pages. Thurley saw as far ahead as he could see. Forever—he would get up at eight, go to his brown office and catch up on the previous day's correspondence, carefully filing away any new mail till the next day. He would teach from ten until eleven, then again two to three. Between he would lunch with Noonan, at Dante's more than likely where they could have draught Michelob. He would leave his office at five going directly to Hermann's to shop, always hurriedly, probably taking a cab if one could be found because Hermann closed promptly at five-thirty. He would be home and in a chair with a drink by six, reading, writing or just drinking except every other Wednesday when he lectured at the art school, or the approximately once a month invitation to dinner by one of three friends who since unknown to each other never alternated their invitations very satisfactorily. Three times in one week, or else not one for months. This schedule varied by an odd faculty meeting, rare sorties to Midwestern conferences, a movie, a play or concert was Thurley's life. When he projected it in his imagination almost every distinction dropped away from the events. It was undeniably true—only the most elemental events of this routine called up any response. He recalled as vivid and substantial only weariness as his body came to consciousness in the mornings, the anxious, ridiculous dash to Hermann's late each afternoon, and finally fear as he dropped into bed at night that the booze would wear off before morning, that he would start up wide awake before dawn in a pool of wet, rumpled bedclothes.

Professor of Comparative Literature. B.A. Harvard. Ph.D.

Sorbonne, Oxford. Somewhere certificates pasted in full-of-truth blue book. At points we diverge, essential points in fact. Always a clean white page to begin on. *Où sont les neiges.* The boy had been strangely unreluctant. Although detached, even cold in a numb, childish fashion, the boy had willingly submitted. First his shoes, then his socks and trousers pulled off by the Doctor's trembling white hands, his priest hands moving of themselves, mechanical but infused with timeless primordial mystery that guided his fingers with a logic more powerful and comprehending than his own being. The flesh presented to his lips, staleness of his own groin floating up to meet him as he knelt. Breath of a dying wino. With this kiss I thee wed, the lean black bridegroom puff of veiled white beside him arm curled into his as they stood rigid with grotesque, confectionery smiles atop the pyramid of cake. Stale cake toppling then as knife keenly enters collapsing with a wheeze the creamy icing. He gave of himself in grudged, thin spasms. The hierophant rose on stiff knees.

The eyes still said I want to go home. That though you have done with me, and I am glad you have finished, I have never begun. The boy stood, his ashy legs quivering, dropping his eyes to stare at the glistening stem of his sex. It too pouted, tipped by an opaque bauble like a runny nose. He bent and gathered his clothes, too grimly absorbed to notice his host as he left. Too quick the host thought, too quick and now the irreparable silence. A swift shadow of fear across the boy's face directed Thurley to his middle, and his white hands buttoned clumsily the fly that still gaped. He tried to smile as he completed this act cursing inwardly the little Italian tailor who had repaired the trousers that hot summer in Naples. He hated his own coarseness, his lapses into natural ease that always produced loathing rather than sympathetic recognition, revealing the brute instead of soiled angel he wished to appear. He had shocked the boy. Ironically the enormity of everything else had simply disarmed him, made him passive. But the sound of the toilet flushing, Thurley's forgetfulness, haste and fumbling with the row of buttons revived a familiar, sordid world of old men, alleys and forbidden deeds. In spite of music, chocolate and the conciliatory, maternal concern of Thurley's voice for another hour the boy remained rigid inside his shell. The last desperate act had won at most his hand to grab the jewel before he tore off into the night.

Thurley knew Eddie Lawson was coming home. It had been a long time, so long that he feared their reunion and had resolved to avoid him. But as the day came closer, he could not conceal from himself the necessity of another meeting. The first and only time he had seen Eddie had been in another city, the seashore. He couldn't remember the name of the bar where it had begun or the exact date of their brief encounter, but some low, sweet jazz, something by Miles Davis, perhaps it was *Green Dolphin Street,* blended with the bar's smoke and darkness and gave to the night's events an identity that would always live inside him.

—You see being a white man you just wouldn't dig. The Negro had leaned close to the white face of his interlocutor. He had swept his sunglasses with a limp, magnificent flourish of his wrist from his sweating face. The Negro was green in the barlight, his thick lips pouted purple. —I don't mean no harm but it's as simple as that, baby. His voice was artistically modulated, from throaty tones to the high almost female whines of emphasis.

Two more drinks were set down. Thurley's white hand dipped then bloomed fluttering green. There was nothing more to say. Afterall the Negro knew, he just couldn't dig.

It had all passed now. That wet dishrag slap of sensation across his face as Thurley had entered the bar less than an hour before. Arctic Avenue, just a few blocks off the boardwalk, from the ocean that he somehow felt he could still hear. It stank, the onion, piss, stale beer stink of every dive in every city three thousand years of civilization had produced. It stank and was full of racket—jukebox music, glass thumping and clinking, chairs dragged, feet stomping, the cacophony of human voices. A din striking him as solidly as the fetid musk of body heat when he entered the door.

It was strange how the darkness made no difference. Thurley still felt hot and exposed as a boiling lobster here in spite of the bar's obscurity. The barfly who had quickly approached him to bum a drink had made his entrance easier than he expected, but their roles had already begun to change. Always like that. The giver always unable to stop giving so that the very act of giving becomes a dependence. Why always like that? Why not smooth and pure? One drink accepted, consumed, fini. Back to your corners. But never like that, even this loudmouthed scavenger deep inside him already and him powerless because he gave first. The Negro's breath again. His mouth yawning for ages before the first word. Purple gums dangling below his upper lip. The horse teeth.

—But we's all bruvers anyway, ain't we? I mean to say under this, he pinched the green flesh of the back of his hand. —All the same is what I mean. He gulped the Guckenheimer's, sputtering as he coughed, wiping his chin with a huge yellow handkerchief produced from nowhere, I ain't nobody's fool you know.

Thurley smiled and turned away. He caught the bartender's eye and in a voice he felt condemning him as he spoke asked for the washroom. It had a sign, but the little electric *M* had burnt out. The door whined on its taut spring then slammed behind him with a furious swoosh. He read the inscriptions. Always tell most about a place by coming here. Not simply how clean, but what kind of people frequent. Here only the crudest sorts. The sensual purity of African art. Phone numbers, names, numerous highly stylized representations of the phallus, something that was either a mouth, cunt or arsehole. He shook himself carefully before re-entering the arena.

It was obvious they all knew. He was surprised one of the more desperate hadn't followed him in. After all why else would a white man be here. He remembered his shame at his body on the beach. He was sensible enough to keep it covered, but the others, the flabby, red-fleshed, shameless others baring their dying bodies. Like sores or wounds out there in the sand. Wrinkled, blue-veined. They made him think of birds, not soaring, graceful kinds, but wobbly, fat bodied anachronisms with atrophied wings dropping feathers as they waddled, smelling of death. Some went by in chairs pushed by straw-hatted Negroes. Some of the chairs were motorized and nothing seemed more majestic to Thurley than a straw-bonneted black boy atop one of these pleasure barges guiding it along the boardwalk. Herr professor was here because he wanted a ride, and so what if they knew it.

The bar had grown more crowded. The Negro had moved off, too drunk even to capitalize on his luck, but others had come. Thurley resumed what he thought was his place by the appearance of a half consumed whiskey sweating on the counter.

—Hey man, you got the wrong drink, that's my friend's drink. Thurley turned towards the sound of the voice. He saw a face, ghostly lurid even in the half-light. The face was shaded by a cap tightly pulled down beneath which two eyes fixed him in a milky stare. He realized it must be a white face, whiter even than his, but distorted into crude Negroid features.

—Excuse me, I left one, and I thought this was it.

—Well it ain't. It's Eddie's. The face abruptly turned away relieving Thurley of the task of finding pupils in the glazed, opaque eyes. He inched away from the mistaken glass ordering another drink.

—No offense, man. The voice had moved from its stool and was now close over his shoulder. You know how it is though, everybody out here trying to get something. Just didn't want no mistake. Thurley listened without looking up, nodding slightly when the voice nudged him. Finally he knew he must speak, that he must say something or the eyes would cut into his back.

—I understand . . . it's nothing. Forget it, won't you have a drink? The eyes made no response, nor the voice, yet Thurley felt clearly and distinctly the man's reply. He felt it in the pit of his stomach.

The hand reached out, long fingers of the same unreal glowing flesh wrapped round the glass, thirstily Thurley thought, as if they drank before the whiskey reached his mouth. The man smacked his lips loudly and grinned. —Thanks Boss, you're all right.

They were side by side now. The albino stranger talking rapidly, passionately in a dated bebop idiom. Not only this language, but his worn hipster clothes showed him to be vintage. Thurley noticed all these things, his shabbiness, his lisp, but most of all the pure ugliness of the man's face gutted by pimples and scars like craters in the garish light. His disgust was aroused by this ugliness, by asthmatic sniffing and wheezing between sentences as the albino labored to say something before the catarrh up from his lungs thickened in his throat forcing him to spit down between his legs. The fitful sing-song voice, the human weakness and need that forced the man to serve up his unpalatable being to other men frightened and excited Thurley as the dish was pushed towards him.

—It ain't nice out here is it, man. It's even hard to breathe. I mean look, every cat in here has got his bag. A bag, that's what life is, a bag. Born in one, carried out in one. Spend the rest of the time gettin' tied up in others. Everything's a bag. Take my friend Eddie for instance. Eddie's a smart cat, but he got so many bags he don't know where to begin. I try to tell 'em, there's only one thing for it. But he just keeps fighting off one so he can get in another. All these cats in here. Ain't one of 'em that ain't in a bind. They's all in that big black bag, and that's enough to kill 'em. You know what I mean?

Thurley nodded, watching as the white aproned bartender mixed a drink. Thick arms, shadows accenting the twisting cordlike veins, violently shook the tin container and clear plastic measuring flask shoved into its neck. Arms like carved black logs trembled with force, rattling the ice and liquid to a storm that foamed out thick and softly crimson from the strainer into long stemmed cocktail glasses. The albino was motionless, his little eyes now opaque, now squinting red and piglike as they caught the light. He seemed to be searching for his reflection in the dim mirror behind the bar. Something shadowy and elusive there behind the glittering bottles, metal and crystal fixtures that would relieve him if only momentarily from the sure image of his ugliness. When the albino spoke again, Thurley felt it was to this ghost, and because of that Thurley listened more closely.

—You know Boss, sometimes I'm scared for Eddie. There's only one thing for it, but he keeps fightin'. A man can't be but so strong. His tones were low, pathetic, he seemed to realize Eddie was the only way of telling his own story. He reached out and took the abandoned drink. His eyes met Thurley over the rim of the glass, smiling a chilly devil smile of recognition.

—I don't know where Eddie is. I guess he ain't comin' back. Why don't we go have some more somewhere else. The blatant, assured tone was of command. He had swallowed his own ugliness and Thurley could not refuse. It would all be simple now, he was obviously a weekend tramp in the weekend city with no place and no one to go to. There would be the night and morning would follow, then the albino would go shake the sun off his shoulders and disappear into another dark cave, sick to death of his ugliness till another like Thurley would come and receive it. They walked out together, touring from bar to bar till staggering and leaning on each other they wound their way out of the Negro district towards Thurley's hotel arm in arm.

—Brother, Brother. Thurley alarmed at the sudden intrusion stopped on the dark threshold of the *Empire Arms*. The albino straightened himself, pulling from him, sidling away from the vestibule door. All Thurley could think of was please no trouble as he extended his arms to steady the listing figure of the drunken albino. Groping in the immense distance between them he suddenly realized his own state.

–Please no trouble. A man had emerged from the shadows. Please no trouble. The man ignored Thurley, moving straight towards the albino who collapsed in his arms.

–Brother, are you O.K., man? He was so intent on holding up his friend that he didn't notice the white man disappear behind the vestibule's outer door. Thurley watched through frosted glass as the two figures stumbled gutterwards, the albino doubled over, dragging his feet, and the slim stranger hunched in the effort of supporting him. He could only see blurs of movement, something that seemed one body violently attempting to sunder itself. From the dark huddled mass a pendent bulk lurched three times, long, hard spasms then slowly was lifted upright. In slow motion one shape sagged slowly to the concrete, lolling dizzily in a slumped sitting position supported under the armpits by the other figure. Slow, methodical movements, exaggerated and prolonged like some surreal ballet. Thurley felt the rising and falling of his own chest, the damp glass pressed against his forehead. Something squirmed warningly in his gut. Both men seemed now to be sitting quiet and serene on the curb. Nothing to fear. No trouble. Suddenly the pane of glass separating them was cold and officious. With a feeling of shame and embarrassment Thurley flung open the door and stepped into the cool night.

–Is he all right? The stranger glanced up, but didn't reply. Thurley knew there was nothing to say, but the knowledge only made him more anxious to speak.

–I didn't know he was sick. One minute fine, walking with me, then he heard you calling, and when he turned around, it was all I could do to keep him from pitching down the steps.

–Just leave us alone, will you please, mister?

–Aw Eddie, he's all right. He's my man. Bobbie baby is swinging. Brother's speech was cut by a series of rapid hiccups.

The sharp, explosive sounds wouldn't stop, and he gasped for breath while Eddie beat on his back with the flat of his hand. Finally after one long spasmodic heave, he was quiet; his chin dropped to his chest and his arms dangled loosely between his splayed legs. Running down his pasty face were tears of exertion.

—Brother's not going anywhere tonight mister so you might as well shove off. He paused, glaring a threat, —Does he owe you anything?

—No, no, nothing. I'm just concerned that's all. He seemed a nice fellow. The two men measured each other in the streetlamp's half-light. Thurley felt cornered, caught. As if some raw, blazing light had come on exposing him. But he could see no more of his antagonist than the vague slim form he had discerned through the glass.

They are tableaued in the arc of a streetlamp. Hotel façade in background. Thurley takes one step then halts peering down at the albino slouched in the gutter. Drunken singing floats out of the night. Thurley kneels and retrieves Brother's cap from the sidewalk where it lies half-in, half-out of the streetlamp's yellow arc. The stranger accepts it, giving the soft felt quick swipes with his hand, then turning it, pats and shapes the material, his fingers extended into the crown. He covers Brother's naked pate and rises fully conscious for the first time of the white man who sways and totters above him.

THURLEY: Are you sure he'll be all right?

EDDIE: As O.K. as he'll ever be.

THURLEY: May I do something to help? (Silence as Eddie looks deliberately from the gutter to the white man and back again.)

EDDIE: You don't get it, do you mister? You just don't get it at all. What a fool you look like standing there asking if you can help. You've already helped him enough. Now get outta here before a cop comes along and we get arrested for bothering you.

THURLEY: You don't understand.

EDDIE: You're right about that. I sure don't. That's why I'm here with my half dead friend in a gutter, cause I don't understand. Why you won't leave us alone. That's what I can't understand. He can't go any lower, there's nothing left to do to his soul so why won't you just let 'em die, let 'em at least take his body to the grave without the prints of your lily-white hands all over it. Go away.

THURLEY: (Moving back, shaking his head.) Please, listen to me. That's not the way it is. I haven't come to prey on him. I want nothing from him it would hurt him to give.

EDDIE: It wouldn't hurt him to give anything. He'd give it all for another drink or a smoke or whatever you had to offer him. That's why he's dying, why he's . . .

THURLEY: No, no, that's not true. We wound up together because I'm like him.

EDDIE: Because you're hungry and the price of nigger meat is cheap.

THURLEY: Watch him, he's trying to stand up. (Both grab at the rising albino, steadying him.)

BROTHER: Hey Eddie, stuff and booze don't mix or I ain't as nasty as I used to be. (He hiccups once.)

EDDIE: Shut up man, shut up and stand up straight. We have company. Get your hands off him white man.

BROTHER: That's Bobbie-baby. Bobbie's just giving his man a hand. He's my ace.

THURLEY: How do you feel?

BROTHER: I ain't bad, but it's kinda hard to catch a breath and my heart's going like a bat outa hell.

EDDIE: Get your hands off him! (Eddie jerks Brother away from Thurley, shoving the white man's hand from Brother's chest. His own arm recoils.) Filth, white filth.

BROTHER: Eddie, Eddie, what's wrong with you man? He's only trying to help.

EDDIE: He's helped enough.

BROTHER: C'mon man, come out your bag. I tell you this is my friend. (He leans, or rather totters towards Thurley. His arm goes around his shoulders. Eddie steps back, glaring at them both, a single vein palpitating wildly in his forehead.) —C'mon Eddie. (Brother circles his free arm towards Eddie in an expansive gesture of reconciliation.) —Brothers under the skin man. Bobbie's all right. (A policeman appears from the darkness. Tall, thick bodied in blue.)

POLICEMAN: What's going on here? These fellows giving you any trouble. (The men separate, Brother drawing towards Eddie.)

THURLEY: No officer, everything's fine.

POLICEMAN: Well, let's get it off the street. These niggers know where they should be after dark. There's room enough in that nigger heaven down there. I suggest you go indoors, sir. They're not to be trusted, one minute grinning at you, the next putting a knife in your back and their paws in your pockets. I know 'em like a book. You fellows shove off. (He disappears out of the arc.)

EDDIE: Your friend has nice friends doesn't he, Brother?

THURLEY: He spoke for himself.

EDDIE: I didn't hear you contradicting anything he said. Let's get out of here Bruv, before he comes back. He won't be so nice if he finds us still here bothering this gentleman. (He spits.) God, sometimes I wish for that knife, and a row of fat white backs.

BROTHER: You're in that crazy bag man. He don't mean it Bobbie, he don't mean it at all.

EDDIE: If you believe me, mister, if you believe that I hate you to the bottom of my soul, you'll be as close to the truth as you'll ever be. (Thurley stands motionless in the light's glare. He only blinks watching as words are flung like stones at him. A whistle blows. Eddie grabs his friend by the elbow, they move off quickly, slouching towards the shadows. A cat meows, there is a clatter of garbage can lid falling. Whistle again. They are almost running. Brother looks back once, halting momentarily to disengage his arm from Eddie's and pull his cap down on his head. They disappear, and Thurley turns slowly back towards the *Empire Arms*.)

An uneasy sense of foreboding made him shudder as the reality of that evening slipped away again into its limbo. Thurley felt the damp glass in his fingers; he stared down at the wet ring it left on the marble. He knew Eddie was coming home soon because Brother had told him. Of course Brother had found Thurley another time back in their own city. Brother was down on his luck and finding the good doctor was a windfall. He almost lived at the professor's house after Eddie had gone away, leaving only on mysterious two or three day jaunts, but always like a cat, there on the doorstep one morning when Thurley cracked the door to gather in his milk.

When they talked, it was about Eddie. His face and the throbbing anger visible in his blood wouldn't leave Thurley's mind. It was a thin face, almost like a skull; eyes had glowered at him from pits dug above the cheekbones.

The old woman lay gazing up at the ceiling. Nothing stirred for the room's one window was shut and the hall door had been locked since the night before. It was dark in the room, dark and close with a faint smell of old rags and dry crumbling plaster. Martha's head lay propped on a pillow, slightly inclining towards one side, towards an invisible shoulder somewhere beneath the bedclothes. Although she was alone she frowned, a sullen, tight-lipped frown, and her brown eyes smouldered as if she was scrupulously ignoring someone in the sombre room.

Morning had come, Easter morning, yellow through a nick in the thick green blind but received no recognition from her. It meant only that Bette would soon be at the door asking in her meek, tentative whine, if Mama was O.K., and could she get Mama anything, and are you ready to get up. It meant the room would soon be flooded by yellow light, that she must begin to stir the barely perceptible bulge beneath the covers that was her body. Some mornings she had to scream. Had to drive that whining voice from the door. –Mama are you all right this morning? Voice so full of tenderness, love, hoping against hope there would be no answer. The key would turn slowly in the lock. They would burst in singing and shouting. Throw the blankets back and laugh at her wasted old woman's body. They would rake Gene's shaving things from the dressing table, throw out the old shoes locked in the cupboard. That was all she had. Shoes of her dead lovers. What they had sweated and bled in. Eugene . . . Eugene! Come here boy. Why don't you put these things away like I tell you. You'll have the whole house smelling like a gym. Look, look here everybody what I found. Two dead skunks. Wonder how they got in the house. Bet your brother Eugene brought 'em in his pockets. Boy, get these barges outa this house. I want you to wash 'em tomorrow. I don't care how many games you have to play. And if they're wet you better not put 'em on your feet and wear 'em outa this house. You need to stay home some time anyway. Your brother Edward isn't out running like a wild Indian everyday, and he still manages to live. Stop that pouting now. You look like a big baboon standing there with your lips poked out. Don't start that either cause I ain't feeling sorry for you, no you'll get no sympathy from me so just get 'em out of here, just get 'em out of here, just get 'em out . . .

–Get out, don't you hear, get out . . . I'm not dead yet.

–But Mama, Mama, Eddie's here.

–Eddie?

–Yes Mama, Eddie's back, he's downstairs, just got out of a

cab. Oh you should see him Mama. He looks so good. So straight and tall. Hurry Mama, please get dressed, you know how much he wants to see you.

–Eddie . . . come back. The woman grappled with her confusion; hazy, shifting levels of reality refused to form one distinct world which she could enter. Don't just stand there you fool, open the door, come in and help me. You know I'm a cripple and can't do for myself.

The blind shot up. Before the old woman could raise herself or protest she heard footsteps bounding up the stairs. Her daughter was helping her; between them the pillows were set and her back raised into a half sitting position. She stared into the open doorway still blinking from the sudden burst of light. Over her shoulders long gray-brown braids hung down like little girls'. The dingy flannel nightdress had come open at the throat, and as she slowly twisted, for an instant the sun highlighted the hollow and curve of her neck making the skin soft and smooth again. Through the doorway her lover would return; she bit her lip to make it stop trembling, to assume a smile or frown because Eddie was home.

His head dropped on her bony shoulder. For a moment her arms went around him, feeling only warmth, the hard male back. Hiding her own face, she felt her features scrunch into the wrinkled monkey mask with its years etched so deeply she could read each line. But tears, squandered too long, then dammed longer would not fall. Her voice was breaking, but gruff as she pushed him away.

–You're trying to crush me for sure with that big head of yours. Looking at him, into *her* eyes, seeing the sun gleam on *her* brow still smooth drew the tears dangerously close again. You been gone a while haven't you son? Are you better?

–Yes, Mama, I'm better.

Her eyes were hard, even cold as she listened to his answer. Almost like looking through him, they shifted, searching for some sign, for an indication of truth beyond his voice. His hands, his nose, the open-necked shirt and tee shirt peeking through. Like him long ago after a bath. Standing nude and shivering at inspection, and her voice, are you clean? Ears, armpits, nostrils, between your legs?

—It's good to be home for Easter, Mama. She shifted in the bed, her light body like a leaf rustling.

—You can see I ain't ready for you yet, Eddie. You go on back downstairs and let your sister make me decent. Least as decent as I can get after all these years. You go down and wait in the living room.

—Sure Mama, sure I understand. But you're beautiful Mama, still beautiful like a young girl. He reached out to touch her cheek. She watched the hand float towards her, the long fingers shaping themselves to the contours of her face as it came closer. She drew back, and it dropped, the shape disintegrating, fingers limp, motionless on the purple spread.

—None of your foolishness. I won't have you telling lies the first minute you're back. Now go on downstairs boy. Bette, get my things, and shut that blind, you trying to burn out my eyes?

—Hurry, Mama, please. *Her* eyes in his pleading face looked down at her. Full, moist, deeply set beneath his eggshell brow. She heard him go slowly down the stairs. Almost tiptoeing, as if afraid to waken someone. Now he's quiet, now instead of before when his crippled mother might have been sleeping. Bursting in here, full of nonsense, of old, worn out lies that make me sick to hear 'em. Lies, lies, lies. I'm all right Mama, and I know good and well in a week he'll be with them hoodlums again. Ain't I seen it before. Didn't his father have the same lies. That Brother and the rest of 'em. Always so polite, always so nice. Hello Mrs. Lawson. How are you today Mrs. Lawson. Hope you'll be feeling better soon. And why, just so they can come here for Eddie, and for her, for her too. As if I didn't know. A whore. I don't know how many. Even that ape Brother probably, grinning all the time in Eddie's face. They must all think I'm blind. Well, I'm crippled but not crazy. Nothing wrong with these eyes.

—Bette, shut that blind.

—I did, Mama, it's almost closed.

—Well close it all the way. I'm gonna keep these eyes girl. They still work fine even if the rest of me is dead, and don't you forget it.

The two men sat silently in the small living room. Eddie slightly flushed on the sagging cushions of a sway backed sofa with springs just noticeable beneath the skirts of its rose-flung cover. Brother fidgeted nervously in a straight backed wooden chair. Outside on the back porch a puppy yelped; there were thuds, bumps and a scratching sound as it flung its body, wildly straining at its leash, driven almost mad by a stranger inside the house.

—Do you know what they call it, Brother?

—Teddy.

—Just like the old dog.

—Yeah, Bette said that was what your Mama wanted to call it. Mrs. Lawson sure loved old Teddy.

—What a fat old bitch that dog got to be. Dragged her belly along the ground. And always fighting. Last time I saw her she had her eye half torn out.

—That's the way she died. That big old sore still raw and ugly when they found her. You'd think an old dog would know how to stay outa the way of automobiles.

—Maybe she was just tired. Besides, Bruv, we're getting old and look at us, we aren't any smarter are we? Brother replied with a half smile, then turned his head to gaze through a window. No traffic on the gray asphalt. Dumferline Street. Beyond, the ground rose steeply towards the railroad bed. Spring weeds filled the hillside, shades of green and gray with sudden flecks of tiny white flowers and goldenrods nodding higher up the slope. In fall it was brown. Stiff, dry stalks the color of ancient parchment. Like needles as Eddie remembered through the window, slowly swaying or loud and brittle when he marched through, snapping them down, clusters of dead flowers that disintegrated at his touch. They rattled, shaking themselves free of some last crumbling seed pod, a colorless leaf or stem. With broken arms or necks they leaned earthward as Eddie tromping through delivered a *coup de grâce* with his manlevelling club. Snow would come and then flying down the hardpacked path on sleds or garbage can lids or just plopping butt or belly down and down, down the slope. Coming home damp, numb, shivering at the oven and her angry voice and blows across his shoulders. Get outa those wet things. Is paying doctor bills all I have to do for you brats? Look at these jackets. Ruined, just ruined. That's it, and this time I mean it. You're not stepping outside till the last snowflake is cleaned off that hill. Just look what you've done to my floors. And always tears, ours, hers, and the next day down, down, down again. Some days, summer or spring days, hiking along the tracks on the hillside. Close as we could get to the country. Filled with grasshoppers and flowers, even trees that blossomed and sometimes bore sour cherries or tough green apples. Just walking. Stopping when we wanted to wave at a train or chase some sound in the high weeds or just climb a tree to see where we'd been and where we were going. The tracks ran past a ball field. Just before, we had to cross a forbidden trestle over a busy street then a straight stretch of tracks high above the field and factories. In a vacant lot between the ball field and McKutcheon Brothers was the Bums' Forest. Profuse with trees and weeds growing in the shells of ruined warehouses. Flat stones ranged in circles, ashpiles, tins, grass pressed smoothly in man-size depressions away from the bare trail, and everywhere glass strewn on the ground. In some places layer after layer deep into the earth of broken glass in a hundred shapes and colors. We always stopped to stone from our perch any whole or only partially ravaged bottles. Sometimes the crash of rocks bright against the littered glass would bring angry shouts, even a bleary eyed derelict cursing or threatening to chase us. Once a black bearded old man in a thick army overcoat pelted us in return, stamping his foot and bellowing as his missiles went awry, futilely bounding into the fields, yards away as we made faces and laughed. In the daylight we would sometimes explore the forest. Unexpected bits and pieces would turn up. But at night when we were allowed to go to a ball game, it was always run, run as fast as possible through the trees and shattered walls, hearing the glass crunch like bones under our feet as we dashed towards the smoking lights of the baseball field. But even as we dashed, Eugene, Brother and I with hearts pounding, I remember hearing them sing, somewhere out of sight, the strange, husky singing of winos.

—Brother, do you remember, a long time ago, that old bum throwing stones at us? Brother stopped wringing his hands, and when his face turned from the window, he was grinning.

—Sure man, I remember that old fool, I told you and Gene we oughta wasted him. Remember how you made me stop after I almost knocked his big head off with one of them stones from the tracks? Boy did those babies sail. I coulda killed the old punk, him standing there tossing rocks like a blind man. Half them boulders he threw he could hardly lift.

At the first tap on the stairs Brother's face changed. The red, albino eyes darted around the room, and he shrunk into himself as if he could disappear beneath his cap peak pointing down and his tightly pressed knees pointing up.

—I think I better go, Eddie. Mrs. Lawson don't like me round here. I understand and everything, so don't you feel bad, but I just better go. He was leaning towards his friend, every joint of his angular body forming a tight V. A stick man and only the tip of his buttocks on the wooden chair's hard front.

—Don't talk silly, Bruv. Of course you're welcome here. This is my house too, and Bette's.

Brother's voice was low, almost a groan. —But I wanna go, Eddie. From the porch the dog's yelps were still furious, but becoming hoarse, and his paws scraped less against the wood. On the hillside the goldenrods stirred, glorious as the sun shone. Cars had begun to pass intermittently up and down Dumferline Street. Eddie thought that if he learned to count the methodical tap-shuffle sequences on the stairs, he could always tell how close she had come and how far she had to go. He rose and went into the hall, patting Brother's shoulder as he passed his chair.

—Someday I'm going to kill that pup. Someday I'm going to strangle him with the end of his leash. He won't shut up till we bring the fool in. Eddie can help me, girl, you let him in. Mother and son faced each other in the dark hall.

—Brother's here, Mama. He met me at the station.

—Brother Small! Eddie felt her thin arm stiffen as he half guided, half supported her into the room. Haven't wasted any time have you? Like you didn't have none of your own to meet you. Didn't tell us a thing, but made sure he knew. Wonder she isn't here too.

—Mama! I knew Bette couldn't come, that she had to be here with you. And if I had let you know I was on my way, you would have worried the whole time. Besides, I just wanted to surprise you. I promised last letter it would be by Easter. And that's today, Mama. I wanted to surprise . . .

—I'm too old for surprises, just like I'm too old for lies. You go sit down now where you were and stop hovering over me like some mother hen. The back screen door slammed behind the dog as he bolted through. His paws raked across the linoleum as he bounded, twisting round in circles, falling and rushing, stopping and starting all at once. One last swirling curvet, rearing and up and down like a tiny horse and he dashed towards the old woman's chair, ears back, tongue lolling, his tail busy as a windshield wiper. Disregarding the stranger he nuzzled his dappled rust body against her soft chair, his heaving belly and one forepaw stretched along her steel braces.

–Get down, fool! Where's my newspaper. There was a howl as the pup bounced back from a swift downward blow. He shied away, then slunk out of range, tail between legs, as the old woman brandished a long, hard roll of newspaper, ragged at the edges and frayed along its seam. It sniffed Brother, then Eddie tentatively, still dragging its tail, one eye always on the rolled newspaper which slowly the old woman lowered. No one spoke and in a moment the pup was gaily nuzzling into Eddie's lap.

–The little fool. Eddie watched his mother's face. Her hair was up now, severely pulled back from her high forehead. She seemed owlish and shrivelled, the old-fashioned, steel rimmed glasses covering so much of her face, the bridge pinching her straight nose, the lenses like blank, indifferent moons over the thin line of her set lips.

–He's just a pup, Mama. You shouldn't be so hard.

–You know all about that don't you, Miss. About being young and wild and hard headed. You know how to look for pity too, don't you? I made many mistakes, and all of them because I wasn't hard enough. I'll make more if I live another day, but they won't be for the same reason. Edward, do your friends always keep their hats on in the house?

–I'm sorry Mrs. Lawson. But you know how I am. With a head like mine sometimes people get offended if I take my cap off. I just stopped long ago taking it off altogether except when I sleep or it gets knocked off ever since I gave up the hope of growing hair.

–She knows, Bruv. C'mon Mama. You know how Brother is. Don't make him feel bad. It isn't a sign of disrespect, we all know that. And you never minded before.

–This ain't before, young man. And it is a sorry sight to see *my son* in *my house* putting his voice over mine. But I'm an old sick woman, there's nothing for me to do but sit still and listen. At least I won't have to listen for long. There was a day when I thought I'd always have a man's voice, be it husband's or son's to take my part. But now . . .

–Stoppit! You know you don't mean what you're saying. You're just upset this morning, and it's probably my fault for bringing on too much, surprising you like this. Now you have some coffee, Bette, get Mama some coffee please, and me and Brother are going for a walk. It'll give your nerves a chance to settle and let me stretch my legs. We'll both feel better. C'mon, Bruv, let's go walk up by the tracks, it's a bright day and the rails will be shining.

–Good-bye, Mrs. Lawson. I know you're glad to see Eddie. I'll be seeing you some other time. He dawdled behind awkwardly in the doorway, turning his cap over and over in his hands. His horsy features, the pink irises of his albino eyes, the pimples, the lisp as he formed his words doubled and trebled their ugliness. The need to touch, to express what he felt, just to hold another still rather than send him reeling back from the milky ugliness held Brother fixed in the doorway. His lower lip hung, his eyes were glazed over with a thin, opaque membrane. Only the puppy shooting after Eddie as he cracked the outer door roused Brother from himself, made him stoop and catch the rust and white spotted animal to turn it back. Its tongue dabbled wetly against his hands, short, playful barks broke the stillness. Brother shoved against the heaving sides and furiously wagging buttocks, overturning the supple body as it flopped into the middle of the room. As the door slammed he heard its simpers and whimpers, its scratching on the door and Mrs. Lawson's angry voice repeating, –Fool, fool, fool.

–You still tired, Eddie? Eddie didn't answer immediately, intent on the sound of their feet crunching in the gravel along the track bed.

–Nothing so lonely as a long stretch of empty tracks. They came together and disappeared off in the distance, almost incandescent, steel polished to a silver gleam by countless wheels reflecting the sun. At the end of the long level stretch, the atmosphere seemed to dance, like a patch of light seen through a flame, wiggling, rising and falling the steel rails merged with a sunspot. Warm and dry now, dust coating his shoes, Eddie thought of rain, of small closed spaces choking him.

−You feel like going as far as the ball park?

−Sure man, as long as you ain't tired. They trudged watching the sun play off the tracks. It was not quite afternoon but the sun seemed very high. It was still spring heat, benign and life bringing, not the sun that sapped and parched, not the sun that was for Eddie the symbol of endless adolescent afternoons groping in a heavy, blinding light.

−Mama looks just about the same, and she doesn't seem to walk any better. If only we could get her interested in something. Just get her to go outside, try to walk up the street. He talked to himself, not looking at the other man who answered anyway.

−Bette gets her on the porch sometimes. It's just been getting warm enough, but I've seen her a couple times already. Brother kept one hand full of rocks, ricocheting the gray stones off the rails with the other. They struck with a loud clatter, sometimes raising a spark, sometimes just bouncing in lower and lower arcs across the tracks. The weeds in the field below were almost waist high. They had been cleared in some places leaving plots of bare earth where cars or trucks were parked. All the trees were gone. Eddie wanted to say something. He knew Brother was hurt, but there was no answer to the vicious ringing of stone on steel that resonated in the air.

Below, the Bows' sprawling shack still stood, the only house on its side of Dumferline. Its weather-beaten boards were lousy with soot, heavy black coal dust that had settled in clouds over the field, when the old steam engines coughed and puffed. None left. Only the clean diesels like bullets cleaving the air. Across the gleaming rails a tall orange crane, regardless of the holiday, slid on an invisible track along the skyline. When it stopped, a long boom arm swung in a lazy arc over the partially constructed factory it fed with huge chunks of concrete and bundles of girders. On delicate strings ponderous vats were gently lowered, lengths of steel clasped in magnetic pincers dangling from cables, bits of straw in a bird's beak. The machine towered over adjacent rooftops; if there had been trees, it would have dwarfed them also. It would brood over the skeletal frame through the night after all human activity had ceased, its stillness in the moonlight never detracting from the animal life it assumed during the day. In fact it seemed more alive because it slept. Eddie wondered if it would be visible from his window, if its gaunt profile like a crooked cross could be seen at night in the haze of flashing industrial neons. FERGUSON'S BLDG. SUPPLY CO.——MC LEOD'S——KRAUSS AND LEECH INC.——STALLEY'S. What new name would blaze on this building? They had glowered beneath a rose, lime and cobalt blue haze on sleepless nights as he gazed through the window beside his bed. Then a train roaring, rattling as if dropped from a great height down on the tracks then just as swiftly swept up again. The old engines whistled, sometimes they left thin trails of white smoke, floating luminous in the darkness. On one one day. On one one day—on one one day—on one one day churned by the wheels.

–Whatever happened to Henry Bow? Brother's forehead creased, he tossed one more stone high and far towards the sun. He remembered Eddie fighting Henry Bow beneath the water tank. Henry had whopped him good and I had to just stand and watch cause Henry could whop us both at the same time if he wanted and two on one wasn't fair anyway. That Eddie sure has some funny bags, even when he was a kid fighting Big Henry Bow like that just cause he said something, just cause he put Mrs. Lawson in the dozens, but Eugene whopped Henry later cause I squealed, then Henry whopped me one day, taking my cap too cause he found out I squealed, in the alley with nobody watching, him on top whopping shit outa me till he got tired. Sure I cried. I wasn't no sissy, but hell it was easier screamin' from the first rather than being like Eddie and trying to fight gettin' in a few licks that just made Henry madder and coming like a bull or ape or some black ugly animal taking little, skinny Eddie apart. Took my cap too, the one I liked and he knew, so he peed on it the black bastard, peed on it and buried it somewhere on the hillside. I could have killed him but better just to start crying and take low than getting him madder and I ain't got no big brother to whip Henry and keep him off, just Alice, just Alice who Eddie always liked and I knew and she liked him but scared and fighting each other always instead. What's Eddie asking now. Henry Bow I remember him, that old shack down there that's what made Eddie think but after all these years and he ain't never mentioned before that name Henry Bow, yes I remember all about Henry Bow with that crazy daddy of his that shot them robbers, Shootemup was what he was called, Sam Shootemup after they came to rob him Sunday cause he sold liquor and wasn't supposed to that day so he had lots of bread that day and they came sneaking down out the weeds two cats thought they could scare the old man, and that he couldn't tell the cops for being afraid they'd take him for selling booze anyway on the Lord's day so down they snuck and like I heard it, he saw them and when they comes in the back door, all the old wood creaking he would of heard them anyway less they waited for a train, a long noisy freight, so there he was just sitting behind the counter all that bread and booze right there but he was waiting and they got nothing but a blast of buckshot and as I heard it told he said I'll give you bastards five to drop them icepicks and get your asses off my property fast as you can go cause I'm going to give one barrel then another straight up your buttholes then Sam laughed and started counting one-two-three and you never seen niggers hauling butt so quick—wham—wham that buckshot spreading out and smoke and niggers screaming he said two punks I never seen before but ugly, boy was they ugly, a yellow one and a big black but both lost all their color looking down that fat mouthed shotgun and lickety-split off they went so I heard Mister Bow tell it and ever since Shootemup's they called it where you used to be able to get booze on the Lord's day.

—Sellin' bootleg whiskey somewhere I bet, just like his old man.

—I can just see that big bully pushing rotten booze. Did you ever notice, Brother, how his hands were always black, and the back of his neck, and shirts? Lot of guys sweat, everybody sweats, but Henry sweat black coal dust. I never forgot the dirty words coming out of his mouth and that look he gave me, like he just knew a skinny runt like me would have to take it or at best go tell my big brother like I was a girl or something that had to run home for help.

—You still was crazy, man. Henry was just too big. You shoulda run off and bricked 'em. I'd have helped you. We'd have killed that big punk, or at least taught him to leave us alone. Just cause his old man shot some hard-up niggers.

—Those dirty fists coming down on me. It was like slow motion. I saw him raise each one, then watched it falling closer and closer. After a while it was like watching fireworks, shooting up, bursting then trailing sparks back down to earth somewhere far away. I didn't even feel it after a while. Just the dirty fist up flashing then down like rain.

—Gene whopped his big ass good when he caught 'em.

—You shouldn't have told, Brother. I had finished with Henry. It was enough; it was over. That time I didn't need Gene to help.

—Sometimes I wish I hadn't. But that's cause of what he did to me over in Carter's Alley. I wish Gene woulda whopped him after that. I remember thinking down there on my back with him whalin' me I had already had my laugh and he was gettin' his last and I wouldn't get no more.

They were standing above the Bums' Forest. Brother knelt to tie his shoe. A train was rushing up the tracks behind them. It was only a tiny red box down the silver threads, but already the rails had begun to sing. Brother turned to watch it grow, to feel terror as it rapidly increased in size and intensity, its roar louder and louder, its form attenuating, growing sharp and distinct like a blunt shark's head with a grim chrome smile. Something aimed at him, headlong, bleating as it rushed across the trestle, some beast shrieking, thundering that for a moment would take him trembling into its entrails. He shook as the train rumbled past, part of its roar, its speed, vibrating in time to its tremendous surging rhythm, a rate his human frame could endure only an instant.

For Eddie it came like a black cloud, shutting out everything—the stunted trees, the weeds and bushes just springing into green life, the dilapidated foundations and brilliant plots of glass embedded in the earth. He was plunged as he looked into night, into chill autumn, a leaf falling night when a fire burned red and yellow under a close, black, starless sky and winos were singing.

Why me here searching? Why not Eugene, who is bigger and not afraid and who is loved? Why do they sing? Why do they drink and break the bottles and scatter glass here where they must sleep? And the other things they do, here where they must sleep. Why? Surely they smell it too. And why so close and yet none of them can I see? Their singing, why is it like nothing else? Not boys or girls, men or women. Not like the choir at our church or Mama when she sings or what I've heard on the radio. Like nothing, but some of everything. If I sing too, will I be less afraid? Will they call me to come join them around the fire over there behind that wall? Should I call him? Daddy, Daddy, Daddy. And if they call should I go? What if the old one in the army coat . . . why did he try to lift such huge ones? If him there and me close a huge one dropped on my head, crushing, mashing me down like the bottles, in pieces mashing me down. Daddy, Daddy. Why me searching these dark woods? Surely Eugene better, he loves Eugene. Where is Brother? Brother would come with me, he loves. These deep woods. Pee smell and piles like dogs only bigger, and I know it's not dogs. Wine smell and sick smell, pools of it slicking the grass or dried on stones and the glass. I feel glass through my shoes, jagged, sharp, cutting edges. Pressing always up and through. Why does it hate, why does it thrust its sharp nose into my feet? They would know me here. All the ones we've stoned. Jumping like cats from the grasses, shouting things at us. In that big army coat. Like squirrels springing out, chattering. Smash, smash. Daddy, Daddy. Mama wants you home. Please come Daddy, please come.

It was gone, and suddenly again the sun shone warm on his back. How deep and cool a shadow can be. How deep so you can walk miles in a small one and be so tired so quickly. The train seemed to suck away all the air. Eddie breathed deeply after it passed, glancing over his shoulder where Brother and the shadow had been.

On one one day . . . on one one day . . . on one one day . . . on one one day. The orange crane was still. Easter only a half day, the ants had descended from the skeleton. Beyond, the neon tubing was gray and lifeless, the names barely readable if Eddie hadn't known them so well. On one one day . . . on one one day.

—Hey Bruv, what you thinking about, man? You're like a statue standing there. You think if you pose long enough someone will take your picture?

—Just thinking man. Sometimes I do you know. Things make me think more than people—things like trains. People's confusing, can't do nothing but think what they said or what they're doing and forget most of that, but things is different. I can think about a train. Trains is always trains.

—Or a cap?

—Yeah, Eddie, you know what I mean. He patted the cap on his head smiling. And I can think about you too, Eddie, I can think about you. He lifted his cap, slowly mopping a ring of sweat from his bare head with a gray wad of handkerchief pulled from his hip pocket. Eddie watched as the sun glinted from Brother's hairless dome, his albino ugliness the sun lit so profusely.

—I'm going home now. Capped again Brother nodded in reply still squinting from the sun in his eyes. As Eddie tromped along between the gravel bed and the high swaying grasses, Dumferline Street seemed far away. A million miles beyond the tops of weeds stirred by a weak breeze. It seemed a shame the trees should have gone. Those few scraggly fruit trees and the one or two others he didn't know the names of. After that certainly the rest too. It was funny to think of himself, hiding out there in the weeds. Had snow ever been there? Behind him he heard stones smacking against the tracks.

The Buick rolled steadily along. Thurley didn't drive fast, but he had style behind the wheel; he gave the impression that he had been driving big, dark limousines all his life. It was a borrowed car. From his more than comfortable income Thurley had never been able to save enough at one time to afford the down payments on a new one. Always something else first, a trip to Europe, an antique, books, gin. For a moment he thought of smiling Hermann. What kind of car did he drive?

The weatherman had been wrong. *Mild showers may daunt the less hardy marchers in today's Easter parade.* Such a smiling voice, with overtones and undertones of the deadliest sincerity. *A high pressure front blown down from Canada will collide with the lingering warm front that has brought us such sunny blue skies. All the Eastern seaboard is threatened with shower activity.* Rain, rain go away Little Bobbie wants to play. He mashed the accelerator, dipping out and around an old Ford, straddling the broken white line as a burst of power shot the Buick forward. Handles like a roadster. Cruising now, a long empty stretch before him. Thurley lit himself a cigarette from the open pack laying on the padded dash. Everything worked. Lighter, horns, wipers, automatic windows, air conditioning, radio, even the square faced clock with Roman numerals. It was like Noonan, big, efficient, a world all to itself gliding along perfectly performing its functions. *Impermeable.* Everything Thurley wasn't. In a flurry, he pushed every button, turned every knob, the car tooted, heated, windows eerily rose up and down around him, music blared, the windshield was squirted and wiped, an aerial climbed then shrunk within itself. Like a child I am he thought, fascinated because the world was once again at his fingertips. Thurley relaxed as he smoked; the car relaxed and sped quietly down the tree lined highway.

Two-forty-five. He would be there before three-thirty. That left time for a few drinks with Al before they went to the chapel. It was a good idea, something that for once he was really glad he had thought of. An Orthodox Easter service. Music and pageantry, what he knew he couldn't resist. Something stuck deeply into the past, something that would reward the intense participant with a giddy headlong flight backwards through time, along one of those fine, vital skeins that like interminable veins feed the present, making it more than madness, making him more than an occasional partaker of its insanity. He had invested so much of himself in finding these paths, in following the mysterious lines as they sunk into obscurity, into the abyss of time. Somewhere, all he could visualize was a cold, brilliant valley glazed with a light crust of snow, all lines converged. The past in one bold epiphany would manifest itself as an answer. Perhaps a footprint in the immaculate snow, or a throne dazzling across the frozen depression. These were his own fancies. He believed that if he proceeded far enough there would be a man, a beautiful, soft-spoken man whose eyes were acquainted with grief, who knew sorrow and had experienced grace, who would welcome him with a hand round his shoulders saying simple things, pure, simple things that exhausted all further inquiry, all disquiet, final, truthful things as they glided back and forth through immense silences. Thurley dreamed of an eternity of these walks beside the soft-spoken stranger. The books he read, and the words he wrote were preparation.

Did he believe? The books, the countless manuscripts yellowing somewhere, each the humble seercloth of some proud beginning. Why do you do it, why do you bother then? Sometimes in the middle of the night the persistency of this question as he lay fully awake and keenly conscious was more horrible than the most elemental nightmare. He had no devils to fear. Once, an edge of his imagination bordered a realm of monsters and devils. It was perdition's scourging pit, the Baptist hell of his father and mother. He had still trembled reading the *Portrait*'s description of hell as a college freshman at Harvard. He was embarrassed and ashamed, never mentioned it to anyone, but still trembled when alone at the hell of his fathers. But that was all past, the devils had become ridiculous or benign, like gargoyles who grimaced and leered from medieval chapels. He was no longer superstitious, but how different was blind superstition from his harrowing disbelief in the mechanical, everyday activities of his life? That overriding doubt and scepticism sapping the vital fluid from his life which he brooded on just as surely as an ascetic priest on sin. Was it conscience?

He swerved to avoid something dead on the roadside. Was it conscience, simply the old religious fear disguised out of recognition to something less unreasonable, less barbaric and shameful? *The agenbite of inwit.* He smiled, letting the quotation drain off the building intensity. *Quotation is as close to reality as they can get.* Was it Stendhal, or was it some aside in the Rostovs' glittering salon? Perhaps even Flaubert. Sounds like a conclusion he would come to after leafing through his trunk of *idées reçus*. A buffer zone now. Peaceful, easy bumps in the limbo of other minds. No sharp edges here. No inbites. Did he seek it on purpose? Did he stock his mind against these threatening moments? Not a cloud in the sky. Do I believe? They must know what they're talking about. Weathermen are scientists aren't they? Conclusions only from facts. Their data resting on reality. Not like us, not the wily humanist playing with the clay of his own utterly malleable, therefore utterly deceptive and unreliable being. I started with a question. I have rallied round me other minds, other words. I am filled to overflowing with parentheses, with qualifications, with ambiguity and paradox. And what have I become, what has become of the question posed? It is armoured, it is inviolable. Hung up by the multifariousness of the *me*. The whine of self-consciousness like Bartholemew's hats that can't be removed. *How shall I presume?* London? Rome? Athens? New York? Cambridge? I have posed a question. Surely it is presumption to suppose I may pose. The inkling of fear. The high fence of hubris stalling our progress. Do I dare, do I dare? How poignant the cross. The seven words. What did he really say? And were they not questions of the highest order? Lost, lost, forsaken is the only answer. To pose an inviolable question. The pride we have in the untampered, the stark, resounding question that refuses to be tainted by an answer. The fierce oscillation ringing between null and void that destroys our souls. And if I pose it, intensely, in a posture of supplication it is enough. I am done, finished, complete. Is it conscience?

I am placated by a weather report. Oh what lovely trees. Serried ranks, a skirt of sunlight beneath, translucent, girding the bare bottoms. How I would love to face the truth, just for a moment, even to be blinded on the tenth step and pitch backwards even into a lake of fire. What could be worse than this machine? Enclosed in its steel guts, propelled by explosions I can't feel the heat of or see the fire. Sometimes it's like looking over a battlefield. Everything dead, stinking to heaven, my task at best to loot the dead, finish the dying.

Of course I believe. How crystal clear it is. I have converted, seen the light, my salvation on the solid rock of the Church. Chartres in the moonlight, its exterior lace. Its towers two unshakable ramparts. The beads, the Hail Marys, the lucid, picturesque ritual. All there in black and white. How many angels on a pinhead? The fierce soldiers of Christ, Loyola's standard cracking like a whip. Cardinal Guevara in his chair. Something strange about the perspective. Like awkward medieval painting, Cimabue, Cavallini, planes of reality distorted or ignored, the Cardinal almost dumped from his chair into the profane living-room. A son of the Church. After so long returning to the bosom. How she would turn over in her grave, her Baptist grave in the family plot. There's always been a Thurley. Dates barely readable on the oldest stones. Magnolias, mimosas languid over-head. The grass and dainty flowers sprinkled through it. It wasn't the veranda any more without her sitting rocking. It curved around the big white house. Flat, slightly sloping from the walls towards the spacious lawn, a wooden railing with carved white posts like attenuated urns, posts that were loose and wobbly at certain spots from being leaned on, sat on or climbed over by generations of Thurleys. How many mint juleps consumed in its shade, how many hours logged in the gliders, sofa, chairs and rockers ranged on their appropriate woven mats. Thurley was there, more easily than he thought possible, out of the speeding Buick and home again, home again.

—Bobbie, Bobbie, look at those knees. He jerked up, im-mediately standing at attention in his bright sailor suit. The blue shorts had ridden up his chubby thighs and his blue socks had rolled down to coils around his ankles.

—Look at you Robert Thurley. We're never going to make a gentleman out of you. His fat cheeks blushed, timidly he raised his ruddy arm adjusting the white collar and matching cap. Now you get in there right away and tell Hattie I said to wash those knees and tidy you up. My, my, if I hadn't known you were mine, I'd think you were one of those little niggerboys from down the road with that dirty face and those knees. In there right now Master Robert.

He marched up the long white steps, and into the house call-ing for Hattie. She came, the model for Aunt Jemima Thurley always thought of her later, bustling and black with that half anxious, half smiling moon of a face peering down at him, always going straight to the root of whatever he was feeling.

—I heard your Mama scolding, Master Robert.

—I didn't do nothing, Hattie, I was just playing. He was on her knee, the strange powder, sweat, clean calico aroma settling around him like a cloud. She was soft too like a cloud, like jelly as he squirmed but really didn't mind the hands and the cloth rubbing his dusty legs.

—What was you playing, Master Robert, coal miner? She smiled down at him, the big moon sinking, showing little eyes that twinkled and teeth. He giggled back. The cloth tickled; her pillowy boobies when he leaned back bounced unsupported beneath the bright calico.

—Sit still li'l mister. Where you trying to get to? He wiggled and laughed outright now, beating a tattoo with the insides of his bare knees against her fat thighs.

—Hey, hey, hey you little rascal, I ain't no rocking horse. He leaped down running out of the kitchen through the long, high hall prancing as he ran trailing the floppy white collar still on a cloud.

Thurley slowed down for a turning, fascinated by the clicking sound as he blinked his signal. Everything automatic. It was actually ages since he'd driven. Always taxi cabs. Taxi cabs like hotel rooms that sometimes gave him that sick, lost sensation in the pit of his stomach. This outing had come to him like a storm. Why not? Haven't seen Al in ages, Easter's a holiday, and the special service was supposedly spectacular, well worth the trip in itself. He didn't need these reasons at all. He had the idea and decided all at once. A positive idea. That alone was startling, exhilarating. But as he came closer, he had to admit it was to Al that he was making his pilgrimage. Not so much spontaneous, but the inevitable climax of a slow subtle process. How often had he thought of Al? At the strangest times, and in a variety of totally disassociated situations over the past few years Al had incongruously popped up, and because he had been involved in other things at these moments, disappeared without allowing Thurley any time to elaborate on his sudden presence. Probably some sort of defense mechanism Thurley thought, to release pressures Al symbolized. Like a dream . . . probably a name for the Freudian paradigm, a word that would explain it, would explain Al . . . a little psychology a dangerous thing . . . dispose of Al. I don't even want to do that, that's not it at all . . .

Just a few more miles, a matter of minutes. Al's cloister. Had he found peace? Teaching music here on a quiet campus. Would that dispose of Al? Thurley drove slowly, cautiously now, repeating to himself the directions he had memorized, watching for road signs, landmarks. *A big Dairy Queen on the corner. Two streets then left. Sycamore, left again. Row of big brick houses, well kept lawns and shrubs, mine a white shingle stuck on corner after these.* Funny the details people pick as substantial, as identifying something or themselves. The car seemed to purr now, Thurley half expected it to be sleeked with a light coat of sweat as he climbed out shutting the door with a solid thud behind him. Still sun shining, birds singing *Oh what a lovely Easter day* as he shuffled up the short flagstone path feeling the kinks quietly protesting in his legs. Like flowers, groups of people, mostly families, sizes assorted from Papa Bear to Baby Bear strolled along the broad, grass bordered pavements. Not a cloud in the sky as he knocked.

Al. Al Levine all aflutter, embracing Thurley, pushing him to arm's length, pulling him close again, his hard little hand and arm furiously pumping clasped into the other's. Like a little boy neatly tucked into his three piece suit, Al made happy, indistinguishable sounds as he hustled his friend into the livingroom.

—Something cold right away, right. Just sit down, there, on the sofa. He moved, pointed and talked with a disarmingly fluttery precision, disappearing and returning with a wooden tray holding two tall gin tonics it seemed all in one motion and breath. Like a nerve end twitching, soft, fluttering Al.

—Wonderful Bob, just wonderful, not another ounce or wrinkle since last time. Here's to you. Cheers! Half a frosted glass tumbled down Al's throat. His Adam's apple bobbed, and he spoke again as soon as his throat had cleared. What a day, what a day this is. You sure can pick them. Ha! It took Easter to bring you though, three Easters in fact, this is the third you know. But that makes it lucky doesn't it, at least between a couple of old occultists like us. Easter! Good old Thurley doesn't miss a trick does he, what an upstage, what an upstage. His twangy but distinct pronunciation of each syllable got the most out of words. Talking to Al was always being on the edge of your seat, listening to a verbal flow that reminded Thurley of a tennis game. The words bounding back and forth, and just one player, Al, serving, returning, bing, biff on both sides of the net. That quick side to side movement straining the neck muscles Thurley felt when he listened could only be compared to a spectator on the edge of his chair enthralled, breathless, hoping both that someone would miss and that the words would never stop bounding high and white across the net.

—You're here, Bob, you're here. It's like all those words thawing to life after the long, cold winter in Paul Bunyan. You know that story don't you? Why it's part of the American heritage isn't it? I mean myth, real myth or as close as we've come —Paul Bunyan, Natty Bumppo, Johnny Appleseed, Mike McGraw, old John Henry, no let's not forget John, last but not least breaking his gut driving rails. Cried the first time I heard that story. You know it don't you? The race . . . that nasty machine laying rails behind him. Chug, chug, like a shadow creeping up on poor black John. Pow. His heart broke. Just couldn't be beaten. Just wouldn't lie down, couldn't stop, so Pow. He took another deep drink, swilling the liquid visibly in his throat.

—Bob, Bob, you're here. He stood over Thurley, a gnome, a

pixie in his immaculate Ivy cut suit. Always dapper, always neat and clean. He stood close and silent for a moment as if he knew he was being appraised, posing, paying his respects to Thurley's admiration. Same Al. Small, delicate, below the neck groomed and tailored almost out of existence. Tight and hard. Even the small head sharp and angular seemed somehow like a knot. His hair was thinning but jet black, still long and slick. It looked painted on his skull, and his eyes and the accentual lines of his face seemed limned with the same hue. Sparkling eyes. Coal black, pricked with spots of light. Nothing could be whiter than his cuffs, shirt front and collar.

–I promised myself to be quiet today. To listen for a change. I want to hear about you, Bob, if it's possible, if there are words I want to hear them. After fixing more drinks Al sat quiet and attentive on a donkey saddle stool, the tray between him and his visitor already dyed with circles and half-moons from the sweating glass.

–Funny how it all comes rushing back, all the closeness and understanding like a kick in the pants driving me right to the edge . . . why Bob, why the long silence between us? Like a pit, or a big hole. It's urgent now, Bob. Everything's come back since I heard from you and started to really believe you were coming. And Easter . . . only you could pull that off. Thurley on the third year returning.

Between them the frosted glasses teared. Like tired horses sweating while their riders, invigorated from pushing them half to death, chat coolly in the shade. Al was like a little boy now. His slim legs in tapered Dacron trousers crossed oriental style as he slipped to the floor from the scooped saddle seat. Something from Greece Thurley remembered, brought back by Miriam, Al's wife, how long ago. It was covered with boldly patched quilting, primitive and striking against which Al reclined his neck and narrow unpadded shoulders beneath the open suit jacket. A boy now, exhausted at the end of a day of hiking or ball playing, content to sip his Coke and listen to the tired voice of any old man who would tell him an old story.

—I'm glad we only have a little time, Al. I really don't have much to say. Just the thought of saying anything begins to fatigue me. And besides how many original or entertaining ways are there to say nothing?

—Probably quite a few. And for some you can even earn a living. Thurley traced a pattern in the carpet. Quick gins began to demand their due. He felt a momentary giddiness, then the start of a soft, gradually unfolding languor.

—You remembered how I like my gin and tonic. Al laughed in reply, tilting his delicate head forward, pouting his lips, blinking both eyes several times in an exaggerated expression of *how could I* or *are you kidding*. Thurley smiled back conscious he was thinking his unrelated, private thoughts aloud. He paused, trying to pull the fuzzy pictures together, then went on more consciously, straining for something both natural and reserved, something controlled that would filter and select through the gray mass of his impressions, to give freely but not all. He searched not only for a place to begin, but for a reminiscence of where they had ended, how far they had been accustomed to penetrate each other's skins in that prolonged intimacy of a few years before. Al was an equal, no talking up or down, all words, feelings legitimate. But even here there were fences and no trespassing signs deeply set. What could they share on this Easter afternoon? Ghosts? Even these brought up problems, because nothing ever really dies. Here they were in this room to prove it.

—How are Miriam and Sandra? That was safe enough, the divorced wife, the beautiful child, so sensitive, so wide-eyed, full of love and belief that stroking her soft brown hair was like running his old man's hand over a razor.

—Miriam's fine so I hear. Still at Sarah Lawrence. The kid writes me once a month. Sweetest letters. God, what a beautiful kid.

—And the music? Thurley was repelled by his own crudeness, his stupid, probing tongue as soon as the question dropped. Why that, why mention the only other thing Al cares for in the world after bringing up the picture of his lost daughter? But the question brought a sort of relief to Al's face. His narrow shoulders seemed to broaden, and he sat taller and straighter. His tone was almost coy.

—Surprises, surprises, Bob. He wrung his tiny, smooth hands. Strange how white and smooth the palms, the backs covered with coarse, jet-black hair. Like a monkey from the back. Al's one visible defect, the flaw in his sculptured, immaculate compactness. Easier to make little people perfect. To mold the limbs and the small faces delicately in miniature. But even there slip-ups, something dangling, out of place, or covered with thick, black hair.

—Something new, something big? Thurley let his enthusiasm run away with caution, he clumsily plowed through what might be open wounds if he had inferred incorrectly from Al's elfish reply. But no, Al continued to grin, to act out a boy carrying a hot, delicious secret.

—Later for me, Bob. I'm saying nothing about me till after I've heard you. You're the guest. You've rolled back the stone, arrived here Easter afternoon upstaging the Messiah. Thurley Anesti. I'm just ears till you finish.

Thurley glanced down at his watch. Less than an hour. Al's insistence began to bother him a little. He hadn't come to confess. He knew that now, sitting in the strange room, Al squatting before him. He wanted to ask him to play something. Chopin, Mozart, something sane, clear, exquisitely structured, like the little girl with flying pigtails who used to run through Al's ramshackle cottage in Maine. That little laughing girl with all her bones showing. No secrets there, and yet something that could never be known, not because it hid itself or refused to be discovered, but because her beauty gave of itself more deeply than anyone could ever ask.

—I'm a fool. A blunderer as always, Bob. Please excuse me. I didn't mean to push, to try to turn you on and play you like I would a batch of L.P.s. But you know how it is. So close so long, then nothing—poof. Suddenly three years later I get a card, and a few days after, you come sailing into my living-room. I wanna know something, anything. It's like an ache, I wanna get inside you, or at least if it's been too long, close enough to feel the old warmth. He rose, his slim legs straight-ened, the creases of the miracle fabric obediently falling into place. He paced about the room, short and for Al slow steps, stopping here and there as if he were unfamiliar with his sur-roundings, examining them as if they were new and great im-portance was attached to a correct and thorough appraisal of the room and its objects. He rubbed the back of a puce overstuffed chair, scanned the elegant eighteenth-century bindings tightly packed in glass bookcases, scrutinized each knickknack and souvenir adorning the flat surfaces, moved his feet tentatively through the thick piled rugs scattered on the floor. His longest pause was in front of a large ink drawn nude over the brick fireplace. Her form was outrageously soft and round. Not cur-licued like a Rubens but thick, maternal curves all thigh, hip and bust like a massive Maillol bronze. She was reposing, sub-missive, an odalisque. Cascading to a scruff of wiry hair her stomach protruded like a melon; her eyes were fixed on this curve.

The march around the room said what had to be said, Al was a stranger too. There had been during the interim nothing to displace fear, loneliness and pain, what they had felt before when together, and what was still all that mattered. Down, down tumbling. Each mask topples, the actor bows, but out beyond the blinding lights there is silence, not a sound, not a cough or a grunt. Panicked, another mask is discarded, still nothing, and another, another, another and another. Still the blank, soundless void. Bowing and stripping the actor dies. Still nothing.

—I'll get us another. Al took a long time. Thurley found him-self staring at the naked woman. Her thighs, breasts, the bush like an animal climbing her round belly. Thurley the bride-groom, Eleanor on his arm. They had gone South to the Thurleys' ancestral pile for the wedding. It was all a show, a sad, desperate show, and as folly succeeded folly, drink succeeded drink, until Thurley had felt the accumulated horror like a wild beast in his guts that must be drowned.

Bride and groom stood on the veranda. Behind them through long French windows the sounds of genteel drunkenness and excess lilted. A hired band, mostly violins, played undaunted till the backs and underarms of their thin white coats were dark with sweat. Waltz after sickly waltz. Only once had some old aunt asked for a country dance—the musicians and other relatives grudgingly complied, the company dispersing to line the four walls of the ballroom each face daring the other to submit to the music's jaded syncopation. Thurley drew his bride closer, letting his hand slip low on her waist till he felt the enormous flounce of her thousand crinoline slips beneath the white lace begin. The music stopped. Only muffled voices drifted from behind the tall windows. Thurley could hear crickets and the dry rustle of the thousand slips. Her gown glowed. Not solid and yellow like the lightning bugs blinking out over the lawn, but like a ghost or a white shadow, amorphous, shifting. Other white ghosts glided in the darkness. Couples taking advantage of the intermission to stroll in the balmy night air, to dry sweat under their evening clothes, or just to find a tree or bush. The musicians stood in a white clump apart, lit for a moment in the glare of a match, huddling close as if for warmth from its tiny flame. Red points of burning ash bobbed.

Eleanor was bored and tired. She wanted a cigarette terribly but she would wait, at least till tomorrow maintain the image unblemished. What foolishness. So this is the Old South and I am by proxy a Southern belle. Proud of it too, they are. This big white barn of a house, the liege lord Thurleys and their guests. Honey, this, Honey that. And always my lovely Bobbikins there to cushion the blows, to spoon-feed them to me and me to them. A regular trooper he's been, held up so well all along. Grinning at the bitch who cooed to me. What a lovely girl, she said, my, my, Bobbie, I'm afraid us pore li'l country gals just don't stand a chance if all the Northern ladies are like Miss Eleanor. His arm around me all the time, yea though we walk, fear no evil. His arm squeezing, so tight I can't breathe.

—It's a beautiful night isn't it, dear? Thurley leaned closer to smell her perfume and hair. Couldn't be closer to perfect. He pointed with his cocktail glass, slopping out a silver glob that splattered loudly against the floorboards. That was my world once, Eleanor. Nothing existed beyond these acres of finely nurtured Thurley grass. You can't see very well now, but you must have noticed already how beautiful the grounds really are. Li'l Bobbie's Garden of Eden. But sans apple tree, sans Eve even. I guess it just goes to show. He used a loaded deck. The snake was enough. The itty-bitty worm in the grass. Look at 'em sneaking off to the woods. Back to nature they go. Can you imagine any man putting his hands on those powder puffs? Down here we make real women, soft, affectionate, one hundred per cent fluff balls. Could any man in his right mind believe there's anything under all those buttons and bows, that there's flesh, live warm flesh. He emptied the glass too quickly, gin dribbled on his chin, —ha, my cup runneth over. I'd better be careful, mustn't spoil our nuptial rites, disappoint Hymen. The bridegroom cometh. Wish this thing I thee wed . . .

—Stoppit, Bob. You're drunk. She didn't raise her voice, just said it calmly, professionally, in the almost bored tone of a physician pronouncing death.

—Aw, Baby.

—Take your hand away please, I can barely breathe. She twisted from the circle of his arm, the white dress rustling as she stepped away. It's getting late isn't it, I mean a decent interval has elapsed since the ceremony. Let's get away from here. I've been on display long enough.

—Not yet, Baby, please not yet. I wanna tell you about my garden, about how it used to be before that nasty old man with the sword drove me away.

—You're not being funny, Robert. I'm tired, I just want to go to bed.

—To bed, to sleep, to dream, that's the rub. Never could figure that out exactly, but then it doesn't matter. I mean the whole speech is simply an elaborate question mark. It's not time yet, the night is young and so are we. He grabbed her hand raising it as he slipped his other arm around her waist, trying to coax her stiff body into a waltz. Swaying and humming he wanted to guide her into the flamboyant steps he rehearsed. Tra la tra la. The night's young, Baby.

She pulled forcibly away. —I'm going, Robert. If you don't want to make us both look foolish you'd better come with me.

—In dulcet tones my Aramantha beckons. Trip, trip fantastic toes. Spinning wildly, his whole body fluttered into a solitary dance. Alone on the veranda he spun and spun, oblivious until the French doors were flung open and on a cloud of cheers, jeers, salutations and ribaldries his name floated out.

Hurry up now it's time, hurry up now it's time, hurry up now.

They had been loaned the master bedroom. The others kept him downstairs an hour, pouring drinks down his throat, patting and pulling, tendering innuendos with each handshake, interminably winking and pinching. The wedding party partaking of a foretaste. Protesting mildly Thurley floundered in the mass of friends and family, somehow for a moment resting on his mother's shoulder, her old throat circled in lace, the green pin an eye on her flat chest, so close he wanted to cry, but quickly whisked away, someone pumping his hand, some arm around his shoulder, the soft, pink smell as he was nuzzled, a wet, flacid imprint on his cheek, violins, the crystal layers of chandelier climbing one another.

Hurry up now it's time.

—Where is Eleanor, where is my bride? Staggering, he made his way into the high, long hall, shedding the voices, hands, the bright, dancing lights of the ballroom. Like emerging from the bottom of the ocean, or being stripped naked he thought alone suddenly in the throes of a valiant effort to maintain his dignity. Look at those knees boy, look at those knees. He would never be a gentleman, never. She must come clean me up. I'll sit still, I promise Hattie, I promise. Who had kissed him, that horrible, horrible kiss. Like death, a drowned woman puckering on my cheek. Never thought it would be wet. Always believed it would be dry, grainy, rasping like sandpaper or a file. There is nothing underneath. Dry, dusty there like old clothes or feathers.

He climbed the broad twisting stairs, slumping at intervals against the graceful banister. When he reached their borrowed bedroom, the light was out and Eleanor lay asleep, a thin sheet covering her nakedness. Like the gown the linen sheet glowed, but incredibly solid, a piece of marble into which had been cut the epitome of female form. All contour, curve and hollow abstracted, into smooth, hard stone. Thurley slowly undressed. As he bent to ease off a patent leather pump from his swollen foot, he was startled by the gown, ghostly white, standing in a corner like another Eleanor. He went to it, for some reason kneeling, pushing his face into the billowing skirts, listening to the slips like cellophane dry crinkling beneath. When he moved away, it toppled in a heap, the sound of silk like a parachute dying. Eleanor did not stir. She had one end of the sheet wrapped under her body and her arm held down the other. Thurley slouched over her, finally naked, perplexed and ridiculous in the moonlight filtering through an open window behind him. He tugged lightly at the crisp, cool material where it stretched tautly on the empty side of the bed. The sheet wouldn't move. At its touch on his bare back he wanted to weep.

—We'd better make it a quick one Bob, not much time before the big show. Al placed a tumbler in his hand. Thurley listened to the ice cubes bumping their glass walls like notes of a miniature xylophone. More than anything he wanted to say his wife's name. He wanted to pronounce *Ele-an-or* clearly and distinctly, nothing more, no story, nothing, just say the word.

But it wasn't just the word, and he couldn't say why he couldn't say it. Words had meaning, something solid to rest on, something which if ambiguous could at least be private and significant. Eleanor. If somehow it could be said in this room, said to Al, it would help so much. Al had a wife. He had lost her, and a daughter too. I said *Miriam* first thing—I asked Al about Miriam. Miriam's a word, Miriam can be mastered even if it's an unpleasant, even a painful task. But my wife, my Eleanor . . .

—Too much tonic in that one? Thurley realized he had been frowning, that Eleanor uninvited sat like a stone in the room.

—No, no it's fine, Al. I'm just a little distracted. It's too much all at once, the two of us alone, drinking together after all this time. Like the wind has blown a door open and it's sucking everything away and I can't close it. Just run round like crazy grabbing at bits and pieces before they're blown away . . . just scraps, pages out of order and half written. Thurley heard the wind, saw the door flapping, the air filled with paper. Somewhere in that snow of fluttering, swirling sheets was one written *Eleanor*.

—Eleanor.

—Whadya say, Bob? Al had been gazing again at the nude. He believed that he had heard correctly, that his friend had said *Eleanor,* but if he was mistaken . . . Excuse, me, I'm daydreaming too now, what was it you said?

—I don't even know myself, muttering, thinking aloud. Thurley concentrated on the second hand idly circling the black face of his watch. *Hurry up now, it's time, hurry up now. Please gentlemen, it's time.*

—What's happened to us, Bob, what's happened? We might as well be a million miles apart.

Was it conscience? Thurley knew some things had not been ironed out, would in no sense ever be finished. The night Al had come into his bed. The three of us, Al, Eleanor and I, romping, sweating, laughing in my bed that hot Italian summer in Naples. First only the laughter comes back; Eleanor's teeth flashing, Al's broad smile and short, nervous titters as she tickled his small, perfect body. I laughed too, loudest in the tangle of arms and legs and lips and teeth and eyes. How many ways were there to do it? Permutations and combinations, the sheets twisted beneath us drenched with sweat. Eleanor's witch hair stringy and matted with perspiration, the way she used her woman's body like a thing she could dispossess. Flopping, rolling, a wheelbarrow, a dog, a pair of scissors, a fountain spewing, and Al's perfect little body quivering, twitching, becoming more and more excited as Eleanor lost semblance to anything human. She dripped, crawled, padded on all fours, mounting and being mounted, screamed, laughed and flung her witch hair. Eleanor's woman's body, prostrate on the bed throbbing, her hands digging at the pulsing clump of her sex, the witch hair in her eyes, her eyes wider and wider, the purring sound deep in her throat, the pink lips opened and closed dripping. And as I doubled over in a corner of the bed, lost my seed, Al covering her, his perfect little legs thrashing like a swimmer, scrambled into her belly.

Thurley spoke. —Do you remember the night in Naples, the three of us? Al was wary, he knew that night was part of their silence. Thurley continued haltingly. It was my idea, remember, and you were afraid, you warned me, pleaded, even refused. You said I was drunk or crazy, didn't believe Eleanor would do it anyway if you agreed. You didn't believe it till the last minute, did you?

—No, you're right, sometimes I'm not so certain now it happened.

—Then you didn't try to go to her after?

—Of course not, she was your wife. That night was unrepeatable, set off from everything else. It was madness almost, but you, we, decided we could handle it. I wouldn't have dreamed of touching Eleanor unless you knew and approved, and of course I hadn't any reason to believe you would have approved.

—Well, there's something you don't know. I didn't really ever approve. I had no choice.

—Eleanor?

—Yes, benign, sweet, innocent Eleanor. How could you be surprised at anything after her performance?

But it wasn't just hers, I mean all of us together, laughing, enjoying the madness and impossibility. Once I got over the initial shock, I guess you could call it fright, I never doubted the closeness of us all. The marvelous way in which everything became valid, the way touching you or Eleanor was like touching myself, the way just letting go made us all so . . . so . . . I'm fumbling now, I can only recall how it was and try to find the right word, the word that would bring it back, make it happen again for you. I can just stutter really, and point . . .

—Al, Al. Still immaculate. Don't you understand, man, there was nothing spontaneous, nothing new or beautiful, just that woman showing me how helpless I was, showing me how strong she could be, and how I had no way to match her, even prevent her from destroying me.

—Eleanor.

—Yes, yes, yes. Eleanor. I laughed, sure, and after a point I really felt a part of something bigger, a force, a fury, I don't know what exactly, but as soon as it was over, as soon as the three of us were sprawled and empty on the bed, I remembered what I had been laughing and fucking away the whole evening; that it was Eleanor's hate, my wife's hate. She used you, Al, just as she did me. We didn't escape anything that night, we weren't free. She just wanted to show me what she could do to anything I called mine. She killed it, Al. That's why nothing can happen. Why we can't talk. He emptied the glistening tumbler. Al had turned away towards the window.

—But, Bob, why didn't you say something? Afterwards, anytime, before now? It was just a night. We're grown-up people. Nothing changed hands in that silly bed. It was madness, wild, drunken madness. You've let it fester that's all, made it become something it wasn't. Hell, Bob, if she was no good, why would you sacrifice what we had for her? What we had was natural, it was true. You know now for sure Eleanor was sick, real help-needing sick. You did what you could; you held on for as long as any man could without going batty himself. It wasn't your fault, you did all anyone could expect.

–Did I, did I? Maybe I did all I could, but it was what Eleanor expected and needed that counted. I wanted to love her so badly. I wanted anything in her to love. But she was closed, she was methodically, eternally shut away from me. And still she wanted something. I guess she hated me because I tried so hard, because I showed her no matter how hard anyone tried, she could never love or be loved. So she learned to enjoy the slam of the gate down on my fingers when I tried to touch. She would let me get close just to enjoy that sound and my pain, keeping some hope alive, letting me think there was still a chance, then slam. She learned my weaknesses too. The ways I couldn't reach her if I wanted to, and if she would allow me. She used her body, she let me sink in till I could go no further then beg for more, beg, beg, beg, till I bled, then she would begin to rail, say I didn't love her, didn't want her, that I played around, then abuse me, say I wasn't a man, that I was still a big fairy, ask why had I lied, why had I dragged her into a lie of a marriage, abusing, taunting till she laughed, wild, wild, laughter that made me want to die. And if I wouldn't come to her, she'd threaten me, say she'd go out in the street and take the first man she could find. That she'd have his baby, black, brown, red or yellow if she could. Eleanor, that was my Eleanor.

–It's getting late, Bob. Would you rather stay, just sit here a while and talk.

–No. I came to see a show. My story just gets more and more boring. I've been over it so many times it's become incredibly tedious. I wonder how we had patience enough to play out such dull, predictable roles day after day. At the time I even began to pray for some overwhelming catastrophe, some violent explosion, for a demon to enter our lives. Somebody who would stir the pot a bit, somebody who wouldn't be afraid to throw in a handful of blood and guts. So intense when it happened, me wrapped up, full of fear and trembling as if I was involved in some mysterious drama, something resolvable, turning on the most minute perceptions and intuitions. If only I had stepped back, relaxed and read the episodes like I would a bad book. I could have seen how banal, how clinical and poor our lives were. Her moving steadily towards wanton insanity and me creeping back on my hands and knees to little boys. Too pat, just too damned pat.

—Bob . . .

—Nothing to say, Al. Just recalling the days of yore. Do you have a cigarette; I want to coat my lungs, I want to give my mouth something to do besides bleat. I came for a show, not to give one.

—I want to hear you out. Will you come back with me after the service? You know I care about you, Bob. No matter how many times you've said things to yourself, it's not like really getting them off your chest. Give us a chance again. Thurley watched Al's nervous movements as he stood and prepared to go. He seemed wilted. Even behind the indestructible Dacron Al was a weary little dwarf. But Al would take Thurley's burden on his narrow shoulders. Al the de-wifed and de-daughtered would console his matrimonially bankrupt friend. Prince Al the Immaculate returned from the kitchen bearing in his eyes the woe of ages. His regal brow was furrowed, he strode, all melting remorse and sympathy across the field of languishing throw rugs insinuating with a grace beyond the reach of art his perfect arm around Thurley's plump back.

Was it conscience?

TWO

· · · · ·

Bette said: —Eddie would you like some more gravy. She slid her spoon into its brown thickness breaking the membrane which like dirty cellophane had formed on its surface. Some more Eddie, she repeated, neither louder nor more insistently simply the words again as she dragged her spoon through the shallow bowl and the thin film disappeared. Bette knew when she began preparing that the tiny Easter ham, two women size, would not make much gravy, nor would it seem a holiday its shrunken redness on the table for Eddie just home. She had be-pineappled its large plate, Libby's slices arranged in rows along the sides, and on its summit brown sugar crust and cloves. Still it had made less than a bowlful of gravy which she spiced and stirred and hoped Eddie would taste. Her brother had been so quiet. When he had returned from the hillside without Brother, it was as if he had been gone another year. Eddie seemed so tired, hardly spoke when he came in the door; just sitting all day till dinner time and then to the table. I was busy in the kitchen, but when I had a minute I'd go in the other room where he sat with Mama. Her in one chair, him in the other. The pup slept beside Mama and I almost believe them too sleeping though their eyes were open, Eddie's always far off out the window and Mama's on Eddie. I'd go in but saying nothing neither me or them it was like a little girl I felt and so silly just standing there in my apron smiling at Eddie till it hurt my face and everything went to pieces and I thought they could feel it and see it too, my face getting sore in front of them because I stood there saying nothing and uglier. I wish

I could have said something. But so strange when I'd go in, felt like I was interrupting them but nothing there but silence, not a word between them. Eddie I should have said how happy we are to have you home, Mama and me are so happy because it's Easter and we have you with us. If I had said it, maybe Mama would be still, maybe she would let me finish, and when she heard, not be able to say different or no. It should be me sometimes who says it. She speaks and because no other voice, what she says is true. I should say things even if she gets mad, even if they are things she doesn't want to hear. I would like to talk about Eugene. Brother can talk about anything. Stories about everybody—about DaddyGene who I barely remember, but when Brother talks sometimes so close, even closer than our real Daddy. Eddie too talked about Eugene and DaddyGene. I wonder why never our father. But I am not sure I could listen; how I can never forget touching him when he had no life. Across miles and miles for days it seemed I moved to touch him that one dead time. I cannot remember another touch, cannot believe he ever lived or held me warm in his arms. It must have been awful to see DaddyGene die. But different because they still talk of him. I am afraid Mama will shout, will tell me not to come in the room again because I stand between them in the way. She makes me know and feel things I wonder if Eddie knows how she makes me feel. It seems he must know with it so strong in that small room, that he would hear her too that way she screams always in my ear to do things and is silent. Bette she is shouting when I stand there Bette get out of this room and leave me with your brother. I felt it so strong he must know. And if he does why doesn't he say no Mama let her stay, why doesn't he say I love her Mama and came to see her too so let her sit with us. I know I must cook. I know I must do things but just let me sit for a moment, let him talk to us both. Mama we need his voice, we need to listen together, to stop the scream that holds us. Let him tell us about Daddy-Gene, about Tiny, about Eugene, and let Brother come too.

It will be like Christmas or a birthday party us all laughing and close, and songs Mama and . . . but Mama don't frown. I know you can't dance. I will sit with you while the others dance. I will be more happy than dancing. We can sing while we watch Mama. I do want to be with you more than the wild dance, we will sing Mama and watch. I am not lying.

Eddie heard her the second time she offered the gravy. He poured from the proffered bowl, wetting the mound of potatoes that had hardened on his plate. With his fork he mashed gravy into the yielding lump then poured again into a depression he had patted into its center. Bette watched him perform the familiar operation. Remembered how happy they could be with food. Not just special days, or particular dishes, but the high-chair glee of texture, smell and sound being devoured by the senses. Oatmeal throwing. Eugene finally huge over Eddie a whole bowl on Eddie's big head. Mama then yelling louder than Eddie and both boys up from the table and into the bathroom. Eddie got the hairbrush too and harder too I could tell as it hit splat, splat and soap in his eyes too as Mama washed out the clumps from his hair. It was then we were so close, and Mama always there and sometimes Daddy. Don't cry, Mama, I'll go down and watch, I'll see the mailman first thing and bring it up to you. Don't cry Mama, please don't; they'll be all right.

Eddie raised his spoon. To Bette it seemed to hang for ages, indecisive, wavering as if his arm was caught between tremendous invisible forces which nullified each other in one small pocket of vacuum. She prayed and he swallowed.

It goes down and how many mouthfuls at this table watched in this room. Bette's eyes, Mama's eyes, the eyes of dead Gene, of my father and eyes of the even longer dead some I recall and others even beyond death have watched. Is Mama showing me her day, trying to cover me with the dead emptiness of her life? Is this all there is Mama, this room and this silence? The pup sleeps at her feet. Bette is busy in the kitchen doing the little that keeps them this side of death. Is it to this I have returned? Is Mama trying to show me once and for all what I have to expect? She has shut me in a closet. There is no light, no air. A feeling I thought only came with death, with the heavy lid dropped and the earth in balls beginning to rain. DaddyGene coughed so much I asked him one day if I could help, if I could buy him medicine. He smiled, then laughed loudly with his head thrown back till the coughs began again. I remember the strong smells of him. What I loved to be close to, his thick shirts, the vest stuffed with pipe and tobacco, the hat of soft felt, high crowned always slick and cool inside smelling of leather and darkness when it dropped over my eyes. His smells so different from Mama's softness or my Grandmother Freeda's sweet, powder scent. Then more came.

—Come here you little rascal. The boy could feel the bones in the old man's hand as it wrapped around his shoulder. You afraid of your DaddyGene now boy. The air was stale with the old man's decaying bulk. His feet, too swollen for shoes, were wrapped in layers of ragged wool socks, and when little Eddie approached, their unwashed fragrance made a palpable ring he must enter to touch his grandfather. Gently in a gesture that was full of the knowledge of his own repugnance, the old man drew the boy nearer to his tainted presence. When his grandfather coughed, the boy shuddered, recoiling from both the violence of the rasping explosion and the tightened grip on his thin shoulder as instinctively the huge fingers dug into his flesh. I've been your Papa, you know that don't you boy. I've been as close to one as you've had. Help your mother, boy. You and Gene better help her. Eddie leaned his head against the old man's shoulder. For what seemed hours in the sour cloud, DaddyGene whispered things he couldn't understand into his ears as the boy stood trembling uncontrollably. At last the voice stopped, the hand was removed from his body, and he stood still. Harder and harder to go to his grandfather after that. Even the room came to be avoided. If he calls I will go, but only then. His dripping eyes that are open but sleep. The sound like choking or sobbing when he dozes in the chair. I go to the store for him. From a knotted handkerchief he produces hot, wet coins. I buy him Five Brothers Tobacco which he chews and spits in the basin I must empty. When I carry it I must be very careful. I always wait till the last moment, hoping that this time perhaps it will never fill, and I will not have to carry it to the bathroom. It swishes when I walk; I am afraid it will slosh out on to the floor, as it sways, lap up to touch my fingertips gripping the edges. There is no other way to carry it. A hand on each side, the bowl held out in front of me. I must watch it, for the redness dances in the bowl, and I must not spill it. The toilet is blood color till I flush it away.

He never changes the baggy trousers or the long sleeved undershirt, and he never moves from the chair. His long legs and bloated feet fill the room and the rattle of his breathing.

Even when finally the deep chair empty, I could not enter the room. I could not sleep till tired out from crying over Daddy-Gene's death and finally Mama soft into our room and the pills and the cool glass of water. Down to sleep. Down to sleep. I thought that feeling was only after death, but here Mama sits with the pup sleeping beside her, and I feel it in this room.

Eddie with a clatter that seemed to him malevolently out of proportion and entirely unvolitional replaced his utensil on the side of his plate after raising one forkful of potatoes hashed with gravy to his mouth. Bette's eyes had left him and she tried to busy herself with the tiny portions of ham, potatoes, succotash and coleslaw she had allotted to herself. His mother's plate retained only a grease smear from a tiny slice of ham Bette had served then hastily removed at a look and a gesture from the old woman. Coffee was all she wanted.

—Will you stay now, Edward? His mother's voice was brittle as the fork ringing.

—Yes, Mama, I want to find a job and make a go of it.

—What kind of job? There's only the mill, and they're firing.

—I can go back with the piano man till something else turns up.

—Moving pianos. You know as well as I do what that means. Sitting here, or in some hangout in the Strip till he calls if he ever does. A few dollars a week if you're lucky. Just something to keep you close to that gang of loafers who all call themselves working for the piano man.

—But he does come, Mama, and when he does whatever he pays is something I can contribute to the food money here at home. Besides it's all I can do till some better job turns up.

—Turns up, Edward, and how many jobs have you ever heard of turning up? You threw away the only good job you ever had. Couldn't stay away from those no-goods for eight hours a day. You could still be with the post office and not talking about sitting in some dirty pool room or saloon waiting for the piano man.

—I've told you why I couldn't stay at the post office. You just don't understand, Mama. The same thing day after day after day. I'd get up in the morning, and the first thing I'd see would be those sorting boxes floating in front of my eyes. I knew that if I lived a hundred years each morning they would be sitting waiting for me. More sacks would come into the room as we worked. Never a feeling of getting anywhere or accomplishing anything. Just sack after sack to be emptied and sorted down the proper slot. That would be my life, Mama. It was like a nightmare, like dreaming I couldn't swim and was suddenly dropped in the middle of the sea. I was caught, trapped, didn't have a chance. So much water around me. Sooner or later I knew I had to go under. Fighting just made the nightmare longer. I couldn't take it, Mama. You just don't realize what it meant to face those rows of boxes every morning.

—You're supposed to be a man, Edward. A man works; your grandfather was up every morning and Eugene though he was just a boy. A man does what he can and doesn't make a lot of foolishness for himself by turning things into something they aren't. You talk like a child. What do you want?

Bette whose wad of coleslaw lay forgotten in a corner of her jaw parted her lips as if to speak. But only her eyes furtive under long, lowered lashes participated in the dialogue. She wanted more than anything to say what was at times infinitely close to the precipice of speech.

We had all said the blessing together; Thank the Lord for this food for the nourishment of our bodies sanctified in Jesus-name for his sakeamen . . . Me, Eugene, Edward, Mama and Daddy when he was home. But DaddyGene never said it, and sometimes even ate standing up which made Grandmom and Mama so mad. I liked it then, all of us together sitting down three times a day. The blessing was written on the first page of our old Bible. I could say it before I could read and made DaddyGene laugh holding the book while I said it. This Easter Sunday there was nothing to say, just the three of us so long at the table till Eddie had finally lifted his spoon. He seemed to like the gravy, but it's getting cold on his plate. He wants very much to say something, but it's like he's almost dreaming or even like he's left the table to find something, and it's only my brother's shadow I see.

–There must be something more, Mama. When I heard the sacks dropped behind me on the floor, believing in something more was the only way I could go on with what I had to do. I'd tell myself there had to be something more than those dead thuds at my back and the slots waiting.

–It's getting cold, Eddie. The old woman, cut off as she still formed a reply, could only stare incredulously at her daughter's interruption. Involuntarily her brown eyes dropped to her son's plate. It *was* cold there, the white plate showing through as a border between each vegetable even though Bette had served him almost all of the succotash, potatoes and coleslaw. Each item was isolated, even the gravy over the slab of ham had spread sluggishly into a discreet solitary pool. She thought of plates heaped high, of men's laughter, their eyes and jaws devouring like bears. She remembered her heroes at the feast. Now her last son, Eddie, was poised over the meagre Easter supper. Cold. Cold. His shadow across the dish, him leaning towards her, a little boy again and almost he understands, almost he seems to be ready to speak. *Her* sad eyes, the delicate forehead you could see the bones so clean beneath. Come, come, son, she wanted to say if only he would . . .

–There must be more, Mama, there must be.

And he died there, halfway. Her lover would never return. Only shoes, only a worn razor strap still hanging on a bathroom nail, only his straight razor still shining on the bureau and the dark mug and brush. Asks too much, he asks too much. Can I fill another table, this flesh dry and bones strengthless, legs tied to cold metal. Can I rise, does he think I can wait for him. There is no breast to pillow his head, no soft lap where he may bow or sit. Can I even stand without the steel clutched tight in my hand. And is there anything to give even if I would give, even if I could forget, is there even time to wait again?

–Cold, Eddie, it's getting cold.

Something roared in the old woman's ears. It rose a crescendo of surging, deep throated sound. Like sea shells clamped to both ears the room possessed her in its blank ubiquitous rhythm. From some unknown source, far out of her own experience and reaching back to a dark communal fund of impulse she sensed the warning of this ocean sound. The deadness below her waist climbed inch by inch to turn her whole body into stone. It was only Bette's hands on her shoulders and the violent rocking of her body back and forth in her son's grasp that woke her to the sound of her own low keening—Nothing . . . nothing . . . nothing . . . nothing . . .

Eddie walked slowly down Dumferline Street. His head was bowed and he watched his feet, playing the old game of snake-in-the-crack, avoiding seams and splits in the broken pavement. Streets weren't fixed very often in his neighborhood so his progress was giddy and irregular as he side-stepped and strode like a wino, like he had seen his father coming home or in anger head for the Strip.

He remembered the other street. When he was younger and his father worked regularly, and they had moved for a short while into the little island of Negro families within the white sea of respectability. Eddie recalled his friend, Joel, who timidly from the others had slipped away to join the dark newcomer.

Half that street was lined by tall, prosperous trees, oaks and wide chestnuts oddly out of place because the sidewalks had begun to crack and large houses deteriorate. Half was brick, the other wood. When only white people had lived on the street, the passage from one end to another had been difficult, but it was a pleasant division reminding some how far they'd come and promising others a rich reward if they just kept at it. Regularly the wooden end was abandoned. No one came there to stay; it was rather a watering place, a station for the transient white families moving up along invisible threads of prosperity. *For sale,* then *For rent* signs blossomed predictably as the chestnuts at the other end. Almost everyone managed to move, if not to the brick and stone of Carter Street, then some other shaded street, road or avenue. But one day the stores and shops began to get too close. Too many strange cars were parked beneath the chestnuts, or blocking driveways. Privacy disappeared and Negroes moved into the wooden end. Everyone else who could moved out, leaving behind a few old people who were too tired to run, a sick, lonely widower who was too proud, and in the corner apartment building the permanent outsiders who hadn't noticed or didn't care.

Beneath the wide chestnut trees, Joel and Eddie had walked. Old Mr. Duncan had chased them one day with a broom. He had called Joel a sneakin' pink nigger, trembling and stuttering as he protected his buckeyes. The widower's porch had been painted again, a bright, tulip yellow this time. Not a brick was out of place or crumbling in his side of a terra-cotta duplex. His lawn was even greener than usual after the rain, its neat border of pastel flowers calm and formidable as a moat. He never spoke to anyone who passed his porch, yet his eyes missed nothing, and from his green and white wicker chair he silently judged. The Corries who lived next door to him were probably at Foxes Tavern getting drunk. If they got very drunk, they would return home and fight, usually icing their evening with a naked wrestling match, all the lights on and blinds up which Eddie and Joel had watched many evenings.

The wide chestnuts were a canopy, then the boys were beneath an oak with its peeling bark. Eddie usually ran up the alley when he wanted to meet Joel at the white end of the street. He would yell up from the apartment building's small back court where the garbage cans stood, hoping he would not run into old Mr. Pope, the janitor, whom Joel called Pops and who always looked at Eddie so strangely. One day Mr. Pope had ordered him to stay out of the court. Eddie had been afraid, but later realized the short, black man couldn't really order him to do anything. Next time he saw Mr. Pope he too called him Pops. The old man had turned away, muttering something under his breath, but after that never another word. Many times as he had been standing in the court waiting for Joel to come down, the Negro boy knew old man Pope's eyes were watching him. He would feel skittish, almost on the verge of running, not afraid of anything the old man would do, but ashamed of what he had done to Mr. Pope. Also those secrets he knew and used on Mr. Pope were secrets about himself and here, where the old man talked and lived with white people everyday, the secrets were in danger.

It was strange, how the trees made noise, yet nothing could be seen moving them. Walking beside Joel, trying to hide and forget till he was past the brick houses, Eddie wondered why he feared an old man and not these very trees under which he moved. Surely the old black man knew no more, nor could speak to the white people more plainly than these trees. In fact, who would listen to him; Mr. Pope too was of another kind, an impenetrable growing thing that neither dreamed, loved, nor remembered. These trees if someone knew how to listen would reveal as much. How Eddie had battered them with sticks to get buckeyes, shuffled through their leaves, carved his name and initials after dark into their thick trunks. Had they seen him crouched at night in the alley, had they seen what he did to himself as he watched the Corries. The trees were tall and surely knew.

One evening snow had fallen. A soft white layer over everything, creating fantastic shapes, making his walk home with a quart of milk under his arm something new. Everything had seemed smaller, a shrunken world, and intimate, a mystery shared that had made him closer to the loaded trees and padded sidewalks. As if everyone was black one morning, or white or any color that covered and completed the past. Church music, like bells at first but then his own church people singing. He had smiled feeling the soft snow blot against his skin. All away, all washed away, closer, nearer. Had the trees seen him then, that night they had dipped so low, and he had walked through a gleaming tunnel? Did they remember green now, and damply beginning to stir how close he had been to joy, how near to weeping? What could he tell the others when he had finally gone home? Yes, I've been a long time in the cold, yes, I have a chill, and you waiting all the time for this milk. But don't sit down, don't open and drink it, go out, no come out with me, there's something you should all see. Just come with me, you don't even need coats, just walk up the street, beneath those big trees full of snow, it's not like it usually is, not like the valley, or the shadow of death, no Mama, no Gene and Bette, it's . . . it's . . . But you set down what you went for and go stand by the gas stove.

His mother's sobs re-echoed in his ears. It was the sound of all despair, totally unanswerable, a sound whose sapless roots drained the substance of hope. Would Alice be home, would she want to see him? He had asked Brother not to tell. Again the same secrecy with her as with his mother and sister. Vaguely he sensed a common motive, something behind this trip home with which he conspired. In a way it was another Eddie, a shadow Eddie who had learned to live unseen. They had talks together, these two Eddies, and from the shadow much had been learned. Grierson had been right, the cure had restored some lost part, but could the shadow be lived with, did the shadow want to live?

Snap! Just missed the poison of that one. Slowly but surely it gets to be my time. Night comes. The air is different isn't it? I mean for you it probably doesn't matter much, but I have bad memories of heavy day air and sunshine that chokes. You see I was sick when I was younger. Always weaker and teased. Too soft because I let their nonsense eat me up. My brother was the worst, I guess because he was my brother and different because he was bigger, stronger and was loved. Not that she didn't love me. No, don't pay any attention to what just happened back there. She was upset. And at her age and in her condition (she was always strong before, tough and not afraid even when twins came too soon after Eugene and died, two more kids without a whimper of fear) it's so hard to do anything about what she feels strongly. I can understand that. Sometimes I feel like I'm in a glove, or a bag like Brother says. You must love Brother, no matter what else, you must love that ugly bastard. No, when she screams and says those terrible things about Bette and about me, it's just something boiling over that has to come. Better in fact that it does. It's her nerves, her feelings using her, like they've been used. She holds things in, so when they come, they have to be violent, tear their way out. I don't mind really. I thought it might be like this. It's Bette more than myself I feel sorry for. She's never had a chance. I helped make Mama what she is. I was soft and easy too long, she held me like she holds Bette now. She needed someone, I mean after Daddy and Eugene had gone she needed someone. So I stayed on and on, doing what I could. But she just got worse, and I began to understand no matter how hard I tried, I couldn't be Eugene, and when she was worst that's all she wanted, that's all that could help her. My dead brother. So I inched away, little by little. Bette was getting old enough to do what had to be done, and better too since she was a girl, and since nobody could do or be what Mama really wanted, I got away. But I did harm, I tried to keep it from her but somehow she found out. She always blamed the others, especially Brother; she didn't understand it was something that had to happen. A man just can't live day after day on nothing. And drinking, after a while you get sick before you get high drinking bad stuff and the belly ache and head throbbing when you wake up afterwards drives you nearly mad and you can't get any help because the thought of the stuff that's made you the way you are is sickening so you just suffer and the world won't turn off. One thing leads to another; what's it matter whose idea, or who gives you the first one, and before you know it hooked. And so what, there's nothing so big it can't be shut out, and after a while the world is only a dream. But sometimes I thought of Mama, and the dream got to be a bad, bad dream. It hurt my guts like drying-out days once did. One morning wind up in a cell, nothing to be had, they look at you like an animal and come to watch when it gets so bad you start climbing the wall. You beat your head on the stones, on the floor of that cage, you try to twist your neck off between the bars. But nothing breaks, nothing gives. Just them like in a zoo so you can't quite kill yourself. I remember how finally sleeping the dreams I had. And someone screaming Mama, Mama in my ear so loud I thought my head would split, and then it was just me in that cage, my own mouth going, calling her. You shiver and sweat and you try to sit still, but pieces of your body flop out and scrape themselves along a razor. You watch them squirming, bleeding and you know it's you and you feel it, and nothing so bad as when they return and crawl back in your guts, full of pieces of glass, splinters and stones.

So she had to know. And it hurt her. She wouldn't say anything. Just be sitting when I came in looking so old in that shawl and legs like sticks in braces. It was her eyes following me.

Why do we have to fight? Don't we understand all we have is each other? I can't believe it s the same place, not the same place as before. DaddyGene was so big in the chair, Eugene and I playing, Bette in the playpen sucking her thumb. It was different air, different colors then, as big as the world, but so easy to move in, to find things, to laugh or be quiet and alone. My little sister, Bette, all lumps and flaps yelling from her playpen, the rows of colored beads alive in her pudgy hands as she squealed and bounced so fast then plopping down on her lumpy seat and up again sometimes crying, sometimes laughing. We could make her cry or laugh, Eugene and I when nobody watched could play her like a game. We knew which strings to pull, which toy to steal, where it tickled and where she didn't like our hands. It was funny how easy she forgot. How she would always smile when we came to her, though we were ashamed and felt we wouldn't be forgiven. On our knees making faces through the bars she'd pat our cheeks, pinch our noses, kiss us till we made funny noises then stamp her foot and jump like a little monkey in her flannel all-covering pajamas with a lump and big buttons in the back. Mama calls her hussy and a whore. She said Brother snuck round the house, and she could hear them at night like prowling cats from her bed when they thought she was asleep. And said Bette had always been that way, that after her father and DaddyGene had gone there was no keeping boys from her fast womanish ways. Coming at night like cats—Bette cried still, she cried not because it was true, but because it was Mama who said such things, and there was no answer because Mama's words would never change. She was there, still there as always and never, never could she be denied.

Things she said about me. Not like about Bette, not warped, crazy things but like my own voice accusing. So why do we have to fight? Did I come back for this, did I go away, did I die for that year just for this? I couldn't expect her to believe quickly. Not after everything she's seen, surely she has a right to doubt, to wait before she opens her arms again. She is an old woman, so much of her life is dead. For her, when they said I was in jail, that I had sunk as low as she knew I had all along, I died. What we had before hadn't been much, no, to move even slightly from her was to destroy almost everything, but after the news, after the disgrace I put to the name of her dead, there was nothing. Can I hope someday she will forgive?

Eddie side-stepped avoiding a pit of nodding snakes. Their throats were swollen, forked black worms darted from bullet heads. How many nights down this street? How many trips along this broken path before a man was old? Stick ball here, a football spiralling perfect as a bird, then dying as it touched his fingertips, his crane legs for once taking the prize. He hoped so badly Alice would be home, that like Brother she would be waiting unchanged, even in the same clothes, as if time were never more than the space between a glance away and back.

He could tell Alice. She would understand how it hurt him to fight, how senseless everything was that kept Mama deep in her own pain.

Alice, do you love? As close as we come to understanding. Lights coming on around me. Same switches, but different hands. Beneath and above like at home, the dirt swatches from countless hands moving in darkness, going too far, falling short. And children who can't quite reach but try. Alice turning out the light. Mama turning out the light. The orderly in white turning out the light. The bartender on turning the light. To sleep they all meant. No more love, no more frowns, no more needles, no more booze, to sleep, to sleep. Alice beside me I never dream. It must be my hand on her buttock as I sleep. I stir never either. Hand on her buttock, sleeping on my belly like when a kid I think because she does too on her belly like little Bette arms and legs sprawled like a frog the big buttoned lump sitting high my hand on it. Strange how deep it seems sometimes. Split deepness if I lift the covers and peek. My hand on the soft mound deep sleeping like a baby. Funny how one fingertip touch can feel everything. The slope of flesh hill, its softness, its deep cleft, even where it goes to fuzz and its soft color one fingertip resting can know. Please be Alice.

Around him lights came on. It was night Eddie liked, his time. He stepped gingerly avoiding cracks, Eddie snake dancer bold and unafraid. Jungle birds shrieked around him, their brazen calls summoning night spirits. Sweet breathed panthers slunk invisible on padded feet, only eyes through the thick undergrowth. Something huge and steel taloned had made a kill and bellowed the blood call to its mate. Monkeys on lace branches gibbered nervously at the moon. Eddie leapt the coiled bulk of a python.

Other nights. The wild chase night and Mama like always waiting. What had happened, when did it begin? Certain things returned clearly. He felt his hand glide into the past, experienced the cold, metallic sensation of that long ago night's coins in his hand:

Eddie had removed his last fifty cents from his drawer. Two dimes, a nickel and a quarter. At the field they'd probably be playing blackjack. He could get in for at least five hands, and he had never lost five straight before. Joel would be there too, not playing as usual, but sitting at the top of the stairwell watching for cops. That was worth a quarter win or lose, and Joel seemed content with cutting the first five pots for his due. Eddie told his mother he didn't feel well and wanted to skip supper, but she was unsatisfied.

—You can't even sit down long enough to eat your supper. You sure do love that bunch of roughnecks, don't you? I don't want you staying away from here late either. I know what you all do down at that field. Don't think I don't know. And don't expect nothing to be here for you to eat when you get home, if you can't sit down with the rest of us, just take your chances.

—I told you I didn't feel good. I won't be wanting nothing.

—But you feel good enough to go runnin' off to that bunch of white hoodlums. Your father and I work hard to keep you in a decent neighborhood, and how do you show your appreciation, by running with the lowest pack of rats you can find. I have a mind to make you stay right here.

Eddie listened and hoped she would begin again and stop soon at a better point to walk out on. After a while, no matter how right he knew he was and how unreasonable all her arguments, his resolution would weaken. It was simply her. His mother loving him in the only way she could that he could not deny. So much had been lost in that short space of silence between them. Strange how first his body, then his mind had become ashamed before her. It was almost as if the words he had learned had made things different. The word for his sex, the word for his tears, his love, his fear. No, nothing had changed, but a subtle alienation made communicating any small piece of himself as difficult as it had once been easy to give the whole. If he could somehow begin, master the first word which would soften her eyes, make her understand how much he still needed and loved. But instead he waited for a cue, a sign she had exhausted herself and would give up again trying to penetrate by violence the thin shell between them.

—Mom, I won't be late. I promise. And I got a quarter if I get hungry later. She was gone before the quarter was produced. He felt it would have been better somehow if she had waited to see it. But now whatever she wanted to believe could remain undisturbed.

Evening hadn't cooled the city. He had watched a long time before venturing his fifty cents. The stakes were only a dime, but he dropped a quarter down on board for show. The streetlights came on, and in two hours he had a pile of silver in front of him and had won the deal. He had been lookout before he entered the game, but now Joel had arrived and took up his regular seat. Eddie's streak continued, paying off only twice in ten rounds and matching the only blackjack he dealt with one of his own. The other players were growing steadily broke and disgusted. Cordigan, one of the older boys, whose blackjack had lost, visibly squirmed each time the dealer turned over his card. Cordigan had big hands with short fingers, and hair had already begun to cover their backs. He watched the Negro boy gather up the cards, raking in a dime from each player who had failed to beat his nineteen.

—Hey boys, don't you think it's about time we had us a new dealer? Cordigan's thick hands were spread out on his knees, a square signet ring, gold and ruby eyed, reflected the street-lamp. His tone contained no question. Beside him the thinner figure of Ken leaned further into the light. His crew cut and windbreaker matched Cordigan's, but no one except Ken ever noticed they were the same.

—I think you're right, Cordy. Yeah, I think maybe you should deal a while. I mean just till things even up a bit.

—What are you guys talking about? That ain't no guarantee of nothing. I got a little hot streak, that's all. Somebody's bound to get blackjack soon.

—Well, I already got blackjack once, and you had the deal long enough.

—It's only fair it should go to the one who had blackjack last.

—But I ain't lost it yet. The cards were in a neat stack in front of Eddie. He looked around at the five deeply shaded faces like masks in the dark stairwell. One cigarette was burning. He couldn't tell how the others had reacted to Cordigan's demand. What his flunky Ken said didn't really matter if the others were not on Cordigan's side. Eddie began to slowly shuffle the deck.

—Never mind that, I mix up my own deal. Cordigan's hand reached towards him.

The Negro continued to shuffle, slowly at the level of his stomach his hands filtered through the deck, his eyes fixed on the ruby eye suspended in the darkness. All other movement had stopped; the glowing cigarette had disappeared; each player sat rigid as the stone stairs on which they were ranged.

—Gimme the cards, kid, you've had it. Cordigan's lips were blue, then his mouth was a black hole in his face. Eddie knew Cordigan could take what he wanted from him, and there was really no question about submitting, but for once in the glittering coins he had won a piece of the white boy he wouldn't give up.

—Sure, take 'em Cordy. I gotta go anyway, I promised my mother I'd be home.

—Did you hear that? Sambo's won everybody's money and now all the sudden he gotta git home to his Mammie. Well, you can go if you want to, but leave the dough. The tableau had come to life. Each stone figure had imperceptibly closed in on the Negro. Ken, Harry, Ronnie, Skeets and Cordigan were all one now, aroused by a magic word that had been spoken. The cards stopped moving, it was suddenly cold, and Eddie feared that soon the streetlight would blaze one bright time then be snuffed out. He was shivering and his hands wanted something solid to grasp. He could feel the circle tightening, it was a belt around his waist, around his head that began to cut the flesh.

It ain't right you guys. Cordigan ain't got no right, Skeets, Harry, you know I'd stick by you. And he knew that he wouldn't if it had been one of them, and he knew they wouldn't because Cordigan . . .

—Cards, Sambo . . .

It was cold in the stairwell, in the arc of the streetlamp, and she knew what went on down there and Joel sitting quiet above. Of the players, Eddie was closest to the top and could make it if he ran quickly. Sambo. Sambo. Sambo. Run Tiger.

He scooped up as much as he could in one hand, straightening and pitching the cards into Cordigan's blue face. Then it was him running, running in a leap over the hedges, handful of money, their heavy footfalls behind, curses and loud breath behind that would never catch him as he stretched headlong into the wind freer than he had ever been, down the street and into the alley with the wind, handful of money singing because they never would catch him. He would easily outdistance them, and this night, heart thumping, he had won the pile and would keep it silver beside him as he slept. It was bright now, moon bright and under his feet the ground crunched and was gone. Cool, clear, he could even smell the wind and hear his heart, till up the steps in two bounds the screen door would slam behind him and he would sleep heart-still until tomorrow when they would find him, beat him, and take it all back.

She was waiting when the door flung open. Almost immediately her words flew in his face. —Where have you been, boy?

—Nowhere Ma, I mean just at Joel's house, just there talking with Joel.

—Talking about what, and what are you shaking all over for? Are you running with those hoodlums again? Look at the time boy. I been sitting here waiting for you since ten o'clock. Why won't you behave? Off with them wild white boys again. Don't you know by now they's just gonna hurt you? Don't you know by now? Since ten o'clock worrying my heart out. Why won't you act right?

—I told you I was just with Joel, Mama.

—With Joel doing what till near one o'clock in the morning.

—I don't know, I mean we was just sitting, talking. I didn't notice at all how late it was.

—Well next time just stay out all night with your white friend. If he can come and go as he pleases, it don't mean you can. Just cause he can run his mother to death, ain't no reason for you both to start on me. Next time you stay out like this, don't come home expecting somebody to be waiting on you. She knew she had to wait, and she knew she would wait again, tomorrow, or the next day, she would always be there.

—Listen to me, boy. Her eyes no longer flashed. As she spoke the animation left her gestures, her features and her voice. The calm and tears that followed were just as predictable as the outburst had been. He watched the one subside and the other gradually take possession of her body. Martha sat down again, sinking into the battered armchair facing the hallway where Eddie still stood. She had nothing else to say, those three hours dozing, snapping awake, pulling the gray cotton sweater closer around her shoulders. She had been a very old woman all that time, she had been very old and grew older, grayer as each minute passed. She railed at him because he had heaped these years on, and now she would cry because only in his young, strong body or in Eugene's could they be borne away. Why was it so hard? Why must she always sit and wait? Staring at doorways, down streets, straining her ears for a footfall, her eyes for a headlight or a figure through the haze. Sometimes she thought she could feel the lines etching their way into her face, she felt things being taken away, felt herself losing the few subdued female beauties of her body that were all of the past she retained, although into that past she had poured everything. She knew for her sons, for the men they would soon be, she could never be a woman. Never create that mysterious, transforming presence for them. She had never been beautiful, never more than attractive and that only to some men, but it wasn't this attraction that her sons denied. Clarence would still come back to her, moved by desire, and it was still something she could believe was uniquely her own that aroused him. At least it was what they made themselves believe, and accepting it as such made it true. What her sons denied was not that she had been a woman, or was one now, but that she would remain one. Her posture in the chair, sweater pulled tightly across her shoulders had been forced on her by them. What she had realized in that chair, and too many times before, was that she was losing the essential, necessary sense of anticipation. Waiting for someone, for something had always been bearable because faith had supported her worst sufferings. In her bed of pain, each time it had been a child she waited for, even when the twins had come too early dying within three days of each other, there had been faith in a next time, in that strong baby, Eugene, already at home. Her faith had been justified, others came, strong, healthy to grow up beside her. Now with her youngest son a different kind of faith was required. There was nothing to anticipate, he had been suckled, clothed, she had given dutifully and unselfishly to his life and now . . . now he would leave, leave her behind just as readily as birds do the dried, broken straw they've outgrown. And what did she have to look forward to? There had been no great illumination, no bliss or unconfined rapture at any point in the long struggle with her sons. They had been conceived, born, and both would soon be gone, leaving only pain. She had believed that someday she would receive her due. Not selfishly something given her in return for suffering, but simply the answer to why she had suffered. The climaxes, the up and down moments of joy and sorrow were afterall too little to believe in. Something told her all these momentary feelings must lead to a complete and final resolution which she by suffering could deserve to understand. But each time she waited, what came, if anything at all did, was never enough. No flash of light, no deep, settled contentment or despair, only the tickled nerve end dance leading her on and on, an animal pursuing the carrot on the end of a stick. There had been love, then God, then love again, and now God up once more on the seesaw holding out this man-child, beckoning her to continue again, to wait. But she was growing too tired, she would sit down one day without waiting just because she was so tired. She would find her sweater, go to her chair and forget time.

She wept now because she had risen to the bait again. She had strained her body and mind, grabbed at the boy as if he was the last thing above water into which she was sinking. But perhaps he would carry her through, perhaps God too was waiting, trying her to the end of her strength the way he tried all his saints. Perhaps too, some miracle would carry her to another shore, a far off golden beach where the sun shone, and fruit hung heavy with ripeness on golden branches. Perhaps someday she would be vomited up suddenly in paradise.

—You know your father's going to be up soon, if he sees you haven't been to bed yet, you know there'll be trouble. She felt foolish now, foolish for doubting, for ever believing that great day wouldn't come. He was still a little boy; he stood the way he always had, like Eugene, waiting for a word or a motion from his Mama to climb up and settle himself in her lap, to be forgiven or reassured, to be freed or received.

—I was just talking with Joel, Mama. I'm sorry . . . I forgot the time . . . talking cause he couldn't sleep.

—Like I did with you when you had bad dreams.

—Yes, like that, only . . . She saw him remembering, realizing what she had said. He stopped speaking, and his eyes avoided hers. She anticipated a word, knowing at the same time what it would be, what it would begin. He took a step towards her, she saw his lips purse, and slowly reappear full and moistened. The word had to come.

Eddie's gaze dropped; the coins were greasy in his tight fist. He quickly turned and mounted the steps as quietly as he could, but Martha heard each stair receive the weight of his body, even thought she heard his breath as he moved cautiously through the darkness. Her husband would be up soon for work, she would wait for him here, in the chair.

Alice the dancer. She had taken reluctant Eddie to the ballet school. All white but them. Never so close to one before, the white girls' arms with light down that covered the flesh when close enough to see. The thought of one in his arms. How his knees had shaken. But Alice really the best dancer. So easy, so free, really the queen as she had soared or pirouetted or stretched her body to the half ugly, half impossible contortions that had names, but Eddie didn't know. Every week on Saturdays they had gone. Hadn't seen Alice much after she had won the scholarship and gone off to school. A rare bird. So ugly Alice was you knew she was Brother's sister, but when she returned something different, something standoffish that made you want to go to her. Alice had come back more beautiful than Eddie had seen anyone. And she had taken him to watch her ballet lessons. The first few times they had talked, nothing much, all they could say were old things, stuff about when they were kids, and what they had said seemed really about Eddie but an Alice who had died and had nothing to do with either person sitting on the glider. Eddie was always with Brother so he had seen Alice often. It was on the porch of the Smalls' frame house where Alice lived and Brother sometimes slept that they would meet. One day she had just popped up and asked so he went with her to the school, met her friends and broadcast his awkwardness.

On benches in the red backed booth of a soda fountain. Eddie, Alice, group of her fellow dancers, coffee, Cokes ranged on a checkered oilskin cloth. His eyes in his cup Eddie had listened. Talk, talk, talk, how they could talk. Everything, anything. Shameless even. What Eddie kept to himself, what he would rather watch swimming in his plastic cup, private and limp like the light bulb reflected on the black coffee's surface. He had stirred his plastic spoon round and round listening. Clara had talked:

–Why it's getting better every day. My youngest sister told me that a Negro had been elected president of her high school class. That's people for you. A few years ago when I was in ponytail and saddle shoes, there weren't any colored students there at all. I bet half my contemporaries believed colored boys had tails. A nervous semblance of laughter passed from face to face. It stopped on both sides of Eddie who never heard or saw it, black coffee staring. Just give people a chance. We have so much in common, and I mean essentials; the emotions, the spirit, the potential for suffering and transcendence, things embedded too deeply to be erased by superficial distinctions of race or religion. I sincerely believe this; everything points to its truth.

Just look around. Take this group—if I say *pain,* everybody here knows what I mean. Maybe it doesn't connote precisely the same words to each of us, but we do share the fundamental reality of this concept, grasp it intuitively as part of the human experience. It's this sort of perception, this community of souls, if you please, that in the end will obliterate intolerance. Clara had shown her bad teeth. Her eyes had surveyed the audience, resting just an iota longer on Alice and Eddie with the undergraduate rhetorician's instinct for emphatic pause. The silence had brought Eddie's head up long enough for him to hear, *Just men and women in the world,* before he had returned to plumb the depths of his cold coffee, futilely fishing for the pinpoint of light with his plastic spoon.

Alice had asked him later why he hadn't listened or joined in the discussion. He could tell she was displeased, even embarrassed. He had felt the good thing between them loosen, the cold, bright aloofness of an unfamiliar Alice returning. They had swayed together on their glider, barely moving, Alice avoiding his face, her hands in her lap. The glider had squeaked, and Eddie felt it all slipping away, had wanted to grab little Alice, pull her hair or take her toy or throw dirt or push her down in the grass. Where was little Alice, old Alice who word by word, evening by evening on the loud glider had been coming back? His new, beautiful Alice. Going, going . . .

—I thought I recognized something different in you, Edward. Something I could respond to. I don't quite know what. Going away has made some things very difficult for me. I suppose I expected too much. But this afternoon, I don't know what I wanted, this afternoon I wanted everyone to . . . to . . . appreciate you. I didn't want to put you on display, but I wanted to reassure myself, I think that's what it was, reassure myself. I wanted to be certain I wasn't fooling myself, that I wasn't just lonely and weak making you something you weren't and didn't want to be. Do you understand me, Edward? It's been hard since I've come back. And in many ways I believe you know exactly how I feel. At least I hope you know, and that's why it's been good to be with you. Why I see you and no one else in the neighborhood. It's not that I think I'm better, it's just that I have absolutely nothing to say to them. I feel like a fish out of water. But I know this is my water, my home, that I can't ever change. And I want so much to have someone to share what I've learned, to have it flourish here. A person to help me keep alive the little something different I've felt grow up in me. Someone to preserve it, to protect it. I don't want to fall back, back into this . . . Her arms had stretched out, wide, wide, wide. She had leaned forward stopping the glider's motion, her arms straining, her fingertips stiff in the effort of expansion. As if the *this* could be embraced, as if she could wrap the *this* in her stretched arms and smother it. She stood, abruptly rising on her toes, her slim dancer's body a cross. As if overburdened by a sudden, immense weight her arms had dropped stiffly to her sides. Eddie had caught her, afraid she was going to fall. He had never been held so tightly.

They had fucked that night in dead Mr. and Mrs. Small's big bed. During the night they had heard Brother come in and immediately begin to snore as he passed out on the sofa. The dancing lessons had continued. Eddie watched and listened . . .

Please be there. Please forgive. Through the shabby streets Eddie the beggar moved. His motion the torpitude of a snail. Behind, his gleaming spore undulated, slowly being devoured by snakes. His margin of safety was diminishing, the sharp tongues would momentarily be at his hind parts. His eleemosynary chalice rattled in his hand. He believed it would frighten away the night crawlers. There was one coin left.

He knocked.

He knocked again . . .

He knocked again . . . and Alice answered. As if from a ghost she shied back. Alice ugly in the half-light. Her flowing robe was something of her long dead mother's. Eddie remembered Mrs. Small vaguely. Mrs. Small who bore white Brother and brown Alice no one would believe from the same man.

Is it my Alice? May I begin to speak? No one will ever know how difficult on this doorstep it is to begin.

—Hello, Alice.

—Hello, Eddie.

—I've come back.

—I knew you would, but I didn't expect you this evening. It was oddly dark behind her. A simple house, a box, wall, corridor. Brother's couch still there, a bulk beneath the window broken-backed. Tiny lamp burning on an end table, only source of light except for the thin stripe along the bottom edge of the bedroom door. Should he try to kiss her? How long had it been?

She switched on more light. Around her pulling tighter the aged chenille robe. Something old, something pink left by a dead woman. Did Eddie really know that?

—It's been a long time. Had you forgotten?

—No, Eddie, not forgotten you or how long either. Please sit down, I was reading, I'll turn out the light. The gown showed her trim ankles, and as she reached into the bedroom feeling for a switch it revealed the beginning swell of her dancer's calf. How long have you been home? I hadn't heard you were back. Does William know? Eddie hated to hear her call Brother *William*; it was like telling a lie. Brother was Brother, he was alive. William was a ghost dwelling only in Alice's mind and here in the house of the dead Smalls. He was suddenly irritated, so vexed that for a moment he forgot the calf.

—Did they cut out your tongue down there or are you just ignoring me? Eddie still stood. Beneath the frayed pink chenille he could see the free mounds of her breast.

—I just got in today. Mama was so excited, things just wouldn't go right. I thought I'd better leave early and let her get her rest, and I thought I'd come to see you. It's you I've wanted to see for so long anyway. Just for a minute, if you're not busy.

—Why come here? For what, Eddie? You didn't come to say good-bye before you left so why bother to come now? Emphasizing the last word, she sunk wearily into the swayback couch. Her eyes were tired, tired Alice eyes, brown staring at sudden Eddie standing awkward in her livingroom.

—Didn't you, didn't you get my note? I gave it to Brother, and he promised he'd bring it to you . . .

—That, oh yes. I received it. William with all the solemnity proper to the occasion delivered it with bated breath and downcast countenance. She smiled, a strange un-Alice smile at Eddie. He shivered and wished for the half-light again.

—I came back because I love you, Alice.

—Like you loved Clara?

—Please, Alice, what's done is done. I made a mistake, I've made lots of mistakes, but it's now I have to live for. Now, when all you have to say is I forgive to begin again. All the time when I was away and just now at home when Mama sat there staring at me, it was you that kept me from screaming, the thought of you that . . .

—You're running from your mother aren't you, Eddie? She drove you away didn't she? Just like Clara, your Mama's finished with her Eddie boy so you come to good Alice. Well, you've come to the wrong place. I'm expecting company.

—Company?

—Yes, Eddie, company, a gentleman caller if you wish. I said I remembered, but you took for granted what I remembered. See if Clara's home, Eddie. See if she welcomes you with open arms, and Mr. Rawlins, and Clara's mother. You'd better try the back door first, don't shock them too much all at once.

—You can't forget can you? One night, Alice, one lousy night. Clara getting her kicks and me like a fool obliging. I didn't think you'd ever know, and even if you did, I didn't see how you could care. She's a tramp, you know that. She just wanted a toss in the hay.

—With her black buck. With you so she could smile and proclaim it. So she could prove her principles with what she has between her legs. No, no I didn't care, it didn't matter to me sitting listening every time she opened her mouth to how real it was, to how meaningful it was, to all the essential truths it demonstrated about men and women. Her glib, bitch mouth so full of praise for Edward, how tender he was, how understanding, how it didn't make any difference in the world what color he was. No . . . It didn't matter; I didn't care.

—Once, Alice, once, I swear it. That's all. I never touched her again.

—Do you think it matters—how many times mattered. I gave you something, I trusted you, Eddie. And all I gave you were willing to trade with that whore for a smell of her white ass. Something rose in Alice and burst. She cried, bitterly and for an age it seemed before Edward moved to her side on the sinking couch. Little Alice sobbed in his arms, cuddling closer, not to him, but to the soft, yielding presence on which her sorrow leaned. Her lost Eddie, home again, home again who whispered.

—I love you, Alice . . . I love you, Alice, please don't cry, please Alice, don't cry. The robe fell away. Her hand which had held it together circled Eddie's neck. It had been long, futile anger. It's closeness choked her, and she knew Eddie far away was pained by its distant force. Intenerating grief. How she buried him beneath the maleflesh she pulled round her like a hood. Eddie gone, dying his way. That night Brother dragged him back, and she knew they had been taking it, and Eddie moaned all night like a child having nightmares; she had watched him tossing in a stupor, his body beside her brother's in the dark room. Oh, for the strength to lift him, to carry him clean and refleshed into her bed. Poor trembling Eddie, the white flesh still reeking from his contaminated body. Oh, to have the arms to raise him, my Eddie, once more from the floor, from the dark room. But how after her can I touch, how can I give again what he had destroyed. Week after week, she saw in William's eyes the cold, unforgiving blame. Eddie had promised, he had tried, kept the piddling job moving pianos; he had been so decent, but after she had refused him, the poison ran through his veins again. Then really gone, not just held off by her anger, the searing anger, the anger supportable only because she believed she had the power to relent, but by the remorse he left solid inside her, like a burning coal when he left, and it was too late for her to forgive. A year could be so long. And after a while the nights are interminable. Worst then when emptiness must be close. When emptiness is a cold, palpable thing you can touch on the sheet beside you. How long? Till like a parade they came. Her lovers. The gates were open, emptiness was a face, a body beside her, long, tall, short, fat, and did it matter afterall that emptiness had a name. She had enough. But they always came back. Like a parade, in shining uniforms, neat, clean, always punctual and well groomed, her men, her lovers, her emptiness.

The robe parted to her waist. Her breasts were powder dusted, in the cleft a few tiny hairs grew. Eddie lowered his head, felt the dark nipple brush his cheek, the faint bumping of her heart. How long had it been?

He eased her down, slowly, slowly, the robe off her shoulders, a faded pink cloud beneath her naked body. He dipped and kissed, his pursed lips tracing the length of her body, the hot house smells kaleidoscoping, filling his nostrils in a hundred shades from her bath damp hair to her ankles. Alice was still serene as he fumbled with his trousers and spread her dancer's legs. Soft and yielding, moist too from the bath he kissed her dark flower. It was all sinking then, layer after layer of warm ice melting. They swayed to the rhythm of their squeaking glider.

—I love you, Alice. In her ear the voice whispered. Her breasts were wet, and a draft chilled them as it crawled up the side of her sweat dampened body away from Eddie's warmth. She had remained silent, forgotten the necessity of tears in the gentle rise and fall of her whole body as Eddie's hard hands worked beneath her buttock. But now a tear seemed to envelop her whole body. It was slick and drying cool where he had pressed down on her. It would freeze to something icy with sharp jagged edges. There would be between them this cold, brittle shell each time his maleness rose from her. Her body would always cry its tear of guilt, of shame, of bitter accusing anger. The emptiness could only have a name.

–Eddie, please get up. He rolled away, propping himself on his knee, his back against the sofa, one long leg stretching onto the floor. She gathered up the chenille robe, Mrs. Small's robe, and turning from him covered her dancer's body with pink. She spoke again, still with her back towards him, a slim column of pink crowned by dark, frazzled hair. You better go now, Eddie.

He was drained. Limp, deflated Eddie, boneless, pastel like a discarded balloon as he slid down onto the couch. Like sitting on the glass strewn ground Eddie felt, his bare ass rubbing against the tough fabric. He squirmed then conceded, melting without the strength to rise. –But, Alice, I love you.

Never turning, only pulling the robe righter as it rode up her dancer's calves, Alice spoke in the room of the dead Smalls, in the room where Brother slept, in the room she had left, in the room to which she had returned, in the love room, in the play room, in the room where the parade formed and the room where Eddie unable to stop her, dumbly regarded his wilted worm.

–Like Clara, Eddie, I gave it to you like Clara. A charity case free of charge on my lunch hour. We're the same now. I can tell her how gentle you are, how understanding. Please leave, Eddie, please get out of here! And don't come back! Please . . . please . . .

First one leg, then the other. It is a delicate balance really, especially when one knee trembles as the other is lifted. So loud sometimes, in this room like a train struggling through a tunnel as I push my foot through these trousers. The belt like a vice.

Where are they? One shoe shoved under the couch. There, I see it. When did I learn to make a bow. It seemed too hard at first. Automatic now, only difficult when I think about it. Alice's back. In spite of her voice I can see by her shoulders she is crying. Cry Alice, cry. Make Eddie cry. Look at Eddie cry. Cry Eddie, cry. Unbending from the task of shoe tying Eddie remained mute.

—Please, please get out. Docilely he shuffled towards the door. Her voice had broken, the second please a partial sigh. The pink shuddered.

I can't go, Alice. I love you Alice.

She hit him once, twice, sharp pummelling blows like a machine thudding on his shoulders and chest. The fury diminished, was finally crushed as he clasped her so tightly her clenched fists dug into her breasts. She struggled to free her arms, to release the terrible pressure his weight exerted on her pinioned elbows. Still fighting she was lifted flailing with one loose arm the steep sides of his boney, eggshell skull. She felt herself lurch as he lurched kicking at the bedroom door which burst open and tumbled them both sprawling onto her bed. He shook her naked body, his hands clamped around her wrists, shook her to a sitting position as his flushed face towered over her, the thick vein pulsating, his mouth working from which no words came. Straddling her he pushed her back onto the orange spread, pinning her wrists so she was powerless. Still her legs kicked futilely, and her head twisted from side to side. Then he was calm, strangely, frighteningly calm as he looked down on her nakedness, the heaving womanflesh stretched helpless in his grip. She lay suddenly motionless, her eyes widening as he stared down. She sensed his poised, inner stillness, the cold implacability of anything he decided to do. In that moment she loved him, loved the doom in his steel hands cutting into her wrists, the crushing, irresistible weight across her belly. Her lips were heavy with desire.

The black nipples, the thatch just beginning where I look

down, the dancer's legs, quiet now behind me, this flesh, this woman on a pink twisted cloud. Did I say I loved, did I shy away from her, did I take her in my hunger and my fear? My Alice. Is she this flesh?

It was all in his eyes, brown, deeply set. It was in every part of him touching her bare skin; he relaxed, the vein disappeared, the grief, the pain returned. Shy Eddie, averting his eyes, stepping down, like from a chair at the cookie jar and caught by his grandmother, stepping down, he backpedalled through the door, bowing almost to naked Alice who rose on one shoulder, hair wild. Softly behind him both doors closed.

It was still black, Eddie's time as he slipped through the dark streets. His sweat, her sweat, whatever else seeps out when people come together uncomfortable beneath his clothes. The fight with Mama, how had Alice known? Quickly, as his long legs stretched in faster, lengthened strides Alice was forgotten. Better to keep her as she was. Let her be like the music of the glider or their shrill singing and chants that were part of games. Rope skipping to the alphabet song. Spelling out your lover. Eddie, timid and frail, had played with the girls. But like the glider, all he could remember was a rhythm, the methodical repetition of rhyming words again and again. How did it go— Alice shouting, pigtails, braces, the thin knobby legs working like a pump, up-down, up-down as the rope swooshed over her head and flailed loud, dry bursts of dust from the pavement. Please Alice don't die. My turn soon, ducking under, knees bent, heart throbbing, straightening in stark terror of the fatal rope's snake touch.

But I must go back. There is nowhere else to go. He hoped his mother would be in bed. Sad Bette too he hoped. His little sister, and why did it have to happen to her? Life had touched his mother, made her old too soon. But there had been other things for her. She had been wife, mother, her years had been full. But Bette, what had she received? Eddie could not answer.

He felt the mist return to his eyes. Alice mist. Alice eyes. For a moment it had seemed that nothing wrong would ever happen again. After so long, Alice gliding beneath him, the love dance. Nothing now. Night now, streets strange and heavy sided, unfamiliar after just a year, a winding corridor thickly black that funnelled him to Dumferline Street where he turned towards home.

Bette waited in the livingroom.

—I'm so glad you're back. Bette paused reading her brother's eyes in the vestibule's dim light, Mama's asleep so shut the door quiet behind you.

Nothing ever changes thought Eddie, settling into the room's one soft chair. His sister was a blur, still standing one arm resting on the back of Mama's chair. Gentle, meek Bette, who if he asked would kneel down to bathe his feet.

—Want a glass of milk or something, Eddie? For her Eddie did wish there was something he wanted, something no matter how small she could do for him, something she could become for a moment that would draw her from the shadowed corner behind the chair.

—No, there's nothing I want now, but could you please turn on the light? It was hard to tell, but Eddie believed she had been crying. Her face was round, fuller than her mother's or Eddie's, more like the broad dimpled face of the dead father, Clarence. But nothing in it inclined towards excess, not his heavy jowls or stuffed cheeks, a completely female statement of his coarse good looks, softened, turned introspective and benign, a placid face even beautiful if caught in the correct light and in the particular repose unique to her kind of understated but perfect features. Unless the light was right her bad complexion would ruin the effect. A splotched, unhealthy type of skin, dark under her eyes.

—What's wrong, Bett? You look so sad.

—Nothing's wrong, nothing to speak of. I guess it's just my look. She looked so old sometimes, drab, loose housecoats down to her ankles almost, her head inclined slightly forward, a furrow in her brow, eyes that never met you, like the lids were too heavy to lift or the thick curled lashes stuck down. She seated herself, a weighty, resigned movement with nothing female in it; her hands settled into her lap.

—It's been a long time, Eddie, are you glad to be home? Mama and me sure missed you. Her voice rose and brightened as the sentence ended, as if word by word it entered her mind from a novel and unexpected source; she seemed surprised and gratified there was an echo returning the sound of her private thoughts.

—I missed you both, Bett, you'll never know how much. It was like I died or the world died, like nothing else existed, that I would never be able to get back home. I even began to believe home was something I had made up. Like the people we used to play with, like Mr. and Mrs. Booboo, remember, Bett? How we'd visit them and talk, and they'd take us places? I started to believe home was just make-believe like that.

—But you know we're real, Mama and me. I mean all the time you were away we were here, waiting and worrying. I prayed for you, Eddie, and Brother used to come around when Mama was asleep to talk to me. It was always about you. That Brother really remembers things. And he's so funny. I was always scared I'd burst out laughing and wake Mama. You know what a mess that would have been. Why doesn't she like Brother?

—Mama's sick Bett and she's getting old. I guess there are few things she still likes.

—It must be the worst thing in the world to be old. Old so you can't remember stories like Brother tells, or so old that the people you know best all begin dying. Do you think that's why Mama's so lonely? Bette's eyes dropped even lower. She rubbed the worn arms of her mother's chair slowly with both hands. —You know, Eddie, sometimes I feel like I'm getting old. When I'm here all day alone, with just Mama and that pup it's awful hard to remember other people, that maybe somewhere a radio might be playing or young people dancing, that there are shows and cars, and new clothes, and houses full of people laughing and talking together. I just have these walls, what you see around you, and Mama.

It was so easy to forget and Eddie felt ashamed because he had. Like a wet rag wiped over a spot, Alice gone, his love like Eugene's shoes left outside so it wouldn't contaminate the room. Only the itch in his groin, in the place he couldn't comfort while Bette sat watching in the room. Was everything so easy to forget, or was it his sister, this room where they had grown up together and the woman overhead asleep? Some special condition, as powerful and basic as *being Eddie,* which submerged all other considerations. Is this what it feels like to lose love, to sit and be sad because your sister is sad, to forget the object of that lost love so utterly that to think of her in this room is to feel awkwardness at the presence of a stranger? Have I returned for that?

–It's so good to have you home for Easter. Eddie started, suddenly, keenly aware of his sister's voice. Its tone, or a word, or just the nonverbal coincidence of some shade of his thought with that which produced Bette's utterance brought them into intimate contact again. Easter was when his grandfather had taken him to hear the sanctified people sing. Bette couldn't go because she was too young and Eugene couldn't be found so off they went, him perched on the old man's shoulder.

–Did you ever hear the saints sing? Bette smiled at her brother's question, her features relaxed and a secret light came from nowhere into her eyes.

–Remember big, fat Tiny, twinkletoes they called him. Brother must have told you stories if I haven't.

–Sure, I remember him being talked about, big as an elephant and black as coal.

–That was Tiny all right, but boy could that black elephant dance.

—Did you see him much? Bette began to lean forward excited, anticipating a story. Brother's talked about him, but not much. And I hardly remember the little he said. Just how he could dance. Bette knew the story from beginning to end, she had heard it rehearsed a thousand times in this same livingroom. But it had become a private, almost mystical link between brother and sister. An experience shared so deeply that its content had become superfluous; they could both fasten on the narrative and wring far more from it than any meaning translatable to an outsider. When Tiny danced, they moved into each other with the joy and fascination of lovers.

—Nothing like it, Bett. You've never seen nothing like it. He was round, huge and round with rolls of black fat. Always sweating, especially on his thick neck and his slick, light-bulb head. Like he had beads on sometimes, or shiny blisters sprouting all around his forehead and neck. He seemed to be crying when he danced cause the sweat poured down over his face, and he closed his little pig eyes to keep the salt out I guess, because if they weren't closed he squinted with a wrinkled-up, unhappy look on his face even though he danced and everybody knew he was happy. I sat on DaddyGene's shoulder and watched through a window. Talk about some colored people. Women with nets wrapped around the little, nappy hair they had, and the men sitting stiff in starched collars, like babies in high chairs with hard white bibs under their chins. But that was only until the music started. Everything—piano, trumpet, tambourines, drums, whatever anybody could beat or shake or blow noise through was in their hands and wagged at the devil. You think those Strip niggers can make a racket! Just go hear the sanctified one day.

Throughout Eddie's speech, Bette had been active, responding to each pause or gesture, squirming childishly in her seat to capture the essence of his words, the urgent masculine rhythms as his voice strained to keep pace with Tiny's dance. But as quickly as it came, it passed. Eddie's cheek dropped to

129

rest on one clenched hand as if content to gaze thoughtfully and silently at a spectacle his words could no longer describe.

—Don't stop. Why are you stopping?

—Tiny's gone, Bett. For a minute Eddie could see him plainly, spinning like a shiny black top, faster and faster, close enough to touch, to hear it turning. Then he started to weaken, wobble, the heavy rolls around the middle dragging him down, he leaned just like a top leaning and spinning slower.

—Don't go away again Eddie, please don't go away again. There was a shriek in the night. First a stab of a yellow light against the tracks then diesel engines back to back rushed past. Eddie's lips moved instinctively, forming soft, reassuring words that if spoken would have been lost in the roar. When the clatter stopped these words had already died on his lips. He rose, moving hesitantly towards her chair, giving himself time to form others, to take advantage of the momentary reprieve forced upon him.

—Eddie . . . He was on his knees beside her before she could finish her sentence. Her moist eyes stared down at him full of fear, full of uncertainty and doubt. Could there be an answer? It was what her eyes asked . . .

—I must go away again. What I felt while I was away was the truth. There's nothing here for me. I'm dead, Bette, the plain fact of the matter is that Eddie's dead. You saw what happened when I tried to talk to Mama. If she saw me at all it was only on conditions that simply don't exist any more. If somehow I could return to her, return completely free of the past, if I could be a stranger, a kind stranger who reminded her of her lost son Eugene then she would accept me. But I can't be this—I've tried to erase my own past, but I can't do anything with hers, with all the long years we've shared . . . Mama can't forgive. Don't you see Bette? You too, you're a reminder of what she wants to forget. She manages to keep you from everything that could and should be yours. She's stealing it away bit by bit, and when there's nothing left she thinks things will be all right, she believes time will stop. That it will forget . . .

—What are you saying, Eddie, I don't understand.

—I'm saying you must get away from here, that I'm going away again, and this time you must go too.

—But Eddie, what about Mama, what will she do without me? You can't really mean what you're saying. You can't really say you want me to leave her alone in the world. She'd die, Eddie, she'd die right away without anyone to do for her, and it would be us that killed her.

—You're wrong, so, so wrong. A nurse could do for Mama. She's sick, and what she needs is a nurse.

—We don't have any money for that.

—We'll get money. That's the simplest thing. What's wearing Mama out is the two of us. She won't let go because it's only on us she can load her pain, and as long as we're close it's all she'll live to do. She'd be better dead, we'd be better dead.

There was a sharp tap on the stairs, another then the shuffling sequence of the old woman's stiff, braced legs lowered one at a time onto a step. Bette was on her feet and into the hall before Eddie could straighten up. Instantly he knew she had been listening, knew his words, finally stated, would bring his mother hurrying to confront him as fast as her withered body could move within the cold, steel bands. His limbs were leaden and morbidly sensitive at once. He felt enclosed in a warm, cloying liquid, the underwater torpitude of his nightmares suddenly remembered and real.

Bette switched on the light just as he entered the hallway. Blinking, shrinking from the light, his mother swayed at the top of the stairs, a ragged gray cloud just beginning to descend. Her eyes rolled wildly, her whole face contorted into something that could have been a mute's furious effort to scream. For a moment Eddie believed she had been stricken again, then as she raised the steel crutches menacingly to point or throw at him, it seemed she smiled, smiled because she knew he was

131

trapped—for the split second she needed he was pinned to his tracks, an animal frozen under onrushing headlights. But the crutch never rose beyond her waist, and her lips stopped working to fall into a slack, idiot repose, as her eyes closed, and she pitched headlong down the stairs.

One look at the lifeless heap was enough. The dull robe discreetly shrouded her; only the metal poles protruded from beneath it and a dangling braid of grayish brown hair. A collapsed tent, with a bundle of sticks within rather than the soft, rounded contours of a human frame. Eddie burst through the front door, tearing into the night, but even as he ran and clamped his hands over his ears, Bette's scream and the puppy's banshee shrieks followed him.

In the street it all came back. Pursued, Eddie fled again through the dark corridor, the Furies writhing shapes his dogging shadow.

—What is your name, sir?

—Edward Lawson.

—Thank you, Mr. Lawson, and where do you live? Full address please.

—I don't have a full address, just a city.

—Family then, we must have next of kin, just in case.

—None.

—Well, is there anyone we can get in touch with Mr. Lawson, in case of some unforeseen difficulty or an emergency of some sort? This will all be kept private of course, and we don't expect to have to use the address you give us, but there is a certain form in these matters.

—Brother Small.

—Excuse me, is that a relative, a clergyman or . . .

—No, it's just a guy. A friend you can get in touch with—in case.

—Is that his complete name, or a title?

—Just Brother Small.

–Thank you, Mr. Lawson. And what's his address?

–The same as mine.

–Just a city?

–Yes.

–Thank you, just as you like, Mr. Lawson. You may go in to Dr. Grierson now. He's expecting you.

–Lawson, Edward . . . 30 . . . unemployed. I'm Dr. Grierson, Mr. Lawson. After a while here you'll probably find your own name for me, but for now Doc will be fine. Sit down, sit down please. These chairs are really quite comfortable, best ones on the whole reservation probably. I thought they'd be worth the extra expense if they'd induce people to come sit in them more than once coming in and once leaving. Nice aren't they? You won't find it as nice in your room. And there's a chance believe it or not that in time you may grow to hate your roommate more than you'll probably hate me. It's not that I'm a bad guy. It's simply that I'm the boss. The hands behind the stones that keep rolling up and down this bloody hillside. Are you a reader, Mr. Lawson? You have an intelligent eye. It says something here in your application about reading. What was it? Yes, hobbies: reading, painting. Fine, that's fine. We have books here, and we can get most any you want on loan from other libraries, and there's an arts and crafts shop. Maybe you'd like to work there. Nothing spectacular. At best stencil a few signs or make posters, probably wind up painting the dining hall. But perhaps something can be arranged. A mural perhaps. Scenes from the life of Christ or something. Well, I hope you like it here, Mr. Lawson. You won't at all, of course. It's miserable, it'll be a living hell, and if we weren't careful to keep the means out of hand most would slit their throats. But the point is there's no need. The gates are always open. Just check out with Mrs. West before you take off, if and when you decide to jump the reservation. She'll have a bunk for you now, and if someone is already there, try to have a little patience with whoever it is. In my experience it's always been so much easier if a chap can stick with one mate during his whole stay. Much better rate of rehabilitation, and often they leave quicker, sometimes even together. But that's far off. You'll have plenty of time on your hands so try to be patient with the other chaps. It helps everyone, especially us here in the office. You must come talk with me about your painting sometime, Mr. Lawson, or your reading. I like to be busy, and you'll learn the virtue of constructive activity here I'm sure. Mrs. West will arrange a schedule with you. Try you on a difficult one at first. See if you can handle it. From your reaction we can estimate something permanent. You'll receive treatments in the infirmary. Mrs. West has maps of the grounds and an orientation booklet. You'll find you'll have no difficulties at all in catching on. Just get along with your mate and be patient. It's part of yourself you have to find here, Mr. Lawson. All we can do here is restore you to yourself.

—Saunders.
—Lawson.
—Just get in?
—Yes. And you?
—Four weeks, that's all, still a beginner.
—Are you going to stay on?
—Today, yes—I don't kid myself about tomorrow. I'll fight that battle when this one's off my hands. Where you from, Lawson?
—East Coast.
—Don't know anybody from out that way. I'm from Detroit myself, motor city.
—Could you tell me which of these beds is yours?
—The one beneath the window. I got my stuff spread all over the closet; I'll shove it to one side so you can put in your things. You get half the drawers too, but I hope you didn't bring too much. It's tight as hell already.

—I don't have much. Just some underwear and a shirt or two. For some reason I thought they'd have uniforms.

—There are overalls and workshirts you can borrow. Like this stuff in the closet here. They clean it free once a week in the laundry if you're interested. Most of the guys prefer street clothes. Cigarette, Lawson? Here, take a light too. I must smoke a million of these a day now, and if it's not one of these I got a chocolate stuck in my mouth.

—Chocolate?

—Yeah, ration of each. Chocolate and cigarettes. We get a couple of pounds of saltpetre a day in our food too. Ugh. Somebody should tell the management that most of the poor studs here don't even remember it's for something besides pissing, let alone care. That's right, plop right down. Your place too now. I gotta take a little stroll for a couple of minutes. Make yourself at home, and if there's anything I can help you with, just ask. It takes some settling in, man, Papa Grierson undoubtedly let you know just how hard it is. Some guy. Pisses everybody off the first time, but he ain't so cool really, just a pill-pusher, pushing a funny kind of pill. Kinda guy you just avoid, loves to hear himself talk. Get to know the other fellows, don't cross anybody and you have a fifty-fifty chance of being a winner. That big room of Grierson's is just a place to get in trouble. Well, I gotta go. See you later Lawson.

—Lawson?

—Yeah, Saunders.

—You know I was just thinking. Wonder why I still call you Lawson and you call me Saunders.

—It's what we called each other the first day.

—But it ain't quite right, is it, Lawson? I mean after people know each other a while they start using other names.

—I'd feel funny calling you anything besides Saunders. Calling you Ron, or Ronald would be strange for me. You're Saunders.

--And you're Lawson. That's the sort of conclusion I came to myself. But it made me think of something else too. It's hard to explain, but you got a good head, Lawson, maybe you can even help me say it.

–Words are not my department.

–I know, but it's not words that I need. It's something else. Did you ever go to church, Lawson? I ain't asking that to be personal, I mean I don't care which one, or how long ago, or anything like that. In fact, I ain't a believer myself. But I did go to church, long ago when I was a boy. With my mother mostly, and sometimes she'd cry and get the old man to go too. But have you been, Lawson?

–When I was a kid.

–That's enough; you'll understand. Well in my church, when the preacher was talking, and he said something really fine, something that everybody understood or that plopped right into the guts of one of the shouting members of the congregation, out would come a loud *Amen*. *Amen* Lawson, you know what I mean, do you remember *Amen?* It was like, like, hell, I can't explain it, but if you remember hearing people say *Amen,* loud and clear, with their faces shining, almost laughing it seemed a lot of the time, then you know the kind of help you can give me with what I want to say.

–Are you going to preach me a sermon?

–C'mon Lawson, you know what I'm trying to get at. What I wanted to say in the first place was things about this place really scare the shit out of me sometimes.

–Amen.

–Wait a minute now. I got more to say than that. The bit about names is what started me thinking. Here I am. One day you just walk in and say you're going to be living with me. O.K., that's simple enough, I don't know nothing about nothing, where you came from, what you do, your name even, and in lots of ways that's good. It's good cause it's so different from out there. I meet a stud here and we're really just two, plain studs. Nobody got nothing going. I meet a stud here and all's I know is that we have the same kick and we're both trying to shake it. Now if you see what I mean, that's good, it's clean, I mean everybody really has a clean slate here. You start over again, like being a baby again or something. But this ain't really the world is it? I mean we're on a kind of island, or in a jail almost. So you call me Saunders and I call you Lawson. It's what we did first, so that's what sticks, that's what's O.K. It don't matter who you are or who I am, Lawson and Saunders is enough. But when I leave here, I ain't Saunders no more. You remember a stud named Saunders, but as soon as I walk through that gate, he dies. Maybe something real good happened to Saunders, maybe Saunders is even straight. But what about the poor bastard walking down that hillside? What good will Saunders do me, huh, what good will all this shit do me on the other side?

—Still hanging on, Lawson?
—Yessir.
—Did you get a good roomie?
—Yessir, but he left last week.
—Oh yes, that's right . . . Saunders, he didn't even warn us beforehand. He was very, very grateful. I remember now, he mentioned you. Yes, I recall it all quite clearly. Mrs. West was quite impressed. She remarked on the change in his attitude, how he seemed even physically transformed, years younger. I think he could have gotten a date, Lawson. She's not bad you know. Just a poor dresser. Good strong legs. He'll have another chance I bet. That is if he fights back at all. He was kidding himself. Look Lawson, I'm going to drop by and see you some day soon. You won't mind, will you? I promise I'll be stimulating. Perhaps we could talk about your painting or your reading. Find yourself another friend. It really helps. And above all don't

brood on Saunders, neither on his absence nor his presence out there. You'll need all the strength you have to keep yourself above water.

Sept 4

Hello Brother:
It's raining like hell here. I don't expect you anymore, but that's something you had to decide for yourself. The fellow I wrote to you about before—Saunders—returned last week and looks pretty bad. He doesn't want to room with me again. Shame can do terrible things to a man; I could feel the pain it caused him when I tried to approach. His hurt is like a bell, something I can hear when he walks past at night. Sometimes I believe it wakes me up. Twice I've found myself wide awake, sitting up in bed in the middle of the night. And both times it was him prowling around when he believes no one sees him. I wonder if anyone else can hear it. Sometimes I wonder if I'm not nuts. The thing that frightens me most is that if I am crazy, I have to stay that way, and even get crazier to ever leave this place.

Dec. 12

Dear Alice, . . . Dear Alice, . . . Dear Alice, . . . Dear Alice, . . . Dear Alice, . . . Dear Alice, . . . Dear Alice, . . . Dear Alice, . . . Dear Alice, . . .

–You learn quickly, Eddie. If I believed in naturals, I'd say you were one. You really feel you wouldn't want to stay on? Not even with the prospect of possibly defeating me one fine day as incentive? I took you for the dedicated, intense type. Not a plodder, by any means, don't think I'm that insensitive to character, I rather intend a compliment to your scrupulous perseverance. The key word is of course scrupulous with its moral connotations and the meticulous solicitude and judgment it involves. I could see you performing many of the most difficult tasks of a civilization. Purifying the language of the tribe so to speak, or its vision, or perhaps something as basic as refining the very heart of the multitude. But now I'm waxing romantic. Chess is an interesting game, ancient and interesting, Eddie. This very set we're using has it's personal history, a long line of ancestors from whom it has received the substance of these final rarified and abstracted forms. What do you think about ancestors, Eddie? How far back can you trace your family, are there any traditions passed down through the male line which the men in your family relish as a sacred trust? It was originally an Eastern game. And in essense it remains oriental, doesn't it? The miniature delicacy and virtuosity that can be displayed in the carved figures, the immutability of the checkered board itself and the rigidity of the movements each piece can perform. Finally, the deliberate rhythmic changes in the disposition of each player's force over which the master's face broods serene. At times the moon, at times the waves. There is a particular beauty when the master resigns himself to the will of the carved jade, wood or ivory. Two minds working furiously, fiercely antagonistic, veiled, subdued, yet all spirit, the dross refined away by rules, by the convention of these little figurines sliding from square to square. Only two words needed and with these two words we can express completely the intricate twisting and turnings of minds engaged, of minds truely communicating. Not the feeble monosyllable *love,* not what the ostriches continue to squeal in spite of thousands of years of disappointment and frustration. That empty signal is forsaken. We move in the eternal dance of *Check,* Edward, and *Check-mate.*

Mar. 27

Dear Mama and Bette:

I will be coming home soon. That's all I can say now, but in a way one of the reasons I'm returning is because at last I feel I have something to tell you. It's a strange world here, suffering and pain everywhere. At any time of the day or night you can hear the screaming of grown men; wild screams like babies crying till they almost choke. You hear men crying like that, and you begin to be afraid that the sound is really part of breathing. That if one stops, the other will, and a man must die. Mama, I'll need your help when I return. I learned a man can only do so much alone, that he has to grab onto something outside himself, whether it be a good thing or a bad one. Deep inside there is only screaming, that or a dull, smothering silence. After we reach that deep, the only hope is to see a hand, or hear a quiet voice, anything outside that can be believed, that is as real as the madness. They put Saunders on a train; some of us accompanied the hearse to the depot. His sister will meet the body in Detroit. You never realize how helpless you are till you see pain in another person's eyes.

But from all this I'm coming home. I'll see you soon Mama, and you Bette, and Brother. You can't believe what strange things come into my mind when I try to think of you all, how in funny ways I can't remember the simplest things. But the winter's over, it's already becoming warm enough for shirt sleeves here, and I hope to be with you to celebrate Easter.

Easter and home. Eddie's chest was full. Burning phlegm congested his throat and lungs; the horrible sounds of the day padded his brain with clumps of thorn bushes. Tioga Street Sanctified in the Name of Jesus Christ Church. Eddie entered and sat near the back, behind a few scattered faithful still unredeemed who waited even unto this late hour for a sign. No lights were on. Only a brace of stumpy candles glowered in one corner, shuddering uneasily in the draft, almost audible like a frightened child's murmurs in the darkness. Eddie wondered which saints were there or who sat alone like he did on a saint's hard bench.

Outside the street was quiet; no traffic sounds and only an infrequent footfall rising then gone in a dying fall, the single, lazy motion of a swing. Eddie wept. In the dark interior alone in his corner nothing seemed more natural. His lament completed a vague symphony he had been creating unaware during the entire day. One by one the themes had first stirred into life, Brother, Mama, Alice, brief, bright flames kindled from the embers Eddie's breath heated, then waning again to ashes that burned acrid in his nostrils and stuck in his throat.

The loud rattle of newspaper unfolded broke into Eddie's thoughts. His eyes, grown accustomed to the darkness, discerned a shape at the end of his bench, a man's huddled figure materializing out of the gloom as if created by Eddie's sharpened perception.

—Piece of bread young man? Eddie was startled. The man had been there all along, all through Eddie's utter submission to grief. A witness authenticated by his gravelly voiced offer of a crust of bread, a witness mocking. Eddie was not aware of how long he sat under the sway of his thoughts, apparently oblivious to the other's sudden appearance. He was shocked and helpless on the bench's edge; his eyes fixed on the apparition as if to keep it real and tangible till the flurry of other thoughts passed, and his mind and voice would be his own.

—I'll keep my bread then, mister. Nobody asked you to sit on my bench. You ain't a sanctified I know. By now the stranger's voice had risen above the original hissing undertone in which he had summoned Eddie's attention. To Eddie he seemed to be shouting in the silence of the sanctuary. Eddie knew the few saints would be staring with shock and outrage at this encroaching corner.

—Please, please be quiet.

—Quiet, who the hell are you telling to be quiet. I listened to your bawling and didn't complain. All the time hungry, but waiting till you finished before I opened my bread. Who do you think you are mister! The man was shouting. Eddie could see him more clearly now, a grizzled old man in an ancient oversize army coat that gave him an enormous floundering indefiniteness in the obscurity of the narrow aisles. The loose bench grated as he arose and stumbled towards the door. As he passed Eddie a wave of heat and pungent wine rottenness enveloped the young man.

—Go to hell you sorry-assed, ungrateful bastard, the derelict shouted from the entrance. All you fools will be in a box soon enough, just like that stiff up there in his waiting for some goddamn angel to come and carry him away. Like grotesque snowflakes they sailed and landed silently, the slices of bread he tossed into the store-front church. The saints near the front began to moan in superstitious awe of this blaspheming vision. A bent woman in black scrambled awkwardly from her seat to kneel before the coffin resting in front of the makeshift altar. As a laugh and more curses thundered from the doorway she rose with a scuttling crab urgency, huddling protectively her thin frame over the smooth wooden box.

—Jesus, Jesus, help me Jesus, the few saints bleated in a confused chorus to drown out the mad laughter. Eddie watched numb, petrified till the wino had gone and the saints' frightened prayers subsided. Why so heavy Brother, why does he try to lift such heavy ones? Eddie watched as they struck harmlessly far down the hillside, why such heavy ones?

The saints had moved closer together. Five or six mourners humming in subdued melodious voices.

Eddie wished for something as solid as the rhythm and words of a hymn. Something which would draw him into the confiding, mellow harmony which the saints shared, something to drive away fear and death from the darkness.

Nearer my God to thee, nearer, nearer to thee, he recognized it of course, even in the monolithic, languishing cadences of the saints. Each note was something they dwelled upon, something tasted and savored, a tangible joy he knew was there but whose substance was lost to him. He could at most recall the joy as a powerful presence—sometimes sweet, sometimes threatening, a presence which had promised him even vaster and more mysterious possibilities as he sat a child in the church. That promise had once burned. Could be taken blissfully into his whole being as once the nipple and cloud of flesh resting on his lips.

To touch the hem of his garment, Eddie closed his eyes, settling into the deeper darkness as he bowed his head. Alice the dancer. The stickiness in his groin had begun to itch again. Flowing from her buttock, the pure, untasted excess of their coming together. Gone to itchiness in his body hair. In this chaste vault with angels singing Eddie scratched because he was alone. Eddie followed in his mind and even to the edge of his lips the hymn they were singing. From his saint's bench he leaned to retrieve the heel of bread hurled in anger by the wino. Pure, untasted. Eddie tore off a piece, compressing its substance in his hands. The ball he formed was moist from the sweat of his palms. He broke it with his teeth into two soft hemispheres. It had been almost perfectly round, and wetting both halves with his tongue he reformed the globe then hungrily chewed it. The wino's laugh returned. The stones bounding down the hillside, Alice so warm beneath his hands, the old woman from the top crashing. She would not taste again, never even this, even the staleness of this crust consumed while the saints sing.

Nearer, nearer to thee.

Eddie rose, turning his back on it all. The candles were nearly dead, but whistling louder to him than the saints' drone. In the street their paltry light was a glare, then nothing as he blinked away their image.

Thurley was drunk, drunk and floundering as he and Al entered the chapel. Al, just as high, had never stopped talking as the two men wove their way through the ivy covered American Gothic buildings of the campus, the scenic route from Al's bungalow to the chapel, and Thurley had been reminded of his alma mater quickly and lost himself in sentimental reveries to which Al's almost angry voice was an insistent counterpoint. Somewhere along the way Al had become lost and confused. Their perambulation came to a lurching, unsteady stop beside an undergraduate residence hall.

—It says Potter over the door, Al.

–Potter, yes. Potter. Named for Israel Potter, hero of Melville's romance. But not really Bob, it's some rich founding father, probably one of your New England respectables I'd venture to say. A fine Anglo-Saxon name Potter, and Potter is just seconds away from our destination.

Just beyond the far corner of the tile roofed building the turf was cut by a narrow gravel walk that curved gracefully out of sight again behind another series of stone dormitories on slightly higher ground. Over this cluster of dull red roofs a steeple climbed into view.

–You understand now, Bob, this is not the real thing at all. Just massed choirs, and a good professional priest singing parts of the Mass. But you get the effect anyway. Most of the hymns we'll hear will be in fact processionals, what the Greeks sing parading through the little village streets on Good Friday behind the icons and candles, but I think they'll come off inside. If we're lucky we can sit close. I like to watch the faces. Especially the kids if there are any. Children singing is one of the few things I still believe in, Bob. Have you ever watched them? My first Easter in Greece it was all I could do to keep from hugging every scrubbed little body. Everyone's in the street. They wait for midnight and the Papa to come bursting from inside the church. *Krystos Anesti*—he shouts beaming from beard to bun. He mounts a little raised platform outside the church and around him, illumined by rows of candles or a spotlight if one's available, the most holy objects are gathered. *Krystos Anesti*—he shouts and the crowds respond—*Alithos Anesti*—truly, truly risen. Oh, Bob, if you could have seen the children. Each face lit up by its own glowing candle. The dark eyes wide and excited. All around maniacs shooting off fire-crackers, in your ears it seems, the sky filled with these great swan dives of bursting colors. You have to see it, Bob. We'll go together someday; we'll climb Lycabettus together and be part of the fiery snake slinking down its sides.

If Thurley had been sober, he would have been embarrassed

by the volume of Al's voice still loud as they found seats in the chapel. As it was he smiled inwardly, happy because Al seemed happy, and the smoke from burning incense rising in the church's transept became for him the exhaust of fire bombs shot off and echoing in the vastness of the distant vaulted arch. Simultaneous with a shush from an annoyed spectator, the solemn drone of a rich bass voice issued from the dazzling altar temporarily valanced with ornate cloth of gold drapery. The shuffle of feet moving to a lugubrious cadence began behind them. A female chorus in long, dark dresses, topped by tunics of white and gold, marched towards the cramped wooden benches of the choir loft beside the bearded priest. Others followed till the cantor was surrounded by a brilliant patchwork of gilt and color. A priest robed in white swung a thurible hypnotically in front of the altar while two small boys, their faces made pale by glowing surplices, passed up and down the side aisles waving their antique copper dishes of incense suspended from chains. Wisps of scented smoke floated in the chapel's dark, drafty insides. The voices of the combined choirs began as a rumble, but quickly dissipated in the corners and recesses of the intricate Gothic interior. The music seemed to flee, to hide, to become lost; it wandered ghostly and was trapped in the dark covered ambulatory, it was exhausted, rising up past the triforium into the rarefied, blazing air of the clearstory where shafts of sunlight smoked. Thurley followed it, his ear inordinately keen, listening to the melancholy plash of music against ungiving stone. Al had become deadly silent, as if he too was constrained to share the music's fate.

A solo woman's voice began a long, aching lament. When she reached the uppermost registers her magnificent control never faltered, the rich tones were undiminished, instead they radiated like a fountain at its peak shimmering into crystal spray indistinguishable from the atmosphere in which it danced. Her song created an unbearable tension throughout the audience. Thurley knew it was an act of pure will, a strenuous exertion of forces within himself he only reluctantly brought to bear, which kept him seated. The woman's solo was too perfect, it arched too highly, even beyond the thick joints of the groined ceiling, and if nothing else, if the effort did not bring the singer crashing down, then at last the song itself would end, and Thurley must plunge from its heights. He experienced an uncanny prescience; he didn't need to look around to know that the others were rapt in fear and submission, to know that Al sat weeping beside him, the tattered remains of his program forlorn in his lap. Thurley knew he must leave, knew he must escape the siren song of her perfect voice foraging like a hungry beast among the stones inside the chests of the audience. Something welled up in his stomach. At first he feared it was a scream, an irresistible ear-splitting scream that would suck away his life's breath as it tore from his body. Then he knew it was sickness. Sour tasting, animal sickness as he stifled a belch, and the fumes rose to coat his throat. Al never noticed him get up, in fact every eye was fixed on the singer as Thurley fled from his seat and hurried giddily on tiptoe up the aisle.

He was barely outside before he doubled up, lunging towards a tree against which he shot out a stiffened arm for support. The gin of an afternoon splattered against the tree's gnarled roots and flecked the thick soles and sides of his cordovans. When he raised his head, he noticed clouds. Deep, gray clouds from nowhere piling up in ranks to obscure the blue sky. No one in sight. Al's voice gone, the priest gone, the woman gone, the choirs and sweet, drifting incense gone. Thurley wiped his mouth. He knelt down and brushed the vomit from his wing-tipped shoes, discarding the soiled sudarium as he arose. A light snowlike shower of blossoms was falling around him. He looked down at his feet and saw the fluttering mounds these tiny petals had formed drifting apart, silently scattered as the breeze curled among them. Although the clouds moved rapidly and short gusts of wind agitated the blossoms, a dead, still calm engulfed Thurley.

The foliage of enormous horse chestnut trees forming a grove around the chapel swayed and rustled, one tree in particular, its shaggy outline flocculent against the dulling sky trembled as the wind's invisible hand dug deeply into its branches. The blanched undersides of its leaves flapped and quivered into view, conical bunches of flowers swayed then released a rain of white petals. Enveloped in his own stillness Thurley saw it all frighteningly accelerated, like a motion picture flickering at the wrong speed, the scene around him became poignant simply because it unfolded too quickly to follow. He felt suddenly weary, suddenly weak and old. There was no way to catch up, no way to remove himself from the unnatural calm. He saw faces looking down on him, grief-stricken, pitying faces obscured by veils. Thurley was stiff and unmoving; the faces passed in procession peering down from a tremendous height, each one tendering only a brief pathetic glance, as if afraid a longer look would draw them into the pit where Thurley was stretched cold, unmoving as stone. Thurley wanted to feel the wind, wanted it to lap inside his clothes and finger his body. The blossoms swam by his eyes. Jerky, uneven movements as they circled closer to the earth. Shuddering it seemed as a puff of air shot them forward, then suddenly dropped its support. It would rain soon, and the puddles would be thick with white blossoms. They would float, mixing with the scum and acrid green to form mottled rainbows in stagnant pools. The air brought its message of rain in a cool draft across Thurley's perspiring face. As he walked, clouds clustered around the sun, and long tree shadows disappeared insensibly into the general darkness.

THREE

· · · · · ·

The powerful engine revving beneath him brought no relief. Thurley drove like a madman, but the faster the automobile sped along route seventy-two, the deeper into a black, yawning gulf it seemed to carry him.

A queasy after-sickness was all that remained of the gin's euphoria; a vitus dance of thought replaced his sensual apprehension of the afternoon's events. He recognized the increasingly morbid content of these thoughts as the black winged drones of a sweeping depression he knew he had no strength to resist. He had to find a room, a room swarming with other men, a dark, whiskey perfumed place where the spirit could drown without thrashing and gasping for breath.

After mounting the stairs, Thurley's progress was impeded by a thick, metal door, and he stood on Harry's bright threshold ill at ease beneath a single, naked bulb. He knew he was being watched, silently appraised through a narrow slit of one-way glass by Ollie, the one-eyed, antediluvian doorman who never forgot a face. As he stood aside, his wizened body straining to hold the door, Ollie screwed the death mask of his features into its customary grimace of greeting which by convention passed for a smile among the frequenters of Harry's Place. Thurley was no stranger to the old black man and his fifty-cent piece dropping with a solid ring into Ollie's white saucer was an ornament left as incentive to other customers but seldom matched between his visits. This model gratuity brought both Ollie's crooked yellow teeth into view and earned the subtle compliance of his bow. With alacrity he depressed a hidden buzzer summoning the steward to a second portal further down the fuliginous corridor. Another pair of heavy doors swung mystically inward, emitting a gust of clotted music and laughter that floated down the dusty hall dying before it reached Ollie's table, chair and porcelain nest crowded by the silver coin. Thurley was inside.

Sunday was the biggest day for Harry's Place. The state's obsolete blue laws which made after hour joints financially practical also added those inestimable second relishes of sin and secrecy, and Harry kept it close to pitch dark so his clientele could savor these virtues. In every corner of Harry's, people felt they were getting away with something. Occasionally to heighten the aura of authority flaunted there were well advertised police raids, usually on odd Mondays when a few paid stooges and forgetful winos were ceremoniously packed into paddy wagons and hauled away. Everybody knew Harry did it that way just to keep the heat off, and to further demonstrate his power over the *man*, the club's bouncer was always a uniformed cop. Thurley was one of few white customers. The reason for this aside from the fact Harry's was deep in the Strip was the women. Although available in various degrees, they were not professionals and a certain fierce etiquette protected them from all white prowlers and Negroes not prepared to go through preliminary gallantries no matter how brief or coarse. The kind of woman who came, the sister, aunt, cousin, neighbor, or even mother of the men, made this code necessary and brutally enforced. Trespasses against it caused most of the incidents in or outside Harry's. Thurley smoothing his way in with heavy tipping and discretion, became a sort of unobtrusive fixture on weekends. One or two white faces could be seen among a hundred or so other customers most busy nights, but they were always the same. Thurley had never approached any of these other white men and gradually had subdued his curiosity about their motives. He valued too much the special kind of peace that allowed him to effectively sink his identity into the darkness of Harry's Place. Always the same bartender, the same stool, the same drink that never had to be ordered. He was simply Bob to the few people who spoke to him, and neither he nor anyone else wanted more.

The weekend band was playing, a local group whose special talent was making a racket loud enough to be heard over the general din. It was always hot in Harry's, and the band leader wore a sweat band around his head. Above it in deep greasy swirls, Indian Slick's processed hair was plastered to his skull.

Indian Slick had a way of moving which disturbed Thurley. After each number, keeping his elongated torso rigid on the piano stool, and his thin arms, bent at the elbow and wrist, suspended over the keyboard, he would twist his head around on the column of his skinny neck to study the audience through grotesquely outsized sunglasses. Something about this praying mantis posture, the frozen intentness of the little Negro at the piano had made Thurley wary from his first encounter with it. When the band broke up for a short intermission Slick joined Thurley at the bar.

—Little word to the wise on this happy Easter day my friend. Let me buy you a drink too, and I'll have one whiles we talk this little matter over. The bartender moved opposite Thurley and his sudden host, immediately acting on the signal for drinks from Slick. As soon as they were set down, Slick raised his glass to his mouth. He sipped slowly, never moving the glass from his lips, gradually tilting the vessel till its contents had been drained. When he finished he began speaking again, taking for granted he had retained Thurley's attention although a space of several minutes had elapsed, and his absorption in this peculiar intaking of liquor made it obvious he was no more concerned with the people around him than an aphid milking a plant.

—You know Brother Small, don't you? Nice fellow, Brother. But Brother got a friend certain people around here don't like, and they have good reason believe me. These people thought you might be able to speak to Brother. Tell him just to stay away from this fellow he thinks is his friend. Brother'll know who you mean; he's been shooting his mouth off about how his friend would be back for Easter. But if he acts dumb, you just say Eddie Lawson, tell Brother we mean he should keep clear of Eddie Lawson and keep Eddie outta here. Now you're Brother's friend and these people think he'll listen to you. I mean nobody's involving you in anything, you can tell him or not, it's up to you, and they don't care if you do or if you don't, they just thought you might drop him a little word to the wise, from the wise. It might save him some bad trouble and I thought you'd like to help him, you being his friend and all that.

—Eddie, Eddie Lawson.

—That's the name. You know 'em?

—Brother just mentioned him once or twice.

—Just take my word friend, Lawson is pure trouble, and Brother's asking for it if he hangs around 'em. Just a word to the wise of course. Now I got to go back to work, friend.

Thurley was sweating. He reached into the inner pocket of his light suit jacket feeling for a handkerchief. His hand met the square corners of a folded piece of paper. He drew it out, forgetting in his curiosity the dampness of his forehead and at the back of his neck. It was a program from the cathedral, a single white sheet folded in half so it gave the contents of four consecutive Sunday musicales. The Easter extravaganza was announced on the first page. Thurley turned it over quickly, ignoring its numerous credits in small print, list of choirs, soloists and the orthodox hymns in Greek characters with translations bracketed beneath. On the third page, after running through the usual introduction preceding the music titles, Thurley's eyes were riveted to the program. Unbelievingly, softly aloud he read *A Cantata, The Voices of Children, by Professor Al Levine, Head of the College Music Department. This new work, directed by the composer, will receive its initial performance.* Al's secret, why he could smile.

Thurley knew in an instinctive flood of confidence that the

music would be grand, would express Al's tremendous talent, his energy and meticulous craftsmanship. But then after a moment's consideration, although he still believed it would be good, Thurley realized good or bad didn't matter most; the point was that Al could stand in front of them safe for a moment, pure as he lifted his arms and began to direct the chorus. In that moment free, the past erased, no past except what was focused upon and consumed in the first swell of singing voices. Soft, fluttering Al at rest, at peace, something that to Thurley always seemed impossible to achieve for himself or anyone else—till it happened. A cantata, a poem, a book, they meant nothing in themselves, anything could be the reason to rise up high. Thurley knew too well the illusion of completion, the crazy idea that the chase really ends. How empty, how desolate the disenchantment could be. Thurley knew he would never willingly be born again, never be a child if one condition was remembering this backside of experience which two thirds of a lifetime thrust in his face. But each time he lifted a pencil or turned a page, this knowledge was a weight on his chest; it strained every sinew of his will to shake free from the taunts and laughter, from the certainty of failure his first step assured. A poem, a book. Too big for the narrow pinnacle, they must topple from the summit to the very depths, and the same inescapable logic that put a man behind a stone drew him after it in its fall. Thurley saw Al loinclothed, his small, perfect limbs toiling. Al Sisyphus reaches the top, balances one precarious second, smiling in the glare of brilliant flashbulbs as angels crowd to take his picture. Al beautiful, poised, with a verve that seems will sustain him however, fig-leafed Al and the depths beneath.

Thurley found his handkerchief. He also replaced the program tenderly inside his coat. He was smiling to himself, the absurdity of his vision, little Al naked, struggling with a boulder up a steep rise was just too incongruous with the immaculate, be-Dacroned back he knew Al would present to the audience as he turned towards his singers. Even funnier was the thought of his own red flesh quivering in the same task. I would need two fig leaves in the garden. Because that's where it began; wasn't innocence just the first way station at the foot of the slope, a place to refresh, to grab a drink before starting up? Certainly nobody could stay there, nobody would want to if they had eyes and a brain, and as long as these continued to function there could be no true desire to return, just moments of utter fatigue when another drink is needed. Once past it, the wish can only be in terms of choosing life or death, to stop or go on. The poem becomes an oasis, a sort of gas station that is only sought because it provides the means of going on, not a destination . . . *an old man in a dry month, Being read to by a boy,* for some reason, as they often did, the lines came to Thurley. They broke into the mild self-satisfaction he felt with his gas station metaphor. Eliot was for him the poet of weariness, of old age. His frightened old men had aged the undergraduate Thurley prematurely, and strangely, they now came back bringing Thurley a poignant feeling for youth. It had all gone so quickly. Between two readings of a poem his lifetime had nearly slipped away. Sometimes it seemed like that. That only a few events, insignificant on any objective scale but emotionally charged beyond calculation had been crowded into a morning and afternoon, a poignantly recent time, so close it seemed that now as he sat in a long evening of recollection something still could be done. But he knew once gone was always gone, time past had no minutes or years. In fact it seemed colors were much more adequate to describe his fast receding day, blues, reds, yellows, violets, a glowing spectrum from blazing white to the black of night.

Thurley spoke silently to Al. But we are not old men. You proved you had further to go, wanted me to hear it and see it. In a way another's triumph can be just as refreshing as my own, but since I'm selfish and weak, it's just as likely to bring pain before its full meaning penetrates. Like the woman's voice this afternoon. I couldn't keep it down, how could I sit still in the presence of beauty knowing what I do. But with you it's different, and your cantata will be beautiful, it must be beautiful, and I will come to hear it. I will not be afraid, and I won't torment myself with the illusion that such beauty only comes from beauty and is only for the beautiful. That's what makes the music of strangers so exquisite, what often makes it unbearable. It seems to come from nowhere, to be pure and unattainable. It seems to somehow make a link with what I've been clumsily seeking and by the perfection of this link seems to exhaust the source. But it isn't like that. It's dirty business, sweating, bitter work, like you've done, Al, like I must continue doing. Strange how wrestling with angels makes us so dirty. You'd think they'd smell of perfume, be soft and clean. But it's you struggling up the hill I'll remember, Al, you with your perfect buttocks and legs straining like they did that night with Eleanor, that I will believe in.

Al disappeared, his familiar face melting again into the noise and darkness of the bar. They had been speaking, he must have been with Al; the words had been important to Thurley, and Al's face had been so close and intent as he listened. Thurley wanted the handsome face and dark eyes again, wanted to express his sincerity in a long, direct look Al would be sure to understand. He must know I meant every word, even down to the bold *I will not be afraid.* How long since I've said that to myself. It's a child's phrase, something said to goblins, to wild animals, to mothers, to other little boys and especially to myself in empty rooms at night with their lights extinguished. Am I really not afraid? What Indian Slick said to me is not to be disregarded or taken lightly. I've been around long enough to recognize the unquestionable authority of some people's words to the wise. Also, another wouldn't have been involved, especially a white man unless something serious was concerned. Brother Small. The name called up no definite response in Thurley's mind. The one outstanding fact about his frequent house guest was the one first surmounted and forgotten by Thurley—Brother's unrelieved albino ugliness. After that Thurley realized he could recall very little. Aside from Brother's pell-mell monologues only partially understood by Thurley, they had no conversations. Brother never seemed to listen to whole sentences. Disregarding the direction and even content of Thurley's speech, except in the simplest question or command, Brother responded according to a logic only he understood. Certain words no matter what their context, and ideas only loosely associated with Thurley's meaning were what he seemed to reply to. Clustered around certain words like *Eddie* there was an endless constellation of incidents which Brother dramatized in his original but disconcerting manner. But by frequently sounding this particular signal, Thurley had gained a familiarity with Eddie at once intimate and mysterious. The intensity of their only meeting had given a spur more than curiosity to Thurley's interest. In a life he felt was shrunken to a minimal content of event and emotion, that rare evening had haunted him, the violence of the young man pinned Thurley down, defined him in heavy strokes as relentlessly accurate as the beauty of the woman's voice.

There had been a Thurley where Eddie saw one. A hungry, preying animal only barely concealed beneath his clothes. But there was more, something Thurley now felt impelled to make clear although he had failed so many times before. Perhaps Al already knew, could already understand, and if he hadn't heard Thurley speak, then after Al's music when they talked again, Thurley would repeat what he had said. But how could Eddie know that beneath his olive suit, within the flushed, white flesh was a consciousness just as acute, just as accusing, just as aware of the beast as Eddie's hate had made him. And if they could meet so powerfully, if the same anger could be shared, could not remorse and the act of forgiveness bind them just as tightly? In this desire to share, to submit to someone else's judgment what he thought he had learned about himself, truth as far as an active, unremitting search had revealed it, Thurley had always been held back by fear. And as long as this fear remained he had to flee.

As he became aware of the music again, Thurley noticed his drink sat still untouched. Around him the shadowy forms of the Negroes like dark, inverted ghosts were absorbed into the narcotic clamor. He stood alone, voluminously robed in a brilliant arc of light, his arms gloved in crimson from the limp fingertips to the elbows. At his feet, supine between the pavement and gutter, the slaughtered offering laved the stones from hidden wounds. A mist rose from the corpse, like cigarette smoke at first, then thickening, congealing to a weighty death's head floating above it. It was a skull, then a full bearded tragic mask in flowing headdress. Slowly the horror began to fade from its eyes, the deeply cut furrows of tension softened and eased, the mouth relaxed its half gulping, half screaming downward slant, the face became younger, the mild, wondering gaze of a youth mortally stricken, the simultaneous disbelief and disillusion Thurley knew was Eddie's face beneath the lamp.

They passed within three yards of him, the albino and the slim figure of his bowed friend, like one body as they slipped through the mass of dark, oblivious jelly. A single blues chord crashed from the piano and was repeated with monomaniacal persistence like a lunatic dashing his head against the ground. The sound increased in intensity till it seemed the blows were struck by feet rather than hands, by someone possessed who jumped up and down with ragged precision to annihilate some doomed section of the keyboard. Like carrion crows towards a death smell a crowd gathered around Indian Slick. Four or five couples streaming with sweat still gyrated on the dance floor. They had given over all semblance of form, submitting to the primitive, insistent force of the music. The couples disintegrated into single, unapproachable entities. Each dancer seemed to be fighting a desperate internal battle, contorting every limb, every joint, pushing his body to an excess and exaggeration of every sense, outraging its reluctant, lethargic core, as if instinctively grasping pure outrage was the only kind of arousal that would raise him to the pitch of the piano's throb. The crowd, dimly sensing the struggle, tried to share the urge. It became a thing of shoving, clapping hands, of patted feet, of hoarse shouts, of popping fingers, of knees and thighs that danced and bumped excited by their own heat and reeking sweat. Clothes would come off, hands would be furtively tucked between legs and buttocks would wink and be pinched.

Thurley's voice was drowned as he called to Brother. He followed the men through a maze of tables and chairs scattered in the rush towards the bandstand. When he reached him they were already seated, facing each other in one of the dim stalls that marked the corners of Harry's Place. He heard Eddie's sobs singularly clear and distinct within the swelling vortex of sound.

Brother saw him first, regarding Thurley from beneath his peaked cap first with a dumb animal incomprehension, then a mute indifference as his pink eyes returned to where his outstretched hand clasped Eddie's on the dark wood. Something sullenly fatal about the turning away of his eyes, something cold and limpid as allegory made Thurley hang on Brother's simplest gestures. He felt exquisitely nervous, attuned to a starkness of meaning that would only be revealed if he carefully attended to the dumb show enacted in this black corner. Eddie raised his face from the table; there was no glimmer of recognition, no sign of resentment, as if a total stranger could be no more foreign than himself to the unbridled grief and pain that ravaged through him. Thurley thought the face peering up at him almost smiled before it was lowered or at least an inexplicable adjustment of the features was caused by some fluid light source playing momentarily upon them. Thurley sat down on the outer edge of the bench on Brother's side facing Eddie. He sat stiffly, folding his hands, gazing at the scarred table top that had a second before seemed a calm, purple sea. He wanted so much to compose himself, to find that peace which would release him from himself, the peace that prevented him from being an intruder but would leave him responsive to the slightest nuance emanating from the two men.

Thurley felt completely inept. His night world had been a kind of game; there was no death beneath the frenzied life of its surface. He enjoyed the vicarious plunge, living on its fringes, feeling the excitement of the music but never dancing. But now the lie failed him because he had something to say to these men a few feet away from him. Indian Slick's insect body loomed up in his imagination. Out of nowhere, out of the poised shadow of violence, urgency and substance came. They *would* understand, and he would understand them. They would know why he had to speak, why he had to come, why the day and the week and the month and the year had to be forgotten so the moment could live. The men he joined in this corner were perhaps more naked and empty than he felt himself. It was not their world which swirled in blackness and heat around the booth. It was the same dark water that had floated Thurley for so long and from so far to the table where he sat this Easter night. They would understand. He could tell them. I come because . . . because . . . I must sit here because . . .

—We don't mind if he sits down, do we Brother? It might do the white man good to see a nigger cry. Eddie sat up, the sound of his voice, although barely audible, relieving him of a heavy load of silence his sobs had not eased. There was nothing pugnacious in his tone, in fact as he spoke the words seemed to belie any kind of construction Thurley could put on them. It was the sound of a man talking in his sleep, of a voice rising from a dream, disconnected from the reality in which another hears it, evocative of some impenetrable state of mind the hearer can only imagine.

—Don't you remember Bobbie? Brother's voice was unreal. He looked up from Eddie, trying to reach the other man.

—Eddie's had a loss. His mother passed today, his first day home in a year. He came all the way here to see her, and now she's had some accident, and she's dead. Brother spoke solemnly, in unhurried deliberate phrases, never turning to Thurley but keeping his eyes on Eddie, trying to make certain that his statement reached through Eddie's silence. Brother's eyes gave everything away. It was clear that he wanted Eddie to believe what was said to Thurley and didn't know how except to hurry on to another question before Eddie could speak. Remember how knocked out I was that night? Bobbie helped you to get me home.

—Yes, he helped.

—And you fussing all the time, Eddie. I ain't got the best manners, but sometimes you shame me. But Bobbie understood. He's all right. I mean if it was just anybody, I'd have chased him away then or now. Just anybody don't have no right inviting themselves to a place they ain't invited especially when men is talking serious, and they got good reason to be serious.

—I remember screaming at you. I remember telling you I hated you. And I did. If I had believed no harm would have come to me, I would have happily killed you.

—And now?

—Now I don't care. Brother's right, he's always been right. There's nothing for it, nothing at all. Get out of here, mister.

—Brother. Thurley blurted out the name like an echo. I must tell you something. The piano player, the one they call Indian Slick. For some reason he told me to tell you . . . certain people don't want to see you two together . . . here . . .

—Not with Eddie! Why that conkeline headed, axle-grease-wearing monkey. It don't concern him a damn who I'm with or why I'm with 'em. Me stay away from Eddie! Just cause Eddie tried to do something for hisself these niggers is afraid of him. Talking when Eddie was away about how Eddie ain't to be trusted, that he'd be working for the Man when he got back. It's that Slick who talks the most. He never did like Eddie. And he don't like me cause I told him to stay away from Alice. I'll do some talking to that chump. Knock his Slick head clean off. Brother rose in his chair as he spoke, shouting almost and drawing deep flushes into his cheeks beneath his ghostly lurid flesh. I'll kill that little junkie.

—Sit down, Bruv, sit down. These rats are bound to be suspicious of me. Just be cool and it'll blow over. You have to get what we need so don't go mouthing off. Be patient man, they'll see I'm still O.K. soon enough. I can't afford to mess up here; it's all I have. After a year I guess I still smell a bit of the Man. He wrinkled his nose, sniffing disdainfully at his wrist, his eyes coldly meeting Thurley across the table. Behind them the noise had diminished. Slick was coming off the stand and the crowd filtered slowly away into arguments about deserted tables and drinks. No one approached their corner, but Thurley felt the space they occupied palpably cramped by unseen phantoms stealthily materializing around them. Within this tightening space, he also felt more alone than at any moment since he had joined the two men. Brother still scowled, visibly at odds with himself, remaining seated when what he wanted most to do was search out his enemy. Eddie had withdrawn into a shell of silent contemplation. That he concentrated severely was obvious to Thurley watching his long fingers pick at the rough edge of the table and the vein he vividly remembered define itself in his high brow. The ease Thurley had felt, what he could almost call an air of familiarity with this man's intensity had vanished. It was as if Eddie's momentary weakness had drawn them together, his grief opening a passage through the calloused husk of his being. An adept at all species of pain Thurley had entered with a surgeon's skill and tact, but now the wound shut of its own accord and Thurley was neither in nor out.

Eddie finally spoke. —Thanks for passing on what you did. Did he say anything else?

—Not really.

—I wonder why he spoke to you. Why he thought you'd involve yourself, even care.

—Cause Bobbie's my friend, and Slick knew I'd bust 'em in his mouth if he started talking that sort of shit to me hisself.

—And you think this man is really your friend, Brother? What kind of friend is he? What does he give to you, what does he take?

—Aw man, now I can't answer that. I don't hardly know what you mean. It ain't like going to a grocery store. Ain't no tags on everything.

—Then you think he gives a damn whether you live or die?

—Yeah, I believe that.

—It's more than I can believe. I killed her, that's all I can believe . . . I killed her.

—Man, man! You killed nobody, you don't even know she's dead do you?

—She's dead. I caused it. My words, my wish brought her down those stairs. I couldn't even look at her. I was afraid of her eyes . . . afraid they would still be open, burning, accusing me . . . she couldn't even speak . . . with her last breath she . . . Eddie couldn't finish, his head fell into his hands, and when he spoke again his voice had an almost hysterical edge.

—Do you know what I just did, what happened when I took my head in my hands? I started to pray. Like a little boy. Like some snotty little kid I started whimpering, *now I lay me down.* Thurley watched the distended pupils grow dim, Eddie's whole body relax as the tightness drained from his shoulders, and Eddie shifted his weight forward to rest both shirt sleeved arms on the table's surface. He leaned closer to them, the eggshell fragility of his high brow bright and frightening. Now I lay me down to sleep. Every night I had to say my prayers, Mama came in and stood beside me to hear. For a long time I didn't understand it at all. Then I began to realize I was asking for things. They told me I was down on my knees speaking to a great and powerful God who had everything in his hands and who could give me anything I asked. So instead of staying in bed when Mama left, I would climb out and ask for something besides sleep and blessings. I kept myself busy all day thinking about what I'd like. Each night I couldn't wait to be finished with the first prayers so I could get down to business. I don't remember how long I believed, but I remember the day I started hating Mama over me while I crouched down to speak to a God who never gave what I asked for. I never quite forgave him, even when I went to church, I didn't forgive. As soon as Mama stopped coming in at night, I stopped praying. But tonight the words came . . . like tears . . . came back. Alice's, mine . . . I can't help them. Do you know the words? *Now I lay me down to sleep, I pray the Lord my soul to keep, and if I die before I wake, I pray the Lord my soul to take.* Then you begin blessing people—one by one—mother, father, sisters, brothers, everybody in the whole world, or special ones, those sick or in need, even animals and things you can bless. I blessed you Brother, almost every night if we weren't fighting I stuck you on the end of my prayers. But they stopped one day. Haven't crossed my lips till now. Maybe it's because I want to speak to Mama, I want her to be beside me in the darkness. When I did feel a sort of comfort, it was her being there and not the words. She always went to Eugene first. And even when we got too old for her to be there, he kept on praying. He's dead you know, died fighting for God Bless America in some stinking jungle on some stinking island doing some stinking job some stinking white man wouldn't do himself. Thurley is your name, isn't it? I don't blame anybody, believe me, Thurley. Lots of people died on Guam. Black, yellow, and probably white most of all. It's the way Gene died that gets me. Being black he had to be a flunky, here, there, anywhere the white man is. So what's it mean—it means he died a flunky. But that's a while ago, isn't it? He's bones now or dust. He died and didn't change anything, and I will do the same and Brother will, even you will. If my head ever goes down again, those words won't come. They came from a long time ago. I had to say them one last time loud and clear so I could be sure they were gone for good . . . make sure I wouldn't get caught alone with them again some night. All that has to be said now is Amen. Say it for me, Bruv. Don't be ashamed. Amen, Brother,

Amen. Say it, man, you must say it. It's finished, don't you see . . . finished, nothing, nothing more . . . Amen . . .

—Amen, Eddie. I said it, listen to me, Eddie, Amen, Amen. Bobbie, c'mon, you say it too. Eddie needs to hear it. Amen. C'mon, Bob. Amen.

It was there, in the urgency of Eddie's cry, in Brother's excited, pleading voice. Thurley heard himself shout *Amen*. Heard the strange sound from his lips grow natural as it blended with Brother's repetition of the same word. Eddie began to laugh, a laugh that made Thurley shudder, then laugh himself, as its bright knife edge softened to diffuse a steady, beneficent glow over Eddie's face. It was finally a rich, throat deep laugh reaching above the discordant sounds of Harry's, a laugh whose power only Eddie knew as it ranged through the immense silences within his breast.

—I said Amen for Saunders once, Bruv. You remember him, don't you? Felt sorry for the poor bastard, he just couldn't take it. A week in the streets and he was hooked again. Just couldn't do with it, or without it. When he returned so soon after seeming so well, it scared me. I decided then to stick it out a whole year, not to kid myself. To get stronger than I thought I'd ever have to be. And would you believe it, this is my first day home, night one and I'm ready. No more strength left. I'm down on my knees waiting. What kind of a man am I? Do you know, white man? You seem to be educated; you're white. But then again you're here too, just about as low as a white man can get, calling yourself a friend of Brother's and drinking Harry's bad whiskey from his dirty glasses, sitting here talking to me, a man even these niggers don't want around them.

—In some ways I believe I can understand. It's an awful thing to lose a mother. I can understand how you feel. A look of panic crossed Brother's face. A look his ugliness made ludicrous. The pasty faced clown, grimacing absurdly, pursued by his shadow.

—Do you really think you understand? Eddie tensed, his face suddenly closer, a flash of heat and light across the table.

—I lost a mother.

—But did you . . . Eddie paused, two words jarred in his mind struck up by the same impulse, words that at first seemed contradictory, then rushed inextricably down onto his tongue so they felt like different ways of asking the same question, and when he used one of the pair, *love,* instead of *kill* her, it contained the meaning of both. Did you love her?

—If I say I did, there are certain things I can't explain, but if I say I didn't, there are more.

—What kinds of things? The question came from a shadow Eddie, a source alien and unexpected whose life Eddie could only observe, blood pouring from a razor slash he could not feel, aware of curiosity not pain as Thurley spoke.

—Her brooch. A gold, green jewelled brooch. Something she felt closer to than any other. She gave it to me when she had become very old and near to death. I kept it in the box that had always belonged to it. A velvet lined box, built up so it had a sort of pillow inside on which the brooch rested. When you closed the box, even though it was very old, a hinge made it snap shut the last inch or so by itself. A soft, muffled snap as the velvet edges came together. I gave it to a little boy a few days ago . . . a year ago . . . I don't know, to someone I never saw before, or will see again and who will probably lose it or sell it if he hasn't already. In a way it was all I had left of her.

—Then she didn't die till you were a man. The question registered in Eddie's ears. The sound of a voice reaching out to meet the other still strangely his own and not his own.

—No, not till I had brought home a blushing bride and Mother had danced at our wedding. Thurley stopped himself on the verge of a gossiping monologue. Something urged him to begin at the beginning, rehearse his one great love affair from the first fearful descent into her body to the culmination of their marriage when Eleanor, laughing hysterically, called him into the bathroom to see the miscarried remnants of his *son* before she flushed *him* down the toilet. It all seemed vaguely relevant, something he ought to share with the voice.

—Where is your wife?

—She's gone. I haven't seen or heard of her for longer than I can remember. She may be in a home somewhere.

—And you don't care, do you? Like that piece of jewelry, she's just gone. Come to Harry's and get drunk, anything you've ever lost can be bought cheaper. A wife . . . a gold pin, Harry has it all. Even God, God's here. That's church music you know, sanctified music, only here you can dance and drink to it. Forget 'em, white man, that's why you're here, and me, and all these fools. Amen, Brother. Tell this white man about bags. Tell him how Harry draws them closed so it's dark and what you breathe is at least your own foul breath. Everybody, everything gone, closed up tight. That's what Harry does. Makes it so everything's gone . . .

—People don't go like that. You can just kill yourself, always part of yourself, not them, they're not what goes. Even if we have to act as if it is, if we have to pretend, have to shut out certain things sometimes to get to the next stage. Love, hate, pity, if there's no one to whom we can tie these feelings they grow too large, too powerful, become something that destroys. What we feel inside must have a release, even if it's one that once was or might have been. That's why we can't afford to ever let go. Even the pieces of other people we've helped break apart. The spirit can't live on air, and especially the air that's inside our bodies. It flourishes when it touches other things—people, work. Thurley began to grow uneasy. He knew he meant what he said, but why now, why to these men? He knew he was generating a rarefied, distilled air, the atmosphere where he liked to believe the still untainted parts of his mind and spirit moved freely. But to bring it out into the open, to hear the high thoughts and exalted feelings transformed into words was like unravelling an infinite tape measure to take the five feet ten inches of his dying flesh. Of course, he thought, it's not wrong to express how I'd like to be, to show that I have an idea what a better kind of life should be, that I think I know the kind of strength I need to live it. No, I can't forget dead things, or things that were never alive. I move among them, like a mole in the darkness, beneath the earth. It is their substance I must burrow through to see the light, to give the spirit somewhere to breathe. I cannot be ashamed, I cannot hold back my little simply because it's little.

—Your mouth's full of words. You say you think you understand. The spirit needs this, needs that. Here's something for you to think about. Some people, the black ones you see around you, they live without spirit. There's just shit and Harry's, Harry's or shit. I despise what you are and they do too. Things about you make me almost sick, but I have to sit here speaking to you, have to listen to you or any other white man who thinks he knows because I can't claim anything better. Because I'm Eddie Lawson—nothing. I've tried the shit today, died for a year so I could have it rubbed in my face again. And Harry's has been here all the time. Harry's waiting for me. That's the funny part. Harry's always waiting.

Thurley felt the words enter, a gust of burning needles, striking, swirling about. His speech had fallen flat. The classroom rhetoric he dredged up could not live in the dark corner. He could not speak again; he wasn't afraid of Eddie's words, only the inevitable silence he knew must follow. Thurley stared into the other man's face, watching the eyes, the blood, the tremors of the skin subside. He had only the vaguest idea of Eddie's character, only Brother's garbled anecdotes and the words passed in two short confrontations. But he also knew nothing would ever be able to separate him from the young man's pain. He must help Eddie. Must get him out. And to where? Of course not any particular place, no place at least through which Thurley discontentedly had passed. No, just free from this choking air, free from the hungers that fed on him. There is the night, the black, all blackening night. We can breathe there, we can lead there and be led unashamedly.

Someone dropped a coin in the jukebox; a woman began to sing, her rasping, heavy voice belting out a current popular ballad. After an initial burst of pleased exclamations, rustling of dresses, chairs scraping, glasses set down, feet shuffling towards the dance floor, Harry's grew quiet. Couples glided, pressed tightly together on the dance floor as everyone seemed moved by the melancholy ballad of lost love and tears.

Thurley listened intently, partly to catch the lyrics and partly to escape the terrible vertigo as he lost contact with Eddie. The voice made Thurley think of Bessie Smith, but it was far from that standard—maudlin phrases that struck him as cliché rather than true, and a voice mechanically amplified through too many echo chambers to retain the suffering edge Bessie always brought out in the blues, that poignant friability always threatening to destroy the singer and the song, the susceptibility to pain that made them one, that made the blues like crying.

The memory of how good it could be made Thurley weak. When he spoke, his voice wavered. —What you said a minute ago, Eddie. About despising me.

—Forget it, it doesn't matter. I'm sick of me, that's what I'm sick of. What I've been, what I am, and the only things I can be. Just leave me and Brother now would you please. There's nothing else to say or do. Just this goddamn night and a morning I don't want to see.

—Amen.

—Forget it.

—Amen, Eddie. Amen. I say that because . . . because there's something left. Even if it's something you don't like, it's there. Say Amen to that.

—You know nothing.

—I know it's been bad. Today and for so long today seems always. And I'm not talking about you, about your pain. I'm

170

saying that it's been bad for me. I don't know what's smacked you down, but . . . I've been down . . . it's true . . . I've been down. But you've got me pegged don't you. A worn out fairy, mouth full of words, rotting on one of Harry's stools. Maybe that's not exactly what you think, maybe you don't even feel I'm worth pegging. No matter what you think, or anybody thinks, there's this . . . this I have to say. The worst is true. Has been and probably will be tomorrow. But tonight I'm more. The music's for me tonight. My music. I'm not afraid. One moment, one morning, one slice of light even if I don't see it, even if it's not for me. No spirit, Eddie, and all these people no spirit. It wouldn't hurt the way it does if there wasn't. You can deny it, you can cut everything off with one of Slick's cures. But you know you'd be killing something that fights back. That wants to live. I don't know what's happened today, or all the yesterdays, but it hasn't been enough to put you out. You're still soft, still squirming beneath the pain and fear. Get through tonight, Eddie. I have a car, I'll take you to your home, or to my place, anywhere you want to go. Just get through tonight and tomorrow . . .

—And tomorrow I'll have the smell of your white hands over my body.

—No, no you must come. I know in some ways you can't trust me yet, believe me even partially, and maybe you never will. Maybe I'll spoil it. But come out of here, I know I'm right in that at least.

He looked at Thurley. It was hard to pick his words out of the deafening roar the jukebox now produced. At first it was only the tone of Thurley's plea that struck Eddie as familiar, then the mad rush of the day's events inundated his imagination with a flood of images and phrases. His own words came back to him. Then Thurley beckoned more clearly than ever across the dark table. He saw Thurley too, swaying and tottering, moments, inches from the abyss. Eddie moved instinctively, grief wide in his eyes, the way he moved towards the mystery

171

of Grierson, the way he moved towards Alice, towards his mother, towards Bette, towards Saunders, the way he always moved with Brother. He couldn't edge very far out of the booth before his arm became taut in the grasp of Brother's who still remained motionless.

—Where you going? Why you running, Eddie. Slick sells the only thing for it right here. There ain't nowhere to go man. You know there ain't nothing out there.

Eddie looked down at his hand crossed by Brother's livid flesh on the dark table. —Let me go Bruv. It's best I go. I don't want to get you in trouble . . . I have to walk out of here by myself. The night, Brother . . . we were afraid of it so long, then it got to be our time. Nothing out there . . . Are they gone, Brother, like the prayers each night, where are they, Brother—Mama, Alice, Bette, and us, where are we . . . Brother stared blankly at his friend, his mind turning . . .

Eddie told me his mother dead then not dead some story about killing her then how she fell and killed herself how he had to have some stuff he said he was dying and had to get to Harry's to find some said he wanted to kill himself crazy he was and said nothing could help but what Slick sells crying almost he said nothing else would help but now I'll be damned if I know talking to this faggot professor and saying crazy things I guess he just must be stark raving.

He watched as Eddie disappeared through the door then felt the weight of a hand on his shoulder as Thurley rose and motioned that they follow. Pulling his cap down tighter on his head, Brother fell in behind the professor almost laughing at the white man's graceless movements as he wove clumsily, bumping and apologizing, among scattered tables towards the door.

He don't look back and we don't try to catch him and he don't try to run away I was scared back there he would get mad and hit Bobbie or say something worse and cause trouble after what Slick said and them niggers don't play games if Eddie hit somebody that's all they'd need to jump him no telling how bad it would be I'd help but then so many of 'em and in that place everybody crazy so I was so glad Eddie just sat and said nasty things at Bobbie and listened and came out here in the night without no trouble though I never seen Eddie so low he went out the door like there weren't no more doors ever for him to go in but it's hard losing a mother is what I hear and I can understand even though I forget and Mrs. Lawson sometimes it seemed better not for her to be the way she treated Bette and Eddie home after a year he was down South where they hang niggers and so bad I hear you gotta cross the street if a white woman's coming funny cause here you see it happen so much nigger with a gray broad and ain't hardly nothing to it see 'em in cars or in some club hanging on each other and Bobbie walking here beside me from down there but walking beside me and even seeking niggers it seems or why else come to Harry's and a nigger like me almost living in his house ain't that a bitch him following Eddie beside me like he don't care what street this is and where we're going deeper where there ain't nothing but black and he keeps walking his eyes stuck to Eddie's back up ahead who don't run or look behind.

—Where is he going, Brother?

Like I might know where Eddie wants to go after all this happening all's I can tell is far from home Dumferline Street in the other direction and soon the tracks we can see and the bridge but first some dark stores and the sanctified church where it's good to listen all day cause they sit there all Sunday and sing their asses off and make noise and sometimes it's louder than Harry's and smells almost as bad Eddie wandering this way I wonder if he remembers Tiny and his DaddyGene and that crazy talk but it's dark now Eddie peeking inside there ain't nothing there to see he should know but like he's looking for someone and what's he got off the pavement something white in his hand looks like bread he's tearing and dropping pieces behind like he's feeding birds or he don't want me and Bobbie to get lost giving us something to follow wherever he's going, he's going . . .

—I don't know, he just seems to be walking and maybe we should leave him be.

—You know we can't; we have to get him through this night, Brother.

And what changes tomorrow like the sun's gonna bring something different if there is a sun tomorrow or if it rains down the gutter some will go but don't change nothing me one day too I wonder how long you drain before you get somewhere it must be the deepest hole anywhere you can fall into or be guttered and blacker than Henry Bow's neck I still hate Slick what he said about Alice just cause she wouldn't and he thinks a chick should be glad he asks but she told him where to take it my sister ain't no whore Alice should be Eddie's girl but there's some things she thinks she knows but don't Eddie loves her I know but Alice is so damned scared that's why she fights like she does so somebody will fight with her so she can be mad and not scared and someday she'll understand and Eddie should be with her now she been so scared since he's gone why I just don't understand why they don't stay together cause there ain't nothing in this world bag ask Brother if you don't believe it nothing to this world bag I know so well cause I been out here and couldn't care less now that I know so I'll just follow Eddie if Bobbie thinks it's best and probably he's right though he don't know where Eddie's going and I don't and Eddie probably neither but he can't look back just walking slow like nowhere particular and no hurry like he wants never to stop but to keep moving in those long slow steps he takes the shadows eat him it seems sometimes a bite of Eddie they take as he moves in and out the black shadows Eddie got a big head like a big egg and it looks so heavy sometimes cause the rest of him is skinny it sitting there so big sometimes it scares me like so heavy it's gonna tip over and fall my head looks bigger than it is but I don't know the last time my hat off only in front of Eddie I remember unless somebody takes it or knocks it but this morning I almost forgot Mrs. Lawson made me and if it hadn't been Eddie's Mama kiss my ass I would have said if it hadn't been Bette's Mama and Bette there too who knows how I am about my cap Mrs. Lawson too knows damn well but sometimes I think she got nothing better to do than hurt me standing there like I owe her something waiting for some words to come to say I'm sorry and after all it was her that did the hurting ain't my fault I got a bald, ugly head she knew better than to say it and make me do it.

—Is he going towards his home?

—Other way where he lives. Nothing down here soon but a dump and the tracks and don't go no further than the ball field after that. Just tracks after that.

—Do you think we should call him?

—He knows we're here. Ain't nobody but fools walk these streets this time of night. Fools and them that lives in the Forest.

—What?

—Bums' Forest—behind those two big billboards under the bridge. Little path through them big signs then trees and grass till the ball field.

—A hobo camp?

—Call it what you like, it's the Bums' Forest . . . I don't like it specially at night and the winos that live there hard up for coins where is Eddie going up between them signs don't he know how them fools are he's liable to get his throat cut.

—Nobody will bother the three of us together. C'mon Brother, we'll catch him now.

Eddie ain't no kid to be running after but this white man thinks he gotta do something though I know there ain't nothing to be done but climb in that one bag Eddie tried to fight but back in this hell it don't matter a year or hundred years ain't long enough and no fight is hard enough cause the bag is strongest and best just to stop fighting till there ain't no more air I'll follow Eddie in here cause I could care less if somebody wants my throat I should say thank you cause it don't do me a bit of good just carry around my bald head and this white man Thurley playing some crazy game about getting Eddie through this night as if tomorrow will be different as if the sun would be a new one that's gonna change something don't he know he's supposed to be educated that chasing Eddie in this black jungle is damn foolishness that even if Eddie lets us catch 'em he don't care if we do cause he ain't running but just going somewhere to hide from the bag the only thing for Eddie is what's good always what Slick sells and keeps the sun off your back I hope Eddie ain't too bad and me and this white man make it worse cause losing a mother is bad and Eddie even thinks it was his fault though he don't really know saying different things and crying like a baby big tears like when he fought Henry I remember or when DaddyGene died I never could understand Eddie crying till he was sick me and Gene cried too but not so much he had to be put to bed funny about Eddie's bags they really cover him and I wonder sometimes where Eddie is like he's gone and I can't find him he's covered and nothing shows not even as much as him still slow walking in these weeds I hear the crickets I wonder how they get so loud if they have big mouths or just lots of them cause I don't believe Eddie knows what he was talking about when he said their legs rubbing make all that noise my legs make no noise through the weeds just wind blowing the trees and crickets doing what they do I guess they gotta holler too I guess they fight and cuss and sing and dance just like everybody me and Eddie did when it was our time but not so much cause I was so ugly and Eddie didn't really seem to care just Alice I always thought he's scared of other girls didn't even know what they were I think him passing up good pussy when Emma Jeanne in the garage and everybody me last climbed on that fat stuff Eddie didn't even know what it was or he woulda' been right there with everybody but I know he did it to my sister to Alice and I always thought I'd be mad when I knew somebody climbed on her but funny Eddie was all right and in a way I didn't even think about it like I knew it would happen someday and we knew it was supposed to be just waiting Alice me and Eddie where is he now these damn weeds up to my knees and getting higher damn bugs I can feel how hungry they are waiting here liable to cut my foot off on this glass everywhere my shoes ain't so good just gumsoles and not even much of that I wonder where Eddie is going and why this white man following damn I'm hungry and cold ain't had nothing dammit I'd like a Hershey bar.

—I don't see him, Brother. Can you see him through the trees, he must have turned off the path. Here . . . he must have turned off here.

Dammit a spider web that must have been where the hell is Eddie going hide and seek now I'm getting tired and it won't be the first time I slept on the grass and here is as good as anyplace I suppose cause I'm tired and any fool can see I ain't got nothing to rob nothing but these rags on my back and these shoes barely keeping out the glass there is Eddie on a big stone and what the hell now look at that white man just standing staring at Eddie well we caught him and here we are in the middle of nowhere on rocks round a dead fire some bums used to keep off the cold both of 'em not saying a word just sitting there and it's getting chilly now the fools are shivering sometimes I think it's me that's the smartest the only one thinks of trying to light a fire on these ashes where is something that will burn quickly a newspaper is what I need to catch these twigs and them just sitting like they's expecting company to come out of this black night dammit they should be looking for kindling but this is enough to start crackle you little bastards get something going to keep Brother warm looks like we'll be here a while with them just sitting looking at the night ain't even a star to be seen like a black roof that's all it is and not too far away up through the trees I wonder how high or if anybody could

touch it maybe Bobbie knows he should know something
teacher he is it seems him always showing me what he don't
know how silly he can be and needs a fool like me sometimes
to tell him things or show him it seems like he should know if
it's too high to touch or if anybody has tried he should know or
maybe Eddie sometimes Eddie knows what you wouldn't think
he knows like what he said about crickets and I wonder how
he got to know such things as I never heard of and Eddie ain't
so dumb though not like my sister Alice who thinks she knows
so much and does know a lot but she should listen to Eddie
and not be afraid to hear the things Eddie knows some of them
so strange I wonder how he found out he says in books and I
believe it cause books is news to me I couldn't care less but I
know when I'm cold and when I need a fire even if I can't
get chocolate and there they sit on those stones neither of them
would have moved just froze to death waiting.

—Thank you Brother, it feels good.

Damn right it does and Eddie knows it too though he don't
say nothing I can see he's stopped shaking and moved a little
closer his face I can see now in the flames big head and the
bones show black and white his face is in the fire everything
dark and deep sunken or shining like his forehead and his eyes
are just sparks little lights I can tell when they move he looks
at Bobbie but away quick like he don't believe a white man's
sitting here on a rock the three of us like bums toasting round
my fire that needs more wood Bobbie kicks a piece toward me
no good it would put out the damn fire but he's trying just little
pieces what I need I don't want to burn the damn Forest down
or attract no attention these bums like flies think cause we got
a fire we got other things and looking for a handout or a drink
I wish I had something myself not that rotgut but what Slick
sells then I wouldn't give a damn about bugs about them
crickets bout bums bout nothing just sit here long as they want
to till tomorrow or the next day even if it takes that long if
Bobbie thinks a night or day will change something and Eddie's

willing to sit I'll stay right with them but it would be so much better with what Slick sells I hope they ain't too mad at Eddie Eddie got it bad Eddie tried to fight his bag and it scares them cause they live off other people's bags and Eddie fights silly fights I told 'em and ones he knows he can't win but Eddie fights and it just gets harder Henry hits harder and it's better to take low and not to make it worse by trying to land a lucky punch his Mama is hard and Alice who's scared and now this white man wants something from Eddie don't he know Eddie don't go that way that Eddie ain't like me I take what comes but Eddie fights and ain't got nothing for Bobbie no not for all the money Bobbie makes Eddie ain't gonna stop being a man not like me Eddie thinks it makes a difference not like me if that's what the white man wants he's wasting his time but that ain't it I got a feeling he wants more wants Eddie to get through this night to wait for the sun to come like it's gonna make a difference . . .

Thurley gazes into the fire: perhaps I will die tonight. Perhaps I am already dead. This is the way it ends the way it begins always will be like this. Men ranged round a fire, the darkness heavy, silence. Perhaps death is on a rock for eternity watching the flames decay other faces. It broods, it chews, it melts, destroying. Perhaps I am dead in this wood. And these devils. Silent devils that mock and change in the fire. How easily they come. The living and dead come to me, throng this wood, this dark wood. They should be wearing robes, or wrapped in flame, something to explain how they move so easily, how they came here. To save him. To save me. What are they doing . . . I ask . . . shapes, colors, old rooms, doors I have entered, beds where . . . she comes . . . but she will not speak, will not look at me, the eyes gone, all features gone, a haze where they should be, but I know it is Eleanor, the hair, the shoulders, the deep pinch of her waist. Perhaps dead. I do not know. Cannot. This boy I must save. Dark boy whose face changes. His eyes

. . . those for a year I remembered. And tonight how he moved through the crowd, through the street and losing sight of him in these woods. I shook, I trembled for fear he was gone. An old man. Perhaps a dead man. And to be dead the need is no less urgent. If I am dead, I still desire. Desire their shapes, their colors. Eleanor whose body I came to fear. What did I fear? Losing him in these woods. Though an old man I still need, still want. Save him. Cling. They glide so effortless through the flame. Does someone have something to say. Each one giving way, waiting for the other to speak. The boy whose dirty hand, who I believed I loved. He gives way, will not speak, defers to the next and all of them defer, all give way, wait for the next shape to speak. How many? How they swarm. How they crowd me. Loved on my knees. All of them bowed to, pleaded with all, but their bodies disappear, they fill me, then they pass, not speaking, deferring to the next to the next. So many, filling up, the dark woods full.

Their thoughts twist in the darkness:
The fire, the fire
I've made many mistakes
Burning . . .
I am sick
Turn to the sound of crickets in the grass
Death is so close my flesh angers the bones.
The fire
But I will sit on this hard stone
Brother stirs it. It licks the darkness. The pup dances
I . . .
On her steel brace.
Am dying.
An old woman, my mother who will never taste again or hear night sounds.
The embers, ashes, dust, a rag . . .
If I could turn again . . . the flame feeds . . . something

must be ending, always ending if the flame climbs, if it eats and cracks.

Upon a stick.

I must turn again. There is Bette. All dead. She watched them all die. How many can the eyes bear? Do the eyes scar . . . will she . . .

Quotation as close . . .

Will she be free . . .

Hattie lifted me. Her eyes were cow eyes, her black hands like new underwear on my body. Where will it take me? I cannot ask.

A chocolate bar

Why such heavy ones, why does he lift

Hattie's breast is round and soft like a pillow. Once I watched it squirm its way free. I did not know what to expect. Then it finally came, finally showed itself black and blacker tipped after flirting so long beneath the buttonless cotton blouse. Touch . . . gone . . . the pain.

Turn again . . .

The fire.

Damn . . . just little sticks.

The Brobdingnags. So big, so close. The smell, the pits in the skin. Gulliver's little box.

Part of myself.

Do I dare . . . on rocks in a circle. Brother tends it. He brought it from the gods at the risk of . . .

Why should Bette have to see it all? Why happen and scar her eyes? Scabs do form, do hide and make ugly. My sister will have to unwrap, turn back the folds, lift the head.

Old.

Like a little girl's hair, Mama's will fall long and straight like a little girl's.

Promised myself a kind of peace. The world hid nothing. I should have been grateful. The worst things . . . could and did happen. I am witness and victim. Truth is only the evidence I have suffered. There can be no more. A kind of peace afterall to step down, to know it has happened, to have admitted the worst. But the others, there are others . . . It begins again . . . always another victim . . .

What were the games we played . . . me and my Alice

Another witness

I remember only songs, only movements, something . . .

Another truth.

Paddy cake Paddy cake Baker's man bake them cakes as fast as you can, Roll them bake them one two three, Put 'em in the oven for Alice and me

Cold

If only till the morning, if Eddie will only stay, if he can stand up in the light and look back on this . . . over it all, through it in the light.

I remember how funny it was. Just nothing, just wrinkles and nothing. Like the back in a way only a small one. Just slits. Ugly Alice held her skirt up high so I could see. I got closer and closer. I looked. She squeezed it, spread it open. I looked deeper. I moved around and she turned. She did anything I asked. Nothing. She said a word I didn't understand. Closer. She bent and I tried to see deeper. Nothing. She said touch. Touch. I said no. Just look. Just see. Nothing.

Rocks, for an eternity on rocks. Alone waiting for morning.

Sometimes I wished it hadn't grown. Hair, coarse, dry and sharp sometimes when I entered. I missed its bareness, bare so I could see. But I couldn't ask, and she wouldn't if I asked, how could I ask . . . begin again.

Looking down at a bird. From a mountainside down on a white bird fluttering over a lake. It was a poem. How I saw it was a poem I couldn't write. That is how you tell how high. When there are birds beneath, gliding white over the dazzling water. How it is serene, unwavering and you see it all in the sudden parting of a cloud. But it is not towards it you can move. Never towards it. The mountain was near the sea. The bird a gull. Streams, froth white, unmoving it seemed far off on the sides of other mountains. Frozen it seemed, veins of ice, but could hear their roar. Could hear thin echo of the sea funnelled up between the steep, rock walls.

My Alice

The summit still in a cloud.

The fire

The loud waters

Love. Love was all silence. Once it meant that for Alice and me. Stillness and silence. There can be a sound, there can be the glider's wheezing, Mama's voice in the darkness when Gene and I knelt, some sounds even begin the silence. Silence is a door.

The fire like pebbles on tin.

Through it are the things you can't say. The things words scare away.

Rocks

I love you Alice. I always whispered, afraid to break the silence. Alice fights. She fights the silence with words. Words like stones.

Morning will come.

What Slick sells

Silence on these rocks and only the fire speaking. Brother. The white man. Why? Where does his white man's mind go at night in this black night in this hole. Afraid. He would cry if the fire went out. Afraid of the dark. Him shaking, fearing black hands from the weeds to carry him away. Leave him. Kick out the fire and leave him.

The fire . . .

Bury it, grind the flame into the earth. We will leave him crying in the darkness. Afraid of the black bogey man. Slick sells.

The clouds part and you understand. The next stage . . .

The white man must have money. Something. If he gives it to us we will not harm.

Lifted, her cow eyes shining. Hands like . . .

His friend . . . Brother believes that the white man is his friend.

Fireflies over the lawn, over the deep cool spaces.

With these hands take . . . what can they take . . . my sister's pain?

Luminous in the corner . . .

Brother will help me if I begin, not hurt the fairy, just take the money. Get what Slick sells. Crush out the fire.

Snow

Please give . . . we won't hurt you if you give and be silent

The voice, the cool hand taking mine. It is a soft crunch beneath our feet. Trackless, pure, closing behind us as we walk. Snow stretches . . . brilliant, snow stretches in some cold brilliant valley. Only his voice, gentle and the snow yielding as we move.

I do not want to hurt. Never again with these hands. Alice beneath me. Almost death. Mine, hers. Mama. Not her. Some heap of rags crumpled at the foot of the stairs. Paddy cake, paddy cake. Bette will lift, like a little girl's . . . falling.

His cool hand

Turn again.

Like color to a leaf whispering, come, come it is time, time to . . .

If only I had stayed. Or never gone. Slick sells. It would have been my pain. I wouldn't have hurt. Wouldn't have killed Mama. My pain neither ending nor beginning, hungry for no life, its red jaws fed with what is mine to give, mine to hurt.

He must see the morning, the light . . . my hand . . . purified through the fire. . . could it touch . . . could it lead through the valley?

Both go. Brother must go with the white man. Me alone.

The fire mine. Its red flame . . . I will feed. Something, nothing the fire lives.

It burns, darkness submits, the darkness abides the cancer of the flame. It feels no pain, the darkness cannot wince, cannot suffer. Night will not lie charred and unrecognized at dawn. It only will have moved, creeping across the brittle earth, its belly unfeeling, enveloping, swallowing all. No pain, no feeling. Unfaltering it will crawl across broken glass, across the razor edge of human cries; the flame does not consume. It does not penetrate the night. It consumes itself or the broken sticks it can drag into its arc. Night is there in the fire, in the core of its blaze, untouched. Night is in the glare it throws across their faces, in the flickering purple horror of the masks it imprints.

Chocolate

Must go away from here. Stop only once to get what Slick sells. Night, night, night.

It cannot be changed. We can only endure till night drags itself away.

No difference. No sun on my back, no night. No on again, off again, again, again days and nights . . . no nights, no days . . . the memories they bring . . . the ghost each hour possesses.

Wait, Eddie's face in the fire. The mask melting, dying, so afraid. Do not go.

Every minute someone rises to accuse. To ask me once again to remember. To hurt them again.

Wait for the cool hand. He will come Eddie. The fire . . . listen to the fire.

Mama.

Could it be . . . through the fire . . . pure again . . . ever pure . . . am I still lying to myself . . . can I know . . . lie, truth, pure . . . only night and day . . . the bird, the lake, a cloud that opens and we know where we are, the summit still wreathed, another cloud, the mask on Eddie's face, hiding, his hands moving as if they could hide in each other. What can I say? Can I tell him anything that is not a lie? Can I say, yes, can I say more than night and day, that day will follow night? Can I say look at me, can I say look at your friend Brother, can I say the snow closes silently behind our footsteps, can I point down to the glistening water, can I fill his ears with the sound of clear rushing water, can I say look, can I say listen . . . listen . . . look . . . darkness and silence

Fire

All the days are one day. Mama will come, she will set down the hot cereal, she will wipe the discolored spoons on the tail of her apron. Bette will be in the high chair. I will turn from my stomach to stroke the soft mound. I will kiss her naked back, I will whisper Alice I love, I will tease Bette, Eugene will tease, Mama will yell, I will take it in my hands fill the bowl with it steaming and hot, I will smell, I will taste, it will all be one, coming in going out, my blue plastic bowl, Eugene's red one, Bette's green, the cold whiteness where I am at last alone, squatting, warmly pouring through myself, the shiny spoon Gene always gets, mine I do not look at till its grayness is coated with thick oatmeal. Bette squeals, it goes on the floor, she turns to me, her lips softest then, no other time so soft, and I loved the sleep still in her Alice eyes, soon, soon, soon everymorning Alice morning, soon soon soon, Daddy will be here, better spoons, and when the chain is pulled all will go away, not left there to be found floating and putrid like you find what the others leave, and they find yours, and locks on the doors, neither be walked in on or catch Mama there standing in the tub wet, shining and cannot look away and she doesn't move and Alice, Alice look, look closer, closer, deeper, not that, just look, all one, soon soon he will be home again, it will be better . . . all the mornings floating, putrid because it is broken, because we do not have money, and it cannot be fixed

Darkness and silence.

All the hours one hour. Bette crying. She will not stop. It

seems her breath will stop soon but crying still and Brother at the door calling. Ball game, ball game and Gene is best, Gene wins always, the hit, the catch, he does it and I wish I . . . there is no time. It is all here, I cannot begin, I cannot end. Bette screams, Brother calls. Mama will be waiting she will be angry because we are late and all the time I wanted to go back before dinner but Gene said wait Gene said finish the game and then she stands at the door she wants to hit and Gene says nothing he ducks in quick while she warms up he is under her arm and in the house and now I have to pass through the door where she stands glaring and does not move. All time, I cannot breathe without the air of all those days rushing down in my lungs, DaddyGene held me Alice held me Mama held me Saunders died.

But I must be heard, must be seen. I must say I am not afraid. These rocks, I cannot let him leave the fire.

Bette screams. She cannot lift. She tries but cannot lift. Too heavy, too heavy for Bette to lift. For me . . .

If he starts to get up, if he moves away from the fire into the darkness again I will grab . . . I will make him carry me through the night. If only I could say something . . . if words were only made to touch . . . if only for a moment I had the singer's voice, the beauty of her voice I believe I could make him understand.

A little girl . . . I must . . . lift . . . help her lift

It will come, it will follow, morning will . . . and the strength . . . witness . . . I have been through, climbed through the night, the darkness . . . I have been there and now . . . now I see

Bette tries, like a little girl's falling, she tries, she raises Mama in her arms.

Floating, a gull over the blue lake.

Bette whispers, I think she is whispering, but it is because she has no breath because she cannot say the word, because it is her mother who lies there.

The strength . . . the light radiant on his back . . . morning

Bette screams. All time. The stone's hard push into my backside, the fire crackling. Daddy's coming soon . . . soon he'll be here. No more time, no more waiting soon soon it pushes, it is hard to sit alone, to feed it, to watch it die, something . . . nothing . . . flame.

If Eddie moves I will cling; he will have to drag me. Hold on even to the edge . . .

They don't move. They cannot speak. The flame crackles. I don't move, don't speak. All time, near then far, near then far, near then far. The crickets stop. We are part of the fire. We are part of the silence. I cannot move. I cannot speak . . .

I wonder how far away it is somebody should know somebody should find out and tell people cause I'm sure they want to know look at them both closer to my fire now and both looking at the flames I wonder what it feels like to burn if it always hurts once your hand is in it deep and if it pops and sparks like wood and if the color is the same and if it hurts and where does it go if you keep it in smoke rises through the trees to the sky towards the black roof where the sun will come if the sun comes tomorrow does it hurt or smell and how high up the smoke kids do it stick their hands right in you gotta keep them away or they'll do it like bugs who get too close and burn up I see why they try once why they want to touch I can see it in Eddie's eyes in the white man's eyes that stare at the flame they want to touch to put them in and see if it keeps hurting I can understand why kids do it cause I want to touch myself just like one I want to put my hand in I want to go to smoke and see how high . . .

Hurry Home

For Judy
. . . I should call this being
In love with you
This skipping backwards
And forwards and quiet litanizing
Of fears

O N E

· · · · ·

"... (meurtries
De la langueur goûtée à ce mal d'être deux)"
—*Stéphane Mallarmé*
"L'Après-Midi d'un faune"

CECIL CRUSHED IN HIS HANDS THE EMPTY
Carnation evaporated milk can. It was red and white and
decorated with a tiny picture of a flower. Every morning
the garbage had to go down. Five floors, fifteen apartments
each left their bundles on the back staircase for Cecil to
cart away. Striding flight by flight Cecil used the stairs because the real estate agency didn't want the smell of garbage in the tenants' elevator. Some mornings Cecil dreamed
while he carted, but sometimes he thought black thoughts
and handled the trash bags as if he could hurt them. Often
Cecil was drunk in the mornings, stumbling up and down
the dimly lighted back stairs, spilling cans and greasy paper,
slipping on the mess he'd made beneath his feet. Cecil
talked to himself, cried, cursed, tried to make his voice echo
in the long stairwell. There were times when, two or three
stories up, he would send one of the tenant's bags crashing
to the concrete floor of the basement. The fact that it would
be he and no one else who had to sweep up the broken
glass, mop the slush, and scrape together every morsel of
refuse seemed not to deter him.

For many reasons November 14, 1968, was one of Cecil's most difficult mornings. To begin with his piles were
bad. The sight of his own blood, no matter what the source
or occasion, depressed Cecil with thoughts of death and dis-
solution. The first time he had hit his wife, Esther, was because she had told him there was blood in the toilet bowl he
had forgotten to flush. November 14 also found Cecil suf-

fering from a hangover. He swore he would die in November, that it was a month sent specifically to plague him with bad luck and worse. He had lost his first girl friend in November, Esther's aunt had come to live with them in November, his son born dead had been conceived in November, etc., etc., as far back as he could remember. As he grew older Cecil tried to remain as inert as possible during that month. For the past few years after attending to the minimal chores that absolutely had to be attended to at Constance Beauty's or now in his capacity as janitor of the Banbury Street Arms, Cecil took to his bed and bottle when the bad month began. Lying in state, he would stare for hours at the patched and cracking ceiling of his basement apartment. Lumps of unfinished plaster reminded him of relief maps, of faces puckered and blistered by burns.

On November 14 Cecil crushed a can and dropped it five flights to the basement. Long after the clatter had burst up through the dark stairwell and the rattling motion of bent tin rolling across the uneven concrete floor had ceased, Cecil stood peering into the tunnel. In another world Cecil heard a door opening. A shadow flitted across his silence, then the light footfall of a voice. *Why did you do that*, once, twice, and perhaps again. Perhaps his own voice asking, feminine, patient, but turning Cecil saw her in the doorway sleeping though she stood. Sleep resting like the red hair on her shoulders, sleep like a topping of snow spread over a dying city. Cecil thought of how they run movies backward, how the can could leap up from the floor, return to his hand and unfold there, a flower opening. It would be fine and easy, no less real than the red hair, the soft robe open at the throat. Cecil could not speak, could only wait for the next sign. The light behind her carried out into the dim hallway, penetrating what should be her solid form, disintegrating hair, flesh, and robe till what Cecil saw was a shaft of brilliance, dazzling, warning him. Sun through her window, through the sheer wrap. Cecil's stare touched her, told her that his hands could be no more intimate, flagrant on her body. He took one step forward, but still couldn't speak, and the light disappeared.

Cecil descended, pausing at each landing to load his burlap sack. There were mornings when the sack became bloated to capacity, and stooped under its weight Cecil was forced to wrestle his load directly to the basement before all the floors were cleared. The bags of garbage he couldn't manage seemed to jeer at him as he passed, make obscene comments about his bent back and heavy breathing. In November there were always more of these mornings than in any other month. Cecil knew he would have to make two trips as he harvested an overflow of waste on the fifth floor. The women didn't seem to care. They pulled the things out of their bodies and laid them atop the trash cans in full view as casually as they would leave a cigarette tipped with lipstick. Cecil had grown accustomed to filth, to the forlorn crusts of pleasure. Cecil no longer made distinctions, no longer judged; he only became angry when someone's carelessness created practical difficulties for him. Broken glass, an overfilled or wet-bottomed bag that spilled when he tried to lift it.

The cigarette lay cold on his lip. Sack would have to be emptied though two floors and their jesters waited below. The woman on the fifth floor on fire in her doorway. He knew her name, and she knew his and nothing in a year had extended that simple knowledge they had of each other. Most likely she didn't even know his last name because as he tried to recall more than the S. Sherman painted on her mailbox, he realized he didn't know what name the initial S began.

Last two floors could wait awhile he decided, closing the double doors of the garbage bin. He cursed as he heard gospel music eking from his basement flat. Damp batwings fluttered against his cheek, brushed his shoulder as he stooped to avoid his underwear and Esther's hanging outside the laundry room. Esther up and at it already. *I've got a telephone in my bosom,* was it Sister Rosetta Tharpe who greeted him as he entered the janitor's quarters. *And I can ring Him up from my heart.* Then piano, guitar, and chorus led by a bass exploding deep. Esther. Esther. Cecil dropped the sack just inside the door, which he had left open behind him.

—You want something to eat, Cecil. He knew the question was *do you love just this small thing about me, this fact that I can fill your belly,* but Cecil shook his head no, that same no that seemed appropriate to all her questions, large or small. Cecil wondered why it had to be said so many times. Tried to remember if it had been more difficult to refuse her at the beginning. It must have hurt, must have taken something out of him that first time, though he couldn't recall what. Esther hovered beside the stove, patient if he should change his mind, as if he could change it. Backgrounded by sweet organ music the announcer was leading his invisible audience in prayer. Esther's eyes were dog eyes, cow eyes, baleful, uncomprehending, while inward worlds revolved in silence. She rubbed her hands on her apron, saying *See sill* abstractly, without volition like an instrument used to project another's voice.

It followed him up the stairs. That Cecil from her lips a shadow as he climbed to the second floor. *See sill.* They all answered to his name, those ghosts he felt each morning slipping into his clothes as he dressed. It was their presence which sustained him, but in November they grew dark and heavy like leaves he needed desperately to shed. Clinging leaves, dead leaves which killed before they fell. It was a pattern, a cycle he had been aware of for years. The ghosts were part of him, his energy revived them, fleshed them, and in turn they hid his nakedness. Then November. Lead skies which leaned but not heavily enough, earth which sucked greedily but would not jerk them down. Autumn when each one took a day to fall, and in its fall was a sliver of his flesh screaming till it touched the ground.

She wouldn't know his name. The red-haired woman could say *Cecil,* could add another ghost, but she wouldn't know his name. He asked himself why not keep walking, why not up past these tithes on one and two and knock at her door. She would have to answer or not. And if she answered, she could only say go away or yes come in. All the uncertainty, the fears, would resolve themselves into a series of simple choices. No gods involved, no turnings of the earth. Just her very human responses, unpredictable but within a limited, unspectacular range. She is afterall only a woman, one who has reached thirty or thereabouts through a course of trial and error, a course in which my intrusion would be assimilated like all other events, growing smaller in significance as it is succeeded by other events, other states of mind. If she is an intelligent woman, she knows all this, she knows my wish to touch, to help, even to hurt, is much greater than any capacity I have to change her. If she knows, the door should . . . but it is November and there is dying to do. I will not knock.

But she is there. A white blur leaning over the banister. Is it her voice or do I smell her, taste her, touch her in the dark stairwell.

Why did you do it. This time he is caught; he must answer. So much red on the pillow, soft red he can smooth or tangle in his fist. He should be brave. The flesh of her he can bathe in as he pleases. The sleep-snow whiteness in which he can ink deeply the heat of his hands, foot or lips. S. Sherman has been waiting for thirty-two years. Not for Cecil, not in maiden lust for the buck janitor who wanders in her dreams, but waiting for that time when need says take a man for the flesh, release the body from its bondage to the phantoms who think they rule and thinking rule. Let a man come to you though his hands stink and you don't know him.

Cecil had hoped it would be red too. That patch of matting unruly over her cleft. But auburn curls around his fingers, the color of freckles between her breasts. Esther's was a hedge you had to crawl through before the meadow spread sunlit and swaying, but these feathers or a tongue tickling almost. I remember once I asked Esther not to move and my ear was on the bush and I listened inside her till we went to sleep. That was early when we believed and there was some point in stopping and listening. There is no point now asking me *why*. Man who threw can plunged with it and cracked his crockery head on concrete. Might as well ask why I died inside her. Why I trembled once, and all man in me ran out like a little boy from a dark room. Can was a bedbug I found in my shirt. Can was the breakfast Esther didn't cook. Can was what I crumpled because I have a hand and because I like to know hand can crumple.

Esther now. There are wheels and they turn and they move her but they are not her wheels. At most perhaps Esther hears chug, chug of washing machine in the basement. Who painted her name on the mailbox. Did the painter know what the initial stood for? May I ask?

Got up the goddamn stairs pretty quick. I don't think anybody saw me go in. Her apartment on the end. Woman turns on her side now, draws her knees toward her chest. Cecil's head on high pillow of her hip. There is nothing in the glance they exchange. A door slamming, footsteps in the hall, and they can smile, his hand can go to her cheek, she can roll languidly on her back.

Esther said she was staying home, a horrible headache, and she had already called them and told them she wouldn't be in. It was strange that she didn't really know. November and the dying. All these years and neither told nor did she ask. She knew he spent days in bed, that he shut off his bedroom from the rest of the apartment and warned Esther and her aunt not to disturb him. She knew certain times were worse than others and perhaps intuitively dreaded the coming of fall and his *moods* as she called them, but rather than look for some pattern, she chose to believe her periods of worried anticipation arose from some soul link between her and her husband. She believed their life together had been preordained by an all powerful force, and since this source was God in heaven, the joining of their lives had to be right no matter how far this rightness might be submerged beneath the troubled surface of their days together. Only after a prolonged battle with herself had she come to realize how God had blessed her. That He had blessed her with a trial. Cecil would be her salvation, her road to humility, the means through which she would finally be placed beside her Creator.

There was a finality, a fatality in it all. Even her Aunt Fanny, coming when she did, that last year when Cecil lived at the law school, fit into the picture, which was now consummately clear. Esther had blamed the old woman, cursed her for giving Cecil an excuse to make the last move from their bed into the dormitory room, where he slept alone. But God made Esther see why Cecil had to move and how in His compassion He had foreseen all and sent Aunt Fanny to take the place of the man she could no longer have.

So much cleaning to be done. One load of clothes up and drying, another in the machine, and still a stack by the door waiting its turn. When everything clean, the ironing to do, then the four untidy rooms in which she felt no one but she lifted a finger to keep clean. Sometimes over the ironing board her headaches seemed to get better. Her arms would move slowly and her fingers grip the warm, black handle.

She could go as slowly as she wanted in and out of the folds of material, pressing, creasing; she could take her coffee and listen to the radio played softly. Gospels if she could find them and best when the slow, sad ones she could sway her whole body to as the iron glided and hissed. She could forget the white heat in the left half of her brain, she could swallow the scream that squirmed behind her teeth, she could deny the damp palms of her hands which ached for the lacerating kiss of clenched fist and fingernails biting deep. It was dancing at the Horizon Room I believe Cecil first said he could feel me hot down there, heat of me coming through my clothes and his clothes. He never said love but he said Esther you are better than you know. You would smile more if you knew the secrets you know. What he said was enough and I couldn't say no I closed my eyes and did it and I hoped in time he would say the rest.

In one corner a rectangle of light trembled on the concrete floor. The patch of light caught the delicate, twisting shadow of the atmosphere—the mobile dust motes and hissing furnace breath—which played across the small window flush with the basement ceiling. Since this window was the only one in the basement and Cecil hadn't replaced the dead bulb outside the rear of their apartment, Esther, her arms filled by a clothes hamper, clothespins, and a box of detergent, had to pick her way through darkness to the laundry room. Though she had made the trip thousands of times and with armloads more precarious than what encumbered her at the moment, Esther cautiously inched her way across the rough floor. She was afraid of falling. Her blood warned her that the fall might never end, that floor and earth would give way, that there were unimaginable distances to plummet through forever. It galled her that Cecil moved easily in this darkness, that with a cat's eyes and feet he could go anywhere he wanted without bumping things or tripping. Even when he was drunk and had just about fallen down the last flight of stairs into the basement, once his feet touched the concrete, his movements would be sober, efficient. The cool, dark air seemed to restore him, to right a balance; he was a fish who had recovered its element, who could stop the frantic writhing of his moment on the sand.

The pain in her head was crisp now, a bell distinct and deliberate, giving form to the hours. It was better this way. Pain just before sleep or pain born with consciousness in the morning was blurred, distorted into *always has been and will be* because pain leaned on the unknown, shared its boundaries with unfathomable stretches of not quite real, of a kind of death. The brain could not focus, could not say where pain came from or where it might lead. Whispers said there is only pain and dream, dream and pain. Esther's feet slid lightly across the coarse grain of the concrete, but the sound grated upon the fibers of her brain. Cecil had killed the rats, but she felt that any moment a squirming, melon softness would give way beneath her feet and the fall begin. Monotonous, ungentle churning of the washing machine seemed to contain a message of assurance; the arc of light around the laundry room door was a sanctuary where all would be fine. One foot then the other pushed forward, toes straining through bottoms of thin slippers to feel their way, test the substance on which everything depended. Night in a strange house on a high, unlighted landing trying to find where the stairs begin. It wasn't far to the laundry room, but how long had she been edging her way on this narrow ridge above the abyss. How long wind chewing the insides of her skull. She lurches through the door, the basket squeals and pushes against her bosom when it is flung upon the high green table and her whole weight collapses on its woven frame.

Footsteps bird quick and light. Little Aunt Fanny hurries from her nest in the home of Cecil Braithwaite to the laundry room where Esther waits strength to pray away her pain.

Aunt Fanny tiny in the doorway, so frail, unreal, she could be a creature of Esther's pain dream, and for a second Esther believes she can think it away, if not the complete dream at least this one transparent image shooed away with an effort of will. But Fanny speaks, brittle, high-pitched like the records that play inside talking dolls.

—Do you want me to help. Do you want me to help. Always like that, twice quick in succession she would nervously repeat a simple phrase as if to assure the hearer that she had spoken, that she could speak. Esther knew her hands were shaking. She buried them in the hamper of soiled laundry. The thought and action were swift, almost a reflex to sudden apparition of old woman in the doorway. Even so, the instant that elapsed made speaking to her aunt possible. Because she couldn't trust its firmness at a lower tone, Esther's voice was too loud in the small room.

—You go back, Fanny. I'm almost finished here. You get your rest. Fanny didn't reply she didn't say I just got up out of bed and don't need or want rest didn't say I came to speak to you to hear myself talking or hear you speak didn't say please, please or weep or stamp her tiny foot she said nothing just twirled her hands at her waist in two tight, rapid circles and nearly smiling walked away.

Eggs boiling in a small pan on a too high flame can make the sound of an angry sea. It must be Fanny at the stove, Fanny whom I've never seen eat other than boiled eggs. Lives on eggs and coffee little old woman under this roof with me. Who am I? Cecil Otis Braithwaite, born October 2, 1933, in the District of Columbia. Suffered under various pilots till earning my own wings ascended to the summit of the law, where it was my job to speak for those about to be judged. Lawyer Braithwaite, third of his race to be admitted and second to finish the university law school aided and abetted throughout by unflagging efforts of Esther Brown, true avatar of that selfless, sore-kneed mother every night scrubbing the halls bright so next morning second generation son could tall stride the shining corridors. Esther on all fours, the solid rock on which I stood *cum laude*. Esther funeral flower weary in the rear of the huge auditorium as pomp and circumstance led me down the aisle, then flower plucked, leaning on my arm second time in the same day down another aisle wedding march we do. On the side of the bed later that night I remember sitting and listening to the clock. Everything before me. Even Fanny gone for a honeymoon week. A new place of our own soon. I sat so long Esther fell asleep; it was no wonder eight years opening those doors it was enough for her to fall through exhausted when entrance finally made. Black pants baggy about the knees and million furrows across back of jacket, they hung limp, suspenders dangling from same hanger on the door hook. I in my T-shirt and shorts sat so long I was stiff when at last I had to move. Eight years but now those two trips down carpeted aisles made everything all right, all right.

It was a beautiful day and they said if life did not begin full, rich, I had only myself to blame. The others liked me as much as they could. Cecil a piece of their education, something to be coped with, to come to terms with, a measure of their powers of self-control, of their intellect's flexibility. They were successful on the whole. Only a few times did they forget, did the eyes in a body turn on me or away. The best is not wasted on Cecil. From the back, from a distance you can hardly tell. Together in our black robes and mortar boards you had to be looking to find him in the class picture. Old Cec. It's not that we don't want him to come, we don't ask him because we know he doesn't want to come; we know he has his own way to go, his own people, his own woman, he is in love.

I heard or perhaps dreamed Esther moving about, the waterfall, her hand finally on my shoulder *come on my sleepy-head baby* I believe I heard it all but kept my eyes shut tight and rolled away from touch from sounds. I'm not so sure about the crying. Dream or Esther when I opened my eyes. She was beside me curled in her robe. The sealed fastness of the robe, the inert mass of her covered flesh I could not go to, could not disturb as I sat awake needing what should be beneath the blue corduroy.

The suit slithered from the door and I was covered and in the street. I saw her no more for three years.

Dear Esther,

You will not read this. You could not read this if some miracle caused these words to appear on a sheet of paper in your lap. Weeks have passed and only notes from me to say I need this or that, five dollars at a post office in a city far from you, money I never wait for or catch. I have assured you that I am healthy and sane that you had done nothing wrong and that you could only wait, just as I was waiting. When I left, I simply left. No destination, no intention, just a move to the other side of the door. I thought for a moment I wanted to see the stars, walk as I often did in the quiet of night alone. Nothing seemed to be on my mind. The moment, and it has been the same moment ever since, carried me with it, drained time of all meaning. I was confused even alarmed when I realized my sense of time, of myself in time had ceased to function, not simply blurred or distorted but blotted out completely as light from a blind man's eyes. Like a man suddenly blind there was panic in my first gropings; I had no means of control, of balance or direction. But more quickly than you would imagine, other senses began to assert themselves, a driving necessity to move, to go on, itself became not only the end but the means of propelling myself through a strange world. I wanted to giggle at the moon. I wanted to run and watch it trying to catch me over the rooftops.

I was afraid I was out too late, that I would be scolded, even beaten if I didn't hurry home. I made up excuses. I began to recall all the demons I'd grown up with. The streets shrank, narrower, darker and I smelled the rot of garbage, of derelict cars, of winos whose outstretched feet you had to step over to get past the corner. But that was only one world. You were there too, Esther. Your door was one of those calling me, one to which I was returning as soon as the moment passed, the moment when all the worlds were equal, each cluttering my vision of the others so I couldn't move, could only wait for some *now* to return.

If someone asked me the date I would look at a mirror, if someone asked me who I was I would want to see a calendar. I won't be asking you for anything else. If this is a bubble, it will burst and when it does I will know and you will know. I know it is not fair to reach back, to lie to you and say there is this much Cecil remaining, this much of him unchanged because he assumes certain rights, perpetuates obligations. I will not write again, not even send this. The black warrior told her fabulous lies. Told her of islands in the sky, men with heads beneath their shoulders. He did not tell her he still searched, that she was the unvisited land he would explore, that he would conquer deftly but with dread, his thick hands peeling one by one layers of silk from her thighs.

The librarian handed him the large, heavy book. St. Veronica was in the center of the glossy dust jacket, a Veronica self-absorbed, palely tranquil against a background of ruddy demonic faces, St. Veronica, whose long, clean forehead and heavy nose gave her face in profile a downward thrust, a kind of humility that pushed her chin against her slender neck, even pulled down the lids of her browless eyes, a face that could be masculine in its unsubtle, almost coarse features, yet a face that absorbed light into its skin, that emphasized the tentativeness, the transparency of the flesh and the fragility of bones beneath, St. Veronica's face utterly submissive yet removed from all the turbulence surrounding her, from the accident of His murder, benign, dreaming His image on the sudarium, loving the relic while the man still breathes and bleeds, Veronica's face in its sublime indifference so startlingly and simply Esther's face.

The work of Hieronymus Bosch has fascinated and disturbed men from his own time down to today. Born in the middle of the fifteenth century . . . Cecil read only this far. He leafed through the illustrations of Bosch's paintings looking for Veronica's face, for Esther's face to be repeated. He also searched for the black men in Bosch. The Negroes were there, they had to be there and in many forms and roles. The Magus, the waiter at the Black Mass, initiates male and female in the Garden, a mason raising the towers of Hell. Cecil found other saints' faces, saints beset, saints despairing, edified, penitent, musing and passive saints, but no face like that of Veronica, no saint's features and expression that said I am waiting, I have this much of you and I am content to wait.

Cecil's face settled onto the spread-eagled pillow of the big book. He sat alone at a table in the rear of the reading room, with his back toward the chief librarian's desk. Back and forth between them two fans cut high in the paneled walls shuttled the heavy air. They were bothersome flies then bees peacefully droning Cecil to sleep in a glade of tall, swaying grass. His corner had the restful gloom of all library corners and the book could have been a convenient headstone in a rural cemetery where all the dead had welcomed him. Miss Pruitt was not quite dead nor did she welcome Cecil. She called Anisse, her assistant, the girl who had given Cecil his book.

—That colored man over there, Miss Johnson, the one in the dark suit asleep. Either he must read or go away. There are park benches more suitable for what he wants to do. Please inform him of the rules of our library.

—Sir, sir. . . . Cecil looked into the squirrel face, the soft eyes, and small lips barely parted whispering.

—Sir, you'll have to wake up or leave. Miss Pruitt sent me over so I think you'd better listen, sir.

—You wouldn't mind if I stayed.

—She wouldn't mind either if you follow the rules, sir.

—But you, I mean would you care if I read or not.

—To be quite honest, no, I wouldn't care. It's a big, nearly empty room, and I don't see why I should care. Or anyone care.

—Then I'll stay.

—But only if you read.

Mirror said time was Cecil when you could not see your face unless someone lifted you to broken glass above the sink. Later you didn't care about image just run, run all day stopping only when tired and maybe seeing dim shadows in a puddle or on the drenched pavement, then one day saw woolly hair and dust that wouldn't wash off you saw colored boy Cecil and really surprised you saw something you had no way of knowing different or worse you saw your face and knew the dust would not change and now you see all things go away but that doesn't go away woolly hair creeps back on your forehead, but only reveals more dust beneath you will always be dying Cecil but that will not die. Cecil's hands rubbed hot then cold water into his face. The library's washroom was the cleanest he'd been in for days, and its cleanliness enabled him to try and tidy his person, to wash, to comb, to straighten the bedraggled clothing on his body as best he could. It seemed proper here in this neat washroom, a possibility that the other foul-smelling ill-lighted jakes had made inconceivable. He wondered why he hadn't thought of libraries before. Perhaps they were rooted too deeply in the other element—books and silent cubicles, alcoves stale with page dust and nervous, muffled breathing as word kindled in dry heatless extinction. Word become flesh become Cecil become invisible opener of doors, lightener of burden, of care, of pigmentation even, transforming mirror Cecil to that which only if you try hard can you find between black parenthesis of mortar board and gown.

Cecil shit and washed his hands again. She had been wearing a loose, green dress, the one who came and spoke to him, who had soft eyes. It could have been a tenuous rapport he sensed or just the ambiguity of his own half-sleep that suffused an aura of intimacy over the conversation. He had asked her name. She was a stranger, but less so than the others. Her green dress.

I should have asked her, Cecil thought, what city this is, what day of the month, of what year. Hearing from her would be somehow appropriate. I know she would tell me what I asked, no more, no less, and that she would tell the truth as far as she was able if I asked her other questions, if I made more demands. Her voice blending with rustle of green dress, perfume. Green color of St. Barbara's dress. Her symbol a tower. I remember a drawing, Eyckian perhaps, in which behind the saint men are erecting (delicately delineated by the artist, bare ribs of tentative form) her tower. Her dress spreads, a lush growing thing, on the hillside, and she gazes up from a book, quill in hand. The workmen, the saint, all motion and activity of the scene arrested, classically static and yet clearly projecting the shape and necessity of their completion like the tower rising from its chrysalis of scaffolding.

Cecil does not see her again. Shadows deepen and the fire goes out behind panes of stained glass. He would have preferred music, but the big books of old pictures had nearly the same soothing effect, emptied him into oblivion.

He saw her framed in the yellow rectangle, naked, not giving a fuck, guzzling whisky from a bottle. Life's done this to me she said and life is your eyes taking me in. All naked pink of me, pot-bellied, saggy titted, clump of hair there and here under my arm as I raise this bottle and don't give a fuck who knows or sees. Window yellow and shadeless, an eye that can't look away, can't blink or shield itself with a tear. Naked lady in the window. Who do you love; who has loved you. Would anyone pinch your melting backside, grin at you. She drinks. It will be morning soon, even now somewhere the light is scratching out someone's eyes. He wonders if the whisky still goes down, if it still spreads and tickles inside the pink flesh. He cannot remember a night that has been different. He has been always walking black, empty streets, streets on which every walker is alone, enclosed in the echo of his own footfalls. Dirty streets even in the blackness, and windows that brush his shoulders. The naked woman drinks, a flesh pillow round her middle, tired breasts that drag, the scraggly beard. Did she see him; he could have touched her, thrust his hand in the yellow frame if the glass had vanished. It was always her street, their street, and he the interloper, the one who is given away by his loud footsteps, his heart beating.

Cecil knew he would see her again. As he approached a rare lighted window each time he thought she would be there again. Something moved her in endless visitations through the rooms of the narrow row houses just as it moved him along the black pavement that was a ribbon around them. She was the fat, pink owner and the exploited tenant just as Cecil was the echo and the sound of his night wanderings. No one had wed them, no one had even introduced them and yet they were blind lovers eternally bound. Cecil and the lady, Cecil sound and Cecil echo, landlord and tenant.

And the street curved and rose and fell and hugged its shadow to itself and became all glass and winking light and slept again and almost died and finally like blood going home emptied into a loud, bright sea. Cecil emerging took the broad perpendicular—Market Street—and walked toward the city's center. After crossing a bridge he turned off into the railroad station. To a congregation of taxicabs and travelers a recorded voice squawked instructions. Yellow tickees for yellow cabs were automatically ejaculated from a blunt snouted machine beside the double revolving doors of the station's entrance. Alms for the love of Allah Cecil thought he heard and reached out to take a yellow ticket. It was freshly stamped: time, date, and serial number. The parrot urged him to take another, for anyone going anywhere to take another and go the best, fastest way. Cecil watched a long, gracefully curved leg slowly draw itself into the back seat of a cab. The beautiful face smiled at the black driver and told him swiftly where it wanted to go. In a moment they were disappearing together into the night.

And after the beginning the end, and after the rise the fall, and after Cecil the calm scalloped breath of a fart entered the Thirtieth Street station. A Family that Strays Together, Stays Together. Buy Bonds, They Did. A Name You Can Trust.

Its always a god they wait for. They wait because they believe, because they have faith. Not many inside at this hour. Sprawled on benches, eating, reading at the snack-magazine counter. Your people wheeling scrub buckets; some even command mopping machines. Someday there will be robots for the job and your people eating or reading or waiting to go.

Somebody was coming home. Somebody cocooned in rich, dark wood. Cecil shuffled across the cold stones of the station floor looking neither to the right nor the left, not down at his unlaced shoes nor up at the distant vault of the ceiling. Cecil obeyed and did not look back, he was to become no salt pillar, no last minute loser of his love, no food for rocks on which the women sat singing. His course was clear. Night waited opposite the door he had entered, night and the group in black beside black limousines. The mourners had been too punctual. They had to watch the cheap pine slats stripped away, the friction build between the mortician's immaculate staff and the coveralled Railway Express men. The shell of yellow boards had no sorrow in them. They split, squealed, and giggled like spring girls being undone. Finally the coffin sat ornate and gleaming under the electric lights that studded the overhang of the baggage porch. The coffin was already a thing detached, mute, indifferent, secure in its order of time. Not the time of the mourners (perhaps mother, father, brother, and wife, perhaps children and grandchildren, perhaps not blood at all but brought by some other coincidence to wait for the train), but the sea time of ebb and flow, of change faceless and forever renewing. Cecil saw there were tears. And the old man with his arm around the thin shoulders of the old veiled woman. The fingers did not stretch themselves upon her flesh. Long, dry hand hung limp against the breast of her black dress, knobby bones touching one another, an animal the woman could be wearing as decoration. It was lifted ever so gently, the polished coffin, which if shrunken would have served as an elegant jewel box for a lady's vanity table. Behind the old couple, young woman and man, other Negroes dressed in black stood at hushed attention. Cecil knew they would soon begin to sing.

Cecil thought the moment had created its own kind of sepulchral silence, a threshold of quiet until the box was in the hearse and the dearly beloved who had gathered could sing it away. But the city found their corner. Cars, trains, buses, the loudspeaker hoarse with the stationmaster's voice, porters calling, newspapers hawked, it all came crowding into the small, quiet place beneath the overhang. Cecil remembered a blind shooting up, the rattling echo of its violent motion that shook the tiny, rented cubicle where he and Esther lay. Surprise, surprise they all said as one after another climbed through the sudden hole in the wall. Cossacks, traveling salesmen, senators, whores, football players, a baboon, a steel drum band poured through smiling and excited. He bolted upright in the unsteady cot. The guests were a flood inundating the room, water rising to his chin. Beside him she was already dead, drowned, the twisted sheet shrouding her lifeless flesh. Light choked him, chewed his scream. . . .

> Farther along we'll know more about you,
> Farther along we'll understand why.
> I want you to cheer up, my brethren,
> Live in the sunshine.
> You'll understand—
> By and by. . . .

Why did you do it. This time he is caught, he must answer. So much red on the pillow, soft red he can smooth or tangle in his fist. Can I tell her Simon is dead, my son Simon out of Esther who has our underwear already up and drying whom I have had to refuse once already this morning. Simon conceived in November, born dead in spring. Simon is why I killed what was in my hands why they grin when I pass. You must hear them laughing, the bags of garbage mocking humped Cecil as he descends the back stairs. You see it has not always been like this. You might laugh too if I produced the diploma, think it was something I bought at a rummage sale or scavenged from the bags. You don't know my name. You might believe I took my name from the document I found, took his name as I took his degree and nailed it to my wall. Hocus-pocus. Let there be Cecil. Because if you are Cecil and you are what it says on the paper then who is crazy nigger I know playing on these back stairs, making noise that breaks people's sleep.

For a somnambulist she moves faster than you'd expect.

Quickly she is down there at my root taking back her own, the loam returned to her lips that I dredged from her lips. Perfect circle. And should I be Indian giver too. Succubus curled at the gate waiting for rain.

Teeth and hair. Immaculate conception recorded three times in this century produced just that, a growth of hair and teeth. Perhaps preserved somewhere in a jar. My Simon nowhere, a dead son not rare at all, to be expected, even predictable, out of a thousand births, two hundred babies will not get past the first month. But I did not have a thousand sons; I tempted the number gods in no way. In fact I tried to be humble, wanted only one son, waited once for one son. Loved all that Esther and I had done together, all we would ever do. So when he came and died so soon . . . So when he came and died so soon . . .

There is a window. From where I rest my head on her breasts I can look through a three-sided window made by her splayed raised thighs and lintel of calf, ankle, and foot crossing them. I can see Simon building a house of alphabet blocks. I can see Simon mashing crayons on a coloring book. I can see Esther washing Simon and me washing Esther and the three of us laughing and splashing naked in the soapy water. The lintel drops, and there is only wide V of two white thighs pointing toward the ceiling.

I will go with him to the park. There will be peacocks strutting unexpected at the sudden turnings of wooded paths, a fountain and a wide basin around it for sailing miniature boats. Simon's boat will lean into the wind, a gleaming scimitar, a swan. I will watch it glide, watch him, grow drowsy in the afternoon sun. I will doze till Simon shakes my knee.

—It was naughty what you did. I'm sure others must have heard the racket. Cecil combed the redness with his fingers. Her hair had become wet and tangled, but as Cecil drew his hand in long gentle strokes smoothness and lightness returned. As if moved by a puff of air a few wisps of red responding to some energy in his hand would rise after each stroke. A kind of magic Cecil thought. You rub your feet on a rug then touch a metal doorknob and a spark crackles. A comb through your hair and it makes tissue paper stick. Cecil waved his hand above the redness. Silky strands strained to reach him. Moon above the tides of a red sea. Cecil's game as he did not answer, as he listened, as he searched for more windows, mirrors, eyes.

—I've never done anything like this before, she said. Cecil thought how everything would have been the first time for Simon, how many *first times* Simon would never have. Why. Cecil wondered if anything like bad luck in November could be passed from generation to generation, if the blood could carry images of dying leaves, still, dark pools, a thousand fleeing wings, if all the sadness of fall sky and earth could be reborn in Simon's heart. What had the child learned in that less than one instant of life. And did Simon learn or did Simon simply have to remember.

—Oh Cecil, if it could have just been me. If I could just take his place. Esther seemed to have dissolved into grief; she was not the lump in the hospital gown and bed, but part of the dense atmosphere, the disinfectant and blood pall which burned Cecil's eyes and nose in the crowded maternity ward.

—Of course I knew a thing like this could happen, might happen to me. But the picture, vague as it was, was somehow quite different from this. When I was a girl, I . . .

—Why Simon, Cecil? Somebody you know named Simon, somebody in your family. You mean like Simon Peter in the Bible? Sounds kind of strange to me. I'm not sure as I like it. No sense in worrying now anyway. Just as easy be a girl.
. . .

As my son died her red hair keeps falling. It is sand through my fingers. Here I lie with this strange white woman and Esther downstairs and Simon dead. She asks *why did you do it.*

All I could think of was Easter and the way all the choirs were singing. You see when you try to answer a question such things come up. My wife and her spirituals. A bunch of us had a group and used to sing. Everything from rhythm and blues to gospels which is not as far you'd think till you've heard a lot of them, then no question of shared roots. Still you know precisely what the good ones want to say. No question about it. In the gospels they are saying I believe and this is the way it is to feel like I do. Easter was old Reverend Reed, but it had to accommodate the song of Schütz as well. Reverend Reed and beside and beneath him on a straight-backed chair Mr. Watkins who was not Reverend because he could not read or write, an ignorant, country black man fast becoming child again as years collapsed the bones of his face, the bones of his sleeping intellect. I saw him on the street long after those days when with Esther I would go to hear the singing and try to make out what words moved Esther's lips as she silently prayed. He was there, Elder Watkins his title at last, Elder Watkins in the remains of a blue vested suit. He still wore the heavy gold chain looped from his watch pocket and the tall black hat with drooping brim. I knew if I had been closer I would have smelled the age, the weariness of flesh and threadbare fabric. Of the million lines that sliced across the Elder's face, I remember those at the corners of his eyes, eyes that seemed forgotten under folds of skin. These lines intaglioed black against dusky black at the outward corners of his eyes could have been the beginnings of a smile. The good Elder Watkins. I could see the frayed ends of long cotton drawers below the blue trousers. The same gray-white cotton showed through rents in the old man's shoes as he shuffled through Casino Way, a loaf of bread under his arm. Good day Elder. Did you know they are singing again, Easter song Elder, by a German you should have known, Heinrich Schütz, who would surely recognize that Jesus shuffle of yours beneath a cross of dignity here in a back alley bringing home the bacon. Man . . . man, do you hear me talking to you. Why will you die, sink down onto the pavement when I turn away? The Elder was on his knees, his hands were clasped and sweat poured down his face in the effort of maintaining with dignity the uncomfortable posture and recalling those sacred cadences, seeking and finding the rhythm that would make the words flow, which would swing that rusty gate of memory back and let the word roam green pastures. It was all there. In the black head sprinkled with salt and pepper tufts of hair. He had learned it all by listening. He was a vessel into which the word had been poured. And if he pressed his knees into the hard boards of the altar platform and strained the muscles of his old neck to hold the head back and eyeballs fixed on Heaven, then the gate would glide back. So I had listened to the old man babble on. Cento of biblical fragments, of scripture, hymns and favorite phrases of all the Reverends he had served beneath. And there were days the Elder found his poetry. The sun shone while rain fell. Devil beating his wife, and Esther of course cried when Reverend Reed thundered over the Elder's prayer, when poor Elder Watkins got carried away and floundered in those deep waters, when his tongue clucked and we all feared now it's the old man's time his heart can't bear these memories, this song that makes him tremble and sweat and stutter, but he didn't die just faded away under Reverend Reed's thunder from the pulpit. And here the Elder was. Like a blind man making his way through this alley. That alley where I wanted to speak, to say Elder I remember you, you are not dead yet, not a ghost yet though you could be the tattered shade of a black Polonius, of ignorance and desperate dignity done to death like a rat.

But I did not disturb him. I went on my way to the Presbyterian church and heard the St. John Passion of Schütz. I believe these things happened the same day . . . Easter . . .

—When I was a girl I hated the freckles and the red hair was just as bad. Somehow they went together. It was *them* that made me ugly. One day if I could just be patient, they would go away and ugly duckling be a swan. A blond swan with clear white skin. She rose and stood beside the bed. Cecil remaining on the bed got up to his knees and pulled her toward him till his arms were tight around the firm, powerful middle of the woman. Strong bones, tight flesh of hips and taut lower belly. Cecil diver plunged into the perfumed depths of her body hair still damp from their lovemaking. His fingers dug into her haunches, spreading and closing the two massy petals of her backside. She moaned, then the moan was a flower blooming, a thrust of naked beauty that was a liquid tongue meeting Cecil's, licking Cecil's, washing Cecil, floating him as seed to the hot inner chambers of his own desire.

And while the tongue was swallowed, another formed in the forest.

Christ lag in Todesbanden. That was another Easter. And Easter in Spain, in Madrid, in Málaga, how many times has the body been resurrected in his name. *Schlafe, schlafe mein Liebster*. Sleep Simon.

And I wanted love so badly I dreamed of encounters under rocks, in the sea slime. My search has brought me here to this white woman's bed, to the aftertaste of her juices in my mouth. If I called Esther at the top of my voice, she might hear me through the three floors and run here to claim me, to take me back below the stairs where she knows I belong.

The room is silent, naked man and woman prostrate in postures of exhaustion. The room shook to the chugging of the washing machine. The room was hung with the damp skins of dead animals. In the room both beds were unmade and a small yellow woman in a rocking chair twirled her hands. The room was empty now, the stacks of clothes removed and Esther on her way through the darkness.

So many things Esther didn't know. Cecil counted, one, two, three . . . on his graduation eve, half enjoying, half dismayed by his secrets. Herbert Philbrick, F.B.I. double agent, led three lives each week on TV in a perpetual turning of tables upon the communist conspiracy. Cecil had been bored by the show but identified with the numbers compartmentalizing the double agent's lives. Cecil defender of the faith: lover of Esther, diligent student of the law, advancer of banner proclaiming *All Men Equal*. Cecil conspirator: lover of love, student of *their* law, carrot wiggled in front of the others *Equal Opportunity Lives*. Cecil Cecil: neither of others, libra, seesaw, see soul, sees all.

Home for a haircut. Sometimes leaving the law school building and university grounds took on an urgency, a one-track necessity like the stinging need to urinate or lose his seed. Today going through the mechanics of his final leave-taking there had been no wistfulness. He had read the instruction sheet and efficiently carried out his tasks. No one had been in the superintendent's office when Cecil had replaced his key on the appropriate hook. Number 203. The last year he had lived among them on the campus rather than with Esther. That was part of his scholarship, a condition which had annoyed him, but which he couldn't afford to refuse. It meant evening and weekend safaris to catch up on his janitorial duties at the Banbury Arms. It meant Esther doing much of his job in addition to her own. He had not told her that the move away had meant his bills would be paid. Instead he continued to collect the money she had been supplying throughout his career in law school. To surprise her with what she would never buy for herself, some gift, some extravagance? Or was it originally for a child? Whatever his intent, his initial reason for secrecy, he scrupulously hoarded Esther's savings.

Someone whom he would probably never see again, unless they bumped in the pomp and circumstance parade tomorrow, had lent Cecil the money for a haircut, and though it was a long way, Cecil had set out on foot for the barber's.

As usual June was hot and got hotter as Cecil got closer to home. Everybody knows how it is now thought Cecil. Information abounds about us down here just as it does about those over there and *that kind* and *them*. We have been measured, quantified by tools so subtle that they tell better lies than most men. And what is the ritual in dying. Does my number when it's up drop or jerk or is it drawn through by a black pencil. And in that room where all our cards are filed does some lugubrious arm in a solemn arc glide over the metal trays till it comes to B then Br then Bra and so on till it has located one Braithwaite, Cecil Otis, then delicately descend, clamp my card in its pincers, raise me, retrace the arc backward till I am suspended over the proper heap of other numbers up. Drops me. Or is there an afterlife, some limbo cabinet in which are housed defunct numbers for a decent interval, for a storage bin repose while all cross references are checked out: tardy credits, overdue accounts, invoices, actions, loans, liens, disposition of estates all are collected, balanced. Books on everything. Why my manhood measures less than it should. Something to do with being lost when I was found, with being made to dance so my legs would not wither, dancing to a cat-o'-nine-tails, with being made to watch and listen while my women did other dances with the sailors. I remember the sun sudden in my eyes, the salt air too rich after the fetid hole below decks. Music began cracking around me and though it tore my ankles and drew flies to the bloody ankle chains, I jiggled my body to make it live another day, to be raised another day to sun and salt air and flagellation.

If I were to write a book it would have no numbers. Sick of Numbers Cecil said almost aloud.

How you doing Magistrate Cecil. The voice and greeting told him he was getting closer and closer. Up from the broken pavement rose the wavering heat. I believe the women wear pants instead of skirts just so they can sit with their legs wide open. She smiled at him from three stories up, toothless witch, her bones held together by an ancient cotton dress; bare throat, bare brown shoulders, she had been waiting for golden hair to grow, to drop into the street, for some knight to climb and release her, but now she had forgotten, only smiled at what passed, even sweaty, haircut needing Cecil below her window she would acknowledge as she did the buses, the dogs and cats, the beer, the grease. Their sea changed forms which dried where they splattered Rorschach blots of I am going nowhere so might as well be here against this building or let it fall where it will right here in the middle of the sidewalk I ain't going nowhere and couldn't care less. Or I am sick.

Handkerchief across his brow, Cecil paused in the midst of the mopping strokes to finger the tight curls of his longer than necessary hair. *What's to it, Magistrate.* To be well groomed essential. An incipient pun in the word groom, its double meaning in relation to Esther and their wedding the next day fixed the word groom in Cecil's mind. Groom, gloom, gloam, gleem, groom, loom, broom, poom. Do you undertake this womb to be your lawful wedded wife. The room was full of men and women attired in black. Some laughed, some cried, others moved among the floral decorations with no expression of emotion on their faces. Black watch. Soon a door would be opened and the mystery would recede. Pipers piping. Gloom pipes. Down from heel and hills pied piper and plague of worms. Bitches hide wombs. Batches fried grooms. The building you see before you is all that remains of the ancient ghetto. We have conjectured from drawings on its walls and instruments petrified in the lava flow that this edifice served as a house of pleasure. Sociopologists have recently discovered municipal records which seem to point to the existence of an extensive number of these bordellos in this area suggesting that perhaps one of the thriving industries of the ghetto was prostitution. No one can accurately estimate what percentage of its residents actually lived from the profits of that profession, and of course there remains the problem of determining primary and secondary participation but modern methods of research and data evaluation are everyday opening up to us the secrets of this lost culture. I wish to call your special attention to the rounded groove in this stone. We have reason to believe that the contour was not carved nor is it a freak of nature, rather we suppose it was worn by the buttocks of long dead ladies of the night who for as closely as we can guess spent thousands of years in this very spot waiting for their male customers.

Sick and desolate of an old passion.

> *Shine, shine, shine*
> *Shine for a nickel*
> *Shine for a dime*
> *Shine for a quarter*
> *If you got the time.*

Boy sang to Cecil, to the sun. Litany of the old street. One-eyed boy with box tucked under his arm, shoeshine rags draped over his left shoulder next to the good eye. He would shine, shine. Better than the sun he would pop and flick and rub till grinning back from the toe of a boot his face would appear. Two-faced. Two good eyes. Boy past, boy future Cecil glanced at the scarred toes of his shoes, the visible coats of liquid polish thinly glazing one another and never reaching the leather somewhere brown and dying beneath. I would my fingers held some musical instrument—a guitar, a fiddle. I would play beside the boy, accompany him along the street. And each time we stopped to emblazon some customer a crowd would gather, watch him pop and flick and rub and they would hear how all this, these smells, the filth, the sweat, *How you doing Magistrate* has not been lost, does not tremble away like hot sidewalks or die like the scream of the siren but lights a corner in a man, a dark huddling corner but one which lives until the next burst of sun or salt air too rich.

Pearl that was his eye. Pearly ball dimmed by the writhing mists cold and gray like curling pattern within a marble agate, agate, cat's-eye explodes from impetus of thumbnail popped against its backside. The splash of sound of color as prizes careen from the charmed circle. Over here boy do this pair of dying shoes. Cecil couldn't even afford the dime shine, but let himself forget one moment. Listened to the jaunty song, met the one dancing eye.

—Ah go on, mistah. Shine make you pretty. She'll like you pretty.

Cecil remembering shook his head no. Told the shoeshine boy with movements of his hands inside the torn lining of his trousers that nobody was home to pay for anything. Cecil smiled whistling the boy's ditty. Shine. Was not so long ago had my own hustle on the street corners. Could pop a rag. Carry a bag. Cecil Otis Braithwaite little boy rimed to himself. Right down there with the rest I did my best. Fever in the funkhouse looking for a five. Rattle them bones. Seven come eleven Nigger goes to heaven. Pay the boss, poor hoss lost. On his knees. Marbles, bones, the grimy coins changed hands. Down and dirty in the street. You ever seen a dog do it. Doggy water is what you make when you shake it. Till it grows up. On your knees makes holes in your pants. Patches. What pirates wear over eyes. Captain Kidd. Popeye the sailor man, did it to a garbage can. One-eyed kid smoking a butt. I would give a million for your song, for your smile, for your lost eye. Do the shoe, do it and you can have everything.

—Nothing, you ain't got nothing.

—Just enough to get my hair cut, and I must get it cut.

—You's all right, my man. For you I'm gonna do it free. A lick and spit just cause you gonna be something someday and maybe you remember Shine that one-eyed boy on the corner.

There were scabs on the back of the shaved head bobbing below Cecil's eyes. He can do it though, can't he. First time in how long these shoes feel wax and a rag. Perhaps the boy heard, could see me all those years ago making my hustle. Scarred bowling ball works so hard. And then the eye and the bad teeth. Long lashes an awning when he lifts his head, when he smiles up at me and one moist, dark eyeball disappears into the top of his head.

Walk a little taller Cecil your shoes are shined. Bottom to top you shall be a better man. The boy's song faded into the dull hum of the streets. Cars passing, doors slamming, the broken talk that had to climb dark stairwells or walk the tepid air between hot brick walls. Going home for a haircut.

—Dat's the man. That's the magistrate.

—He ain't no magistrate, ain't no man. He ain't nothing.

—A big faker.

—Yazzuh, a big, black humbug thinks his sweet ass got wheels.

—Give the boy his quarter. That's his due.

—Mister magistrate of nothing.

—Humbug magistraitassed uppity nigger.

The voice had been hidden on cat belly beneath the cool rot of some decaying stoop. The voice could not be heard above the drone of flies or maggots inching their way along the particolored spills of rusty garbage cans. It was more quiet and humble than the short puffs of air Clara fanned up under her dress to cool the damp kiss of her loose thighs. It might have been a roach snoring or the scurrying rodent feet that panicked at the dark, pulsing cat shape prostrate beneath the cool rot of some decaying stoop. Cecil didn't believe the light tread hardly heavier than air, but almost before he could disbelieve, the needle point bore into his flesh and then too late to do anything about, wings and thread legs perched on his arm drinking, drawing up the blood from his heart.

—Pay the boy, magistrate.

Cecil counted the coins in his hand. They were holy beads he fingered, trying to squeeze some metaphysical life from their dull, round shapes. The introit, the Angelus. He told them one by one, entranced, anxious, dreading the sum, the full circle.

—How much do you want.

—We want you, magistrate.

One-eyed boy moved to the edge of the group that was gathering. The rag was still, both eyes glazed and unseeing.

—I've done nothing wrong.

So then this cat they call the magistrate starts to fidgeting. Like he knew all the sudden niggers weren't there for no play. No, man. He commence to counting and looking around, down at his feets, cross at the boy, side to side at all them hot nigger faces.

—I have done nothing. What do you want.

—Boy said he did them kicks of yours then you walked away without paying him nothing.

Then the mag says slowly looking from face to face:

—There is some misunderstanding. The boy did the shoes because he wanted to, because he felt like it not because I promised anything in return. Ask him if you don't believe me.

—Shine, is he lying. If you lied to us, Shine, I'm going to have a piece of your ass myself. And as if busting one head was just as good as busting any other them niggers starts to grunting and pawing the ground and Big Tony shakes a fist big as the shoeshine boy's head about one inch from that blind darky:

—I mess up that other eye for you if you lying.

But the shoeshine boy ain't for no shit and out comes his razor:

—Nigger you lay that hand on me and you gonna draw back a nub. Now Big Tony ain't no fool and when he sees the boy one eye all lit up and that blade standing tall and clean he cools his heels and grunts but don't move one inch closer.

—Put up your sword into the sheath. The mag stood there like he really was some kind of special body and strangely enough the boy did put back his knife in his pocket and all the rest didn't barely move just froze in they tracks like waiting for another word.

Ich hab es euch gesagt, dass ichs sei, suchet ihr denn mich, so lasset diese gehen.

—Let him go. If it's written that blood must flow, I'm sure it was meant to be mine.

—Well did the mag cheat you or not.

The shoeshine boy spoke and when he did it was like words from a rock. Both eyes was dead cause he didn't blink just stared straight ahead with the dark one and the light.

—He ain't no friend of mine and if his shoes was done it was cause I expected a quarter.

Everybody had crowded round now like they do when theys the tiniest excuse just to get close to each other and make heat. Off the stoops, outa the shade, from corners, boxes, kitchens, windows facing the street all them gathered round magistrate Cecil and the one-eyed boy.

–Don't worry friend it's me they want. They'll always want me. Go your own way. It is done; I am delivered.

–The man is crazy. Like all I got to do is give free shines. He ain't no friend of mine. Out here to get what I can. Give nothing away, asks for nothing. Shine for a nickel, shine for a dime, shine for a quarter if you got the time.

–Let him go.

Wine smell was high on the air, especially you could smell it on the cat's breath who sidles through the people till he got right next to the magistrate and splat with the palm of his hand loosened some jawbone and made Cecil spit red.

–Who you telling what to do, nigger. You is in trouble if you don't know it.

Magistrate Cecil shook his head, swiped his hand cross his lips and commenced:

–I have only said what had to be said. If I've done wrong or said something wrong tell me what it was.

So there was the mag soft talking and trying to move down the street with all them niggers crowded round him. Close as white on rice. He was like a stick being carried away by the gutter or a leaf in the wind. Kinda in a daze it seemed to me I don't mind saying I felt sorry for the cat. Afterall he come to grief just trying to do some of the things most of us would do if we could get together the right shit at the right time. Who wouldn't like to walk through this jungle with his nose high like he couldn't smell the scum and even if the filth could rise up to his nose his nose held so proud and holy it couldn't be touched or hurt. Always that piece of suit and some kind of rag tie you could tell Cecil thought something of hisself and wanted to make something of hisself. The way he talked when he would talk. A book caught in his throat or a spoon shoved up his ass he dropped each word like an egg that hurt him to lose and like if he didn't get it out just right it might crack and be yolk all over the front of his shirt. He did keep a clean shirt. Holey and frayed but Esther did keep the nigger clean. Everybody knows what a fool that woman is. Thinks she got a good thing, she thinks when his day comes he's gonna be a big man and all her slaving and saving pussy just for him will pay off with loads of gravy and goodies ever after. Too bad that child don't know magistrate Cecil will drop her yellow ass quick as he gets the chance. Same old story every time. Some good woman hauls a cat up, kills herself doing his dirt, then one day he says goodbye, goodluck, I got a younger, sprier, prettier hen. But getting back to what I was saying, off they went with Cecil in the middle leaving that shoeshine boy singing on the corner.

–Never seen a fool like that. Like I'm out here for my health. Free. Did that nigger say I said free shine. In the boy's fist a quarter from the hand of Big Tony from the pants pocket of Cecil from the vest pocket of Henry Gitenstein, thirty-fifth in his class at the university law school.

TWO

· · · · ·

"Ole Rileeh walk'd in wahder"
—Leadbelly Song

HARBOR BELLS TOLLING, DING DONG PIPING
whistleshriek ou whee, ou whoo, *Bee Ohh*.

Heaving subaqueous heaves and shudders the land like a table rolled from beneath a magician's horizontal assistant in a demonstration of levitation left the ship by inches till miraculously Cecil was afloat.

Seaborne.

Stubbornly groaning and wheezing that lingering menagerie of cranes, lifts, drydocks, tackles, and slurring chains was put to sleep. Only blinking lights now that studded the shore in formless profusion, lights identifying the prehistoric reptilian shapes only if the viewer abstracted his iconography from some mythic overlay that isolated horizontals, verticals, pairs, and triplets and with the astronomer's irrepressible metonomy yclept this Orion, that the Dipper, those eyes there the dinosaur who spewed my trunk into the hold. Cecil had watched the loading, the lowering, awkward beasts and thick men who tended them. Handle with care, with fragility. Made in Japan. Maid in Germany. Union maid.

Flags and flowers and the scurrying crowds chased by whistle toots up and down the gangplank. Kissing in the corridor. A door slamming farther down the passage. Summer sailing and all's well bluesea beckons a band plays. We are going to war, we are conquering heroes returning. Beneath our feet the Trojans in chains hold their breath. Some of the slaves are sick with anxiety yet hold the curdled fear behind their teeth, choking themselves because they fear a greater torment than that of their own suffocating insides.

Embraces become more public, more passionate. I expect those red quivering fingers there to slide from the waist that cleaves to them down down past the pinch to the blooming fullness there to pat and fondle and at last raise the skirt push down the panties and a cheek in each fist down to the marrow squeeze, down to the deck drop and never even be missed. I am seeing machines that line the dock, boxes, crates, vehicles drawn to shining attention. I see acrobats on the swinging ropes. I see a tall lady with an upraised ice-cream cone toasting the emperor. I see in what must be the west how fast the sun drops. A moment ago one side of the city was brazen, each window molten with the heat of its own brilliance. Buildings that were ingots of blazing bronze, gold, and copper. This against mauve of flocculent clouds trimmed in gold. Now purple bellies higher more somber, gray of sky meeting gray towers of city. Monuments in a humble churchyard vying for attention, crowded, vain, a ragged silhouette of withering stone.

Winking now, they offer constellations, significance to be deciphered. I see rivers, flotsam and jetsam. I hear myself hissing, a candle drowned.

Dear father, father in whose black home I see so many stars blinking, tell me, father, do all journeys commence with such questioning, such tumult and confusion.

Some sign. A comet cutting deeply through the blackness, red meteors glowing in its tail. Here we are drawing the sea closed behind us, white, ghost churning, invisible ripples outward, then nothing. Sea zippered shut in our wake. A sign would do, anything you could do for us since afterall we are launched, we cannot bargain, hold out for an overwhelming demonstration. Assure us not of a special destination, but that we are destined, intimate no portion, just that there has been an apportionment.

Why did you do it.
—Sometimes you are very much like him, Cecil. Below the Alhambra they sat talking in a café, Cecil and Webb remembering rooms in other cities, other worlds.
—You mean your son.
—Yes, like him.
Around the fountain a room grew. Circular the pool, circular the benches, circles blunted to octagons climbing one within the other to a vaulted ceiling. Fountain splash trifling like someone peeing in the sea.
—And is that why I'm here?
Windows in the white walls. Pictures like stained glass depicting pageants, saints. Windows Netherlandish framed in thick gilt and gold. The dozing, gray museum guards.
—I can't answer yes or no to that. I think at times you're here purely by accident. When I say you are like him I don't mean in any obvious way. The first time I saw you I was aware of no similarities. At most he was approximately your age when I saw him last.
—And your son, he was black.
—Color yes, but even that was quite different from yours. Darker in fact. Anyone could see he had Negro blood. But his build, most physical details differed from yours.
Above them in the Moorish castle a room and a fountain. Fountain was a pride of roaring lions. Tribute from some oriental monarch to the conquering black kings. Onyx lions whose throats spewed twenty foot geysers which cascaded to white turbulence in the center of a deep pool. Continuous gut deep reverberations, lions growling hunger, anger in a marble sepulcher which echoed their yearning. Stalactites hung, ice transformed to marble dripping from the arched ceiling. Where the black kings laved their bodies, underground, surrounded by magnificence, symbols of obedience, of power, the coolness and rectitude of geometry, symmetry celebrating the peace within themselves.

—And the picture made you speak.

—The "Adoration." No more than it made you answer. Not until I knew you for a while did I begin to sense important resemblances, points of contact.

—To your black son.

—Yes, my black son. But in the museum, in front of the picture, the first time I saw you, what drew me to that particular place was the Bosch painting you were standing beside. Then I saw you and . . .

—You said there was a better version in Madrid.

—Something silly like that, and the rest followed. The rest was easy after such a foolish intrusion.

—I was nothing, no one, nowhere. It was impossible to intrude on *me*.

—So you said yes to my proposal. Let me take you to the Prado "Adoration." Three thousand miles away. And here we are.

—No strings attached.

—And still none. You have your return ticket. I've given you sufficient money to make travel or other things feasible. But here we are, still together. No strings attached.

—Cecil sees the world. Cecil white man's burden.

—That's how I mean. Like him.

—You didn't know him, you've admitted that many times. You say you only saw him once. Or that you've seen him only in your imagination. You contradict yourself continually.

—I don't know you, Cecil. But like him you've decided to wrap yourself in old sorrows. To be a kind of walking, talking *lest we forget.*

—But it's just that quality that makes me needed, makes me loved. Earns me expense paid vacations to Europe. I run into the nicest people, people just begging to be reminded.

—The word bitter keeps wanting to be said, but I'm sure

saying it about you or him would only be another way of turning my back.

Cecil stared; it was the look he had given the Magi.

—And if I go now, Cecil, will you promise me that you'll follow on the day I asked?

—Why then. Why not a day before or after. And if we split up now, we might as well keep going our own ways. Break clean just as we met.

—I tried, Cecil, honestly I tried to tell you why. But the reason, the story, is so incomplete in my mind. It would mean much to me if you would just do as I ask.

—One week from today. The end of Semana Santa in Málaga.

—It's very important to me that you come.

—I'll go back to Madrid. I'll wait six days then I'll go to Málaga. But why Málaga . . .

—Why you Cecil. Why me. Why this table three thousand miles from where we started.

—Then you'll be leaving tonight.

—Always leaving it seems. Running somewhere.

—Or away from somewhere.

—You are like him.

—You've given a lot to me.

—Please. Just come. Nothing has been given, much is lost.

Cecil's eyes had been dazzled by the Prado's black king. The long neck of the Magus, the richness of his garments and the elegant page by his side. Not a man who had just happened, who had yesterday learned of bright colors, precious metals, the dignity in the folds of a robe. The Nativity was alive in a way the other one hadn't been. A final statement of the theme, repose, assurance, simplicity.

To say yes. Yes yes yes yes yea saying again yes yes again to say it yes yes yes yea yea saying I am yes. . . .

I will go yes as you ask. Of course I will go. Image of

235

image in water. How one is upside down will not stand still is deep yet floats on the surface is really neither down nor up nor does it end or extend that still image of itself above water.

I was on a ship. The land moved away. When it rains or when I stand beneath a fountain I am underwater as the image is neither under the water nor on the water but shadow of that which is itself still shadow.

On that promontory My Friend is the seemingly impregnable citadel of the Black Kings. Defied all of España till on a White Horse Iago Matamoros cleansed the dark plague from dis Land.

At the foot of the hill, barely visible from the ramparts of the Alhambra a café called La Gloria, consisting of twenty-nine chairs and a kiosk, reinvigorates those who are about to ascend and those who have descended from the fortress. Cecil alone.

Es muy bonito aquí, no señor.

I read: potpourri of architecture. Additions made throughout its existence. Each incorporating prevalent style of period of construction. Succeeding kings each attempted to make personal impression on structure. Can be viewed either as combination of many individual parts or complex unity reflecting not so much definite plan as a continuity that has the shape of history rather than logic. Restorations, additions, buildings razed, left partially constructed one century, completed the next. A tension between new and old if not completely satisfying aesthetically, at least vigorous, realistic, and honest.

So in the shadow of the walls I dream and drink gin. Webb is gone; my promise is gone. I review the history of the Moors in Spain, the Reconquista, the pogroms. They say the gypsy quarter at night is exciting, authentic. Brown bodies, brown wine, brown music. Not brown of business shoes but that black tinged, red tinged blood-brown of gypsy skin.

Of all punishments the poet said the greatest is to be blind and in Granada. These words inscribed on the castle's walls. A high thick wall that secludes the intricate, almost effeminate gardens, where bearded black kings were wont to stroll with maidens carefully selected from the cowering red-roofed houses below. Maidens chosen as scrupulously as chargers—color, gait, fineness of teeth and mane being not the least of qualities ascertained. Maidens who would feel the subtle silks of the East for the first time on their skins. The scent of orange blossoms, lemon blossoms, frankincense, and myrrh languid through the delicate trees and shrubbery, scents which alternately lifted then pasted to their soft skin the diaphanous, caressing fabrics that had been arranged on their bodies by smiling eunuchs. Maidens whose eyes widened afraid of some pagan sacrifice when led past the roaring onyx lions till down through cool subterranean passages they were put at partial ease by steaming baths and sherberts tingling through their warm insides. So strange that black hands, gnarled bark-backed warrior's hands could be so soft and smooth, could intoxicate the white tenderness where silk parted silently.

Why did you do it.

She tossed me an artificial rose. I had a table close to the platform on which they danced. El Cinco Flamenco. Two hundred pesetas to enter, one fifty a drink. Cab driver who took me to the gypsy quarter screamed he had been cheated when I refused his first tabulation.

I closed my eyes and heard a jackhammer ripping the sidewalks apart. Their gypsy heels clacking, clacking louder and louder, ball and chain striking feeble walls which collapsed in a dust wheeze of weariness and gratitude. *O lay O lay. Baila Hombre!*

237

I kissed the Rose.

Gave it later to a saucer eyed urchin who wandered into the bedroom just as my pants and drawers finished wobbling up my legs to embrace my bare ass. I gave the rose and an *adios* to pass on to her mother, who had disappeared as soon as her ablutions at the bedside basin were over.

Esther, In my fashion.

First but not the last it began my tour, my quest. Don Cecil, undertaker of perilous journey, seeker of knowledge. Knight of the rose made flesh, the carnation.

The narrow ship plies backward and forward relentlessly. Someone, even if only part of myself, to talk to.

Notes on THE PRADO—April 19

Luis Tristan 1600
> Sad upgazing saints—Santa Monica, Saint Llorosa

Hericlatos crying

Juan de Juanes—pyramids—in background leering mustachioed faces. Martyrdom of St. Esteban cycle—sun draws apex of pyramid toward it.

Cena de San Benito—austere, dark, frugal cubicle of hermit. Brown shadows. Two studies, old men's faces—drinkers, cups in hand.

Zurbarán—little color, muted shades, chiaroscuro, browns, grays; simple like monks' habits he paints—bold relief effects—objects in isolation because of monochrome planes of color, blackness of background—relief almost—one red cup startling because it comes in midst of gray, brown, black darkness. Unnerving—fresh blood in an empty room.

Ribera—much in common—only red appears in large amounts—the only "color."

16th cen. anonymous—Judith con la Cabeza de Holofernes —Esther's body—nipples, breasts, torso exact—widely spaced breasts, pronounced cleft to navel, flatness of abdomen to pubic mound.

St. Sebastian's martyrdom? Santa Catalina. A city, an automobile, almost Simon—St. Simon?

Mural painters, 12th cen.—Angels with eyes on hands, feet, wings. Saints with curiously tilted heads, as if just hanged. Impossible contortions—angles of limbs, hands, feet inhumanly flexible—supple like the fins of fish—repeating the undulations of some fluid, invisible medium.

An old woman who has a potato breast, wrinkled, brown plantlike tendril droops from tip. Old man prostrate in a tentlike hut—attended by two demons, snakes, toads. Old woman with burning hair—dogs—cats— monster in saucer hat, veil, trunk protrudes beneath.

Pieter Brueghel—"Triumph of Death"—1520?–1569— dogs eating dead children—army of skeletons at gates of city. Man hung from crotch of tree—man chased by black dogs, he guards his genitals.

Head of goose—phallic, pallid, fondled by a cherub same color. Gooseneck like a snake crawling into bottom corner of frame—sheet music—a violin—Virgins

My Pietà—one I drew from wall of church—D. Crespi— Jesu Cristo Difunto

Teniers—monkeys

Clots of tourists meander by. I think it is not a desire to confront the paintings but the language of the guide they follow. The sounds he makes are reminders of home and simple concerns, the common accents of native speech which each can share though the members of the group are strangers in a foreign country, trespassers who at best conspire among themselves beneath brittle canopies of sound maneuvering through the corridors and galleries. Is there a guide for me, will one come along who knows how I must withhold my assent until I translate any language into that black subterranean one which is my own. I am unprotected. I am tempted by French, Italian, German, Spanish, any and all of these bursts of sound seem appropriate as they float by. Not a linguist, nor a citizen of the world, just equally a stranger in all the tongues parading past.

And the pictures. Can I move among them without the aid of some impossible interpreter.

It is different, alone this time. I am calmer but more desperate. With Webb as guide I seemed to have some purpose. We were in Europe because something awaited us. It seemed almost as if we had a timetable and appointments to keep. But now that I know he is waiting for me, I have no sense of purpose, no feeling of urgency or direction.

I think at times I am on the edge of a great awakening or at least a realization. Something to do with understanding Webb. What do we share. Where have we been. Always backward, always to the past. I associate museums with him, certain rooms in libraries. When he is on the verge of talking about himself, I feel he has begun with a tacit *Once upon a time*. His self-revelations come like chapters of a nineteenth-century novel, shaped, interlocking with that pervasive sense that life owes some unpayable debt to literature. I think of Proust in his corklined room, but a Proust who has lost the thread of his own experience and reads rather than remembers. Perhaps because I have so little past I know of, I am jealous, or at least hypersensitive to what Webb has accumulated. Perhaps I am intimidated by his continent of archives and documents.

This is my last trip, however, to the museum. When I see

Webb again I am afraid I will be impatient with his stories. I dread enough the mystery of my own past without entangling those longings and memories with another man's dream of himself. There is nothing I want to return to. That is why I am here, a stranger. I need no more temptations, no gods to serve.

The "Garden of Delights." I am a horseman in the enchanted circle. Others ride beasts magically corresponding to their species of damnation. Leopards, lions, camels, oxen, bears, hogs, deer, unnameable eclectic mounts, haunches of bloodhound, head, chest, and forelegs of an eagle, pelicans on a goat's narrow back, mounts and mounted leisurely around a charmed circle in whose center a still pool with naked women standing thigh deep in dark liquid. Black and white women their slim bodies exposed in provocative poses to the circling riders. Surface of pool broken by hands and arms of couples who copulate submerged like frogs. But the riders are barely aware of the pool and women. Some are burdened with monstrous, outsize fish, others are aroused by the closeness of nude male flesh, the sensuality of the beasts they ride or some narcissistic game they can play with touch, smell, taste, feel, and sound of themselves. Birds hop, perch, ride, fly, hover, drink, eat, sing, and screech within the scene. It could be the procession toward the ark in its profusion, its universality, yet that image modified perversely so the pageant of life projects its greediness and absurdity rather than an orderly, calm progress toward salvation. Men and beasts in an arbitrary hierarchy, even an arbitrary stability of form amuse themselves as best they can within the closed circle of the sensual dream.

I hear one of the maidens singing. The black one who sits on the edge of the pool, the one with the graceful peacock on her head. She elegantly holds a piece of fruit aloft, either beckoning or considering its plausibility before devouring it. She says come play with me in these warm dark waters. Hurry, hurry she teases. She asks if I am a man or simply another of those riders round and round again.

Cecil didn't want to sit. Standing in the circle of green tables and chairs that surrounded a striped refreshment kiosk he gazed slowly upward and outward relieved by the brilliant afternoon sun and serene stretches of blue sky. As usual Bosch had disturbed him. Even the ridiculous Spanish title bestowed on him—El Bosco—with its associations of chocolate milk, cookies, and talking cows in Cecil's mind did nothing to dispel the foglike gloom that seemed to seep from within the canvases. An adolescent reaction, or even more, the primitive revulsion of a child. Some threat seemed contained in those apparently chaotic, incomprehensible masses of movement and color Bosch had created. An undulating ridge in the background or a color rhythm would suddenly assert itself, begin to dominate a composition. And this order, this moment of pure insight when the kaleidoscope gathered itself into a pattern, would make the nightmare world of demons and evil in which the vision existed surge forward full-blown into life. Cecil could hear Bosch. The screams of the dying, the damned, those already whirling in the vitus dance of hell. Today the moment of insight had been almost unbearable. Even now in the open air, in the sunlight, slight tremors passed through his body still echoing the tumult that had spilled from the "Garden of Delights."

Finishing nearly half his glass in a clumsy gulp, Cecil blotted the beer foam from his lips. He believed that only a madman could truly understand Bosch, and that only a man periodically insane could have painted all he had painted. Bosch had studied the crippled and deformed. He knew a madman's eyes, the blank, expressionless stare of the living dead. He knew how they sat and stood, what they dreamed. Bosch awakening from his madness to paint, fascinated like Dostoevsky by all manifestations in other men of the raging darkness he feared in himself. Perhaps searching for something to prevent another plunge, or perhaps just feeding the hidden demon while it sleeps.

—Heya, buddy . . . why don't you sit down here.

What struck Cecil was the way the burly man seemed to surround the table at which he sprawled alone. The man's red elbows leaned on the table's damp surface. He was hunched forward so that his Hemingway beard covered the backs of his hands. If the round table had been twice as large, Cecil would still have felt he crowded the man.

—Cross there . . . to the museum?

—Yes.

—Something, ain't it. Yeah. I go there myself. Lots in that place. Say, could you spare a man a fag. Cecil pushed the opened, silver case toward the man. Already he had become familiar with the strange bright object, its incongruous richness was natural in his fingers. One of the hands emerged from beneath the beard, and thick, blunt fingers dug out one of the offered cigarettes.

—Nice case. If I was the kind of guy that kept things, that's something I'd get to keep, a nice cigarette case. One with a lighter built in. Yours got a lighter . . . no . . . but you know what I mean anyway. After you give a broad a fag you snap the case shut, solid like a Cadillac door, then press some button or something and up jumps the fire. All this time you're still leaning in her face smelling her hair and she's leaning in yours and she's impressed like hell. Everything in a fancy silver box. She knows you're the kind of guy gets things done. Efficient. Right down to business type and silver . . . but I'm not the sort to keep things.

–If you don't mind me saying, before I called you over, looked like something was bugging you. None of my business, I know, but it was noticeable as hell to me and I wasn't doing anything so I figured I'd call you over, figured you wouldn't mind me mentioning what I saw.

–I don't mind. I wasn't even aware of what I was doing.

–Not what you were doing. You just looked damn strange, like you were being chased.

–That's close.

–Just telling you what I saw.

–You did see a man running. Something inside the museum. It had the power to drive me out here to the street.

–Made you almost choke on your beer.

–I was thirsty.

–That's what I said. And you can believe what I say though I don't think much of talk. It's my eyes that work for me, and half the time I'm not listening to other people . . . just watching. Tells me more than words. When I talk, it's about what I've seen, not other talk. World's too full of people talking about other people's talk.

–You probably have a point.

–No, no. The point is you don't know anything about me. And you don't know if what I say works or if I work it. You've only heard me talk. Watch me. See what I do. That's the point.

–I've seen how you can use your eyes.

–A good beginning. I'm Albert, friend. The man rolled the cigarette between his fingers. The red, freckled forearms and thin biceps exposed by the rolled shirt sleeves were unattractively disproportionate to the man's brawny trunk. Cecil thought of a beetle's dark hulk darting along on stick limbs. Cecil lit a match, but then hesitated an instant, intimidated by the combustible looking mass of reddish beard. Smiling the man leaned toward him.

Albert drew deeply on his cigarette, exhaling a light

cloud of smoke. His brown eyes were moist and bright as his smile broadened; he pointed a thick finger at them.

—Ha. Eyes, man . . . eyes. They'll tell you what there is to know. I warned you, I'm a watcher. Did you think you might burn poor Albert up? The bearded face moved back. Smoke curled up again, this time from wide nostrils. The features lost their animation. Cecil saw a middle-aged man, a man with a rather scruffy ginger beard, a hairline already receding far back upon his square brow. The man's skin was coarse and weathered, its permanent ruddiness as close to tan as alcohol and sun could change nordic white. Cecil imagined that the beard hid square jowls that had begun to sag and go flabby. A peasant face. Brueghel. Lots of beer, sausages. A man on the downhill side of prime—limbs beginning to shrink, the limacine middle expanding, flesh disintegrating into the beard.

The eyes lit again. Catlike Albert rubbed his broad back against the metal slats of his chair.

—You didn't say what was chasing you.

Cecil realized for the first time the size of the eyes. They were tiny; their brilliance not their size dominated the face. Lines sharp and precise marked their corners. A swatch of dark brow above and purplish flesh beneath made the eyes seem deeply inset.

—Believe it or not I was frightened by a painting.

—Painting, huh. Why not, why the hell not. If you're the kind of guy that gets frightened, why not a painting.

—You've never been frightened.

—Well shit, man . . . never by a painting.

—By anything.

—Not a painting. That's what we were talking about . . . paintings, right. Hell, of course I ain't a fool. I mean there's some things in this world a man moves for. I mean a tank or eagle shit if he sees it coming. Stuff like that any fool moves for. But that's not being scared, it's not being a fool.

—But what about something that can't knock you down or dirty your clothes. Something that . . .

—Something what?

—I was trying to get you to answer a question I don't even know how to ask. If you have or haven't been afraid, doesn't matter. I'm going to have another drink. Can I get you one?

A man and a boy sweated inside the striped kiosk. Neither saw him till Cecil placed two glasses on the counter. After a moment the man raised up from the block of ice he was chipping into a small sink, nodded at his customer, and looked disgustedly at the daydreaming boy. Shouting, he slammed the pick once more into the ice then kicked and cuffed the boy toward the counter. The boy cringed as each of his clumsy movements in the tight enclosure brought another outburst from the man and a violent thrust of the pick. Cecil wanted to catch the boy's eyes. To smile at him or wiggle his tongue at the man bent over the sink, anything that would draw some part of the boy out of the cramped box. But the boy hid his eyes beneath heavy, black lashes concentrating on the awkward movements of his own brown hands as they opened and poured two bottles of beer into two glasses.

When he turned again toward the table, Cecil saw the bearded man was gone. He felt relieved, conscious of his entire body responding to the sky and sun as it had after being released from the vault of the museum. Cecil looked down at the two cold glasses in his hands. The second was a joke, a dream, joke glass he would drink himself or pour onto the pavement. Then he heard the already familiar voice:

—Put 'em down, man. Albert ain't gone nowhere. And hey, get another. Albert was in the middle of the broad **Paseo del Prado**. Bearded Albert one arm around a long-legged woman in a short, tight skirt continued to shout and curse as he returned through snarled traffic.

–Bringing a friend, my friend. Bringing Estrella to meet you.

Estrella's long legs were bare. As he approached with a third drink Cecil watched her cross them, leaving most of their slim length uncovered.

–Estrella . . . this is my friend.

–*Buenos días* . . .

–C'mon, none of those bows and that *buenos días* shit. Estrella ain't *señora* to nobody. This old girl is what you call *puta, puta,* man, and that means whore, tart, bawd, streetwalker, pussy, fucky-fucky in any language. Right 'Strella. The woman smiled at both men; she wrapped long fingers around her glass nodding to Cecil as she raised it to her lips.

–Strella, Strella baby. You got drawers on today. Albert's thin arm slid under the table. Cecil felt the sudden bump of ankles against his as the woman started in her seat. Albert's visible hand was quick and caught the flashing purse she aimed at his head. His eyes sparkled, coughing spasms of laughter shook his thick body.

–Strella you got as much down there as I got on my chin. Hissing something between clenched teeth the woman jerked her arm free. Beer lapped onto the table as she pushed her chair away and swung her legs out into the open. A perfunctory tug at the black skirt was the only way she qualified the nakedness exposed to Cecil. Tossing her head in Albert's direction she spit loudly into the gravel.

–Whore acts like she got something down there I don't know about. Well I can tell you, my friend, she's done better tricks for me with those lips than spitting. One thing I can say for her. She knows her business. What's she sitting around here with it hanging out if she don't want somebody to pay attention to it. She must think she's in godblessamerica where they can wave it around like Old Glory and not get it touched.

Cecil lit the cigarette he had given to the woman. Her thin lips were painted mauve.

—Whatta tell you. Her eyes ain't left that silver case since you pulled it out. If I was the type guy who kept things, I'd have one. Yours don't even have a lighter and look at her . . . like a moth after a flame. Kill herself to get to it. Go on. Grab a little pussy yourself if you like what you see. I'll be damned if she does more than smile and let you dig in.

The woman was a sphinx as Al talked. Wine and brandy succeeded beer and somewhere in the progress from bar to bar, woman disappeared altogether, an unnecessary mouth, an evolutionary dead end in the efficient movement from sober to not sober of Cecil Braithwaite and Al, his thirsty appendage.

Foot tapping to guitar music, mouth full of chewed peanuts, leaning on his elbows Cecil nodded, his features screwed up a moment as if swallowing a belch, but then he was smiling, a giddy, silly smile.

We were children running on the beach. Old grace. She was French, German, Spanish, Russian, sun tanned and dark haired a body I had known so well night long as she lay breathing cocooned in sleep beside me but now we trotted at the sea's edge teasing the foam flicked rushes setting a hard pace, splat of our feet lost in surf's crashing.

Wind beat our faces, sucking out breath. Legs still good but this hungry wind empties the lungs. Down we go sprawled on the sand. Rolling into the sea it takes us gasping, sputtering with a sudden swell. Hands and knees high we scramble out. Down again, bronze crosses on the white sand. Words taste salt as tongue moves across ocean wet lips. I am mystified by the language we are using. Wind cools the off side as we sit up, blinking back the intense sunlight. When we run and splash and die a bit on these sands, I am as alive as I have ever been. I have been alive only this once, pushed dripping wet from the sea. But we are singing an old, old song, song older and bigger than born or unborn. Are we the first or the last two.

Up a rock El Moro mounts, gleaming sea birth. Atop and pissing a parabolic stream caught by the wind. I promise myself to spurt thusly into seven seas from seven continents. At rock's base breakers crash, rumbling over the coral reef, gaining momentum and fury as they sprint the last blue gap and extinguish themselves brutally on the black rocks. Can't help laughing as spray reaches my face, as my stream ended and breakers in heat rushed to thud and die beneath my feet. Laughter, loud, rolling over the muffled explosions below, I was as high as I had ever been. El Moro's bare feet find niches on the rock's slippery surface. I grab at her hand, pulling her up so we could laugh together. Peals of it mocking the ocean's dull thunder and its thousand deaths, trembling together till spray and wind managed to chill us in the brilliant afternoon.

You leave in order to lose to find.

Es muy bonito aquí, no señor. El Moro grins. His awe-giving jack boots reflect the bar's brass rail, grind the sea shells and peanut shells and sawdust.

—*Sí, sí, amigo. Cerveza.* And you lisp glib tongued the Castilian lisp blackly bellowing San Miguel with proper intonation and from the bottle after wiping rusty lip with heel of hand gulp one half of contents to wash down the shot of gut eating brandy.

—*Felipe Segundo. Uno más, señor.* An arm went around the powerful shoulders and a voice, a stranger's voice whispering something about slowing down about how one mortal sin in Spain is to be drunk and show it. Cecil conqueroo turned to meet the challenge. The stranger's eyes dropped to a glass the waiter had deposited, twin to the one clacked down in front of Cecil. If the man saw the belligerent flash of El Moro's hawk eyes, or the sudden combat tautness of neck and hand, he ignored them. Sweet booze looseness eased the conqueroo. It was Albert's red arm upon his shoulders. Albert who was speaking.

Albert was an expatriate from southern California, whose sun he had often followed across the border into Mexico on liquor raids. Marijuana and *señoritas* for a five buck, crowded car hop on weekends. Thick necked, square shoulders, a big man whose imposing exterior had begun to soften. Hair on hand backs; Dutch descent. Tales of South America with its Latin propensity for hot blood, political revolutions, dark-eyed *chiquitas,* massacres. The dead stretched in rows across an empty field. He had a picture of it; a smiling general all teeth and brass two minutes before he was machine-gunned. Album of violence. Uniforms. Bravado. High black leather boots, Sam Browne belts, a peasant grinning with a pitchfork. Albert, tow-headed, very young posing with heroes who pledged land reform, but brought tyranny. Always sun. Dust rising behind a vintage tank. Rubble. Smiles. Albert armed, posing with the deposed. Jailed. Front tooth out grin. A pumpkin. A hairy-handed Dutchman, rectangular, wooden dikes inside his belly and chest. Spain. Last resting place of the Hemingway breed. Oh, the good old days. Blood. Spirit of the revolution! Gone. Whores commercial, timid bulls, a brash, mustachioed little man stamped on deflated currency. The sun. Yesterminute. Albert disgusted. His Swedish wife home again, home again with her admiral father who never liked him in the first place. Just left her one day. Couldn't take it any longer. We had two kids, blond, plump as *Blutwurst,* he presented another photo. Always the little things. Fine when we were alone. When we could come and go as we pleased. Always together—nights in tents, under stars, railroad stations, a barn. Scandinavia produces damn good women; they learn early up there what it's all about.

But the brats, they made it different. Impossible. Little things like hours, silly obligations, give in, give in. It's them now. It's their turn. Live for them. So I just left. Five years now. She's still young; I was the first. Twenty years difference between us. Probably your age. Since then I haven't been doing much. Just drifting. Munich to Madrid. Sometimes like a ping-pong ball, sometimes like a feather. I've been trying to write a book. It's my last hope. But it won't come. Just little spurts. Anecdotes. Not even stories really. Pieces. Like me, bits and pieces. Jew hater, lover of a Jew. Munich to Madrid. Like an old train stuck on one unfashionable milk run; hoping at best to be taken off active duty altogether. Retired to a pasture. To rust and be climbed on by children. Hulking shell of a toy, all movable parts removed for salvage. Not even the dignity of a hole. Tears in my beer, huh? Just a passing fancy really. Just seeing you, hearing you talk about the things I know so well, seeing you looped on this gut rotting brandy. Echoes sometimes. I'm an anachronism, friend. There's a certain security in this. Last of the race. A dinosaur. Determined not to change, not to compromise, to go down brilliantly futile and obsolete. Then seeing you, my kind perpetuated, takes away the vestige of pride left in being unique. I'm sorry. Just one of those whore evenings. Why doesn't one of those greasy bastards sing? When you want quiet, can't keep them off the top of the barrels, stomping, clapping, yelping like castrated coyotes. Get up there and sing you cunt mouthed Castilians. The good old days. Yesterever. Now you only have to yell fuck Franco to clear a bar. Scared. All the proud little greasers scared. Sing somebody. Sing or I'm going to get on that barrel myself and curse your ancestors.

Nobody hears. Nobody cares. Just a row of backs and

asses staring out at you. Sorry, it's just . . . sometimes it's like this. I mean not even somebody to fight. You know you're the first colored guy I've ever really talked with. To be frank, don't think much of Negroes. About in the same class as Jews, except a little better because they don't have as much money to spend. I guess it's more true to say I've never known any. Don't really care one way or the other. A few general things against them though; couldn't depend on them in the war. Bad outfits. Not worth a damn as fighters at all. That was an accepted truth at the front lines. But after what we've been talking about, maybe I can understand some of the reasons why. Hell, I guess it was tough. Especially then. Catching hell from both ends. And your generation or rather in particular you, if you're any indication, you're saner than any of these effeminate scatterbrains I see making the grand tour. Sick, pasty faced, pimply bastards. Not one ounce of blood in a dozen of them. Afraid, that's what they are. No background, no roots. Saucy and fresh, ready to throw mud, smear disdain. Tear everything down. Every man that's ever done something is a square, an incompetent. They discredit every real personality that's ever existed, the ones who have built this world that the punks piddle around in. They try to bring the great men down to their level because they know they can never rise up. Afraid. Smart, rude mouthed little punks vomiting undigested wisdom, covering everything with their filth. I can smell it, feel it. That's what's killing me. Everything tight, no spice, no freedom, no place to go. I feel sorry for you. It's gonna be worse for you. What was your time, when was your age? At best a counterfeit nostalgia for one you never had. Maybe mine, maybe one that never did exist. Alone. Not strung out between two worlds like me. No improbable Colossus of Rhodes, no, you can't even plant your feet in a small doorway. Nothing. I feel for you.

Just a question of going back for me, burying the young man, the only thing I can or ever will be, but you can't bury him till you get to be something else. A question of standing up. Looking back and seeing what happened. That's my story. What I have to write. This mess, this world about to lose its guts, I don't care about and don't care to understand.

Albert's face. Far away, coming from eons ago, heroic, immaculate, armored in his own strength. Mountain tall, his will implacable as man leveling club at his waist. A child rushing heedless, headlong, believing wholly in a brash trumpet clarioned in the crystal air. Believing. In love with the simplicity which rolls all the world into a ball, carrying him with it out of the trenches, and across no man's land to pile up singing on intricately wound clumps of barbed wire. Selfless, immersed, or squat and unconcerned as barrel on which someone has begun to dance. In the café. Albert rehashing forever. Cheap brandy resting on odors of the rancid *bocadillos* hung in bulk on the wall or bite-sized in open dishes lining the damp bar. Lyric almost, Albert's self-conscious keening. A surprising delicacy, eloquent as each snowflake that dies to make the ponderous drifts.

Albert loving. Releasing from behind the stolid dikes a sheaf of photos he kept with him always, stuffed inside his offensively bold, open-throated plaid shirt.

Ashes, ashes, we all fall down.

Wail of flamenco from the jukebox someone had turned up. Albert's voice *sotto, sotto* as if music were a dark curtain hurrying to enclose the drama. Cecil swayed, either inwardly or with his body rocking. Not the sickening lurch of the stricken ship, but the dance of bare treetops in the wind. But a proper metaphor was nautical, was that natural correspondence of boat to medium, the exchange of self-centered gravity for the water's embrace, its rhythm and power, its eternity. To be a captive. To be the drunken boat, to release as Cecil knew he had released all illusion of control.

Albert explained that the background song was the chant of a prisoner, a condemned man, who had killed his unfaithful mistress and her lover, but from his cell shouted that he would do it all again, take his revenge even in the face of God and of greater punishments than his captors' could possibly threaten. Al could anticipate the singer's moods, his laments, the warbling screams, whines, animal modulations of voice which re-created scenes from his story. Flamenco passion, echo of the conquering east still brooding over the land. Cecil was uneasy. Incongruity of Al seemingly moved by the ghost music of the exiled *moriscos*. Or perhaps just the sadness of the song, the lonely voice, the utter isolation of the soul trapped in a cage with only a memory of betrayal to dream.

But El Moro had come to town to laugh to drink and fuck and forget. At home an uppity nigger, thinks he's smart, all dressed up, Magistrate Cecil parading down the street like he owns it. But here, El Moro. Whatever else they think about the dark foreigner, they remember in their blood that he once had the upper hand, that they paid him the conqueroo's tribute, that he was a teacher.

Song is finished a second time through. Cecil wants to speak, to tell Al . . . or is it just a desire for a monologue of equal time.

—It's funny how you carry that black crap inside you. Like the time I wandered around in Granada needing a haircut. Walked past the damn barber's ten times. Looking in, trying to figure what he'd say, if it was O.K. for me to go in, plop down in one of his white chairs ignoring the fact that I was black and had kinky hair. All that crap churning inside me—afraid, embarrassed, mad at myself for being these, for being different, mad at him, at every white man for making me uncomfortable and mostly just shame that I couldn't bring myself to walk in and sit down. Well El Moro finally said fuck it and went in. It was like nothing, I waited my turn, got in the chair and he sheared me like any other sheep. A little conversation. As much as I could manage with my eighty-two words of Spanish. American. First time in Spain. Thank you. No more. Good. Paid and gone. Painless. Just me, carrying all that bile inside myself. Cecil Braithwaite Transporter of Plague Incorporated. First three thousand seagoing miles free. Guaranteed safe delivery.

El Moro cannot see across the waters, yet from the other side they see him. Voice of his dead son; Esther's voice less than ghost but living, beckoning. Her dowry.

Why did you do it.

Al's eyes are glazed, two antique, polished coins laid atop the closed lids. The bodega's interior had gone to mist and black impenetrable smoke. A bier is launched and the mourners on the shore's edge are dark silhouettes, miniature skyline of a fog-shrouded city. Is it proper for the dead to speak when spoken to. Gentle rhythm of the narrow ship. Cecil cradled serenely by beer, brandy, and wine. Being here is being nowhere and everywhere. The passage is everything. Destination as unreal as that quiet city already lost in the gloom.

It is afterall part of me. Trader Al would have made his fortune camped in some calm inlet; he would have hacked back the jungle with his heavy Dutch hands and built a limbo village of cages beside his spartan hut. Warriors would appear with other warriors in chains, with children and females huddled together in the shadows of the men. Al would Dutchly wheel and deal. Sampling now and then a Negress to reassure himself of the quality of his product. The Great Western Civilizing and Trading Society with branches everywhere. I was the burden Albert chose to carry. Mongo Al, supervising the middle passage from darkness to light. But I am tired of travel, weary of dancing once a day to whip music, nine-tailed cat songs. I grow old, I grow old. And must I remember older sorrows, nakedness, hunger. Did they come bearing gifts. Was it wrong to squat catatonic and die staring at the sea.

There is a storm. I am angry beyond anger. I hear the splash of bodies heaved overboard to lighten the ship. Some go unnecessarily because a frightened sailor miscounted and disconnected one black wrist from another. Waves, thunder, and wind, but the doomed in one last futile triumph are heard above the tumult.

I am tossed, tumbled, enraged. But storm settles and for better or worse some survive. Albert burping beside me survives and I buy him another drink.

The men move on. Festival time. Relentless flogging ends for a thirsty week and the streets of the old quarter are full.

El Moro dances:

Rosa. It had to be a Rosa. What other name goes with olive skin, high cheekbones, flashing eyes and white teeth. The whole bit. My twelve-year-old gypsy of the incredibly happy smile and jet, never-ending hair. Dancing together flamenco style and the crowd loved it. We sent some kids to buy more wine and passed it all around spudie-udie. Fifty pesetas slipped into Rosa's hand, the first touch. Always. Gypsies shouting—*olay, olay Rosa. Baila hombre!* El Moro *baila.* And I must have fled to find this street.

El Moro battles:

—Should I hit the son of a bitch.

—Forget it, man, there's too many of the enemy.

—C'mon we can take 'em. You ain't chickenin' out on me, are you, Al.

—I'm right here, man, but there ain't no win. You hit him and every little bastard in the cave is on our asses. You know they carry scimitars in their pockets. And we bleed, my friend, we bleed.

Albert, the nuns have cloistered your bowels. Up there on the hill, in jars, are your intestines and balls swimming in alcohol. A preservative you know. But Sister Angela Maria Duessa. Her guts blew away. Dried up, and one day a little dusty cloud descended from under the folds of her many black skirts. Spoof. They were gone. She told me it was a kind of warm leaving. A pleasant, very intimate closeness then separation, warm, almost like a fart.

—Next thing I knew the fascist sons of bitches threw El Moro in a cell with a bunch of gypsies. Smelled like a zoo. All those greasy little bastards, piss and barf all over the floor. Musta been the drunk tank. Smelled like hell. Stale wino pee smell. And I ain't in there a minute before one of them starts vomiting. Splattered on my boots. I pushed him away and he fell. Straight down. He musta been real drunk cause splat he buckled right in the middle of that steaming shit he just finished bringing up. Then three of 'em was on my back. I was whippin' hell out of any I could grab, but somebody got to my face and scratched me good. Son of a bitch tried to tear out my eye. Look. I'm gonna get a tetanus shot tomorrow. Just like animals, little filthy animals— gruntin', sittin' around in their own shit.

—How'd you . . .

—So this weasel beneath one of those plastic toreador hats he smiled a yellow toothed smile and began to beat me. Goddamn Civil Guards. Heavy, flat sounding blows across the cheeks then a hollow thudding noise as leather coated stick slapped against my groin. I was so ossified didn't feel a goddamn thing. Just worried a little about how close he was coming to my gonads. Wino laugh. Pain no part of me. Remembering it would all be over in a few minutes, like reading in a newspaper about atrocities being committed in another country. Laugh saved my balls. Everybody started laughing, all them in those cartoon hats laughing away. Then they kicked my ass out of jail.

El Moro loves:

Keep off the grass said a boot to the drunk who woke with pain and found sun in the sky overhead, fountains of the square dry, nowhere to be found those gaudy lights or music or the swirling dancers so many whose hands and backs and cheeks he had touched or where was it I kissed her, hot tongue probing deep in my throat and a bouquet of hair, all black, elastic yielding, it was hot there and wet, popping back the nylon panties snapped against my wrist. I think I remember a doorway where from my charger I leapt down, her with one arm lowering from his flanks and then I began to forget and how much petticoat, won't those ruffles ever end. I began to forget the frills, the scalloped edges, all wet they were her lips and inside me something not me moved hot like an animal in my mouth and if I am very still the blood will stop, nothing no nothing will I feel nor will these hands push and pull, popping elastic too tight here anyway for a whole hand, *señorita,* squirmita, I could love you on these stones, no one will enter this darkness, but first my armor, let me remove these obstacles, obstacles, obstacles so hot and dry like the skin of a dead snake I found once, forgotten where it lay, where it lay forgotten kick, kick me again—*Olay*—I am falling. I give up, please forgive, please don't kick, forget, forgive, I promise never again. O father, father forgive me, forget me, let me forget that I have skinned, that I have sinned, forget me Father, no more please for I am dying, do you hear me, dying, you bastard, pop pop pop soon it will break and room for five fingers, can you take five fingers I remember once there was a girl we all went to her in a car and when my turn she smiled over a clump of weeds and she was wet and purple and something had been eating her flesh and left raw running wounds, she winked and beckoned hurry, hurry from behind the weeds her mounds of fat and sunken like a patient on a table slowly opening, closing, the bush winked a bird flew out and died on my head, streaking my cheeks with something, with blood, sweat, or perhaps its white, dainty excrement, and I ran from the room but that was then and now I would have shoved my foot up the hole and shut the door if she screamed like she did as she straddled the gleaming machine strung out in pain, having her uterus scraped but better a quick pain than one looking at you everyday, a dusky, kinky haired one from her womb so let me hold your hand as you writhe and please be careful Doctor for in this moment I am bound to love, bound to love as you catch the drippings in a pan, pan getting filled God where did it all come from one black bastard made all this mess hold my hand and don't cry, it is better than seeing it grow, than hating it more and more each day, oh how they wail and shit and scream and the pain growing everyday please believe what I say Esther that this is best that I love that I will never let go your hand though it burns and squeezes and drains feeling from mine bone against bone you grind it and wriggle on the shining machine wide open will it never stop coming, never stop never let me sleep I must get up and turn it off don't be afraid I'll be right back, Esther, then we can sleep I will tiptoe and turn on the light only a moment, just for a moment on then it will stop we will be able to sleep and dream and dream and dream.

And if he hits me there I will be a choir boy. My voice will not drain away into gonads and hairy cheeks. I will always respond to the master's flaccid wrist. Higher. Higher. It is so beautiful here, is it not. Ruins of a Moorish castle on the left. Best one in Granada. Right above you, madam. Yes . . . black. Black kings. I don't recall exactly when, but long ago. Arabs and niggers. Long ago. But that was before the pill. Perfectly safe now. No pain. No more calls from a pay phone telling me to put in my diaphragm. I'll be home soon, dear. Do you understand. I came to find to lose. The fear. Fear of what's on the other side of the door.

There is to be a celebration the last night. Oh sure I'll be there. Meet you at the hotel. Bells on. Cap and bells. Celebration in the gypsy camp. An ox is to be slaughtered. *Cristo Negro's* hands dyed crimson in the sacrifice. The streets will be crowded again. I must hurry . . . find my place . . . find Rosa, the singing . . .

The plain which is the threshold of the city curdles with the stench of unburied corpses, dead men rotting in the sun, bodies with soft insides already pulpy and boiling, heat blackened dead wandering through the maze of shanties and hovels, through impermanent, weather ridden heaps undignified by stone or monuments, the human soup laced with rag and cardboard and splintered boards that seeps from the city in an ever widening pool. The poor of Madrid, compressed between hot, dry clay, and the heavy sun into bronzed bricks that will build pyramids to honor the Emperor. It is one more canvas to observe, a *pièce de résistance* after chasing El Grecos in the low hills surrounding Madrid. Toledo with its Alamo, Thermopylae don't give up the ship Alcázar and the villa of the painter who perhaps could not see straight. I wanted to remember names —the paintings, the chapels which housed them. But it is the narrow streets which I recall, afterimages of heat white when I blink my eyes. The favella is a giant rancid sponge, sopping wet that clears the blackboard. I smell and I taste and the postcards I had dreamed are in shambles.

Suddenly as if to say you cannot forget everything, I noticed that in the distance the horizon seemed lower and an El Greco sky was forming.

Rain, it would rain in the city, on this sick plain. But not rain of Verlaine's ballade, not a human rain that completes a mood, but just water, feverish and exhausted water that had dropped then spiraled invisible back to clouds only to drop again and be sucked up again from puddle and sea bed to drop again. Water that already had tasted the dead and would return this knowledge to the land. Rare, pummeling rain that drenched Cecil as he sat listless in the tourist bus lumbering down from the hills into the city.

Rain or sweat tepid inside his clothes. It was hard to tell, to understand. Speaking out would make a difference, clarify things. But to whom. Would the dead comprehend his obscure language. Would a few downtrodden songs chanted in chorus relieve them of silence, and of distance. But if the vehicle paused Cecil knew he would keep his seat. His destination was no more this teeming shantytown than it was the teeming hard city. Estrella, Webb, lying, extravagant Albert who had caught Cecil in childish dares. Estrella's scent still strong on his body. Webb. The Webb. Follow the leader.

The night air made Cecil shiver involuntarily. He could see no stars above the fluorescent blue shimmer cast up to rooftop level by the neon lighting. His hands were in his pockets. He didn't really watch where he walked, letting himself instead be jostled along by the light pressure of the crowd which was taking the long way home through San Jerónimo's narrow, twisting streets. Like the fish and mushrooms frying on open air grills, Spanish spit and crackled around him. He expected to see a fight beginning after each explosive exchange, but only saw bright teeth and eyes, smiling men and women with hair groomed and shoes shining no matter what they wore between these extremes. The women were colorful schools of fish, self-contained, outwardly indifferent, discussing their curiosity among themselves in whispers as they glided past. Clusters of men attached themselves quietly, a natural condition of the seascape, making no obtrusive signs of possession or even of the right to approach. Lone females would appear in force later, though they often traveled in pairs. Cecil noticed a few already drinking alone in cafés or surrounded by laughing groups of bare-armed laborers in the cramped interiors of bodegas.

Estrella would soon put in her appearance with the rest. Would anything be different this last night in Madrid. Albert waited for him, not far away Albert waited, certain like the woman was certain that he must come. Each day Cecil had promised himself he would not go to Estrella, but at some point during the night he would find himself in a taxi rushing to her. Once in a drunken dream he had mounted her, ripped the sore of her from within his bowels, heaved up his rage and need in one humiliating assault after another upon her flesh. He had awakened sweating and impotent in her bed to the reality of her laughter and her fingers kneading the dough of his sex.

She lived with her mother in one of the government housing projects near the Plaza Monumental. The women kept their small apartment very clean. Bedroom, kitchenette-dining room, and a sitting room. The last was Estrella's pride. It contained a thick pile rug, an overstuffed sofa and chair, a glass topped coffee table, a television set, and most of the time her nearly blind, senile mother. One night Cecil had sat with the old woman close to three hours waiting for Estrella to return. The mother had been silent and expressionless the entire time. An occasional blink was all Cecil had noticed until the television station had ended its transmission and the room was plunged into darkness. Then except for a slow belch which had relieved the stillness, Cecil could have been in a room with a corpse.

When Estrella finally arrived that night she had company. The sailor was drunk. He swayed in the doorway, disconcerted by the light Estrella had switched on and the two people it revealed sitting wide-awake in the dark. Cecil couldn't make out what the man muttered to him, but understood the leer at the old woman. Estrella's mother did something to the thousand lines of her face, screwing them into the grimace of taut exertion she must have believed still approximated a smile. It was her greeting to all her daughter's men, as constant and forgetful as the vertical lips of Estrella's nakedness. It was what had greeted Cecil the first night and what had been repeated just as uncomprehending each night since.

Estrella had kicked off her heels and padded across the rug to turn off the television. As soon as her daughter and the sailor left the room, the old woman curled herself into a corner of the couch and lowered her head onto a shapeless pillow covered with yellowed silk. Her snores were not loud enough to smother the sounds from the other room while Cecil waited.

This last night he wouldn't go. If the old fear returned, he would bury it in some other whore.

Cecil thought it strange that only one woman had sung to him, to him alone as part of their love-making.

Cecil walked to the end of Ventura de la Vega. After a few more steps, he could see the bright sweep of the Puerta del Sol. In its center twin fountains sent up high, swaying jets. The wind that had carried dark clouds over the hills whipped ragged skirts of spray around the silver columns. On the long awnings of sidewalk coffee bars and in huge letters on the thick, blunt buildings that faced the plaza the names of the beers they drank, the clothes they wore, and the banks that owned their mortgages smiled down on the people.

Cecil made his way from island to island of security till he finally arrived on the other side of the impossibly wide plaza. He wondered how long it took a cop to learn to control the countless streams of pedestrian and motor traffic which converged on this arena. He was dazzled by the sudden onslaught of motion and brilliance. It was entirely different from the intimate activity of San Jerónimo, from the ambiance that had allowed him to linger over his meal, the wine, his thoughts. Here cars careened at a pace that could kill. And they came from all directions imparting their urgency with violent trumpeting and shrieks. Wide, bare spaces hostile and forbidden to those on foot isolated the cramped plots of safety. Once Cecil had wanted to dance between the fountains, El Moro naked except for a cop's white sun helmet and Sam Browne belt. The memory of that first day made him shiver. He thought he felt the chill prickle of white spray blown onto the back of his neck. As if pursued by a dark shape materializing out of the night, he entered a bar.

The bar was too bright; its harsh, yellow light had weight and substance. Cecil could feel it like a swarm of insects settling on his skin.

—*Felipe Segundo, por favor.*

—*No hay, señor.*

—*Cuarenta y tres . . . grande . . . doble.* Not quite certain which word to use, Cecil placed his hands together then moved them slowly apart. The old fish story. Bartender smiled, nodded, in a moment delivered a tall water glass three-quarters full of brandy across the counter.

Where Cecil stood the counter was glass. Behind the glass on shelves were displayed a variety of confections. Farther along beyond the glass case the bar was stone-topped, with a flat wooden edge facing outward. Saucers containing the snacks that seemed to be essential for Spaniards when they drank were ranged on the marblelike slab. Cecil could distinguish slices of squid, varieties of sausage, mussels, boiled eggs, anchovies, cheese, pickles, tripe, crayfish, peanuts and olives. The contents of the other dishes were unguessable, but seemed to be devoured at the same rate as the ones Cecil could recognize. Men were shoulder to shoulder the length of the bar. At the rear of the long, narrow room mirrors extended the bar and the line of men forever. On the sawdust strewn floor heaps of crayfish shells and legs had collected under the footrail and banked against the spittoons. Like breakers, clots of sound from the far end of the room gathered force then hurled themselves toward the street. Saucers and glasses slammed on stone, the cash register's incessant ring, the excited jabbering of the men, washed over Cecil. Through the open doorway Cecil was surprised to see sidewalk tables belonging to the bar. When he had entered, he hadn't noticed the green metal tables or the well dressed people around them. He bolted his drink, then cautiously picked his way through the tables and the milling crowd away from the Puerta del Sol.

Albert had said he would be there most nights, that he would explain, justify. It was a short walk to Calle de Jardines and Calle de Jardines was a short street. In the middle of the block was a shoddier than usual bodega Al had named. The bartender proprietor pointed out to Cecil the name of his brother, Manuela, which was listed among many others on a disintegrating bullfight poster. A gray, cracked mirror two feet long and a foot wide was the only other embellishment of the wall behind the bar. A bead curtain separated the private and public halves of the owner's dwelling. Against the wall facing the bar three empty wine barrels served as tables and chairs. The predominant tone of everything was dull, dirty brown. Plaster dust rained continually from the exposed beams of the low ceiling, and with gestures, grimaces and a few words of English, Carlos, the owner, complained bitterly about his lungs. He made it clear that he didn't get enough sun. That the tall *pensiones* across the street were too close and he was dying in their shadow. But he could not leave because the men always came to drink, to sing, to eat his rotten *bocadillos* and dance on the tops of the empty barrels.

The rain finally came. Somehow the night grew even darker. Calle de Jardines seemed to be in the storm's center. Before Carlos shut the crooked door Cecil listened to the flurry of panic, the rapid footfalls, banging shutters, women's shouts at the heavy drumming of the first big drops. No matter how long or ominous the threat, it was always like that when rain descended at night on the city.

Albert lumbered through the yielding curtain, his ham hands fumbling with his fly.

—I ain't the only one doing some pissing. Sounds like the whole heavenly host squatting over this town. He smiled round the room and crossed himself. Hearing his rumbling voice several Spaniards looked up from their wine, saw the pious gesture, and repeated it.

—Figured you'd be here sooner or later. I see you beat the rain.

Ignoring the voice Cecil reached for a narrow tumbler of brandy Carlos had poured. Quickly it was inside him and racing for his belly. New and raw the cheap spirit was a ragged current sending heat back up into his throat. The smell and taste lingered. He could always tell when a sick night was coming. Early in the process of obliteration one drink would be like this; his senses would recoil, the bile rise warningly in his throat. Some nights he knew his body would refuse the outrage.

—Prithee, Cecil, why so pale and wan?

—I don't feel playful. Let's come to the point quickly. What you said . . .

—Trimmings, Cecil. Trimmings are all. Just being my usual protean self. Saint, sinner, dunghill of flesh, suave courtier. Whichever you like. A man for all seasons. Even for rainy nights in Madrid. Tell Uncle Albert whatsamatter. Rain, rain go away. Cecil wants to play.

—I said I'm not in the mood.

—What mood then. If not versatile, I'm nothing.

—Just don't be the fool. Let me drink another drink and try to relax. There's not much time. No time. I leave for the south early tomorrow. You relax, be quiet for a moment, then please say what you have to say. Cecil recalled Bosch, the demon at the saint's ear. What had been said. Webb's face appeared, ghostlike, at once vulnerable and distant. The promise. The artificial rose the dancer had thrown Cecil in a clip joint later that night.

Rain splashed the cobblestones and swirled in gutters. Already from ancient, tile roof spouts rivulets cascaded.

The men moved to the back of the bar. Albert buddha-like draped the lotus of his buttock on one of the wide barrels. Between his feet a nearly full bottle of Felipe Segundo rested. Cecil stood, his back almost against the lisping curtain. Leaks in Carlos' front door let in stabs of cold air and oily snakes crawling under the door began to twist through the cracks of the stone floor.

—What did you mean when you told me to relax. Dammit, man, I think in the whole universe there is no mass which has more inertia per pound than I do. Like here I am sitting on this barrel. If there was wine inside this wood, it wouldn't be any more relaxed than I am.

—O.K. so maybe you're relaxed. But what you're doing, what you said had just the opposite effect on my nerves. After your story, those crazy warnings that first night, you knew my curiosity would make me come here. Now it's late, now I want to hear everything. Or at least the rest, why you wanted me to see you again.

—I wanted you to talk to Albert some more. To hear some more of his stories, get to know him, maybe even tempt you to forgive him. There is much to forgive, and shame, betrayal. I wanted you to bid Albert a fond farewell; I wanted you to listen again, hear me say why you can't see Webb. For your sake and his. I knew the cigarette case, saw his initials, but I knew it was his before I saw them. I guessed he gave it to you, I told you I knew him once, and you told me the rest. You told me lots I'm sure you don't remember. Not hard to figure even if you had said nothing. He wants you to meet him tomorrow in Málaga, last day of Semana Santa. Jesus Christ, man . . . I repeat: get your ass away from here as fast as you can. Albert kids you not. Stop the mothering thing.

They were pig eyes, scared pig eyes at last recognizing the butcher. The body would be stuffed in the vat it now so cockily rode.

—No sense, no sense to it all. This place . . . Webb . . . me here . . . the rain . . . you and that ridiculous beard. Matted with every conceivable filth. Do you ever wash it.

—No, my friend, not me. You didn't come here to insult poor Albert. Besides I don't always hide from the rain. You're exaggerating. I stride naked into it and angel piss makes me clean. The beard too. That and all the other hairs with which I'm festooned. But you don't offend me. I see a bigger picture. It's not me you resent or the occasional flea who might reside upon my carcass in a dry season. I see deep, dark forces at work. The worm, the mole, things that crawl, creep, and burrow underground. They're blind when they strike out in the light. You do not offend me. And do not apologize. I see your hasty, and I am not being spiteful if I say nasty, words hurrying back like so many boomerangs to rankle in your bosom. Do not apologize. I see the big picture.

—What . . . just what do you see.

Albert snatched up the bottle of brandy, a red slab of hand wiped across his lips.

—You know what I think—this purple-bellied bottle is half the secret. Cheap booze and donkeys. Every country has a secret—you know, something special that holds it together and makes it what it is, makes Spain different from Germany and Germany different from England, etcetera, etcetera. Well, without cheap booze and donkeys the bottom would fall out here.

—What do you want, Albert.

—Look at them. The spics. Big, brown flies, flies heavy like when the weather turns cold. So damn easy to swat them then, I give up the sport. Swollen with the offal of what they've been. Nothing worse than those buzzing bastards when they slow down and begin to die. They don't swoop down any more, just fly over something and collapse. Hara-kiri for that one last sniff, that last chance to rub their legs in shit, to buzz-buzz and drag their wings across your donut. Look at them leaning on the bar. Like they all just shot their load seventy-five times in a row. Making love to Carlos' booze. Queen Carlos. I used to think that he worked for them. But my eyes told me no. My eyes watched them begging for what he has, my eyes saw how they loved him, how these flies think he is the grandest, cutest, stinkiest dungheap in the world.

—Grow yourself a mustache. Get out in the sun and bronze that shit-brown skin of yours. Make it black if you can. Then get sandals, a beret, and clothes like those you see them wearing. Go to the outskirts of town and find one of those donkey trains, the kind that don't have people with them. When you see one like that, let it pass till the last little old donkey's ass is about a yard away. Then just fall in behind. Donkey trains go round and round the earth forever. Somewhere, somebody's building a big hole. People-less donkeys will take you right to it. You know those sacks they carry. They're full of dirt, nothing else, just bags of dirt from that big hole. When the hole gets deep enough and wide enough this country's going to slide right through it. Then the rest of the goddamn world. But this country first cause they own the donkeys. Like water going down a drain. One loud fizzle, a burp and nothing left. Just the donkeys circling a void loaded down with sacks of nothing.

But you go and see for yourself. The hole ought to be big enough by now to let you and everything you want to take with you get through. Of course I can't say if it's small enough to keep out all the things you don't want. Been a while since I've seen it. I'd go again, but I get tired looking up a donkey's asshole.

Cecil poured more brandy in his glass. It was innocuous now, sending no messages to his brain. Outside rain blew in sheets through Calle de Jardines. From roofs water drained downward to find the smooth depressions it had been licking for years into the pavement. A baby's sharp cry, distinct and angry, floated from a high window, fading till it blended with the rush of wind and water.

—I don't know what I expected, but I'm certain I was wrong to come here tonight.

—It's damn wet outdoors. There's a lot to be said for being dry . . . and high.

—Just tell me . . . no, tell me before you drink or pour the bottle. Was there a son? Who is Webb looking for?

—Who? There was once upon a time a young man. Webb fathered a bastard on his black mistress, Anna. Webb has been waiting years for the boy to come to him. He still believes somebody would travel three thousand miles to say God knows what to a perfect stranger. When I met Webb, he was searching for his son and paid me to help him. It didn't take me too long to figure out the situation. I had fallen into just enough madness and money to keep old Albert going in his declining years.

—And Webb. You feed his delusions. You attached yourself to him just like you did to me that night.

—We search. When I saw you with the case, I was scared to death. I thought to myself what the hell's going to happen to poor Al if Webb has really found what he's been looking for. It was tough with Webb in America. He wouldn't take me along, but I knew he'd be back. But I was damn sure he'd be alone.

—And I am to be this son to Webb.

—You are whatever you want to be. He's waiting. The streets are full, but he will find you if you go.

The pig eyes widened.

—Cut me in whatever you do, please. But for Albert's sake, for your own too, just forget about Webb. What'll happen if you go to Málaga tomorrow. What could happen. He needs his dream of a son, not a son. And could you act out the part he'd want you to play. Could you stand up under all that guilt and remorse he'd want to lay on your shoulders. Could you forgive him every day a hundred times a day for the woman he betrayed, for his blindness and unfeeling hands. Whose life would you be living. Come on. You're a sensible guy. Stop this before it goes any farther. You can't change what he is now so give him back his ghost. It's the only decent thing to do. Let me lie to him. Let us go on playing the game. Go home, Cecil. He isn't as rich as he seems. We just barely make it. Leave us in peace.

One by one the children die. It is this fact that makes the sun unpleasant on my back. I can hear the sea, the wind and the gulls. The pages of a book rippling. Sand thick in the air covering everything.

When the sand beetle begins his climb, I will kill it. He came from nowhere, armored, prehistoric, and after sunning himself, is ready to crawl over the yellow mound of sand. Beetles crack like nuts. Nougat centers surprisingly white. I raise my fist. . . .

Someone said no Charles no panic almost in the voice.

But there I was on the edge dreaming of the long plunge, of the scream that would leave me breathless.

—Doctor. Dr. Webb. I have a lady, Doctor. Would you please come in. The room is so small and the company unpromising I know you wonder what you're sitting next to—cancer, flu, hemorrhoids, morning sickness. Then starched white the saving angel comes: Next.

You cross the threshold.

—It's going to spoil everything. Don't the fools understand what's at stake? Everything we've worked so hard for. Sometimes I lose faith, begin to think that we've been wrong, that the crackers know what they're talking about. Blind rage, ignorance, and bloodlust. Killing and looting now of all times.

—But how do you expect people to understand?

—I don't expect everyone to understand. Not yet anyway. We're just beginning to make progress. The men who count are finally reacting, money and power slowly pledging themselves to our ideal.

—And you want . . .

—Patience. That and nothing more. After all these years, and the time and effort so many of us have put in. Delicacy is the key. You can't imagine how important it will be to find an appropriate language for the most fundamental questions.

The train passes through a broad, green plain. Nothing taller than nodding grass as far as the eye can see.

The little staircase was so flimsy and treacherous that Robinson did not often go down into the crypt where the mummies were.

First the shadow then the white hand touches the page. He turns down an edge. There is sand in the ridge where the pages meet. From his hand yellow-gray grains cascade. Whisper then hiss as a mound is formed on the spread-eagled book.

Bardamu Bar Damn you Bard an Mew

Meanwhile Old Ma Henrouille kept things going on in the depths below. She toiled like a nigger over these mummies.

It scuttled black and shining within my reach.

—Like everyone else, I suppose, I just want to feel that I'm free. I wouldn't know what to do if somehow I were turned loose.

—But you are, you know. *Loose,* as you call it. Now, this instant, what keeps you from getting off that stool and walking out of here.

—Doctor, you realize . . . of course you must realize . . .

Someone running in the wet sand. Feet sound like flippers. And children laughing. Perhaps a game of tag. The sea lapping up and swirling round their ankles. The sun.

Stop chewing your pencil, Charles. Charles, did you hear me? I said stop chewing it . . . you mustn't . . .

When Charles received her letter, he thought of the word *disdain.* Anna had taught him to spell the word: *disdain* not *destain* as he had written it twice in the short story. He had been annoyed at first, wanted something more from Anna than the schoolmarmish quibble, had to exert tremendous control over himself not to shout or strike out when he saw her precise handwriting and the little bracket she had inserted in his manuscript. Until that moment he had never felt so distant from her. The penciled correction was a rebuke pure and simple. Her chiseled word *disdain* over the chaos of his own barely legible scrawl could never be removed. At the periphery of his resentment had been something that for a long time afterward had managed to remain remote. But now as he slid his finger into Anna's letter, he remembered the whisper of fear, his gradual recognition that something profoundly disturbing had elicited his disproportionate response, that the word *disdain* leaping up at him from his page had intimated all that would subsequently take place between Anna and himself.

Slowly he cut through the blue airletter. To Charles Webb watching his hand clumsily part the dotted folds the whole progress of his life in time seemed no longer or shorter than this passage of his finger through the paper. In fact the ragged edges seemed to him a perfect metaphor for the wake he had left in time. But his trail had closed, a knife cutting water. So it had seemed with Anna; with all things. He knew the letter he spread on his desk would affirm this truth. Anna would be a different woman altogether, mother, wife, tourist, after twenty-five years making the much delayed and longed for grand tour. Would she ask him for travel tips, for hotels, restaurants, a list of good people in each capital to visit. Perhaps in her careful handwriting grown more ample, more decorative, more *feminine* in twenty-five years, she would tactfully offer to secrete the grave of the past, landscape over it a green, cheery memorial park by introducing her husband to Charles and the progeny she knows he'll just adore. He was sure at least the letter would announce her imminent arrival. Nothing short of such a drastic removal could have caused her to write after twenty-five years of silence. Perhaps her husband was dead. Perhaps she herself was dying prematurely and had chosen some bit of beach, some set of strangers to die among. The consumptive ebbing away in the brilliant sunshine. One final, corrupt tug at life. The street boy who would crawl from her death bed and strip the jewels from her corpse. All these morbid fantasies took their turns in Charles' mind. What Anna had been to him had climbed back into its limbo after the word *disdain* had flickered then faded from his mind. His random thoughts, the little plots he could fabricate were an attempt to establish a mood, a tone that would give import to the reading of the letter. As it lay on his desk, it was curiously insignificant. A vacuum surrounded it, nullifying the possibility of any response, making it impossible to treat the flimsy piece of paper and its words as a reality. Anna and what she chose to set down on paper belonged to a dead time. The man to whom these words were addressed and to whom they might have meaning had ceased to exist.

With resigned respect and solemnity as if a priest were crossing the arms of a corpse Charles folded the blank flaps of the airletter back upon its body. So long to reach him. So many dead addresses canceled. But finally in his hands. After glancing down once more at the two strange names on it, Anna's and his, Charles tucked the letter into his back pocket.

Charles often suspected that it was an affectation on his part to keep the tiny *salle de bonne* at the top of Hotel St. André des Arts. Years had passed since he had written anything that would justify the keeping of a studio. The tomblike room with its steeply sloping ceiling, the tortuous staircase that led to it, the sudden bare walls and boards of the uppermost level contrasted theatrically with the worn but still pampered elegance of the four floors beneath. But the room had been cheap and elevated enough to temper some of the street sounds so Charles had found it suitable for his purposes. Though it no longer served any vital function, Charles felt that its former services deserved some lasting reward, some monument, so instead of relinquishing his lease he indulged his sentimentality. At one stage the room had been for assignations, but much sooner than he was willing to admit to himself, the labor demanded by five flights of stairs outweighed the titillation he received from what was vaguely erotic in the room's shape and seclusion.

Of course, as he perpetually reminded himself, the room would be just the thing for any friend passing through the city. But as he crossed into Rue St. André des Arts moving toward his studio he knew it would be empty, and that it had languished tenantless for longer than he cared to remember.

M. Jacques, the porter, greeted him. At one time Webb's association with the short, bald man had been almost conspiratorial. When women had shuttled in and out or the American alone would spend days locked up in his loft, M. Jacques' professional curiosity had been aroused, and he had enjoyed fabricating a secret life for his guest, a history documented and enlivened by significant nods, winks, gestures, the intonation and emphasis in a *çà va* or *bonne nuit* in the lobby. M. Jacques compiled volumes listening to the tread of Webb and each new companion upon the stairs. Shy, certain or uncertain, leaning upon each other, or a leader and follower, rhythmic in step together or the stumbling wine dance and finally in the quiet darkness of the hotel, from high in the vault of the stairwell the closing of the last door. M. Jacques was now nothing more than polite. Like the bells in small Paris shops he registered Webb's entrance with an automatic echo of cheerfulness. The porter's mind never left his thick ledger and its ornate, close-columned calculations.

Through the room's one window a dull light like a coat of yellow dust broached the obscurity of its interior. Webb stood in the doorway, aware of his heart and lungs, of the machine's dependence on its finite, vulnerable elements. His cot, his writing table, his lamp, his chair. Charles pulled the string that dangled from beneath the hood of the gooseneck lamp. The lamp tilted forward as it always did, but just before its equilibrium was lost Charles laid the palm of his hand against its fluted base. The thick metal was cold. A ridge of dust came off on Charles' hand. Acrid smell of dust burning rose as the bulb heated under its tiny reflector. Its circumscribed glow only accentuated the room's shadows. Charles engaged in the familiar struggle with the window, finally wrenched free the inside metal retainer and using both hands pushed out the double panels.

Traffic sounds of nearby boulevards reached him rather than the morning activity below. Like its residents some Paris streets awaken early in the morning, but others who find themselves busy most of the night and sometimes till dawn arise leisurely, refuse to acknowledge another day's beginning, resent the sunlight's intrusion or the premature striking of a footfall through their corridors. On Rue St. André des Arts the arrival of shopkeepers in their long blue dusters, the rattle of the three-wheeled milk wagons, the postman's boots were interlopers in the somnolent morning atmosphere, activities that had commenced only in the dream of the street, which continued its slumber.

The writing desk had one small drawer. Turning from the window Charles opened the drawer and drew three notebooks from inside. Two black, one red, they contrasted boldly atop the desk where he laid them side by side. Quietly as if to conceal the movements from himself Charles took the few steps that were enough to examine each corner of the room's interior. He stopped beside the cot, stood glancing down at the counterpane, attempting to distinguish its faded pattern from the mottled shadow patches imposed by weak light coming in at the window. Abruptly he dropped onto the bed, raising a puff of dust that writhed through the narrow band of sunlight floating beside his dark figure. Charles closed his eyes and leaned back against the wall submissive to the confused flow of his thoughts, not yet admitting the inevitability of certain images, events and personalities, pretending that the plunge into his memory would not be structured by his particular fear and desires, but some arbitrary, soothing logic of the unconscious itself.

Charles Webb, his head now resting on a thin pillow rooted from beneath the dusty counterpane, his body bowed to curve of unresisting springs and sagging mattress, became a thing inert, as bereft of volition as the instruments he had disturbed by entering once more his cave of making. The window, the lamp, his chair, his bed, the bright stripes of color across the desk top. Other caves to enter, dust to disturb. Anna, the word *disdain,* stairs to climb ever so slowly . . .

The red notebook had begun as fragments, and its shapelessness had frightened Webb. It had been too real. Knowing Anna, knowing himself equal impossibilities. So what could the words do but mirror inadequacy. First the red notebook had contained only his words, but later with an ocean between them, it had gradually been filled by Anna's letters, his answers sent and unsent, his impressionistic meditations and snatches of verse. Webb remembered how seldom he had reread the pages after they were covered with words. Fear again. Anna lost somewhere in the words, himself smothered.

I was afraid of words as we had been afraid of crowds. Saying *black woman* and *white man* destroyed Anna and Charles. They would miss cues, botch lines, two novices inept and nervous before an impatient audience. Black and white. Not only losing the stage personality but floundering unanchored to any identity at all.

Did Anna want to die. Did she want to be released from the words. He could not write them. *Black. White.* Instead he preserved fragments. Warmth of bodies. Hands touching. The park and dying leaves. River running brownly. Twilight. Dawn. Shadowy transitions. And he did not reread. Did not try to order or make whole. Young man's words that were disguise as much as discovery.

He knew one day he would repudiate them. Hate them. For their fear, the lie of Anna.

Turning the pages now, drowsy with age, with the room's ancient familiarity, with words and words written since the red notebook had been laid aside, Webb felt time and distance collapse. That last summer on the riverbank she fed me grapes. We watched the emerald-headed ducks glide past trailing their dun mates and children. She said you have not forgiven and I looked away, tried to focus on the far shore, the sailboats and racing sculls. Wanting her so much, so near, all of her within me, as her deep black eyes swallowed my image. A moment the notebook should hold, should balance and preserve. But how in words. I spit seeds on the grass and she leaned backward, black hair a frame, eyes risen to white clouds and blue sky. She was beautiful and I knew I should lean down and press my lips against hers. Here on this bright, summer day. River, sky, trees and grass and sun.

Her words defined my hesitation. She said no one can learn to forgive because forgiveness can't wait. Like a lie. You know at the instant you are asked if forgiveness is truly given. All you can learn later is that perhaps you should have forgiven. She was up on her elbows again, hair dripping almost to the grass, her face still slanted to the sky. She said that's why I don't think we can forgive them and I'm sure they won't forgive us.

He would not read on. Not try to remember. The young man's vision betrayed itself. The constant irony of the thing withheld cruelly revealing all in its absence. Words an elaborate masquerade defining the wearer with more precision than his naked skin. The young man was a pedant, a liar, a fool, he was ignorant, illogical, afraid, and Webb's list grew as he had read, but in spite of these defects, or perhaps because of them, Charles Webb envied the young man. What was the final most difficult fact to accept had been that just as a saint's clairvoyance rested ultimately on his belief in God, the young man's vision had a still center which gave his words a transcendent authenticity—his love of Anna. Nothing Webb had written since had captured that reality.

May was the month in which he had received Anna's last letters.

Dearest,

Please do not be angry with me for taking so long to write. I know it has been a long time because I count in my heart each hour of each day we are apart. You are probably smiling because you think I'm telling a silly lie or that I'm just silly. But I'm telling the truth. More times than I can keep track of, a thought filled with you drops down like a cloud and covers me. Not a dark, unpleasant cloud, but gentle and caressing like your hands over my skin. For a moment I'm lost to what's around me. I actually begin to float upward, lifted by my dream of you. Then some lifeless detail, a word or object suddenly cries out that it exists, that I must turn and pay attention. But in a way, I suppose I'm grateful for the petty details that accumulate to fill my days. Time would be unbearable if I had to remain suspended between the dream of you which rushes so close to being real and the distant reality of your presence which remains unmoved by my desire.

This seems so little to send after such a long while. But soon we will talk forever. You'll get sick of all the things I have to say. You'll want me to keep quiet. Aw Shut up! you'll say in exasperation when I tell you for the thousandth time I love you.

Anna,

I fear the very intensity of our love. From the distance of a year its heights seem unattainable, the day to day reality of its existence in words, things and actions is lost beneath a golden aura of recollection. The idea of being with Anna again is just as impossible to conceive as the lonely void had been before we were separated. Your image of perfection, the rhythms and emotions it revives have broken away from the limitations of particular individuals, times, and places. It is no longer the love of Charles and Anna, but *love,* a sublime, universalized condition that no one can approach or call his own. Being here, I can't help thinking of Proust, of Swann and his Odette. So you and I won't be able to shut our eyes and will into being our former love because that love or more importantly its transfigured image can only exist in our minds. To myself I admit all these things, reaching and dismissing countless stages of sobering skepticism and somber faith. Not enough can be said, and there is nothing to be said. Battered between these alternatives I also find it increasingly difficult to write. What has been spontaneous, self-justifying, has become for me an enormous crisis of will power, a labored, compulsory task for which I have neither words nor spirit.

Dearest,
    There has been a long silence. By far the longest of all. I could not stand still, Charles. I have been growing. But more of me goes into this letter than ever climbed the stairs to Billy's room. Past the smell of onions, salami and burnt grease, the step somewhere in the middle that groaned and threatened to swallow me. Always dark, voices, sometimes the jukebox of the sandwich shop beneath Billy's room. Why after the party was over, and being taken home did I say yes. It was late, I was tired. No special attraction. Had we danced at the party? That I couldn't recall. But he offered a ride home and late and rather than walk lots of us piled in but finally just Billy and I so I said for some reason though I was tired and had barely seen his face yes I would stop.

    How many times did I go there? Would it be better to say once, to be able to say just once and I was weak and please forgive. Or should I say to you to whom I must be able to say everything: that I went back, learned to rely upon those trips to Billy's room, learned to stop questioning each button undone, each layer of reserve melted in his arms. That I learned to stop torturing myself, buried the guilt and shame. Would you understand.

    Please come home this summer as you promised. I will be here, I will be yours in a new way, I believe a deeper and fuller way. I will have changed and you will have changed. It will be a new beginning; it can be the start of our forever.

Answer (not sent)

The key is her handwriting. She can adopt various types of handwriting just as she can choose and sustain the disguise of a life style. What I have always been uncertain of was the number of removes each one of her poses put her from the truth. Now I know the problem is and will always be that her conception of the truth consists only of the sum total of perspectives contributed by her styles. There is no layer which cannot be peeled away either by me or someone else. There is no fundamental reserve that cannot be disturbed. Each pose has some corner of the truth, but no point exists at which the discreet units form a unity. When Anna has wished to be the satirical correspondent, up popped material upon which she could exercise her wit and spite. When she was depressed, enough of the chaos weighed upon her, enough of the world's cruelty and emptiness blunted her sensibilities to justify the most severe stoic meditations. Her desire for a new dress, her concern for her figure, her hair, stray cats, children allowed her to launch unashamedly into the most feminine epistles. Each slot, each pose that could be validated, verified on its own terms made the gathering of the whole implausible, the effort of consolidation and appraisal less urgent. In fact as she had gradually realized she could withhold, could crowd out the inevitable evaluation indefinitely. That part of her, that life which included another man, his bed and the lovers' hours they spent together had for her no more relevance than any other of the lives she had lived. And it could be, she decided, the last of which I learned. Perhaps I would have never learned.

Another letter to be added. Twenty-five years and his hand must copy out Anna's words, end the story in the red notebook:

You came but didn't stay. You made love to me as you would to a whore. But that didn't matter. You couldn't stay for long, we couldn't continue looking past each other's eyes each time our bellies were stuck together. And though it was not love, we created what love might create, what only love should be allowed to bring into the world. Your son is a young man now. Today I told him your name. He knew many things about you before that. The better part of you, what we once shared. But I am dying. I can neither lie nor leave certain things incomplete. The boy should not be left with shadows, with rents in his past. It will be up to him to pull the pieces together. I have been fair. Of you he knows more good than evil. But of course that is meager fairness, perhaps the greatest unfairness to you both. I know I will not live out the year. The doctors are honest and fair. Sometimes I wish I had followed you, had put my life in your hands. Surely the bitterness passed off. Surely your wound healed of itself, and you remembered more of me than the transgression of that stranger to us both, my flesh.

I cannot visualize you any more. Sometimes I pretend to see you in him, but that trick is shoddy. He has never known you so the most important things, what I would want to see, could not be transferred, reborn. And you haven't even known he existed. You chose the kind of break we made and I respected your choice, your right. Perhaps I should have sent a picture or his name, revealed his existence before now. But I was waiting for a moment when everything inside me would be calm, detached, entirely distinct from any memory of you and our love. I see now I have waited for death. I believe someday he will try to find you.

Semana Santa was ending. Tonight the final procession bearing *Cristo Negro* would weave through the warm, spring night drawing behind it a brown cleansing river of gypsies through the streets of Málaga. The evening like others for Webb would begin with cocktails under the awning of a café, with the small boys who knelt beside you to find their faces in your shoes. Webb would sit and observe, then stroll along café lined streets to be observed. Simply a matter of time. God in his abundance would provide fuel for every fire.

Webb did not live until those first moments in the street, until the tartness of the iced gin brought sudden clarity and amplification to his senses, until he was certain again that everything he felt was real and would die. From the glassed in terrace of his hotel, he had watched the first night's festivities unfold. His moment of certainty had not come. Perhaps it was the harsh lighting and round tables with their drooping skirts of immaculate glowing linen. Perhaps he lacked all assurance because he sat alone at his table against a back wall able to see only the top of the lighted fountain which sprang from the main square below.

He could arouse no enthusiasm that first night for the seemingly endless courses brought by his white-jacketed waiter. Around Webb the other diners had seemed spurred on, first by the canned music provided by the management, then by the carnival enthusiasm of the band playing below in the square. Silverware clattered against china, metal lids of warming dishes reverberated like tympanum, talk was vociferous, laughter exploded between mouthfuls. Through the glass wall Webb could see the harbor, a cluttered pattern of masts illuminated against the blackness of the sea. Closer, blinking from color to color through a pastel spectrum, the crown of a fountain swayed unsteadily in the air. Gradually the room dimmed and emptied till Webb, who had moved to a table beside the glass, and his waiter, a blur and a red dot as he stood smoking in a corner beside the bar, were the sole occupants.

—*Uno más, por favor*, Webb asked the darkness, vaguely guilty because he knew he was keeping the waiter overtime, preventing the man from joining the crowd down in the street. The sentinel moved slowly, ice from a bucket like bones cracking, the musical bumping of cubes against glass walls. The drink was set down. In the man's face Webb could see no anger, no expectation or impatience. What the night might mean to him, the singing, dancing, the women in the streets, did not reach his eyes, was as concealed as his opinion of the drink he served his last customer. The man may prefer to be here, to be earning the large tip I must leave, to be avoiding the noise, the confusion below. Webb preferred to believe that, but either way desired some sign from the man, something beyond neutral passivity that would spell out an explicit relationship between them, define it so it could be forgotten, no longer intrude. The waiter's restaurant English and Webb's tourist Spanish, however, made the possibility of spoken understanding remote, and the waiter withheld from his features and gestures any expressive movement. When and how he had finally risen from his seat at the window, Webb didn't know, but in something that seemed like a dream he remembered the body of a young sailor that was somehow the body of the waiter, and the white waiter's jacket that somehow had become part of a blue naval uniform whose brass buttons embossed with anchors were being undone by Webb's hands to kiss the cold, saltiness of drowned flesh beneath.

The last day Webb boarded the crowded bus for Torremolinos. A seventeen mile bus trip down the coast took over an hour; the delapidated vehicle made innumerable stops picking up anyone, anywhere along its route, fortunate enough to make themselves seen in the roadside clutter and dust. To Webb it seemed impossible that the sea could be less than a mile away paralleling their route. No breeze penetrated the dust. In the sunlight's glare Webb imagined he could see the tightly packed layers of dust and air forming a solid, inert mass through which the rumbling bus must plunge. The engine wheezed and sputtered straining its dust clogged lungs on the slightest grade or when it lurched into motion again after picking up another clot of peasants, the brown peasants Webb saw as forlorn, indistinguishable from one another or from the dusty loads which they carried. The occupants of the bus were silent; only the animals slowly suffocating within the press of human bodies muttered weakly their sounds of terror and distress.

Webb could not stand still. Like the others who had boarded too late for a seat he was jostled violently as the bus careened headlong over the rutted highway. Since he was taller than most of the passengers his drunken motions were more visible. After each particularly vicious thrust, Webb would find some dark face staring intently at him as if the white man had caused the collision and directed its force. But before the eyes could trap him Webb and the accuser were driven apart just as suddenly as they had met. Webb knew, unlike him, the Spaniards who filled the bus carried no comforting images of sudden relief once the bus reached its destination. They saw no expanse of cool, blue sea, no golden sands stirred by breezes coming in off the water. They would walk away from the beach and the lush resort hotels that fronted it, toward the shantytown that hid itself from the gleaming island of shops, banks, and restaurants. Their eyes told Webb he was an intruder. Asked why they could not be left alone, why even here they must be reminded that nothing is theirs, not even this hot cramped space that carries them from one job to another. Webb realized he was offending them, that in his blue cord suit and madras tie he should have taken a taxi between the two towns, a vehicle that preserved the necessary *détente* between two alien forms of life.

As if to cut off his escape, to fuse the passengers into one unnatural whole, a new wave of heat dropped like a blanket around the bus. Webb wanted to take off the jacket that lapped against his skin like a wet rag, but such an extravagant movement was impossible to arms pinned at his sides. The pools of moisture that had formed in every cavity of his body began to overflow and crawl like insects inside his clothes. His eyelids dripped and blurred his vision. If he could have seen the floor of the bus, he wouldn't have been surprised to find puddles forming around his shoes. He was in kindergarten again, his face on fire, unable to move from his seat while the other children laughed and pointed at the pale liquid spreading beneath his desk.

The bus had slowed, finally coming to a complete stop when a flock of goats being driven toward the sea blocked the highway. A thousand collar bells began their high-pitched jingling, delicate goat feet clattered against asphalt. Webb looked down on the black and white wave of animals driven past the front of the bus. Their tiny horns were frozen ripples in the bobbing surface of lean backs and pointed heads. Sitting cross-legged on a donkey the leering shepherd appeared unnatural because no tuft of beard sprouted from his chin or horns from his forehead. With the racket and dust came the rancid smell of the animals, detaching itself, inundating the bus until it harmonized with the garlic, olive oil, excrement, and sweat that reigned in concert.

Webb shut his eyes, wished for some means to deprive all his senses just as abruptly. The bus was motionless less than a minute, the herd of goats did not contain all the goats in the world, but for Webb the moment was an eternity. He was tossing in his bed, feverish, unable to sleep. Distance drone of heavy bombers, the apocalypse thick in their bellies. Anna weeping. *Too late. Too late.*

The engine coughed and jerked raggedly into life. One last straggling black kid bolted past the wheels and the bus clambered again toward Torremolinos.

The Tower of the Mills. From Barcelona southward the coast was dotted with what had once been Roman military outposts, then fishing villages, and finally emblems of the good life in the sun that brought French, Germans, Swedes,

Dutch, Englishmen, and Americans streaming to sun, ocean, sand, cheap living, and each other. Pedrigaleho, Castelldefels, Sitges, Tarragona, Málaga, Marbella. The view always the same. A stretch of white sand, the shimmering blue of the ocean, a modern high-rise hotel flanked by the perpetual construction of a newer, bigger, brighter, more lavish accommodation. From Paris there are six flights daily to the Costa Brava and the Costa del Sol. Webb remembered the brochures, the posters, the fresh tans of the clerks in the travel agency. Champs Élysées. No, it didn't matter that he wasn't a Frenchman, still eligible for all cut rates, discounts, package deals, I know just the thing . . . it's a lovely . . .

From the square Webb walked down a narrow street crowded with restaurants and bars. Signs were usually trilingual, English, German, French, and sometimes Spanish last, inviting the stroller to eat, drink, wear, smell, hear, feel, possess what was displayed in windows or walk through the low doorways covered by swaying strings of beads and submit to the lure of darkness on the other side of thick cool walls. The paved street became rutted, then gravel, and finally earth packed tight by the passage of countless feet. A crumbling stone balcony overlooked the beach, and twisting down from this platform a staircase even more dilapidated than the decayed landing was cut into the rock. Webb could see figures moving beneath him, two-way traffic slowly negotiating the steep weather-beaten stairs. Scrawny children, dark ragamuffins with stylized saucer eyes played on the staircase, skipped along its precarious edges, and scrambled over sharp, broken rocks. A group would swirl by Webb's legs, threatening to topple him, or in a tangle of arms and legs plunge them together helplessly down the stairs. At many of the landings, cut deeper into the less solid rock or constructed of an incredible variety of odds and ends on outcroppings, what must be the homes of these gypsy children came into view. Webb could discern no possibility of ventilation or light in these warrens, only the scooped out entranceways like drooling mouths, littered with refuse and filth. Occasionally a shriveled old woman or one nursing a child too young to climb the rock staircase would be squatting at their holes. They smiled toothless smiles as the children's bright eyes smiled, even muttered wearily some automatic greeting as the children always sang out when strangers passed. Webb could not put his hand into his pocket, felt ashamed of what he would draw out. The sea breeze had begun to refresh him and at every other turning of the staircase he could see crackling with sunlight the ocean spread across the horizon.

Webb walked along the beach dreaming a Prufrock dream of himself. Semana Santa was almost over. Málaga would become a staid city of cautious, middle-class Spaniards, and Torremolinos would shed its spring skin of faces for the summer crowd. Nights would become as hot as the days and the days too long. The endless gin tonic of an afternoon would flow.

Webb dreamed of a young man. Saw not sandals tied over his feet but bare flesh, from the tough soles of his feet curling in the hot sand to the strip of black cloth that hugged his narrow hips. His bronzed legs naked and strong, pounding the sand in a sudden dash to the surf as their power lifted him high into the air, bounding, floating till the cool water rose with a shock against his chest. The playful fight with the sea until he was no more than a black dot seen from the shore.

Webb removed his sandals, rolled his trousers to the knee and padded along the damp sand. He had stuffed his tie in the breast pocket of his cord suit jacket slung over his shoulder, and his white batiste shirt was open to the waist. The sea was a dull roar in his brain; water lapped against his ankles coolly, rhythmically. Slowly the sand was sucked away from under his toes, the imprint they made pushing deeper into the strand. Webb stared at the brilliant sea, the subtle bands of color descending toward the horizon, tried to locate the points where green became blue and blue purple. But the play of light and atmosphere danced continuously, never allowed his eyes to find end or beginning. A shudder passed through Webb's body. He was aware of the strain on his eyes, of the sand that tugged at his feet, the horizon meeting somewhere behind his back. The damp shirt was clammy against his shoulders, chill, threatening like a sudden draft from an unknown source.

Sea girls combing. Webb back-pedaled carefully placing his feet to avoid the quick foam-edged rushes of water that chased the bottom of his pants. Farther up the beach a low white building painted in hulking red letters across its front *Bar Genymar*. A cluster of red and white umbrellas promised service outdoors, a shaded chair facing the sea, an iced drink. He would come.

Too many bodies littered the sand. Webb picked his way, erratic, cautious like a crab scuttling among the flesh mounds. He chose a table closest to the sea and sat half in, half out of the shadow of its striped umbrella. The gin was called Green Fish, was raw and cloying, made Webb tremble as the first long gulp settled unsteadily in his stomach. For the first time that day he allowed himself to ask questions, to have a past. To ask what future that past implied. Gin said you are an old man. And tired the old man replied. Place names came to him, automatic, insinuating, a list he had been forced to memorize and must always upon demand be prepared to repeat. From the tall glass fumes, incense rising. Dream of Anna in the White Mountains. A steep green hill. We tumble down, accelerating as body pitches over and over within the earth carpet unfurling. Wind whips the high grass, hisses, falling we land in a heap. We are alone. Beneath the sea. We are its creatures. Green hills, deep caves, always a seascape where the land flattens into blue distance and the eye can go no farther. Said to be the lair of the dragon. Benign now, turned to stone, baking in the sun. Wind whips. Her shaggy sweater is covered with dry grass, straw clings to her black hair. Smiling she whips, her fingers comb. Blackness floats. I see it spread against a pillow. A hand smooths it, touches her dark face. She is beneath me. The long strands are wind. I bury my face in the black wind. She begins to cry.

Her son would say to her the white man never loved you. Her son would say I loved only my words about her. My son would say I loved nothing. He would find notes to him written in her books, notes that were written while he was still a baby, even before he was born, while she carried him, she would have begun a record believing someday that if he read the books she had loved and saved he would understand. She would write the story of her love, her submission, her trust and belief. And how when she was loved no more, she had let me leave without a word. He would know she had given everything to me, that I had touched greatness only when I touched her and that when she died I still didn't understand, didn't have the faintest idea of what had been given, what had been lost. That he had been lost. He would know I had lied. That my paintings, music, and books were a monument of lies, deceit. He is my son. What I had planted in her black flesh. He had no name. Over her body I will offer him my name, but he will spit on the floor and laugh, louder and louder. Then he will say . . .

The voice was Al's, rousing him, shattering the mirror.

—Hail Charles, full of gin. Blessed art thou among men for Albert has found you. Wrinkled and puckered into a second grotesque face Al's naked belly hung flabby-jawed over skimpy red trunks. The red hairs of his chest, bleached and curled, were incandescent.

—Why did you leave me, Charlie. And come back without a word. I was worried sick. Above the shaggy beard his smile arched to his ears.

—What a lucky break this is. Dammit. I was nearly going nuts with worry so I decided to get some sun and sea. They relax me you know. Nothing like being near the sound of the surf at night. Whales own lullaby. I'm snoring in a minute and sleep all night just like a baby. You know what I mean?

From the sea a squealing girl was lifted. Two hands clasped her waist momentarily suspending her above the billowing breakers while she screamed louder and thrashed perfect bronzed legs. The hands ducked her again in an explosion of foam.

Webb knew his voice would falter if he attempted to speak immediately. He took the plump hand held out toward his, wagging as it wagged, accepting its presence as he did the image of his dying body each morning in the mirror.

—I won't ask you why, Albert. I'm not prepared to listen and I doubt that I would understand what you would call reasons. I won't ask why, just how, how did you find me.

—You might say I didn't look. Just went about my own business and—poof—here we are, face to face.

—Did you follow me?

—Let's drop it, Charlie. A coincidence is a coincidence. Don't you know I got better things to do than dog you.

—It's simple of course. You've seen him. And we waited here last year. Almost exactly to the day. Where else would I be. And you. The vulture . . . just minding his own business. Just hanging black in the sky. His own business.

—Now wait, Charlie . . . wait. You're going a bit hard. I got feelings too. His bulk swallowed the chair. Like some part of Al already digested and organic, the metal legs he straddled propelled his lobster body closer to the table where Webb sat.

—Look here, *señor*. There is hardly any sense in which I'm

an outsider in this. I cry like you do when we don't fine him. I cry and spend the blood money, not one peseta into the sea where I promise myself it will all go. Just because you feel so damned bad is no reason to believe all the grief in the world belongs to you. I cry, Charlie. I figure you came here to mourn. My eyes tell me at least that. If you'd open your windows you'd see Al is a mourner too. And that other thing. The sting . . . remorse.

Al's face disintegrated into broken spirals of color and motion through the bottom of the tall glass as Webb drained the last of his silver gin. What did it matter Webb asked himself. Here we are again. This fat, red-bearded man and myself. Both ridiculous, both obscene. It was laughable afterall. The classic pair, umbilically joined. The knight dragging his squire across endless plains of La Mancha. But who is who. Which one the deluded fanatic.

—Charlie, I hope you're listening. Al leaned forward, digging the legs of his chair deeper into the sand. His tone was measured now, his voice calm, conciliatory. After calling for drinks he folded the ham hands on the round tabletop.

—There seems to me something you're not willing to admit. Like it or not we're in this together, and when I say *in* I mean from the bald soles of our feet to the toppest headhair. You think the boy will come, don't you. You think too that maybe all these years he has been hiding from you, or leastways from something you caused. All what I say is true, ain't it, Charlie?

Webb's answer was half a nod, a barely perceptible downward dipping of his head toward the sweating glass of gin.

—And if the boy is disgusted, lost, or scared you did it, didn't you? You made him into whatever he was, if he was anything. But if we don't find him I gotta face the failure too, don't I? It ain't something you can do alone. In fact you don't have the right to do it alone. We'll go back to town together. We'll wait together. The rod and the staff. That's the way it has to be, it has to be this way, Charlie. And Charlie . . . Cecil ain't coming. He ain't coming to meet you. He's going home, Charlie. I sent him home. He won't be here, Charlie.

—I had so much I wanted to tell him. And now, here, we would have time; so much time. Do you know what's happening, Albert? I am an old man, I am dying, Albert. Tell me he is coming that I am not dying. That Anna . . .

—Hail Albert full of grace.

Hail Albert full of grace.

Hail Albert. Hail Albert.

—Come on Charlie, the night is young. The shoeshine pimps are just hitting the streets. Let's get a good shine, Charlie. And give them a fabulous tip. Let's get good brandy and sip under the umbrellas. The show will be pretty as it always is. Loud, wild night show for us. Let's get away from here. Maybe buy a new tie or a kerchief or something bright. Feel different in new things, in bright new things. Come on the night's so young.

The woman was arrayed in purple and scarlet, and bedecked with gold and jewels and pearls, holding in her hand a goblet of bronze brandy in which she dipped her lips then I my lips then she anointed her fingers and with fingers she wet my member and the short curly hairs perfumed with Felipe Segundo. Onto my back I settled received by the blood-red bedspread as I would be by a mother's lap. Soft and drifting my peace was such I could float any place I pleased, to Paris, to Rome, back to those cities in America, forward to the deep couch of earth in which I would sleep forever. Estrella, whore that she was, had no scruples concerning my brandy letch and seemed either drunk herself or wooed into a compatible urge because she alternately wet and licked my liquorish stick with a rhythm neither hurried nor mechanical, a slow baptism of damp fingertips dragged lightly the whole length, quick dabs at my scrotum and body hair, then the languor of her tongue undoing the lubrication or to be more precise supplying a new balm from her moist lips. I watched her. When she moved it was on all fours, crouched like a beast. She would drag the tops of her thin breasts over my naked flesh. Her body was neither voluptuous nor skinny. It had to be both: meaty round buttocks, drooping pear breasts thin till the pendulous diamond-tipped bulbs that scratched parallel lines into my skin. Estrella. Al did not exaggerate when he sang your skills, five nights waiting for Webb and five different women you were for me. And this last meeting, this slow removal of all of Cecil through the tube at which you drink reveals a lore in you Estrella old as memory as old as lonely men in cities, ancient craft passed down through generations like the concourse Egyptians had with the dead, how they could preserve, make lifelike, extract the brain through a nostril just as you exquisitely diminish me through my root's blind eye.

World must have stopped hours ago. I listen and hear only your breathing, the lapping of waves on a shore thousands of planets away. Life must end after stillness like this. Not simply my life in time but all the tumult and clamor in the streets, the jungles, the seas. Surely a judgment has been brought upon the earth with this revelation. The blood of all the saints and martyrs ready to burst from my groin.

Dawn came. I am undeceived. Dawn of the last day, always comes again or tomorrow or however you perceive of never-ending. We stand naked at the window. Madrid sleeps below us, gray, misty, undisturbed except for the whining of motor bikes, the waspy, angry buzz of machines as unhappy as their masters at being routed out to thump along the empty, early city streets. My hand goes around her waist. Fingers spread concave at the deep indentation. So here we are Estrella, the last two. A new beginning. Sounds you hear are machines so accustomed to early rising and hitting the streets that they perpetuate the ritual although their masters are no more. Or perhaps it was machines that dragged men from their warm beds. A new beginning. Sons and daughters from your loins. The first few will be indeterminate, kaleidoscopic leavings of many men from many nations, amalgamated children we will welcome but finally the all clear and I can begin to sow a new generation. Adam to Zachariah, Alice to Zenobia. We naked two framed in this dusty window seven stories above wet Madrid. We will name one Webb, for mystery and cunning and the past. Pola, Hans, Martine, Xavier, Carlos, Ingrid, Karl, Vladimir and name after name but do not think Simon.

I pull her closer, fingers in the rib grooves. A cage I could shatter if I squeezed with all my strength, brittle curving bone, her narrow waist. But I relax and let my hand drop, curl it round toward me, past the softness of her flank, the molded contour of belly to springy hair. She is humming. How far away is the city. How dead.

We turn from the window and our eyes meet, her whore eyes and mine bloodshot, raw. I think the gray dawn light is a blessing, a conspirator because we hold the glance an unnecessary instant and the cracked lips of her whore's mouth soften to a smile.

She is padding a step or two away yet far enough for me to take in all the incongruous body. Emaciated in shank and back and shoulders, two lumps of rump which jiggle giddily on the bone with each step. Straight rail of body which breaks at knees and deep waist to kneel as if in supplication but down farther beast on all fours rummaging beneath the red skirt of the bed cover. Surprising the breadth of beam in one who standing has boyish hips but spread they do to matron amplitude. I bend too and tug the sprig of beard exposed at hemisphere's base. She is up like a cat, bird-caging her fingers and feinting plucks at my groin.

—Estrella.

I want to take her by way of her plump buttocks. It is painful, dry and tight. I relent and leave her folded over the edge of the bed. The softest part of a woman, those two cushions on either side the ragged joint. Inside the thigh, but outside the eye. When she is standing, at the bottom curve of the haunch, that momentary fleshy hesitation before thigh sweeps dramatically outward. Cradle in which the life gates purse, tender vale, unfringed yet redolent of the tangled forest.

My love, Estrella, whom I leave to do the bidding of others. To perform for others.

Estrella come. Let us sit our nakednesses together here on this bed. Let us forget that the city is dead, that we are the last two. I memorized a poem once. If you could understand what I'm telling you, if you knew the poem was really a part of your Sacred Book, you would be scandalized, perhaps even turn me away. But we speak different languages, so if I recite quietly, solemnly, the words will be just so much billing and cooing, particularly if I punctuate the verses with caresses, kisses, even come to a full stop between stanzas so I can dip quickly into you. But no, listen. Let me go all the way through. I'll be selective. Only the most relevant passages, although all of the prophecy is more than appropriate. Such a memorial is the least we can do. A dirge between the pavanes we dance. You stare wonderingly. Perhaps titillated or even bored by the prospect of another sensual game, one more fancy, one more debauchery from my fertile imagination. But no. Relax, cuddle against me while I lean back against this ornate headboard. Is that some astrological sign carved in the center. A sun with stylized, horny rays projected outward. Some creature of the zodiac, a constellation, the universe itself? No, nothing more mysterious than your taste, always poor or bizarre. But we are in mourning. No levity, no tickling of groins, no lip love-making. Just my lips speaking and yours still. The queen is dead.

I will call this farewell or elegy to a dead whore:

And the merchants of the earth weep for her, since no one buys their cargo any more, cargo of gold, silver, jewels and pearls, fine linen, purple, silk and scarlet, cinnamon, spice incense, myrrh, frankincense, wine, oil, flour and wheat, cattle and sheep, horses and chariots and slaves, that is *human souls*.

> The fruit for which thy soul
> longed has gone from thee.
> And all thy dainties and thy
> splendor are lost to thee,
> never to be found again!

> Alas, alas for the great city
> that was clothed in fine linen,
> in purple and scarlet
> bedecked with gold, with jewels
> and with pearls!
> In one hour all this wealth has
> been laid waste.

> Hallelujah! the smoke from her
> goes up for ever and ever.

If I had been wise, a flatterer, Estrella, I might have sung for you the Song of Solomon. Visited your breasts and belly with heaps of metaphor. But you understand that you don't understand so what matter if I speak my farewell bitterly or like a spring morning. I am leaving you and leaving him. Which works out to be the same thing. Unless his story changes radically. Unless he is a Janus in disguise and hides another face beneath that distinguished long white hair. Perhaps one is there, one facing forward, lips I can speak to, that would speak to me. But I cannot take the chance.

One kiss more, a wrestle, a handful of your powder puff and I'll be on my way.

Home

Is always a street on which I happen to be walking. On which to some great extent I am lost as I am lost along this Madrid street.

Little light on the whorizon. Silent distance. I will walk toward that myth of earth touching heaven. As good a destination as any I can perceive, as any revealed to Cecil in this last consultation of his whoroscope. I am drunk and funky.

Behind the jumbled silhouette of buildings a true horizon must stretch. Walk to the edge of the city, to the favella's musty plain. I will gaze far out to the low hills which will be blue as morning light spreads over them. The gypsies will still be sleeping and I will move as stealthy as a dream among them, stepping always closer to that quiet distance.

The whore rising from her bed and I am helpless because I see Esther's bare back and I remember that the nightmare is irresistible that my sleep is troubled more and more by images of Simon scraped from her womb and the horror deceives me so that I must live it believe it feel myself gouging him out from her body. Fantasy of my son dripping into the pot.

But I know I did not kill him, wish him away, that of all things I dared hope for, I was most fearful hoping for him. Esther tried to do too much. Her body was just too tired to carry him any longer. And I followed the law, I slaved as she slaved learning the law. I was learning, learning so much for her and for him. But something broke. He could not wait and I dream I am responsible for his terrible coming. I am masked, a white aproned butcher who drags son from mother while some part of me holds her hand and whispers love.

I did not kill him. Dream is perverse. Perverse as the illusion that somewhere I could lie with my back on the hard ground and have blue sky and clouds against my chest.

Sun is rising and I will shock those eyes I meet in these narrow streets.

Cecil Otis Braithwaite, barrister-at-law, put to sea one day during the spring month of April, 1966. On the hot deck he stood resplendent in loden green, Tyrolean knickers with vest to match aching only for his first glance of Africa. Never did Cecil's wet gaze stray from the opaque screen of soggy atmosphere except to fasten upon the shrieking gulls that hovered over the ferry's stern. The birds were masterful in their lazy glides catching updrafts and currents of sea air that suspended them serenely on lax W's of wing. Unhurriedly, the gulls would dip to scavenge garbage thrown overboard by the stewards. Low over the waves they skipped like flat stones, nibbling, screeching, beating away competition with rapid flourishes of gull-wing. I too white-bellied and fleet-winged have danced upon the foam sang Cecil to himself. I remember when I was a swan and met this languishing maiden she stroked tender of feathers my long neck and oh so phallic head-piece and it's been so far away I forget now just how we consummated but it was good Cecil blushing lied to himself. If it wasn't me a close friend anyway. Someone took a picture, and though I admit the likeness isn't great, it could be me.

Cecil heard a pig rooting in the narrow companionway where he stood, but when rumbles grew louder and closer and still no fat back in sight, Cecil realized he was hungry.

This here narrow boat carries goats not pig iron he heard Leadbelly explain to the tickee man. Horizon still hid in mist. No green African hills or giraffes visible to Cecil's straining eyes. Algeciras to Ceuta. Someone, a wronged Jew I seem to recall, left the gates open one night to Tarik the Moor, and his band of merry hawks. A bridge here Alexander commanded but ferryman's union stymied the erection which grew no further than huge stones stacked in either edge of the strait. Still to be seen on a clear day when the sea is low. But Cecil saw nothing. Neither weeping Alexander, nor Ilyan weeping in rage, nor the daughter of that wronged Lord of Ceuta weeping in shame, nor Roderic villain weeping for joy while nuzzling his weeper into fat thighs of the Jew's daughter. Cecil heard only gulls scolding and pigs grunting and old wood groan and fart under his feet.

Anisse looked different with her clothes on. Cecil would have preferred that if she had to dress at all, she dressed like a man rather than try to disguise broad, square shoulders, flat chest and backsides beneath the most outrageously feminine frills and flounces. If there was any canon of beauty which vaguely complimented Anisse's physical attributes, Cecil felt it had to be found in plane geometry. Atop Anisse his fantasies had been of surf boards, of sleds, of unknotted pine slats, of flat, honed surfaces scudding his prostate bones. Freckles for breasts, a squared valley between her jutting hipbones. Cecil wanted to sand her. Finish smoothing the tabletop where ribs made slight indentations, and plane away lumps on either side of the navel. Anisse redolent of mothballs and gin raises high one straight ankle and slips boot through the first rail. Like the sea her inner thigh is blue veined. Cecil turns out the light and God is merciful. The flaunted thigh, young again in darkness, shies from its mate till compass spreads to an angle of eighty-four degrees. Limber at last, the forked tongue engages Cecil in earnest conversation.

–I grow old, I grow old, should I eat my sausage rolled or pat it into patties.

Cecil tries to remember how to answer a question. The process is too difficult. Better if I just keep quiet and listen.

–I thought one day I would just stop. You know what I mean. Just have no more urge. The natural conclusion of a natural process. I hoped that as I lost all power to attract, I would no longer be attracted to attracting. But Rome wasn't crushed in a day; it fell into gradual disrepair. And I despaired over regretting over loss over obsolescence over gyres that cycled me phased me out. I feared a rocking chair, a porch on long summer evenings alone, I feared drool and difficult bowels, despair. . . .

She is not flirting—she is climbing the rail. Cecil stirred from reverie fuzzily considers the possibility of action. A board balanced on its edge, she has been swaying there an hour. The boa goes. She goes. Cecil squeals barely audible above the wind, *Stop, don't jump,* but Anisse is already shriveling from sea cold. Cecil, too, is suddenly salty-eyed as he dreams of Anisse sea changed, scaly and supple-tailed, of hair growing and her chicken voice gone to pure nightingale. Anisse rock candy calling over the sea come and get it.

There is no Africa. Only curtain mist and sea split by prow. Cecil is afraid to approach the rail. A tiny man with a big mouth screams *Man overboard. Man overboard,* inside Cecil's chest. Through the spiraling echoes a pig roots for food. Cecil will not release the voice because Cecil knows, in spite of her freckles and plains, Anisse is not a man but a woman, and in spite of the fact that she is a woman, she doesn't want to dance at the end of any more hooks.

Salt sea. Smell of vinegared privates floating in brine.

Metal sea stairs narrow and unsteady Cecil winds from upper to middle deck and into the ship's bar. He is tired of waiting for Africa, for gulls to speak. He is asked for a cigarette. No burnoose but Arab nevertheless who is close to Cecil's face and whose smoke lightly expelled is a warm shadow on Cecil's cheek. I am taller than the Arab and I speak better English. Cecil nods as the man puffs and emits English in a throaty, French-spotted phlegm of regrets, losses, orotund hopes. He is the prodigal returning; he will be welcomed, understood, loved, be a man again. The Arab explains how cold the foreigners were and how greedy. The back of an Arab hand wipes an Arab nose. Cecil's brandy comes and for a moment he believes they are sinking, that sea crawls darkly over the portholes. A lurch makes glass tinkle against his teeth. My teeth are better than his. The Arab has been away many years, but still he knows a man who does wonderful things with foreign currency, who does not exchange but multiplies dollars, pounds, and French francs into stacks of Moroccan dirhams. Just give him my name. Do not trust the others. They are robbers, cold, greedy.

Another cigarette, tent folds, and Arab glides away. Son of Allah. Of Africa too, but I seek the black kings. Andalus. Ilyan smiling promised Roderic: *I will never feel satisfied until I bring thee such hawks as thou never sawest in thy life.* Tarik avenger came giving his name to a rock. A country with delightful valleys and fertile lands, rich, watered by many large rivers and abounding in springs of sweetest water. Lime trees, lemon trees, and most of the fruits of earth grow in all seasons, and the crops succeed one another without interruption.

Some say it is a triangle of land. Some say it is the tail of a bird, a peacock's tail lush-eyed and brilliant. Others are silent upon the matter, but spread themselves darkly over the land building mighty towers, abstract, geometrical forms within whose ramparts there are gardens and vaulted ceilings of crystal. The land provides and we straddle it as we do our horses, our women.

So Cecil crosses the sea to see where it all came from. He has cleansed himself. Expiated his sins by committing fornication within the dry husk of an old woman. He has promised to wash his hands and feet, to cry out impurities from his eyes before he touches the African soil. If it were allowed, he would plant himself in the sand. Stand like a flag that claims possession, satisfied to be forever possessed. I am part of it. It is part of me. The closer I draw, I realize how impossible all else was, how all that past melts like a wax casing as I am nearer and nearer the flame.

When I left this land, I rode a white horse, my beard was thick and my sword studded with jewels. Then I was a doctor; I looked to the stars and learned all manner of things of mind and body, but with the rest I remembered fear. Then I took to tinkering. I made swords and countless, ingenious toys. Though I built on a larger scale at times, I began to keep a garden and learned to cook. *Matamoros* came on a white horse and pitched me from the land. I was herded into ships which my blood propelled, and I was sold as chattel in another world. I had no garden and after their rutting time even my women laughed. I worked harder than I should have just so I could sleep. In the end I learned to sleep while awake. They called me night.

Sea sways, curdling where ship slices its wound across the strait. Algeciras to Ceuta. Iago matador goads the black bull. The moment has come, and somehow the silence of the vast crowd, the sudden intensity of the sun leaning closer to the arena, the light glinting from specks of blood dotting the pink sand, the matador's conspiring smile inform even the bull of the moment's arrival. Toro knows. He would bellow, but the sword is too close, too real. Under the sun he is wax melting.

Felipe Segundo. A religious fanatic. A collector of Bosch. A moralist who kept the Tabletop of the Seven Deadly Sins in his bedroom. A king of Andalus, the Netherlands, and the New World. A brandy to the waiter who served Cecil and knew none of these things. *Cinco pesetas.* Down the mothering hatch. Mouth not eyes the soul hole. Word made flesh made liquid made Cecil's guts cringe as gulping all three ounces he hurriedly secreted one more revelation. El Moro. Sons of hambone where you been? To a bar-b-que. Pig bones roasted and toasted, juicified with hot mustard ketchup pepper salt tabasco sugar onion pickle soul sauce. I got the shit all over my white shirt and under my fingernails.

—So this cat said to me *Work in your garden.* Well you know what I told the mother. You know where I told the Malcolm Frazer to go.

—So this big, tough-looking fag jumped up from the table and just like he was in full drag leans over and in a high, squeaky voice says if you don't like it, you can kiss my pussy.

Soul hole. Cecil would find a job in Constance Beauty's straightening parlor. Cecil would make it. Jive his way through one set of real and one set of false teeth. Cecil had been a singer, a dancer, a cop. Cecil had bootlegged and pushed shit, played a little semi-pro basketball and baseball, even got to Florida one year with the Dodgers before a near fatal indiscretion with one lighter and brighter than himself almost ended all careers. Cecil had been a bank clerk, a high school teacher, and had sold Watkin's products before finally finding the law. They had just laid the cornerstone of that new office so long in coming when Cecil retired from the service of the Lord. Justice.

—No, I don't know much about hairdressing, Miss Constance, but I have good hands and a strong mind and I'm willing to learn.

–Well it coulda been worse, Sister Esther. He coulda started workin for Process Pete where all them sissies and hoodlums go.

The narrow ship plies backward and forward relentlessly. Duty free so Cecil took a bottle for himself and remounted the corkscrew twists of staircase. Clearer now. Veins of blue wider in the sea. At first blinking in the sunlight and spray Cecil couldn't decide whether Africa rolled across the horizon or was just some cloud of fog and mist being pushed seaward from the land. Behind him Spain and Europe had disappeared. From the bow white water churned outward in undulating waves. As sky brightened the sea became a tabletop crowded with glistening crystal and silver. Cecil hadn't asked her to come and for each other they hadn't done much, but in a sudden surge of sensibility and regret, after tilting it to his lips, he tossed overboard the half empty bottle of Felipe Segundo and hoped the sea would carry it in the right direction.

THREE
· · · · · · ·

. . . We consist of everything the world consists of, each of us,
and just as our body contains the genealogical table of evolutions
as far back as the fish and even much further, so we bear
everything in our soul that once was alive in the soul of men.
Every god and devil that ever existed . . .

—Hermann Hesse
DEMIAN

WITH THE AID OF A POCKETBOOK EDITION OF Webster's *New World Dictionary* Esther Braithwaite began her memoirs:

All alibis are anonymous. Any act allows arbitration among antagonists. After admitting accidents, amorality advances. An axiom assures acquittal although adversity attacks antecedents. Africa awaits. Before babies babble battles begin. Boiling blood builds bastions. Battering behemoths besiege bulwarks. Brawling bunches board boats. Cruisers, canoes, corsairs, clippers carry crowds. Crazed children cry continually, cough catarrh. Caesar ceases cutting cheese. Decrees: Denizens destroy. Deserters die. Dissenting dregs, drab, dirty, disgust diligent dissuaders. Do dwarfs dare deceive? Everyone endures education. Eager egos elucidate entire etymologies. Empty. Easy essays enslave. Electricity emits energy, earnestness enacts ennui. Encourage excitement. Everybody errs even famous fakers. From freedom fear forms. Foolishness. Forget free food. Forge felicity's formulas. Freeze flippancy. Fallacious fanfares, fragile faiths fashion fearful foment. Feral fecundity forever.

Gabriel, God's gadfly, gaily goaded good genitals. Geriatrics germinate gelded gifts. Gethsemane's ghostly gestation gores gizzards. Gravestone grass grows greedier gazes greenly, grinning gulps gristle. Guillotine gypsies. Harass heathens. Here Heaven hurts, Hell helps. Hurry home, hurry home.

Esther sought the word from Alpha to Omega. Cecil's last chance rested in her hands, but her hands were palsied by ignorance of the word. Cecil must be a saint, join her in the posthumous fire dance or at least that's how she saw what the poet had called fiery, angelic consummation. The death of Cecil in some faraway land had to be put in the proper light, illuminated as the selfless sacrifice of a saint in his foreign mission. Oh Cecil, why did you do it.

Esther practiced. She grew to love the dictionary, and each word was something to fondle and caress, a new life that came into existence when she had copied it out, memorized its meaning, and could add it to the litanies she chanted each night in her bed.

liberal: 1. generous   2. ample; abundant   3. not literal or strict   4. tolerant; broadminded   5. favoring reform or progress. *n.* one who favors reform or progress.

liberal arts: literature, philosophy, language, history, etc., as courses of study.

liberality: 1. generosity   2. broad-mindedness.

liberalize: to make or become liberal.

liberate: to release from slavery, enemy occupation, etc.

Liberia: a country on the West coast of Africa founded by freed U.S. Negro slaves: area, 43,000 sq. mi.; pop. 1,600,000.

libertine: a man who is sexually promiscuous.

liberty: 1. freedom from slavery, captivity, etc.   2. a particular right, freedom, etc.   3. *usually pl.* excessive freedom or familiarity.   4. leave given to a sailor to go ashore.

libidinous: lustful, lascivious.

libido: 1. the sexual urge   2. *in psychoanalysis,* psychic energy generally: force behind all human action.

libra: (L. a balance, pair of scales), the seventh sign of the zodiac.

Style was another problem. Solved by the simple expedient of finding the proper word for the proper place. Esther studied the meaning of *proper* and the meaning of all the words in its definition quite carefully. She even began to study the words used in the definitions of the words that had defined proper, but she stopped because she believed by then that she had learned the meaning of proper.

On the morning of October first, her pen still shaking, but her determination unflinching before her awesome task, Esther began the canonization of her lost husband.

They say love is a many-splendored thing and my Cecil, son of Zion that he was, splendiforated the bounteous goodies of his loving heart universal. He has been in Your service, dear Father, since that first day his eyes opened and his cute, hairy bottom was slapped by good Dr. Stebbins who wore thick glasses and has loved colored people for longer than any of us can remember. He may be departed by now, bless his soul, but it seems proper and fitting such a fine white man and educated to do the medication of the lives of God's children should bring into being Your servant, Braithwaite christened Cecil Otis that long ago but doesn't really seem so day of October 2, 1933.

He was healthy and refined. Such a child that comes but once into the world to parents couldn't help but edify the indulgence and wonder of Mr. and Mrs. Braithwaite. Cecil came late in their union but You move in ways beknownst to Yourself alone so they asked no questions just demonstrated their gratefulness by the tedious care lavished on that crown to their aged heads. Being advanced in age I suppose they could not easily descend to that proliferating, childish world of their only begotten son. Perhaps here began that endemic trait so significant about Cecil and all saints who must find their own lonely paths through life far from beaten tracks and madding crowds. With his milk (not mother's for the paps of Mrs. Braithwaite had long before gone out of production, but formula made from condensed Carnation milk) the infant Cecil must have imbibed the chill of older lives on the gentle downslope along with those childish dreams that have characterized him since. Faunlike, unresolved, Cecil must have felt that languor of being two so well epitomized in the French by the poet. Half-playful boy, half-goatish old man fearing for his powers but with still something left neither he nor I am, was or will be quite sure of.

I find this section of Your servant's life entangled with skeins of my own eden of early existence. I am tempted even here to anticipate that twined destiny You ordained in Your all-seeing wisdom. I was one of many, but I, too, was a child of old age born twelfth and last to a humble preacher and his second wife. I struggled to orient myself between two worlds, and not seeing the light took on the prancing, coltish ways of the children because beneath the somber black coat of my father, and behind those stiff shirt fronts ironed hard by my mother I did not sense the infinite music of Your presence. They were good people as You well know, and I am only sorry I do not have that choice again, a chance to walk with those good old people today. And so You saw fit to use the same mold twice, shaped my clay and Cecil's with the pattern of Your fond intentions.

I am distressed when I find how little I know of these early days of Cecil's voyaging in the world. From what reports and witnesses I can gather he was on the surface then just as he was till the last moments to eyes not privy to the secrets of Your grand designs—ordinary. But there is a *look*, an almost imperceptible aura of being in the world but not of the world which radiates its effulgence like a halo to other initiates. In my despondency, in the weakness of my flesh, it was to this ghostly radiance that I looked. I would watch him sleeping, pine away in my secret bowels for his touch, for a word. But in the time of my direst need, when I feared my blood would burst its fragile walls, Your presence would be made manifest, and that oh so precious, that worth waiting for an eternity better part of him would upbraid and calm my spirits. Showers of golden honey would inundate me to restore sweetness and tenderness, and I would dream incense dreams so real that the fragrance of frankincense and myrrh would seem to cling to my fingers when I awoke in the mornings.

How sweet it is to be loved by You. And Cecil knew it Father. For You he crossed perilous seas, for you he went seeking untended flocks in a hostile world. He was a brave man. When I told the others where he was gone and why he went, they were not surprised. I thank You for preparing, unknown to them, that corner of their hearts where they know all things are possible with belief. Cecil had been a man among men, he had raised himself high in the world's esteem, but little did they know, and I must confess I, too, did not guess how distant from the exalted glory of his true vocation this worldly success had left him. Though he was only the second of his race to finish the law school, that brilliance he displayed, that ability to outshine the best white men was only humble preparation, toiling in the field which barely tested his greatness. His soul still slumbered, not even dreaming of its trial, of its strength.

That morning I found him gone I confess I was a woman, Father, the most forlorn, pitiable creature in Your wide dominions, a frightened, grieved woman alone. I cried and prayed, beat my head against the floor in futile rants. I was lost to the wisdom of Your ways. Uncomprehending I wanted the time of my need to be Your time to move, to grant my desires. But all things, the best things must come to pass in Your own good time. I was Job demanding and you chastened me. You who took Your son from us in spite of all the good women kneeling at his torn feet. I shook the filth of a puny, sinning fist in the face of Your benignity and compassion. And after the horror came to me I curled my body like an unborn child on the hard floor, trembling because I expected Your wrath, because I had lost sight for a second of the cherished presence of You which had sustained all that I could call life in my body for so many years. I had cried and cursed because Cecil didn't come back. Because I knew that door would never open unless I went to it and turned the knob. I was a little girl on that floor, Father, till Your infinite, divine mercy lifted me and restored what I did not deserve. Cecil's halo, that better part of him made a brand in my soul.

The building of Your Kingdom on earth is like the gentle lapping of the sea against the shore. Souls of men are those almost invisible motes of silt carried to the land with each fluid caress of the waters. Many are delivered by the sea and rest for a moment till that unresistible force which brought them jerks them away. But some, Father, blessed with Your grace, are deposited and stay. To anybody looking all them grains look alike that the water brings in. But some are chosen and lo and behold in Your good time a golden beach stretches brighter than the sun. So Cecil dropped unnoticed. Had his moment with the others. But now all eyes through my humble efforts and the magnificence of Your design shall see him in the true blazing light of his sainthood.

It is no easy road, and it is no accident that some are picked. They used to play ball, all the boys in the neighborhood on Sundays would go to a clearing in the woods, behind where the old sawmill used to be and play baseball with their shirts off. Girls being girls would follow the boys down there behind that shell of sawmill and sit like they was interested in who was going to win. Some of the bigger boys was heroes and always hit the ball clean to the high weeds and could have gone around the bases seven times with their sweaty chests poked out like roosters cock-a-doodling but in those games everybody won. Cause when they were finished some went to swim in the crick and wasn't one swimming suit among that whole mixed bunch that went so you can imagine what kind of swimming those sweaty boys and shameless hussies did. The others weren't no better. Taking their business private into where the strong boys hit the long balls or finding corners in that ruined sawmill or its wrecked out buildings. And it was the Sabbath to top all. I know it is hard to see such a Sodom as educationary for a saint, but there I was one Sunday the first time I snuck to see for myself what I could never get to learn much about from the other girls before one would giggle and blush then all of them giggling and blood high in their cheeks so many hens cackling before they got much past saying *well we watch 'em play* before one would start up.

Wickedness was rampant when I arrived. No innocent ball game ever because there on what they called home base where one stood with his big stick a flaming box that looked familiar burned. Excuse the expression but it was a box of sanitary napkins right out in broad daylight flaming for all that mixed crowd to see and nobody enjoyed it more than those giggling girls, backs just out of church clothes that must still be warm in a closet or across a chair where most of them sloppy hussies probably throw theirs. I was shocked, but like a new fish I had no better sense than to leap for the naked line. There I was almost comfortable in a few minutes, laughing with the rest and waiting my turn on the nasty cigar the boys had made.

Then He came and got me. Your militant Angel Michael with his wings high on his back overshadowing us all. My good Daddy in black and starched white with his hackles risen high as I ever seen them round his tight collar. He was that avenging angel snatched me round my bare arm from the midst of sin. He roared like some mighty bear or lion. Before his wrath even the most shameless scattered, goats and sheep alike tramping on one another to get out his way.

And his hard hand on my bare arm gripped tight and hot like Your word grasps my heart. I cried out not in agony I know now, but in understanding, the hurtful recognition of Your strait and narrow path.

He switched me. I felt the air and sunlight rush real fast up between my naked legs, and knew ankle to bloomer, they were exposed to the world. Though it seemed his hand still deep in the flesh of my arm, it was underneath the new red skirt and my two best slips clearing a path for his serpent switch to chastise my loins. I tried to run, but stopped when I heard everything ripping away. If skirt and slips came away I knew his hand would be free to rip away that last cotton between my shame and the world. It was like everything hushed. His roaring, the trees, the sky, the ground I wanted to open and hide me from the others. Just that switch whistling and me sighing too scared yet to cry or scream each time it bit the backs of my bare legs. Not even tears to comfort me. I just stood there in the red, hot pit of sin, stood till I felt myself sagging in the middle and had to go down like an animal on my hands and knees in that field. And when the devil came wretching up from my insides, Daddy pulled the skirt and slips down over my hips, helped me to my feet and let me lean on his hard body till we was home again.

Thorn and blossom, Father, both teach the meaning of the rose. And if the instrument of Your knowledge must blister the flesh, surely it is better received here in earthly fires and in a time that has beginning and end.

Whenever Cecil raised his hand to me it was as Your instrument. I had caused him to sin, to make profane vows. Even in the hours of his darkness Cecil could perceive the load of sin he gathered unto himself, that weight which grown tenfold he would one day have to remove with raw and bleeding hands. As You forgave me my weakness I forgave him the lash, the blows, those hateful, bitter words. On my knees while I earned the pittance which kept life together for us. I prayed each night that he would be delivered from those harsh, secret burdens my love could not remove. I wanted so much for him to move with joyous strength, upright, untrammeled vigor as a true pilgrim fulfilled his tasks and journeys. But the cleansing of his soul rested in Your miraculous hands. I was Martha, going the way of deeds. I always thought of my reward in terms of Cecil's success, in the maturing of my love whether it was returned or not. I asked for no promises. I lived with him as helpmate, as wife, never asking more than the knowledge in my soul that I was achieving Your appointed task, though my duty took me along darksome, unfrequented paths. I knew what some called me. It was difficult and trying at times. There were those who were affronted when I sat beside them in church. I was called harlot, fool. I did not explain to them. You chose a blind man, a whore, even the dead to illuminate your mysteries. My worldly life was public and misunderstood; my life in You was for myself. And Cecil.

But he was a scoffer. I almost smile when I think upon the breadth of Your mystery. How sweet it is. I feared for Cecil's soul, even felt my belief threatened by his blasphemy. I forgot the unfathomable limits of Your mercy, Your redemption that can pluck a sinner from the very jaws of Hell's mouth. Never, never too late. There is no time where You move. Even with his hand an inch from the doorknob, Cecil did not know it was You who called from the other side.

Promises to keep, the fruit You planted in my womb was an earthly promise. Cecil said he wanted that son, that our union needed no blessing but that child. And when I carried him, Cecil ministered to me the way he must have tended Your faraway flock before You in Your wisdom called him to Your side. He was gentle, knowing, cared only for those parts of himself which could somehow enter into my needs. I had only to ask and he gave. I knew the love of one of Your saints. Not for myself, but for the life I carried I asked Cecil for a name. Like the promise in my womb, the promise of a name was given. Two names in fact given to the child yet unborn who Cecil knew would be a boy. Simon Braithwaite. But then You took him. Born and died too soon, prematurely without stock for this world. A pure soul spiraling back to its Creator before even earthly love could soil it. We mourned. The day of our intended marriage passed. Cecil did not speak, barely moved from my bed. Then still with no sign of life beyond the immediate motions of arms, legs, and hands that moved him from place to place, he went back to the law school and his dormitory room, promising he would return and marry me when he had finished.

He did. I remember how strange it was to be with him again. It had been nearly two months since I had seen him. I did his work in the building as best I could, as I do it now to keep this poor roof over Fanny's head and mine. With my arm locked in his as we walked down the aisle, he felt no closer, no more real than from my seat in the back of the auditorium; something not Cecil he had seemed marching in the long, black gown toward the platform where a tall man passed a ribboned scroll into his hand. A long day and I was wet beneath my dress. I wore the same white all day. No fancy bridal gown, but a saint's white cotton I had sewed myself simple and cleanly over the silk slip I saved so long. He remained a stranger when we got back to where we stayed. I had cleaned everything. New sheets, a new picture on the wall, one of the old Italian ones I knew he liked. It was Jesus at the foot of the cross. I knew he would like it because once in a church where we went to hear music he had pointed it out. Said he tried to draw it once himself. But he didn't even see the picture I don't think, and I was so tired I just couldn't sit up with him no longer, just sitting saying nothing in the black suit. He made me think of the dead child and his staring not seeing anything just made me more tired than I already was so I pulled my robe over the new slip and lay down on the cold, new sheets and went to sleep.

He must have turned off the light before he left because I remember just before falling into sleep a red wall like a sheet of flame close up against my eyes. It's like that when you have to shut your eyes against light while you're going to sleep. But it was dark when I woke up alone. Blind shut, door shut, light out.

I dreamed he touched me. I dreamed unmaiden dreams of wind in my hair and against my thighs. I was in water and Cecil from nowhere like a hawk plummets through the air, I saw a dark cliff where he leaped from and he was a bullet about to slam into where I was floating and I knew the spray would dazzle, would burst and make ripples and circles and flowers in the water.

He snatched me, Father, from the brink of perdition. I knew then he was Yours. That Your love would not deny what should be mine. I find I falter, Father. I find the words are not proper. I am a dark spot of ignorance in Your luminous world. I forgive him, Father, forgive him, I am wholly Yours. I ask only to be brought to rest as he is resting against Your bosom. Sometimes I hear his voice. Sometimes it says I am coming, wait. Sometimes it calls me to find him, come to him. I am at times desolate. I find myself again prostrate on the hard floor. But doubt does not throw me down, doubt does not send me to my hands and knees. I want to go down even farther, I want to crawl through the dark earth for you, Father. Forgive. Batter my heart. He died for You, in Your service. For You, for me he did it.

They are singing tonight. When the song is over I will testify to Your goodness and grace. I will tell them how

Cecil served, how he served to the limit of his strength, gave what only saints can give. Do not renounce him. Let them hear my fervor, my words. He is in Your hands, Your hands.

ESTHER BRAITHWAITE

April 19, 1967

What you gonna do when death comes creepin' in your room. The song was a funeral chant, same words repeatedly dragged over a slow, heavily accented rhythm. Words moaned, slurred, stretched so that the beats of the melody thumped with the relentless, painful irregularity of a cripple weaving his way home along a dark alley. Esther found a seat in the rear of the gospel tent. Against the mournful cadences an electric guitar twanged some message of its own. Ridicule, resignation, either the urgent thrusts of a soul being born in spite of everything or the futile challenges of a spirit already on its knees.

THE JOURNAL

March 2 "And did you see the island which is inhabited by men whose heads grow beneath their shoulders. A friend of mine once described it to me." Is he afterall as mad as I want him to be. My Uncle Otis and myself. How many times have I tried to ascertain once and for all the definite point at which his madness begins and the fence rises which is the bulwark of my sanity. He of all people to be the first to whom I spoke. I returned from another country and hoped to find something familiar in him. Was I looking for myself, a mirror.

March 3 It appears that I will be able to remain. It has been almost a year. Not even church brings Esther here. Nothing will take me back to her world, to the Banbury Arms.

March 5 The time is six in the evening. The sky is salmon pink. Birds browse above the threadbare sleeve of river. I can see the melting silhouette of a barge being pushed by a tug. Can they find the sea from here, can they walk on water till the other side of the earth. I am the pied peeker issuing a proclamation. It is safe here for no one listens, there will be no temptation to follow. The sky is salmon. A glob of silver and blood flecked flesh squirms to be liberated. Once, twice, a thousand dashes of its sharp snout against the unexpected rock that glistens blackly in the stream. And it flops weakly till stunned, only its tail quivers, butterfly wings weighed finally by a gush of current, then moving only because the water moves. I am afraid to walk on the water. Of the pale, floating condoms that may still carry life.

Esther was with me when I climbed the stairs to the top of the monument. Oh say can you see. She giggled and spun round full breasts that buffeted my chest light yet full so full I had to press all of her into my arms. Consuming, losing that sight of myself, of the city, of her strong shoulders and the billowing dress she shouldn't have been wearing. We looked down together, side by side, and I asked her if she needed my eyes too, so much to see she smiled and closed both hers saying no you take mine and tell me what we see.

Dinner on the town. Night and getting chilly but we still roamed at home in the city's heart, its steep sided glare scooped out of the darkness. Put your hand in mine. Whistle. We bought a bottle of wine against some future thirst, walking till her feet hurt and my thighs heavy. Bridges. I think we crossed several, over water, buildings, streams of headlights chasing each other. Trees and a place to walk soft under foot; bridge now arching like a roof above spreading the quiet of its shadow so no one could see us. Beer cans tinseled by moonlight, patches of trash that were snow tufts littering the ground.

Esther shivered in my arms. I stopped fumbling with buttons, the flimsy things beneath her spreading dress. No point in letting the night run up under her clothes, nor my hand part of night of the cold disturbing her reservoirs of peace and warmth. The bridge curved above. Traffic a sound distant but within like the roar of a shell clamped to the ears. She said it's warmer when we keep moving so we walked from the shadow toward the river, but though nothing seemed to stir, a chill breathed by the water floated out to meet us, wrapped around her thin calves and took her through the dress as if the flowered material was only another layer of bare skin. Arm around her firm shoulders I took a few steps away from where we had been, inching, edging along the metallic band of water that was not dimpled but sculpted by the diamond-cutting edge of moonlight. Toward the far dark trees, the heavy growth tangling into the water's edge where river turned and was lost. A few steps barely audible her breathing suddenly bird rapid and fragile as her body pressed more closely to mine. I tried to remember to forget, to talk above the night. It was Dowson that finally came in sputters and fragments my mind unable to focus clearly and my lips trembling so the words were painful to speak. Shivers passed between us indistinguishably mine or hers but I could not laugh as we both laughed when in bed naked belly to belly some ambiguous gut rumble oozed from our stillness. Night long in love and sleep she lay. Cynara. Surely, surely I have been faithful.

March 6 The darkness of the ceiling and the darkness of the floor rush to meet each other on the bright face of a wall. One shadow climbs, the other drops, and the colors of the wall disappear. Innocence is a sense of expectation, a belief that certain events will occur, events which are inseparable from personal needs and aspirations.

> I have spent my time
> In pursuit of a fast happiness
> Chasing springs I have never seen
> All those springs happening before me
> Because I was young.

It doesn't matter what we accumulate, eventually it takes on a sentimental value. Is it because we know we must die alone, amid things? Newspaper reminisces over a seeker, an innocent:

"I remember a gentle dreamy young man who started out on the theory (common to schizophrenics) that he had a divine mission to save the world—it's never clear what from. But first a female soul had to come down from God and unite with his soul. There was no sign of this happening, so he liberated one himself, very neatly, with a carving knife."

For the innocent, desire and attainment have not become separate ideas; he feels there is no need to qualify his wish. Until a man has gotten up from the bed of his love-making, pulled off a contraceptive, washed his penis and flushed the whole wet glob of his seed down a toilet, many ideas about copulation can exist that this afterlude banishes forever. The morning after, the moment when flesh parts and there is remorse, sometimes panic. It's different then to wish for love again. Some people forget quicker than others. Some never forget. Rilke good on the instant of separation. How it is difficult to believe anything has happened.

March 8 The Cobra Room. I have been here before. Too familiar too soon. The music, the faithful languid round the magic circle. Lights go on in mirrors, twist around the glass rims. My name is wanderer, seeker. Agamemnon of the whittled host. To my lips soliloquy rises then falls, whispers then lisps in silent, faultless frustration. I am a discard of my mother. Something she grew inside herself and lost in a grunt. Heave ho. The hatch is down, the wave is on the rock, the music is a lullaby. The bar man watches either pleased or annoyed I cannot tell what if anything plays across thick lips, through the eyes that are cat yellow and opaque. Of course I will have another. The season is upon us. April in Paris.

March 9 Sometimes I am very sorry for what I have done. There are times, less numerous, when I am not certain what I have done and why I should be sorry. Leaving Esther and the rest, betraying the people whom I have loved. Or what love meant to them.

March 10 Uncle Otis had told the story this way: Ilyan (some say he was a Jew) was governor of Ceuta, faithful vassal to the mighty Lord Roderic. Ilyan's charge was the keeping of the gate; he guarded the very navel of Roderic's dominions. Poised where he was between east and west Ilyan received tribute on his island bastion from both the sleek, dark horsemen of Africa and the sumptuous envoys from Roderic, though remaining unswervingly loyal to his master. In fact Ilyan's allegiance was a legend men swore by.

Fly in the pie. Ilyan had a beautiful daughter, soft-thighed, innocent pride of her father's eye. Ilyan hoped humbly, but with a sense of the gratitude owed him, that his master would take into his court as handmaiden to the queen the daughter so loved and doted upon yet willingly sacrificed if for her ultimate benefit a lasting union could be achieved with one of the noblemen who formed the king's glittering circle. With overwhelming cordiality but pleading with regret the cumbersome official maneuvering that necessarily surrounded such an undertaking Roderic acknowledged his vassal's request and the matter seemed destined to rest forever in the stagnant swamp of court bureaucracy till Ilyan, infatuated with his scheme and almost desperate with fear that the ripe beauty of his virgin daughter would fade unnoticed and unadorned, journeyed with the maiden to the court on a contrived mission there to let all eyes see his only child's nobility, grace and irresistible beauty. Her appearance in court did what the decades of service and imploring letters to his master had not accomplished. Soul warmed by an inner glowing light and his daughter left under the protection of the king, the faithful governor returned to his rocky island.

In less than a year the arduous journey was repeated. Into his arms the old man took what remained of the fair girl-woman, weeping as she told her sorrow, her dishonor, of the bloom gone never to return. The king welcomed his servant, ravished him with delights of the court, called his loyalty solid as the rock in his trust and publicly put his arm around his vassal's stooped shoulders. Swallowing the black bitterness Ilyan smiled at the peacocks and birds of paradise fluttering around him. He copiously thanked his host, repledged his vassal's oath and as if blind to her red eyes and swelling body took his daughter and bowing returned to the east. But not before, in the height of merry-making, promising an exotic gift as a small token of his gratitude for the king's welcome. Knowing Roderic's and hence the court's passion for the hunt, Ilyan promised to the revelers *hawks such as they'd never seen.*

There were meetings. His gates were opened and from the east those swift, hawklike men sped into the soft underbelly of Roderic's land. Their thrust was headlong, irresistible, and up and down the ravaged countryside widows and virgins wailed echoing the sound of his daughter's shame, a sound Ilyan had not been able to drive from his ears. Tarik leader of the dark horsemen who gave his name to the betrayed rock between east and west could not understand why Ilyan wept when messengers returned with joyous tidings of victory. Afterall the old governor had offered the gates.

March 12 My hands have not changed their color. I still desire the concealed warmth of other bodies. How can I tell it then, measure face against face, compare the dark shapes: shadow to form. When I left I had no destination. Now I can say that to myself, return and retain that fact in my conscious mind. One suffers to learn. If it is the will of gods which makes things fall out and not the single stubbornness of each living man, then was it necessary to leave? Aren't all voyages redundant, superfluous. On the rented bench of the Paris park, cowering from the pigeons of Trafalgar Square what did I know which I had never known. The world is a small room inside me. No one enters, no one leaves.

March 12 I return to the museum where I met Webb, to the picture. I hear the water running, kiss of air driving the thin jets out of the circular pool. Splash of water returning to the pool's opaque center and rippling outward over the bright pebbled bottom to a border of black marble circling the fountain. Ceiling is high, octagon within octagon rising, trapping footsteps that resound against the marble floor. Eight walls, four doors, four black benches curving around the pool. One wall crowded almost by "Christ Carrying the Cross" which dwarfs two dimly colored paintings of Bosch that flank it. Neither is convincing, not the "Mocking of Christ" with its insect demons and flat gold background nor the "Adoration of the Magi" whose blubber-lipped black king is caught in a burlesque pout. Only one face haunts, Magus standing in carmine gown, the face of the prodigal returning, the vagabond peddler who has tarried and lost his shoe. Faint hint of a beard, of exhaustion around the eyes. Too many days on the road, in the wind, gazing after the chimerical star.

Water climbs and falls, ragged pinnacle of straining drops, then noisy as it troubles the marble basin. I do not think Webb touched me. Only his voice, solicitous, gentle, the promise to perform miracles greater than those hung on the eight walls. There should have been seven walls. I would build a room around a fountain, a lion spitting seven streams high in the air, the beast high on a pedestal whose form would be the smooth backs and graceful buttocks of seven buxom maidens. My king would roar his water magic in seven directions toward seven walls and on each wall the portrait of a sin. Not clustered small on a table top but spread floor to ceiling I would have mad Hieronymus do me Lust, Avarice, Gluttony, and the rest twisting round my fountain.

If you are very quiet and listen only to the water a stillness comes over this marble room. It is a monument, a sepulcher for those bones forgetful of the illusion of flesh. Hard, black benches force admittance, kiss the ischia as in some persistent buggering embrace. The room is full of guilt. Of the sound of urinals constantly, futilely flushed against corruption. He said suffer to learn, he said suffer to lean, walk across the water.

So on that day when it should have still been Esther my new wife on my arm and the sunlight on broad stairs and boulevards and columns I stepped instead acolyte to Webb's phantom lore across the void.

Rogier van der Weyden—"Christ on the Cross"; "The Virgin and St. John."

Gerald David—"Pietà."

Two St. Jeromes and a partridge in a pear tree.

March 14 Franz Fanon: *Wretched of the Earth*. He characterizes dreams of oppressed natives. Dreams are always of muscular prowess, of action, aggression. Counterpoint to behavior native must exhibit for colonial masters. In life, when awake he must be a tree, but night liberates. "I dream I am jumping, swimming, running, climbing. I dream I burst out laughing, that I span a river in one stride, or that I am followed by a flood of motor-cars which never catch up with me."

March 14 It happened a long time ago or at least it is far enough away that I feel it no longer. I think I was a young man in Spain. El Moro. The heat was white and stretched in wavering piles like snow. I could set the scene further . . . detail the music, wine . . . how the castle's geometric walls were sheer . . . the tableau of workmen, their berets, and rope belts, sound of bread chunks breaking, shrill birds fishing in pools of dark moss that floated the dilapidated walls . . . the way far below among the red roofs donkeys jingled past going nowhere. But I am uneasy, impatient at certain times of the year, the fall to be particular, beginning in September I cannot raise my spirits, see or celebrate. As if the fabric that holds moments together slowly begins to tear and disintegrate. Time becomes separate, disjointed fragments leading neither forward nor backward, isolated instants that wheel sickeningly in drunken, futile circles. A hawk wounded, dying. A voice calls *it is time, it is time, it is time,* but I am only the dream of myself and the voice strangles in its own reality.

Only a coincidence, but time is *emit* spelled backward.

March 19 There was a park near the law school in which I liked to walk. In the park were trees, grass, diles of sog phit, bare feet, pregnant ladies, benches, checkerboards, old men, a commemorative rock from the battlefield of Gettysburg, a basketball court, sliding boards, cracked cement walks, trees, benches, women who expose themselves when they sit, dogs being walked, the sound of surrounding traffic, black children running down, across, and up a steep-sided gulley in the park's center. At times Cecil was also there, especially when September was more than half finished and the cruelest month close enough to touch, to smell the deadening fumes in the air, to hear the dry hand worrying the trees.

Park of all my springtimes, park various as existence itself, the only way to go for Cecil in his premature, suffering moments. (Sometimes late at night, after the booze and talk among imminent lawyers, there would be a wooziness of exhaustion and floating languor that suddenly for a moment became still, quiet, and in that moment an inkling would come of what a better life could be, might be. The body is left behind. Something rises and surveys. Wisdom, affirmation, peace—all the blood running home in a brilliant tangle toward the sea. Corridors of time echo the black sound of a footfall. You are removed—full of dimension yet dimensionless. You are not measured, but the measure. No distinctions remain. You are accepted, full, filling. But that too was a parklet, an oasis those *sometimes* till human voices . . .) He named the trees after generals, didn't count the blades of grass but addressed them collectively as the multitude. His generals were impartially chosen from all nations, all times. Included because they had done other jobs in addition to generaling, were emperors, presidents, writers, a philosopher, even a homosexual proving that, taken as a group, generals are pretty much like the rest of us Cecil expressed to the multitude one day, but they only nodded.

Consolation was when shuffling through the early dying leaves a rustle could be sustained that held his thoughts high enough so he could see them, a gilded spider web strung against the sky. Remember how the corners of the windows near the steeple's top were molten for an instant. As if once more the glass had been born in fiery heat or was phoenix going home again. Then he had looked in an open window: dark, high-backed benches, stone walls, faint musk of old, damp tapestries hung too long away from the sun. Pipes of an organ. Walking faster while the glimpse entered him. He could have been caught peeking, asked to come in, embarrassed or embarrassing. So he tried to find the brazen images again. But light in the corners was gone, the metallic gray of dusk glazed them sightless. The fire had dropped lower, suffused to brilliant, unexpected patches at rooftop level and along fences, in the chrome of automobiles, or in blond halos insectlike hovering above dark forms. Thought was whistling old tunes, forgotten, truncated tunes, which were never completed because never more than half-learned. He could not whistle, nor recite the words of any entire song. It was melody decayed, enhanced, added to, subtracted from, multiplied or divided by other fragmentary gusts of music. He thinks in the darkness of thought, the complicity of his remembering and not remembering. He imagined speaking to Hannibal and Hannibal answered. Or he spoke to Hannibal and imagined the tree's response.

This park or rather parklet which Cecil enjoyed had no fountain. Statues (a verdurous Dickens being stared at imploringly by Little Nell), but no fountain. Paris parks are built around fountains and Cecil's one reservation about the park near the law school was because of water's absence and the absence of Universality which the presence of water guarantees.

Sometimes he wished the gulley would be inundated. He would warn all the black children, then help them off with their clothes so they would be ready to splash into the water after they had careened down the steep slope. But water still could be a problem. Insects, disease, the repulsive colors of stagnancy. The vision had really not been of a tiny lake, but of the sea. Of pot-bellied, large-headed, grinning pickaninnies galloping across hot sands and being taken by the salt sea. The grass is greener? What is sea green, sky blue? What are colored people? Wine dark sea?

The park was amusing when he was lonely. Either it or walks by himself (along the river front, through the city's eighteenth-century streets) or hunched in some theater seat hoping the camera slips that the censors slipped, that in one sublime frame the hair pubis will appear dark and tangled like the lowering forests beyond which barbarians live their rampaging lives. Time was when woman real, woman flesh private, obtainable over time at slight discount filled my nights. Not those fantasies orchestrated by snores, grunts, and wheezing silence of old men, starved men, with hands in their pockets or hands strayed to past time, time to come, prostitutes, substitutes, the stale familiarity of their own private parts when the getting was good. Getting better all the time I can walk among the trees, along quiet streets in strange neighborhoods. I can avoid the warm, yellow lure of other lives framed in unshaded windows. Walk, mind my own business. I must read Robbe-Grillet. His book about a voyeur. French movies, blue flicks, girlies, stags. When you've seen it all somehow the titillation ceases, there is something funny about the holething.

The young lawmen called her Briar Patch because of the abundance of curly pelt protecting her lower middle. A bush it was (and burning one of them revealed, blue ointment in hand). All of them agreed it was unique and after much consultation Cecil was summoned and permitted to judge and agree. In the darkened room he peeked beneath the shade across the fifteen feet or so that separated the law dormitory from the nurses' blindless windows. She was best seen from Carpenter's bedroom, and when the show began, he called the others to take their turns. Not only Briar

Patch but her roommates performed. Cecil laughed because the others did. Cecil went down on hands and knees because the others did.

March 20 Dante's Bellacqua, condemned in Purgatory to sit beside a rock and dream over his life forever. His punishment for sloth while he was living. Cecil as Bellacqua at the window? beneath the trees? beside the fountain? Now.

March 20 Nightmare. Early morning. Dampness, soft sucking earth. A thick tailed, heavy muzzled, gray dog. Tree like flame. Yellow leaves in the center, gradual deepening of color till leaves at periphery of tree's outline are flame red. Unnatural rapidity with which leaves fall. A multicolored, swirling snow. Movement of leaves gives form to the wind. Like hair blowing can be urgent, disdainful, flustered. Tangible motion, something that is swift, invisible being born. A shark's inevitable meandering that dramatizes the medium's presence.

March 24 It is spring, earth rendering spring again.

Morning April 19

So spring comes again.

> "Silent as a mirror is believed
> Realities plunge in silence by"

My journal is strangely blank at this season. I believe I was once accustomed to write poetry. Spring made a lyre of me.

When I get up it is birdsong and walls gleaming that should be but are not quite opaque to the sun. I know it shines, that the day brilliantly begins. I have plans, desires. Quickly as God is my witness I shall begin to undo what has been a winter of slothful discontent of faltering and hesitation. Urgent this need to be fated, to be hooked by the taut string.

If that is me staring back. I heard my feet pad, across the wooden floor. They must be large, fleshy. I always wear a T-shirt when I sleep, only when another's nakedness looms beside me do I strip away the last covering and even then I know where it is while we rub and romp and sweat and when we are still and either one or the other has cleaved and turned away I reach deftly for it to cover my sleep. An old pain, fear of night chills and stiffness. A physical fear of what it might be like to waken stark and unprotected, the ache too late to dread already inching through deep back muscles. To shiver and know it is too late. The fear is that which comes at the end of dreaming after the crime is irrevocable and I am a captive.

I cannot remember having the dream last night. Peace plundered. Perhaps changing as the seasons changed. No longer March dream of violence, rage. Have you held a life in your hands, twisted it, darkened it till something not life slumped from your fingers. Oceans of blood whipped by the moon and winds rush headlong to crash against the skull's echoing walls. The body lies there divided from me. It has been prepared: laved clean, suffused with the ripe glow of its own fullness. She is not beside me, not behind or in front of me nor lying motionless neck awry at my feet. Someone has combed her hair, demurely crossed her ankles and laid her hands softly along soft hips. More than ever the image beyond reckoning. I would crawl to her over seas of broken glass. More living than ever (how wind stirs the web of short, curly hairs) I know she is more alive than ever but I am caught and condemned, have been chased breathless and cannot speak while they say guilty of death till death do you part till death.

My big bare feet. Someday I want to meditate on my

body. I will study it, then logically divide the several king-doms. Write an elaborate description of each member. Toes, thighs, knees, fingers. Measure everything precisely, designate color, texture, even count the hairs, chart their relative frequency. I would leave a plan, a map. No, they will say, this one is not an undiscovered country. He did not lose himself in a futile chase after the seemings and changings of the mind. His record is a real one, his exploration valid. He knew himself and now we do too. Someday they may reconstruct me. Homo sapiens c. 1950 (extinct). This model based on writings of Braithwaite, Cecil O. pioneer in science of Self-Knowledge. When a coin dropped in the slot I become animated, immortal. I am programmed to act out their image of their swarming hotblooded ancestors. I am speaking a quaint English and my exaggerated, frantic movements are those of a nineteenth century Shakespearean actor.

From the mirror. If I am the pure form of myself, the super reality of me then how am I to treat you and the million forms you take. And do you diminish me. And when you are in her eyes is she killing me. In a crowd am I losing something invaluable, irreplaceable even in the stares that do not see. Gathered round me like a flock of ghosts. Imminent children of the imminent father. I am what.

You see

In the mirror

Returning do I create a mind looking back. You have a white T-shirt just like mine. Do you sleep in it always.

Hair grows after death. As do fingernails. Even after death to be shaved, manicured, pedicured as if something still depended on the living as if it does now. I have been tempted to grow a prophet's beard, to forsake soap and water. I am a cliché unto myself. Saying, doing the same things, the blood things I can disguise but not change. What was never thought and only poorly expressed. Sum of being.

Another said when it's poetry you cut yourself if thinking of it and shaving. O O O you Shagspearean rug cuddled round my chin. The storm, the hot gates, cold steel, warm steel, steel too hot *señor* you are about to burn.

> Roses are red
> Whiskers are blue
> Poetry's your face
> Looking at you.

Not bad for an im-prompt-too. I could rhyme forever, never ever lever sever fever. Eye rime. But this is bathtub shower shaving poetry. The kind calculated not to bite. Am I rite. You see when we are talking of things serious and wish to communicate I believe there should be rules to facilitate the message. I propose more silence, a quiet stretch after each speech as Cooper reported his Indians to observe at their council fires. I would propose that no one speak until he can rime his first line with the last line of the preceding speaker. i.e.:

> 1st speaker: And so I conclude.
>
> (*Pause*)
>
> 2nd speaker: Perhaps you wish to delude . . . is all I have to say.
>
> (*Pause*)
>
> 3rd speaker: I agree, but would put it this way . . . etc.

Etcetera. So it would go. The improvements in verbal discourse would be immediate and profound. First each speaker would have to listen closely to his predecessor in order to earn the right of reply. Secondly the pause would make him organize and ponder his reply. Third the spirit of poetry, wit, and repartee would preside over even the most traditionally pedantic and unimaginative occasions for speech. A new class of rhetoricians would grow up. Imagine the impact of a speaker in the Senate who could end a perfectly appropriate and reasonable argument for abolishing war with the word zebra. From such a context would arise the golden age of Philosopher-Poet Kings. Great men who could only be followed by silence or consent.

Steam rises. I see only shadows, lemur eyes lost in deep sockets. The flesh melting. But if I lose you, if you die, another, another will come. Steel is the temperature of my blood. It is congruous, her soft hand that caressing glides down my cheek, a finger traces the bottom curve of my chin, my throat.

You are so easy. I do not cringe, shy away. I have been waiting for you and now I kiss your finger that is crimson tipped.

Spring is all things blossoming. Sudden bosoms and bare legs, that corpse we planted last fall. All the young men who have learned to cower and die who have not learned to ask why they are dying, whose chests will be heavy with medals, ribbons, and flowers tropically lush and quick in the loam of gristle and blood. Spring before summer and summer sin heavy because we cannot forget. The chorus of Argive elders, ghosts of winter, snow clump preserved in the high shadow of a mountain we had not intended to climb. What is their foreboding what unseasonal talk of prophets long dead of omens fore-telling and fulfilled long ago. Certainly they did not expect all this to be gained without loss. Without sacrifice. They murmur as if they never knew someone must pay for spring. Each spring. All the time I suppose they thought it was the early dying ones, babies, young men. They grieved, they were assiduous in their lamentations, they made a song of mourning and dressed in dark, choral robes. As if they didn't know that would not be enough, as if all things did not have to suffer. As if they believed the suffering and sacrifice were over. But here it is spring again, all things relentlessly blooming and the elders wonder why they are not touched, not made whole, why roses do not blossom at their lapels. Why age does not drop away.

My face is smooth. Mexican hairless. My fingers draw blood wakes. Five knives slicing forehead to chin. How long do you want to live. Can you repeat yourself. If I carved ever so carefully, surgically flayed away one layer, what would I be. And if I lopped off an arm or a leg. My head?

You are the sum of parts. Some Cecil replaceable, others mysterious, inviolable if you are to remain whole Cecil. Chemistry of addition and subtraction. What became of Cecil in her eyes. The steam. *Give me your heart my love* must be looked on with even more suspicion than before. Discreet, vulnerable parts. The shame of obsolescence, the purring intimidation of better machines. I am a nest the young have flown. I am dry, the dull bits of me are carried off by the wind.

If the walls let in light then perhaps within me is not as I had imagined. Styx dark. Black capped waves restless lolling above the black sea invisible against the black sky. Years, millions of years of distance to be traversed, the black sun weeping on the black land. Perhaps instead the flesh is an infinitely subtle prism, perhaps the blood laps multicolored, multifaceted, jewels within a kaleidoscope. Perhaps I could live there, float on my back in warm amniotic waters quietly fascinated by the circus of lights.

It is the flesh, the body I fear for most. To be handled, to be molded like putty into a mask of repose, to have cosmetics applied to restore color, to be falsified, violated, shaved and washed and manicured even after I have lost the power to be ashamed, to decry, despise, cry, or laugh over the ritual. To have other hands do mechanically what I have done with agony and determination, because I saw the doer, what he must do. That meeting of eyes when mine do not secure his image. Coins on my eyelids. To be as powerless as a child who has his favorite toy taken away, the mirror taken away, the ghosts locked in the machine.

No poetry but anyway the blood blooming sudden buds on my upper lip. I am closer, magnified. I am watching the jet's shadow stumbling beneath me on brown plains. The shadow grows gradually less distinct, a blur, then nothing. Red ball of sun sucked in a matter of moments below the broad, flat plains. Patchwork, colorless quilt, monotony broken only by the irregular gashes of dark rivers and straight, shaved highway bands dissecting the dun and gray on which low clouds cast their illusory forests of shadow. (A square of toilet paper drinks the blood.) The land is mute, humble, acquiescent to the elaborate swirl of a partial cloverleaf, to the symmetry of baroque, concrete curves. My man's scarified skin magnified ten million times. Approaching Chicago. I have seen the epidermis pictured thusly. A patchwork desert of unimaginable, rutty distances. Ringworm of psoriasis twisting dramatically through the submissive tissue.

Blue in the distance. Am I hovering dead over the land. What is dying on the ground.

Carefully I clean my instrument. Beneath the glint of stainless a fringe of hair is obdurate, will not be dislodged by bursts of steaming water. I will not use my fingers in the dangerous slot. Already I am looking for blood spots on my grainy upper lip. I can see the Virgin where she always is, stony on a pedestal that leans her precariously toward the earth. She is white, or better, a dingy gray standing in someone's backyard. I have chased children from her. Their rocks had snubbed her nose so a buddha's profile stares vacantly at someone's back porch. I think she is lifesize. A boy had to reach up, to plant the fatigue hat over her cowl. A graceless, stubby virgin yet artistically placed among the high, rotting fences, spilled garbage and heathen weeds. I have seen the moon on her forehead. A white smile.

Hail Mary. I must remember to watch her when rain is falling. A gray day when the slants of rain are thick and distinct, when the water seems sent to cleanse. I could take a picture of the drowning Virgin, of her gray indifference. That would be before she ascended to the kingdom. In fact the precise instant before her trip when human all too human the deluge began and she without brolly or rubbers. Absence of rubbers (prophylactical contraceptacle as found in most dirty men's rooms) has been the bane to Virgins time out of mind. *Stabat mater dolorosa.*

Your hands along my cheeks. Take my face, mother, as if a prayer had suddenly dropped from heaven and wedged its thick way between your steepled hands.

Dogs, cats, and children go in and out of your shrine. The sky is a roof to your temple. I have seen you all hours of day and night but never have I seen you asleep nor ever preparations to disrobe, bathe, and lay you down in the cool weeds. It is your stony duty I suppose to remain as you are, weather the weather, flinch not from dog pee, cat pee, boy pee, or even those small hands that fondle your stony breasts for a second before they seek to topple you. The boy who brought the hat also moved his hands in and out of your stone robes. Adoration. Would you take a black lover.

Sweet Life. Sweet Simon son. Laid to rest one day of spring, invested in her silence in her flesh soil embedded was my son. I can dream of rivers of freshness, of sunshine holiday. Blue coming in at my window tells me all that season has not been forgotten. Charged blue like something glowing in a child's paintbox which he goes to first and spreads indiscriminately over the printed designs in his coloring book. Pretty, pretty blue.

But you would not recognize the color, the day. No seasons for my son. I am sad but perhaps at some level deeply relieved. There has been and will always be color. The last rot of the last man will be vaulted some season of its passing by blue. And warmth and snow in passing. Things that fall will kiss and cover, brush by and race the heap to oblivion. All this glory to the insensate, the putrifying last trace. So your eyes, your nose, your lips have missed no rarity. My son I couched you within her, November, and wish I could say the day, the hour, because I was desperate. You were not to be simply the glue between Esther and me; we needed no bond or perhaps knew no bond could hold us together if not that identity of will and blood we had become. No, you were to be something better. A contradiction I suppose to the way the earth seemed to be turning, to what I knew myself to be and all starving men to be. I wanted you to be full, complete, not a living hunger or a word written in the sea. I was oppressed. Three hundred years I had been stooping and dying, the life urge dribbling out obscene and curdled like white insides from a squashed bug. I could go no farther. Backward nor forward, neither side to side, just stand and dance in my chains, teeth showing not in joy but agony as my ankles were rubbed to slender, trembling roots ready to snap and end the jiggling dance forever. I studied the law.

All so simple. Someone always there to whisper *Cecil you are not real.* That is no body swaying but sunlight glancing from steel braces caught in the shimmering heat. Do not weep or moan. You are not there. You are not real. Smoke.

Cecil, let me tell you how it is. This girl, young pretty and white, she come up to me smellin' good, wearin' nice clothes, trying to smile. I want to help is what she said. Then all the sudden she got puffy pigeon breasted grew ten feet and sprouted these stiff gold tipped wings. So I begins to move a little closer but them wings start rustling, humming and glowing around her. She gets brighter and whiter and them blue eyes crackling so I freezes and stops thinking what I was thinking. Wonder where the white girl went.

And can you imagine asking someone to dance and actually dancing in a crowded ballroom when you are a black face and there are no other black faces in the world.

Well, to be short, simple, and to the point, Simon, greed, fear, hate, and ignorance, the outriders of the End, stocked the land. The best people were already being suffocated by the high, thin air of impending doom, the premature apocalyptic putrefaction in the bodies of the people. The best men hadn't slept for years. Echoing through their consciousness night and day the death keen of King Agamemnon lacerated ear chambers where rest and comfort should reside or the sea sound of echoing forever.

In my desperation you died. All thought of providing more fuel for the fires of hatred and destruction was impossible. When we loved it was always with walls, the rubber sunk in her womb or the drooping dunce cap crowning my root. And though in my fury and need I coupled often with her, still when alone I would grasp it in my fist and shake and choke as if this one time this final brutal separation would be the last. I waited for a drop of blood, an excruciating pain or sense of relief, some sign that all potential for life, all possibility of providing one more black victim had been wrenched from me. I cleaved life from our thrashing and flesh need. Only violence gave our love-making depth, an added dimension. A thousand, thousand times you died and in my frenzy I was a cannibal feasting on the flesh you could not become.

But early one November, again I regret the lack of detail, in my desperation death brought you forth. Impossible conjunction, nature's mistake as much as ours, you were conceived.

Simon, can you ever forgive.

Of course it was spring. A day not unlike this maybe. Across the land there was mourning. Men and women in black march among the tender, blushing colors of life tentatively renewed. Spring is never certain. Always the possibility that its delicacy, its ethereal forms will not make it, will be false, cruel omens not of summer and life but of that unrequited yearning in men's souls that leaves them shivering on street corners in thin clothes at the mercy of sudden arctic winds. Maybe, just maybe, is the moan beneath the rush to enjoy, maybe it won't come, this will be all that we will get. Hurry, hurry.

But the mourners were stately, solemn in their pavane beneath mimosas, tulip trees, pink and white early blooming ones. The king was dead, long live the king. At this impossible moment, at this almost melodramatic gyre of epochs cycling to a still point and prophesying in their dying pinpoint glimmer the configuration of the future, at this death/life, black/white, peace/violence, love/hate extravagant, metaphorical, metaphysical moment of truth you could not wait, you chose to rupture the membrane, the sheerest curtain retaining wall of all, Simon, you began.

Was the timing perfect; sublime in its irony and false promise. With the portents running so high and prospects darker than the thought of black men when it first occurred to Mister Whoever is Responsible for All This Shit, what would one expect if not a life for you that touched the outermost edges of tragedy and farce. A life that would be the fullest sounding board of human experience. And so I rejoiced. In spite of myself, after the most profound sleep and death, life was being resurrected. Life as a thumb in the nose at impossibility, life as a redemptive, unquenchable force outside of me, outside of things. But Simon my son you came too soon, never even got a breath of fresh air.

I am willing to go on. I will breathe, shave, fuck. I will be a man of all seasons. But I will not undam those squiggles of other Cecils, other xy Simons in my loins. No, the black man was not meant to be. Ask them, any of them. *You are not real.* And unless some God comes down and starts to kissing this black clay again it will crumble and blow away ungrieved, unfollowed, and without remorse.

Bitter, am I bitter on a spring morning Sweet Life alive just outside my door. That cannot be. Surely I have learned to forgive. Afterall Cecil Otis Braithwaithe. First of his race to do, to be, etc. You proved something, Cecil. You are in fact the only one of your race. There is only one black man in the world. Love him. He has no brothers, no look alikes, not even dogs to be loved in the bargain. Just say *I repent.* Just say *I forswear all rights and privileges.* Just say *They are not real.* Real is Cecil, real were those fine white men your classmates and what they do and what you will do as practitioner of the law. Nothing good comes without sacrifice. Christ paid for our sins. Let *them* pay for their own. Don't you know *they'll* only drag you down, eat you up, Cecil. Being one of *them* is as impossible, frankly, as is being one of us. That's fact, it's written. I kid you not. Just look at the realities of the situation. Whose sins do you care to die for?

Choice one: *Them*—dying for their sins is dying for nothing since they are unreal. Proof of this unreality is a choice you can make, a choice which can make them unreal. Forsake nothing.

Choice two: You—you are one of a kind. You will be treated accordingly.

Choice three: No choice: an illusion founded on a misapprehension of your other choices.

Now to go through this picking and choosing routine every morning is time consuming. In fact it makes you very inefficient, in fact it is a leaning toward choice three which is of course an absurd choice even in some ways more absurd than choice one since at least a blind, dumb passion for martyrdom bogus or not could be argued as a reason though not justification for choosing *Them*. Why teeter-totter like a mindless child? The assurance of company on the other end of the seesaw board? Could be a rock, a weight set there to fool you as well as wear you out. Come man. Choice two, choice two is unavoidable. Everyone likes to be thought of as unique, don't they. One of a kind, treated accordingly.

They are testing the sirens. In my book there will be a siren. Shoooooeeeee. How does one represent a siren sound. I need it. What better background for the Armageddon scene. And its fitful foreshadowing wails that will be a leitmotiv through the novel. Wheeeeeeeeeeeeee. The scene in which my hero is walking through the park contemplating suicide and he whistles a dirgelike keening monody that is picked up by the mournful wheezing of a factory horn then the whine of a jet till finally a throbbing banshee cacophony swirls around him in ever widening circles and his breath dragged by the tail of his whistle is sucked from his body and he is nearly hysterical till freed by the rumbling of a trolley car that wraps him in its trembling nearness.

For a movie sound track not a novel. In my journal when I want to catch some mood, make some point, I wish for the MGM orchestra. A crescendo here, violins soft in the background, there and there a trumpet salute. And pictures. I cut them out and paste them in the journal. But my novel.

There is no novel. I have a vivid imagination, and countless frustrations. Therefore I retreat to illusion, fantasy. Call my imagining my novel. Journal as close as I get. But not even journal, more like . . . like nothing but fantasy, illusion. My notes to Simon, my prayers unaddressed and unbelieved even as I pray. I write my novel with my backside as it puts down roots in dusty movie house chairs. My book is all the things I spend so much energy preparing to say to someone but never do to anyone. I am seeking the one word book.

The *mot juste* which ends all imagining, all squirming, all encounters with the eyes of old men in cages beneath lurid marquees. Cecil.

> Birds fly good days or bad
> Birds fly because they are sad
> Bird or his heart thumps at my window.

Window. Skindough, shindough. Chin though. Pause. Something maybe. Pause. Scrunch forehead. Dig deeper worry lines.

Bird won't shave my chin though.

Cecil's face is clean. He leans toward the window. Virgin still there, smiling in the sun. He can hear the children coming.

Afternoon April 19

Terrain spreads rusty, grease splotched redolent of barbeque, fried chicken, dried blood, waiting to be blasted, cooked, done by these allegorical hands my brother. Currycomb through layer after layer then somewhere cringing beneath (last layer of scales, sores, turf to shock a phrenologist) is the roots' base, skull wall thin but hardy Walt would you feel it if I bite steel teeth into your cranium. Yeah, yeah I know it hurts but that's the treatment, brother.

At the door is Gin Brown with Pepsi-Cola and chow mein.

—Hey Clyde baby, you got to do this thing.

I should have been a camera. Pretty pictures and no memories. Snap. Snap.

. . . and this is Walter Willis' head, before and after. Quite a difference, eh. Like between being seen in a Cadillac or in a Ford. How many pimps you know drive Fords.

. . . and this is Walter Willis, first potato of the day dropping in the bubbling fat. Let me advise you of something Walt. These hands about to be violently laid on your head are the hands of a man who has scaled Mendelian ladders time out of mind from tiniest spoor of salty rot past sloths and killer apes past Pithecanthropus and your Neanderthal experiment. Walter I have highwayed my way straight and narrow to this last whining spiraling exhausted dead end. I thrived, I fed on green pastures, pastures new reserved for the experiment I was. In the beginning was my end. Like those anthropoids that dropped from the trees too soon and could not learn the reptilian lore. Swallowed as the earth bathed in fire and ice. No canines, Walt. They had to chew and grind all day to survive. Daisy eaters, pansy eaters, eaters of the rose, daffodils, lilacs. They drink no blood, Walt, had no wine no Tiger Rose Thunderbird Pio Manischewitz Gallo Virginia Dare grapes and so they salvaged nothing from their dispossession only when they were dying did the high flying days return, vestigial, blurred, nostalgia as being devoured, a predator relieving the hot secrets of its bowels, glazed monkey eyes of the victim on his back last thing being seen was thick trees swaying, swaying through a mist.

Like this forest I have raised atop your head. Crested in front, a crown of tarred feathers for the king.

—Brown, this shit is cold and the other shit is hot.

Mr. Gin Brown unnerved because unbaptized because dry trembled in all regions of his body, those seen and unseen, he stood on the porch of the Big House waiting for Marse Jim, never a hungry water bug caught black and ugly in the middle of the kitchen floor was more petrified by sudden revealing glare of light than Gin Brown needing this drink bad and thought he had made a hustle but cold hot food and warm cold pop flopping if only I had that one that straightening one pull me together get me together get it together that one that one.

—G'wanne Gin Brown. You ain't nothin', nigger.

Brown bent to catch the dull thud of dime on the checkered linoleum. No, he don't look disgraceful down there trying to get his shaky yellow thumbnail under the coin's edge. You blame a piglet belly-sloshing his way through mud to get to the titty.

Wine dime now or wait and get enough together for gin. Brown tottered at the threshold; the dime burns through his clenched fist. Dime wafer offered to his lips.

Blood, Walter.

—Whisky kills you, wine make you crazy. Pays your money, takes your choice.

—Gin do both.

—I know when Gin Brown make one hundred and thirty-five dollars a week. Long bread.

—He got too good for his old lady. Put her down. Always in Oscar's. Fast cat.

—Fast. That nigger was Speed hisself. Dance his ass off, too.

—Good old lady. Would'a made something of Brown.

—Put her down. She always called him Clarence. Oscar'd tease her. *Is Clarence here? Don't know no Clarence* Oscar would answer grinning in his dark place, but all she could see was his eye through the peephole. *Is Clarence here? Don't know no Clarence.* And then finally she would have to say *Gin Brown Gin Brown is he in there, please, is he in there.*

—Dance his ass off.

—And Oscar would turn laughing. *Is there a Mr. Gin Clarence Brown in this establishment.* And everybody would laugh and know she was on the other side of the door and Oscar would say *Nobody by that name here.*

—Made something out of him.

—I seen him count it one hundred and thirty-five clean. Thirteen tens and five ones that's how he'd always get it. Bet dollars one at a time to learn his luck then nothing but fading tens till his gone or everybody else's gone.

—Fast Gin Brown.

—Speedo Brown.

—Dancing Brown.

—Ten dollar Brown.

—Pay the boss poor hoss lost.

—Ten you don't ten Brown.

Ten can't wait, wine dime gotta do it cause used to it got to get together.

You are Walter Willis and for seven dollars and fifty cents the difference between being seen in a Cadillac and being seen in a Ford.

—Clyde baby, like how you mean, No.

The laying on of hands. Cecil Braithwaite touches the hair of Walter Willis. Gingerly at first then down to the red roots chafing, greasing, handfuls of slick wool stiffened by an occasional wire bristle. Knead, finger tips on skull. You can feel the tar wedge its way beneath the fingernails. You remember popping string beans, the perforated belly bowl and when finished handfuls lifted and then cascading lean and lumpy sound of rain back into tin bowl. The white oleo in bags. Lard white but a red bubble on the side of bag and you burst blister red seeps, spreads beneath your fingers like a bland dawn sky into which color oozes, blood bubble squeezed till everything is soft yellow. I am buttering your dome. Pure vegetable coloring no one will know the difference. Which twin is bologna. A lady never tells. Only your hairdresser will know.

There goes Dr. Sylvester. Dr. Alonzo P. Sylvester in his Continental.

Constance Beauty's was filling up. On the floor dark irregular matting of martyred locks. On the ceiling gleaming white tiles. On the walls mirrors, mirrors ricocheted the room from plane to plane, doubling, tripling, devouring. The shop had seven chairs and often all seven would be occupied wafting their tenants in lifts spins twists and bends, positioning them so each customer could be subtly accosted by comb, heat, and chemical. On this spring morning April 19, 1967 at 11 A.M. five chairs danced, four black sheep being shorn, the fifth transfigured to a wolf.

Hot already. Sticky enough outside and the shop predictably ten degrees worse. Five attended customers, five attendants in white, three customers waiting and eight spectators kibitzing in various attitudes. Constance Beauty's was one large rectangular room, its glass doors opening in a short side. A curtain separated the back room from the arena, and as needed potions, balms, and unguents were fetched from the other side of the drape by the white coated acolytes. Only Process Pete's was competition, and long ago the two shops had partitioned the territory, not by a geographical division with its inherent difficulties of border watching and dissident minorities within the artificial boundaries, but by a simpler economic expedient—Process Pete's charged $5.50 and had to itself beginners, one shot artists, the indigent and transient needing a blast, in short those who really couldn't afford the luxury, but were hooked or in the process of being hooked, those who had fallen from good times and those who would never reach them, while Constance Beauty's $7.50 price catered to those who liked to give the impression they shared none of the crimping necessities of Pete's clientele.

Cecil spun his chair catching for a moment the sublime repose of Walter Willis' sweating face. The rivers of perspiration were appearance only, deceptive in their hurry and confusion; what Cecil saw beneath the film of change and impermanence was soul, pure soul. Walter, head afire, scourged of the flesh, Walter spirit supine at the foot of the swaying lotus trees. Oh how happy you have made me.

Dreaming Cecil soaked and singed absorbed in momentary flights of fancy which he communicated to the tarry jungle of Walter's head. Under Cecil's deft fingers Kilimanjaro rose, the horns of a bull, cuckold's horns, the Eiffel Tower, the twin peaks of Marilyn Monroe, anonymous buttocks and phallic symbols. Consummately these artifacts were created atop Walter's brain and just as resolutely when they had reached a formal perfection, a leveling cruise of the comb extinguished them forever. Dead without a trace, a phantom world above Walter's skull, a *tabla rasa* afterall was said and done. Cecil thought of ripple making, that other transitory art he had conceived. Since the artist can only call the process of creation itself uniquely, truly his own in a manner that not even the finished, public manifestation of that process is his own, the most pure art and the one perhaps most satisfying would be the most ephemeral art, the art that was all process, all unfolding, all experience, the art which removed the necessity of an exportable, finished product. Not a new idea certainly, but novel and revealing to Cecil as he sat beside the still Italian lake and tossed pebbles into its sunclean surface. Each pebble, depending on complex relationships among force of contact, angle of incidence, size, weight, shape of pebble, and countless other factors mysterious enough to form an art, produced a distinctive ripple pattern upon, within, and beneath the quiet water. Sun golden bands crept outward from the initial brilliant ring. The possibilities were endless and the challenges a limitation not of the medium but of the imagination of the challenger: size of rings, speed of rings expansion outward, perfection of rings' shape (a badly thrown pebble splashed so that the circle's shape was pitted, distorted), more than one pebble would be thrown at a time to achieve subtle rhythms, interlocking patterns of ring with ring, shadow with shadow. And a moment after the pebble had struck, after the creator's eye had been delighted or depressed the entire effort silently passes to oblivion.

Fulfillment rarely and if it comes at all, unified too closely with the process to be exhumed, made a monument. The creator whose canvas will always be naked, unresolved, ready. The black, bright lake kissing Cecil's mood but gone before the embrace.

Before the laying on of hands.

Suppose I made of your fleece a wedding cake. Seven tiers, Walter, and on top lovers arm in arm. You would have to let your hair grow even higher before I could attempt such a masterpiece. Let it be ten feet long, each strand a bamboo pole stiff and erect. The world would wonder why. Why so tall Walter. Why so tall. There would be talk, betting pools but finally the day you entered Constance Beauty's, talk and smiles would cease altogether. They would gather in droves outside and invitations to the privileged would allot the inner space. Cecil of ripple fame would at last divulge an example of his heretofore transitory art for the delectation of the public. Until Walter's hair went back home or was rained upon or he forgot his stocking cap and mashed the sculpture while sleeping, the multitude could experience in their midst a frozen artifact of the most essential art.

Seven spiraling tiers each like the Grecian urn decorated with a frieze of classical scenes. Seven ages of man the theme, culminating in naked Adam and Eve resplendent on the crown, their proud private parts promising a new beginning, a continuation of the cycle. Walter, the ebony Atlas, would balance it on his head. And each day the world floating elegant, graceful and precarious down the Strip. Niggers knowing to fall back, not to touch, to look but don't leap as the world is carried past.

Cecil ripple maker, coiffeur supreme. Creator of an art that has no past or future, no tradition to be sustained or transmitted infinitesimally modified to generations unborn. No corpse poised along the chain of straining, uplifted hands.

Ripples begin and ripples end. Ripples are made then gone. Cecil is a ripple playing through the increasingly recalcitrant hair of Walter Willis. A wind ripple that in slow motion disturbs and stirs the fleece. Swirls, mounds, caves, a landscape exists then doesn't exist. A past is either present or not at all. Walter sleeps.

—Here comes the Continental again. Drop top with four doors.

—Nigger has all the money in the world. Least all the money down here the number man ain't got.

—You talk about pills doing a job. That nigger done scraped away just about as many babies as he brought into this world. Charges $300. Wish I had a dollar for every fixing up he's done.

—You think you'd get tired of looking up pussy.

—When redeye stopped winkin' back I'd get tired.

—All pussy's the same.

—You's a lie and a grunt. You sure ain't been round many if you say a fool thing like that.

—Black, white, brown, yellow, I been all over the world when I was in the war and up holes every place I been and I'm telling you pussy is pussy.

—Smells different according to race. And white ones ain't so hairy.

—You got it ass-backward fool. Them German girls and French ones got hair niggers ain't even thought about.

—That's European women not white.

—You are one dumb nigger. Never been out of the Strip, a chitterlins and cornbread coon.

—You sure think you know something. I been places. All over this goddamn city. I know something you don't. Where

I'm wanted and where not. Who my people is and who ain't. I don't kiss no man's ass just to get his white smile on me. And the stuff he's tired of put in my hands like I's supposed to thank you boss thank you boss and shine his shoes. And European ain't white.

—And you are not the descendent of an African, I suppose.

—Oh no, here we go again. Africa this and Africa that. And black, black, black. Nigger, you're makin' me tired of being black. Robes and bushy heads.

—Why don't you be white then. Go on, be like Willis. Watch when he gets up out that chair with his good black man's hair all straightened and waved. He won't be black any more, Willis paying $7.50 and he's Tony Curtis.

—Seems like it would fall apart. A car without no top and four doors.

Cecil combed and curried, smoothed and patted. The reddish brown roots of Walter's hair were invisible, hidden beneath a coat of glistening, contoured jet. Roots were where a bad job showed. Like shining the toe of a shoe and leaving the sides cracked and dirty. Getting at the roots was probably the most painful segment of the treatment for the customer, and a minimal singeing of the cranium would be rewarded by the well-heeled *cognoscente* with a generous tip. Cecil's caution in dealing with Walter was perfunctory. No sadism, but no financial considerations either to crystallize Cecil's concentration. He burnt and wandered, swimming in what was now a din of voices within and cacophony of activity outside the glass walls as the Strip sprang into full, loud life.

From the Avenue Record Mart the Staple Singers entertained the mothers who were shopping. Later it would be the Temptations, James Brown, Stevie Wonder and those stars of lesser magnitude who would hover above the Avenue, a radiant canopy for the teen-agers returning from the mountain where the piper leads them six hours a day five days a week forty weeks of the year. But in between spirituals and dancing music, the dispossessed were serenaded with their own special kind of music. Late risers, nonrisers, the men who would make the action after dark or men who had been flung by the action onto these barren afternoon beaches would listen to a potpourri of cool jazz, West Coast jazz, blues, oldies but goodies, dead musicians, throaty dead singers, the static on bad recordings lacing their voices like the night club smoke and unerasable tinkle of glasses, low warm talk, Lady Day's last live recording.

Sleeping, somnolent rhythms. The sudden screech and crash of a subway, a match flaring in an alley, a bottle crashing to the pavement. Knife sounds, hurt sounds, sounds that were taxis' wheels gliding to rendezvous. Cages locked, cages flung open. Litters drawn by matched leopards, stretcher-bearers in white. Constance Beauty's.

Constance Beauty's had a jukebox. But on principle it never competed with the Avenue Record Mart. No more than the Establishment envied Process Pete's its medium to full house, its register ringing $5.50. Afterall some presiding, ulterior force guaranteed the smooth running of the Strip, perpetuated the profound rhythm of its identity. Chord and Dischord. Advance and Retreat. Violence and Peace. All factions, contradictions, extremes not extinguished but harmonized, not blurred but made compatible by a force whose nature Cecil could not plumb. Was it blackness, some secret experience of the race, blood knowledge ineradicable. And would it always be so or could this knowledge run thin, exhaust itself in one mutation of genes, one black coupled with white or black ridden by deeper black. Was the Strip a ripple, blackness itself and all its secrets a larger ripple in the infinitely slow, infinitely bored game playing of time wasting time.

Cecil's fingers slowed. He walked away from the chair, eyes straight ahead on the drapery, the only surface that did not return his image. Though he focused narrowly on the velvet curtain and though his ears strained to be stones on which the breakers of sound would crash and subside, Cecil could not turn back the sensuous reality lashing about him. Smell taste touch sight sound all his and not his. He was their excuse for being and they were his excuse for being, for calling this memory Cecil and that one Cecil, and all those things Cecil upon which he had no claim. They claimed him.

A Swiss lake, or was it Italian. It didn't matter because what did matter was how aloof in the quiet, in the stillness in the abyss illumined only by pebbles' bright plunge. The moment said . . .

Do I shuffle, do I try to hide as through the gantlet passing of mirrors and eyes I am afraid of seeing myself in them but want to be there want to know I am someplace seen that I am substance, that the sea parts in my passage, that between knife prow cutting and fan wake Cecil can be seen Cecil is neither one nor the other neither becoming nor gone as a foamy wake is gone. Must I see myself in them to know myself to believe myself. And when I awake from dreams must I always fear the larger dream, circle within circle, Chinese boxes forever insidiously, diabolically enclosed, ripples within ripples.

The deep voice from the jukebox made him start. But then quickly other voices, the bitter-sweet Miracles, Bill Smokey Robinson *et al.*, the lilting, swinging rhythms yet always that trailing edge of poignancy of loss and regret barely concealed that was the Miracles' style. *Tracks of my Tears.* Afternoon music. Who played it. Cecil saw no sign. But the Miracles singing, the tile, the mirrors, matted hair on the floor.

Because the singer smiles . . .

They smile

What I am is what I feel now. What else, how else. But Webb took me and pointing said this, all this is yours.

Museums, whores, all the beauty he thought was me, all

the beauty he thought. And I was young. I could kill the dragon, release the golden dream, find the cup, the maiden, the castle, the home, the father, the seeking. Ruins, ruins we all fall down.

See a clown's face
An entertainer

And though I have made mistakes, he confessed, though I have betrayed, even slaughtered believers, in fact had least tolerance for the best men, though I have been wrong, there is beauty in struggle in a past no matter how gory, how defiled because it is a past a child to the man and though your body is among those gored and defiled . . .

But the blue song inside

And though she suffered at my hands and though he forsook me and disappeared . . .

His eyes remembering

You are not my son not my flesh but heir to my dreams to that better part of me laced with greed envy bitterness and fear though it is still a better part . . .

Ghost tears
Old sorrows walking down his face

Walter Willis yawns and stretches, receives Cecil's final ministrations and with serenade rather than coin of the realm tips the magician. Poets pay that way, why not Walter. Briefly Walter beside the chair and new Walter in the mirror coincide, couple, exchange places.

—Kiss my ass, Clyde.

Night April 19

Go back. Go back. No matter where Cecil found himself sooner or later the admonition to return would slink then dance to his ear. Go back. Return. Reprise. Repeat. About face. Again. Return. The direction was clear, but destination, even point of departure impossible to grasp. Ring the changes. Sea changed. Sea-borne wrapped in hazel mist, swaddled in pea coat, balaclava, rubber boots the boy stood on the shining deck. For he is a Charlie good fellow. He is afterall a victim of circumstance, of circumvention, of circling, curling woolly locks. And keyless Cecil weeps at the command. He retrieves from its hook the tiny brass bell. Ring a ling. Ring a ling. Life buoy. I am held up by the waves, they fondle my arching prow, they foam wash me. Why are the niggers moaning. Why do they fear this voyage home. Ring a ding ling. Lifeboats in order. The deck is clean, the hold hosed down. They should shit less when they don't get much to eat, provisions are low. Do not cry my brethren. Tell Martha not to moan. We are going back, we are going home.

Uncle Otis, please tell me a story. Listen to a story. Beneath the cautious street lamp that slipped an arc of salmon pink around his shadow, Uncle Otis stood resplendent as if in a suit of lights. Wary Cecil approached.

—I am confused, that will be apparent. I want to start at the beginning. . . .

—Why me.

—It's necessary.

—Who besides you could benefit from the telling.

—You are an amanuensis, a recorder.

—A pawn then. Benefiting not at all. A plaything. A device. Taking advantage of your old uncle.

—A necessity. A necessity because so far there has been no story, no telling, and I must begin. You see, when I walked out of the door that evening, I had no idea. I was just . . .

—Taking a step.

—A step then another and another. Somehow it led to

him and the need to tell and I suppose the need to return, to begin. My mind plays with me. Retains, withholds according to a will that is seemingly beyond me, outside of my control. I feel exploited, manipulated by a force I cannot fathom. And yet I am the meaning of the force, if its reality can be known I *am* the force. But he . . .

Dark night. Listener chews his gum. Itches near his groin but will not reach down. Sees Cecil in a tree.

–You are waiting for a monologue.

Nod (anything, nothing, beginning, end, motherfucker. Just do it).

–The night I left I didn't touch my wife. No good-bye anything. Kiss, caress, word. Just Cecil gone into the night. If I could tell you about that night. How it felt, how much I lived in the first few breaths of black air maybe the rest wouldn't be necessary. Remember what I'm trying to get to. Why I had to go through the door. Perhaps I was just sorry for myself. The bad luck. Perhaps that long flagellation, that impossible lifting of Cecil by Cecil, the learning of the law, that see, hear, smell, taste, touch, say, be no evil monkey I had become chased me through the door. None of these, perhaps. Just blackness seeking blackness, beaten by blackness. All those Cecils *I couldn't be* calling the ghost I had become. Promises. Promises. The ones I made and ones made to me forgotten if I got through the door. Well as it turns out those first few breaths of black air at the beginning had in them all I would ever learn. Now it becomes a word game. Shuffling them in and stretching and straining and exploding till I can say it tried and I tried but it was not quite it, not the word because something essential still missing still asks to be propitiated by another word.

So night is this which is unavoidable, inevitable either as it bursts through the narrative or dies one of its seeming deaths just out of reach but always always there. You see I could call myself night or call this night my foreknowledge and thorough knowing of myself but that would be to make a rounded, full tale I have never lived through, nor anyone lives through, until knowing that rounding will not come the need to erect it comes into being and then a scaffold rises as much air and space as it is orange, cool tubing and we say out of courtesy there it is, the emperor is so well dressed today.

As I recall I kept on my wedding suit. I must have put the jacket over my arm as I walked because the day had been so warm that night made no difference same heat but different because it seemed stale, walked in, sweated in like someone else's sheets you find yourself trying to sleep on but they already have given all they have to give, exhausted those frail possibilities of habitation and they either smother you or expose you refuse your measure within the ghost mold of the one who has already been there. I walked and tried to find some cool empty place but of course I did not have within me any sense of seeking or search just the inertia of one foot after the other it must have been hours or days I walked out reserves I had not known I possessed, I tapped resources of purposelessness I had resigned myself long before to being born without I stitched oblivion with unknown, untiring steps as if there were a state of undreaming between realities and I could plunge deeper and deeper once I stumbled into it.

I have no memories, no images to share. Have you watched the caged animals leave their cells in some distant gazing that is through you through walls an irresistible, hurtling stare until you can see fur dissolve and teeth crumble and the high stench incense burning for one departed, lost even to itself far away in jungle, cave, or black river you are dizzy and fear disintegration because some part of you is in that stare, swept with it beyond cage and sensory evidence that all is here and well and organized as it should be to the end of that longing that roar of the eyes dissolving lion flesh or ape flesh your flesh and ridden home where the blood waits to be consumed. As if I could become the sound of my feet, and in the same way physical energy can be drained, I walked until what I was, what I had been began to collapse and run away in salty streams beneath my black suit.

—The meaning of this is that I need you to listen. Authenticate.

—Piece together.

—Not that. Not help. There are no pieces. I could accept fragments, shards. No. Just listen. Listening assures me that something has transpired. That I began and ended. Something in between.

—But that night was nothing, was steps. You see why you must simply listen. Add nothing, make no effort to construct, construe. I told you night was everything, that it was me, that it was the story. Now I call it nothing.

And it was nothing. Can a man listen to himself going to dust. Surely an instrument delicate enough could record the *gigue* of ashes to ashes. A thunderclap when heart beats one last time, how that note would linger, the accumulated resonance of ten billion remembered beats, linger like clarion knell over wing fluttering palpitations of near silence as nothingness gestates within the meat and bones slowly gnawing, gnawing at substance, molecule by stilled molecule meat to matter to bad breath in a wooden box. Fetus of nothingness full blown in one gasp swallows all memory all trace of ever beating ever alive something gone nothing. There should be applause when the music finishes, wing systole and diastole, but no man can listen to his own dust and no other man could clap in such final silence. So I didn't even listen to those footfalls I know I was, but I know I was walking toward nothing and perhaps beside me umbilical I drew him or he drew me two in one trace one echo we *moved together* because those words can mean from immense distances from no knowledge of one another though nearly touching back to back two nodes on a huge circle we began to approach a confrontation, each drawn steadily, magnetically around the circumference of the invisible circle, or the words mean side by side, juxtaposed, paired, twinned, walking two peas in pod as invisible to them as the circle around which they move together.

No one face or voice or building or street can I recall. Only when I stopped or seemed to stop did I begin to take account, to estimate where, when, why. So you must keep in your mind that this is guesswork. Reconstruction after no facts. A long time somewhere because when I stopped, I smelled, was filthy, bedraggled. I had a beard. My feet felt as if they had been bound in rawhide to stunt their growth. I could not talk easily. A kind of hoarseness, an unfamiliarity with movements of tongue and lips, with the shuttling of spit and breath at the proper intervals. A craving not for food but for water. Nausea faint, slightly threatening at the thought of food, an inability to even conceive of individual foods because some effluvia haunted my throat and I could taste and feel its stirrings in my belly, a gaseous distillation of all food, the essence of food which was the color wheel of all foods spun at a rate that blurred the spectrum to an oppressive gray. Whirling total presence or absence of everything I had ever tasted. But water I thirsted for. Needed like I had once needed a god, cornucopia of abundance to refresh everything from dry lips to soul's desiccation.

When I found a fountain I drank deeply. Teasing, compromising myself with cool, extravagant mouthfuls, swishing the water over my gums and teeth, enjoying the plash against my puffed cheeks before I spit the too much out. I had visions of all the cowboys and legionnaires I had seen rescued from the desert. The rescuer's sympathetic but firm refusal of more than a mouthful. The exemplary caution; too much too soon not good.

Then I continued to search for water. This too a paradigm, a compression of the story, like night contained everything so does searching and water. Where did it all end. By the sea by the sea by the beautiful sea. And begin. With the *Mayflower* or even sooner Dutchly planted in this land. *Desire* the ship.

Not only something to drink, but a place to be received, embraced, revitalized. I could cleanse stains from the flesh, whitewash my soul. I was sea-borne as I knelt at the fountain, baptized as I dipped to drink again. Water washed me, rivered me home. I found something was shouting inside me, some excitement unbearably titillating yet promising an impossible, excruciating further titillation. All this in a few mouthfuls. And then simply, dully the first step was over. I was through the door.

And on the other side a consuming thirst. A day blue but overcast and the hour must have been early because I remember being nearly alone as I walked along a beach. Gray sand, warm, full of jagged shell fragments then sleek like an animal's wet coat, gleaming sand pocked with debris. Puddles of foam like soapsuds quivered where they had been deposited by the lapping waters. Frothy and white, some strange animal form, ephemeral, perhaps deadly, miniature glaciers that slid almost imperceptibly back toward the waters that brought them. Wind sculpting the suds the way a man toys with the foam on beer. I was there dreaming of a sea plunge, of drinking and bathing of sun and breeze of salt smarting in eyes and lips but clearing, cleansing old wounds. Though it was early, riders had been there before; deep half-moons carved in the sand, dung heaped so neatly I thought someone must have aided nature to build the golden pyramid near the water's edge. I didn't see them till I had walked two hundred yards or so away from the water. Sand was loose, I floundered, my steps were heavy and awkward as if my body suddenly found itself imposed upon by an unfamiliar gravity. Four riders on shaggy maned, long tailed mounts and a black boy behind them straddling a donkey. The horses bunched together, a frieze of motion against the seascape. They pranced, stylized almost, one body in relief and many tails and manes and legs beside and beneath it to give an illusion of other bodies. White breakers beyond, rippling, prancing, churning to touch breast against breast, to plunge together in one synchronized flurry of arching mane and tail. Splash of hoofs as they crash into the surf, troubling a sea mist around slender ankles. The riders held their reins laxly, giving the mounts full head. And the course of the band and the trailing donkey was erratic, aimless yet rhythmically attuned to the same miscellaneous certainty of the waves rushing to the land.

I stood and watched them until they disappeared. Horsemen on the sand. Riders to the sea. Phantoms who left miraculous indentations and golden piles upon the beach. I asked myself how real they had been, if I had only seen whitecaps dancing across the blue water. I now knew the form revelation must take, and yet I was no nearer, still thirsted, still had some aching reservoir to fill.

Magic water rubbed across my face and the litmus change of young to old man as I watched in a mirror.

Fountain trinkling in the vaultlike room. Pebbles that were pearls. The master crucified on the wall.

So when he asked . . .

So when he asked I didn't even hesitate. Of course I'll go. Night and water there too. I actually thought that thought because the pool into which the fountain dribbled was rimmed in black marble. I had learned to read things, to put them together according to the subtle yearnings, the incalculable forces expressed in what they had lost to become individuals. Or at least some such facility enabled me to be impractical, to forsake my characteristic fear of obvious consequences and embrace the immediate, assuaging effect. But I must not be too analytic, precise about a state that will not bear much precision. I said yes and the rest followed.

—So you went.

—Yes, across an ocean with him. Seemingly in tow, humbly mounted, almost careless about the course, yet like the black boy on the donkey a guide of sorts, and of course like him responsible.

—My prosperous, ambitious nephew, Cecil. Do you remember who gave you that name. In whose namesake, Cecil. Who brought you out of the darkness. I could tell you stories, stories about your name, about darkness, about being dipped in a pot of colored water like an Easter egg. But I know you are impatient. Got a train to catch, don't you. Pay no mind to your Uncle Otis who gave you your middle name. Crazy old coon, gonna die soon.

Cecil Otis pumpkin pie/ Never knew he had to die.

Singsong lament tired on his lips old man leaned against the lamppost. Long, straight spine picked clean of flesh only seven stark vertebrae climbing its sides, the pole drew night closer to the salmon pool.

—There will be a time when you recall all this. How I stunk and my breath so bad you kept backing up as I spoke, and how I tried to move closer to you so as not to have to shout. You'll remember me shouting till I got hoarse and you moving away but never far enough so you missed what I was saying. Like a beating you know you deserve so you don't fight back. Let me tell you something. Like I told it to the whore spitting and wiping her mouth trying to get the pee sting out. If at first you don't suckseed . . . is what I told her after wiping and zipping and ready to go out the door. You should have seen her sputter and spit. She came at me finally, clawing, tearing, screaming to get tooth or nail planted in my black hide, but I was tough and quick, not a mark on me. I batted her butt-naked on the floor and dared her to move. She knew she had crossed me. Turning everybody on behind my back then coming nibbling at me like she was loving and obedient. Mad as she was, I took a chance, though I knew it wasn't a big chance and unzipped again and sprang it in her.

—That name, Cecil, is a slave name. It means hard of seeing. So saying the old man picked from his dusty neck an intruder.

Dies Irae. Tempus fugit. Etcetera.

The hard shell cracked between pressure of thumbnail and first finger.

—Did you see the smoke, nephew. I done the little bastard more good than he was intending on me. Soul mist rising to join the atmosphere then floating till it finds some new form to seep into. Maybe an elephant or a horse he'll be next. Something grander than either one of us two-legged monkeys. Sometimes I think this pole is leaning on me. I feel like if I move away it will come toppling down. When I was younger, I used to love to climb utility poles. You know they have spikes driven in so you could giant step right to the top. From up there things were a lot different. Course you had to be careful. Wires and humming and black boxes I never dared touch. But it was good just sitting secretly up there where nobody could touch you. Sometimes I even thought no one could see me like I had really disappeared from the earth. You mounted those spikes with long stretching steps. Up until the sky closer, the wind louder like sea shells on your ears. I was scared sometimes, but really sorry they didn't make poles no taller.

—I'm going to go back to her, Otis. Nothing has changed. Never will. What they did to me that afternoon. I'll do it. She'll be my wife.

—There are days now when I feel like climbing. I believe I could get up, but the coming down would be too much for these dry bones. I can see the niggers gathered here laughing they asses off at the crazy coon hung up on the utility pole. I had a dream once. I was talking to a dog, nothing silly or unnatural seeming about it, we was just talking. I don't remember how it was whether he was standing or I was on all fours, but anyway we were looking in each other's eyes and having a damned interesting conversation. I remember now how it was. He was on a table, a big stone table and stretched out talking in a dignified voice. The strangest thing was when he finished I stroked him with a big ax. Not vicious or violent or mad at the creature, just did it looking straight in his eyes, and he never blinked or cringed. It seemed the only thing to do when he had finished talking. Butchered him afterward, real professional, like I knew what I was doing. He looked kind of pretty, the way well sliced roast beef looks pretty when I had finished and arranged his skinned parts on the table. Put his still thumping heart in my pocket. It was warm against my thigh as I walked away. When I finally got to the top of the pole (which is why I'm telling you the dream) I was naked and the heart was gone but my leg was moist and stained red on the thigh. When I woke up I had wet the bed.

—Esther is going to be my wife. Not a lawyer's lady, but my wife.

—That's what you said just a minute ago.

—You have nothing to say.

—Don't doe-eye me. After all you're a man aren't you. A man who knows so well where he's going that he's always in a damned hurry. Too much of a hurry to listen to a dying old man.

—You'll be standing by this pole when my children are dead.

—That's what I mean a hurry. You're counting your children already. Geronimo is what them paratroopers say in the movies when they's throwing they asses off into the wild blue yonder. All Otis has to say is Geronimo.

—Geronimo was an Indian chief. Also a holy man who lived in the desert with a lion. Who was buggering who I never could learn, but one went to heaven so it must have been true love. Then there are niggers call themselves lion-men, Masai lion men. I won't speak too harshly of that heathenism. One might be my great granddaddy prancing around the jungle roaring till his throat is sore. Geronimo is the last word said by a hell of a lot of men.

—I guess I've got what I came for.

—Did you ever want to be a blind man? Something about the mouth and mind seems to be improved by being eyeless. And fingers become better. When he jabbed the brooch in his eyes he knew what he was doing. The only way he could understand, could *see* what had happened was darkly. That's why they are afraid of us. See darky run, run darky run. They understand what they've done; it's not me but them that can't forget. Cecil.

—I have some scripture for you. One of the woolly balloon heads gave it to me yesterday. He was talking about roots and past and the pendulum swinging back. Told me to come to the Temple, get off the corner and come to the Temple to hear how wrong I've been done. He thought there was something being said that I should hear. I laughed at the bushy top. If I went in their Temple, it would be as a speaker. I could talk about roots and past about a black world and black men the woollies had to forget before they could begin their ranting and raving. Someday before I die I may tell everything, tell everything then climb up my pole and watch the walls come tumbling down. My voice would be a host of trumpets, relentless and shattering. Tarik and his hawks would raze the city, gallop through here like ten thousand dusky Gary Coopers. A

trumpet and a drum. Drum made from skins of the
martyred. Black skins stretched taut again after wrinkling
around the starved bones. On the first note they would
rub their eyes as if awakening from a long sleep. Their
bodies would be tired as if they had been journeying for
days. But the sleep haze would go and the exhaustion would
flee before the drum and trumpet. Surely good music would
follow them all the days of their lives. Globe trotters come
on to Sweet Geronimo Brown, scourge of the earth. Hawks
such as never seen before.

Otis hesitated, hand on the first rung:

Onya manas. Then like a madman I will shower flowers
in all directions. Whatever I see I will worship. Horsemen
gone to a pure cloud of golden dust. Sons of Light cascading over the earth like sun after the storm. There are more
worlds than one. More to come and many we have forgotten, but they are all One.

He begins to climb:

Lila, is it only this? Does God exist only when my eyes
are closed and disappears when my eyes are opened. No, I
am not blind and still the rumble of the horseman saturates
my heartbeat. The Play belongs to Him to whom Eternity
belongs, and Eternity to Him to whom the Play belongs.
Some people climb the seven floors of a building and cannot get down; but some climb up and then, at will, visit the
lower floors.

Otis is enthroned:

Pitha. I hear the humming, feel the damp throb beside
my groin. As from a tall mast silver threads glide off into
the night. All things converging, power, peace. My hand is
on the black box.

Cecil reads the crudely printed card handed to him by his
uncle.

*And slay them whenever you catch them, and turn them
out from where they have turned you out; for tumult and*

oppression are worse than slaughter. And fight them on until there is no more tumult or oppression. Koran 2:191;193.

Shower flowers. Cecil cringed inwardly as he watched the trembling old man search for something in the periphery of darkness. Perhaps it would be a large, bruised petal his kneeling uncle would lift toward him.

—I can't find the bugger. Big one he was though. He would have popped loud as the crack of doom. Felt him crawling down my arm and brushed him off before I thought what a treat it would be to float another soul for my anxious nephew. I remember the preacher navel deep in a swampy creek ducking the black bodies while the sanctified chanted on the shore. I would not walk in the water. I hid till the others had to go, then watched from a tree them being dunked like donuts in that coffee-colored water. Maybe it was crystal clear once and gone sour from scouring souls. I think some believed everything would come out white; sin, ass, and giblets if they prayed.

The man stood tall now, no longer shaking. Cold wind in which he shivered passed to the night. Looking at him Cecil restrained the urge to scratch, disgusted by the silent life teaming within the old man's clothing. Like old skin he cannot shed, that is corrupted but will not molt Cecil said to himself staring at the rags loosely hanging on his uncle's body. Suit of lice.

—You are my namesake. You are the only one who came to see me when I had the run-in with the police.

The visitor's window, thick dull glass. The swaying sheet of ticking in front of which the prisoner stands. Proximity of all the windows. Snake house in the zoo. How one must shout to be heard, confusion of all voices attempting to reach behind the glass walls. Babel, din, bedlam. One must bend his ear down to the talking grill. In this position impossible to see prisoner's face, to be seen. Makes communication faceless, mechanical like talking long distance on the phone. Difficulty in hearing, in being heard, seeing, being seen brutalizes the interview. Someone had begun to sing a hymn. Otis crying.

—I could tell you stories. I have a gift. I can handle flame, touch men where they burn and not be burnt myself. I could write their epitaphs. Yours would be Geronimo.

The old man's performance visibly tired him and when he was tired, he seemed to Cecil to smell worse.

—When I rub my eyes it is to see you better, Cecil, to make sure I have returned. How long have you been here. Or rather how long have I been here. There is a distinction you know.

Cecil was annoyed with himself for believing the pole had leaned, had been about to crash down before his uncle's hand returned to steady it. Esther was waiting.

—I once knew a dwarf. Well not exactly a dwarf, but a child who was not really a child but an old man who had grown up too fast, in a matter of months from twelve to fifty then died of old age right there in bed. He said they called it progeria, growing up too fast, all life passes like a film at the wrong speed, days are hours, months, days, a year might stretch to a week. His mind was storm but some days there was calm, he could talk a moment. I lost my job at the hospital because I did nothing but hang around at his bedside waiting for the lucid minutes. His voice would come from far away, a man's voice from the wrinkled old, new bundle of flesh he had become. He said:

—*In me all things occur with unbearable intensity. Never a pause for my emotions to rest, for some experience of my blood's growth to become quiet and calm before the next tumult begins. My whole being races, is scourged by time. Always losing and dying without even the illusion of possession. I cry because I cannot have this illusion, because it is an illusion, a nothing, and yet you are blessed because you have this nothing. I cry for an illusion, for deception, for a lie to deceive me. I cry because I must tell myself this lie would be better than my body's truth. I cry because I am not made to live the lie.*

I didn't dream this dwarf man, neither his clenched baby fists nor the choked, panting of his voice when he spoke. He wearied me nephew. I grew tired watching him die so quickly, just as your hurrying makes me lose my breath. Go, go to her and the rest. You see me here, where I have been, what I brought back and what I have. They laugh at me and they'll laugh at you. They see in us only themselves, and because they are what they are, can only laugh at themselves. I kissed the dwarf when he slept hoping I would be infected.

Cecil did not look back once his legs began moving. He knew it would be a pillar of fire and that he should be turned into salt.

At midnight when Esther was sound asleep, her Aunt Fanny quietly slipped from bed, dressed in the darkness and tiptoed into the kitchen. The old lady had heard everything. Her niece home from the revival tent, the padding of her heavy body on bare feet across the boards of the rugless bedroom floor, the bending squeaking bed, sobbing and snores. Esther had flushed the toilet twice in the short time before sleep. I don't know what she could be doing but I hope she has left everything neat because the others will soon be here.

When the lights came on sudden, so bright after Fanny's noiseless gliding through the hall, there was a scurry of sleek-backed roaches returning to their nests. Not really many nor overpowering just enough to make some things, the wooden backed sink, shadows along the oven door that never quite closed, move that weren't supposed to have life of their own. Fanny watched one disappear beneath the blue fluff ball of her slippers (given by Esther at Easter); she looked back behind her callused heel to see the crushed nougat but there was no spot upon the floor. Not enough left in me to squash a bug. No wonder I'm so hungry (Esther screaming eat, eat) terrible pains in my belly, and moving nimbly the implements were gathered by her knitter's quick fingers. A pot and lid for rice, skillet for the fat meat and big boiling pot for the kale. Implements chosen and displaced, Fanny rummaged in the cupboard and icebox for contents. Lined them on drainboard: Uncle Ben's Converted Rice, fat meat on waxed paper, cellophane bag of kale. With a blue-striped cup water was carefully measured into the pot and pan. Skillet sat warming on a low flame. All in readiness the cook squinted at the hissing gas jets to gauge the heat generated by the fine yellow flames.

A moment for coffee which she made by stealing a cup of water from the large pot. Greens wouldn't miss that little bit of moisture she naughtily tapped. Hadn't missed it all these years she had been preparing supper and borrowing her water for instant coffee. Can hardly wait. Turn off the flame a moment while she drinks. These men home later each evening. Thin legs look strange naked for a change since she had left the opaque stockings hanging on chair back in her room. I wish there was something I could sing, that I knew the words of (Esther hates my songs). If she ate now the men would not like it. Not as if they'd make a fuss or anything of the sort just that them out working all day and having no womenfolk about they appreciated that restful hour at the dinner table and her eating as well as feeding them after that long day in the fields. Her men. Her Henry and little Henry and Thomas and Amos and Benjamin. All men and all twice her size. Dark, strong men and her high yeller as anybody in the valley. They liked that too, their woman with bright skin and eyes that were green in the right light. She could tell how proud her husband and big sons so she would sip her coffee, watch the pans, and wait.

Benjie would play with that braid. How pretty your mama's hair Henry said to the boys and they looked funny and didn't know what to do but little Benjie right up on my lap and took it long and silky in his hands. Henry knocked Thomas to the ground when he heard the boy had sassed me. I cried with my Tom, and Henry just standing there shaking.

All day I have so many things to do in this house I'm just so busy keeping it clean and my hands full with all of their things I never think about food must go all day sometimes without passing crumb to lips but then soon as I start to getting their supper ready I get so hungry I feel like these pots full of food won't hardly be enough for me. (Eat Fanny eat, you'll starve to death, fool.) But wait I shall, light the fire, listen to the simmering and boiling and turn the fat meat till its brown and . . .

When Cecil entered he used the same key he had used three years before to lock the door when he left. He heard no sound, saw there was someone in the chair, and for a long moment the insides of the familiar janitor's apartment trembled giddily before his eyes refusing to believe him, to be believed. The body in the chair did not turn. Twig arms and legs told him the form was not Esther's, never in a thousand years would her flesh wither as close to the taut bones. It was Fanny, Fanny grown even less substantial than the doll creature he had remembered. One waxen arm was stretched onto the tabletop and the other was lost somewhere in her lap. Her hair, lusterless and dry, thinning but still with its longest strands reaching far down her back was loosened from its accustomed braid to spread faintly like weeds beaten by wind against her thin back. Nothing moved.

The table was set for six, orderly, meticulous, as formal as the battered china and dull utensils could carry the effect. A tall pitcher of water stood in the center of the table and at the head a frayed Bible beside the fork and paper napkin. Fanny still hadn't stirred and deciding she was asleep Cecil switched out the light then moved quietly past the stove. He left the old woman where she sat, head slightly slumped, one arm stretched to the coffee cup, the other buried in her lap. He remembered swiftly. The element had frightened him, seemed impossible from a distance to manage, like the sea when he thought of swimming alone at night. Terror, shivering, unimaginable phantoms would wait for his foot to break the restless surface. He would be swept away, screaming. But once there, surrounded, submitting the element would care for him, buoy him, reminisce with its hands on his body of peace and a soothing control. Plunge, unhunch the stinging shoulders, glide. He was home again, he would be welcomed.

It was his darkness, his room. He knew where things were, believed nothing had changed, and so it hadn't, and he moved efficiently, not unduly cautious, not afraid of butting into things, upsetting what might be precarious, disastrous. The door he had opened, never to return or to return in a moment or to simply open and see the other side. It moves on its hinges. Is he coming or going, is it opening in or out. The bedroom's one window, cut high in the wall was barely above ground level. To see in from outside you had to move very close to the glass or kneel down. Cecil could see the wooden platforms that supported the outside garbage cans of the ground floor tenants. April moonlight curled around the bottom of the aluminum drums. *Walpurgisnacht*. A black cat with arched, prickly back should suddenly appear, a flood of gray rats thud in terror from the cans. In the harsh theatrical moonlight framed by the narrow window all things seemed possible, begged for some ominous display of the black powers.

Esther's plump buttocks claimed a moondrop. She must have been sleeping when she struggled from beneath the covers because the night was neither hot nor humid. Cecil sat in a straight-backed chair aware of clothing that was draped on the seat and backrest. A moonspot, then moon modeled to the deepened cleft. Wherein joy of my desiring. Stirred. Cecil strained his eyes in the darkness. What would there be to see. Perhaps something I had seen before, perhaps I could see more deeply, she would lead me where to look.

Cecil in the chair, Esther sprawled naked on her naked bed. Moonlight, starlight, the silvered drums trembling imperceptibly as mute, indifferent spirals twist through them eternally. So Cecil dreamed.

The Lynchers
. . . .

To Hiram Haydn—
bless the affinities

The author wishes to acknowledge Herbert Aptheker's collection A Documentary History of the Negro People in the United States *(New York: Citadel Press, 1951), which served as the source for many of the quotations in this novel's "Matter Prefatory."*

Matter Prefatory

And entering in [a river], we see
a number of blacke soules,
Whose likelinesse seem'd men to be,
but all as blacke as coles.
Their Captaine comes to me
as naked as my naile,
Not having witte or honestie
to cover once his taile.

"The First Voyage of Robert Baker to Guinie . . . 1562"

Everye white will have its blacke,
And everye sweete its soure.

Thomas Percy, *Reliques of Ancient English Poetry,* 1765

I Would Willingly Whisper to You The Strength of Your Country and The State of Your Militia; Which on The foot it Now Stands is so Imaginary A Defence, That we Cannot too Cautiously Conceal it from our Neighbours and our Slaves, nor too Earnestly Pray That Neither The Lust of Dominion, nor The Desire of freedom May Stir those people to any Attempts The Latter Sort (I mean our Negro's) by Their Dayly Encrease Seem to be The Most Dangerous; And the Tryals of Last Aprill Court may shew that we are not to Depend on Either their Stupidity, or that Babel of Languages among 'em; freedom Wears a Cap which Can Without a Tongue, Call Togather all those who Long to Shake off the fetters of Slavery and as Such an Insurrection would surely be attended with Most Dreadfull Consequences so I Think we Cannot be too Early in providing Against it, both by putting our Selves in a better posture of Defence and by Making a Law to prevent The Consultation of Those Negros.

Governor Alexander Spotswood, 1710

And while we are, as I may call it, Scouring our Planet, by clearing America of Woods, and so making this Side of our Globe reflect a brighter Light to the Eyes of Inhabitants in Mars or Venus, why should we in the Sight of Superior Beings, darken its People? Why increase the Sons of Africa, by Planting them in America, where we have so fair an Opportunity, by excluding all Blacks and Tawneys, of increasing the lovely White and Red? But perhaps I am partial to the Complexion of my Country.

Benjamin Franklin, 1751

They import so many Negros hither, that I fear this Colony will some time or other be confirmed by the Name of New Guinea.

Colonel William Byrd, 1736

Ibos pend' cor' a yo (Ibos hang themselves)

Old Haitian saying

From New London [Connecticut], Feb. 20th past. By certain Information from a Gentleman we are assured, that some Weeks ago to the Westward of that place, a very remarkable thing fell out, (which we here relate as a caveat for all Negroes medling for the future with any white Women, least they fare with the like Treatment,) and it is this, A Negro Man met abroad an English Woman, which he accosted to lye with, stooping down, fearing none behind him, a Man observing his Design, took out his Knife, before the Negro was aware, cut off all his unruly parts smack and smooth, the Negro Jumpt up roaring and run for his Life; the Black now an Eunuch is alive and like to recover of his Wounds and doubtless cured from any more such Wicked Attempts.

Boston News-Letter, March 3, 1718

I'll tell you 'nother funny joke 'bout Henry Johnson. He had to clean up most of the time. So Mrs. Newton's dress was hanging in the room up on the wall, and when he come out he said to old Uncle Jerry, he said: "Jerry, guess what I done." And Jerry said: "What?" And Uncle Henry said: "I put my hand under Old Mistress' dress." Uncle Jerry said: "What did she say?" Uncle Henry say: "She didn't say nothing." So Uncle Jerry 'cided he'd try it. So he went dragging on in the house. Set down on the floor by Old Mistress. After while he run his hand up under her dress, and Old Master jumped up and jumped on Jerry and like to beat him to death. Jerry went out crying and got out and called Henry. He said: "Henry, I thought you said you put your hand under Old Mistress' dress and she didn't say nothing." Uncle Henry said: "I did and she didn't say nothing." Jerry said: "I put my hand under her dress, and Old Master like to beat me to death." Uncle Henry said: "You crazy thing, her dress was hanging up on the wall when I put my hand up under it."

From *Lay My Burden Down*, B. A. Botkin, ed.

In fact the only weapon of self defense that I could use successfully was that of deception.

Henry Bibb, *Narrative*

. . . I remember Mammy told me about one master who almost starved his slaves. Mighty stingy, I reckon he was.

Some of them slaves was so poorly thin they ribs would kinda rustle against each other like corn stalks a-drying in the hot winds. But they gets even one hog-killing time, and it was funny, too, Mammy said.

They was seven hogs, fat and ready for fall hog-killing time. Just the day before Old Master told off they was to be killed, something happened to all them porkers. One of the field boys found them and come a-telling the master: "The hogs is all died, now they won't be any meats for the winter."

When the master gets to where at the hogs is laying, they's a lot of Negroes standing round looking sorrow-eyed at the wasted meat. The master asks: "What's the illness with 'em?"

"Malitis," they tells him, and they acts like they don't want to touch the hogs. Master says to dress them anyway for they ain't no more meat on the place.

He says to keep all the meat for the slave families, but that's because he's afraid to eat it hisself account of the hogs' got malitis.

"Don't you all know what is malitis?" Mammy would ask the children when she was telling of the seven fat hogs and seventy lean slaves. And she would laugh, remembering how they fooled Old Master so's to get all them good meats.

"One of the strongest Negroes got up early in the morning," Mammy would explain, "long 'fore the rising horn called the slaves from their cabins. He skitted to the hog pen with a heavy mallet in his hand. When he tapped Mister Hog 'tween the eyes with that mallet, 'malitis' set in mighty quick, but it was a uncommon 'disease,' even with hungry Negroes around all the time."

From Lay My Burden Down, B. A. Botkin, ed.

Dear Brother: . . . It was a sense of the wrongs which we have suffered that prompted the noble but unfortunate Captain John Brown and his associates to attempt to give freedom to a small number, at least, of those who are now held by cruel and unjust laws, and by no less cruel and unjust men. To this freedom they were entitled by every known principle of justice and humanity, and for the enjoyment of it God created them. And now, dear brother, could I die in a more noble cause? Could I, brother, die in a manner and for a cause which would induce true and honest men more to honor me, and the angels more readily to receive me to their happy home of everlasting joy above? I imagine that I hear you, and all of you, mother, father, sisters and brothers, say —"No, there is not a cause for which we, with less sorrow, could see you die." Believe me when I tell you, that though shut up in prison and under sentence of death, I have spent some very happy hours here. And were it not that I know that the hearts of those to whom I am attached by the nearest and most enduring ties of blood-relationship—yea, by the closest and strongest ties that God has instituted—will be filled with sorrow, I would almost as lief die now as at any

time, for I feel that I am now prepared to meet my Maker.
. . .

John Copeland, fugitive slave captured with
John Brown at Harpers Ferry, 1859

Petition from Kentucky Negroes, March 25th, 1871

To the senate and house of Representatives in Congress assembled: We the Colored Citizens of Frankfort and vicinity do this day memorialize your honorable bodies upon the condition of affairs now existing in this the state of Kentucky.

We would respectfully state that life, liberty and property are unprotected among the colored race of this state. Organized Bands of desperate and lawless men mainly composed of soldiers of the late Rebel Armies Armed disciplined and disguised and bound by Oath and secret obligations have by force terror and violence subverted all civil society among Colored people, thus utterly rendering insecure the safety of persons and property, overthrowing all those rights which are the primary basis and objects of the Government which are expressly guaranteed to us by the Constitution of the United States as amended; We believe you are not familiar with the description of the Ku Klux Klans riding nightly over the country going from County to County and in the County towns spreading terror wherever they go, by robbing whipping ravishing and killing our people without provocation, compelling Colored people to brake the ice and bathe in the Chilly waters of the Kentucky River. . . . We appeal to you as law abiding citizens to enact some laws that will protect us. And that will enable us to exercise the rights of citizens. We see that the senators from this state denies there being organized Bands of desperaders in the state, for information we lay before you a number of violent acts occured during his Administration. . . .

1. A mob visited Harrodsburg in Mercer County to take from jail a man name Robertson, Nov. 14, 1867.

2. Smith attacked and whipped by regulation in Zelun County Nov. 1867.

3. Colored school house burned by incendiaries in Breckinridge Dec. 24, 1867.

4. A Negro Jim Macklin taken from jail in Frankfort and hung by mob January 28, 1868.

5. Sam Davis hung by mob in Harrodsburg May 28, 1868.

6. Wm. Pierce hung by a mob in Christian July 12, 1868.

7. Geo. Roger hung by a mob in Bradsfordsville Martin County July 11, 1868.

8. Colored school Exhibition at Midway attacked by a mob July 31, 1868.

9. Seven persons ordered to leave their homes at Standford, Ky. Aug. 7, 1868.

10. Silas Woodford age sixty badly beaten by disguised mob. Mary Smith Curtis and Margaret Mosby also badly beaten, near Keene Jessamine County Aug. 1868.

11. Cabe Fields shot—and killed by disguised men near Keene Jessamine County Aug, 3, 1868.

12. James Gaines expelled from Anderson by Ku Klux Aug. 1868.

13. James Parker killed by Ku Klux Pulaski, Aug. 1868.

14. Noah Blankenship shipped by a mob in Pulaski County Aug. 1868.

15. Negroes attacked robbed and driven from Summerville in Green County Aug. 21, 1868.

16. William Gibson and John Gibson hung by a mob in Washington County Aug. 1868.

17. F. H. Montford hung by a mob near Cogers landing in Jessamine County Aug. 28, 1868.

18. Wm. Glassgow killed by a mob in Warren County Sep. 5, 1868.

19. Negro hung by a mob Sept. 1868.

20. Two Negros beaten by Ku Klux in Anderson County Sept. 11, 1868.

21. Mob attacked house of Oliver Stone in Fayette County Sept. 11, 1868.

22. Mob attacked Cumins house in Pulaski County.

Cumins his daughter and a man name Adams killed in the attack Sept. 18, 1868.

23. U.S. Marshall Meriwether attacked captured and beaten with death in Larue County by mob Sept. 1868.

24. Richardson house attacked in Conishville by mob and Crasban killed Sept. 28, 1868.

25. Mob attacks Negro cabin at hanging forks in Lincoln County, John Mosteran killed & Cash & Coffey killed Sept. 1869.

26. Terry Laws & James Ryan hung by mob at Nicholasville Oct. 26, 1868.

27. Attack on Negro cabin in Spencer County—a woman outraged Dec. 1868.

28. Two Negroes shot by Ku Klux at Sulphur Springs in Union County, Dec. 1868.

29. Negro shot at Morganfield Union County, Dec. 1868.

30. Mob visited Edwin Burris house in Mercer County, January, 1869.

31. William Parker whipped by Ku Klux in Lincoln County Jan. 20/69.

32. Mob attacked and fired into house of Jesse Davises in Lincoln County Jan. 20, 1868.

33. Spears taken from his room at Harrodsburg by disguise men Jan. 19, 1869.

34. Albert Bradford killed by disguise men in Scott County, Jan. 20, 1869.

35. Ku Klux whipped boy at Standford March 12, 1869.

36. Mob attacked Frank Bournes house in Jessamine County. Roberts killed March 1869.

37. Geo Bratcher hung by mob on sugar creek in Garrard County March 30, 1869.

38. John Penny hung by a mob at Nevada Mercer county May 29, 1869.

39. Ku Klux whipped Lucien Green in Lincoln county June 1869.

40. Miller whipped by Ku Klux in Madison county July 2, 1869.

41. Chas Henderson shot & his wife killed by mob on silver creek Madison county July 1869.

42. Mob decoy from Harrodsburg and hangs Geo Bolling July 17, 1869.

43. Disguise band visited home of I. C. Vanarsdall and T. J. Vanarsdall in Mercer county July 18/69.

44. Mob attack Ronsey's house in Casey county three men and one woman killed July 1869.

45. James Crowders hung by mob near Lebanon Merion county Aug. 9, 1869.

46. Mob tar and feather a citizen of Cynthiana in Harrison county Aug. 1869.

47. Mob whipped and bruised a Negro in Davis county Sept. 1869.

48. Ku Klux burn colored meeting-house in Carrol county Sept. 1869.

49. Ku Klux whipped a Negro at John Carmin's in Fayette county Sept. 1869.

50. Wiley Gevens killed by Ku Klux at Dixon Webster county Oct. 1869.

51. Geo Rose killed by Ku Klux near Kirkville in Madison county Oct. 18, 1869.

52. Ku Klux ordered Wallace Sinkhorn to leave his home near Parkville Boyle county Oct. 1869.

53. Man named Shepherd shot by mob near Parksville Oct. 1869.

54. Regulator killed Geo Tanhely in Lincoln county Nov. 2, 1869.

55. Ku Klux attacked Frank Searcy house in Madison county one man shot Nov. 1869.

56. Searcy hung by mob Madison county at Richmond Nov. 4, 1869.

57. Ku Klux killed Robt Mershon daughter shot Nov. 1869.

58. Mob whipped Pope Hall and Willett in Washington county Nov. 1869.

59. Regulators whipped Cooper in Palaski County Nov. 1869.

60. Ku Klux ruffians outraged Negroes in Hickman county Nov. 20, 1869.

61. Mob take two Negroes from jail Richmond Madison county one hung one whipped Dec. 12, 1869.

62. Two Negroes killed by mob while in civil custody near Mayfield Graves county Dec. 1869.

63. Allen Cooper killed by Ku Klux in Adair county Dec. 24, 1869.

64. Negroes whipped while on Scott's farm in Franklin county Dec. 1869.

65. Mob hung Chas Fields in Fayette county Jan. 20, 1870.

66. Mob took two men from Springfield jail and hung them Jan. 31, 1870.

67. Ku Klux whipped two Negroes in Madison county Feb. 1870.

68. Simms hung by mob near Kingston Madison county Feb. 1870.

69. Mob hung up, then whipped Douglass Rodes near Kingston Madison county February 1870.

70. Mob takes Fielding Waller from jail at Winchester Feb. 19th, 1870.

71. R. L. Byrom hung by mob at Richmond Feb. 18th. 1870.

72. Perry hung by mob near Lancaster Garrard County April 5th, 70.

73. Negro hung by mob at Crab-orchard Lincoln county Apr. 6th, 1870.

74. Mob rescue prisoner from Summerset jail Apr. 5, 1870.

75. Mob attacked A. Owen's house in Lincoln county Hyatt killed and Saunders shot Apr. 1870.

76. Mob releases five prisoners from Federal Officers in Bullitt county Apr. 11th, 1870.

77. Sam Lambert shot & hung by mob in Mercer county Apr. 11th, 1870.

78. Mob attacks William Palmer house in Clark County William Hart killed Apr. 1870.

79. Three men hung by mob near Gloscow Warren county May 1870.

80. John Redman killed by Ku Klux in Adair county May 1870.

81. William Sheldon Pleasanton Parker Daniel Parker Willis Parker hung by mob in Laurel county May 14th, 1870.

82. Ku Klux visited Negro cabins at Deak's Mill Franklin county robbed and maltreated inmates May 14th, 1870.

83. Negro's school house burned by incendiaries in Christain county May 1870.

84. Negro hung by mob at Greenville Muhlenburgh county May 1870.

85. Colored school house on Glen creek in Woodford county burned by incendiaries June 4th, 1870.

86. Ku Klux visited Negro cabin robbing and maltreating inmates on Sand Riffle in Hay county June 10, 1870.

87. Mob attacked Jail in Whitely County two men shot June 1870.

88. Election riot at Harrodsburg four persons killed Aug. 4, 1870.

89. Property burned by incendiaries in Woodford County Aug. 8, 1870.

90. Turpin & Parker killed by mob at Versailles Aug. 10, 1870.

91. Richard Brown's house attacked by Ku Klux, in Hay.

92. Simpson Grubbs killed by a band of men in Montgomery county Aug. 1870.

93. Jacob See rescued from Mt. Sterling jail by mob Sept. 1870.

94. Frank Timberlake hung by a mob at Flemingburg Fleming county Sept. 1870.

95. John Simes shot & his wife murdered by Ku Klux in Hay county Sept. 1870.

96. Oliver Williams hung by Ku Klux in Madison county Sept. 1870.

97. Ku Klux visited cabins of colored people robbed and

maltreated inmates at Havey Mill Franklin county.

98. A mob abducted Hicks from Lancaster Oct. 1870.

99. Howard Gilbert shot by Ku Klux in Madison county Oct. 9th, 1870.

100. Ku Klux drive colored people Bald-Knob Franklin county Oct. 1870.

101. Two Negroes shot on Harrison Blanton's farm near Frankfort Dec. 6th, 1870.

102. Two Negroes killed in Fayette county while in civil custody Dec. 18, 1870.

103. Howard Million murdered by Ku Klux in Fayette county Dec. 1870.

104. John Dickerson driven from his home in Hay county and his daughter ravished Dec. 12, 1870.

105. A Negro named George hung by a mob at Cynthiana Harrison county Dec. 1870.

106. Negro killed by Ku Klux near Ashland Fayette county January 7th, 1871.

107. A Negro named Hall whipped and shot near Shelbyville Shelby county Jan. 17, 1871.

108. Ku Klux visited Negro cabin at Stamping Ground in Scott county force (White) & Ku Klux killed two Negroes killed in self defense.

109. Negro killed by Ku Klux in Hay county January 14, 1871.

110. Negro church & school house in Scott county [burned?] Jan. 13, 1871.

111. Ku Klux maltreated Demar his two sons and Joseph Allen in Franklin Jan. 1871.

112. Dr. Johnson whipped by Ku Klux in Magoffin county Dec. 1871.

113. Property burned by incendiaries in Fayette county Jan. 21, 1871.

114. Attack on mail agent—North Benson Jan. 26, 1871.

115. Winston Hawkins fence burned and notice over his door not come home any more April 2, 1871.

116. Ku Klux to the number of two hundred in February

came into Frankfort and rescued from jail one Scroggins that was in civil custody for shooting and killing one colored man named Steader Trumbo.

On Lynching

. . . The crime which these usurpers of courts of law and juries profess to punish is the most revolting and shocking of any this side of murder. This they know is the best excuse, and it appeals at once and promptly to a prejudice which prevails at the North as well as the South. Hence we have for any act of lawless violence the same excuse—an outrage by a Negro upon some white woman. It is a notable fact, also, that it is not with them the immorality or the enormity of the crime itself that arouses popular wrath, but the emphasis is put upon the race and color of the parties to it. Here, and not there, is the ground of indignation and abhorrence. The appeal is not to the moral sense but to the well-known hatred of one class to another. . . .

For 200 years or more white men have in the South committed this offense against black women, and the fact has excited little attention, even at the North, except among Abolitionists; which circumstance demonstrates that the horror now excited is not for the crime itself, but that it is based on the reversal of color in the participants. . . .

Now where rests the responsibility for the lynch law prevalent in the South? It is evident that it is not entirely with the ignorant mob. The men who break open jails and with bloody hands destroy human life are not alone responsible. These are not the men who make public sentiment. They are simply the hangmen, not the court, judge, or jury. They simply obey the public sentiment of the South—the sentiment created by wealth and respectability, by the press and pulpit. A change in public sentiment can be easily effected by these forces whenever they shall elect to make the effort. Let the press and the pulpit of the South unite their power against the cruelty, disgrace and shame that is settling like a mantle of fire upon these lynch-law states, and lynch law itself will soon cease to exist.

Nor is the South alone responsible for this burning shame and menace to our free institutions. Wherever contempt of race prevails, whether against African, Indian or Mongolian, countenance and support are given to the present peculiar treatment of the Negro in the South. The finger of scorn at the North is correlated to the dagger of the assassin at the South. The sin against the Negro is both sectional and national; and until the voice of the North shall be heard in emphatic condemnation and withering reproach against these continued ruthless mob law murders, it will remain equally involved with the South in this common crime.

Frederick Douglass, 1892

I was struck by a question a little boy asked me, which ran about this way—"Why does the American Negro come from America to fight us when we are much friend to him and have not done anything to him? He is all the same as me, and me all the same as you. Why don't you fight those people in America that burn the Negroes, that made a beast of you, that took the child from its mother's side and sold it?"

William Simms, May 11, 1901, during Filipino Insurrection

. . . More than 500 persons stood by and looked on while the Negro was slowly burned to a crisp. A few women were scattered among the crowd of Arkansas planters, who directed the grewsome work of avenging the death of O. T. Craig and his daughter, Mrs. C. P. Williamson.

Not once did the slayer beg for mercy despite the fact that he suffered one of the most horrible deaths imaginable. With the Negro chained to a log, members of the mob placed a small pile of leaves around his feet. Gasoline was then poured on the leaves, and the carrying out of the death sentence was under way.

Inch by inch the Negro was fairly cooked to death. Every few minutes fresh leaves were tossed on the funeral pyre until the blaze had passed the Negro's waist. . . . Even after the flesh had dropped away from his legs and the flames were leaping toward his face, Lowry retained consciousness. Not once did he whimper or beg for mercy. Once or twice he attempted to pick up the hot ashes in his hands and thrust them into his mouth in order to hasten death.

Each time the ashes were kicked out of his reach by a member of the mob. . . .

As the flames were eating away his abdomen, a member of the mob stepped forward and saturated the body with gasoline. It was then only a few minutes until the Negro had been reduced to ashes. . . .

Memphis Press, January 27, 1921

I watched a Negro burned at the stake at Rocky Ford, Miss., Sunday afternoon. I watched an angry mob chain him to an iron stake. I watched them pile wood around his helpless body. I watched them pour gasoline on this wood. And I watched three men set this wood on fire.

I stood in a crowd of 600 people as the flames gradually crept nearer and nearer to the helpless Negro. I watched the blaze climb higher and higher encircling him without mercy. I heard his cry of agony as the flames reached him and set his clothing on fire.

"Oh, God; Oh, God!" he shouted. "I didn't do it! Have mercy!" The blaze leaped higher. The Negro struggled. He kicked the chain loose from his ankles but it held his waist and neck against the iron post that was becoming red with the intense heat.

"Have mercy, I didn't do it! I didn't do it!" he shouted again.

. . . Nowhere was there a sign of mercy among the members of the mob, nor did they seem to regret the horrible thing they had done. The Negro had supposedly sinned against their race, and he died a death of torture.

Soon he became quiet. There was no doubt that he was dead. The flames jumped and leaped above his head. An odour of burning flesh reached my nostrils. Through the leaping blaze I could see the Negro sagging and supported by the chains. . . .

. . . The mob walked away. In the vanguard of the mob I noticed a woman. She seemed to be rather young, yet it is hard to tell about women of her type; strong and healthy, apparently a woman of the country. She walked with a firm, even stride. She was beautiful in a way. . . .

"I'm hungry," someone complained. "Let's get something to eat." . . .

"Gov. Whitfield won't have a lick of luck with any investigation of the burning of Jim Ivy." So declared William N. Bradshaw, of Union County, Mississippi, admittedly a member of the mob that for forty-eight hours sought the Negro accused of criminally assaulting a white girl near Rocky Ford, Miss., Friday morning in a statement to the *News-Scimitar* this morning. "And furthermore," he continued, "not an officer in Union County or any of the neighboring counties will point out any member of the crowd. Why, if he did, the best thing for him to do would be to jump into an airplane headed for Germany—quick. Sure the officers know who were there. Everybody down there knows everything else. We're all neighbors and neighbors' neighbors." . . .

Memphis *News-Scimitar,* September 1925

When the two Negroes were captured, they were tied to trees and while the funeral pyres were being prepared they were forced to suffer the most fiendish tortures. The blacks were forced to hold out their hands while one finger at a time was chopped off. The fingers were distributed as souvenirs. The ears of the murderers were cut off. Holbert was beaten severely, his skull was fractured, and one of his eyes, knocked out with a stick, hung by a shred from the socket. . . . The most excruciating form of punishment consisted in the use of a large corkscrew in the hands of some of the mob. This instrument was bored into the flesh of the man and woman, in the arms, legs and body, and then pulled out, the spirals tearing out big pieces of raw, quivering flesh every time it was withdrawn.

Vicksburg, Mississippi, *Evening Post*

I had rationalized my environment, but it had rejected me in the name of colour prejudice. Since there was no understanding on the basis of reason, I threw myself into the arms of the irrational. I became irrational up to my neck . . . the tom-tom drummed out my cosmic mission . . . I found, not my origin, but the origin. I wedded the world! The white man has never understood this magical substitution. He desires the world and wants it for himself alone. He considers himself predestined to rule the world. He has made it useful to himself. But here are values which do not submit to his rule. Like a sorcerer I steal from the white man a certain world which he cannot identify. . . . Above the plantations and the banana trees I gently set the true world. The essence of the world was my property. . . . The white man suddenly had the impression that I was eluding him and taking something with me. They turned out my pockets but found there only familiar things. But now I had a secret. And if they questioned me, I murmured to myself . . .

Frantz Fanon, *Black Skin, White Masks*, 1952

Every organization, then, involves a discipline of activity, but our interest here is that at some level every organization also involves a discipline of being—an obligation to be of a given character and to dwell in a given world. And my object here is to examine a special kind of absenteeism, a defaulting not from prescribed activity but from prescribed being.

Erving Goffman, *Asylums*, 1961

Slavery was the worst days was ever seed in the world. They was things past telling, but I got the scars on my old body to show to this day. I seed worse than what happened to me. I seed them put the men and women in the stock with they hands screwed down through holes in the board and they feets tied together and they naked behinds to the world. Solomon the overseer beat them with a big whip and Massa look on. The niggers better not stop in the fields when they hear them yelling. They cut the flesh 'most to the bones, and some they was when they taken them out of stock and put them on the beds, they never got up again.

When a nigger died, they let his folks come out the fields to see him afore he died. They buried him the same day, take a big plank and bust it with a ax in the middle 'nough to bend it back, and put the dead nigger in betwixt it. They'd cart them down to the graveyard on the place and not bury them deep 'nough that buzzards wouldn't come circling around. Niggers mourns now, but in them days they wasn't no time for mourning.

The conch shell blowed afore daylight, and all hands better git out for roll call, or Solomon bust the door down and git them out. It was work hard, git beatings, and half-fed. They brung the victuals and water to the fields on a slide pulled by a old mule. Plenty times they was only a half barrel water and it stale and hot, for all us niggers on the hottest days. Mostly we ate pickled pork and corn bread and peas and beans and 'taters. They never was as much as we needed.

The times I hated most was picking cotton when the frost was on the bolls. My hands git sore and crack open and bleed. We'd have a little fire in the fields, and iffen the ones with tender hands couldn't stand it no longer, we'd run and warm our hands a little bit. When I could steal a 'tater, I used to slip it in the ashes, and when I'd run to the fire I'd take it out and eat it on the sly.

In the cabins it was nice and warm. They was built of pine boarding, and they was one long row of them up the hill back of the big house. Near one side of the cabins was a fireplace. They'd bring in two-three big logs and put on the fire, and they'd last near a week. The beds was made out of puncheons fitted in holes bored in the wall, and planks laid 'cross them poles. We had ticking mattresses filled with corn shucks. Sometimes the men build chairs at night. We didn't know much 'bout having nothing, though.

Sometimes Massa let niggers have a little patch. They'd raise 'taters or goobers. They liked to have them to help fill out on the victuals. 'Taters roasted in the ashes was the best-tasting eating I ever had. I could die better satisfied to have just one more 'tater roasted in hot ashes. The niggers had to work the patches at night and dig the 'taters and goobers at night. Then if they wanted to sell any in town, they'd have to git a pass to go. They had to go at night, 'cause they couldn't ever spare a hand from the fields.

Once in a while they'd give us a little piece of Saturday evening to wash out clothes in the branch. We hanged them out on the ground in the woods to dry. They was a place to wash clothes from the well, but they was so many niggers all couldn't git round to it on Sundays. When they'd git through with the clothes on Saturday evenings, the niggers which sold they goobers and 'taters brung fiddles and guitars and come out and play. The others clap they hands and stomp they feet and we young-uns cut a step round. I was plenty biggity and liked to cut a step. . . .

In them days I weared shirts, like all the young-uns. They had collars and come below the knees and was split up the sides. That's all we weared in hot weather. The men weared jeans and the women gingham. Shoes was the worstest trouble. We weared rough russets when it got cold, and it seem powerful strange they'd never git them to fit. Once when I was a young gal, they got me a new pair and all brass studs in the toes. They was too little for me, but I had to wear them. The brass trimmings cut into my ankles and them places got miserable bad. I rubs tallow in them sore places and wrops rags round them and my sores got worser and worser. The scars are there to this day.

I wasn't sick much, though. Some the niggers had chills and fever a lot, but they hadn't discovered so many diseases then as now. Massa give sick niggers ipecac and asafetida and oil and turpentine and black fever pills.

They was a cabin called the spinning-house and two looms and two spinning wheels going all the time. It took plenty sewing to make all the things for a place so big. Once Massa goes to Baton Rouge and brung back a yaller gal dressed in fine style. She was a seamster nigger. He builds her a house 'way from the quarters, and she done fine sewing for the whites. Us niggers knowed the doctor took a black woman quick as he did a white and took any on his place he wanted, and he took them often. But mostly the children born on the place looked like niggers. Aunt Cheyney always say four of hers was Massa's, but he didn't give them no mind. But this yaller gal breeds so fast and gits a mess of white young-uns. She larnt them fine manners and combs out they hair.

Oncet two of them goes down the hill to the dollhouse, where the Missy's children am playing. They wants to go in the dollhouse and one the Missy's boys say, "That's for white children." They say, "We ain't no niggers, 'cause we got the same daddy you has, and he comes to see us near every day and fotches us clothes and things from town." They is fussing, and Missy is listening out her chamber window. She heard them white niggers say, "He is our daddy and we call him daddy when he comes to our house to see our mama."

When Massa come home that evening, his wife hardly say nothing to him, and he ask her what the matter, and she tells him, "Since you asks me, I'm studying in my mind 'bout them white young-uns of that yaller nigger wench from Baton Rouge." He say, "Now, honey, I fotches that gal just for you, 'cause she a fine seamster." She say, "It look kind of funny they got the same kind of hair and eyes as my children, and they got a nose look like yours." He say, "Honey, you just paying 'tention to talk of little children that ain't got no mind to what they say." She say, "Over in Mississippi I got a home and plenty with my daddy, and I got that in my mind."

Well, she didn't never leave, and Massa bought her a fine, new span of surrey horses. But she don't never have no more children, and she ain't so cordial with the Massa. That yaller gal has more white young-uns, but they don't never go down the hill no more to the big house.

Aunt Cheyney was just out of bed with a suckling baby one time, and she run away. Some say that was 'nother baby of Massa's breeding. She don't come to the house to nurse her baby, so they misses her and Old Solomon gits the nigger hounds and takes her trail. They gits near her and she grabs a limb and tries to hist herself in a tree, but them dogs grab her and pull her down. The men hollers them onto her, and the dogs tore her naked and et the breasts plumb off her body. She got well and lived to be a old woman, but 'nother woman has to suck her baby, and she ain't got no sign of breasts no more.

They give all the niggers fresh meat on Christmas and a plug tobacco all round. The highest cotton-picker gits a suit of clothes, and all the women what had twins that year gits a outfitting of clothes for the twins, and a double, warm blanket.

Seems like after I got bigger, I 'member more and more niggers run away. They's 'most always cotched. Massa used to hire out his niggers for wage hands. One time he hired me and a nigger boy, Turner, to work for some ornery white trash, name of Kidd. One day Turner goes off and don't come back. Old Man Kidd say I knowed 'bout it, and he tied my wrists together and stripped me. He hanged me by the wrists from a limb on a tree and spraddled my legs round the trunk and tied my feet together. Then he beat me. He beat me worser than I ever been beat before, and I faints dead away. When I come to I'm in bed. I didn't care so much iffen I died.

I didn't know 'bout the passing of time, but Miss Dora come to me. Some white folks done git word to her. Mr. Kidd tries to talk hisself out of it, but Miss Dora fotches me home when I'm well 'nough to move. She took me in a cart and my maw takes care of me. Massa looks me over good and says I'll git well, but I'm ruint for breeding children.

After while I taken a notion to marry and Massa and Missy marries us same as all the niggers. They stands inside the house with a broom held crosswise of the door and we stands outside. Missy puts a little wreath on my head they kept there, and we steps over the broom into the house.

Now, that's all they was to the marrying. After freedom I gits married and has it put in the book by a preacher.

. . . My husband and me farmed round for times, and then I done housework and cooking for many years. I come to Dallas and cooked for seven year for one white family. My husband died years ago. I guess Miss Dora been dead these long years. I always kept my years by Miss Dora's years, 'count we is born so close.

I been blind and 'most helpless for five year. I'm gitting mighty enfeebling, and I ain't walked outside the door for a long time back. I sets and 'members the times in the world. I 'members 'bout the days of slavery, and I don't 'lieve they ever gwine have slaves no more on this earth. I think God done took that burden offen his black children, and I'm aiming to praise Him for it to His face in the days of glory what ain't so far off.

Mary Reynolds, Louisiana, from *Lay My Burden Down*, B. A. Botkin, ed.

ONE

· · · · ·

SOMEWHERE he was singing. Pure, effortless tenor rising to the mellowest, highest note possible a sweet tenor ever sang. *Nearer, nearer my God to thee* shaping his lips. His eyes closed, head tilted so that the nape of his neck sank into the white choir robe and his throat from which music issued curved thick and fluted from stiff white collar to out-thrust chin. Yet he did not strain, could have been sleeping, so easily, smoothly did he form the notes. Then it was gone, the rest of the choir sweeping up his solo in their gusts of rich chanting.

She saw him sprawled in the soft chair, mouth open, head flung back, pasted to that perpetual grease spot on the slip-cover. The rug did not quite reach the corners of the room and two legs of the soft chair dug knurled toes into the linoleum. His arms dangling where they had slipped from the thin, tattered arms of the chair, one big hand empty and from the other, inching as fingers relaxed, a brightly colored paperback book. She stood motionless until the book slapped against the scarred border of linoleum. He did not stir and she stepped noiselessly from the room.

When he awakened his neck hurt and his eyes watered, blinking into focus. The necessity of a gunfighter's eternal vigilance jostled into his thoughts and he wished he could be like the Pecos Kid, one eye always open when he slept. A surge of good feeling, of warmth reminded him he had done something well, or had something pleasant to anticipate. Orin Wilkerson recalled the climbing, the crystal note. But when he grunted up from the chair, clumsy sections of himself clattering and bumping like freight cars shuddering into motion behind a steam engine, he knew music had been left behind. No rhythm to his footsteps as he shook the cocoon of sleep from his body. Dust and smoke and moss sliding down. In piles at his feet. You want to wipe the sleep fog from your skin the way you dry yourself with a warm towel after a shower. Work shoes still on his feet weighing as much as they do at the end of the day, though this day is barely beginning.

He is suddenly cold, a swift, enveloping chill. Door or window open he knows, though he can't see it. He would call her but if it is morning she may be asleep and perhaps she slept right through and I can tell her any lie, choose the decent hour I came in and just too tired so went to sleep downstairs on the couch. Even as he forms a probable fiction he knows she will be sitting in the kitchen, aware of everything.

And she is and she asks why did he bother to come home for the hour he did. He wants more from her. He wants her calling him out of his name, calling him *Sweetman,* treating him like he's still in the street or like she wants him gone. He shivers again in the draft, his voice aching the no sleep, the endless fog hours reeling inside him, wasted and still to come that he must set in order for the small woman drinking coffee at a gimpy table. Does the table tremble too in the same chill waves that pass over his flesh, is it cup rattling against saucer that he hears chattering inside his jaw. She stirs her coffee very slowly, spoon the elongated fin of a meandering shark circling its prey in the brown liquid. Some slops into the saucer, mutes the bone rattle.

—Don't lie to me. He thought she would repeat the phrase. Please, don't lie to me, the *please* a softening, a breach he could enter and take her wronged softness, but she did not admit him did not repeat or request, demanded simply, once, that he not lie. And he couldn't. But circled the small kitchen in his work shoes, saying nothing, avoiding her eyes, careful not to step on land mines, or over sheer cliffs, tentative till he found a safe path through the blue and gray squares of linoleum, then repeating his steps exactly, not stepping on a crack, not breaking his mother's back, circling till he realized he was a spoon held in orbit by a giant fist whose knuckles were going white. And each time the hand forced him deeper into the floor, scoring the faded covering, burning down through lathes and plaster and beams, opening a hole to hell, a lopsided oval through which his wife would tumble with him.

In the kitchen a silent, curdling postponement. Pocked walls breathing sourly, patient mirrors of everything and if peeled layer by layer paint to paper to paper to paint to paint you would see old lives crowded as saints in the catacombs. Their children's hand prints crawling up the wall. The low border when it was a third leg to hold them up, the grease streaks from the boys' slicked down heads as they leaned back cockily on spindly legged chairs sneaking smokes and trading lies around the kitchen table, up near crease of ceiling and wa l, splash of roach where she told Thomas not to squash them even if he could reach that high. Once blue, once yellow, hopelessly white, blue again, now the rosette paper meant for somebody's living room. All layers seemed to hover near the surface, dark ghosts scratching through the faded blush of roses. The walls would never be disguised again. They would regress now, shedding skin after skin, betraying the past.

She realized how easily it could all disappear. Everywhere in the neighborhood buildings were being torn down. A wall could look so pitiful when everything around it had been stripped away. No ceiling, floors missing, no outer walls to protect its pink or blue from the bleaching sun. A room was just space, just emptiness bounded by paint and plaster.

Standing in the emptiness she liked to call *her* kitchen, where she reigned if nowhere else. Cooking and serving their meals. First two to feed, a neat ritual she could give herself to wholly, chiding him playfully to remember to bless the food, then three, a quiet settling down together, boy an image of his father, so pleased with himself, so grown when his seat hiked by a pile of cushions and phone books was pulled to the table, four, five, finally six, four, three, two again . . .

sometimes, but not the same two, not the same sleepiness, the anticipation, the gently fumbling progress through the dishes, the down hill glide of simple chores always easing toward the bed they shared. Not a circle. Not the same two. A steep hill you climb then tumble down. One.

If she would only cry. Orin wanted her to be the girl sobbing, the rich damp earth in which he had first planted his seed. Not spring but deep winter, snow clouding the mounds of garbage heaped on the curb. Rooftops stayed prettier longer than the rest, gleaming white crust unbroken by tires or footsteps though it too would gray in the fine, clinging soot constantly rained from thunderheads huddling blackly over the city. Summer hot in the room because furnace either overheated or sent nothing except pops and grunts up through its pipes. One day the room covered with soot, every surface, the edges of the oval picture frame with its sepia portrait of a moustachioed black man, doilies set out on the coffee table, in shoes under the bed, coating the waxy looking plastic flowers she had arranged in a water pitcher. She cried. And it was hell hot in November and we got as naked as we could, finally alone, finally together someplace where we didn't have to worry about somebody's footsteps or a door flung open. You are my sunshine. She was a stranger to me in her flesh, the places shaped by bones close under the skin, springy hair in the heat frizzled and damp on her head and curling thickly, innocently from her belly. Lighter places the sun never touched where veins showed, and the skin though mottled was one piece, a covering over flesh and bones that did not break into sections the way clothes make women breasts and waist and ass and legs but moulded one whole curving animal moving together, brown and supple.

It rained between us, stinging hot, cold, sweet, sour rain we trapped between our bodies, that we drank deeply into all the openings of our flesh. Rain dance an oozing sluggish rhythm then heat lightning and thunderclaps and tropical downpour threatening to wash us away, tugging our island to pieces, whipping up the sea that lapped icily like shadows. Her sobbing in peace, contentment and release as we lay side by side on our wet backs staring up at the blazing sun and a blue sky through which white clouds rushed. Smouldering, only hands touching, utter stillness until once every thousand years a huge cool drop of rain spattered against our nakedness and we shuddered. Then we were Mr. and Mrs. Wilkerson. If I had seen these walls and floors, the loneliness tottering from her womb, the years which her thighs flapping like tired pigeon wings opened and closed, the dark passage, time and time and endless hours, could I have seen her sitting in this kitchen her body either aged not at all or decaying flabby under the robe twenty years too soon would I have been so young once, so eager to enter and take her hand and walk on, keep walking and whistling and children laughing unseen in the corners and stumbling and walking in the darkness still while her ghost drinks coffee and there is nothing to say that is not a lie because I began so young and eager and she . . .

She leans, one hand holding the robe to her chest, and reaches toward the radio. Wrist is thin and ashy. He remembers the cold. He has removed neither the second sweater nor the quilted jacket, feels instinctively for the duck billed cap and when it is not there scratches loudly in the nappy thick hair above his ear. He feels silly, countrified, one monkey picking another's fleas from its red behind. As if the hat on or off made a difference. Little boy's hat he wore each morning to war with the rats. Cap should have been there so he could sweep it off and bow low in one elegant gesture. Honey, I begs your pardon, I shorely do ladychile I shorely does ma Lady Honey Lamb lighting up her regal frailness, wrapping her bright shoulders in furs and pulling lace up around her delicate throat, I do declare I don't know what got into me Honey Lady forgettin a thing like that. Prince Beauregard down on one knee, her pale hand withheld then graciously, haltingly tendered while the heavy lashes subtly flutter, dark butterflies above her lowered eyes.

All's well ending well. To be forgiven after the worse.

But ain't coming this morning in this kitchen ain't no need standing around waiting neither.

—You might as well take this. Something in your belly besides whatever rot you've been drinking all night. No way to take the mug of coffee she poured but in a fighting mood the way she'll fling it at you so catch her eyes an instant as you glare over your shoulder hard and mean like staring down a dog you just kicked and making sure he has no notion of sneaking back to his feet and coming at your heels Just the head swiveling round on the tight neck. Hadn't even heard her move from her chair but she is beside the stove pouring hot water from tin pan into the hulking mug. Steam. All those stories about mean nigger bitches throwing boiling water on the cool daddies who did them wrong. But she fills the cup and sets the pan back on a burner. Her body still has curves and soft places but you wouldn't believe it seeing her wrapped in that robe. Robe looks dirty. Like she cooks in it or sits around all day drinking. Know it's not. Just washed and ironed so many times color whipped out of it. Yellow or white or tan.

Mug is on the table. Me on one side, her standing across on the other. As far as she's going cup says sitting there like a bomb or a rat she's caught but don't want to pull from the trap so leaves it out for me to throw away.

—Woman, why don't you get a new robe. His eyes are lowered though he is almost shouting. Better pick it up by the handle or burn my fingers. Steam.

Her back is to him. She takes up little space but seems crowded between table and the stove which she now faces. Oven is probably on, she's probably standing there so the heat can run up under her night clothes. Her shoulders are shaking. Even through all the sweaters and jacket he can feel the cold. Maybe she is laughing. He looks down into the blackness with its aura of curling steam. Careful not to spill, to hold it steady and put one foot after the other carefully out of the kitchen back to the chair for ten minutes of blowing and sipping and feeling the tickle of warmth worm through him before he hits the streets again.

• • •

—So I took the wife downtown to see The Prime of Miss Jean Brodie. Wasn't much else playing just shoot em ups and the usual cops and robbers bullshit and I heard about this movie being pretty good all about lesbians and what not it was rated X so I thought mize well let the wife get out we got clean my old lady looking nice as she wants to we jumped in the car and went to see Jean Brodie. Movie was something else. Full of people we had to sit where the usher took us. Two old white ladies sitting behind us running off at the mouth through the whole damn thing. I got tired and turned around a few times but the old hens kept cackling getting all excited humming and tsch-tsching during the finger fucking scenes when the broads naked and laying on each other. Let me tell you now I was steady digging that action on the screen and I didn't need no silly old white ladies clucking in my ear like they didn't know people played sticky finger. Lights went on and my old lady goes to the powder room them bitches still jabbering behind my seat I started to get up and tell them something but I hear *Are you ready to go* one bitch up the other kneeing hell out my seat the bitch finally gets up turns her broad backside right up against my head and cuts loose. Blat. Easy and loud like it was nothing farting up against the back of my head. Lawd. Barupp. Loud just like that. Now you know. Man, I couldn't move. Just sat there not believing she had done it. Lights on and everything. Natural as if she was saying good-bye. Cuts loose on my head and said *let's go* to the other white lady and went on about their business. Talk about a nigger being hot. I was so mad I couldn't do nothing but sit there. Nasty old heifer. Barupp. I had to tell my old lady when she got back. She cracked up laughing all over the place but I didn't see a damned thing funny behind that action.

—Sweetman you look like somebody done farted on you this morning.

—Go on nigger, I'm tired and evil today.

—You getting too old to take care of business all night and work all day.

—Hysterectomy—that means they ain't got nothing inside. Her function is pissing and that's all. Fucking's over with.

—You wrong man. Today, you're wrong.

—Naw, they take all her insides out. Sensation and what not but ain't good for nothing but pissing.

—Who you telling. I used to go with one. She fuck you to death. Better than ever.

—You talking about a partial.

—What you call a dildo.

—In France some cats making them. Whatyoucallit, what models in the windows. Matchikins.

—Mannequins.

—Yeah. I saw in a movie where he making them with hair and skin that feels like the real thing.

—You have to be a weird cat to lay on something like that. I'd rather jerk off it come to that.

—Some weird shit.

—Buy anything in them stores back of Market Street. Dildoes in any shape and size. And color.

—One, she had fixed up real nice. You know like a handle grip she musta had twelve rubbers wrapped around it. Before I started messing with this trash I worked in a gas station. You run into all sorts of strange bitches working in a station. Bitches out there get hold of the old man's car running around doing they business burn up all his gas and ain't got no money. White broad in a fifty-nine Caddy convertible. Fill it up check the oil and water. So I do it up nice. Gas and two quarts oil. Wipe down all the windows. Come to seven dollars and forty-two cents. Went round to the driver's side and she just sitting there. I guess you want some money.

Rolls down the window cutting her eyes at me staring big as day. Then she say I don't have a dime. Lawd. I knew what's coming next. White bitch don't even blink when she say But I got plenty cock. And I'm thinking seven dollars and forty-two cents you better got a whole lot of cock. I drives her into the garage and pulls down the door. Bitch already had her drawers off and laying across the back seat. I knocked it out and she scooted round the side to pee. Whiles she gone I still thinking bout my seven dollars and forty-two cents. Naw, I wasn't finished. Hard as my money comes. She switches back I turns out the light and we in that Caddy again taking care of business. You know when she drove outa that station she hand me seven dollars and forty-two cents just as nice as you please.

—Some strange shit out there in the world. Some weird bitches.

—Weird ain't the word. Let me tell you about this other bitch. Always be some change behind the seats and on the floor. Two, three dollars every time she bring it in. Her old man own the factory across from the station. You know the place I mean. Right on down the street. She bring it in almost once a week to be washed. A white Lincoln. She leaves it so I means to check it out good. I found some dimes and quarters down in the seat so I said shit go on and do it right I had the seats out the muthafucka and copped a five dollar bill. I was searching my ass off and had about nine dollars and some change. Decided I try to get in the glove compartment. I'm fiddling around struggling and prising till I got the muthafucka open. Man, I didn't know what it was. Looked like a handlebar grip offen a bicycle. This bitch musta had twelve rubbers wrapped around it. I commenced to thinking and said to myself she jugging herself with that thing.

—A dildo. What you call a dildo. I saw a bitch doing herself with one. She was into a weird thing. See her all the time up in her window. You know it was up on the third floor so I couldn't see nothing but her head and shoulders.

I couldn't tell what she was doing. But she was always there and always had that one arm going and gazing off into space. I could just see the shoulder from my window so I didn't pay it no mind. Figured she's shucking peas or squeezing margarine. Just sitting in her window with that shoulder I noticed always going up and down. I got to wondering more and more about this shit so one day while my mama was out shopping I sneaked up on the roof and crossed over two, three more so's I could look right down into her room.

—And I shore nuff gonna question her about that tool she had fixed up soon as she came back for her car. But I got busy with one another thing round there and missed asking her. Took me till next week fore I got to it but I asked her what she doing with that grip. Seems her old man ain't no good. Lawd. I told her ain't no need to be doing all that. You got a good man standing right here ready. I tore that pussy up. You better believe it. Her old man had to take her down to Florida. Moved out his building across the street. She got hot pants behind that action I put on her. Man's gonna need a chain to keep her home wherever he goes.

—The bitch got her legs cocked up wide as hell on the bed and working away at herself with a dildo.

—Be some hard work.

—It might be hard but she working that thing good and seemed to be liking it all right. All the time gazing out the window.

—That's damn hard work.

—Some weird bitches out here.

—You run into the damndest shit working in a station. Sometimes I don't know why I quit to come on this garbage job.

—Bitches out here is something, man.

—Riding to work about five thirty and it was cold's a muthafucka. Hawk was whipping them streets to death. I was on my way to work minding my business. Bitch scared me. Jumping out from behind a parked car. I had stopped for a light. Had my radio on and heater going I was all warm and couldn't care less. Heard tapping on my window. Bitch shocked shit outa me. So I rolls down the window. Grinning with her bad teeth she says How far down you going, Daddy. How far you going, girl. Get on in. Thought the bitch going to work. Bitch wasn't going nowhere. You know she was out there cold as it was hustling in the morning.

—Man, you oughta give the broad a few dollars and send her off that corner. Hustling at that hour. That's a hard up broad.

—I took er on down the station. Went in the garage and got her up on the lift.

—Childress, you lying now.

—If I'm lying, I'm flying and my feet sure ain't got no wings. I'm telling you just like it is, Sweetman.

—On the lift.

—Shit yeah. Drive on the platform and hike the mutha-fucka right up. Get that bitch up in the air and knock out that pussy.

—You crazy, man. You go on knocking it out and you gonna rock the boat. Capsize the mothafucka and you, car and broad hit the floor.

—Naw. I know that lift. Locked our ass tight in there we do all the rockin we want.

—Gotta rock a hell of a lot to bring a car down off one of those pneumatic jacks.

—After a while we ease on down. I takes her for some breakfast and the bitch be telling me how hungry she been and shit.

—Man, you saw that woman out there freezing you ought to give her a few dollars and sent her home.

—We finished eating and I say good-bye girl and don't you know the bitch start hemming and hawing and talking some off the wall shit. I . . . I . . . I thought you was going to give me something. Damn. Told her I did give her something.

—That's what you shoulda told her.

—I give her something, warmed up her behind real nice and bought the bitch breakfast besides. I told her you better go on girl, get out my face with that gimme something shit. Hustling in the cold at that hour.

—Was she clean.

—You damn right she clean. Rode up on the lift and spread them legs. She was real clean.

—Shit. Childress, all you know is your motherfucking dick ain't dripping yet.

—That was years ago, man. When I was working in a gas station. I'm still flying high hard and clean and that trifling whore probably dead by now.

—Good old days in the barracks. People with funky asses and feet who don't like to wash. Scrub them with lye soap and dry them in burlap. Stings for days. They remember that shower. One cat was good at picking out farts. Everybody be sleeping away and it be dark as a muthafucka, cats steady snoring and braaack somebody cut loose. If they find the Johnson out he goes. Don't matter how cold it be outside. But it be dark in the barracks, couldn't see shit. DePetrie could find the Johnson in the dark. I'd tap him and he'd still be half sleep and we lay there quiet till the cat popped again and DePetrie say it come from there pointing in the pitch black. Find that Johnson and out his ass would go.

—There be some cats can't help it. This boy he have the kind of feet be sweating all the time. Behind all the perspiring the cat have some funky dogs. But he keep his self clean and nobody say nothing to him. But them non-washing dudes. Out they go. Everybody jump on they ass. The lieutenant come in talking shit no passes cause the joint funky. You know you got some hot dudes. Whip on them that don't keep they ass clean.

—DePetrie find him and out the Johnson go. When you pulling duty and be walking outside the barracks you can hear it all night. Cats be in there blasting away. Hot dogs, potato chips, eggs, beer, and if they had beans in the Mess Hall, good gawd amighty. Blasting away. Barupp. Braack.

—Barupp. I couldn't believe the nasty old heifer. Got up

out her seat put her ass in the aisle and cut loose as much as if to say *Blatt. I'm going now. Good-bye, Mr. Nigger.*
   –How you know the bitch was clean.
   –It's best in the dark. You got to do it when it's dark . . .
   –Like digging jazz.
   Why you think people like it dark when they listen to jazz. Somebody had asked me that in Harold's. In the middle of all the nasty talk they did each morning. Like nobody really ready to git out of bed yet and they are still there dreaming all the pussy they've had or smelling and fingering their bodies or the body they've caught for the night. Coming to Harold's for some extra sleep. Talk and whiskey a woolly gray blanket over their heads. To each his own. But why should it be dark. First of all the dude that said it just knew he was right. People want it dark. Need it dark. And you don't dance either. Almost solemn as a sanctified church. But, hell. That ain't so solemn. Shoutin and signifyin and prayin loud enough to be heard in the street. I would have liked to hear Harold answer. Come up with some of his three years at Morgan State these are the facts of the matter shit. He'd be wrong but at least you have to beat him down and think before you open your mouth or he'll make a fool of you and everybody laughing till you can see somebody getting terrible quiet and tight jawed and then it's time to beat on somebody else. Even in the morning these dudes will fight. Fact is they probably fight sooner in the morning. Everybody still sleepy or sleeping and running down what they want to be not what they are. Like don't rap on my man's new coat if he been working like a dog to get the coins together even if he looks like a damn fool in it. After he starts cursing it himself, talking about how much it cost and wishes he had his coins back then you can beat on him. But these cats still dreaming at Harold's in the morning.
   Because maybe jazz dreaming too. Or those listening dreaming of leather coats and big cars and fat thighed sisters. Don't know what a man playing jazz could be thinking. Does he want the lights out? I remember the piano player Chil-

dress knew and he came on down to the bar and we all had a drink. Just jiving. The cat was stone folks. Natural and we're rapping like I known him my whole life. Only thing his eyes redder than any eyes I've seen. And he blinks. Take the cover off a skillet with two eggs frying and see them kinda soupy running together before they firm up only these eggs was a pinky red bloodshot and each time he blinks top's off that skillet somebody turned off the fire because they are just sitting there undone and getting no better. He must have seen me looking. Said bitch broke my motherfucking shades. And I understood everything. How jazz men always on the go always moving from town to town and probably have plenty women but keep none of them actually happy so when he calls or knocks on the door the woman feels good but she is mad too because she knows here he is and something real nice is going to happen but sure as morning the nigger will be gone and god knows when he'll be back but sorry assed bitch that I am I'll get up and fix him something to eat and be hurt when he leaves and let him take enough of me with him I'll open the door next time and be opening it for him when others knock or call and them running through me like water because I'm waiting for him and he may not even come back but so good when he does I could kill him. So after he's been good and then getting ready to go she smashes the gold rimmed dark glasses to the floor. Her nail catches in his cheek when she rips them from his face. He knows it has to come to this and no way to change it because this is just the way it has to be if you move from town to town and try to have a little something going each place. But the bitch ain't supposed to fuck with my things. But this is the way it has to be so he doesn't really try to hurt her bad. He blots the sting on his cheek with an open palm and quick like an answer to the trumpet's riff same hand slaps her to the bed. She thinks for a second she is in hell, that the devil is standing over her, eyeless, his stare is so vacant. She thinks he will lean down and scrape his eyes from the back of the broken glasses, and paste them into the rawness above his cheeks. Watching that act worse than the death. But he blinks, doesn't even look down because he knows what he'll see, crumpled on the floor. No sense in saving the jagged pieces. The way it has to be he just walks out saying nothing the way he came.

I am staring at his eyes and he has nothing to say except what he did. After all some things are plainly out of your hands so they are just there and people being what they are can't help noticing. You say a few words and they either understand or no sense in trying to say more. *I coulda killed that silly whore*. And tomorrow you'll find new shades in this city or another city and there will be nothing to say.

Childress said he had met the piano man in a bar one night. They just started to talk. The cat wasn't jamming just sitting at the bar. Childress didn't know him from Adam but they talked for a long time. Sees him now every time he's in town. The cat's real together. He's been around. One of the best at his trade. Childress didn't know much about music except that some of it got to him especially near the end of the night at the Vets and he thought he was over with some mamma, but since he had talked with the jazz cat Childress say he into his music. Dug the way the piano man played no matter what he played or who he was jamming with. And Childress didn't make a big deal behind knowing the cat. I mean he didn't *I want you to meet my man* loud enough for the whole place to hear and back slapping and tugging at the piano man's elbow like he was some fine bitch Childress was turning out. They both just kind of slid off to the side of the bandstand, at a corner of the bar where the waitress sets her tray and nobody sits. Tight with Childress and Childress say *this is Sweetman my main man*—everything's okay and I'm talking with them.

Cat was from the South. And he laughed about the home folks and country ways. Childress had only been there during the war but they understood one another about how you had to laugh at some of the shit or be dead or crazy. But they didn't talk that much. One would say something and they'd laugh or grunt or make some other noise or repeat a word several times each taking a turn and doing something a little different with how he says it. They didn't want to be in one another's way so lots of space between sounds. Just the bar noise to fill in and little ripples of music from the jukebox somebody had turned on when the set was over. The light wasn't very good anywhere but it was almost black where we stood. Childress and the cat seemed to get far away. Not like they tried to make me feel I shouldn't be with them. It was like I was slipping into a deep thing someplace they might take me but where I'd be alone. I remembered how Childress talked about the cat's music. I thought about moving so fast nobody could see you pass but to you the moving would be very slow, drifting more than anything else, like in water or a scrap of paper sailing. Listening to jazz in the dark. The waitress made her order. Funny stuff like frozen daiquiris, lady fingers, sloe gin fizzes, and it had never seemed so funny until just then. Little kids running to the ice cream truck. Half of them ain't got a damned cent but they's running as fast as the pickaninnies that have dimes in their fists. Candy ice cream cake. And the bell tinkling and some Jew or dago in a frowsy white coat parceling out the goodies. I could see that summer day and me racing with the others and worried somebody would snatch my money or whatever I bought. Right in front of my eyes though I was deep somewhere in the talk of Childress and the jazz man, deep as in a black woods but a summer day I could look at floating like a balloon or closed in a glass ball. The kind you turn upside down and snow falls over the little church and people inside the glass. Snow drifting down lazy. You shake it and down again just as lazy over the house and people.

—She got a nice pair of tits.

—Yeah I was digging.

A small light below the level of the bar haloed the spot where the waitress paid her bills and picked up her orders. I didn't need to look to see her features then her tight white blouse modeled in the glow. His voice made both. Two smoked circles of glass had grown over the jazz man's eyes.

They were home again. I did not see them but I knew shades patched the rawness, that he needed them and they slide into place as real as the waitress switching her tail away from the arc of light.

But I be damned if I know. Badass jazz blowing cats traveling from town to town shooting down the locals, doing what they can do best blowing away, gunfighters only not at high noon but doing their fighting in the dark when all the lights out. Time I was in Camden trying to get into something my man Childress and me stopped for a taste in some little hole in the wall. Drinking gin in the middle of the afternoon getting friendly and loud talking with all these strange dudes after a while you get lost could be West Hell or Camden or round the corner from your crib for all you know niggers and gin kind of insinuating wrapping you round till you comfortable and floating with whatever place you be. Sitting there talking away and before you know it you been to New York City and Frisco and Deetroit and Chicago and China and West Hell and back all round the world drinking gin messing with white folks and cutting niggers and somebody smoking a reefer in the toilet good Nam grass a young dude with a black beret slanted on his head and the dude talking a funny game going to change the world you begin to believe his hat is straight and him leaning forty-five degrees he has a purple hand the bones sharp and the skin of his fingers like crusty canvas over tent poles offering you a toke on his shit you take it from him and drag the way it's supposed to be dragged though you don't like tobacco and only smoke once in a great while raggedy weeds like he's offering the dude running down his revolutionary game like you still there when you pull the door closed after you step into the midnight bar everybody bigger than when you left they are moving faster and their voices gathered in a box somewhere near the ceiling that weaves them all together into a riff chasing the juke.

And the riff is people passing me like they going to a fire. Black faces blurring into white. Horns and plate glass windows and sad-eyed mannequins dead for fifty years staring at their own stiff reflections. You thought you were the lizard scuttling fast as four legs could carry you but the others without even trying leave you behind or high heel tramp their way right through you. You are jazz being played in some dark room. In the late afternoon street, sidewalks glinting a shower of golden flecks that swim before your eyes, sin kisses, you are a ghost losing his way. Somebody bumps you and you want to crumple where you are. Be another spot of spit, sweat or wine staining the sidewalk, flat on your back looking up pant legs and mini-skirts. Smell the soft underbellies of the bloodhounds chasing you. A cop is exploding in the middle of an intersection. At any moment the brass and blue and icy leather will tear apart the thick body puffing itself up to hold them together. I can see his belly straining to reach the billows of blue serge.

Because somebody is asking me last week how I am today and they are getting an answer. A lame, wrong answer but the social worker knowingly shakes her head and believes it, and here I am ass over ears bumping along chased by a gorilla riff.

So it must be the dark that does it. Darkness necessary. Like Childress said not so much that the cat was famous or supposed to be the best at what he was doing but that he knew the cat and that's what he heard when he listened.

• • •

Outside Harold's, city still dark or at least not light yet. We flowed out into our cars. Fuzzy edges still pretty much like they were when we went in to have our morning drink.

–Later, you badass bunch of sanitary engineers.

You have to go over a bridge to get to the depot. As a matter of fact the depot is kind of under the bridge you go over. Always in the shadow of the bridge so sometimes like you are going into a cave. The crews would be rolling in all at once thirty, thirty-five minutes before the trucks had to go out. Day didn't start till half hour after punch-in time. Union got us thirty minutes for changing, getting the equipment together. A good crew could get a truck ready in ten minutes and most came to work dressed to go so after punching in we had twenty minutes to bullshit and pass around a taste if anybody brought one. You could tell where people was at by the taste they offered around. Like Clarence bring a fifth of Bali Hai once or twice a month and be doing good then one day up he jumps with a pint of Cutty Sark you know he either done left his old lady again or hit the numbers or both if he come along with something top shelf for a couple days in a row.

When is this shit gonna cease. Orin Wilkerson swore softly under his breath. Somebody had killed the pregnant movie star. All that good, white pussy doing nobody any good anymore. A damned shame. Somebody crazy did it. Must of been to look at her fine as she was and in the condition she was and cut her down. Goddamnit. He saw them scurrying around him. The men he saw each morning. He thought he knew them. The way you know Clarence or Clisby who has that Continental he loves and nothing else in the world. But you see them hustling and bustling round here these last ten minutes, cursing, all those raggedy clothes they wear like space suits or second stiff, greasy skins they all look pretty much alike. Then again before the rush they all talk the same shit. Drinking and fucking and how badass they are or whatever team in whatever sport they are following on T.V. Some just sit quiet though. And some only speak when asked but when they put in their two cents you know they're happy to get it out and all they needed was an opening. I think I know them. Can call most names. Then I try to image one of these sorry assed dudes with a knife in his hand going to carve up some white movie star. Standing in her big living room where she paid more for a rug than he can for an automobile, where a picture tacked over the fireplace would buy the whole house in which he's renting three rooms.

I can't figure it out. Had to be somebody just like one of these. Or me. Not that half these niggers ain't stone crazy.

Got to be a little crazy to be out here before the sun even up wrestling with garbage cans and chasing rats. Or doing whatever you have to do day after day to keep food in your mouth and the Man from taking away every stick you got including the roof over your head.

All that ain't crazy as you have to be to get in a car and drive up to somebody's big house and cut them up like you would chickens on Saturday night.

Paper tries to make a story of it. Tell what was done, who did it how many bodies and ages and how much money but you take all the pieces and it still don't add up. Still don't tell me how one of these men I see every morning walking around me and laughing and shouting and drunk and getting in my way could do it. And it has to be one like them. Unless an altogether different kind of people in the world. Kind that can breathe in your face and shake your hand and talk the shit you do while really they never stop scheming and hating and looking for the chance to pull some woman's drawers down and slice her up.

I know there's people crazy sick. I mean so bad nothing you can do but keep them locked up. But too much is going on. And gets weirder every day. And the ones they catch seem hardly different except they did the thing that makes the newspaper full of blood. Getting so that strange shit is regular as rain. Nothing more to do about it than you can about rain. Stay indoors when you think it's coming.

–Let's make it.

–Hit the road, Jack.

–Do your dreaming with your arms wrapped around some fine garbage can. They be smelling good this morning. Make your joint hard.

–Let's make this run, youall. No time to be bullshittin.

• • •

Not quite dawn. Morning an echo over the city. Not an echo idly repeating, but drawing into itself all senses and details of the hour and returning them sea changed, un-accountably harmonious. Steep hill to climb, sharp right at the crest you are on the bridge under whose arching shadow we gather six days a week. Caught in a web of steel and con-crete, sharp angles, the hurtling, whiney thrust of the ma-chine. Somebody in the cab is fresh from a woman. Among the other odors of three large men cramped in a small space that special, sweet stink every so often pricks a nostril open.

—Poontang. Don't want to catch none of you niggers sniffing at his fingers.

River below. City panoramaed on all sides. Lights are warm. Not the high yellow or icy coal of night or the blank, sun blinded glare of day. Somewhere in between. Everything mellowed. As if after being together so long, silhouettes and sky had worn down the harsh, cutting edges of their conjunc-tion. Dawn middle ground. Time Orin liked best particularly here on bridges, bridges which at this hour did not pace businesslike over the void but merged the shifting masses of water land and sky. And time. He never looked at his watch when the truck began its run. The motor turned over when the time clock at the depot reached precisely the half hour and he would mechanically glance at its bland, white face once to admire the synchronization. Then time left him as it seemed to leave the echoing stillness of the city. Since it was not night and not day and all he could hear see smell and touch confirmed some floating middle ground he felt no need to measure the transition, to rush away from its gliding full-ness.

Did the others know how far away they were? That this bubble had left time and might never be trapped again. The motor would sputter and cough in the thin air. Rainbow fish would ripple past the windows. He wondered how a fly felt resting in the damp vault of an immense cathedral. A flea in the belly of a whale.

—If you want to sleep go right ahead. But I ain't gonna listen to your snoring. Cat's gonna come in here smelling of pussy, dreaming and snoring like just cause I'm driving I'm the only one with a job.

The vehicle clattered at the end of the bridge. Steel plates used to reinforce the bridge surface had been loosened by the pressure of heavy traffic and flapped when struck. Jolt and crash were no more inevitable than Childress:

–The muthafuckas gonna come clean apart one of these days.

Broad snout bloody with the last crumpled barricade the truck and crew highball to their rendezvous with the sleeping city.

• • •

It was March. Long afternoon walks that begin in warm sunshine end in shivering, rapid steps home again toward the indoors. Three men had talked in the park till the sun's waning and a chill wind sweeping off the river had driven them out of the bare trees to a bus stop. The park had been deserted. Ground snow blotted, still stiff, crunching underfoot when you stepped from the gray path beside the river. Grays and browns, dull city colors reflected in the water.

The men continued to argue as they waited beside a trembling aluminum pole festooned with bus route numbers. The city's avenues were broad, exposed, good for pomp and circumstance parades, for displaying monumental architecture, good for cannoneers to sight down in the best Napoleonic tradition. Bad for people whose clothes are thin and few. As the men talked their bodies shuttled in the wind.

–Hey Littleman, how come I got to be tween you and the wind every time you start to say something.

–Stand where you please, Saunders.

–I'd get behind you cept you don't make much of a windbreaker.

–Your mama breaks wind.

–How come little dudes always the first to jump bad and call the dozens. Must be cause they know they's put on earth to get they asses kicked.

—Every dog has his day. And the earth keeps turning, the days keep changing.

—I could say something about the dog that had you, since you started that mama stuff. But I don't play the dozens. Dogs and days. Listen to him, Wilco. Littleman thinks he might get lucky some day and whip somebody. That's why he tries so hard to fuck with people. Playing percentages. Figures if he gets whipped enough times he's due one of these days to get him a win.

Thomas Wilkerson wanted to speak. Say words which would dull the cutting edge of the talk. Talk had been brutal all afternoon. Pick. Pick. Pick. Both men on tangents of anger connected only when one decided to strike out at the other. Always tense when they spoke of the plan, but today circling through the gaunt trees of the park, never really warm under the deceiving blue of the March sky, his companions had seemed ready to explode. Littleman absolutely committed to the plan, teasing and slashing at the others with the authority his readiness gave to him. Saunders resentful because Littleman had something he needed badly and would relinquish it only on his own terms, terms Saunders must submit to. Wilkerson still fumbling, unable to see the plan except as a joke or enormous threat. So Littleman piped and they paid. And the chill air made them brittle as glass as they bumped awkwardly in the music he played. Wilkerson wanted words to make them all laugh, forget a moment the violence that drew them together. But Littleman spoke first.

—Still just like kids. Still shy away as soon as we get to a serious issue and I ask a question that puts your backs to the wall.

—I wasn't the one started playing the dozens.

—It was a fool like you who invented the dozens. Some darky done with his cotton picking, picking his nose and toes and had nothing better to do than insult the fool darky lying next to him in Mr. Charlie's hog pen.

—You sure don't like niggers do you?

—What am I.

—A sorry assed, runty nigger who don't like hisself.

—The hawk is a bitch. I'll give somebody bus fare if they stand between me and that wind. Wilkerson knew his words weren't enough. A flickering match in the wind's bluster.

—What about Littleman, Mr. Hall, here. You gonna give him a whole fare for covering only half your chest. Course if he didn't have that bear rug on his chin, he could ride for kiddie fare.

—Leave him alone now. You don't know how far to carry a thing, Saunders.

—Everythin's gonna be all right. I surely don't need you to tell me how far to carry anything. I got hands and feet good enough to get me out anyplace my mouth puts me. Which is more than I can say bout some folks.

—Saunders, you know it's my pity for you that keeps me from smashing your skull. Several times today you asked to die. But I see myself in you, that meanness in you and in myself I can't do a thing about. But the meanness may be useful, after all. It saved your life today. Be grateful . . . be grateful . . .

—Littleman's getting hysterical.

It wouldn't go any further. Saunders' voice was subdued as he spoke and a barely audible *only funning anyhow* meant nothing else needed to be said. Wilkerson was learning. If they were going to talk about killing they had to believe in each other as killers. Which meant they had to recognize the point you don't push a man past. Perhaps with the others it was always a ritual of testing, rubbing the raw, morbid places which had to be ready when the time to kill came. Wilkerson could not believe that he was ready. If he had wounds the others could prod, he had managed to conceal their seriousness, even from himself. When they talked of the plan he gave his assent not as a killer, but as one who was beginning to understand why the others must kill. And why he must choose to aid them.

Gray pole quivered ringing hollow as the little man rapped its base with his cane. Height of a twelve year old, heavy head and shoulders done in a heroic manner then stick legs added by a clumsy apprentice.

–Let us forget the diversion. Let me return to the question you wanted to hide from.

Littleman's skin was that lightish brown that gets ashy in the cold. Eyes glazed too, wet in the cold, wide as if blinking were a sign of weakness. Rigid, distant as if he were not responsible for his voice or the light tapping of the cane which punctuated his words.

Bus wheezed to a stop beside them. There were clicks, jingles, rumbles, hot, stale breath in the face. Scattered seats were available and each man found a place, a silence among strangers.

• • •

Graham Rice lived in the basement. Two rooms and a kitchenette that shared crumbling brick outer walls with sixty other units of various sizes and shapes known collectively as the Terrace Apartments. Since words and particularly names fascinated Rice, he had developed the habit of looking for meaning behind, within or because of the patterns of words which confronted him in his everyday life. Words could reveal the significance of the past, prefigure the future, make a running commentary on Rice's present existence. The word science Rice had perfected was his history, religion and consolation. His own name was a mystery to be studied, a node at which countless lines converged. Rice. White food. White on rice. Rice of weddings. Soul food and Chinese food. Rice paddies. The East. The South. Uncle Ben. Ho Chi Minh. The Rice Bowl. Machine guns. Football games. Etcetera, etcetera he thought always some new consideration. Tentatively he had decoded these bare outlines of a plot: that rice was the sustenance of the poor man, the oppressed; that it was white because it came from the white man, the crumbs from his table, so much lotus for blacks and Chinamen to fight over while in fact both groups were themselves being consumed by the white devils' trickery. And Graham Rice was a vehicle, a manifestation of this knowledge of duplicity and oppression. In the very kernel of his being he understood exploitation and as a new Rice, a conscious, revolutionary Rice he would feed his knowledge to the masses, in fact become food for their souls. Graham was just a slave name, literally a cracker name, bestowed in ignorance to degrade and confuse him.

Living in the Terrace Apartments worried Rice. Not because of the building's deathly calm, its smell of old newspapers, not because he had to hide from the tenants while doing their dirty work, not because a Jew owned it, but because Rice could make nothing out of the name. Its significance utterly eluded him. None of its connotations or denotations aroused the slightest reverberations in the eighth sense he had developed. Even the obvious made no sense. No Terraces decorated the brick walls and the building's shape was an undifferentiated flat roofed box. The nothing name wasn't an overwhelming difficulty, more like the just discernible murmur in a tooth, the pre-critical worrisomeness that says things will get much worse, indeed.

Rice had forgotten to buy a new box of rice. When he turned Uncle Ben on his head, a short whisper of cascading grains barely covered the bottom of a cup. A few darker, fatter particles had also settled to the bottom of the package and speckled the tiny bit of remaining rice.

Shit.

Chicken and no rice. The wooden cabinet above the sink was easy to assay. Salt, pepper, flour, lard and hot sauce. Beans and sugar in pudgy, rolled-top bags. Not even a can of soup.

Shit.

Rice broke the tape and folded back the bloody paper. Chicken by itself. Wrinkled, yellowish skin looked forlorn, needing a cushion of rice and a blanket of brown gravy. Chicken was to last three days but without rice to pad this evening meal, the bird would only last two. Just won't cook more than a breast and wing tonight. That way it'll have to last. I won't be able to pick at it in the icebox. It was a small dead bird when you got to cutting it up and thinking how each piece is gonna look floured and crispy. Good thing I got those six extra wings.

Doorbell made him jump. It seemed a response to the sawing incision he began down the center of the breast.

Heavy, loose handled door scratched open finding its customary furrow in the kitchen linoleum. The three men arguing loudly carried Rice with them into the center of the room.

—Who you gonna cut. Rice saw he still had the knife in his hand. The chicken was back in the box, but the knife with its lacy, serrated edge proclaimed him guilty.

—I was turning a screw. Fixing the light switch just as you came in.

—That's a pointy knife for turning screws. Saunders winked at Littleman and Wilkerson.

—Little screws.

—I bet they is. Don't let us interrupt, brother, go on do what you doing. Just come to get out of the cold. Saunders rubbed his hands together.

—Cold.

—Yeah, the hawk. You know like he's flying high. It's a bitch out there. And speaking of hawks and such things, you ain't seen none in here, have you?

—What.

—I mean hawks, pigeons, ducks, chickens, birds one thing another like that.

—The man's busy. Didn't he tell you. Why don't you look for yourself and leave Rice alone.

—Hey.

—Hey is right. Look what Butcher Brown done laid down.

—Saunders, that's my dinner.

—All of this. Paper rattled, the plump chicken was undone.

—Shit.

—Now you wouldn't send these hungry brothers back into the cold just so you could hoard this bird for another week or two. You know that ain't right. You know that bird needs to be in our bellies tonight and not sitting lonely in your icebox. Littleman was already rummaging in the refrigerator.

—You know Littleman can cook up some chicken. Com'on Rice. Put some tunes on. We ain't come empty handed. Got some stuff that goes good with chicken. Goes good with any damn thing.

—Gentlmen, I accept the office of Steward as well as Cook. You will be delighted to learn I have uncovered a cache of Rolling Rock Premium Beer to lubricate our repast. And half a dozen succulent, virgin angel wings.

—Shit.

• • •

They sprawled greasy mouthed and high as if the floor was the seat of an enormous, steep sided chair and a giant hand had helped them slide gently down the green walls to join two stereo speakers and a rack of paperbacks leaning between them. One of the books was spread-eagled over Wilkerson's groin. In between snores he muttered in the direction of a copy of *Believe It or Not*. Thelonious in San Francisco dropped quietly, painfully onto the machine. After the glare of Archie Shepp's ear and throat filling insistence, it seemed you could count to ten between each note Monk chose to touch. To Littleman Monk playing in this quiet, thoughtful mood was what classic meant. Knowing where you're going, how to get there, and being in no hurry. Patient, pure, simple notes saying *I am here because this is where I belong and nothing else would do.* Angela and that summer five years ago in Atlantic City. She'd go as far as the head of the stairs each morning, naked under her black raincoat, hair messy, sleepy-eyed. Little skinny girl playing grownup in her mama's clothes. Golden skin and black coat saying good-bye honey don't be home late honey and watching me make my cripple ass way tapping down the steps. I think she believed I might fall and she'd have to come and dust me off, straighten the little man up and point him in the right direction. We bought two records and made love to them that whole summer. She told me she could play the Rachmaninoff or anything if she practiced and I believed her as we moved to that music or Monk Alone which I thought would be harder to play the way he did because it was just him and some way he made the piano feel like she made me feel and no one since the same way.

Rice still had a wing to eat. It was only right he thought, his prerogative he thought to take the first, last and as many pieces in between as he could. So he was there with his plate as Littleman turned out the crisp, golden brown nuggets. Meat white and juicy when you bite inside. Saunders made the white meat red with hot sauce. Ate the skin first, peeled it like he was skinning a piece of wild game and then saturated the exposed flesh so it looked as if skin had been flayed. If uncouth meant anything it described to Rice the black, loud talking man who ate his chicken like a beast. Rice didn't want that last wing but he knew Saunders had been ready to pounce. Almost a responsibility so Rice spoke up and claimed his right. And Saunders bad-talked him anyway.

I'll eat it after this Rice promised himself reaching to take the smoke Wilkerson held toward him. A long greedy drag, I got almost as much as Saunders could suck up into those pig nostrils of his.

—The nigger won't eat it. Just took it for spite. But Lenny Saunders am too clean to be bothered. Flying too clean.

Wilkerson knew the music by heart. At least it seemed he could run ten bars ahead of Monk, hearing the music once as he sped past it and a second totally different pattern of sound when the notes caught him and bathed his curled body. Or backward, hiding till the music knew he had escaped and rhythms waited for him to resume the chase.

Monk died into Reflections. Last cut, last record on the stack.

Littleman flopped onto his belly. Wilkerson's eyes tracked across the bare floor. Dust balls, a safety pin, islands where the film of dust had not been disturbed. Littleman miraculously made whole, a normal man from this angle on the floor because his legs disappeared somewhere behind the thick shoulders. I am a fish sidling across the floor, a merman belly scrunching my way to where the restored Littleman has risen up to his elbows and challenges me with thundering eyes and swaying fist to arm wrestle.

–Thomas Wilkerson come give my ego a lift. Their open palms met, a violent, exaggerated thud. Clenched fingers were knots pulled tighter and tighter.

And if I could whip the little dude in this game, would I? But that's not the question, it's not holding back but seeing how long I can survive. Languor goes out of both, smoke glaze replaced by sweat, chicken, beer, pot, funky sweat which is a sheen then melts and collects, then dribbles as faces contort and shake. Littleman's beard is a live thing, a shaggy sponge drinking moisture from his face. But lips are laughing are sputtering when sweat seeps through moustache and black eyes tell Wilkerson exactly how much they are winning. Wilkerson begins to groan, to cry aloud, something part despair, part shouting down of Littleman's grunting, the machine-like pants that slowly form themselves into a word, *down, down.* Wilkerson heard the panting of dogs and women in labor, saw thighs grinding and buttocks bouncing smelled his own sweet farts and felt the soft parting, the rapturous release. Hmmmmm.

–Timber, timber, motherfucker. Slowly at first a tall tree in the wind, then strengthless but still erect, Max Schmeling after the Brown Bomber delivered, a wall slammed broadside by the black demolition ball, all stays gone, brief pitiful totter, maybe, maybe you won't die after all, then down,

down for good, good and hard, knuckles rapping on the bare floor, *down, down* Littleman still panting as if the rhythm and strength would not leave him, as if the victory were only partial, as if the hand embraced so tightly by his iron must be driven through the floor, driven to some sub-terranean rendezvous with *Down.*

The others had watched silently, not knowing how to be stirred, Rice nibbling at the wing, Saunders flexing his fore-arm as the balance teetered one way or the other. On his feet Saunders felt he had moved too quickly, covered an immense distance at too fast a pace. His knees wobbled, he was getting angry, half afraid to look down at his legs be-cause he knew they would be naked, the knobby knees shaking, his pants down around his ankles. They all laughed at him. Everybody in the stands, the same bitches who had squealed every time he galloped to the finish line first. But here he was, one bad day, his guts bringing up stale wine onto the cinders, his cool busted because he had roared out too soon, responded to their cheers and burnt out in the first 220 of the city championship quarter mile race. Riggy got me. That stiffening death at the back of the thighs, that lead tightening the calves so you can't lift them just hobble on like a Buick is sitting on your shoulders, just stagger to that tape that ain't no more cause all the mothers with they silk asses and cardboard numbers burned past you and took your win away. Last race. You bend till finally had to go on one knee. Cinders biting into the skin but don't matter would bury my face in that shit if I could. Everybody saw my knees shaking and so damned funny I lost, only once but I lost, I lost they will always say the big one.

Saunders felt the queasiness pass. Better now, leap from down to up must be delicately negotiated, he took four slow, short steps and bent, pushing the stack of records up the shaft again and the first disc plopped down and began to spin. The tone arm jerked and floated, deliberate, aloof, settling easy as a bee in a sunflower. Music made. Jazz Mes-sengers doing it. Columbia Avenue, South Street, the Jungle,

Senorita ohh laa la all mixed up in one bag. Staring at his stockinged feet Saunders watched them do quarter time an intricate cha cha step. The moves. He saw black sock transformed to spit shined patent leather. Square toed, buckled, perforated with intricate designs. Eyes doing double take from her brown ankles to hips and down again to his partner's red high heels following his lead. Moves. Catch her eyes hiding under drooping lashes, wink.

Saunders dat datted the staccato signature of Blakey's Cubano Chant. Trinidad by way of the Gold Coast. A naked brown girl, high breasts and fat butt wiggled to the rhythm. In her hands golden bananas that rattled like marimbas when she shook.

—I'm hungry again. Littleman was a grotesque puppet leaned against the wall, half a man bent in the middle with doll legs splayed in front of him that would never move unless someone tugged the invisible strings. Hand across high damp forehead his eyes dismissed Saunders' plaint even as lips buried in the beard answered:

—Chickee all gone, beer gone, joints all rolled and gone to heaven. Party's over.

Rice chewed cautiously, shifting the dry mouthful of chicken as best he could without allowing his cheeks to puff. He was afraid the wad he maneuvered might contain bones. Chicken bones could kill you. You don't even give them to dogs because the bones split and splinter like glass, become spears inside your soft guts. He wanted to get the mush down as fast as he could. He knew Saunders watched him, would abuse him for such a sloppy last ditch mouthful, so he had to get it down quickly. But he didn't want to die. They all were regarding him now. Accusing, stern faces. Eaten his chicken and now they were ready to hurt him for having his share of what *all* belonged to him.

Molars ground something hard. Bites tongue trying to dislodge the brittle morsel from the pack. Should I spit in my hand when I get it. Saunders. Bones.

Bones mean . . .

—Well, are you with us or not. Business time. It was Saunders' voice, crisply, impatiently, the way Littleman could ice his words.

Rice coughed, shavings of chicken flesh gulped and sprayed as Saunders whacked his hand down twice on the host's back.

—Little in-die-gest-nion, das all bothering the man. He ready to take care o business.

—Saunders, why do you try so hard to be a nigger, a sambo black ass field ignorant darky.

—What are you, Littleman? You want I should Speaka da Engleesh like a good wop, or sing Danny boy, or put ski on the ass end of all my words. Do you want me hunki-fied or spickified or maybe through my long Jew nose or like a Kennedy or collitch professor. I talk like your people, like your mother and mine been talking a long time. Is that what you don't like. Is you uptight with them.

—I thought we were ready for business. Wilkerson shouted to be heard.

—We've been through it all ten times in the park. I'll tell Rice what we've decided.

—I thought I . . . Rice was defeated but he could speak again squeezing the fistful of chicken balled in a sodden napkin.

—Wait a minute, Rice. Listen first. You'll get your say just like we promised.

On the floor again only this time ringed in a tight closed circle in the center of the room.

— . . . the crucial thing is to insure ourselves against fail-ure the most likely kind of failure and we've all agreed that the human factor, the four of us and what we must each do will put tremendous pressures on all of us. Therefore . . .

(run it down, brother)

Therefore we must build safeguards into the plan, minimize the possibility of individual cop-out by maximizing the cer-tainty that the one who fails cannot hurt the others and will himself be absolutely dealt with . . .

Wilkerson listened closely. The cloak and dagger intrigue, Littleman's lapses into grade B spy movie language at first amused him, but now as words and imagination drew closer to action, he had grown hypersensitive to nuances he hadn't dreamed existed. The wrong words could contaminate everything. He remembered making fun of Rice's notions. But the deed did have some magic relationship to the words. That was why Littleman was so angry in the park, why he became pedantic in his references to what they were doing. What they said they were doing was what the act would be. It had to be precise, it had to be *lynching a white cop*.

Lynch. Wilkerson remembered how he had laughed, had believed Littleman would laugh at the joke with him. But now he knew better. Littleman had never uttered the word *lynch* in jest. After Littleman had decided to recruit the others, each step had been carefully calculated. What seemed an idle, stray comment would be picked up later, embellished, repeated ten times in the space of a few days. Some lewd or comical suggestion would gradually lose its ridiculousness, establish itself in the meandering reality of their talks.

—What this town needs is a good old fashioned lynching. The real thing. With all the trimmings. It would be like going to church. Puts things in their proper perspective. Reminding everybody of who they are, where they stand. Divides the world simple and pure. Good or bad. Oppressors and oppressed. Black or white. Things tend to get a little fuzzy here in the big city. We need ritual. A spectacular.

—And they could put it on satellite T.V.

—In living color.

—Now I'm not talking about grabbing just any old body and stringing him up to the nearest lamp post. That's not it at all. We must learn to do a thing correctly, with style for immediate appeal and depth for the deep thinkers, the ones who concern themselves with history and tradition. I mean a formal lynching. With all the trimmings. And that's a world away from the crudities of your poor white vigilante necktie parties. I would eschew that western model, go to the South where tradition means something.

—When I talk about lynching, I'm talking about power. Down home the ones with the power are smart enough to know that people are hopelessly forgetful. Give them a little wine, a woman and from one day to the next they can't keep it in their heads that they are on earth to serve and die. The woolly heads even forget whose earth it is. Here's where power comes in. Power must always be absolute. When it's not absolute it's something weaker, imitating power. Which means if you have power in a situation you can do anything you want to those whom you have made powerless. You must be prepared to assert your power brutally and arbitrarily if it is to remain pure. In fact you must periodically expose the fundamental basis of your relationship to the powerless. The most forceful and dramatic means are most effective. If it's a man over his woman, he beats her because she bats an eyelash; if it's a king over a subject people he systematically slaughters their first born. A master exercises droit de seigneur with the women of his slaves. The white citizens of Talladega Mississippi lynch a black boy. And so it goes.

—What could be more dramatic? A great artist must have conceived the first lynching. As a failed poet myself I envy his sweet touch, the sure hand that could extricate a satisfying, stable form from the raw fantasies of his peers.

—Mr. Neegro, swinging in the breeze. You recall now, charred blacker than you ever were in life, pea brain boiled away, monkey bowels carved to souvenirs, you recall now with nothing else to do but dangle in your cherished idleness, who gives and who takes away. Who made you in darkness and who can come in the black hour of the wolf to unmake you. Forked log swaying in the heavy air, black pendulum tolling power, power, power. White power.

—You better believe that poor lynched darky blinks his message like a lighthouse through the misty countryside. Beware. Nigger beware. If the whim took us, we would burden every tree in Dixie. In our dealings with you we are constrained only by the limits of our imagination. Imagination which we possess in abundance, fertile, subtle, co-ercive. Witness your brother, our sport with him, how we make poetry from our power.

Littleman rambling on till the outrageous and plausible were linked in his metaphors. Often Wilkerson could walk away with a slightly condescending smile, amused because he had found the ravings of a madman so entertaining. But he knew a sharp razor did much of its work before the flesh felt its bite. His suspicions became increasingly palpable, he felt himself awakening from a deep sleep, stunned and helpless.

—You know I'm right. One lynched nigger more or less doesn't change anything. The symbol matters, the ritual. The point is to get it all out front. To say this is the way things really are. Will stay forever.

—Nothing is co-incidental. There are no accidents involved. All tactics and all roles are ordained within the master scheme. A passion play is what it's like. Only more engrossing because with each enactment a fresh sufferer is delivered to the mob. Real blood. Undignified screams and writhing. Maybe even more holy and sanctified since each actor is bound to his role not by some compact with a distant, abstract deity, but by the same circumstances which tie man to wife, children to families, families to the community which they have created. When Rastus burns there is a communal hard-on. Whites right, standing tall. Pine tree straight, snow clean, gleaming big and power swollen like an Empire State Building right here in lil ole Talladega, population: white—7,000; mules and niggers—8,000 minus one.

—Power. Neck stretching power.

—Cops standing around watching. Every damn body in the town knowing the open secret. Nobody from the outside knowing more than they can decipher from the mutilated, swaying corpse when they come upon it in the woods. No one must ever be prosecuted. Complicity. Conspiracy. From the littlest towhead red neck in progress to the fattest, cigar smoking most respectable cracker in the big house on the hill.

–What poetry.

–Do you think niggers could ever get themselves together enough to do a lynching in the grand manner?

–You know if it was done right, if tradition, nuance, imagination were consulted, the victim would have to be a white cop.

–And in the middle of the afternoon. And everybody standing around. Not looking at the beast but eating chicken from picnic baskets, sitting on fences munching watermelon. Dancing, singing, playing ball. Blasé as could be.

–In a big city. With black cops all around. Music blaring from the record shops. No white faces in sight.

–You wouldn't take his clothes off. Nobody would give a damn about seeing his pot belly and flabby ass. Leave him in his obscene blue uniform. Pour a sack of flour over his head while the noose is being fitted. He'd be sweating so much the flour would stick like it does to a wet chicken breast you're dipping to fry. Pasty, dough face screaming for John Wayne and the Texas Rangers to rescue him. Bleating Mercy boys, begging for mother, marines, yelling that the Jews did it. Red eyes vainly searching for some of his best friends out there in the crowd.

–Cart him away in a white sack with Nigger lover stenciled in eight inch letters. Throw it on the garbage heap at the city dump.

• • •

When Wilkerson left the others in Rice's apartment he had welcomed the cutting bitterness of the wind. It hurt him, defined him as Thomas Wilkerson, an old friend he has known for ages, a nice fellow whose eyes sting in the cold, whose hands and feet get numb even though he walks fast along the dark streets. Wilkerson could deal with the cold. No matter how badly the hawk whipped him it was like Littleman's hand, the reassuring challenge of flesh on flesh.

Thomas Wilkerson reflected upon Thomas Wilkerson, remembered there had been for him many nights like this cold March one. Time collapses and all those Tom Wilkersons stand side by side, compare notes, forget how many years had intervened between the lanky, self-conscious boy and this last lanky, shivering Wilkerson. How could he continue to work at what had been given him. His father's slow suicide. The deadening ache the Sweetman had become for his mother. How could he explain to the others what time had done. Perhaps he should listen and they could tell him. When you were thirteen the nappy headed kid began to say in his man-boy voice you thought nothing of stealin empties from behind Klein's store and cashing them in to get money and pay the girls for taking their drawers down so you could look. And the melange of voices began to tattle, scold and accuse, a babel of times and places that restored Thomas Wilkerson to himself.

Because once through the door and into the street he had been a stranger, some foul afterbirth of the smoke and talk and bloody promises compacted in Rice's apartment. The others would probably stay, sleeping on Rice's floor the way they often made themselves at home in Wilkerson's front room. But he had to get out. Escape. Leave the room though he knew he couldn't shake off Littleman's words.

—It's not as impossible as you might think. All the elements are present. The oppressors occupying army in their blue and white skins. Our people finally awakening to the nitty gritty of their situation with hundreds of years of anger and frustration to purge. In fact the dice are loaded in our favor. All we have to do is set the game in motion. Sevens will fall for us all day.

Streets were dark. Most houses seemed to have no curtains, just drawn shades, smoke gray over the windows or cat eye yellow where the odd light still burned. Nothing of spring in the night air. The hint of change he had felt in the park had died. Winter squatted with the finality of the first snowfall.

–Pick a day. Preferably a holiday that has special meaning for black folk. Sure enough there will be some kind of memorial program. Most likely to commemorate a martyrdom since the best black men have all gone that way. Now suppose on this spring or summer day, has to be warm to bring our folks out, there is more cause than usual for the community to be hateful toward the Man. Suspicious, let's say, of some outrage. Perhaps a sexual crime. Maybe a white cop beat up on one of the whores that pay him protection. Let's say this rancor is in the air and nobody has seen the woman for a day or two. You know how that would be the number one topic. How everybody would build their own version of the story. How after telling lies all around about what they know and saw and how they heard about it before anybody else, the storytellers would have to believe the tales themselves. Then a story appears on the front page of the Black Dispatch. Mutilated body found. Think of the turnout for what would ordinarily be a jive little program where a few Toms get high puffing out one another's sails. People would be in the streets. You could be sure that every hustling organization would want some of the action. Try to get a speaker on the platform to run down their answer. It would be an event. Snicks and Muslims and Rams. Every damn body wanting to capitalize one more time on some poor bitch they wouldn't have given a Band-aid to if she walked by bleeding at the throat. So here's all these hot, bothered niggers. Waiting for a chance to bust loose. Hoping for a speaker to say the word they need to catch fire. Of course whiskey will be going around in some quarters. The young boys will be sweating through their head rags. The good Naacp brethren who sponsored the service in the first place will be looking for ways to slip through the edge of the mob and move their automobiles. A goddamn regular Fourth of July powder keg just waiting.

Wilkerson had wished for some ghost of the high to gently becloud him. Or Monk's music to seep from one of the cold windows. Only Littleman's words came hard and brittle like sleet in the chill air.

—*Imagine just for an instant, if we could channel all that energy. Get to the people before the fever dissipates. Reach them before they explode into each other and bring the ambulances, fire engines and paddy wagons down on their heads. Suppose that for once we could put before their eyes the real villain. Now I don't mean some long winded string of epithets, no screaming condemnation of men far away and safe. Not hoarse words or silly puppet gyrations on a speaker's platform but the real thing. The criminal delivered up to them.*

—*Here's the one. This particular white man in his bold blue hunting suit is the one you all been talking about and looking for. No you haven't read in the white papers what he did to Clara Mae. Not news when some part time pimp cop slices up a black woman. (Crowd gasps) After all he's white, he's the Man. He's been serving her black meat to his customers all along. (Glory) She was his property. He had absolute power over her to do as he pleased. And he did as he pleased. Cut her the way you would a dead chicken. Why, I don't know. Not my business to ask why. He's the Man. (Motherfucking man) Why shouldn't he leave Clara Mae soaking in her blood. He paid rent to the landlord on Clearwater Street where we found her. Clara Mae owed him everything and it was his right to take back what he wanted. So he killed her and left her lying in her blood till the rotten black meat began to stink and her neighbors opened the door. (God rest her soul)*

—*Here he is. You won't see his name in the newspapers. Nor Clara Mae's name. Same old story, people. The Man gives and the Man takes away. This is not a guilty man. He's the judge and jury and we could hardly expect him to convict himself. I say he ought to go free. His hands are white. His eyes are blue. If that's not innocent I don't know what is . . .*

—*And the voice goes on signifying, insinuating. It's like a prayer meeting. Some old sister in the amen corner shouting back at the speaker. Blood of the lamb. Somebody weeping Oh god hunkies did it to my sister too. The walleyed junkies getting nervous at all the heat and rage they feel building around them. Picture it.*

—Then the speaker says something like . . . Go on brothers and sisters. Ain't nothing happening here. I thought we had a criminal, a guilty man, but we all know which color is right.

—Somebody dumps the sack of flour on the cop.

—Everybody go on. Mind your own business, people. Party. Nothing's going on. I thought I saw a white man next to me. A white man who had slaughtered a black woman after feasting on her body like a beast. But I don't see nothing. I don't see anything at all.

—Speaker's eyes roving the crowd. The black cops feel his gaze touching them. He peers through their blue shrouds. Burning through the ice. Entering like a camel through the needle's eye, weighed with the mass of black bodies encrusting his words.

—I see nothing at all.

—Crowd has begun to drift apart. They see and don't see. Clots of people form, seemingly intent on some business of eating or singing or talking which brought them together. But the platform is the still center of the constellations.

—From it the speaker's voice is almost an apologetic drone. Dully urging his audience to ignore him. Forgive his presumption. His mistake. At times his words are curdled in terrified screams from the throat of a man who cannot understand he no longer exists.

—Finally no voice rides above the crowd. Things are like they always are on a normal, loud Saturday afternoon in the neighborhood. Speaker has disappeared. His ghostly mistake hangs unnoticed, a piece of lumpy laundry twisting in slow, diminishing arcs.

The shower of words passed. Real or unreal, outside or inside it drenched him and shivers twitched from head to toe till nothing remained but the cold night and Thomas Wilkerson, shoulders hunched, head down, on his way home remembering himself.

Wilkerson recalls a bird he had seen in the park. Plump, red breasted bouncing from branch to branch, top of a bare tree quivering as if its dry limbs just weren't ready to endure spring so soon. Sky had been clear and blue at noon. Simple blue charged with brightness, cracked into intricate designs if you peered up through the naked branches. Those images come and go, do not displace the voice and smoke and grease popping.

On his bed Wilkerson reads for as long as he is able. *Gavrila Ivolgin.* Ganya. It is impossible to keep up with the Russian names. He turns down a page, three creases, the way the kids begin folding jack-in-the-boxes. Just before sleep comes he repeats the page numbers, hazily attempting to reconstruct what he will underline the next day when he has his hands on a pencil.

He had still many years of playing the fool before him. A profound and continual realization of his own mediocrity and, at the same time, an irresistible desire to convince himself that he was a man of the most independent mind, had rankled in his heart ever since his boyhood. He was a young man of envious and impulsive desires, and he seemed to have been born with overwrought nerves. He mistook the impulsiveness of his desires for strength. In his passionate desire to excel, he was sometimes ready to take the most reckless risks; but as soon as the moment for taking such a risk came, our hero was always too sensible to take it. That drove him to despair. He would perhaps have made up his mind, given the chance, to do something really mean, for the sake of getting what he wanted so badly, but, as though on purpose, as soon as the moment for action came, he always seemed to be too honest to do anything that was too mean. (He was, however, always ready to agree to any petty meanness.) He looked with disgust and loathing on the poverty and downfall of his family.

When his eyes open the dream of the lynching is still there. He does not know if he has slept ten minutes or ten hours, just that the room is dark and the dream is fresh. He wishes for a tape recorder beside the bed so he could speak into the machine before fear distorted the telling. He needed to keep everything blanked from his mind, begin telling the truth into the microphone.

• • •

He is being peeled from the dream. It drops from his consciousness in rotting, musty shreds, the bandages of a mummy unraveled after black centuries of sleep. He is exhausted by the effort. Luminous hands of his watch form an upside down V. Five thirty in the morning. Less than two hours before the first bell. They were before him already, forty-five souls with folded hands, fuzzy headed, dark-eyed, fallen black angels, dropped prematurely into a lake of fire. Sulphur tanned, smelling of soot and gas, ephemeral substance that will not survive the brazen underworld. Oh yes, suffer the children to come. Or wait little tarbabies. Daddy's putting on his white shirt and tie. I will be with you soon as I get respectable. Must brush my teeth. Clean the beer from my breath, the fumes of hashish shake from my brain. Get it together little darlings so I can steal you away to Jesus.

Thomas Wilkerson rose. One foot on the floor, knee on the bed and some anchor stronger than either limb still fouled in the scarlet tangle of dream. He began to ambulate. Across the cold floor barefooted to a sink where he turned on water, dipped his face and tossed handfuls of the wetness against his skin. Cold then hot. Day is the dawning of a roar between the ears. Water continues to run into the chipped sink then splashes into aluminum kettle Wilkerson tilts so that the spout receives the flow. In and out the same hole. Hot water going in, coffee coming out frothing as it rises in the cup heaped with brown powder and white powder.

Wilkerson sleeps in his shorts and undershirt. When he urinates the shorts go down rather than fumble with the slit.

Very yellow it is perhaps the beer or greasy chicken or probably some fatal impurity in the dream smoke he will die a horrible choking death, penis bloated, throat raw, unable to cry out because the yellow bile floods to his throat and there is nothing left inside, just the gritty yellow pulp that once was organs, just the bile slooshing when he walks.

Shorts go up when he is finished, settle, full of the spreading cakes of Thomas Wilkerson, onto the crumpled bed. Someone should clean everything. Shorts, bed clothes, the coffee stained T-shirt, last but not least Wilkerson's own hairy ass. When you are a baby someone comes and lifts your legs. Undiapers you and wipes impurities from the cute, chubby bottom. Then they stop coming. You get ashamed. Your hind end becomes very private, secretive, something to forget about, be avoided, a shameful thing. So no wonder it grows weary, drags, loses its proud curves and declines as Wilkerson declines sourly, flaccidly to drink his coffee sitting on the side of the bed.

Body make its overtures, belches, farts, regrets old pains it must exhume each morning. Body exhales its staleness a thick scent through pursed lips till the room is full to bursting. But the shape created is not round and smooth like a balloon, it is uneven, bulging in places, shadowed, dark cornered, harsh with right angles and sharp inclining planes. Room choked with hissing spiral of his breath, confining him, settling that torpor over his thoughts and movements.

Wilkerson thought of the children, the rooms growing around them, the furry eyes pushing back shadows and finding nothing has changed.

For the children he would raise himself from the bed, undo the pall by snapping on all the lights in his two rooms. He would shit, shower and shave for them. And pull a clean shirt from its cellophane. Clean white breast beneath a suit that needed pressing. Dark suit of course, all his functions merged within that darkness. Whether priest or undertaker or judge or mourner or dead man, the subdued tone appropriate. Wilkerson would pull on his black socks, wedge his way with the aid of a strip of cardboard torn from the backing of his laundered shirt into new black loafers.

He sees little Andrea's hand go up. The other children laughed before she could begin speaking. He knew almost all their names. Handles to pick them up and set them down gently. Why was her harelip so ugly? Why did it trap her? You want to tell them not to laugh but a voice you own chuckles with them, tickles from within, teasingly pulls at the stern mask of your features. Andrea Palmer. The children. Their voices reach him in ripples of crooked singing. He walks up and down narrow aisles listening, a hand he doesn't own patting Andrea on the head. He stares at the pale creases furrowing her skull. Her hair is pulled tightly away from the parts, forming taut mounds spotted with flecks of dandruff, a dull gray Vaseline sheen where it reflects the ceiling lights. Her mother lovingly patting' down each strand. Pulling the pigtails tight. Andrea Palmer remembers the busy fingers in her hair. The welcome annoyance of so much attention. She forgets the hanging lip. She raises her hand to answer a question.

Accent lines of bare scalp crisscross atop her head, an elaborate pattern perhaps she has never seen. He wants to touch her. Trace his finger through the grooves.

Wilkerson turned with the pages of his appointment book. Who had decided to represent time in these perfectly congruent squares. A grid of red lines crossing one another at right angles dividing the page into equal compartments, name of the month he had penciled in *March* underlined above the grid, the letters S M T W T F S in succession heading each vertical column, in the corner of each square a bracketed numeral, from 1 to 30. That was March. Predictable, orderly. All Thursdays separated by six days. The last Thursday (31) followed by two blank spaces which meant March had ended but the pattern would persist, other compartments would succeed which differed only because they were arrayed under the heading April, a month which necessarily begins on Friday, the blank space which had no number in its corner on

March's page. If you were a good teacher, you planned ahead, accepted the calendar's impeccable vision of the future. You made notations in the squares. Each Monday would bring a test. By Thursdays the papers would be returned to the class. Your promptness and regularity themselves a lesson to the slovenly children. Reward the children who had conditioned themselves to acquiesce to the logic of the squares. Be grateful to those who did not deviate, who arrived on time and did not disrupt the schedule, did not let chaos ramble through their compositions and examinations. Wilkerson drew a heavy line around the vertical column of Wednesdays, outlined five days to form a horizontal crossbar. Rewarded those like himself who had chosen a shape and moulded themselves to it uncompromisingly.

But who had ordained this bland equality of days, months, hours, years. He knew children had to be crushed to believe it. He knew it was a weariness in himself and most men which acknowledged the rightness of the pattern. Somewhere they had lost the urge or the skill to resist. He was beginning to become convinced that self-discipline, maturity, courage, reality, truth were all synonyms for what he now called weakness. Yet didn't he hate his father's life because it seemed accidental, shapeless, best represented not by ruled lines but by a child's aimless drawing all swirls and lumpish climaxes, sprawling giddily, ripping the paper on which it is scribbled.

Were there only two choices? Either cage time in the red lines that marched across the page or like his father in his lost weekends abandon any illusion of control. Littleman believed all men were trapped. No choice existed except to reverse or destroy the particular historical process which at a given time determines the life of individual men. He would see my father and me as equally unredeemable.

Perhaps he is right. I believe in his plan. It may free men for an instant, create a limbo between prisons. But can the instant be extended? Can it support life and a society? I don't think Littleman cares. I don't think my father cared when he felt the need to escape. He could run and that was enough. He blessed the legs and hands that could carry him away. To the high of music, laughter and smoke, the peace of emptying your pockets and sleeping where you fell down.

But while I am full of Littleman's plan for escape, I still resent my father's humble breaking away. I question his right to make one woman suffer yet am prepared for a circus of bloodletting when the plan triggers anarchy. And though I conceive of myself and the plan as a fulcrum turning history, how much further will I have moved it than my father moved it?

But these are not questions to be answered. They are soft laps to lay my head in, to hide from what calls me.

Though the date has been circled many times, he scores the paper again, marking the day of the lynching, defining its square once more in an enveloping ring. A noose he thinks. A wound through to the next sheet. If you lifted June, the day of the plan's beginning would not rise with it but remain a ragged, black wreathed patch on the wrong page of the calendar. Leave fluttering June with a gaping hole in her belly. The day was a thing apart. A hole in time destroying the meaning of the calendar. A mouth drinking the ink from each page. Order, logic, thin red stripes spiraling through the whirlpool, accentuating motion, beginning and ending no-where like lines on a barber's pole. You cannot reckon time with the squares. They are swallowed too quickly, tumbling end over end, flashing past in a blur like the cars of a train speeding through the windows of the speeding train you are riding.

He turns backward in the book to March. A neatness, order in his jottings. No mention of the plan. Most of the notations concern the children, his pupils. Books for them to read. Presentations on current events he wishes to connect with their history lessons. Reminders to himself of faculty meetings, luncheons. A list in the margin of books read and movies he would harvest in the future. Tanya's name appearing. The references to her as businesslike as all others. His eyes running over the page. No mention of father, mother. Wilkerson was annoyed that the information tediously recorded yielded almost nothing about its author. The most startling characteristic of the writer was his uncanny ability to fit all he had to say within the space allotted by the calendar's framework. Like a well trained child filling in a coloring book he did not let his crayon slip over the thick boundary lines. It was as if some stern parent watched over his shoulder, ready with a stinging ruler to rap the offending hand. Wilkerson had once seen a journal Littleman kept. They were both drunk and Littleman had wanted him to read a poem. The loose leaf notebook passed to him had been opened to the wrong page. Nothing in the jumbled pencil scrawl suggested poetry. Wilkerson turned three leaves before he saw a staff of words centered on the page, slanting like a barbell between two opaque clots of run on prose at the bottom and top of the sheet. Littleman had asked him to read aloud, so laboriously Wilkerson deciphered and intoned. Surprisingly the lyric was regular; two interlocking rhymed stanzas with diction faintly archaic. What was described was the castration of a bull framed ironically by images of soft white hands and maiden tears. He read the poem four times before he approximated the version Littleman wanted him to decode from the chaotic manuscript.

Littleman had said:

—Yes, that's good, that's the way it's supposed to be. Just the way you did it then. Now do it again, please, like that so I can remember.

But the next recitation was no better than the first three. They began to argue, Littleman name calling as he snatched away the notebook. They drank more wine and passed on to the plan.

And though she kiss the black, heaving flank.

Upon the wound lay lily hands . . . These lines were all he could remember. And his disjointed impression of the whole. Quaint. Obscene. Funny. Pathetic. Then the one word. The sure word vivid as the lines he recalled. Transparent. You see through to the man. There is a man writing this poem. Either a sign of amateurishness or of genius. With Littleman's poem an aesthetic judgment not possible or necessary at the time. Just the unavoidable discomfort Wilkerson had felt as he stared through the words at the human shape.

—Today I want to tell you how the leopard lost his spots . . .

He looks at his watch. A half inch crack in the crystal runs diagonally from 12 to 2. He is dizzy. The scarred face of his watch is his face, bruised, lined unaccountably. He is afraid to ask why. To turn time over in his mind.

Still early. A clear March day. Unseasonably warm weather predicted for the rest of the week. Perhaps shirt sleeve warm. The urge to linger outside after dark, to talk and laugh on the street corners, cluster around somebody's front steps and dream lies, tell lies, hear the old stories again. His people. The fathers and mothers of the children he tended five days a week. And where were his children while the night was being whittled into a thousand shapes by the elders' voices. Would they be listening at windows or wide-eyed hunched in the shadowy doorways listening. Were the stories for their ears or was it better that they disappeared into their own darkness, the alleys and vacant lots, at the periphery of poolrooms, sandwich shops, the record store with the loudspeaker outside singing as long into the night as anybody seemed to be listening. When did the children learn to wear night like a badge.

But the children were not alone. Somebody went to them in the alleys and vacant lots. Somebody filled their heads with visions he could not budge when the chidren came to school sleepy-eyed, sated.

Man we killed some good grapes some fine pluck man, we be high as a muthafucka man we be flying behind that stuff we be sniffing and chewing and drinking and poking and man Mary Lou got nice big legs man anybody can get some of that shit.

—Today I want to tell you an African folk tale of how the leopard changed his spots. Lame ass shit. Jive muthafucka.

—We gonna lay at Larry's. His mama be working till six ain't nobody home we gonna get into some nice shit. Yeah man we got some bitches coming.

        All together, baby

Sunny March day.

            Albums, baby. You know. I dig albums not that doo wah ditty shit. We gonna git nice behind jazz.

Mansa Musa

Night time.

Fuck it man.

March day. March day. March day. And after this March day another and another. And after those days.

Still early. He tilts his wrist so the scarred crystal does not interfere as he reads the face of his watch. If he hurries he will catch Tanya at Dewey's. She takes her breakfast there every morning. A quiet antiseptic coffee shop. Far enough away from the school so that it is not filled with school faces, but close enough so that a ten minute walk gets you to the front door of the school building. They never talked much over the coffee and rolls, the spatula of scrambled eggs and home fries with which he would begin some days. But when they walked to the school building he felt as close to Tanya as he ever did. Just a few minutes together, but so sane, so private coming as they did before the onslaught of the children, the bells, the classroom walls. They never lingered, never played at lovers kissing in the empty morning streets, but he sensed in her stillness as they clattered together along their special, usually deserted path of back streets that the time they shared was not inconsequential for her. He tried not to worry the mystery, did not question too closely what he believed was special about the brief passage between Dewey's and the school yard.

Though they spoke rarely as they walked, one morning damp and chilly, the broken sidewalks blotted with dark reflecting pools, the sky mottled gray like sheets slept in too many times, he had let his fingers go instinctively to the point of her elbow guiding with the faintest touch her step up a high curb, and still without realizing how far he'd gone he pressed her arm against her side, letting his fingers circle it, pulling her toward him so they bumped awkwardly, swayed forward another two steps before he remembered how she mocked couples clutching in public, her distaste for the sentimental formalities of courtship, and remembering her disdain he squeaked . . .

–I seen Mr. Wilkerson making love to Miss Tanya right out in the middle of the street. . . . Yes, lawd . . . in broad daylight.

He thought she smiled. No stiffness when they had come together. A perceptible yielding. Perhaps she understood the morning as he did.

–It's a miserable day. Did she know he said what he did because those words were the only way of telling her yes the weather is oppressive, what we left and where we're going are unhappy places, but if there is an endless list of things gray and distressing, there is also you, a pair of eyes and ears and legs walking beside me and all the warmth holding you together and so I can speak I can smile at your eyes when I point to the emptiness surrounding us.

–Don't you get the feeling sometimes . . . or rather more than a feeling, a certainty . . . you know you could change everything about your life. He watched her as he spoke.

–You would want to do that. She spoke to the air.

–Many things I would change if I could. But I'm not talking about for better or worse just a knowledge coming, the experience of utter detachment. Like . . . like dice. Dice scooped off the floor and wrapped in somebody's fist.

–I didn't know you were a gambler.

–Dice don't decide, don't know how they'll fall. They are just suspended. Out of the game awhile. If they were seven or two or twelve before it doesn't matter. When they tumble from the fist they . . .

–Somebody picks up the money.

–Sometimes in the morning when just the two of us . . . I lose my bearings. Or maybe I just wish I could lose my bearings. Continue walking.

–Where.

He was going to say somewhere new. He was going to say where doesn't matter. What mattered was her power to lift him in her fist. He had much to say that morning as they approached the iron fence enclosing Baxter Junior High.

But the clamor surrounding the building was a signal for small talk; they maneuvered through the early arrivals, protecting themselves with a wall of earnest, professional conversation.

Voices of children. Swelling traffic noise from the broad street that fronted the school building. Sleepy-eyed sentinels with white Sam Brown belts trudging to their posts at the busy intersections. Mrs. Davis the crossing guard in her heavy clogs and the dark blue cape shrouding her shoulders, a giant bat resting its heavy wings, hooded eyes neither open nor shut as she leans against the light standard.

He had said too much that gray morning. His father believed you could jinx things. Brag them out of existence. You never talked outright about your good luck; you never said directly how much you wanted something to occur. Great need was a crime or a sign of weakness, and his father's law had been admit only what does not incriminate you. Wanting something too much was the surest way of guaranteeing you'd never get it. Be cool. Be cool. Even if it comes don't shout, don't grab. It may blow up in your face. Never turns out to be such a big deal anyway, once it's in your grasp. So never mention the morning. Don't try to pick up the conversation where it ended. You too guard the silence. Just sit in Dewey's red booth and sip your coffee. Walk beside her till you get to the building. Enjoy the complicity without asking if it is complicity, if it's mutual, if when she plunges into the life of the school she feels the transition, if she is aware of how well you work together fooling the others, pretending nothing has happened, nothing has been shared before you are among them, full of business, each getting his set of keys from the board, and striding without a backward glance in opposite directions.

Time to catch Tanya if she stopped at the restaurant. He would have to hurry.

A wave of fatigue and nausea overtook him. His knees buckled. Wilkerson was forced to sit on the edge of the bed. Hunching forward he pressed his fists into his forehead, rubbing his knuckles down against the bony ridges of his cheeks, grinding the flesh around his closed eyes, then allowing his hands to fall limp from his face, his elbows to slide from his knees so his arms dangle full length along his body. His eyes burned. For a second there were short streaks of blue and yellow and white. He was afraid to straighten his body. Afraid his soupy guts would drip from the hole in his belly he held closed by doubling over. The sickness passed. His muscles were deadened, flaccid, but had not disintegrated. His head throbbed but would not explode.

He looked in the mirror. No wounds. No scars. The eternally seedy cheeks, the eyes bloodshot but familiar. Still time to reach her. The subway. The transfer to a bus. The little newspaper vendor who would look past him. Get off a stop early, cross the street. See the window, the red and white stripe of Dewey's sign, the blur of movement within. She will be sitting alone. Not even needing the prop of a newspaper to indicate how absorbed she is in her solitude, how uninterested she is in company. The black waitresses do not like her. Her long fingers and perfect nails. Soft cloud of hair framing her face, a reprimand to the heat and grease with which the others have disguised themselves to serve the white faces coffee and doughnuts. And though she is dressed simply, the rich unobtrusiveness of her shift, her coat, the shoes she wears mock the stylishness of the special purchase each girl has made, the extravagant investment that must be worn long after its elegance is outmoded. She sits minding her business, business which her hands and eyes, her voice as she orders or politely acknowledges, hold aloof from white customers and black staff.

He sees Tanya in the red booth, feels the arms of the turnstyle bump against his thighs as he enters the glass wall.

The metal is cold and he brings his hand to his cheek. He hears the rattle of cups and saucers. Orders shouted at the kitchen. He finds his eyes again in the mirror. Still time. Still time to go to her. He would begin to explain the plan.
Still time.

The water stung his hand. He mixed more of the cold tap. Sink was a bowl. Barely enough border to lay his tooth-brush, the razor, set the can of instant lather. Sometimes his father had shaved in the kitchen sink. He would watch from the drainboard where his father perched him. His mother didn't like it when they did that. The way she didn't like it when his father stood beside the icebox to eat rather than sitting down. Father said he could see better in the light that came in over the kitchen sink. He said it was better for shaving than lightbulb light in the windowless bathroom. One day his father brought home a fragment of cracked mirror. Hung it in the kitchen so he wouldn't have to cart out the one from the bathroom. Which had meant going into the bathroom where she was probably bathing somebody or changing a diaper and she would want to know where was he going with the mirror. He'd break it one day carrying it all around the house. Half the time she'd have a baby in her arm and he'd leave the mirror sitting all over the house she'd have to tramp around carrying a heavy baby looking for the mirror, why didn't he leave it in the bath-room why can't he wait till the bathroom's empty, shave where he's supposed to shave why can't he wait in such a damn hurry anyway where's he going so fast no money any-way to go anywhere why can't he just leave it where it is. So he brought one home and hung it by the kitchen win-dow and I would watch him from the drainboard. And the water so hot it would steam, I wanted to put my fingers in he said too hot. I cried and he said go on if you don't be-lieve me. And she heard me squeal when I ran my hand un-der the faucet. And she screamed at him and I wanted to get down. It was wet under me. I felt it coming through my clothes. My hand didn't hurt but I wanted down so I screamed and they were at one another and I wanted down. Finally she carried me from the kitchen because my feet were bare and glass all over the floor from the mirror she'd torn down.

And it is so easy to remember. His father had a flare with the long razor. Wilkerson winced because straight razor was chill death, nigger throat cut death even in his own hand, raised to shave his own face. He toweled his cheeks. Rinsed his hands and dried them.

He stared at the face of Thomas Wilkerson. Mr. Wilkerson impatiently awaited by forty-five fifth graders in home room 109. He was shabby. Somehow the shadows never scraped from cheeks, chin and above the lip. Never new and shiny. As if the dark contours and hollows had been quickly gone over with a thin, cheap paint. Never really clean or fresh. Not quite but almost a seedy reflection. An old man on a park bench whose indolence in the spring sun seems selfish and desperate. He would not try to catch Tanya this morning.

If you stood on Forty-third Street in the middle of Clark Park, you could catch either trolley. You could see far down the tracks and either go right or left depending on which showed itself first, the 13 at the top of a slight incline, white whale brow first, then slowly descending a curve that revealed its white and green flank, or the 34 a flat, floating cream blur that skimmed above the broken silhouette of parked cars on Baltimore Avenue. Both took Wilkerson below the ground into the same loud tunnel and unreal light. Trolley trapped within the echo of its clumsy sprints, its wheezing, swaying halts. Catacombs of the city. These caverns and the subterranean islands of light madly careening without purpose or destination. These tunnels would be the burying ground of a martyred race. Packed thick, barely leaving room for the screaming hearses, tiers of the dead would peer blackly at those who for the moment were alive.

You blink when you find yourself released. You are relieved because for some reason you were not kept below. March sunshine glories from concrete, steel and glass. You were cramped and now you are dwarfed. Nothing is man sized around you. Speed of the cars is threatening, would crush you if you stepped into the flow. You blink and look down at your new shoes already dusty on the filthy pavement. You are undeceived.

You would whistle, you would about face and walk against the grain of those bodies hustling you forward. But there is no place to go but where you are going. You clutch the transfer in your hand. Put your back against the wall and hope the bus will be on time, the next step toward the children can be taken.

Although it must be over a thousand mornings now, the vendor does not raise his eyes in greeting. He leans against his blue newsstand, aproned, capped as he always is. Runty man with hair on his hand backs, hair you can see curling up his forearms when in the summer he wears a Los Angeles Dodgers T-shirt. It would be so simple to notice the vendor, to speak to him so the next day he would notice you. A thousand mornings and the man has yet to remember or to make a sign of remembrance. And if you bought one of his papers. From out of town so the transaction wouldn't be ordinary. An expensive one and give him a dollar so he would have to make change. Let him keep the nickel, perhaps. Each morning give him a dollar and he hands back the Times and three quarters. In twenty weeks he will have earned a dollar. He will smile and remember. But why all of that. Why can't he see you just because this morning has happened so many times. Up out of the black hole, across the street, standing back against the wall so as not to impede urgent pedestrians, staring at his bearish shoulders and hairy hands, the rituals of shuffling, counting, giving and receiving, the muttering sounds he makes, ghosts of his strong hawking voice that drew customers to his blue box until they didn't have to be reminded, just came and knew he would be there, shuffling, rhythmless dance as he gives and takes muttering.

But there is only one of him. One capped and aproned boy/man peddling papers and each day so many wait here where I wait. Obvious why he doesn't remember, why he can't remember. In fact most days the wait is short. I am only unnoticed a short while before the bus comes.

I pledge allegiance to the flag of the United States of America, and to the republic for which it stands, one nation under God, indivisible, with liberty and justice for all.

Forty-five black throats finish. Go their separate ways again, coughing, laughing, talking, sighing, burning, hungry, dry, sore, angry, silent, full of sleep and want, stale with unbrushed teeth, with soured food, with rotten teeth and sore gums.

—Africa is a continent. For a long time it was thought of as the Dark Continent. Civilization looked upon its inhabitants as savages, wild and untamable as the ferocious beasts with whom they shared the impenetrable, jungled land.

Now Mr. Willkerson tell them like it is. Tell them how greed overcame fear and how, after such a momentous push forward of Civilization, overcoming scruples was not difficult at all. Europe and Africa embracing in a Brave New World, peopling two Americas with spangled children. Sing Glory. Sing blessed art thou Fruit of that Loom my orphans.

—We must learn not to shy away from the truth. Africa was dark only in the darkened minds of those who approached her with dark intent. When you come to steal, the past of your victim is of interest only in so far as that past may promote your plundering. But Africa lies swaddled in history and you are part of its past, heirs of its legacy.

Now tell it Wilkerson tell them heirs is anonymous for victims. How you trembled purchasing the luminous dashiki. how its exotic swirl of colors is buried deep beneath your cellophaned white shirts. Tell them how yes the first African you met, black wallflower at an AKA dance, answered politely in English reeking of stiff upper lips and cricket and faggotty blazered, red-cheeked boys, —No my good man, I have never seen a lion, outside of a zoo that is.

Off the smart alecky big lipped bastards for months after

this foray, this sincere attempt to come to terms with my past.

—Benin, Mali. See golden cities my children, see black people in stately, flowing robes glide across the spotless streets, see their poised, quiet shadows rest upon golden walls of sun baked brick. Every man a prince in sandals, striding with effortless grace as some men have been said to walk on water without disturbing its surface, raising not a ripple in the yellow dust.

And though the ghost of a white giggle is restless in your throat, bury it with the full mouthed sound of Mansa Musa, Lumumba, Kasavubu.

—Your history is black, your heritage dark but that does not mean it is negative or nothing at all. Africa awaits you as a full mooned, humming night awaits only your coming to fill it with meaning, with the knowledge of your own being.

—Learning was esteemed. The black scholars of Timbuktu were fabled for their learning and lore. Listen to the black voices from your past, let them raise the veil from the Dark Continent:

Our land is uncommonly rich and fruitful, and produces all kinds of vegetables in great abundance. We have plenty of Indian corn, and vast quantities of cotton and tobacco. Our pine apples grow without culture; they are about the size of the largest sugar-loaf, and finely flavoured. We have also spices of different kinds, particularly pepper; and a variety of delicious fruits which I have never seen in Europe; together with gums of various kinds, and honey in abundance. All our industry is exerted to improve these blessings of nature. Agriculture is our chief employment; and every one, even the children and women, are engaged in it. Thus we are all habituated to labour from our earliest years. Everyone contributes something to the common stock; and, as we are unacquainted with idleness, we have no beggars.

—Olaudah Equiano goes on to describe the physical beauty of his people, their cleanliness, the chastity of the women. Yet Olaudah was kidnapped from this Darkness and made a slave. Only through uncommon perseverance and good fortune did he manage to survive the fatal Civilizing process. His voice in an adopted language speaks for countless brethren whose stories died mute within them. Olaudah's slave name, Gustavus Vassa, a Roman.

Fair weather will continue. Temperature much higher than average for March but the nights deceptively cool. Cover up. Don't forget a coat if you'll be outdoors after dark. Time is . . .

Bell between my temples. Their faces sleepy and impatient.

—Mr. Wilkerson, Walter Brown, he ain't comin. His little brother got hit by a newspaper truck and he's home cause he keep crying.

Giggles sputter from a corner. Foolish to cry. Silly if you cry. You know Walter Brown ain't here cause he found a way to get round coming. You are annoyed, envious. You laugh at staying home to cry.

—Was he seriously injured.

—Nothing wrong with that nigger. He ran two blocks to tell 'em his brother got knocked down.

Roll call. Time is their names one after another. Either here or not, X or O. And one day, if you could live that long, not one would answer. In fact the room would be empty and the columned book uninterrupted in its droning monotone. What was the little brother's name. Who would note him absent. In what kind of book. What color, what symbol mourned him.

—Andrea Palmer.

Andrea Palmer is Andrea Palmer a leaf shaking in the wind, a face that goes to smoke. Does she still have that sore beneath her lips. Is she already dreaming again or still at home lost in dream.

—She here, Mr. Wilkerson.

She sink lower, lower than that if she could, if she could hide the lip sore beneath the edge of the arm rest, she would sink that far. She is doing her best. Obedient the black arm sticks up, antenna, periscope splitting the horizon, as much of her self she dares risk in an alien element.

—Today we are going to talk about Africa. Africa is a continent. Who can tell me what the continents are?

Who can name three?

On the board:

> N. America
> S. America
> Austria
> Africa

In it so many times yet when alone I cannot list this room's contents. Just as I cannot pledge allegiance or remember the words to the Star Spangled Banner unless I am in a crowd, threatened by the other voices. Trying to list the things.

The children scatter to lunch. I am alone in the room. It would be easy to remember the lynch dream, bring back the horror and pleasure.

—Are you going to eat? Tanya called from across the corridor. Nothing feminine in her voice, nothing suggesting I am woman and you are man and an invitation to lunch is the smallest part of what I am saying. She was tall and the bright colors she wore seemed brilliant streamers wrapped around a stately column, column topped by spongy cloud of light brown hair. Her features moulded from skin barely beige contradicted the colorful Afro print and hairdo. Green eyes, long, thin nose, lips full but tensely held as if denying the fleshiness they could release. Tanya whip slender and elegant beneath the soft umbrella of hair. She seemed oblivious to the swarming confusion of the lunchtime corridor, picking her way by instinct through the children, unconcerned yet untouched as bodies scudded past, deliberate, never faltering a step till she stood beside Wilkerson.

—More nerve than I have. Wild Indians going to knock you down one day.

—I hardly think so, they know who I am and I know them. No reason for either of us to get in the other's way.

—That's what you always say. But they know me and they know one another and that doesn't stop the pushing and shoving and bumping. She answered him by taking a step in the direction of the lunch room. He forced himself through the oncoming stream of students so that he could walk abreast of her. Things he wanted to say seemed impossible in the clamor. Perhaps because the words were less important than how he wished to say the words, how he wanted his voice to be an instrument rendering through rhythm, pitch and timbre those things he felt which had nothing to do with the meager stock of words he could use in trying to reach her. But subtlety was pointless in the loud current of dark children, free for a few moments from constraint and self-imposed silence, liberated among their own kind with whom they could trumpet and bleat the warm, violent messages of the herd. Wilkerson suppressed the urge to take her slim, perfectly manicured hand, to squeeze warmth from her long fingers which always felt like a bundle of twigs in his fist. He would shout over the other voices, you are beautiful Tanya and we are in love on this island slowly navigating the crowded corridor. You are a palm tree and I am tall enough to stare down into your deep eyes almost hidden beneath the canopy of perfumed fronds. Shout all of that and more to her as they strolled hand in hand to some rendezvous of sunshine through the barred, chained doors at the end of the corridor. But no, we barely exchange a glance as we arrive at the intersection and take the left turning through a steaming kitchen to the teachers' dining room.

—How do you feel about tonight? Or should I first ask if you're still coming? Pipes running the length of the room gurgle and squeak overhead. Each time the yellow door opens a gust of kitchen and cafeteria noise blasts into their conversation. They are alone only a few minutes before others join them.

—Sorry to break in on you love birds. But you got plenty time to get together outside this jungle. Be damned if them kids don't have more space to eat than we do. Stuck in this hot box behind the funky kitchen. I bet if there was white teachers here they'd find someplace else for them to eat. Out behind the kitchen always been good enough for de darkies. And niggers is niggers be they doctor, lawyer, butcherman or sorry assed teachers. Whole thing is nothing but a zoo anyway. Least they ought to provide us with uniforms so we wouldn't have to dirty up the few rags we can afford to buy wearing them in this godforsaken dump. Yeah. Uniforms whips and guns. Ought to pass them out tomorrow. My animals know I got a pistol even if it's not in view. I tell them first day. They better believe it too. The way them fools carry on, you better believe I won't let any of them get up in my face and start wolfing. They carry around everything from hat pins to meat cleavers and I'm having none of that. If one so much as rise up at his desk, I tell them I'm not going to shout or use my fists. I'm going to walk out the door, or run if I have to, but when I come back they'll know I'm for real. Blow one of their crazy heads off. Just like they do to one another every chance they get. A goddamn zoo. And Charlie paying us peanuts for keeping the beasts off the streets, out of his part of town.

The voice continued, but was lost in a cavern at the pit of Wilkerson's belly, a cave where his own voice often settled, curling in the void, swallowed but indigestible, a reeling fog that by inches could fill his whole being with gray sickness. He knew the fury that was building in Tanya. She would not internalize it, not poison her guts but listen hungrily to the speaker's words, fascinated by his performance the way a boa constrictor intently observes the trembling vulnerability of his victims. Tanya savored every one of Edward's words, his bitterness, greed and hate moulting in ragged syllables, piling in heaps around his chair. As if she knew he would be punished and that she would be instrumental in his undoing, she slowly, seeming to discern him marginally if at all, picked at the tuna fish salad and emptied her coffee cup in dainty, poised mouthfuls.

Yes she would come tonight as they had arranged, to meet his parents. Be it for better or worse the girl brought home to Mama. She nodded her assent refusing at the same time to commit herself to more than the mechanical recognition of her barely tilted head, a motion more displacement of eyebrow than nod. As if the whole matter had been previously settled and pointlessly, tastelessly injected by him here among the sordid voices, in the cramped, stale space. But she gave him nothing more to go on. Was her disdain directed toward the others who had settled at the table and their interruption of what should have been an intimate exchange or was she telling him of course she would come to his home since coming to his home could not possibly be construed as anything more than politeness or indulging a child in his ridiculous whim. Home to mother.

• • •

Wilkerson did not realize how far he'd been till the rustling of the newspaper called him back. You read paragraphs then sentences, finally words are the largest unit you can concentrate on, but they too begin to break up, are black shapes flashing in figure ground reversals, counterpoint to whiteness of the paper, blots themselves disintegrating as ink explodes leaving the newspaper blank, a snow bright mountainscape. Your eyes are wind blind and you glide lazily down precipitous slopes, dreaming in the arctic stillness, till in the distance a hiss of glaciers bumping vast flanks, massy clouds of ice whispering thunder as they pulverize mountains in their passage, a rumbling deep in the skier's throat, that sets his veins on fire because the white cliffs are beginning to crumble around him.

Falling to his lap. Wilkerson recalls the last sense he had made of the printed sheets. Paper crackles and sighs as if it is burning. *Thirty-eight Books Written in Prison by Monk. Buddhist monk Venpitagedera Gnanasheeha, released after thirty-eight months in prison, wrote thirty-eight books on Buddhism during his confinement. They included two written in Pali, two in Sanskrit and the rest in Sinhalese, the native tongue of Ceylon.* Gnanasheeha. Chewing the silence of his cell. Digesting it and shitting treatise after treatise hot and funky on the dank floor. Shapes of the guards' faces, ballooning in the corridor's pastel darkness. Your rice, traitor Venpitagedera. May it be laced with elephant urine and may your bowels curdle when they kiss it. The monk chewing wood from the top of his pencil. Writing night and day till the cell is crowded with universes and Gnanasheeha squatting in the darkness smiles with pity at the iron cage outside his world and the trapped creatures within it who stare longingly at the jade river through which he floats.

Wilkerson remembered that he still didn't know the basketball score. Turning the front pages, skimming news, amusements, social notices, he had been anticipating the score, but denying himself the ultimate pleasure until he had done his duty. Perhaps less sense of duty than need to diminish painlessly that superfluous block of time remaining before he could lose himself in the business of getting ready to meet Tanya. Surprisingly a rout. His favorite team, favorite because he could become more involved rooting against them than he could rooting for some other, had been knocked out of the playoffs. Which meant their season was over. Which meant endless, redundant baseball games dragging through till pro football began to gobble prime time again. Sports made it worth owning a color T.V. Not too proud to accept the Empire's circuses. 154 to 120. They hadn't been beaten much worse than that all year. Wilkerson was just as happy not to have seen the game. No joy in seeing his favorites stomped in the manner they so richly deserved. He liked the issue to be in doubt. To be so absorbed in the frenzy of the action that he could actually forget his prejudices. It was best when he didn't know whether he wanted a shot to go in or miss, whether he hoped the referee would call charging or blocking. Then he could feel the anxiety, the thrust of both teams, the tangle of guts and bodies could ensnare him and dribble him up and down the court as if he were some objective seismograph. He was there drinking at the source, at the core of the action as it radiated from deep, underground channels. What pulsated through the players were forces they had no means of reckoning and the best at their best moments simply abandoned themselves to the rhythm.

And this pitching of the earth's innards produced scores. Things you could discover the next day in your newspaper. And was the score a simple minded reduction of all that had happened or did the numbers record a further, truer rhythm? Was the score saying no it never ends because this is how far it is at the moment and obviously since there are so many scores to be tallied the Game goes on.

Season ended. But the playoffs continue until a temporary champion crowned. The King is dead. Long live the King. Banners will hang from the rafters. With dates and scores. But in a back yard or under a street light the King is practicing, or unborn yet first feels the rhythm, the grappling of earth snakes as he is spilled, a spangled arc, a perfect shot swishing through shy fallopian tubes.

Score at the moment was zero to zero. If it could be called a game that he played with Tanya, if in fact what happened between them was tangible enough to register anywhere. When he could be honest with himself, Wilkerson admitted that the sole evidence of any attachment between himself and Tanya was the blank sheet of yearning he worked so hard at filling, but which remained empty, omnivorous as the sea.

He folded the newspaper neatly, re-establishing each section so the pages ran consecutively and placing the sections in order. He had daydreamed and read longer than he should have so now a slight edge of urgency would have to propel him through his final preparations. Happens so often must do it on purpose, not allowing myself to get ready till it's just about too late. Now the tasks take some concentration, some eye for efficiency. I can think about what I'm doing even though each operation is mechanical and mindless. Vaguely excited, challenged to get square peg in round hole. No time for wasted effort, no Yo-Yoing thoughts backward and forward. The fresh shirt from his drawer, the ubiquitous suit brushed then draped on his body. But no. Something different. The tree arches gracefully toward him smiling. Rich with tropical breezes and fruit sweetness the fronds brush his lips. He pulls the dashiki over his head.

Somehow enough. Nothing more to do. Only pick at his hair in front of the mirror. Worn long before long became fashionable and if fluffed out and shaped and seen from an angle that hid the inroads of balding forehead it could be mistaken for an Afro. The shirt was decisive. He could leave now in plenty of time, forgetting his game, his ritual, the score.

● ● ●

–Let me do something to help, Mama.

–You sit still and don't worry me. Nothing to be done. Nothing here to do it with, anyhow. This kitchen as empty as something can be and still be a kitchen. The few dishes is out and pots is on the stove.

–There must be something.

–Sit still I told you. Whatever's done here, I'll do and do my best so's if nobody don't like it that's just too bad.

–Nobody's said a thing about not liking. Everything looks fine.

–What you here for so early, anyway. In that wild shirt telling lies to your mother already.

–It's ten after seven and you told us to come at seven thirty. Are you tired of me? Isn't this still my home?

–As much as anybody else's. You can use it for a whistle stop like the rest. That makes a home I suppose. A place to sleep and eat when you're in the neighborhood.

–No that's not it.

–No, it ain't. You're right. Need a fool tied down to the raggedy boards. No. I'll get it together like I always do. For him or you or the rest when they decide to stop.

–Mama, wait. I'm a man now. I have my own life. I get

busy and don't come as often as I should. But you know . . .

—Nothing. I lived fifty some years and know nothing. Head just as empty as this kitchen. Cut me open all you'd find be a mess of old clothes and dirty dishwater. Everything else I gave up cause I didn't know any better. And if I walked around the corner who'd so much as know my name.

—I'm bringing the most important person in my life to meet you this evening. Doesn't that tell you something?

—I'm doing the best I can. I've laid out the dishes and got this place as close to clean as it gets. I'm waiting to see this lady though I hardly know why you didn't carry her here yourself stead of straggling in first one then the other like strangers if you think so much of her. Could at least walk through the door with her.

—I explained already. This is the way she wants it. She is a very strong, independent woman. That's one of the qualities I like best about her.

—Don't seem natural to me. Strong and independent don't mean she supposed to be traipsing through the streets at night like a man.

—It's a little thing, Mama.

—Did you want it this way? Is you all going to leave at the same time?

—What I want isn't the only thing that counts. You should understand that. A man and woman . . .

—Just stop there. No more "man and woman" talk. I know better than I hope you ever will what counts and who counts and how I don't even bother to ask myself anymore what I want. Do you see your father anywhere in this house? You might say I wanted him to be here. And I knew when I asked him and told him what you wanted and what I wanted that I might as well be asking that sink to turn into an airplane and fly me out of here. This night like all the rest.

—You don't think he'll come.

—Do I think he'll come. To tell the truth I try not to think about things like that at all. Almost two days since I saw him last. He might remember you and your ladyfriend are supposed to be here and he might not. If he does remember, I suppose he'll intend to be here. But I know his intendings don't mean much. When your father is out with his friends they call him Sweetman. Sweetman cause all he drinks is gin. Sit at a bar all night ordering gin. Gin and gin and gin. Mr. Sweetman your daddy.

—Nothing has changed.

—What did you expect? Maybe you're getting like him. Maybe you think something will change if you stay away long enough. Did you think you was coming back to the Ritz? Your mother in an evening gown ordering her maids around. You've just been away that's all. And while you've been gone I've gotten older, tireder and poorer. Your father's still drinking hisself to death fast as he can. He's ashamed to look me in the eye, not so much cause of what he's doing to me. I was never very much to him. He's shamed because he knows I know what he's doing to himself.

—And you can't stop it. He can't stop.

—Maybe you need to go away a while longer. You don't like what I'm telling you or what you see with your own eyes. Leave now before you see and hear too much. Before the lady comes. Both you all come back in ten, fifteen years. This rag of an apartment building will be dust and we'll be dust and you can say what you'd like about your fine family.

—She'll be here any moment. The reason she's coming is to see you. You are all I have and she is all I have and I want to bring you together.

—Sure enough a pitiful world.

—Mama, help me make the best of it. Let me help you.

—Things is ready as they gonna get. I saw your father two mornings ago. Him standing where you are, big nigger half sleep on his feet, a cup of coffee in his hand. God knows where he is now. Just as well he don't turn up tonight.

—He's my father. I want him here.

—You wanted that woman here too, didn't you. Wanted her on your arm as you came through the door into a fine, sweet home. I know plenty else you wanted. And none of it resembling this old, bitter woman and dingy room. Why do you have that bodacious shirt on and hair sprouting all over your head? What do you have to be for her? Who is she to be strong and independent? One thing I was happy about when you all was born. All boys. No little soft, sweet girl I had to lie to and pretty up till some man came along and showed her just whose world it really is. I had boys and was so relieved I didn't have to die three or four more times trying to patch together soft, sweet girls have to walk the world like I walked it. Now here you is, a man, waiting like I'm waiting for somebody to come through the door. Going through changes I've been going through all my life. You, my son. Telling me she's strong and independent. It's pitiful. You looking to do her part in the kitchen. Coming early to sit in the kitchen. Woman talk. Wearing some wild man clothes and hairdo. Just what he got that's worth one evening of waiting. I asked myself that one day. You know what the answer is. And I'm talking about waiting for Mr. Sweetman, your father. The answer is nothing. The answer is he's never given me a thing and never will. What I hate is how I missed my chance to go out and take for myself. I know what you're waiting for. And it ain't never going to come walking through no door to greet you. Whether she comes or Mr. Sweetman himself big as life sauntering into the room. What you're waiting for is what I waited for all these years. Myself to get up and walk out.

—Could I . . .

—No, don't touch me. And don't you dare feel sorry. I'm crying over you just as sure as I'm talking about myself. I'll go on doing the best I can.

—I think I love her.

—I don't understand that. Time and poor and hate and hurt I know something about, but I don't know love.

—She's beautiful. Tall and slim. She has an artist's hands. Her eyes are green with a gray cast. Not dull gray but a special kind of gray light if you can picture that, gray that sparkles through green mist. I've known her a long time. She is intelligent, poised and decent. We teach in the same school. She won scholarships and worked her way through college. Lost her parents when she was very young. Everything she has she's earned for herself. Not an easy life. Passed among relatives, living in institutions when there was no one to take her. Learned to scuffle, fight for what she wanted. We're a lot alike in some ways.

—Except she don't have to take you home to see what's left of those that brought her into the world. She's the lucky one, maybe.

—I didn't have to bring her here.

—She ain't here yet. Smart gal. She arranged it so's she could change her mind at the last minute. You must have scared her away talking about us. What did you tell her? She must have asked. Did you tell her to wear something old, to eat before she came.

—Why are you saying these things. You know they aren't true. Who do you want to hurt? I'm proud of you. And you know you're the best cook in town.

—Sure, sure. Give me a batch of tough greens and all the ends of meat the white man throws away. I'll make a feast. Guts and feet and tails. Scraping, pounding, cleaning, boiling. I can make bones fit to eat. Stretch food for one so it will last a week for three. All my secrets that come from having scraps to work with or having nothing at all. I'm sick of my secrets.

—You know you can cook. You can't keep from smiling when I say it.

—I'm going to slap you boy. Lying to me.

—Then everybody who ever ate your cooking's just as big a lie.

—When do they get it? At funerals or weddings is all. And full of so much booze anything tastes good. "Thank you Sister Wilkerson," "God love you Sister Wilkerson," niggers nodding and crying, eating, drinking, laughing, as long as people got something to feed them and pour down their throats. It's free besides. Course they like it. And you standing there grinning like everything I've been trying to say to you is going to get chewed up and disappear in the first mouthful of chicken and rice.

—And gravy.

—Yes, fool, gravy.

—Crackling.

—Crackling.

—And did you fry the giblets?

—Livers under that saucer keeping warm.

—Remember how we'd fight over who'd get the liver. Putting in claims early on Sunday morning, then starting the day before we'd get in our claims. You got so mad you threw it out one Sunday. Right in the garbage pail and all three of us half grown boys standing around it crying.

—I remember that. And I remember how I felt trying to slice a pie, or divide ice cream or slice meat or count out french fries and eight or ten pairs of eyes froze on my hand waiting for me to slip up a little to the right or left so somebody would get cheated and start to scream. I remember how it felt, sure enough. Trying to make one half of what we needed do for us all.

—But those were good times. We laughed a lot too. We were all together.

—Now you're all gone. The babies and Sweetman who made them. What's her name?

—Tanya.

—It's not a bad name.

—You'll like her. She's strong, Mama. Strong like you always were.

—Strong. That's the biggest lie you've ever told. You get the door. Least I can do is serve what little I put together without burning it. Go on Thomas. She's at the door.

—Thomas. Tom. Tom my school teaching son. Only one to inherit his daddy's brains. I brought her a present. Something I picked up on the route. Good as new. Flowers for your lady. White folks ought to be shamed, the things they throw away for old.

—Why don't you have your key, man.

—Key. My key's right here in my pocket. Key to your heart, sugar.

—Then why you lean on that bell like you don't have good sense.

—Oh, you talking about some door key. Seem to have lost that one. Must be in the truck.

—Or somewhere . . .

—Surely in the truck, old lady. But I'm home ain't I now. To see Tom's princess. If she's fine, don't leave her alone with your daddy. Sing sweetness in her ear.

—You make somebody drunk they get too close to you.

—Woman, you ain't said nothing but nasty to me since I been here. My head hardly in the door and you pickin.

—Nothing came in that door but a drunk man fit for the bed. Don't even have sense enough to shut the door behind you.

—Mama.

—Don't get in our business. Just move out the way so he can stumble past and fall down cross the bed like he always does. Coming in here with some rotten flowers you stole from a garbage can.

—Weren't in a can. In a box. Still had ribbon round it. And nice tissue paper inside. I open that box and they smell fresh like just cut. I say to myself Tom bringing his old lady home so why don't I keep these. Put them on the table in some water to stay fresh. Brighten up things a little. Or just put the whole box ribbon and all in her arms when she come through the door. Let her see we know how to be fancy with the best. So I grabbed them up before anybody saw how nice they was. Little envelope fell out. They was to a woman. You can never tell about women. Something nice as these she just tossed out must have been soon as they came. Bitches is something. Childress talking the other day about one who came to the garage he used to work at. Ain't you going to gimme something she said. I believe anything anybody tell me bout a woman. Thomas, where is this fox got your nose open.

—Should be here any moment. Thought it was her when you rang.

—Now you know you can't keep no fine girl letting her run around at night by herself. Should have picked her up in a taxi. Young man in your position ought to have his own automobile anyway. A big one like I been telling you. Let her know you ain't afraid to spend money. Flowers and taxis and nothing but top shelf.

—That how you keep your women, Sweetman.

—Use my name when you talk to me, woman. I got a name.

—Ain't it Mr. Sweetman. King of the bar stool. Flowers and good whiskey for all his women. That's how you keep me ain't it. Hauling my ass around from one fancy place to the next in a taxicab.

—Shit. You gonna call me out my name and bad mouth me like some common whore. And your son standing right here.

—Get out.

—You ought to be shamed.

—Leave. Go on back to wherever you've been. Don't need you here tonight. No more nights.

—Go on. Talk. Talk. You're gonna be sorry for each mouthful. Sorrier and sorrier but you just keep talking. Let him take it all in.

—Nothing new. Nothing he don't know. He was born and raised in this hell-hole. God knows why he's back tonight or why he'd want to bring a woman he cares anything about here.

—If it's a hell-hole, you set the fires. And stoke em for all you're worth. Screaming at me like you're crazy. Standing over me when I'm sleep cursing me. Throw food at me the way you would at a dog. And laughing when you know you've drove me so far I can't go no further.

—Laughing. Did you say I laughed. I wish I could laugh. Could feel free of this pitiful life for one minute so I could open my mouth and eyes wide and laugh. But I'm past laughing. Crying too.

—You ain't past being knocked down if you don't get out

of my face, fool. I'm going in to put on some clothes. We's
having dinner with Thomas and his lady.

—One of us is not going to be here when she comes. I
swear to god one of us is not going to be in this kitchen.
Now take your choice. I'm staying or you're staying, but not
both. You can walk over me or throw me out the window.
But I'll fight you till I can't stand up. And if I can't move
you, I'll crawl out myself. Now get out. Leave us alone.

—Thomas, you can see how she does it. You can see how
she traps me. I could break her in half. And she stands there
challenging me, asking me to kill her. Won't let me in my
own house. Picks and pulls, tears at me. Trying to do something nice. For you and your woman friend. I bring flowers.
I want to get out of these filthy clothes and wash, and pour
everybody a drink, and just sit down like people supposed
to do. That's all I want. Just to be . . .

—You're drunk. You smell of the streets and the women
you've been sleeping in. You can barely stand up, swaying
there with that mashed, dirty box in your hands. And you
just want to sit down and be like people. Over my dead
body. I won't let you insult them or me. Mr. Sweetman sure
enough. A rag man. Something barely recognizable for man
in my kitchen.

—You ought to thank god I ever come back to this trap.
And your terrible mouth. So much hate in a skinny little
body. You bitches is something else. You bitches will ride a
man to China and if he don't break, stomp him when you
get off his back. God damn motherfucking blood sucking
wenches ain't no wonder I got nothing never had nothing
bled like a stuck pig to keep roof over your heads and food
in the children mouths.

—There ain't no children. Only your grown son listening
to your mouth. Hearing you threaten to lay your hands on
his mother.

—Fuck it. Fuck it. Fuck it. This is my goddamn house and
I'll be goddamned if I ain't staying. You or no other bitch
gonna move me.

–Thomas. The door's open. She's standing there.

–Tanya.

–You trifling bitch look what you done. Decent people won't even come in your house. I ought to knock you down.

–Thomas don't wait. Pay him no mind. Go on away from here. Get her away.

• • •

Wilkerson knew she would not be running down the stairs. Nor would there be tears. He doubted that Tanya would have raised an eyebrow in recognition of the scene she watched from the open doorway. Nothing new for her. No names she hadn't heard before. The threats for all their vicious promise would echo hollowly since she had often witnessed the next step, the laying on of hands, the blood and bone and teeth swelling the words. She would be descending the spattered stairs in graceful, long legged strides, pausing on dark landings to be certain of her bearings, never brushing the dank walls, her fingers resting on the soft, unsteady railing only long enough to assure herself that she didn't need its support, that she had oriented herself in the sighing middle of the staircase. And she would be cat quiet. As if she could will her senses to give no evidence of her passage. She did not exist, warm, tall and elegant within the ramshackle building, just as its stench and darkness and peril could not touch her. She could will that. Could free herself unblemished from his parents screaming. And the squalor shadowing her down the steps to the street.

He could catch her easily. He could call and she would halt in the darkness, listening to his hurrying footsteps. She would slump against him relieved beyond words at the sob of their bodies coming together, melt for the first time. Forever. Throbbing pained heart against throbbing pained heart. Naked together in their need and helplessness. He would confess without saying a word to the crime that had left mother and father trapped at the top of the rotting stairs. She would proffer her guilt, cool balm to his burning. Her stiff sin of denial. Unnail the dark boards in which she had neatly coffined her heart. Everything fallen away except the small, vital heat of their embrace.

He stopped on the second floor landing. Muffled voice of a white man imprisoned in an electric box leaked through the thin door of 2 C. Wilkerson would not send her name booming down the stairwell. If at all he would drop it lightly, a crumpled piece of paper spinning. But not even that. He could not call and he knew he would go no farther. He had not seen the woman outside his parents' apartment. Perhaps it was not Tanya. She hadn't answered when he cried out her name. He had been looking at his father's face when his mother had spoken. *She's standing there.* But he was caught by his father's expression. Father's face for an instant utterly empty, emotion gone, features gone, opaque as eyeglasses glazed by the sun. No face at all. Or every grin, grimace, leer, frown, twist, convulsion the face had ever known suddenly reappearing, present simultaneously in a blur of time collapsed and exploding, his father recapitulated from fetus to reeling Sweetman. Face unlined or the horrible blankness of infinite scars creasing the skin, face is the sum of all contortions forced upon it from the first day. The plane of his father's face a frontier, available this instant in a way it had never been before, something beyond it beckoning, real, accessible if the first step would be negotiated. A wildness and peace, a still center in the hurricane's eye. Your father is a door. You may, if you dare, walk through his face, his life, what he is; what is unimaginable will be revealed.

The smell of death is all that clings to your father's eyes as they return to his face. They had been so far away, in South Carolina, and Washington, D.C., on Okinawa, in Chicago and Pittsburgh, cane sweetness, steel stink, gunsmoke and bulldozers piling the cords of corpse wood. Pungent women, soap, beer, gin, cornbread and sweet potato pie, a black breast soothing its swollen nipple on his lips.

Gone so long the eyes limp back to his father's face and the other features marshal meekly in their places. The face of a drunken, confused man of fifty-five returns. Frontier closes as his lips cluck on a swallowed curse. As death reeking eyes travel to the door *Thomas. The door's open. She's standing there.* And my eyes lose his, unlinking clumsily, giddy, the way I'd feel when he set me on the floor after spinning me in his arms. I hadn't seen Tanya there. I might be chasing anyone in this darkness. I'll run up behind a perfect stranger and she'll scream *murder, rape* and doors will open, people will laugh and throw bottles or she'll kick me in my groin, clawing with long fingernails.

If it had been a stranger at the door, hesitating only to be entertained by the ruckus, then Tanya may still be on her way. If I wait I will meet her. I should have waited outside the building, anyway. Escort her up the stairs at least, even though she'd let me know I had reneged on part of our arrangement for the evening. Meeting here on the second floor would seem co-incidental. An accident which it almost is. Chasing a phantom Tanya I bump into the real one. She might like the irony, the story I could fabricate. So I'll wait here. Make her laugh. Then the lie about dinner. Why we have to change our plans and eat with my family another time. But she will know I'm lying. But I will let her know I know that she knows I am lying. A necessary and half admitted lie. One I am asking her not to believe, but to honor, respect.

I am standing in the guts of a huge machine. Behind each door energy is being generated by the friction of black bodies. I can hear them bumping and rubbing. I hear the low purr, the white voices from another dimension which by subtle magic orchestrate the movement in the rooms. My people are laughing and crying. Radios and television sets giggle at their antics. The building trembles. Through my shoes I can feel molecules unstable, shifting. Something not me leaks through the soles of my new black shoes and becomes part of the doomed structure. The building begins to rain on my shoulders, and the something which is now obviously a crucial part of my being rains down, and black people shredded by futile motions behind their thin doors join the rainfall. I am breathing dust. The engines I hear are grinding flesh and bone. Gray pink powder sticks in my throat. A vast crematorium, slow, plodding, but foolproof. Lights go out one by one in the stairwell. Not sleeping but emptied of cargo, of fuel. Dust of my parents floating past my eyes. Perhaps Tanya's. Perhaps my own.

She's not coming. Or has been here and will never return. Perhaps she could have saved us. A chill to ease the burning.

Urge is to smash the doors. Pull the tongues from the lying machines. Tell them to go, to get out before it's too late. Go. Go, brother. While the front door's still open. While there are still no barricades and sentries, while the Man is content to strangle your dreams, while he is too busy with the yellow men to ring your bodies with steel. One door after another kicked down. Like gunshots echoing. Fourth of July, Bastille Day, Dien Bien Phu, the message loud and clear. Shatter the silver screens, cut the plugs, join me battering down the doors. Ray Charles singing "Unchain My Heart."

Tanya will hear the tumult. Return. Lead with her laser eyes and iron will. Beside me. Mounting to the top floor. Take them in our arms. Away.

He did not want to be seen lurking on the shadowy landing. A door cracked, breathing yellow into the hall. Someone was leaving and voices crowded the front of an apartment, vaguely excited, loud enough and close enough so they passed through the walls. Wilkerson could hear their words clearly. Milton promising to come back later. Bring a taste after he made a little run. Laughter. Wilkerson exploded like a sprinter. Quickly gliding through the slice of light. On his tiptoes until halfway down the last flight of stairs.

T W O
. . . . .

WILLIE HALL watched the brown body rise, the powerful legs scissor-kick in midair, the explosive force which had launched the player diffuse to graceful control of body and ball as the leap ended in a glide to the basket, the shrug of the net as the basketball fluttered down bouncing onto the court like an echo to the shooter's contact with the asphalt. The player's momentum had carried him beyond the goal and landing in a crouch on the balls of his feet, he spun, barely glancing over his shoulder to record the ripple of the net, the ball's clean drop through it, before he loped back down court to defend the opposite basket.

Besides two teams on the court both sides of the playground were lined with players waiting a turn. Littleman knew the role of this chorus. How their signifying and cheering could whip up the action. How reputations were made and dismantled as the bystanders with the words and noises they made participated in the game. There were no passive spectators. Within the area enclosed by the cyclone fencing everyone's blood was up. Even at a distance Littleman could sense the energy, could feel the rhythm of the game tighten his own chest, accelerate his heartbeat. Littleman thought of gut bucket jazz, of the sound of the ocean as sudden pauses in the game would be marked by a crescendo of angry voices, deep, male voices disputing a foul or an out of bounds. To a stranger the anger would seem violently out of proportion, four pairs of sweat drenched bodies immobile while a wiry, barechested player in red trunks with at least three pairs of sweat socks taped high on his calves, bands of color just below the knotty muscle, has the ball under his arm and is stomping toward the sidelines. A bearded taller figure whose star studded jersey is soaked dark, deep blue in a bib-like yoke beneath his chin mimics the other's walk, stalking behind him bending to his ear to narrate a version of the foul. Both turn flamboyantly on cue and parade to the center of the court where red trunks, unconvinced but wearied by the other's teasing monologue, slams the ball high off the asphalt.

—That's the last fucking thing you're getting. I ain't giving up shit else.

The game resumes. Splat of the ball dribbled, grunts and yells as the players jostle for position under the backboards, work themselves free for shots and passes. An older player, chunky, bearded, head shaven clean bulls his way through the lane for a lay-up. A lean, black boy guarding him springs high, his hand at least a foot above the rim, but all he can do is slap his palm against the metal backboard because the other's shot has already looped around his flailing arm and ricocheted through the goal. The entire standard, orange rim, steel poles, the perforated metal backboard continue to shudder after the action has passed. Littleman liked the way the thick, yellowish man had made his move. No waste of energy. Everything for go, nothing for show. The man was past walking on air, past the rubber legged dunking and pinning shots on the backboard which made the gallery squeal, hoot and shake their heads. But the man knew the game. How to conserve his strength, how to use his bulk to offset the spring of long muscled jumping jacks he contested for rebounds. A kind of fluid inevitability when he drove for the basket. He was going to get his no matter how high the others jumped, no matter what impossible refinements their skills brought into the game.

Sunday morning, barely ten thirty, but the sun was already high and the court crowded. A rainbow of colors, jerseys advertising high schools, churches, hamburger shops, real estate agencies, garages, clubs, colleges, a few emblazoned with pro or semi-pro names, but dominating these was the spectrum of flesh tones from dull ivory to glistening black, the wet muscles highlighted by brilliant sunlight. Littleman wondered how they had survived, the sleek muscles, the strength, the pride, how did it bloom again and again, how were these men so real, so richly full of life. Where did it hide the six days a week they were trapped in the decaying city? How did the vigor, the beauty disguise itself, how did these men slip into the nonentity, the innocuousness demanded of them as they encountered the white world. Black men playing basketball. Less than half of them were high school or college athletes. Most had to be classed as dishwashers and janitors or men who carried mail, men who scuffled to make ends meet for themselves and their families. Yet here they were. Playing this game the way it should be played. Sunday in the playgrounds as far away from this earth as the sanctified people in the storefront churches just down the block, singing and shaking their way to glory.

Willie Hall forgot for a moment why he was here. Relaxed into the game.

The man was coal black and dripping with sweat. He had stolen a pass and streaked away from the others, the ball pushed in front of him in long, exaggerated dribbles so he seemed to be chasing it although his fingertips expertly controlled its speed and direction. He must have heard the footsteps of the pack behind him, but he never looked back. Not a question of eluding his opponents. The breakaway lay-up was his to score. Only a matter of how he would do it, how much imagination he could bring to bear, how much style in the execution, which laws of gravity, momentum, which human limits he would deny. Aside from striped Adidas sneakers and white cut-away shorts, his skin, chiseled by sun and moisture was naked. Lip of the rim hung ten feet from the ground but he propelled his six feet and inches toward it, ball cradled in one wrist and palm, soaring till his fingers atop the ball stretched over the basket and jammed the prize home.

Somebody did the bugaloo. Somebody said *Shit yeah*. Another brought both hands down in a sweeping arc to slap the upturned palms of somebody saying *Do it Darnell*.

Willie Hall knew why he was not jealous. He felt his crippled legs high stepping up an invisible ladder toward the sun. Thrust, parry, thrust. Give one. Get it back. You just had to say ooowhee when a nigger got it all together nice as that.

Littleman heard Wilkerson's voice before he felt the hand on his shoulder.

—Lots of talent out there. It's a damn shame. With a decent break lots of those guys might have been college players or even pros.

—Too good for that. Wilkerson would not know what he meant but Littleman turned from the game saying no more.

—A good day for our talk. I like to walk on days like this.

—Let's walk toward the river then. Down Lombard then back up South. I like the contrast. Primes the anger.

—You mean black and white.

—At least that. Always that but I can be a little more specific in this case about what bothers me. Littleman was moving in his peculiar shuffling gait as he talked, tap and shuffle along the pavement, a pace Wilkerson could match with a casual saunter. Sounds of the game faded. Stillness. Then bells of nearby church steeples. To the left, visible beyond the fenced-in vacant lots which marked newly leveled areas destined for urban renewal, the historic buildings, Independence Hall, the Mint, had been cleaned and restored.

—See all this. Littleman's finger jabbed at the elegant red and white of the monuments, the expensive facades of the town houses lining Lombard.

—Marble, concrete, stone, brick. Money and tradition. Look at this and remember what's over there, just through these walls. Not even a hundred yards away. People are insane. Two hundred years and they haven't learned a goddamn thing. They want to rebuild a lie. Colonial architecture. They want to hide their heads in the sand. Don't they know it didn't work in the eighteenth century and it surely won't now. They want the Enlightenment, the Age of Reason, as if they don't know what those delusions cost, who paid for their leisure and elegance. How many black bodies were cast into the sea to finance what these damn merchants call culture.

−Look around us, Wilkerson. I wish I could teach every black boy on South Street what I see. We can't let them do it again. Order, right reason, the white man just under God at the apex of creation. The buildings foursquare, proportioned, what they call classic because they think they are reproducing the harmony of dead Greeks. Divinely ordained order. History, progress stopping dead because they believe they have all the answers. Fountains and squares and columns, the best of all possible worlds. Sublime order. Everything, everybody in its place. That's what they dream. What they thought they planted beside the water. So they preserve these remnants of the eighteenth century, have an urge to produce an exact replica of every error and misconception. What should a black man feel walking down this street, the Liberty Bell almost close enough to spit on, the fat, ugly boats full of money laying down there in the Delaware. What should he think when he knows about South Street over the other shoulder. South Street giving the lie to every promise, every pretension of the architecture the city is restoring. On South Street you see what really happened. Here is where it began, what they wished might happen, but there is reality, the twisted guts, the filth, the million ways to be crushed. South Street like a sewer to drain off what they don't want over here.

More bells tolling, taking into themselves chunks of the silence and liberating a sound which accented the stillness. Steeples poking above the huddled masses of row houses, an occasional church gray and isolated framed by the emptiness around it. White fencing like that cordoning the demolished city blocks closed the end of the street on which the men walked. Below them a muddy slope spilled down to Front Street, Front the broad, dilapidated perpendicular to Lombard, across which a fringe of low buildings and rusted machinery edged the sluggish river. Nothing moved. They leaned on the fence at least two minutes before a car rattled along the wide, potholed roadway. Littleman spread his fingers on the two by four railing. The river could not reflect the clear blue of the sky. In spite of sunshine the scene before him could be painted with browns and grays. Even the few cars picking their way over gulleys, humps and the railroad tracks that intersected the street were dully nondescript.

–It must have been beautiful country once. Littleman had returned to the pavement and moved toward South Street.

–I mean with all the trees and water. When everything was clean. Like when it was just river and forest and hill and valley and nothing had a name. If we were fighting for some of that, I'd feel better. Sometimes it's damned hard getting excited about winning a piece of this action. Not much left besides the money they made selling the land. I guess that's why so many just want out. A new start somewhere else. But I'm not sure what they'd do. I mean would our people kill the animals and trees and pour cement over Africa. Is power always just a rope nobody can play with too long before they hang themselves. You think about these things, don't you, Wilkerson. I need you because there is this silly ass part of me always wants to sit back and observe, do nothing but talk and think. A part that's past caring about anything.

–I know what you're talking about. Sometimes I think there's nothing to me but the part you're describing. What goes on inside my head, just because it's the head of Thomas Wilkerson becomes more important than anything else. The worse kind of selfishness.

–It's not the selfishness that hangs me up. Who am I. What I am. I'm smart enough to see much more to despise than to fall in love with. I'm not afraid of loving myself. My mind worries me because I can't trust it. It's lazy and preening. And because those things are unacceptable to me, my mind has learned to deceive. Put me in a trick every time. I used to write a lot. Writing cleaned me out. Cleared the bullshit.

But it takes too much time. I know what's important to me
and writing is an extravagance I can't afford. But I still have to
get the words out or they'd spin around and spin around and
give my mind no peace.

—I can listen.

—Yes, I know damned well you can listen. You're a
gentleman, you can listen till I'm tired of talking.

—And gentlemen are buttholes, right.

—Don't get salty. I was paying you a kind of compliment.
What's out here. What kind of world are we in now. We've
crossed the barricades. South Street stretches far as you can
see. This street means they are killing us, whittling away day
by day, a man, a woman, a baby at a time. And most of us
just sitting on our asses waiting our turn. If you see this and
understand this, doesn't it become obvious that we're all mad.
The killers for killing and the victims for letting themselves
be killed. That's the total picture. Now to be called a gentleman ain't half bad. I mean a gentleman's a pig, and he's
crazy like the others are crazy but at least he hasn't murdered
with his own hands, at least he's not dead yet. In an insane
world those are not small blessings. You're an ostrich with
your yellow ass sticking up in the air but for the moment
nobody's after it and maybe you can even believe your head
will find something down there in the sand.

—You're beside me walking and talking. What's that make
you?

—Makes me sick if you really want to know. Makes me
weak and sick. Right now the best I can do, the only way
I can walk calmly through the pillage and the dying is to
believe I have an answer. To believe that on a specific day,
just a few months from now these filthy walls are going
to crumble, and we'll be able to stand where we are and see
a cleansed plain, this scab of a city peeled back so air can
get to the wounded land.

—And then.

—Then I would prefer to be among the dead.

—A martyr.

–No, you're trying to make me sound silly. I wouldn't even want to be a memory because it won't be a time for memories.

–Do you believe anyone would have the strength to start all over if the new day, the emptiness ever really comes.

–Shit. That's the kind of thinking I want to get rid of. I don't need to think about then. Look at what's here. How real it is. Don't you remember what you saw a few minutes ago. Brick and stone and money and marble. All that's still there. You can peek through these ruins and get a glimpse. Let's think about now. About what ails now. Let's make sure this won't be here tomorrow. Then let tomorrow take care of itself.

They were past the wholesale shops, the seven day a week hustlers that congregated at the river end of the street. Through this gauntlet of merchants, then a strip of specialty shops, natural foods, nostalgic junk, arts and crafts galleries catering to the young white people who wore their hair long and the frontier clothes of their ancestors. Bunting stretched over the street and archly lettered signs proclaimed a renaissance. Storefronts were relatively cheap and the whites who felt themselves bohemians, outcasts were attempting to establish an islet of sanity, an oasis which would nurture their life styles here between the businessmen and the troubled black sea. Wilkerson wanted to linger. Stand in front of the displays of painting and photography, handle the trinkets, smell leather, incense, perfumed candles, but Littleman tugged at his sleeve.

–These people are fools. They'll be the first to die. And all this crap they're making, all the bullshit they're talking will go up in smoke. When Hitler and his boys decided to clean up a country, do you know who caught just as much hell as the Jews? Gypsies. The rootless, the transient, the people who had cut their ties and roamed the country trying to mind their own business. These people were automatically criminals. And machine guns were judge, jury and executioner every time the Nazis found a flock. Shit. If black people don't kill these babies their own people will come and root them out. And the smart ones among them must understand. They know they're lambs waiting for the slaughter. Yet they bring their women and children here and whine about love.

—At least they're doing something they want to do. And some are producing beautiful things.

—Look closer. Nothing but crap. Do you think they really want to be down here with the niggers. Do you believe they want to live in these old roach traps and wear raggedy ass clothes and eat shit. Do you think this is what they really want and are happy to be here. Shit. They want what everybody else wants and as soon as most of them get kicked in the ass enough times, as soon as they spend a winter with no heat and stand for days in clinic lines waiting to get the rot cleaned out of their bellies and off their skins, soon as they find out what this nigger street means they'll fold up their tents and slink on back to being white.

—Now we're home. Just a few steps, and, shit, we came the long way, just a few steps and we're on the other side of the moon. Do you believe it, Wilkerson, do you believe we've stood for this shit as long as we have. Jesus fucking Christ. If you listen, you can hear niggers dying around us.

—And you think we can change this.

—Are you still so unconvinced? Why is it so much easier for you to doubt than believe?

—You said you wanted to talk. That's why I got up and met you this morning. Why we're here. So you must think there's more I should know. More convincing to do. I'm not like you. I can't speak to crowds, I have no grandiose plan for the future. I have no desire to lead anyone. Hard enough getting myself together.

—I have to get you ready, baby. Get you ready. But you won't be ready till you believe the plan. All the talk in the world can't get you to believe. I can tire you out, but I can't force you to believe. I knew better than to make the mistake the white man has. He had us weary and exhausted, beat down as far down as down goes, but that didn't mean we had accepted his lies. I'm ready to begin talking to you about details. How we kidnap the cop. How we stage the main event in the streets. For me it's just a matter of putting the pieces together. The plan is whole, real, imminent. I'm concerned with incidentals. With making the parts happen, with making you real.

—You believe we can do it.

—Do you believe what we're seeing this morning? How simple and concrete everything is. Do you see the next step? How vulnerable the lies are that hold this mess together as it stands. Do you realize how we have all the evidence we need to expose the lies, to shatter the arbitrary balance and order. Nothing but an alley between two alien forms of life. The whites are just a few paces away living in a manner which makes a mockery of our suffering. Two people in a fifty thousand dollar town house, eight or ten rooms to stockpile the loot they've acquired. And babies on this street sleeping in drawers, on the floor, in the same bed with their mother and whatever man's come to help her through the night. It's an alley we can cross, we can cross in numbers. Nothing in the world can stop us if we decide the barrier is not there anymore. If we all die at least the lie will die with us. When have we ever risen up as a people, united, resolved ready to die together. Never, never once in our pitiful history. A sane man looking at us from the outside would wonder what is so precious in our miserable lives that we cling to them in spite of hundreds of years of degradation.

—We must strike and strike so desperately that our example is stronger than the lie. We must say No, you cannot define us, you cannot set the limits. No, the flunkies you pay to keep us within bounds are not enough. We must show how the cops are symbolic. How they are too few and how these few can be made to disappear. We will lynch one man but in fact we will be denying a total vision of reality. It's been easy for them too long. Some are almost convinced they understand us, some believe we are transparent, that they can kill a nigger or beat a nigger and scare the rest out of fighting back. Some think they can toss us a few coins and fill our heads with dreams of catfish and watermelon. So many books, so much talk, so many experts and explanations. And they're all right because they're all wrong because what they see is what they have created, what they want to see. The plan begins by sweeping aside what is past. When we lynch the cop we declare our understanding of the past, our scorn for it, our disregard for any consequences that the past has taught us to fear. We also deny any future except one conditioned by new definitions of ourselves as fighters, free, violent men who will determine the nature of the reality in which they exist. Or die in the attempt. There won't be a South or a South Street for these new men. They won't be taught to bow before the symbols of their humiliation. A Liberty Bell, a white hand holding the keys to the kingdom. When did the bell ring. Who did it ring for. I was on a boat while their liberty bells were ringing. All I heard were pipes and whistles calling us on deck to exercise, the rattle of chains when we danced, the life buoys pealing in a foggy harbor three thousand miles from my home. The auctioneer ringing a bell so the buyers could stampede into the pens and look at our dicks and teeth. And I've been listening ever since. To bells and bullshit.

As if Littleman demanded their noise to punctuate his speech the antique bells clanked and gonged, floating over the littered corridor of South Street, hanging like a rainbow of sound into which the black churches sent up their tithe of bell music, tambourines, organ, drum and piano or just the rejoicing voices of the saints in the storefront houses of worship Wilkerson and the crippled man strolled by.

—Wilkerson, the plan's as simple as death. When one man kills it's murder. When a nation kills murder is called war. If we lynch the cop we will be declaring ourselves a nation. Only two responses to our action are possible. They must attack us or back off and either way they must recognize our sovereignty. Since the total community gives its sanction in a lynching, mass retaliation, undifferentiated slaughter of community members is the only suitable punishment and that means in effect a declaration of war, an acknowledgment of the separateness of the community. If a white woman was molested or a slave struck his master and ran away, the South reacted by killing any niggers who happened to be handy. No question of justice, of catching the offender. All black men were responsible and the rules of war meant all were guilty. Now suppose after we lynch the cop they attempt another kind of action. No retaliation at all. The symbolism of our act is too obvious to be ignored. In fact if they don't declare war, they are accepting the rightness, the validity of our rejection of their lies. They are saying yes you are a nation and we accept the truth of your nationhood, your right to establish your own law and justice. Yes, our soldier was an outlaw when he crossed into your territory. Either way our community becomes defined, becomes separate. No half measures will be possible. We are incorporating their understanding of history and power into our plan. We are saying crystally clear in the language they invented: We are your equals. Accept that or go to war. No more pussyfooting. No more slow attrition of our best men. No more battles in which only one side is allowed to fight.

–As simple as death. But you're not ready yet because you're afraid to die. You think of dying as some complicated trip with millions of arrangements to be made before you go. Most people are like you. But I've been alone a long while. I understand how easy it is to disappear absolutely from the face of the earth. You don't owe anyone anything and nobody wants to go with you. You just go. Men, races, trees, bugs, rocks. Here and gone. So we get hung up in this little squabbling between black and white, a fight over land that's going to be worthless very soon. A struggle so goddamn wearying that we forget how arbitrary it is, how irrelevant to larger movements, the flow of history in and out of this moment. We talk around the solitary issue at stake. We avoid putting the whole mess in terms of life or death. They know that, they know we prefer the worst they can do to death. We think they own death because they have bombs and soldiers and cops and rope. Every black man carries a fear of death in his heart, a fear of death at the hands of white men. Each is isolated by his fear of death. It's that terror we must release our people from. But first I must carve it out of you. What is anything worth if you've given up to others the single significant choice, the choice which proves something has value. It's not much but we all have it. The decision to make some arbitrary event or choice worth your life. Can you die for the plan. Can you be prepared at any moment to forfeit your life to the plan. The plan must be worth your death and if necessary a million others. What's at stake is blood, and we must let them know clearly, precisely that we mean business. We must teach them the blunt, blind energy of the plan. But first we must believe. We must radiate belief, glow with it like avenging angels.

Littleman nodded at the men around the ramshackle shoe-shine stand. Six or seven sitting and standing, exiles from another planet huddling close to the wreckage of the elaborate machine which had dropped with them from the heavens. They projected confusion, their eyes and hands moved at the wrong speed, evidence of a subtle deterioration of hidden, vital organs. Sucking on bottles of sweet soda pop, chewing candy bars. Two had climbed onto the platform and occupied the customers' seats. The jaunty angle of the goosenecks on which their feet rested exposed the raggedy soles of their shoes. The men luxuriated under a glossy picture of crisply blue Mediterranean sky and the peaches and cream curves of a naked blonde stretched on white sand, under the shade of a patchwork overhang, under the crumbling brick and gouged windows of a ruined building, under a hazy blue sky through which shafts of sunlight smoked.

• • •

Its cyclops eye bloodshot and spinning, the squad car hovered outside the entrance of Woodrow Wilson Junior High School. Donohue and Harkness listened impatiently to the long string of sputtering static emitted from their two way radio. They glanced stiffly at one another and at the dark watches on thick straps circling their wrists. The windows were up and the air inside oppressive. Air conditioned patrol cars were part of the new law and order bond issue stalled while city hall politicians played both ends against the middle. Sometimes, cruising in this section of the city, Donohue felt he was an astronaut orbiting alone beyond the earth. He felt the astronaut's profound detachment from all things familiar and real, a growing bitterness and fear at being deserted amid the cold immensity of the stars. Only a metal shell between himself and extinction. That his partner sat beside him offered no consolation. In fact Harkness impinged upon his privacy, the necessary, final privacy that would allow a last wallow in tears, farts and blasphemy when Donohue finally knew without a doubt that his mission was unsuccessful, that he would never return.

Though other red cars and personnel carriers, each with its team of special riot commandos were stationed around the school, Donohue could not shake the dreadful sense of isolation intimidating him. He was a defensive safety alone in the hinterlands of the immense stadium bowl, waiting for the streaking ends to attack his position. Where the blue of his uniform creased against vinyl upholstery, cool rivers of sweat drained down his back. And the weight of the gun at his waist. Foreign as the creep of some other man's erection against his thigh. At times he believed he would bring on a hernia if he tried to lift the revolver from its sheathing.

His eyes sought Harkness. He wanted to ask him if he was afraid. But Donohue could only concentrate on the harsh angle of his partner's nose, the bird's profile and thick, black eyebrows. Harkness whose cheeks always looked like they had been sanded shiny after a clumsy razor dug out each whisker. Moonscape. Donohue could not admit fear. His mission was after all beyond fear; he had contracted to operate in a void where humanity with its doubts and fears was the first thing left behind. If he confessed to fear, he would be compromised. All the power that had focused to rocket him into this foreign sphere would be sacrificed to his weakness. He would plummet back toward earth, farther than any man had ever fallen. Cremated in an instant by the same laws of energy and momentum that had been harnessed to place him where he sat, safe for the moment, uncomfortable but secure within the steel capsule.

A voice crackled from headquarters. Waiting was over. The normal pull of gravity was restored. His limbs lost their granite monumentality, slid easily onto the pavement. Boots sent up pleasant shivers through his shins, buoyed him with steady crunching assurance at each stride. *Get the crazy black dwarf off the fucking school steps.*

White helmeted, eyes invisible behind thick sun tinted visors, wearing superfluous gas masks with long wrinkled snouts curling like a nightmare incarnation of the word shouted by the crowd of children, the police moved purposefully, businesslike into formation. A wedge of bodies, indistinguishable one from the other, incredibly obscene in their mirror sameness and identical gaits, the spawn of some amuck geneticist spilling from laboratory vats onto the city street, unreal in the sunlight, threatening in the way ranks of lead soldiers threaten, stiffly alike with their grotesquely painted faces and right legs suspended in the air forever.

They marched, an overgrown wind-up toy, scattering the audience that had ranged itself on the front steps of Wilson Junior High to hear the man who now stood alone, framed between corinthian columns ornamenting the building's ponderous facade. Brown, bearded figure at whose heart point of the wedge seemed aimed, statue rigid, a puny Samson whose arms could not stretch between the false columns, could not bend them inward and topple the temple upon his mechanical tormentors.

The arrow reached him. Its point blunted as the speaker flailed his cane like a scythe about him. Two policemen fell who had underestimated the strength half a man could retain in his stunted body. Speaker striking with fury, waist high, blasting the truncheons back against unarmored blue bellies. Desperate with rage and impotence, ringed by blows, the dwarf crashed his cane down on the cushioned steel helmet of patrolman Donohue, who lay crumpled on the cold stone, wind slapped from his guts by an earlier blow of the cane now splintering harmlessly on his gleaming headpiece.

Those who had detached themselves from the rear rank of the phalanx and had stood with shotguns cocked, some aimed at the brief melee and the others sighted down the steps at the screaming children, rejoined their comrades. Nearly as perfect as it had mounted the steps, the formation descended. If there were wounds or blood, they were not apparent. Only to one on his knees peering into the center of the wedge would a few faltering legs of the centipede be visible, and the dull sparks of metal scraping stone. Sparks from the braces of the little man dragged lifeless from the rally.

● ● ●

Willie Hall had never been able to explain to himself why he came to the seashore resort. The city was a place where people displayed their bodies, and it was with something less than enjoyment that he exposed his crippled legs to the sun. Night life was plentiful. The bars shoulder to shoulder on a long stretch of Arctic Avenue, then the gleam of Kentucky Avenue with its fanciest Club Harlem and satellite, almost as expensive joints, and finally scattered at the city's edges roadhouses from plush to honky tonk. But bars, restaurants, traveling shows that filled the huge barn of Convention Hall with every sort of hustler and hick imaginable were definitely not what attracted Willie Hall since he could barely afford to drink through a two day weekend in the cheap gin holes that he frequented. Though it was surrounded by architecture that compounded the uglinesses of ostentation, parsimony and greed, though rashers of bodies baking in the sun were a fleshy barricade through which he had to hobble to touch it, perhaps the sea was why he took the bus to Atlantic City the two long weekends a month his job allowed.

Willie Hall strolling on the boardwalk. Metallic wheeze of his armored legs slow shuffle, tap of his cane on the wooden promenade. Scowling above the leonine beard. As if the sun perpetually in his eyes.

Willie Hall drawn to the sea. He prefers night vistas, alone, staring outward into blackness. There is no horizon, no time. From nowhere dull gleam of breakers dancing into being. Steady pounding, a pulse, a giant steel ball slamming into the meat of the sand. Booming and walls crashing around him, city laid waste, crumbling to dust, luminous shivers rising, walking the black depths into which he peers. Willie thinks of his fist smashed into the purple of his palm, the silence of his cell shattered as blow after blow strikes, his arm a piston, rhythmic, tireless, the sea beating the land, his heart beating, the wings of some gloriously colored bird relentlessly ascending, fanning with its beating wings the smouldering city below.

Wrapped in chains the squat shape worked its way from the water toward the boardwalk. Moony night. In the shadows and needle light it could have been a sea creature, swift and sure in its native habitat, but hopelessly unwieldy in the damp sand. A walrus. A snail. All sense of proportion gone where sea and land come together under the moon.

He is grunting or singing tunelessly to himself. Barely audible above the water's roar. Seabeast keening for its lost element. A gospel song dim in recollection. Willie repeated the same few words again and again, varying the lyrics by modulations in the tune, faster and slower, deep or rising, imitation of crude instruments taking up the melody, or the notes passed in steps from dark bass to high wailing of the deep breasted women. To a listener all the richness of Willie's memory would be an embarrassingly inadequate attempt at whistling or singing, but for the man groping from sea to shore, country people in a country church he could revive only with these snatches of words and music, these uneven mumblings of song were all the family, the home, the child's glow of peace and innocence he had ever known.

Willie stopped when he realized he was not alone. After the figure had taken a few more steps he realized it was a woman. Long bare legs, a loose wind blown dress. She continued toward him so steadily he thought she must not have noticed him yet. Night on a deserted beach and she was a woman alone, him a strange man. A wave of resentment was hot in his throat. Perhaps she saw him all too well. Broken man, tethered to braces and cane. Barely as high as her chin. Why should she fear him? Then he wanted to hurt her. Remain concealed in whatever pocket of shadow he stood. Leap out and strike her down with the leaded cane. Pin her body to the sand. A man taking what he wished.

Her voice was husky in the night air. Morning voice stiff in its first venture at words.

—A beautiful night isn't it brother. Of all the fucking things to say Willie thought to himself on this beach in the middle of the night. Of course what else would make more sense. Is there anything at all to say to a little cripple bastard you just happen to meet on a beach nobody supposed to be on anyway after 10:00 P.M. if you can read the signs posted everywhere.

—My name is Angela.

She's trying to make it easy. Legs ain't so skinny up close. Her face in the moonlight modeled in broad planes, like the face of an eroded statue, its painted eyes plucked by the birds, its features superfluous to strong harmony of bones, of contour and volume, firmly suggesting the skull for which flesh is ornament and glaze. She was handsome reduced to these elemental patterns. A strength of line, a fullness in her face. Willie Hall imagined his appearance in the dappling moonlight. Beach was a pocked moon crater. Shallow dunes with scalp locks of coarse grass, the amputated humps of an army of dwarfs just like him. But his shoulders sloped clean, his arms could even be said to ripple from his polo shirts. Her eyes were on him he was sure, but he couldn't see the downward cast he hated so much when women looked at him. Perhaps there, but mercifully obliterated by the night. For the first time since he had begun his night walk he felt the chill which had gradually and now completely absorbed all the heat of day.

—The hawk's flying. Aren't you cold?

—I don't think so. At least I hadn't been aware of the cold until you spoke. I was sitting up there, under the awning where they store rental chairs and umbrellas. It's lower, out of the wind.

—Somebody will shoot you for trying to steal the Man's beach chairs.

—No one can see me from the boardwalk. And nobody ever walks down on the beach this late. If they would, they could pass a foot away and not see me snuggled in one of my cozy lounge chairs. It's a place where I can be sure I'll be left alone. Me and the sea. And I get a kick out of think-ing that I'm using those two twenty-five an hour daytime luxuries as long as I wish for free.

—But now I know your secret.

—We're even. I peeked at you when I knew I shouldn't be looking. You stood by the water a long time. And I sensed that you wanted to be alone. Thought you were alone.

Willie Hall smiled to himself. Asked himself was con-cealing his expression necessary in this half light. He was thinking of all the times he had ended his night staring at the sea by taking a hearty, long winded piss into the waves. He hadn't felt the urge tonight, but wondered what the girl would have thought if she had peeked at that particular finale to the ritual. He wished that he had pulled it out. Shown her from a distance the healthy ramrod of his man-hood. A stiff, strong dick. Functioning as well as that of any seven foot basketball player. But the clumsy prepara-tion for such a simple act. What if she had witnessed that.

His three legs carefully balanced in the wet sand so a free arm could liberate his pisser. Fear always in his mind that he would begin to topple, steel and wooden tripod failing him and uncontrollable stream spurting everywhere as his hands go out instinctively to brace his fall. Memory of the days before he turned his rubbery legs into muscle he could sometimes depend upon, when he had to sit like a woman on a pot.

—You watched me.

—It was so strange to see someone here. I've come often and never a soul. I decided I would just get in your way. Risk saying something. Even if you were annoyed. Or walked away.

—Or worse.

—There's worse?

—There are people who kill and maim. Who live to hurt. Werewolves at the full moon. Frankenstein monsters.

—They don't act like you were acting.

—They don't look at the sea.

—Not here and now. The sea calms people at night, doesn't it? I mean if you came full of anger or anything doesn't the water make those feelings much smaller. It shrinks everything.

—If I were looking for loonies I think I might come here first. Madmen have a thing for water and the moon.

—Do you think so?

—I think you are a strange girl.

—Because I like the sea? I get lost when I come here. I mean so much of it rolling in, always rolling in. When I sit in my hideaway, it's like I'm a little baby sleeping only I'm awake and can enjoy every minute of it. That's why it seemed so right to approach you. You were part of the feeling I had. You were something like a dream I could get up and speak to. She was closer. If he extended his arm, he could tap her on the shoulder with his cane. One step forward and he could bring her to her knees with a sudden blow, swoop down and circle her with arms she could not resist. A dream from which she would not awaken.

Sea chill. Black water lapping at black land. White bones glowing.

—My name is Willie, Willie Hall. He did not add that everybody back in the city knew him as Littleman. That most if asked could not say what his given name was. He tried to smile, forget the darkness, the sea voices shouting *Littleman, Littleman.*

—Willie. I wouldn't have guessed, Willie, but I like it. It's fine. Any name would be fine. Her voice told him she was smiling, maybe even laughing.

He remembered the whore laughing his name. On one of his first excursions to Atlantic City, when he thought he could take pleasure trips like others took them, he had been drunk, hungry for a woman and found a bar where women could be purchased. One had come to the booth where he sat propped, the illusion of a whole man since his braces trailed off into obscurity below the table. She said yes and they got up to go. Outside when he turned to face her she was laughing. Drunk, uncomprehending, he began to laugh too.

—What's your name little fella? He answered mechanically, his name part of the laughter he thought he was sharing with her.

—Willie, huh. Well you's a game little fella, Willie. You had me fooled in the bar. Thought you some big strapping Papa, and I was hot to get turned on myself. You know a lady likes to enjoy her work sometime. Ha. And I was gettin ready for a good one. Out you hobble cane and all. I wondered why everybody looking at me funny when I sat down. Out you hobble and I nearly dropped my drawers. My smooth talking Papa ain't hardly big as a minute. Kiss my ass I say then I can't hardly keep a straight face walking behind you. Signifying Otis back of the bar chessy cat grinning at me. Game little man. Scrambling outa there like you in a real hurry. Into something, I guess you thought. Well, now we out here, you can forget it. Janice ain't for no freak tricks. Straight fucking all this girl gonna do. That's why I stay away from them white boys.

–I'll give you all the fucking you want, sister.

–You ain't gonna scrape my knees with all that metal you got wrapped round your legs. You a freak trick, honey, that's all there is to it.

–How much.

–Ain't no how much to it. Go on up the road. You find somebody up the road do what you want.

–I want you. And I can pay. Extra if you want me to help you forget the inconveniences.

They haggled in the alley. Finally compromised on a figure that left Littleman with only bus fare and loose change. She insisted on half of the amount before she took him to her room. He counted out the bills. Lips mouthing the arithmetic she snatched the payment, stuffed it into her bosom and took a step backward.

–You telling me what a badass cocksman you are. Well, if you so bad, catch my black butt and you can have all the pussy you want. Laughing, she backpedaled two long steps, turned and was gone up the alley in a clatter of high heels. He shouted but whiskey slowed his movements. His mind was spinning, unable to sort any pattern from the swirling merry-go-round of images. The whore's fleeing figure, comical like a duck sprinting, broad assed, skinny ankles, big feet in minnie mouse heels, striding tight legged till she tugged her skirt to the middle of her thighs. The echoing laughter. His cane lazily turning in the air, unaimed, jerking itself from his hand and flying of its own volition, a drum majorette's baton end over end till it banged harmlessly into something metallic, missing the woman's back by six feet, but stopping her laughter long enough for *Cripple freaky motherfucker* to be flung over her shoulder.

Her voice full of smiling. Would this one turn and run? Awkward slow motion in the sand then clattering down the boardwalk. Laughing his name. He was close enough to make her pay.

–Would you like to sit with me a while? Under my private awning? In Mr. Charlie's expensive chairs?

Sea roar. A hissing progress up the beach toward the greater sheltered darkness where she led him. He could not tell if she moved so slowly because the loose, heavy sand burdened her woman's steps as much as it did his scuttling or if her pace was a way of holding his hand.

• • •

Weekends together in July, then the room they shared during August when Willie quit his job to be with her. At first Angela kept her job selling hamburgers eight hours a night in a drive-in restaurant to supplement the few dollars Willie could salvage from his odd jobs. After her shift was held up twice in ten days, Willie had told her to leave the plastic fishbowl with its glowing dome and crackling neon, its propensity for drawing insects and stocking capped bandits from the sultry darkness. He tried looking for steady work but even in a city where swarms of migrant black laborers became bell hops, porters, dishwashers, bus boys only long enough to amass a stake that could pay the back rent or buy new clothes for the boardwalk and bars, or simply extend their season in the sun away from the oppressive cities of the North and familiar dull poverty of the South, where the brown-eyed, lithe college men played a laughing game of musical chairs with the coolie work available to them, swapping jobs, three men alternating in the same position, hired, fired, retired, rehired, by one employer in one week, even here in this carnival city where open jobs popped up like metal ducks in a shooting gallery, Willie Hall was insulted, lied to, pitied, tittered at, ignored when he presented himself as a candidate for work. At five o'clock after confronting countless faces waiting behind the help wanted signs he returned to the hot room at the top of the stairs on Baltic Avenue. Angela lay on the bed sleeping. Her honey colored skin was damp from the heat.

They had been awake almost the entire night before.

Money was just about gone and Willie knew something had to be done; he would have to force himself to meet the mocking, condescending eyes which would stare at him like he was a beggar extending a tin cup. He had been through such interviews a thousand times, heart pounding, dripping with nervous perspiration. Anger so rampant inside that he could barely control his speaking voice. Almost as if their judgment of him, palpable in their eyes and words, forced him into being the helpless stuttering idiot they conceived. No matter how hard he tried his words sputtered, tumbled, bordering on incoherency because his replies were so distant from what he actually felt, who he was. He swallowed pride, independence, surrendered the image of himself as a man infinitely superior to the red cheeked functionaries at the back doors of kitchens, or gum chewing secretaries with piles of spray starched hair who parroted, barely looking up from glossy magazines, "We'll call as soon as something opens up." The dammed eloquence of his indignation made his lips tremble; his tongue heavy as he replied, straining not to be what his guts told him he must be.

The humiliation of the coming day had already begun as he sat on the bed, back against the wall that served as a headboard, naked in the sweltering heat, the lights out, Angela alternately sitting up beside him or curled, curve of her back and buttocks softly awaiting him to cradle his head. But he could not go to her. Sopping wet. Hot night only partially responsible since Angela's skin was cool to his touch. Rancid boiling of his insides that coated his body with sweat. He anticipated walking the pavements, his body dragging beside him, an obscene animal on a chain he could not let go. Voices full of lies sending him down the next street, up an alley, to a vacant lot ten blocks away. He saw the atmosphere wiggling above the asphalt, the chrome and plastic hotels, rising like diseased exhalations of the surface miasma. Even the broken, old men could wheeze comfortably to themselves when he passed *there but for fortune . . .*

Willie knew the next day, could cite intimate details, quote

clipped conversations with lackeys who avoided his eyes. He
had been there before, was there now as he sat sleepless in
the bed he was transforming into a puddle. Angela must be
aware of the stink, the rankled nerve sweat, fetid as a rotting
tooth. He was on fire with stink and apprehension. Her back
was to him, she appeared to be sleeping, but in the stillness
he could discern her quiet sobbing. He stroked her bare
shoulder and she answered.

—Another planet. You might as well be on another planet.
Willie. Do I have to tell you how much I need you now. Do
I have to scream loud enough for another world to hear me.

He buried his damp shaggy beard in the floating coolness
of her hair. Brutal sobbing racked her body. For a long while
they lay just so, the tears he could not loose from the steel
that held him together pouring from her eyes. His heavy arms
around her, sliding up and down her body, kneading fistfuls
of her substance, stealing the symmetry of her long, straight
legs to remould the absurd foreshortening of his own. Finally
his fingers shaped to the slope of her back he turns her to
face him. In a fluid arc her shoulders rise and she is atop
him, a jiggling perpendicular straddling, squeezing him in the
powerful thrusts of her hips.

The next day had come again. She had walked with him
to the head of the stairs naked under a black raincoat. He
descended to meet the dragon, was destroyed and now
climbed to the room again.

Exhausted by their night, the coupling that had seemed
to go on for hours, the dull day waiting alone, she lay on her
belly, honey colored skin slightly damp, black hair piled on
top of her head. It angered him that she had not pulled the
shades. He saw her exposed to the eyes of another man, the
secrets of her body shared with a stranger. Late afternoon
sun flayed the room of shadow and illusion. He scanned
their nest. Wrinkled, graying sheets on which they had
thrashed half the night, another swath of soiled linen draping from the bed's bottom corner to the floor. Both sheets
smudged with patches of dull yellow. Two rickety cane

chairs, one with its seat gnawed away, a tall wooden end table with newspaper wadded under one leg to keep its wobbling at a minimum, a doorless closet where clothes were tossed, hung, piled on boxes and shoes that littered the floor of the shallow recess. Angela's scratchy record player beside the bed, Thelonius Monk spinning crazily at 78 r.p.m. on the turntable, Rachmaninoff leaning against the dusty baseboard. Tone arm was limp, content in its silent repose. Willie Hall examined minutely the nakedness of the woman he had returned to. In the harsh sunlight her skin lost the gold night glow. Almost no colors at all, a yellowish wash, uneven, splotched with darker regions where the skin was not tautly drawn. The curve of her buttocks that had arched rainbow perfect, fruit lush in his guiding hands was faded to mottled, lumpish immobility. Beckoning darkness of cleft and hollow no more mysterious than the yawning closet with its shaggy disarray.

And yet the stirring in his groin. As if a hand had reached down, grasped the sleeping tone arm and sent music irresistibly swelling through its blunt head. The same urgency of the night before. To mount and be mounted. To spend himself, to root out the terror and fear. Change all those things he knew would never change. But more. Not just change himself. He must annihilate the force that slapped them together, stuck man to woman, Willie Hall to Angela. After a day of futile trudging, of voices and eyes dismissing him, he was dizzy with lack of sleep, hunger, need. But he must rouse her. Fight the day again on different terms. Whip what had whipped him.

He pulls the wounded shade. In stages it rattles down, in stages he collapses, steel and flesh on the bed where she is stirring, turning toward him.

—Nothing, he says.

On one elbow, her eyes still hooded, her whole body yielding, soft as the droop of her breast leaning toward him she echoes

—Nothing.

He knows she will always be there. That some things cannot be changed. He will go down the steps tomorrow morning. Surely she will pad behind him, the black coat draped around her she will go as far as the top of the stairs and he will ask the questions all over again.

• • •

He is going down the steep steps. Mr. Jones is coughing, catarrh thick with melted liver and lungs. Deep snores from Sister Rosamond's room. He wonders if his landlady, the widow Mrs. Carter, is sleeping alone or has the cat-eyed slickster from the first floor tiptoed up to pay his rent. Angela still a warm blur clouding his thoughts. Image of her sleepy eyes caressing his back as he creaks down the stairs merges with the spiritual he hums to himself. Song and woman shredded by exploding whirr, iron jaws masticating heaps of garbage tossed in a truck by brown men in brown aprons. The beast screams, its teeth grating and grinding, as if its roar could arouse the men who move drowsily back and forth, automatons on a conveyor belt, between the clutter of cans and the hungry truck. Too early for the drones to speak civilly to each other, they limit their conversation to brief, violent exchanges with the machine, each container of refuse expelled with vicious force to splatter against the rotating iron teeth.

The gospel song hovered, a refrain whose words were repeated endlessly but whose melody danced through infinite variations. Angela's barefoot tread, her face shadowed, looking down into his. Strong bones, counterpoint to the machine's savage rending, complex fugue of sounds receding, struggling for dominance. Whirr of the truck now reinforced by the workers' voices rose finally an insistent monotone absorbing the last scraps of music.

—Let's get this shit together.
—Let's make this run and split.

—Woman don't want me gone all day.

—These be heavy mothafuckas first thing in the morning.

—Heavy and stinking.

—I do believe half these cans stuffed with bodies.

—Cheaper than burying.

—We ought to get the checks undertakers get.

—I read in the paper about undertakers joining a meat packers' and canners' union.

—I'd join a beauty parlor union if it would get me more money.

—Union ain't shit. If you're Black stay back. That's how the unions talk. Always have.

—Two kinds of people. Haves and have-nots. Those that have guns and those unprepared to defend themselves. You can forget unions, Naacps, Kings, Kennedys, meetings and marches.

—Union eat you up just like the Man.

—Out in California they have drive-in funeral parlors. Bodies laid out behind big picture windows. You just drive by and pay your respects. Don't even have to get out of the car. Saves dressing and pulling a long face.

—Don't want my dead ass up in no window. Just don't sound right. When I die my soul is God's and the dust supposed to go back to dust. It's a sin laying up in some window.

—Man, when you're gone, you're gone. They could put you in a jar of pickles and you wouldn't know the difference.

—That be some funky jar.

—Jew pickles funky anyway.

—You know, I bet the Man wouldn't hesitate to use dead niggers any way he could.

—Black buck fertilizer. Makes your garden grow.

—You think that's funny. I know in my heart that if somebody proved to the Man's satisfaction a dead nigger was twice as valuable as a live one, in a year or so they'd give out nigger hunting licenses.

—You're crazy.

—The truth is crazy.

—Come on, you all, I want to be out of these rags by noon. I got business to take care of.

—Then get your ass outa the truck. Uniondriverass wannabebigshotnigger.

—Lawd, lawd.

—Guns.

—You better believe I got mine.

—It's a sin.

—But do you know how to use it. And why you must learn to use it. Organization. Nothing will work unless the brothers can get themselves organized. That's the white man's secret. It's not leaders. Kill one president and you have fifty more just like him ready to step into the office. Defeat one at the polls or shoot him at breakfast. You just kill a man. It's the total system keeps us down on the bottom. Offices mean organization. You can't shoot an office. That's what the brothers have to learn. Pool our skills. Organize.

—First it was Liberia, then Garveyites, then the Communists, now you have some other half baked system and prophet going to lead us poor, ignorant black folk to the promised land. I got news baby. I'm neither poor or ignorant. I'm doing all right and my children going to do a lot better than me. The Man knows we're here. And he knows we got something going. I know. Don't bother to Tom me. That's your bag. I know where I'm at. I'm not fool enough to wait for somebody to give me something, I'm going to fight and demand. But within the law. I got a son fighting in Asia to defend the law and my rights within it.

—That's the way it has to be.

—Niggers killing Chinks. And proud of it. If you ain't ready for integration I don't know a Kneegrow who is.

—Heave Hucking Ho

—Biff Bam. I got a whole barrel of rotten gizzards and kidneys.

—It sure nuff do stink.

Going to Kansas City
Kansas City, here I come

Song shattered by song. Lead me. Guide me. Along the Way. Lord, if you lead me. I

I will not stray.

Lord.   Let   me

Walk

Each day.   Each day.   Each day.

Hammer blows pounding, pounding. Skull is an echo chamber. Brain cells cannot feel pain, lack sensation. But pressure builds. Numbing, bone splitting. Eyes sees flashes of red, blue. Gleaming egg on the steps. I try to squash it with the cane.

I am sinking. Down. Sinking.

I am dreaming or hallucinating. Nightmare lethargy. I want to move my finger but the pain is unbearable. I think my hand is stirring, but as it shifts slightly on the white shroud it crumbles from my wrist. I am breaking apart. Each effort to revive control costs excruciating pain. A crippling loss.

But I am already a cripple. The deadness below my groin. If they have tortured my body . . .

Have they . . .

Siren returns. I am tossing on the metal floor. Somebody's booted foot on my belly, keeping me in the center of the aisle, between the rows of blue knees. Sometimes he prods and nudges with his steel toe, sometimes the foot under my ribs shoving hard, almost lifting me from the wagon's bed. Urine smell. Slimy runnels in the uneven surface on which I'm stretched. Another foot explodes in my shoulder, its follow through scraping my face. My beard gives stiffly. Matted, wet. I am rolling, bouncing. The feet shuttle me between them. A game. Wrists being slowly severed, pinned behind my back with a bracelet of razors. I cannot move my arms to brush the thick moisture hanging over my eyes, making me almost blind. I see everything through a burning glaze. Sweat, blood, spit. I shut my eyes. Something dribbles down my cheek. Siren spilling over everything.

Then utter quiet. Bright light. I think I can hear the filaments crackling as they cook. I am naked, bathed in sweat. I see a black face. Kind that plays Ethiopian eunuch in hollywood epics. Cannot read his eyes. They are yellow and bloodshot but tell me nothing. Broad nose, thick lips, almost bald. Stripped to the waist. So perfectly black and enigmatic he is perhaps an angel.

—I ain't got an idea how to get these off. Silence is broken by a scream. After the pain passes I realize the scream is in my throat.

—Nigger still has feeling down there. The lips, thick as if in a perpetual pout have not spoken. I see plainly they are the underflesh inverted, perversely displayed. Slack face unreadable as before. Not a quiver of emotion as the words disintegrate.

—Leave him like he is. That'll do for what we want.

Another ride. Only this time within a metaphysical vehicle. Pain. Of course it was my physical body they assaulted, but the senses have their limits. Much of the time I floated beyond these. Metaphysical because the most difficult times were those in which I could contemplate myself as a helpless object of their whims, myself as someone who would have to bear the damage, the scars of the encounter, once, and if I emerged from the torture.

I awakened in a hospital bed. I had been injured in a fall down the steep steps of Woodrow Wilson Junior High while resisting arrest. I had been fomenting a riot. Had instigated an unlawful assembly. I was technically under arrest although a motion for bail had been made and a bond posted which would release me on my own cognizance once I signed the proper papers. I recalled the other signings. Confessions to a thousand crimes I scrawled my name to on demand. I wondered where they were filed. Who I had maimed, murdered, suborned, kidnapped in their depositions. Among the present relevant charges was assault with a deadly weapon, with intent to kill, a police officer.

Today is Saturday. I was surprised that I had lost track of only seventy-two hours, all of which I purportedly spent in a coma in this very hospital bed. For a moment I almost believed them. Was ready to accept the whole pain dream as hallucination until my body began to throb with the nearly unbearable truth of its bruised nerve endings.

—Quite a tumble you took, Mr. Hall.

I didn't say fuck you, you smiling jackass of a white coated fraud. I didn't say I'm going to get you Mr. Doctor and the rest of the hunky bastards who put you up to the lie of a diagnosis you grin at me. I didn't say that or anything else.

—They sure put a whipping on you, didn't they brother. Saunders stood at the foot of the bed. He moves quietly, assassin's feet thought Littleman who hadn't seen Saunders until he heard him speaking. Mauve Italian knit, white zigzag stitch ornamenting the soft collar. Dark trousers with a light gray pinstripe, snug around the hips, flaring to stylish bell bottoms. Littleman brought the figure into focus. An instinctive process he had to perform consciously since his fall. Belled bottoms and stubby shoes as elegantly italianate as the shirt. Littleman, flat on his back couldn't see below the other's knees yet he was familiar with the appearance the other scrupulously maintained. Not the flashy pimp, hustler weakness for visible richness or the narrow shouldered, bird chested mimicking of Madison Avenue, Ivy League junior executives. Saunders' clothes fit him well. Always suggesting the trim raciness of his physique. Colors distinctive, assertive, but never calling attention to themselves. Littleman felt clothes were the only area in which Saunders demonstrated taste. Though loud and rowdy in his mannerisms, not choosy about what he ate, drank or where, he maintained a consistent fastidiousness about his dress and person. He was proud that he could change his underwear twice a day, that what he wore beneath his clothes reflected the color combinations of his sleek garments.

—The man sure put a hurt on you. Littleman wondered how many times his visitor would say the same thing. Yes, they beat the shit out of me and if I didn't know it you'd sock it to me your voice crowing almost saying little motherfucka I told you so, I tolt you somebody gonna do you in real good. Voice complimenting the cops on a superior manifestation of force, a good professional job to which he is bound to give credit. Saunders in tailored blue and brass and leather for a moment whipping instead of being whipped, letting himself admit yes they have something to teach me yes if I ever get on top I will use the tactics they have so painstakingly labored to impress me with. If the tables are turned I won't forget the simple logic and efficiency of the system your blows have internalized. Saying also chalk one more up for the Man. He's way ahead, a front runner showing his ass but I'm measuring the distance, marshaling my strength for the stretch. Saying many will fall, will absorb the punishment meant for me but I'm still untouched, they haven't gotten to me yet and when they do the hurts are going to be passed out in both directions. Saying to the victim on the bed, chump, brother, martyr, fool. Saying next time, last time, wait.

Littleman had not attempted to stir, grateful that his present position in the bed produced no more than a dull ache. He heard his breathing, rough, nasal, broken like snoring. Swollen face in the hand mirror the nurse had held for him. Eyes hidden in bruised pockets of flesh. Perhaps Saunders thought he was sleeping.

—I guess I'm not as pretty as I usually am. Littleman wanted to smile but hot pincers tugged viciously at his rib cage and the pain reflex contorted his face. Battered mask in the mirror which she held reluctantly, snatching the glass away before he could find the face he knew as his own beneath the lumpy caricature of human features. Would it matter. Could Saunders distinguish smile from wince. Saunders didn't need a welcome smile anyway. He appeared when and where he wanted assuming his presence spoke for itself, asking no more warning or recognition than he gave.

—Pigs usually swing that rubber hose with more circumspection. Don't like to leave marks. *Circumspection*. The word incongruous in Saunders' speech, a loose end like his spotless underwear. Wasn't simply ostentation. Words such as circumspection frequently laced his conversation. Employed always with accuracy, a sense of verbal nuance, but simultaneously mocking the words and himself as he used them. He communicated his awareness of a larger picture, the sense of irony he felt at being trapped in a language whose formal modes excluded him. When he said circumspection he was playing an intricate game, reverse slumming, burying black dogs at night in the white only section of a cemetery.

–You don't understand, Mr. Saunders. Mr. Hall unfortunately tumbled down the front steps of Woodrow Wilson Junior High. I don't know if you're familiar with that institution, it's in the Ghetto, you know, All Black, an Urban Inner City School you know. Well, there must be six, seven hundred steps. Mr. Hall was lucky to arrive at the bottom alive. He of course sustained a knot or two in his resistance of our gallant boys in blue. Though minimum force as always was employed some few pats and taps were necessary to subdue him. A pity he had to trip over one of the fallen officers. But you know he's a cripple and had lost his cane.

–I heard about you, man. Musta been a bitch. Bending your cane on those motherfuckas' heads. Too bad they got them riot hats.

–That's what I needed the last few days. A goddamned helmet.

–Where you been, man. Soon's I heard what happen I called Wilkerson. Rice heard and called me. We called cops, hospital, everywhere we could. Nobody would say shit. Finally got that lame ass lawyer Cecil Braithwaite. He ran his civil rights bullshit down to the police chief. I heard him soft talking this that and the other law to the Man. All the while I knew they was somewhere beating you or you dead already. Finally on the second day they said you was here. On the critical list. No visitors. I figured then they had decided not to kill you. Or at least not this round. I didn't figure you'd look as bad as you do though.

–It's bad. But they didn't kill me.

–Wilkerson ought to be here soon. I thought he be here fore now. Cat's in a bad way. His old man, you know the one they call Sweetman. He ain't been acting right. Wilkerson says his mama wants to leave him. Wilkerson been trying to keep them together but he says his old man just won't do right. Out in the street most of the time. Just about come apart when he had to get his daddy out the drunk tank last week. Got Wilkerson shakier than he usually is. I don't know about the dude. I mean Wilkerson's all right as long as things ain't tough but when this deal goes down ain't no room for shucking and shamming.

Easy and impossible to take it all in. Saunders' words, the mauve shirt, the room's shifting and tossing, remember how to open and close the proper valves, pity, hardness, sorrow, cool, feeling yet not feeling so much that sanity is destroyed. He saw Wilkerson's face, his quizzical expression break up into soft planes of vulnerability. Wilkerson seldom spoke of his parents, but he was black, had started poor and made a humble dent in the system, had a profession. What was unsaid in his case could be pieced together from the general phenomenon Littleman had observed. Second generation son with his catch as catch can affluence, sorry for his parents, sorry for himself. Sorry because they gave him everything and nothing. Sorry because he respects qualities in them that transcend the cramped physical poverty of their lives, a poverty he doesn't change because he isn't that far out of the woods himself. Sorry because reverence is a cheap way of quieting his guilt. Wilkerson's scared rabbit nerves, his stiff white shirts. Sweetman. What could Wilkerson give his father, tell him about life. What had Wilkerson learned. Except how to deny in himself the force that had generated him. Perpetually mourning for what. For whom. Black veil, black folds, curtains, sheet, silk, sea rustling, sighing . . .

–Hey.

Room revived. First its astringent odor. Then walls of appalling sea sick green. Nostrils absorb the dominant ether pall, begin to discriminate the subtler smells of sickness gliding in from the ward, the uncontrollable bowels, stale bandages, sour exhalations of cells and nerves collapsing. Blood. His bed swathed in white. Halo of aluminum tubing so a curtain can be closed around him. Brown man in a mauve shirt lighting a cigarette. Smoke curls around his head. Hands suspended in front of him, cupping a match, holding it there forgotten as he stares at the bed. Another curl of smoke twisting from the well of his fingers. Word mouthed with the cigarette still squeezed in his thick lips so that the word too is squeezed, nasally grunted.

–Hey.

Black waves have parted. Saunders is real before him. His gestures and movements have regained their normal speed. No more exaggerated, stop time slow motion weaving. Saunders is a creature of the upper air. Acts like it now. Drags up a chair and straddles it. Calls back over his shoulder.

–Wilco.

Wilkerson with Rice at his side enters from the fuzzy edges of Littleman's field of vision. Blinking, he cameos them clearly, his three friends, colleagues, fellow conspirators.

–Oh my God.

–It's for real Rice, baby. Maybe you better call a cop. Or a doctor.

Ignoring the exchange between Rice and Saunders, Wilkerson moves closer to the head of the bed, looms over the prostrate Littleman.

–You all right?

–What kind of question is that, man. You sound silly as Rice. He's been beat bad. He talks sense a minute then gone. Drifting off like he's a somnambulist or something. I might as well not be here half the time. He ain't dead. That's about all I'd say. Except he looks like death been dragging him through a briar patch.

–I'll survive. I hurt now, but I intend to get up out of this bed. They're not as smart as I thought. If they had real sense, they would have killed me. They shouldn't have gone this far and left something alive. Is my cane here?

—I don't see it. But we'll get it for you. Or a better one.

—Liable to be holding it for evidence. Exhibit A. Dangerous weapon. Headache stick used by one evil, pugnacious nigger trying to break up the police force.

Wilkerson smiles. Not so much in appreciation of Saunders' bantering as from relief. He sees his friend alive, a momentary brightness in Willie's eyes that could be the indication of a smile beneath the distorted features. With difficulty words are formed above the beard.

—Poleece farce.

—Ain't it the truth.

Littleman's outline is taut beneath the sheet, Egyptian in its rigid symmetry, childlike in its inadequacy, feet poking up, leaving one third of the bed, from toes to tightly folded corners, a chill emptiness. Wilkerson winced. His friend forlorn in this strange, outsize bed. A dramatic scaling down, prophet reduced to helpless dependence in an alien atmosphere. Not visiting the land with the black plagues of his vision, but propped up by pillows, ringing bells to summon nurses who feed him, wash him, sit him on a can while he moves his bowels. But Littleman struggled to smile; he punned. *Poleece Farce.*

Where was the grand scheme now? Why had Littleman's words frightened him, why was the hanged cop a bloody reality? Why did he dream about Littleman's words? Wilkerson stared down at the man in the bed. Where were the words now. The threats that had seemed imminent possibilities. The scale. The withering scale. They were challenging something so vast that in one bed of one room among its infinite beds and rooms it could contain the anger, the rage of Willie Hall, not simply contain but swallow. His screaming defiance diminished to the sound of a pin dropped in the ocean.

Wilkerson wanted to weep for Willie. For all the Willies and Sweetmen and shadows like himself dreaming puny dreams, alive at best in some muted fantasy underworld, lying, cheating, even killing to avoid the simple truth. How they dream of dignity, of vengeance, of confronting the immensity that dribbles out their portion, portions which barely fill a box, a can, a paper bag, the cold sheets of a hospital bed.

It was silly. They were all phantoms. Wouldn't it be nice, wouldn't it be right to cradle Willie in his arms? Rock him. Sing to him. Quiet his fears of lightning and thunder, or storms raging and still to rage. Isn't that all there is to do. Whisper comfort. Ignore one's own trembling and confusion. Sleep Willie, everything's going to be all right. The way my father came to me. Be Willie's daddy. Sweetman rocking me to sleep. Maybe drunk, maybe just come from the women who were breaking my mother's heart, maybe not there at all but a memory of that time he did come, pungent, taller than the storm. My arms around the heavy shoulders, laughing together.

Then the horrible reversal. Saunders laughing. The nurses and attendants outraged or snickering. The preposterousness of it all. My father hiding from the storm. And when he's not cowering, dying by inches. Butterfly spurts of drink and lonely women. I see him plainly he has become the child. Within my father's shrunken shadow there are no quiet recesses. Because I see him differently, I try to believe I have changed. I pretend I have outgrown the need for misty dependence. Yes, I look at Littleman and know he is powerless, that his plotting consoled me only because I had a desperate need for consolation. Nothing intrinsically worthwhile in what he had to say. I stand over him. Larger than him, than any vision of my future he can project.

Why am I here? Not out of courtesy to pay my respects. No simple sentimental proddings of friendship for I am sure that Littleman is not a friend. Too much at the root of Littleman that I hate and despise, too much I would not inflict upon anyone other than myself. It was the need. The need to be comforted though there were no comforters. The need to embrace my father, though for years I had accepted and tried to accustom myself to the fact that I no longer had a father. To hear the sweet voice again. To go down in softness and repose.

—Wilco, you trying to stare my man into good health. Move back so he can at least breathe some of this pig fart they call air.

Littleman nodded below him. His heavy head lolling on the pillows, his eyes blinking, pupils bleary when they were exposed.

—We can only stay a minute or so longer. The nurse at the front desk said . . .

—Who gives a fuck what she said. Lying bitch probably got instructions to do everything she can to make Littleman uncomfortable. Short of killing him. If there was that qualification.

—Do you have to yell like that. They'll send someone in to put us out.

—Now that would make this little visit just fine. I wants one of them paddies come to put me out. Saunders wanted his words to carry and the last three, *Put me out* were a challenging crescendo broadcast to all corners of the hospital. To Rice the words were two loud nigger drunks stumbling from a bar.

—Won't you ever learn. And don't you see Littleman is trying to sleep.

—I been here longer than both you and Wilkerson. And me and my man were doing fine before you came. Now if he's sleeping why don't we all just get the hell out of here. And if he ain't, let's say what's on our minds. Not go creeping around like we's in a funeral parlor. Littleman ain't sleep, and he ain't dead either.

—I can hear everything you're saying. But I don't feel like talking. Head throbs even when I move my mouth.

—I wouldn't leave for nothing. How many times we gonna get this little nigger in a room and him with nothing to say, with nothing to beat our ears about. Seems like lately Littleman been talking to me more than my own T.V. And I be steady digging T.V. He done cut into some of my favorite shows.

The room was quiet. Saunders and Rice had both settled on chairs at the foot of the bed. Wilkerson remained standing opposite them. Littleman's eyes continued to blink slowly, masking his attentiveness, but his head was averted to Wilkerson's side of the bed. Across the stiff planes of the sheet Littleman creased with his body the others seemed also to be making a subtle demand.

Wilkerson realized he must speak. That for the moment Littleman had been forced to abdicate his role as leader. Wilkerson understood that the conspiracy up to this point had been only the words of the voice in the bed. That if it were to survive Littleman's temporary demise, he, Wilkerson, was to be the bridge, must take the next step. Clearly his words would commit him and the others in a way they had never been to the fantasies and arguments Littleman initiated. This would be an action. An affirmation that something did exist even when the dreamer was awake.

—We must begin to move quickly. Spring will be over before we know it. Littleman will be ready when the time comes. But we must begin without him.

Someone else was speaking. Not Thomas Wilkerson. Not that aimless, turned in upon itself joke he had learned to despise. Not predictable Thomas with the Midas touch which turned everything to silence. The speaker, this new unfamiliar version of Thomas Wilkerson, so direct, so forceful was a wonder, but a wonder betrayed even as he metamorphosed from the ashes of the old. Tanya's face. The face of his father. His mother's face. The children. They should hear him now. He should be talking to them. Leading them. Perhaps he was. Perhaps the bloody plan would be a step forward for them. Littleman believed it was the only step possible, the necessary action no matter what followed in its train. But such thoughts were too big. They betrayed the speaker. The new man of action could not spiral away into ifs, shoulds, the dizzying possibilities of history, of plans other than the one he had chosen to act out. Action kills. Thought kills. But some kinds of death were preferable to others. Action, thought, both still born. But one gets you out of a room, onto the street, bumps you into other human beings. Tanya. Sweetman. The children.

–Obviously we can't talk here. And the three of us shouldn't meet here again. But those inconveniences needn't deter us. I can draw a blueprint of the plan. Study it as I go, Wilkerson. Make sure you are certain you understand each step. I'll be out of here for the nitty gritty. You better believe it. I need a pencil. Something to write on. We can't wait. We've been through it all a hundred times.

–I know the plan. We will begin.

A stream of images raced through Wilkerson's mind. Readiness. Ripeness. Hamlet throwing off the dark mourning. He heard bugles, drums. Saw a rocket burst from its mooring, the steel chrysalis drop limply away.

Father coming apart. Mother on a cross. Woman in a cool ivory loft. But you move. You speak. The plan is real. Let Littleman sleep. We will take the necessary steps.

• • •

Saunders was looking for Raymond. If he found his brother, a good chance Raymond could lead him to Sissie. Raymond, Mary Lou, Porter, Reba, Jacob, Rowena and his own name, Leonard, though of various fathers his mother arbitrarily registered Saunders as the last name of them all. As far as Saunders knew five of his mother's seven children still lived. He was not sure meeting them accidentally on the street he would recognize their faces. He believed he could capsulize a life history for each one although the accounts would be bare outlines, and the facts probably a bit confused and the stories would not necessarily be attached to the correct name. Prostitute, dead in the war, doing ten to twenty armed robbery, married to a preacher in Detroit, moved west haven't heard from in ten years. Before his mother had died he would listen to her tales. She was long suffering, broken by so many old pains and deprivations, the doctors at the clinic felt it superfluous to name her affliction. She had slipped gradually into incoherent fantasies, reliving her past on at least two distinct levels. She was a pitiable black woman done to death by cruel, lusting men who had forced children upon her and fled back to the darkness from which they had crawled. She was a respectable, church going lady, soul saved, declining into a satisfied old age, proud of the children she had launched successfully onto the seas of life, mourning for the doting father who had tragically died before he could share the peaceful years his hard work and stead-fastness had earned.

When she passed, Saunders had been fifteen, somewhere near the bottom middle of the brood as far as he could work out. Only three, Raymond, Mary Lou and he stayed with their mother. He alone had spent time listening to his mother's stories. Perhaps, he later conjectured, her stories had amused him, perhaps since he realized they were the Saunders' sole legacy he had been hoarding them, seeking an advantage over his brother and sister, perhaps he had experienced a momentary victory watching the hard circumstances of his past shredded, destroyed, refashioned according to the whim of a frail, babbling woman old before her time. Any or all of these motives could not explain their long sessions together, his fascination as she unraveled version after version of the family history. Sometimes so fraught with self-pity and despair she keened at him, stopping for long shaking sobs or pausing, eyes fixed on some object in the room, to weep steadily a half hour or more as if she were alone. Once as he watched she had passed from wailing to quiet crying then knelt beside an imaginary bed and mouthed a prayer of thanksgiving to a generous god. Still crying softly she had pantomimed the ritual of shutting down a large house for the night. Turning out lights, locking doors, pulling shades, tiptoeing into rooms where children slept, to cover them and plant kisses on their foreheads, finally returning to the bed, kneeling again, praying again but this time a bitter blaspheming tirade, cursing creation and the cruelty on high which had given her breath and so little else. Saunders had not been able to look away when she, her body heaving, her hands tearing furiously at her hair and clothes, began to undress. If she had bloodied herself, as long as the wounds were inflicted with her own hands, he knew he could not stop her. Would not intrude on what she had earned the right to do.

They had always called him cold. He knew why then. A numbness in his limbs, an icy wind swirling through his chest. Cold and nothing else as she frantically stripped each garment from her body. His mother stretched naked on the floor. Cold. She could have been a strange corpse on a slab rolled out from the morgue's cold storage. Her flesh so arbitrary he could have taken a scalpel, if prodded by his curiosity, and sliced down to the clockwork innards. His mother's body, female because someone had snatched something from the point of her groin and left a hairy emptiness, female because someone had taken two fistfuls of flesh and hurled them with such force against her chest that they had flattened and stuck.

Spraddle legged on the floor. Last act of the family chronicle she endlessly recited to him. Termination and beginning. On her back to receive another lover, to birth another Saunders, to welcome madness and worms. Hunched over her were swarms of bulky shadows she cooed to and called by name. Her bony hips pitching. Her palms and loose backsides slapping on the gritty floor.

Saunders sat rigid in the musty, dull box that was their home. His mother rose unsteadily from the floor, the memories suddenly gone, the complaints of her joints and puckered flesh already a dull buzzing in her temples. He could see the miseries inching back covering her like a chaste robe. Though he had violated her privacy, crept into her dream, she retained the power to restore dignity to herself. Below her clothes was skin, beneath the skin another layer of hurt and memories stretched over her frame, clothes without buttons or zippers, a mottled, camouflage suit. Her suffering excluded him, baffled his seeking.

She gathered her scattered things unhurriedly, eyes bright with a sleepwalker's tranquillity, meeting her son's stare several times, chatting with him all the while in a nonchalant tone of his father's passion for chitterlings and her reluctance to fill the house with their nasty smell when expecting nice people for Sunday dinner.

Saunders walked toward the Red Cap luncheonette. If Raymond wasn't there, no point in seeking further. Logic was simple. If at home his brother would be sick or sleeping, if in a bar, high, if away from the neighborhood, engaged in some hustle that would render him invisible till he returned. The luncheonette was where business had to be transacted. There Raymond would surface, lucid, calm, scheming.

It was easy for Saunders to picture his brother's life. Streets on which he walked treacherously familiar. Faces and storefronts changing but remaining the same. On the corner Klein's had been burnt out and a smoke odor clung to the blackened stones of its foundations. He remembered the crashing of huge plate glass windows, the crunching fragments under his feet as he had stumbled through the glut of broken, overturned and unmovable appliances searching for something to fill his arms. Only a few summers back. Klein's, the liquor store, a few other insignificant scabs had been peeled away. But all that seemed a thousand years ago, children breaking their favorite toys in spite. Scabs torn away while the cancer continued its ravages deep inside the body. Nothing had changed. Saunders knew the life, believed he could submerge himself again, move as efficiently as lethally as he once had.

Something about his memories was nostalgic. The rhythm which had moved him, his instinctive responses like an insect or flower to the subtle play of light and energy. He didn't have to think to move; life had been a series of appearances and disappearances, of being someone or no one, and it all happened simply because he was Lenny Saunders and couldn't be anything else. The streets, the bars, the faces. Saunders was revisiting himself. But he had grabbed at one of those unpredictable hooks that occasionally disturb the sanctity of the medium. From the bland, blue-eyed sky a job in the post office, the alien chemistry of a half forgotten caution *Make something of yourself* causing him to seize the opportunity, cling to the hook as if it were salvation. Rise and go away. Perhaps to make room for his brother back here on the street. He didn't know why he worked in the post office or why Raymond had become a mirror image, thief and hustler, of his own days on the street. Saunders was certain neither one of them had a choice. The deal went down. Skinny white fingers, manicured, sandpapered at the tips, laid out the cards and if you were a joker you joked, a king you reigned, a spade you couldn't scrub away the blackness of your ass.

Sometimes the sameness was sweet, was good to come back to, a woman always there, soft legged when you needed her. He could go down in it again. His reflexes would come back. He could learn the new names of the faces. Forget going to the Man eight hours a day, forget time clocks, supervisors, the post office routine learned in two days then endlessly repeated. He could respond again to subtle tugs of the environment, fixing him, spangling him, a bright piece of glass in the kaleidoscope swirl. He could be Raymond. Offer Raymond in exchange one hundred fifty dollars a week, a decent apartment on the quiet periphery of the neighborhood. Good clothes.

But he was not here for trades. No sweet bait for Raymond. Just. *Where is Sissie?*

And Raymond answered:

–No good bitch still fucking for that paddy cop.

All Saunders needed to know. He did not waste an instant studying the ghost his brother had become. The thin body, unhealthy skin, gaunt eyes were beginning to shiver into focus, the ghost was almost his brother, something about the way it carried its shoulders, the right one higher than the left like a shield it would talk safely behind, but when he had heard what he came for, Saunders was quickly far away, gone as suddenly as a stone smacking the still surface of a lake, disappearing as it explodes the perfect reflections held in the water, rippling shadow of Raymond blurring outward into larger and larger concentric circles till the circles themselves dissolved.

Sissie could be used. Yes. And should he feel remorse because she would be killed and mutilated? His brother's woman led like a cow to the slaughterhouse? No more remorse than she felt abandoning Raymond for a surer, more competent protector. No more remorse than Raymond would have felt if he had known he was dooming Sissie and her pimp cop when he spoke to his brother. In Raymond's voice had been the bitterness of betrayal, the frustration of one who has had the final insult delivered after an eternity of injury. Anger and hatred so deep that he was ripe for killing, but the delicate balance had not been tipped, murder was in his blood, but not the specific death that would avenge him. He could not kill Sissie and the white cop without losing his own life. Raymond preferred living, keeping the shell intact no matter how rotten the insides had become. In some form the flesh must survive and its bare maintenance seemed Raymond's sole concern. Saunders knew his brother's capacity for emotional death was limitless. Raymond had been ripe, sure handed, laughing. He had said, *Brother, I'm getting it together. I'm going to walk tall through this shit and when I get out my shoes still be shiny*. Watching his ragged descent was like seeing a drunken man dragged by his heels down a steep flight of stairs, the skull cracking as it bumps from landing to landing. Always further to fall. Life guaranteed that. Perhaps not a bad bargain. If you feel you've hit bottom, you're wrong. His brother would continue to survive and the seeming bottom on which he was now floundering wouldn't seem so bad anymore.

Perhaps Littleman wanted to show the bottom could be reached. After the white cop was lynched, the old lies could not be believed any more than the corpse could strut its beat. Lynching the cop said we can fall no further, we give you license to kill us, but we are going down no further. Things have come to this. We have chosen and here swaying in the breeze is our decision. You will die or we will die but we will not submit.

Perhaps that was what Littleman meant. But this was no time to try and figure it all out. Sissie could be used to get the cop. By taking certain steps she had lost all power over her life. She was dead already, a puppet in the hands of those whose whims controlled her, a doll who could perform certain lifelike tricks, simulate when the proper strings were pulled, *love, passion, desire.* Now he would steal the strings, and after she had wiggled her necessary dance, he would snip them.

• • •

The rain came from far away. Light but steady he felt its weight accumulating in the creases of his raincoat. Glancing skyward, his gaze was cut off abruptly by the blackness which seemed clamped like a lid a few feet above the tops of the highest buildings. The rain assured him privacy. He had parked two blocks from his destination. In spite of the rain he enjoyed the thought of filtering through the usually crowded streets silent and alone. At intersections the light posts were hooded with dim cones of yellow through which slants of rain blinked. Other than the rain's patter, the occasional hiss of cars along the streets, there was quiet, the yellow hush of the street lamps pervading the neighborhood.

Moving by instinct, surer than any memories could have been, Saunders negotiated the narrow streets where ten years before he had hunted other human beings, preying on them with the unquestioning regularity and rectitude of a bank clerk arriving promptly each morning for work. He realized he hunted still. He must stalk the whore who had supported his brother. Study the habits of his quarry, decide when, how and where she could best be struck down. He knew it would be easy. She was already dead, part of the submarine world which floated the city, but that with its tall buildings, grinning signs, its frantic hurry of business the city denied. Sissie would be vulnerable a thousand times a day. Ten Sissies would have to die, cut down in some mad ripper's crusade before the newspapers would react, the police conduct a rigorous investigation. Saunders had recently read a story about Jack the Ripper and now, strangely, here he was in his English mackinaw shrouded in rainy fog, gliding along deserted streets to a rendezvous with a prostitute whose violent death he was planning. Saunders had promised himself that he would read more about the Ripper. The notion of Jack reforming his society through murder had surprised him. In movies the murderer was always a beast, a dark villain the plot trapped and executed. Perhaps the reality of murder was never that simple. At first the idea of killing someone already a pitiable victim had been distasteful. Then Littleman showed him how Sissie's life had been stolen, how she could not forfeit what she no longer owned. Since she functioned as a puppet in the oppressor's system, taking her life would be a minor act of sabotage. He hadn't pushed Littleman to answer the next question. Wouldn't all sufferers who submitted, who allowed themselves to be used rather than striking back at the users, wouldn't all of them be guilty, eligible for slaughter, his sick mother if she were still alive, one of the most guilty since she had endured to the breaking point and past.

Rain collapsed about him, gathering in the broken pavement, sleeking the street where cars wheezed past, staining his eggshell coat with darker patches. From far away. Rain had always seemed out of place here. He remembered himself as a child watching it bead the rusty fire escape, gather in pools at the mouths of clogged drains, drench the back of an apartment house visible through the kitchen window. The outside of the next building had matched the one in which he lived, thick shouldered twins lurching on one another for support, derelict, diseased, frescoes of soot and pigeon shit decorating the flaking brick, old men breathing rank poison into one another's faces. He had watched. Struck by the foreignness of water dripping from the sky. Fascinated that the rain came at all to this world of black faces and crumbling buildings. Rain not an intrusion. Rather a simple mistake. Something that belonged to white people, which had erred in its course and dropped reluctantly in the wrong place. Like the white voices and faces on radio and television, the brittle faced teachers who raced away when the dismissal bell rang.

In the darkness, rain and solitude his thoughts were a nagging companion. He had a job to do, and that for the moment was the answer to any uncertainty imposed by his imaginings. Too many questions made men cripples like Wilkerson. Littleman's runty legs could not make him the cripple Wilkerson was. Yet something new seemed to move Wilkerson. Perhaps Wilkerson finally understood what it was all about now. Maybe he would have a glimmer of determination Saunders had not detected before. Maybe he would start acting like a man. At most Wilco could be stubborn in an argument, even get angrily self-righteous if he thought his opinion was being ignored. But that was when they talked. Something lacking in the man. If their words had suddenly become things and what had been said had to be backed up with action, Saunders guessed Wilkerson could not be depended upon to follow through. To do as he said, to not back down were instincts like the others remaining strong from Saunders' years in the street. He suspected part of his distrust of the teacher might have something to do with Wilkerson's education, the manner in which his trained speech and thoughts subtly erected a wall around him. But Saunders could dismiss this thought quickly when he counted the many ways there were of being smart and how the flaw in Wilkerson prevented the man's intelligence from concentrating its force in all but a few narrow areas. Wilkerson was often not much more than a fact man. He had information. Could spurt answers before the contestants in the T.V. quiz shows. A good machine could do that. Maybe more than facts comprised Wilkerson now.

But Saunders would not mistrust him less for any vein of iron which surfaced in Wilkerson's voice or will. The flaw ran deeper. Back at least to the days when a fair skin and a soft voice meant goodies from the kitchen rather than hot fields all day and gruel when the sun went down. The whiteness in Wilkerson's complexion and features that yellow niggers like him wore so proudly in their mongrel faces, would always earn them crumbs from the Master's table. In Wilkerson's pale face Saunders was confronted with the image of the raping white devil astride black women.

Saunders asked himself how little of the enemy remaining was enough to taint. When the deal went down, when it was kill and be killed would Wilkerson make a clean break, could he shed white man's ways, white man's blood. Saunders scorned white blood. Throat cut, slopping the gutter red, he would rather die than have the sickness from a white man's veins enter his black body. He recalled Big Red, Malcolm Little, pouring the burning lye into his hair, how reading that scene had caused him to plummet backward, relive his own experiments with evil smelling brews cooking his good black man's hair. His cool when, rag tied around his gleaming stew of grease and dead hair, he went forth preening, to rob and beat the kinky topped brown people around him.

If Raymond were right, she lived in the second row house from the corner. It couldn't be the houses on either side of the one his brother had designated since they were signposted and boarded shut. At least every other house in the row had been condemned. Where no boards slanted across the windows, chunks of glass were rooted, jagged and uneven like crudely carved teeth in the mouth of a pumpkin. Nearly all the dwellings seemed deserted. Down the block dim rectangles here and there cracking the obscurity. Coldly glowing, glass like fresh snow banked on the thresholds, glass crunching under Saunders' feet as he moved close enough to the second house to peer through a low window into the dark street floor. The window moulding smelled of damp, rotting wood. A sludge of weary paint and filth glazed Saunders' hands where they pressed against the window frame. He called into the gloom. The front window of this house was boarded like its neighbors, only more subtly from the inside, a sheet of uniform darkness, thick cardboard or wood painted black, backed the cracked fragment of glass which ended a quarter of the way up the frame. He drew his hand back quickly, wiping his fingertips on the wet bricks. Glass was loose. A good shout could bring it crashing down at his feet.

He stepped back, mounted the first step, called again. On the second step still hearing no answer he stretched to his toes peering through a vacant slot where once a vent had graced the top of the door. He heard footsteps, then saw an unstable glow of light moving toward him. It was flame rather than electricity, solid, tearshaped like a match but burning too strongly for a match. It responded to drafts inside the house, twisting as it drew closer.

—Who's that. A woman's voice from the bottom of a well.
—Leonard Saunders.
—What you want. Voice husky, challenging. A tough assed tone that would make killing her easy since it said she knew the danger surrounding her and had prepared defenses, defenses she was cocksure of.
—I'm Raymond's brother. He gave me something for you. Easy to scheme and lie at her.
—Don't want nothing of his. And I ain't got a thing for him, coming or going. You get on away from here. They spoke through the closed door. Saunders could see the wavering light play through the vent. He pictured the woman inside. She would be holding a candle in one hand, the other hand would be on her ample hip which was jutted toward him pugnaciously. She would be pouting, angry at the intrusion, at the strange voice from the night calling out names

that never had, or no longer existed for her. He sensed her woman's parts, lips, breasts, thighs denying their softness and roundness, promising instead with eyes that cut at him through the locked door that she was a rock, a cast iron figurine set down to forbid his entrance. He sensed her weight wedged against the door. If necessary at another time he knew he could crumple the old wood with one swift blow of foot or shoulder. But not now. He filed the information, recording also the desolation of the adjacent houses, the unlikelihood of interruption from anyone who lived on the block, the imperturbable stillness that would swallow the sudden splintering of a door, the one or two screams Sissie might trumpet before she could be quieted.

—Raymond gave me something for Lisa. *Yeah, the bitch live over behind South Street with her bastard she call Lisa.* He hoped the timing was right, that the unexpected name confused her, allowed a part of him to insinuate itself through a crack in the wooden barrier. Her daughter's name a key.

—He gave me some money for Lisa. He heard metallic clicking on the other side of the door, a deep wheezing sigh, a string of muttered epithets in which his brother was damned copiously, the whole business of locks, keys, doors and chains cursed. Could have been the sounds of a robot undressing, Sissie lugubriously stripping away the tin and wire that secured her body, and Saunders half expected the door to open upon a massy ebony nude, lewdly posed to recompense him for the payment he carried in his pocket.

In the flickering candle light a scrawny silhouette split the partially opened door frame. He saw a cadaver's face, saffron skin gouged out by black shadows, eyes and mouth empty pits.

—Give it to me. The voice demanding, fearless as it had been through the door, issuing incongruously from a small figure facing a stranger in a dark doorway.

—Mama.

—Damnit Jewel, can't you keep that child quiet a minute.

A little girl's cry for her mother had come from somewhere, but as he strained his eyes to sort out shapes in the darkness Saunders could see nothing. The room could have been full of people, things substantial as she was, or else the woman at the door could be conversing with squeaking phantoms. Saunders could not see beyond the ghoulish icon and dancing flame below it. But his foot was in the cracked door. He had to go farther.

—He said to give it to Lisa. Nobody else. He wanted to match the terseness of her words. Give no room for qualification or doubt. If she barred his way curtly demanding, he would make her come to him, drop a cold take it or leave it in her lap and wait for her whore's greed to respond.

The child's cry again, sudden, breathlessly desperate as if its mouth had been wrenched from a stifling hand. Light cascaded from an outflung door, a yellow wind cleansing the room. Saunders could see a tiny figure outlined against the blur. After hesitating an instant, it rushed into the room. The blind charge of the child carrying it past the candle into Saunders. He recoiled from the hard bump of bones against his legs, the frantic groping at his trousers. He heard a panicked whine, the rustle of another collision and could see as the dim halo of the candle lowered, stick arms grasping stick legs, a plaited head burrowing into the scantiness of the woman's short dress.

—Jewel, you ain't good for nothing. The inner door slammed shut but the woman with the candle continued to yell over her shoulder stooping simultaneously to gather the child into her arms.

—Lisa. Lee lee, baby. I'm right here. Mama's going nowhere. Hush now, Lisa. Open the goddamn door you simple woman.

Seemingly forgotten, Saunders fell in behind mother and daughter. If the three women noticed him when he entered the second room, no gesture or word betrayed the fact. He felt invisible. He was one more piece of battered furniture standing beside the door.

Kerosene lamps lit the crowded inner room. Two cots, a table, three chairs of bent chrome tubing each with plastic covered pastel seat and backrest. Not one was intact. They had been bent, sliced, gored, oozed their stuffing like neglected rag dolls. A curtain drawn across the entrance partially screened a smaller room opposite the doorway where Saunders stood. In this alcove Saunders could make out another cot and what seemed to be the shattered bottom of a toilet. A sink, its exposed pipes irregularly snipped away, gaping holes in the plaster above and below it, dangled limply in the far corner to his right. Atop the sink's scarred drainboard sat the rusty base of an alcohol burning stove. Around the room numerous excavations similar to those framing the sink had been dug from the plaster and floors. Somewhere in the shadows water pinged methodically into a pan or bucket. The house had obviously been ransacked, everything of value carted away, even to the iron pipes which would at best bring pennies in a junkyard. The burner on the drainboard, the kerosene lamps, the gutted sink implied that all utilities had been shut off, that like its neighbors this shell had been condemned.

Though physically dissimilar the three women seemed somehow related, as different as crawling and wings but issuing from the same shrouded chrysalis. The girl who had run into Saunders' legs sat subdued, melting into the loose springs of a cot. Though the iron bed was low, only the toes of her sneakers dangled as far as the floor. She wore elastic banded slacks, red, filthy, rolled several times at her ankles, and a short sleeved candy striped cotton shirt whose bands of color around her torso emphasized the frailty of a rib case he could encircle with his hands. Large eyes, hair tightly braided into a profusion of pigtails, delicate brown hands cupping her chin, one thumb slipped furtively between her lips. Her body seemed shrunken so that it occupied the smallest space possible, but her eyes did not reflect her timid posture, they were wide open, preying, independent of the room, of the quiet face lodging them. If they expressed anything it was cool neutrality saying everything will be absorbed, nothing revealed. Saunders knew the girl had been crying minutes before, that she had flung herself desperately, headlong into the darkness and had been frightened by a strange man's hard, unyielding legs. In the room she had watched mutely as he had watched the bitter, violent screeching, her mother's hands shoot out to shove the older woman skittering against a chair. But the slack mouthed serenity of the features as she sucked on her thumb and the hungry blackness of the eyes were unchanged, articulated only a bottomless capacity for more. Saunders thought of the African fetishes with their unflinching eyes of tin or bits of shiny stone, their potbellied wooden bodies nearly invisible beneath nail studded skin.

The woman called Jewel, plainly the oldest, though of an indeterminate, beyond fifty age, all distended bosom and belly balanced on bony, razor sharp ankles that protruded incongruously from the wide girth of her long housedress, had turned her broad back to the others, screening one of the kerosene lamps, adjusting its flame so a humped sail of light billowed on the wall she faced.

—You gonna go too far one time. You gonna go too far, she muttered into her corner. Her shoulders were trembling and her words broken by a wheeze.

—You ain't so goddamned high and mighty. The woman stuttered when she spoke. Saunders could not tell if she always did or if her rage twisted her tongue.

—I ain't such an old fool as you think laying your nasty hands on me. Saunders guessed at what she was saying. Her clucks, slurs, the asthmatic sighs made her speech opaque as a child's. She was a witness he hadn't counted on. A possible complication. Two deaths uneconomical in the logic of the plan. Was she the child's nurse, a relative, cousin, aunt, mother to Sissie? Her eyes glowered as she suddenly turned, dismissing him at the same time as a thing familiar and predictable worth no more than passing contempt. Saunders thought she had eyes like a pigeon. Bird eyes and bird legs old bitch cocking her head so it aimed at what she wanted to see.

When she spoke to Sissie again she was whining. Like the child she drew herself in, shrinking to a soft, quivering ball inside the shapeless dress:

—I ain't staying here if you don't treat me no better.

—And go where? Where some worn out thing like you gonna find it good as you have it now? Sitting on your ass all day calling yourself taking care of Lisa. Him slipping money to you on the side so's ycu can stuff your fat mouth while you're spying on me. Don't think I don't know. You tale carrying, loose tongued old witch. You tell him every breath I take. She's gonna tell him about you, too, Mister. So give Lisa what you brung and git out. I don't want to give her lies nothing to feed on.

She was short, trim. Nothing like the fleshy idol Saunders had imagined. A hint of her daughter's eyes, large, round, disguising their hunger not with the other's neutrality, but with a constant, surface animation, the fire and ice of her moods playing across her eyes so they were never still long enough for him to gauge their depths. Her hair was cropped brutally short. In slacks she might give the appearance of an adolescent boy, but in the brief dress she wore Saunders admired the completely feminine texture and grace of her legs. He measured and classified her with the word petite. Deceptively inconsequential at first glance, revealing soft curves, perfect proportions if your gaze lingered. Saunders could imagine her, a wig of flowing, luxurious hair crowning her model's figure. She would look as soft as the pampered redbone girls his new post office job and status made him eligible to court and fondle. Yet he had heard her mouth, seen the springy strength of her arms manhandle Jewel.

She probably looked best in the dim light of bars where she picked up her tricks. In the morning waking up beside her in a strange room the charm would be lost, gone with the shadows, the lazy glide of a high. She would have been a mistake, there would be an urge to hurt her. Feeling her perfect body twisting in your arms would have teased out a private itch, made you believe you could find something you had given up as lost forever. In the morning, what had begged you to cradle it in the strength of your hands, would be cheatingly undersized, your hands would want to throttle.

In the weak light of the oil lamps she could have been anyone young and pretty. Women Saunders had known slipped noiselessly into her face. Only the lonely smack of the dripping ceiling confirmed the room's presence, the now of the three women whose lives had been consecrated to the plan.

—Lisa, that man has something for you. He says it's from your daddy.

—Is she Raymond's child?

—Nobody else's. Though I guess he don't do much bragging on it. Not even to his brother, if you is his brother. He don't lift a finger to help her get along. If he sent something by you, it's the first penny he's give her. Easier for the nigger if he believes she ain't his. But he damn well knows she is.

Saunders searches the girl's face for a trace of Raymond, of himself, for whatever links the Saunders' scattered seed, dumb to one another though they are. She looks more distant than before. He wishes the girl would speak. The proof of her right shoulder raised like a shield. Sissie could be lying. Trying to wring an extra nickel's sympathy for her bastard. How many times had Sissie sold the child to her lovers?

—Sit up straight. And git your thumb out your mouth. Mister, if you got something to give, give it and go on your way. Of all the women in the room the prostitute's face bore the closest resemblance to his brother. She had the female counterparts of his clean, even features, fast welterweight's physique. And his brother's hooded eyes were once like hers, liquid, full of heat.

—She ain't gonna get up and come begging to you. We don't need nothing he can give us that bad. You tell him I don't need nothing from him and I'm just letting her take this cause it came in her name. So he don't need to be creeping around here to hear her say thanks. Or me.

The room stank. The longer he stayed the more its squalor

oppressed him. Stinking pipes, stinking plaster, woman stink, wood stink, the rain methodically filling a cup with water, the cup patient as it overflows, the brackish contents crawling over the unswept floors. The child, perhaps his niece, patient like the cup, receiving the words, the stink till she is filled to bursting. Just a matter of time. The derelict shell of a house. The girl's skinny body scooped out, looted, abandoned, fit only for desperate transients. For trespassers. He started toward her, fumbling in his pocket, fingering the clipped bills. He didn't care what he pulled out. A ten the biggest he had. No matter what his hand extracted he would give. He would return his hand to the pocket only to draw more. For a moment he thought of shoving everything into her outstretched hand. Couldn't be much more than a hundred dollars. He had bet five times that on one roll of the dice.

He saw the wrinkled money slowly consumed by flames, the cop's wet thumb riffling the notes. No sense in throwing good money after bad. He couldn't buy the girl away from this house. If that much money existed, he had no idea where in the world it might be.

He paused before her. He saw Lisa was shivering, had a snotty nose that probably never stopped running in the damp, chill room. A sorry assed, wasted little black gal. Not the first he had seen. Already she knew the trick of looking past him, through him, just as he had taught his eyes to see and forget in the same instant.

—Here, baby. Sounded too much like what he'd say to her mother, his joint placated, smiling as he dressed beside the flimsy bed. Not an urge to save the child, but an impulse to free himself, pay and be gone. His sudden generosity a sham. As his fingers flipped through the bills he knew there had never been a chance that he would come away with empty pockets. Good money after bad. He could not fight a lion with a stick. Crazy Littleman taking on the whole police force with his cane. When the time came Saunders would be at a desk, pressing buttons, watching miniature mushroom explosions on a video screen as red squad cars disintegrated.

—Raymond sent this honey. You use it to get something nice for yourself.

—I just might wipe my ass with it and send it back to her pitiful daddy.

Lisa avoided brushing his hand when she took the money, then held it at arm's length, an insect plucked from some intimate place of her body. She crushed it in her fist, the extended arm petrified, unable to release what she had trapped, to acknowledge what it was, where it came from, the heat and dampness sliding through her closed fingers.

More to do, more to learn, but he wanted out. They would take care of business. If the old crone in the way, she would die too. And the child. Lisa. Swallowed by the bed. Her outstretched arm still rigid, waiting for someone to snatch away the strange paper from her grasp.

—Raymond said he's sorry and he'll try to send her what he can from time to time. A foot in the door. A way to enter when the plan sent him on an errand.

Sissie. Jewel. Lisa. Wipe all the silly bitches off the face of the earth. Walls were pressing in on him. Had to get out. He could feel them ignoring him again. A man out of the night. Business done he was gone forever. That's the way it was with nigger wenches. The stink. The chill. Too familiar to Saunders. The bare routine of their lives resuming behind the door as it slams in his face. Muffled voices already squabbling as he picks his way through the black front room.

• • •

They are watching me all the time. More than before they seem to be controlling my life. But what do they see? What do they touch with their knives and needles and rubber gloves?

The plan proceeds while I lie here. To their eyes I am helpless. Once the fuse is lit nothing remains but the waiting. I am content to wait in bed. I wonder what will reach me first. Gunfire, explosions. Door bursting open and who will enter. Hearing it begin will be enough. Whether I am carried out a hero or a corpse.

I awakened dreaming of Angela. Strange how the need for luxury never completely leaves us. The condemned man rankled because the vegetables in his last meal are cold. A symptom of unquenchable vanity. My need to recall the interlude with Angela. To possess her in a dream even though my mind recognizes the absurdity of an Angela where I am now and with what I have to do. Angela is part of that summer. I needed her body to feel like a man. I knew something was missing and she appeared to be a piece that would fit. I am able to recall moments when we were liberated by an illusion of wholeness. My dreams are still confused by those accidents. Dreaming, I treat the luxury as something earned, something that should persist. I forget how useless Angela would be in this stinking hospital. How hopelessly she would be entangled with the plan. In my dreaming I am like a man who would slit a flower's throat, tuck its bloom in his lapel, then weep when it withered.

They watch me but I will reveal nothing. They might as well be observing a catatonic idiot, waiting for him to break into sociable conversation. As far as they can see I have no concourse with the outside world. No telephone, no T.V. or radio. No other patient in the room. I will have no more visitors. Send nor receive letters. The movements of my body communicate nothing to them. I have reduced my motion, even the blinking of my eyes, to a minimum. I co-operate with them to the extent of swallowing the food and medicine they bring, nodding at the doctors' inquiries, facilitating as best I can the rituals of pissing, shitting, having my body washed. Beyond that I have systematically concealed from them any indication that I am still beset by the collection of vanities they associate with humanity. Of affection toward them, toward myself, toward any other individual or group of human beings I wish to seem as innocent as a dead man.

I write at night. During the day I soak the pages in a basin.

The water gains a bluish cast as the words dissolve. I dump the sodden unreadable remnants into a waste basket before I go to sleep each afternoon. The writing is a conscious attempt to retain my sanity as I lie here imprisoned. My dreams such as the one of Angela are an unconscious safety valve, but I believe they too can be brought under control. So much of my life that was formerly haphazard I have subjected to the dictates of my will. What I am, all I wish to be is a finely honed mechanism functioning within the plan. The only parts of me, of what I am or do, which I would not willingly release, are those indispensable to the plan. Thus I relinquish easily the pleasures of a body, an identity, my scribbling.

Appropriate that my papers will not be read. No longer difficult to destroy them, to watch the words leak into the water or blend with the yellow pee when I amuse myself by shredding them into the urinal. I wonder if one of the drones has the job of searching my garbage. If one has to dry the pee stained bits of paper and try to piece them together. A scholar whose duty is to know everything about me. Oblivion for my words appropriate because my people have always written their history with their mouths.

Just before I awakened I was listening to Angela and she was telling me why she hadn't met me as she had promised. I passed under the archway of City Hall. I sat on a low stone wall in the open courtyard at least an hour before the appointed time. In ten minutes I was despondent because she hadn't been driven as I was to come early. I counted the clumsy turrets, read the bronze plaque beside the West arcade. Finally four o'clock, the appointed time. Then five numb rings of the tower bell separated from one another by eternities in which I held my breath, disbelieving as long as I could the inevitability of the next gong. I made a circuit of the four broad walkways North, South, East and West that emptied into the courtyard. I felt completely unsure of myself. Invented ingenious mistakes that I might have committed. Entertained the possibility of any error, tortured myself for one stupidity after another rather than admit the most likely circumstances. Was she dead? Had I forgotten the hour, the day, the year? It had been over fourteen months since I'd seen her. We both had laughed at the idea of a rendezvous in the middle of the city at the castle of the bureaucrats. We joked that we might not recognize one another in a crowd, with our clothes on. At five thirty it seemed feasible that I might have seen her and not remembered her face. I tried to recall all the young women I had seen that afternoon. I felt a surge of sympathy for Angela, regretted how deeply I had injured her when our eyes met and I had turned casually away to search other faces in the throng. I reasoned that since I had been an hour early she could be two hours late. Perhaps she was testing, teasing. Watching me from a window high in the tower. The rush hour crowds thinned out. Pedestrian traffic through the arches diminished to a few footfalls echoing on the brick and stone. An old man tied down the canvas flap on his cart and wheeled his load of unsold pretzels wearily, stoop shouldered through the sun dazzled needle's eye opening onto Market Street. He was probably going to the row of penny arcades where sailors and prostitutes congregated. With Angela beside me I could have smiled at the women and their shiny purses, the young men whacking away with miniature twenty-twos or jamming the knobs of the shuddering pinball machines. Alone I would not go close to their corner. A slow, burning rage, the only cover I could draw over my loneliness, would make me grab one of the rifles, rip it from its mooring and fire into the passersby. She was not coming. I took hours to form that sentence. Say it to myself. The next sentence came instantaneously. I will never see her again. But seemed just as final, just as true.

In the dream she was explaining why she had not come.

—I don't think love's possible anymore . . . love . . . not in this world. It demands the best of us. And we're not used to doing our best. The best is never asked of us. At school, when I work, when I talk to my friends or family the same deadening half-ass effort is always enough. Nobody really wants more. They're frightened by it. Don't go too far, don't try too much, go part of the way and we'll bridge the difference by smiles, clever talk, build a world which makes a virtue of our mediocrity.

–In you there was an intensity which spit upon the world I had known. You had an anger, Willie, a rage that drove you, held your world together without lies and compromise. I felt your anger from the first moment. It was rigorous, total, it began to clear my head. Make certain things possible again. And when I felt you giving something to me that was not hate, but just as pure, just as consuming, I began to hear and see things again. A new world opening.

–I had been hiding for a long time. You don't know my middle name, do you. Rowena. Angela Rowena Taylor. My initials if you please spelling in capital letters A.R.T. An endowment. A legacy from the good Dr. Taylor my father and Marie Eleanor Taylor née Hudgins, my impeccable school teaching mother. I could play the classics at ten. I was invited to parties in the best homes. Even little white kids came to the Taylor house to celebrate my birthdays. If I was not exactly a prodigy on the piano, I was a prodigy of politeness and punctuality. My oiled braids so long I could sit on them. I could read, talk, sing and spell better than anyone in our integrated class. I learned to cheat early. Learned a clean starched dress and shiny hair was what my teachers responded to when they read my compositions. I stayed top middle outstanding all the way through, maintaining with countless shortcuts and deceptions a bright, polished Angela for the world to measure and admire. Of course I despised this heroine. And though I still don't have a very good idea of who or what I am, I could keep the perfect Angela miles apart from anything that seemed to touch me. And I was touched by books and music, people who carried themselves in a certain way, a special way which proclaimed this is all of me, everything I am held apart from the world, no lie, no split to deceive others or myself.

–My parents were proud. I won a scholarship. At the prestigious school they were ingenious enough to name in every sentence they formed concerning me I met Teddy, Teddy the poet, Teddy the mad white boy who could put into words all the anxiety, the fear, the uglinesses I felt in myself. I was dumb. I thought I was different, unique, and here by the grace of the gods was one more exile, a rare one like myself. Teddy ate me up. He broke apart the bones and cleaned the silly meat off them with his yellow teeth. And always his little pinky elegantly greaseless, pointed at the ceiling. He was ugly beyond my fondest dreams of myself. After they cut his leavings out of my belly I stumbled around for almost a year feeling sorry for myself, loving anybody who'd pity me. I thought I had spun free from the Taylors. I worked. Went back to school at night. I liked the feeling of independence, of being one Angela. I'd go along for a month or so fairly content with myself, working, studying, close to a few good friends. Then the whole show would abruptly go to pieces. Shattered by something different each time, but each time utterly demolished. I'd want to die. Job, books, people. Nothing mattered but the overwhelming sense of failure. The certainty that I had betrayed myself. The Angela I had buried, had denied for so long, still eluded me. In the moments of depression there seemed no doubt that she was gone forever. The only decent, honest thing to do was not mourn, not try to forget, but die, destroy the shell, the mockery. I hid. Sick and alone. Waiting for strength to return to the routine I had established. After a while the difficulty of returning was too great. I couldn't go through the explanations, the lies it took to get back into people's good graces. I finally cut myself off. Lived like a kind of ghost waiting for the fits of suffering to come. At least during the suffering I was real. My life was substantial enough to be painful, to be a burden I wanted to remove. When I was a ghost, when I believed people could look through me as I looked through them, I consoled myself with the thought that next time the utter desolation came, I would not be a coward. I would recall the emptiness, the frustration and rid myself of them once and for all.

—I haunted the beach so an instrument would be close at hand when the time came. When I saw you that first night, I thought you might be a suicide. I wanted to watch it happen. I saw your braces and cane. Took those for a motive. I wouldn't have tried to help you. I was too excited, I knew a door was opening. I would follow you. I would be changed. Then you came up from the water.

—When we said good-bye I really believed I would see you soon again. That a year could not possibly make a difference. I would return to school, feel better about myself and bring someone back to you who might someday match your strength, your intensity. I thought I could make it. Be someone for you.

—Now you know I couldn't come. Without you close I failed. I see Teddy again. He came back six months ago from New York. A novel he wrote there will soon be published. I can be the Angela he understands. I have grown up to despise myself at least as much as Teddy despises me. You didn't offer me an easy way. You did not tell me what I had to be for you. I would have floundered. I would have come apart. I was frightened because I saw the best thing in you was relentless, demanding. In many ways it is a sick, evil thing, but it is the best of you. I could not come back to you and wait for it to expose me, for it to grind me into bits. I am more afraid of dying than anything else, and the best thing in you is death.

She spoke this last waxen, rigid, dissolved to a hovering mask. The uncertainty, the vertigo of the lost rendezvous returned to me. Who had been speaking in my dream? Had I heard simply what I wanted to hear, stuffed conveniently into the form and voice of Angela for effect? A theatrical production staged for my benefit?

Had I invented a life for Angela? The story seemed too authentic, too independent of me. Something real somewhere and mystically transmitted. Or simply a letter I had both repressed and committed to memory. If I doubted the dream, why not doubt the total memory of Angela, accept the interlude as fiction, a prop, an anchor created by a lonely man? What proof were those hours of waiting beneath City Hall? What proof was Angela's face divided among a hundred women at whom I stared? Rather than accept the fact of her non-existence I cling to her through strands of remorse and bitterness. Now I conjure another vision, fashion one more visitation so I may continue to believe. I am almost tempted to accede to a miracle. Angela telepathic, filtering her voice through molecules of air and matter so it reaches me, undimmed, full of truth in this antiseptic closet.

Perhaps Angela is all the poetry left in me. For what it's worth. Not much at the moment. A sonnet won't lift me from the bed. No metaphor will hold the bed pan or change the shitty tailed gowns. If there is orderliness, precision, cleanliness, rhythm in the world, they are most visible in an action, a plan such as I have conceived. Formulating a rite totally consistent with the logic of history, yet harnessing the blind rush of events, opening a momentary wedge so a new myth can shoulder its way into the process.

The gods of fire, of wine, of blood are not co-incidental. They are the faint impressions of mortal men blown up a million times. History is a consuming, crackling fire and time is a vast bland screen and all that men can understand or believe is the play of shadows, the outlines of men or nations caught for an instant before they drop into the flame and ascend in shapeless smoke endlessly climbing the screen. Most men read the smoke, most men pass so easily to oblivion they are the smoke. But some are free. Are gods because they print themselves against the screen. Then the smoke readers, the smoke itself cannot ignore them, will never quite be the same again.

To free the Black God I will drop the hanged cop into the fire. The contorted silhouette will flash darkly on the screen. There will be no turning back, no hiding in the shivering smoke. The lynched white cop will not only be an ineradicable element in the future, but it will seem as if he and his lynchers have always existed, patiently waiting to be perceived, a mystery to be worshipped.

To tear such a hole in history. To assist at the birth of a God. These are worth any sacrifice. I would lie here a millennium, if my organs continue to function, calm as a sail waiting for wind.

A black boy cleans my room. He is gangly and tight lipped. A vacant look in his eyes, which seem fixed six inches beyond his wide brogans. The animal taciturnity and sullenness white people associate with laziness and stupidity. They cannot conceive of the discipline, the self-denial such a mask demands. It is that discipline I seek to divert from self-effacement, from obsolete survival techniques. This boy could play a part in the plan. Could serve as a link between me and the others outside. He has learned to wear his brown skin like an impenetrable veil of ignorance. He moves freely here in the gut works of the enemy and no one trembles when he walks by. He is treated as a drone whose imagination could not possibly go beyond the routine prescribed for him. Like the three boys in Atlantic City who held one job simultaneously, alternating each day in the tasks of sweeping and washing and carrying out garbage, called by the same name, paid with one check, their trinity opaque as father son and holy ghost.

But the Man is wily. This boy may be a plant. A good loyal darky praying for tales to carry. Or he may be a scared one. Hopelessly unmanned already by his dependence. As frightened of me as he is of the haunts and bogey men he learned to dread in the tales his mammy whispered to him.

I will not make the first move. I have leisure to study him. Gauge his usefulness.

—Do you smoke.
—Uh, huh.
—I've never seen you smoking.
—Ain't supposed to smoke in here.
—Why not?
—That's what they told me.

—And you didn't ask why.

—Don't matter to me that much. I go on up to where nobody bothers me. There plenty places to smoke.

—But you don't smoke here.

—I don't want no trouble.

—Who would see you?

—Nurse maybe and the supervisor comes round some time.

—What would they do if they caught you smoking?

—Something . . . I guess.

—Do you think you'd lose your job?

—I don't know. People always coming and going.

—What you're saying is the job ain't shit. Right?

—I suppose . . . in a manner of speaking that's what I might be talking about.

—Then why do you give a damn about the rules?

—I don't want trouble.

—Trouble's what you got already with their piece of ass job and rules.

—It's better than nothing. Lots of people got more trouble than me.

—Like me.

—Maybe. I know who you are. I was at Wilson when you trying to make your speech.

—You look too old for Wilson.

—I don't do too good in school. They keep me back but next year I be too old they got to pass me. Don't matter anyway. I be tired from work. I don't hardly go to school now and I ain't planning to stay much longer. Don't make sense when I could be out working full time.

—You're working now and you can't even light a cigarette when you want it.

—Least I can buy me a pack now and then . . . and help out my mother.

—There's a pack in my drawer you can have. I don't think it's even open.

—You don't want 'em.

—I stopped smoking.

—Doctor make you.

—No. I make my own rules. I look in worse shape than I am. You know what I mean.

—These your cigarettes.

—Yes. But wait a minute. You can have them all but first I want you to light one. Smoke it here.

—I ain't supposed to.

—This is my room. I make the rules. I want you to understand that. You can have the pack but you must smoke one here, now.

—What if I don't want no smoke now?

—Are you afraid? If you are, I think you should ask yourself what it is that's scaring you. You'll see matches in the same drawer.

—I got my own.

At least once a day during his shift he comes in here and smokes. We both look forward to it though I'm sure for very different reasons. From a distance I enjoy the faintly stale, rough aroma of the tobacco. The first few times he was stiff, perhaps felt bullied. Now he takes deep drags, seems infinitely relaxed as he exhales through his nose and lips. His mannerisms with a cigarette remind me superficially of Saunders. Yet the boy is not taut enough or abrasive enough to be a Saunders. He doesn't have the assassin's skin which fits too tightly over the bones, the unsettling efficiency of gesture, the face crowded by extra shadows that appear to move independent of any light source.

He talks more freely. I am almost positive he can be trusted. Be of use. His name is Anthony. That's what I call him though he says the sound of *Anthony* is strange. He is Tony everywhere but here. And school. A Miss Collins with whom he is infatuated. A white teacher of social studies. She calls him Anthony, displays posters of black heroes on her classroom wall. The class listens to recordings of Paul Robeson, of Malcolm X speaking, they read Richard Wright and Eldridge Cleaver. She has drawn him in. Many days the only class he attends is hers. Of course he can't really read the books, but he listens, watches her as with a shining face she reads her favorite passages. He hears the cream skimmed off the top, sweet, heady in her young, white woman's voice. He is taught five and dime moral lessons. A mortician's version of the bloodily martyred artists is displayed for him, all powder, paint and rigid smiles that reek of formaldehyde. What grasp does he have of history? Of the larger context that destroyed the black men whose words and music are now being exploited by their destroyers?

I tell him stories. The full biographies of the men with whom Miss Collins claims such intimacy. Occasionally he understands. Sees them. Sees her. But the dumb black boy is in love. He returns.

Yesterday I played a game. While he in his painful style rattled on, huffing and puffing on one of the cigarettes I make available, I reached up to the cord dangling beside my headboard and pushed the emergency button. For some reason, perhaps because I signal so infrequently, a pink baby elephant uncomfortably trussed in white nylon immediately responded. The nurse was inside the curtain pulled across my door staring at Anthony some moments before he was aware of her bulging presence. He was deep into a tale about a classmate raped by a teacher in the girls' room, when the nurse shouted at him.

—What do you think you're doing. Put that out this instant. As she stood in the doorway, fat, flushed, breathing heavily, I wished it had been Miss Collins. This nurse was too easy. Ugly already.

—Don't put it out, Anthony.

—Out this instant or I'll have the supervisor in here. You . . . you don't interfere. I don't have to take smartness from your kind. Didn't you hear me say out. She screeched the last command, her voice no longer feigning any sort of control or rational authority. Her words bubbled and boiled as absolute in their stridency as the power she believed supporting them.

—Why must he put it out? I am the only tenant. He has my permission. No one's afraid just because you raise your voice. Call the supervisor. Bring him in here. The boy was lighting the cigarette for me.

He was slow. Confused. I had to say *Thank you, Anthony, for the cigarette,* extend my arm before he stepped over and handed it to me.

—He lights my cigarettes all the time. I have difficulty doing it myself.

—You . . . you people stick together don't you.

—Black birds of a feather. Is that what you mean?

A slow but irresistible wind pushed her from the room by inches. She knew she was going, knew she had no choice, but stubbornly planted her heavy feet, squared her broad shoulders and fought as best she could, spitting threats, face saving phrases of rule, regulation and privilege, rote-learned from her manual.

When she was gone and the curtain sighed back across the entrance, it was like some thick, viscous fluid had been drained from the room. I didn't mention her, asked him to go on with his story. I wanted him to see how she was an absolute irrelevancy, a hulking glacier unable to comprehend the end of the ice age as it slides into the sea. Though she had departed without determining my reason for ringing, he knew I had summoned her and almost belligerently asked me why.

—To demonstrate something about their rules. To show you what I said earlier is true. This is my room and I set the rules. I did not recite for him the most obvious lesson: they are trapped just as circumstantially as we are by the rules they have chosen. I knew he had enjoyed the nurse's discomfort, her absurd floundering. In the space of a few seconds he had seen how ruthlessly lines must be drawn. After seeming to betray him I had treated him to a show of his own force, the power we could wield together. How utterly we could exclude her, dramatize her foolishness. At some level he must have laughed. If for the moment he understood nothing else but the liberating power of that laughter, my little game had been exquisitely managed. I could deal with his mistrust later. I could sermonize on the parable another day. His muteness was not a sign of stupidity, it was the organism's compensation for an inner life tumultuously astir.

I think I can use him. An unexpected boon. I had reconciled myself to being excommunicated. After the unforeseen circumstances of the rally and my *fall* and this imprisoning bed, I had no choice but to resign myself to passive participation in the plan. I had conceived it, launched it, but would have to entrust its implementation to the others. Doubts pound at me of course, but the scheme is much larger than any individual involved. That's its grandeur, what insures the inevitability of success. History has provided a raging sea, a flimsy dam, the corrupt village within hearing distance of the waters but refusing to acknowledge its peril. I have seen the total picture, examined in detail each element without losing the sense of the basically simple configuration. I know the dam will not hold. Its solidarity is a myth as transparent as the myth which describes the water as low and placid on the other side of the wall. I want to inundate the city with a dream of drowning. I want to flood the gutters with the sticks and mud depended upon for salvation. The vision of the end may be simultaneous with the end, but that is not my affair. I have divined the means by which the vision can appear. It is ironic that I need no more than a few hands to help, someone to lug a bucket of water, another to tote a sack of wood and garbage. Flat on my back I can direct the charade.

The boy, without disturbing the logic of the plan, may provide me with a window on the proceedings.

The metaphor is almost too obvious. This boy as a messenger, as youth entrusted with the secrets of the plan. Our link with the generations to come. He will not understand the words, not realize they contain the possibility of death and resurrection.

Careful above all. My vanity must not be allowed to jeopardize the undertaking. I have steeled myself against its promptings. If Angela walked through the curtain and said we may have the best moment of our time together extended for an eternity if you leave with me, I know I could refuse her. I must weigh my motive carefully in this case. Are there practical advantages in communicating by courier with Wilkerson? Is Wilkerson's conviction deep enough? Is Saunders cold enough? Rice stupid enough? Had the endless rehearsals of the event in our talk established the plan for them as clearly and purely as it sits in my imagination?

The last time we were all together I drew a diagram. Step by step from the kidnapping to the lynching and disposal of the body. I couldn't have forgotten anything. Wilkerson nodded assent, said he saw no problems, understood everything. Yet we were inhibited. They are always watching me. I wouldn't be surprised if the room were bugged, if some lackey who has earned the honor of spying on me isn't dozing right now in front of a closed circuit scanner beamed on me. The possibility of surveillance is enough to make the strictest cautions necessary. Except for Wilkerson's one visit when everything is in readiness, the others cannot return here. We did not talk of the plan on the single occasion they thoughtlessly arrived together. The drawing had to suffice. And Wilkerson's reaction to it was limited to what would pass as casual conversation.

Though the plan reduced itself with mathematical precision to a series of incidents which I numbered and circled, though the beads would be strung together by the immutable logic of history, and though the events were no more or less than anticipations of the rhythm of history prematurely externalized, the plan retains a minor, co-incidental dependence on the conspirators. Timing is most important. I'm sure I am the only one whose sense of the timing involved is faultless. In this bed I have become the plan. I have emptied myself of everything but what is necessary to the plan. My pulse is its pulse. I have been content to lie here blind, deaf and dumb to the only reality which concerns me. The boy could restore my senses.

The first task is to be sure of him. I will have him carry a message that is his death warrant if he gives the slightest cause for suspicion. Tell Wilkerson to have Saunders shadow him, watch for a sign that he intends to betray us.

Meanwhile, more preparation of him I can do. I have often regretted all of my fellow conspirators were as old as or older than myself. But I had to work with the available material. We are not quite ancient. Rice, the eldest by two years, is just thirty-six. We are, however, at least a lifetime away from the college kids and the children mimicking them. Our extra life consists of disillusionment, the string of failures and deceits that disqualify us for a better world if by some miracle a better world began tomorrow. The others can wear their hair and clothes differently, sing, shout, call one another brother and believe themselves identical with the new wave, part of a new world, containing and contained by it. We have lost any vision beyond a wavering faith in something better than the misery we have lived through. We are certainly not any part of a vision of something better. We are not even vessels of transition. The men I picked to carry through the plan can gauge change only by its distance from the wreck they have made of their lives. Change must destroy them. They can't call anybody brother without inviting them into a room contaminated with the . plague. I am appalled by Anthony's ignorance, but once as we discussed some trivial matter, he shouted at me, as peremptorily, as uncompromisingly as I had ever heard him speak. He said it's always better to tell a person the truth. Never, never is telling them a lie better for them than telling them the truth. I raised the obvious objections. Offered concrete examples which I thought proved the ambiguity inherent in the word *truth*. The virtual impossibility of differentiating truth from falsehood in many complex situations. How truth could be a superfluous value, outweighed by other considerations. He dismissed my arguments summarily. Said he had been lied to all his life, and if he could change any one thing about his life, it would be to remove the web of lies told to him for his own good.

I was astonished by his innocence. How it furnished him with a clarity all my cogitation and cunning had not achieved. Parts of Anthony had flourished in the ooze. If light had not penetrated to illuminate him, neither did it tarnish or corrode. The torpor of his barely realized life was often repugnant to me. I had struggled long ago to exorcise from myself the demons of sloth, fear and self-denial I saw rampant in him. Yet he sat teaching me, flung open doors that made me shrink from the sudden light they exposed. I had killed an Anthony in me, rejected his weaknesses and strength. Though in many ways I had been Anthony, his life now was unimaginable. I could only react with sudden flashes of awe and despair.

—Anthony. Suppose a great leader, a black man like you, discovered a way to turn this country inside out. Suppose he knew how to free black people once and for all from their oppressors. He could do this but first he'd have to lie. Offer his people all the things most think they want, cars, clothes, big houses, promise them possessions in order to rally support, to prepare the way for the liberation. Would you tell him not to lie? Would you tell him to allow the suffering of black people to continue because hearing lies from him would be worse than the beating, stealing and killing they are subjected to every day? Would you say freedom is not worth that lie on your lips?

He pondered, his face vacant of any sign he had understood or even heard my question. When he answered it was blandly, as if he had no idea his life was staked on the question.

—If I be working hard for a car and when I do everything I was supposed to do somebody give me something that ain't a car I'd be pretty mad.

—Even if somebody gave you freedom instead?

—That's why people lie. So they can give you what they want to give you and not what you want. They lie to keep you from taking.

—You don't understand freedom.

—Maybe not. I don't know much about anything. I ain't hardly supposed to.

—You're right. There are blinders over your eyes. But whose fault is that?

—Whose fault don't seem to matter. I just know I got to get along with what I have. I'll make it. Lies ain't helping.

—You said you heard me speaking at Wilson. Do you know why I was there? Why they were scared? Did you see the army they called out to silence one man? They were frightened of my voice, no matter what I had to say. The barest chance that you might listen or any of the others listen, even to a pack of lies is a threat to the Man. The Man controls everything you see and hear. To play the kinds of games he does with your mind his power over you must be absolute. An outside voice, a desperate act, so barefaced and brutal they won't be able to cover up its significance. These are the only ways of penetrating the veil. For a while the impact of Watts burning or revolutionaries kidnapping and ransoming a judge are raw, crude sources of energy. They are answers in progress to the questions you have been afraid to raise. They make you angry and ashamed because you realize someone else is paying your dues, doing your dying. For an hour or a day or a week you are changed. Your vision of history is concrete, unobstructed. You understand the white man's power, its intimidation and threat. Then most of us are only too grateful to have the veil restored. The radio television and newspapers begin their juggling act. Words are invented. A cast of cartoon characters appears with their roles clumsily stenciled on their sweatshirts. They are grossly inhuman, and slide neatly into place, Humility, Virtue, Innocence, Evil, the same old refugees from a morality play shuffling through the same tired situations. We have seen it before and we assent wearily. What we thought was new, daring, perhaps even liberating, is after all cowboys, Indians and the inevitable blue coated, blue-eyed cavalry speeding to the rescue.

—It's that simple and you hear me but you'd still prefer a car to freedom. Don't shake your head. I know better than you do what you're thinking. They've put it all there for you to think. You are the history they have manufactured. Tony. Anthony. Exhibit A. A monument to their success. Do you have any notion of what you really are? How many carbon copies of you walk the streets of this great nation? You all spit and scream and fuck in the same way. You duplicate your teeming, cramped hives across the country. The resemblance is disgusting. The unanimity. They have a wind-up key stuck in your ass so far it tickles your brain. Your nose is wide open and I can see the key twisting. I see you now and I know where you'll be tomorrow. You're that safe, predictable. They have you on a tight schedule. The stages are clearly marked and you'll go through each with a blindness and enthusiasm. You'll think they are you. Till one day you'll reach the last stage and perhaps a glimmer of how you've been cheated. Of what a clumsy, repetitious trap they've made black manhood and how eagerly, foolishly you've performed your paces. Do you think it's a co-incidence? Do you believe there could be such undeviating failure and frustration without a program? Of course exceptions exist. There must be exceptions. But almost to a man the energies of those successes are made accessory to the white man's control or superfluous to black people's freedom. With the Man's million eyes and ears, the images of *now* they bombard us with, they have forced us to lose a sense of before and after, mistake their programmed version of our present lives for history, inevitability. Only a violent reversal will do. The fabric they have strung together must be torn apart. One sudden rent and every thread will unravel. The smallest and largest lies will go at once. After the chaos, if nothing is comprehensible at least nothing will remain of what once was thought to be solid, real, forever. That is freedom. Metaphysical revolt.

—If you prefer I will call it an automobile. A house in

Scarsdale. A Brooks Brothers suit. I will call it Black. I will call it Pan African Unity. I will call it God. Scream revolution. Armageddon. I will metamorphose it to the comeliest dream you have ever dreamt. Kill you with it if I have to.

I realized I had lost him. For three or four minutes I had been shouting at no one in particular. I was rankled by this burst of vanity and ego. Ranting to please myself with the sound of my words. The boy could have been insulted as well as confused. All my patient preparation of him would be wasted.

I attempted a smile. He wouldn't look at me. I felt my own skin lifting. I saw what he must see. A battered half man flat on his back, chained to a bed, screaming freedom. The irony oppressed me. He could not remain in awe, puzzled by such a creature. I couldn't allow him to dismiss me as loud and powerless, a clown to laugh at with his friends when he left the hospital. I thought of disclosing the plan, of offering him a role. I began to hint of dark, portentous events. I reassumed the part of master, seer. I drank in his attention, it rose so palpably to his eyes, his lips relaxing from sullenness.

Then I stopped. Just short of disgust. I had been wooing him. Not for the plan—I was on the verge of betraying it for any paltry gesture of affection from him—but because of a vain, selfish urge for comfort, for luxury. But of course the plan was everything. And if I was the plan as I had conjured myself into believing, what prompted the urge? Where had I hidden it from myself during these weeks of abstention and self-denial?

I would have been overjoyed at that moment if the inklings of a plot I had revealed to him were transformed to poison coursing through his system. Nothing less than watching him shrivel to a lifeless heap would compensate for the injury he had forced me to inflict on myself. I knew then my mind was infinitely treacherous. I could deny or convince myself of anything. In my desolation, a prisoner of their violence, their bed, I could attach myself as hungrily to this hard-legged, thick-headed black boy as I once had to Angela.

Saunders would have to kill him. My life, the lives of the conspirators, the plan itself could not be dependent on the boy's ignorance. How much had I actually divulged. I could dispatch him now if necessary. The razor blade under my pillow. Draw him close to light a cigarette for me. Make him bend till his pimply throat is in reach.

–Do you understand what I mean? How a few men with the proper insight and unflinching resolve might change things. They wouldn't necessarily have to be great or unusual men. People like you or me I'm talking about. If some coincidence put them in the right place at the right time and they acted with all the determination the situation demanded . . .

–No, we must talk about history first . . . before you could understand. . . . You . . . must understand the rules in order to break them . . . if you understand fully . . . there will be no rules but the ones you make as you act . . .

–Supervisor told me not to be hanging around here. I been here long enough to be done cleaning.

–Then you better go . . . we can talk tomorrow.

Whatever advantage he had gained, I could win back. The plan was safe. He could only go as far as I explicitly led him. He could piece nothing together from the generalities, the suggestion that my world does not end an inch beyond my fingertips, nor is it bound by the curtain and three walls that contain my eyes. I had not chanced the plan in the game I played with him. I had merely been fortified by the plan's power. Felt its strength well up within me, refusing to be belittled by what the boy with his untutored eyes thought he saw. Pride moved me to entrap him again. Pride flowing from my knowledge of the plan. I had toyed with his life and possibly my own, but the plan had never been in jeopardy.

If all has gone according to schedule, and there is no reason to doubt it has, Wilkerson should come here in two weeks. By now Saunders should know the best way to ambush the girl. Her lover will be annoyed the first day she is missing. The second day he will be angry and on the third start searching for her. We will assist him in his hunt. He will find his whore and his doom together. We will hold him until it is time for him to make his grand entry on the platform. He will be drugged to minimize his fear, any chance of untidy panic. The rumors will have circulated. Her mutilated body will have been discovered, described. He will personify the guilt of a million jailers and executioners. The sharp crack of his neck breaking will be a thunderclap above the mob. His body will convulse with explosions of piss, shit and bile at the moment of truth, all the rottenness inside the man suddenly decorating the blue uniform.

Perhaps the sack of flour should wait till then. One last mockery of the man's image of himself, one more coat of white dusted over the foulness.

Then . . . then. The horror. The outrage. Everyone knowing the truth. A heave and explosion as the dam splinters, the earth recoils from the first onslaught of mountainous waves.

I dreamed I was lying on a rock. The rock was on a narrow point of land jutting into the middle of a lake. Twilight. A full moon preserving the color of the sky. Only a few of the brightest starts were visible against the pale turquoise. One pinpoint of light directly over my face as I lay with my back pressed into the stony contours seemed to be moving. I thought it might be a satellite, or a plane whose altitude negated its screaming engines. The darting shadows on the sandy strip of land, the constant rush of water across the rock strewn tip of the point and slapping rhythmically along one smooth black edge, the nervous rustling of trees sometimes in concert but also one tree at a time quivering alone in the grip of a giant, invisible fist, something about this ceaseless animation that extended even to the sky where scudding clouds made a star seem to move, placed me outside of time. I thought I could listen forever to the water, watch for eternity the changing shapes of the clouds rushing overhead or the fire and blood streaked setting of the sun blazing molten through the purple clouds piled on the horizon.

But everything stopped. I felt a birth. A god donning skin. I believe a man must be conceived twice. To exist, a man must first be imagined by other men. The mind of at least one human being must become a breeding ground, must nurture some possibility of itself in the quiet of spirit and will until the thing it could never be has a throbbing potential life. The spiritual incubus will then float immune to time and space in a vast blackness whose dimensions are only suggested by the phrase: there is nothing it does not contain.

Soon, since time is superfluous and a second or a millennium are both soon, the incubus will unite with a human form. This is the second accidental birth. A sputtering urge to rebel that seemed lost in the flesh of a slave tossed overboard to lighten a Spanish galleon in a stormy sea will be reborn wire taut and indestructible in the soul of an infant whose first home is 125th Street, a drawer in a vermin infested bureau. As there is no fixed interval between the two conceptions, neither is there continuity of nation, race, sex. I sometimes feel that animals, plants, even a rock with its slow thoughts that need millions of years to form exude a spiritual exhalation that is realized in man shape. After a certain type of man is imagined he may be reproduced endlessly, all variation co-incidental details of the flesh. A god is created when the will and spirit of the many focus repeatedly on a lack, an emptiness each senses in himself. The collective energies are projected with such force that the god achieves an existence whether or not a co-incidence with flesh has occurred. The imminent messiah remains incomplete, however, until he has been a man. A man for a day or a lifetime, a man long enough to converse with some storyteller who can spread the news abroad.

Though the many create the possibility of a god, one man must dream a human guise the god can assume. Stretched on the slanting rock I know I watched the Black God pass to manhood.

I was aware of the transition first as an absolute stillness, then a flood of patience, an unquestioning certitude. All that seemed to move around me—water, light, wind—must come to rest. Motion was imperfection, was form seeking form, continuous dissatisfaction. I don't know how long everything stopped, but it did. Not peace, not rest, not quiet, or stillness, or oblivion, nothing I could anticipate. Just a stop, a space between. Not an abrupt cessation or a hurried pause. Just everything stopping, kissed to sleep by the God's touch. He was not there. Then He was there. All I could comprehend of the transition was that it filled the space between not there and there. Filled it so completely that nothing else existed. Water, moon, stars, heartbeat. When I began to breathe again and the rhythms of the finger of land crashed around me once more I knew I had assisted at the birth of a God. I could see the earth as fatally afflicted, see its dance of forms as a futile attempt at curing its disease. Though I could visualize my own existence as one of an infinite number of mirrors reflecting the earth's fitful struggle, I could be composed, in fact accept my own mortality as blandly as I did that of the stone I rested upon. The God was father and son to me simultaneously, revealing gently, compassionately, the way only flesh can, that I had been born and would die, that these arbitrary limits were as far as the flesh could go, but his coming, clothed in flesh, was a guarantee that these limits were fitting, ordained, that the parenthesis which contained me was not entirely opaque at either extremity.

The dream ended without a revelation of the God's precise human shape. My contentment was spoiled by a worrisome curiosity. I wanted to be able to recognize him if I passed him on the street. Despite all that had been revealed, I resented what had been withheld. I wanted to see the face, the body, the vulgarized form of his mystery. Perhaps Anthony or one of the conspirators, a face teasingly close and unreadable. Perhaps some tall, straight, brown-eyed handsome man who would stride from the crowd, roaring like a lion as he feeds upon the body of the lynched cop. Perhaps a baby sleeping on its black mother's breast while the woman quietly weeps. Whatever, wherever, whoever, I can no longer doubt the spirit has been released and received, a new man born.

I cannot trust the boy. Perhaps I should say I cannot trust myself with him. At some crucial point I might ask too much of him, put into his hands words which could destroy us all. I will wait for Wilkerson. I can subdue my curiosity for ten days. If some drastic modification of the plan is necessary, Wilkerson will certainly consult me. The boy tells me it's getting hot outdoors. School will soon be dismissed. Old people will be squatting on their stoops, women hanging from their windows, young boys gathered around the newest, sleekest car on the block basking in its elegance, daydreaming, telling lies in which they function with the machine's speed and brute force. In spite of the oppressive city scape framing the scene, I see a street momentarily pastoral. Something in the old people's faces, the skinny children idly abandoning themselves to motion, to crying, to any stick or bit of junk they find on the littered curbs, the vacant lots where one rotted tooth has been razed from between its monotonously decaying neighbors. I hear the music I always hear on such a block. The houses leak the same heady perfume of manured fields. I sense discontinuity, inappropriateness. A mass of people have been displaced. The stumbling rows of houses cannot contain them. They spill onto the streets and the streets cannot hold them, the people keep slipping away. Rivers are in their eyes. They disappear behind luxuriant trees. Run across wide, grassy fields. Superfluous clothing falls away. Their arms and legs are sculpted by a wind that never aired these streets.

But a sense of another life, another world asserting itself in the midst of the fallen city dims in each generation. Only rarely does the teeming life glimmer across the surface of the things I see as I walk down our streets. Perhaps I dream it to the surface. Need to forget what rots and stinks and dies around me.

I see a man walking down the block weeping. He stops at

each grouping on the front steps or sidewalks. He makes the vacant eyes meet his. He stares until the only sound between his face and another is his hand reaching out to touch. Silence a wake behind him. The old walls dissolving soundlessly to dust. The people joining hands. I visualize him at times moving in this manner. In certain moods I prefer that to my image of him bronzed, bare chested outside the city gates, his trumpet raised, and ten thousand trumpets echoing his first note. The walls tumbling. Smoke, fire, thundering apocalypse. The blind given sight. The lame walking. The rich man guillotined by a razor shuddering down to close the needle's eye.

My strength is slowly returning. I do my exercises faithfully, flexing my muscles, holding them tense for sixty second intervals. Beneath the sheets a silent, unobservable recovery. With help I believe I can walk. I grabbed the boy's arm as he swept under my bed. He couldn't free himself. He laughed because I was smiling. He treated it as a game but I knew my sudden show of force surprised, even frightened him. They all believe I am helpless. Perhaps the boy knows where they keep my braces and a cane. Is he ready to recover them for me? He might call it stealing. I must tell him a story about Frederick Douglass. Explain how it's impossible for a slave to steal from his master.

Anthony described a ward on the seventh floor. It had been a refuge for him. A place where he could smoke undisturbed since the inmates of a particular section on that floor couldn't have cared less if Anthony was lighting a cigarette or putting a match to a fuse which could blow him and the ward to bits. They call it the Sanitarium. It contains the madmen. The staff has incorporated a phrase into their jargon. *You'll be sleeping on the seventh.* It's a humorous catch-all used to characterize anyone whose speech or actions don't conform to the rigidly observed hospital routine. According to the boy most of the staff considered me a good bet to be sleeping on the seventh. A few thought I was not there only because I was too dangerous, too criminally crazy for their benign loony bin and that I would be transported, as soon as I healed sufficiently, to a padded cell in the state institution. I was sure the rumor had been purposely started. Such a reputation would serve as a moat around my prison rock. The authorities are clever. They are determined to exile me, isolate me from any aid I might receive from my people. They don't miss a trick.

I was encouraged because this piece of scuttlebutt came from the boy. He was truly beginning to serve as a pair of eyes and ears for me. If I thought they would not be replaced, I would ask him to locate and dismantle the camera and microphones that make this room like a fishbowl.

It seems the nurses on the seventh floor are very liberal. One of the few places the boy felt he could relax and talk. Most of the patients are harmlessly insane, immured in psychoses that blessedly protect them from this world. They are as docile as plants and their inner turmoil if it exists is opaque to the nurses as they water, change the soil and move their charges in and out of the sunlight. The others receive heavy sedation. Doses so large that many never move from their beds. The nurses like to show off their prize patients, have them perform. Since Anthony is available and has a big smile he often serves as an audience. There was one old black man who on command would spit shine your shoes with his tongue. A girl of thirteen who had been raped and brutalized by a street gang sang sweet lullabys to a non-existent baby she rocked in her arms. Anthony would smoke and quietly listen to the gossiping nurses if the patients were all resting. The seventh floor had been his favorite spot before I came.

Through him I gained a familiarity with the hospital. I knew which part of the floor I was on, had a fairly detailed map of my surroundings which I could depend upon if the occasion for speed and stealth arose. He knew nothing more of the plan, but he understood that my situation was precarious. I let him connect my speech at Wilson with threats to my life I anticipated. I embroidered upon the fragment of speech he had heard. He admitted he hadn't gone to listen. The rally simply had freed him from the monotonous routine of his life. A rally brought bodies together. I wrote the outline of the speech I had planned for that day on a paper towel. He promised to study it, repeat the guiding ideas to me the next day. No satisfaction came when he faithfully parroted my words. I demanded more, tried to draw him out.

–I ain't ready for this.

–You mean you don't understand.

–I'm tired. It took me a long time to say those words you put down. And I still got a lot of work after I leave here.

I saw him sitting in Miss Collins' class. Listless, bored. A student to be diverted to the vocational track. Incurious. Inherently lazy. A dull thing who would never learn the correct answers.

–Are you stupid, Anthony? Who has convinced you of your stupidity? I thought he shrank from my question. Visibly cringed as he took the butt from his lips and let it drip from his fingers into the pool of dust and trash he had swept into the center of the room. He stood motionless, the broom a third leg rooting him to the floor. I half expected a hole to open beside him, a gurgling drain that would suck his body and the dust together into the cloacal darkness reigning beneath the foundations of the hospital.

–I'm tired. If I didn't stay tired, I'd be crazy.

–Maybe crazy is preferable to hiding. If the others are right, I'll be sleeping on the seventh to keep you company.

–Company don't do much good up there.

–What I wrote down frightened you, didn't it? You understood the message perfectly well, what it asked of you. What it would make of you. But you recited the words with no more feeling than you'd give the ABC's. You pretended to be ignorant of what you were saying. You were protecting yourself.

–Like I said. I got lots to do. And I'm sleepy already. You don't do nothing but lay here in the bed. Plenty time to just think and write anything comes in your head. Plenty time to do nothing but worry and tease me. I'm gone on about my own business now and you tend to yours. I do what you ask me, but what you ask ain't really what you want. You always want more. You always asking for one thing when you want another. You just want me in the habit of doing what you say.

—You're forgetting why I'm here.

—Cause they whipped your head at Wilson.

—At Wilson. Wilson. Wilson, Woodrow, twenty-eighth president. Racist fucking bastard wanting to found a League of Nations. Goddamnit. Yes, at Wilson Junior High. Some lily white League it would have been. Perpetuating his name. Perpetuating the tight assed little Miss Collins who mangles your dreams. Yes that's where you saw me. A crippled bastard they broke into even smaller pieces. At White Woodrow Wilson. White Woodrow Wilson Junior High filled with black bodies and black sweat. The stones ooze white pus. Do you know white is the sign of death, of extreme putrefaction? The orientals have known that for thousands of years. And every day you are driven like cattle into the rotten white barn. They whipped my head at Wilson. And my balls and my back and my hands and parts I didn't even know I had, they whipped me at Wilson and didn't stop for days. So long I lost track of time they got me good at Wilson, whipped me enough to last for the rest of my life. Why? Do you know why? Because I came looking for you. For you who came looking for some fat ass to rub up against. You who hides on the edge of the crowd, not listening, not caring who is whipped or why. You who would watch and cheer whatever spectacle was provided. At Woodrow Wilson I got a head beating and you think that makes me a fool. That you're safe because you keep your distance, hang around the edges. You with that silly broom when you ought to have a rifle, be killing yourself or killing them. You weren't reciting a nursery rhyme a few minutes ago. You had in your hands a recipe for liberation or death. One or the other. Doesn't matter which comes first. But one or the other is coming and

I tried to tell you that. But they whipped my head and dragged me away. And you sulked home with your tail between your crusty legs. Cowering like you cower from any words which don't put you to sleep.

I must have been shouting because a nurse and an orderly rushed into the room. From the corner of my eye I saw Anthony disappear, a black slinking shadow the others would take no notice of. I knew they would come to my bed. They would flood my guts with some tranquilizing poison. As it crept through my system I would become calm as a daisy. I considered the razor blade I had tucked away. Each day I concealed it in a different spot. Always instantly accessible, it could be in my hand before they had time to react. I thought of the nurse's pudgy arm slashed from elbow to wrist. The syringe dropped from numb fingers. Skin nerveless puckering back from the wound, a red path through her flesh, my wand striking, like Moses plowing a furrow in the white sea, my people marching down the bloody highway.

Instead I let them drown me. After the needle's bite everything was extremely funny. Shudders of laughter, a velvet undertow dragging me down.

THREE

· · · · · ·

RICE heard it first on his favorite radio station, the one with all talk shows and news so you could stay informed. He heard it just after the announcer gave credit and a twenty-five dollar bonus to the lucky informant who called in a story worthy of a flash bulletin. You got a fanfare, twenty-five dollars and your name on the radio just because you were lucky enough to be on hand when something happened and had a dime you could drop in the box to call the station before anybody else did. Rice envied the lucky bystander. Jealousy made him pout because during his entire lifetime he had never been witness to anything newsworthy. Certainly nothing worth a flash bulletin. Once he had come upon a man squashed on the pavement. But a crowd had already begun to gather and somebody officious had covered the head of the suicide. He expected no more men to plummet out of the sky and fall at his feet. The only thing he knew that other people might want to know he couldn't tell because it was a secret. He would never be interviewed. Never get a check or a plaque delivered to his door.

After describing the twelve alarm warehouse fire and honoring his informant the announcer had detailed a murder. He said the victim was Wilbur Childress and the suspect being held Orin Wilkerson of 6540 Simon Street.

Rice was indignant. The old man had no right. Just when they were on the verge of trying to make things better, he had to go out and act a nigger. Cut somebody to death. And his son about to become a hero. Rice was angry. Could they allow Wilkerson to continue as one of them? Bad enough with loud Saunders. Rice doubted for the thousandth time his own wisdom in joining the conspiracy. He had never been enthusiastic about the plan or the role it allotted to him.

There never seemed time or occasion for him to have his say. Rice could plainly see how the others were using him. He resented Littleman for his bullying and co-ercion. But as long as they all thought of him simply as a tool Rice felt in control of the situation. He could, in fact, stay a step ahead of the others, even Littleman, because they underestimated him. With Wilkerson compromised by his father's crime, Rice felt himself clearly as the number two man, just behind Littleman. Saunders had always been out of the picture. A thug for the strong arm duties, replaceable as soon as his usefulness ran out. Now when the revolution came, the son of a convicted murderer could not be placed before the people as a leader. Rice knew Littleman would want to remain behind the scenes. And since Littleman thought of him as spineless and weak, someone easily manipulated, he, Rice, would be the logical person to head whatever provisional government the revolutionaries instituted. Littleman would believe he had a patsy, a puppet who would respond mindlessly to his whims. Well, Littleman was not the only one who could plan.

Twenty-five minutes later the bulletin was repeated. A report from the scene of the fire, and in its wake the murder item. Rice caught every word this time. No mistake. Wilkerson's daddy had killed a man. Drunk and fighting in some vacant lot. Though Rice condemned him and all the lost creatures like him, he couldn't help feeling pity for Wilkerson's father. Like a child, really. Grown men with families, out in the street acting like children. Wilkerson would be crushed. It was a damned shame. A black man like Wilkerson trying his best to make good, to be somebody and he has to worry about his own kind pulling him down as much as he has to worry about the white man. Niggers are backbiters and spoilers. Ones at the bottom have no better sense than to try to keep everybody down. . . . You just have to cut them no count niggers loose and go on about your business. What his mama said, and a million times he had seen how right her advice had been.

But he was stuck with the others in the plan. Even though Rice believed he would turn it all to his benefit, that he would come out on top, he hated how the plan exposed him to the ugliness of the other conspirators. Saunders' boisterousness, Littleman's devious cunning and now the cloud of murder hanging over all their heads because of Wilkerson's father. A smart man shouldn't let himself get too connected. And the plan was all about connections.

Well, he would call Wilkerson and tell him about it. Wilkerson would still be at school. They'd call him to the office. Rice would make his voice urgent, let them know it was an emergency. He would be the first to tell Wilkerson even though no check or plaque was forthcoming.

● ● ●

Wilkerson watched the dish cloth twist in his mother's hands. Her knuckles whitened, the rag was an infected organ she had dragged from her body. The children's faces had been displaced by his mother's face. But she grew younger, vulnerable, more like the children while he talked. Wilkerson had left the school building moments after the call from Rice. He had checked with the police to verify Rice's announcement, then had rushed to his mother so she might hear the news first from him. He didn't understand her eyes. Suddenly young and innocent and untouched. Where were all the years, all the weight she had been carrying. He didn't see his father in her eyes or even himself. Wilkerson hated the drone of his voice, but could find no better way to say what had to be said. Before he had finished he was certain she knew more than he could tell her. She knew and she didn't know. He must stop altogether or wedge himself brutally into her consciousness.

Wilkerson realized he was in the wrong place. She had been telling him to go, to leave her and find his father. She appreciated his coming, his love, but she would be all right, she would work out a way of understanding. But her husband, his father . . .

Go get him. Go get him, Thomas, and bring him home.

Down the steps. A million times down the rotting steps of his parents' building. So many times, he had forgotten the pee stench, the crumbling wood, the softness suddenly underfoot that could send you spinning into other worlds. But you descend knight errant tippy tip down the steps and into the streets you've forgotten too. And the caves beneath the street. Bold hieroglyphs spray painted on the subway walls. Puddles. A blood red trickle leaking from under the platform into the murky bed of the silver rails. Muck and cigarettes. Obscenities five foot tall decorating the crumbling plaster walls of the station. You wait for the roof to cave in. The rumble of trains to be swallowed by the groan of shifting earth.

Then at the courthouse you had to wait in line again. Like you did for groceries or tickets to a ball game. His father was just a few yards away locked in one of the cells. Wilkerson glanced around the small, square waiting room. Green walls freshly painted, but already pencil scrawled, inset benches lining three sides, women and children in watery pastel colors. Cowed by the dead green walls that were window bare, coldly glowing. The women fretted over children absent and those who shuttled from lap to lap. Conversation was subdued, marked by sighs and long pauses, by the sudden departure of animation from the women's eyes.

Wiggling her narrow hips toward one end of a bench and scooping a sprawling pile of infant's bottles, diapers and miniature clothing toward her lap, a young black woman made room for a newcomer. It could have been his mother who brushed by him as he stood just inside the door. Same age, same size, a brown suit like his mother would wear here, the familiar scent as she made her way past him to the bench, adjusting her skirt around her knees, sighing as she sat. Her will expiring, a perceptible afflatus stately rising, Wilkerson believed he could see it reach the ceiling and blot itself to soot. Picking nervously at her brown outfit, but firmly in possession of her corner of the bench, she was stiff in the semi-circle of women, her eyes fixed on a child crawling across the gray green concrete floor.

A voice squeaky and singsong like the voices of his students softly chanted a nursery rhyme.

> *This is the church*
> *This is the steeple*
> *Open the doors*
> *Out come the people*

He watched a dark skinned girl build the church, then the steeple with her long, bony fingers. When the gates opened her ten fingers, each tipped by an oval of pearl, galloped into the ribs of the boy standing pressed between her knees. He giggled and squirmed as she tickled him under the chin and ran her hands down his body. He was laughing aloud though his pudgy face was still streaked with the tears of a moment before. His mother played the finger game again. Church, steeple, the explosion of scurrying people. Perhaps it would be that easy. Open the door and his people come laughing through. Free. Free. Free at last. Scrambling through the out-flung gates.

Twenty-five feet away the cages began. Barely room for shoulders and hips in the passageway between the waiting room and the barred steel door. When your name finally was called you pass through the first steel door. On the other side a guard calls your name again and lifts one layer of your skin with his eyes. The guard holds an oversize key ring. He sifts through cast iron keys that clank dully against one another like cow bells. Oiled steel hinges, sliding bolts and latches, keys jammed home but you are barely fifteen feet from where you started. The floor is stone. The guard mumbles, and though you do not turn to meet his eyes again, you hear a number. In a dream you repeat the number five, you say it to the guard who has already turned and left, slamming the steel maze shut behind you.

Moment of panic. Wilkerson realizes the deception worked upon him. He had been tricked into this dungeon, locked in, and now the grinning guard was throwing away the keys. No way out. Never see sunlight again. Never another human face. Guilt stinking through his pores. Of course they knew about the plan. Of course his role in the conspiracy had been discovered long ago. Rice was an informer. He had tricked Wilkerson into coming here. Meekly led to the slaughter. Laughter rattling the bars. One of the cops patting Rice on the back, buying the traitor a drink. Wilkerson's helplessness made him shudder. Not a thing he could do, they could beat, maim, torture. He saw Littleman's bloated face, the eyes closed by lumps of bruised flesh. He saw himself, a toothless madman giggling in the hooded corners of his cell.

Wilkerson forced himself to stop trembling before he stepped to number five. Free men and men in cages, men separated by arbitrary inches. He must face his father across the incalculable space. Perhaps it would be easy. His father would come forward, bow to his audience, grin as his cell is unlocked, as the farce ends. Guards stripping off their paper uniforms. Childress, the victim, wiping ketchup from his shirt, the cardboard bars of the jail set no longer menacing as house lights go up.

—Thomas

—How are you, Daddy

His father's heavy eyelids drooped once, but quickly popped up again. Then his gaze steady, deep and naked, greasy-eyed like a dog.

—It'll take some time but I'll be all right. I don't need a lawyer or putting your mother through a trial. You save the money and trouble and worry of it all. I'll just go to the judge and tell him I did it. I just want to say I took his life and here's mine, take it and be done.

—You know it doesn't work that way. We're doing everything we can. You should have called us so we could have started sooner. I talked to a bondsman just before they said I could see you. He thinks he can work out something we can afford. You ought to be home tomorrow.

—Where is your mother?

—She'd be here if she could. But the rules allow only one visitor a week. And I wanted to let you know what had happened so far. What I could manage about a lawyer and bail. Mama said she wouldn't be able to remember anything once she saw you. She knew she'd just break down and make things worse so we thought it best for me to come. I know you're upset and worried. And I know how anxious you are to get out of here. I wanted to relieve you in any small way I could. If things don't work out tomorrow, maybe they'll let Mama come in. Your hearing is tomorrow at noon. We'll both be there in the courtroom.

–No that's not necessary. I appreciate all you all doing. But I don't want to see her here. I don't want her in this place.

You slowly recall what you came for. A man is framed in the viewing window. Behind his head a sheet of striped ticking sways. It is a curtain he had pushed through to begin his performance.

–Daddy, I don't know what to say. Wilkerson had sorted through countless definitions, had many words for what his father had become. But no satisfaction came in saying: *drunk, philanderer*. In saying the worst, trapping with a word all that was formless and unmanageable about the man who had entered his mother and left him there to live. In a cell now. Murderer staring back at you through the thick glass partition.

–Nothing to say, but I was hoping you'd come. I was worried about you. Hadn't seen you since that night at the house. Orin Wilkerson bowed when he spoke to reach the metal circle that allowed words to pass between visitors and prisoners. Bare patches show his scalp. As if a fist had rubbed hair away. Forehead still smooth, sun rich brown Wilkerson had always envied, coppery brown that had been fumbled by the genes, transmuted to pallid tan in the son's complexion. Father's cheeks needed a shave. Thomas Wilkerson clambered onto a chair, chubby legs dangling precarious for an instant but worming his supple body till he stood upright, bare toes curling on the wooden seat, hands grasping the chair back, eyes riveted on the mirror image, on the soapy luxuriance of his father's chin, the gleaming razor and its lisp through white foam. Cheeks did not have the tautness of the brow anymore. Age was the eyes, nose and mouth growing smaller in the face, losing their dominance to encroaching folds of flesh. His father had a way of shifting his lower jaw so it jutted to one side. When he had the migraine headaches, you could almost hear his teeth grinding, hear the pressure building inside his skull, pain which he fought silently, grudgingly, tightening his crooked jaw.

Twitch in the pebbled cheek. Excess flesh betraying him. Cheeks could not exercise as the hands did, could not grasp the cans and hurl garbage into the rumbling trucks. Hands could die with their toughness intact, ropy veins binding them. His father's dark hands. Mother loving hands. A man nearly twice his age who could probably lift twice as much. If he challenged him, fought him wrist to wrist the way he fought Littleman, the calloused fingers would bear him down. A child for them.

—Daddy what happened.

—I wish I knew. God knows I wish I knew. The grate through which he spoke distorted his voice, made it quaver, fade, a long distance telephone call from a foot away. Wilkerson bent, resting his elbows on a well rubbed shelf below the window like offering his ear for a kiss in order to make out the words. He had never heard his father's voice shake. Perhaps on the other side the visitor's voice sounded just as uncontrolled, perhaps the speaking grill was meant to cheat the speakers, to reinforce the distance and isolation of the prisoner's world.

—I try to put it together, but it don't make sense. Just sit here with a terrible ache. I try to figure out what happened and nothing comes. Like I ain't had no life outside this jail.

—He came at me with the knife. Childress was drunk. He came at me with a knife. My back was up against a wall. I couldn't run away. And he had stopped playing. He was coming at me for real. Nothing I could do but grab for my own knife. So fast I didn't even have time to think. Got the knife in my hand and had to open it with my teeth. He was so close I shoved at him with the knife in my hand.

—I tripped trying to get out of his way. We were in that lot on Collins Avenue, the one near the show. We had hustled through the route. Barely twelve o'clock. Radcliff had his car parked there and we were carrying a can of gas to get it started. Me and Childress and Radcliff. I bought the gas and Radcliff was supposed to pay me but Childress screaming Radcliff better give him the money because I owed him. And Thomas, I swear to God I didn't owe him nothing, but he got mad. I told him Radcliff was giving money to nobody but me and Radcliff said I was right since I bought the gas and I didn't have anything that day anyway, hardly enough to get me a taste of something after work but Childress he just keeps shouting and getting madder. First he tells Radcliff he's gonna take his money from him, then he's on me talking about money or cutting me so I get tired. You know how he is. Childress always jumping bad, talking about who he's gonna cut. And him hardly big as a minute. But that bad mouth of his I told him to go on back to the truck before I broke his arm. He went running and when he came back had his knife open. I backed up. He's pulled it before and waved it around so I hardly paid attention, but he kept coming. I could see something in his eyes I never seen before. And he wouldn't say anything make sense. I kept trying to talk to him. Backing up and saying wait a minute, man, wait this is your man I remember trying to get him to say something but he was staring wild right in my eyes and circling with that knife. I knew he meant business. Too late, he was too close. I tried to run but tripped over a log. I was down when I got it out remember opening it with my teeth and pushing myself up and him on top of me I shoved with it in my hand and fell on him.

—He said I'm cut bad. I was up and my knife on the ground somewhere. But he didn't move. Just said that one thing *cut bad* slumped over on the ground. Radcliff told me he had been hollering the whole time at both Childress and me and hollering to get the others to come and stop it. I hadn't heard a thing. Radcliff had his arms around me I think when I was standing over Childress. He didn't need to do that. I wasn't mad at Childress. He didn't need to hold me. I thought I was cut. I was wet and sick feeling. I saw the broken glass, the garbage spread all over that vacant lot and the sky getting dark. And then it all just goes to pieces. I know we put him in the car to drive to the hospital. We took him and I was in the back seat with Childress holding his head.

—If I could just understand a little bit better. I keep seeing Mamie Childress and the kids. What they must be thinking. He was my friend. My best friend. I don't know how many times I've been in their house, eating their food, drinking their liquor. I could always talk to Mamie. Say some things I couldn't even say to your mother. And she used to talk about Childress. Tell for an hour what a wrong, no good nigger he was then cry for fifteen minutes cause she loved him so much. Now he's gone. She got kids hardly more than babies. Why did the little nigger have to get so mad about those pennies. Happened so fast and now he's dead. I was trying to get away. Shoving out at him. Don't matter what they do to me. You know his head was on my lap while we were driving to the hospital.

—White faces when we got to the emergency ward. *A stretcher, we need a stretcher*. And one answered wait a minute mister we decide what's needed. One looked at Childress. There wasn't much blood. While we were riding his head seemed to get heavier and heavier.

—They eased him out when the stretcher finally came. I was afraid to let him go; then I thought they didn't want to take him. They had to talk first. Him dying and they wanted a story.

—I was sick. I vomited beside the car. It was on my jacket and when I had to talk to them I could see what they were seeing, an ignorant razor fighting nigger, stinking of sour wine.

—When the questions were finished I sat and watched a clock while Childress died. Didn't take long. I was staring at the face of the clock but I couldn't tell you where the hands were pointing. I just heard somebody say dead. Radcliff had been trying get Mamie on the phone but stopped and came over to me when he heard Childress was gone. He looked at me and I knew he was saying man, you got to call now. But I had no voice. If Childress was dead I wanted to follow him. Just stare at the clock a while longer. The minute hand jerked from black spot to black spot.

—We carried a dead, nothing nigger in that hospital. They opened his shirt and saw a hole in his black chest. The juice run out let's throw this one away. Dead they said. Him and the other playing nothing nigger games. Stab for a nickel, stab for a quarter. The nigger juice runs out. And he got heavier instead of lighter. Snoring like you did when you had asthma. I thought of rocking a baby. In the car with the horn blaring I thought maybe there was man still in me. Maybe the whole situation was one I could handle. I thought about our children and his children. I started crying when I thought of you all looking at us, two grown men, two ghosts in the back seat of a car. Nothing to say to your eyes. Nothing to say to him. Just his head lolling, getting heavier. I wanted to hide in him. I wanted all that was still alive in me to fall off my shoulders and give him back his life. I wanted to be dying in his arms, but all I could do was cry like a baby. And cry because I was crying because I was so pitiful in your eyes and their eyes and had nothing and he had nothing but I was so pitiful because I took his, stole his little bit from him and it was so little so silly in my arms. Where could he be going. Why did I have to be left behind to speak for both of us.

You are standing in a narrow corridor. Your father has stopped speaking. A jerkiness to his words and movements. You cannot see down past the third button on his lime green shirt. You think the shirt is one you received from an anonymous colleague in a grab bag Christmas party at the school. It was too big and you seem to recall disliking the color and giving it to your father. And how grateful he was. You look down the narrow passage, barely open parenthesis between concrete and steel and you see other people carrying on conversations with invisible partners. Studying their faces you can make up stories about the prisoner on the other side of the wall. Faces of the women from the waiting room. Mostly young. Almost all black.

Corridor is loud with voices, reeks of indignation and regret. You stand among them doing your little dance of gestures and words truncated by the partition. All you came for within reach. If your fingers could press through steel.

—I been steady fucking up. I knew but I just kept it up. Now this . . .

Both know he must go on, but the words fade, will not penetrate the glass wall, they return, deflected to the source, silenced within the green shirt.

The lack of privacy becomes obscene. The men content themselves with a simple exchange of information. People are shouting all around them. Wilkerson saw himself listening through a crack in the bricks of another man's house. He could slide along the row of windows, peer into each frame, hear at random the lonelinesses of the trapped men. Would it be to him they were talking. Did it matter who spoke or who listened. Didn't they all talk only to themselves. His stomach tightened. For a moment he was on the other side in a cell standing before a yellow, opaque square. Madness of all the visitors' voices an incoherent jumble tittering through a hole no bigger than a pinprick. On the walls were painted gross caricatures of human mouths and ears, lewd graffiti mocking the prisoner while he sowed his anguish through the one way glass.

—I only talked to the lawyer a few minutes but he sounded encouraging. He'll see you in the morning before the hearing. He said not to worry. He said . . .

Wilkerson could not tell from the eyes whether his father listened or not, if the busy words had reached him or lay in broken pieces littering the concrete floor. He heard rattles and clanks, then footsteps, heavy, methodical, time, death, the executioner, black theatrical footfalls pompously fore-shadowing the end of the interview. The sound seemed to pause, enter and resound within his father's thick walled cell. Nothing more to say. Just stand in the corridor and wait for the stones to stop shuddering, his father's voice to climb from the stillness.

• • •

How is he, is he all right. His mother half whispered the words. Although her voice was barely audible above the groan of static haunting their connection, Wilkerson talked till the end of his dime, pressing the greasy earpiece tight against his cheek, afraid to ask his mother to speak louder, more clearly because he knew he would be asking too much, that her words, feeble as they were, could disintegrate any moment if a straw upset the precarious balance between speaking and sobbing. Wilkerson recalled coal black Reverend Watkins swaying above the makeshift pulpit. When you tells the Lord's truth it fill up our mouth and the back of your throat and telling it hard as a woman birthing a ten pound child of God. Wilkerson promised he would go to her as soon as he could. He lied, said he didn't have another dime. Speaking was like handling the clothing of someone newly, abruptly dead. He had to weigh each word, let it run through his fingers, touch it as he resolved a rationale for discarding or keeping each obsolete possession.

—I'll see you soon, Mama. His last words swallowed by the metallic burping of the machine, lost in the yawn of emptiness ending the connection.

Drinks in an anonymous downtown bar. The subway surface car rattling underground then emerging into the sirupy light of early dusk. His stop was a few blocks beyond the tunnel, aboveground beside the park. Wilkerson couldn't return to his apartment; he picked a bench and sat down to wait for night.

Darkness settling was a plug opened to drain life from

the park. Wilkerson detached himself from the bench and shuffled to a playground in the center of the park. Usually teeming with kids when he passed during the day, now the outlines of sliding board and monkey bars, unbroken by the tumbling forms of children, were skeletal in the fading light. Wilkerson stepped over a low stone wall surrounding the play area. Tanbark inside the compound was soft under his feet. He stroked the metal pipes of the jungle jim. Perhaps made by the same people who made the steel of his father's cell. Wilkerson remembered climbing up a similar contraption, the forbidden kiss, lips pressed against the smooth, money tasting chill of the steel, he always had stolen when his mother looked away.

The sky was light enough to frame the twisting leaves if he stared up through the tops of the trees. In spite of the heat he was almost shivering and the shaking leaves seemed to be part of his skin, black, brittle, hoarsely rustling fifty feet above his head. Someone was pounding on a congo drum. Wilkerson had watched two people: graceful silhouettes, a black man, trim and tall, a white woman in a mottled red and yellow tunic shuttle between the thick tree trunks. They had seemed to move closer together as they walked, finally merging perhaps and swallowed in the same mouthful by the darkness. The drummer wasn't good. The instrument would die on him. Refuse to move another inch beneath his fingers. But he attacked it again and again, half in, half out of a wedge of light suspended from a pole farther down the walk from the bench he occupied. Before the couple disappeared they had stopped beside the drummer and the tall figure had hit the drum a few licks. Obviously he had known what he was doing. Drum quickstepped to the rhythm he had chosen. Sweet and insistent. Music made the sultry night warmer. The man had lost himself in the drum only long enough to make the owner self-conscious, to say you got a long way to go, baby, to catch me and I got a fine bitch besides and here you sit beating your meat like a fool on this drum head.

Easy for Wilkerson to identify with the clumsy apprentice still knocking himself out in fits and starts of shallow rhythm. He watched the frenzy of the drummer's hands, how the light blurred their movement. Dull axe blades hacking at a log. Apart from the drummer the park was empty as far as Wilkerson could see. No dog walkers. No baby strollers. No Frisbees. No thump of basketballs on the asphalt. No yells from the hollow where interminable games of softball or touch football kept the ground slick and brown. Just the two of them. Drummer in the semi-darkness of the bench, Wilkerson surrounded by the low, sinuous stone wall of the kiddies' playground, resting his back against the monkey bars.

Two days before, a community fair had been held in the park and from where he sat he could see trash piled high on the curb. A man, a woman and a child were picking rags from the debris. Wilkerson was too far away to tell what they decided to keep and what they tossed back on the heap, but the woman had accumulated a sizeable stack of rags which she kept draped over one arm as she bent to sort with her free hand.

They were sifting through the rags of the rags of two days before. Good citizens had raked the carnival's remains to the edge of a sidewalk bordering the park. Somebody had tossed the unsaleable second hand clothing on top of the mound of trash. When her arm got too full the woman would pass her load to a man Wilkerson took to be her husband, standing in the shadows. She was wearing shorts and a sleeveless sweater so nearly the entire length of her arms and legs was naked. Her body would be silhouetted in the glare of on-coming traffic when she stretched her arms above her head to assess a garment in the cold glow of a street lamp. She was slim waisted between the fullness of breasts and hips and as she rummaged efficiently through the leavings, Wilkerson's hands went numb compressing the nothing squeezed between them.

Rags flapping when she held them aloft. Wilkerson

thought of proud sails being tested in the wind. The child stopping his forays into the junk to inspect as she inspected, deadly serious, discriminating, knowing what she wanted.

Lights had come on in all the buildings circling the park and they made the few square blocks of grass and trees a world apart, an island of deeper shadows and uncertain footing best avoided until the sun rose again. The booze haze from late afternoon drinks had worn off. Wilkerson felt his senses quicken, night sounds distilled and amplified by the open spaces around him. He could not name the sounds, the trolley did not hiss or glide or shiver or rattle or clank. But the sound found his ears and shimmered in his chest and he heard it fully, richly, had that shock of recognition and discovery he experienced when matching just the right word to the thing he needed to understand. Another trolley car at the opposite end of the street revealed itself to him as metal striking metal, not the banging of the clumsy steel car against the steel rails, but cymbals slightly muted, brought together once on time, precisely pitched, then slowly opening to release the singing lines of force trapped between them. The sound was visible to Wilkerson as it crossed the park, rippling the pool of darkness in which he sat. As the shimmer spread Wilkerson resisted its subtle tug, the death by drowning it suggested so pleasantly.

In the city, there was always a reservoir of noise faintly roaring in the distance. Even in the middle of the night in the empty park Wilkerson had heard the noise of the city's rough breathing as constant as ocean crashing on the sand. The roar could never be silenced. A siren's whine or the surge of a jet would emerge from the gray rumble and dominate while it passed, but such explosions were as close to silence as the city ever came.

As suddenly as it had descended, the clarity passed. Trucks, cars, planes, sirens, trolleys, the wind, the drum, the leaves, his own breathing were again a frustrating muddle. He was alone in the park and nothing made sense. Not the wall, or the bones of the playground equipment or the fumes of alcohol belched up from his empty stomach.

The man hunched over the drum was insane. Not a dedicated apprentice but someone who would always mangle the drum, warp it into his image. Only a madman could allow himself to thump out again and again the same fractured pattern. The man stuttered on the drum, he could not finish a phrase. He would stop and begin again, stop and begin again. He would whip his hands to bloody stumps rapping out the beginning of a measure they could never resolve.

But was the drummer mad because he didn't fear for his hands, his sanity, his life, was he insane because the reality in which he felt himself rooted granted him a serenity beyond anything Wilkerson could imagine? Was insanity torment or when you stopped tormenting yourself about those things you couldn't change?

Wilkerson couldn't ask the drummer how it felt to be insane any more than he could have asked his father how it felt to kill a man. Yet he needed to know. He needed to understand.

The bondsman had promised he would swing a deal. Have his father out by the next day. Tomorrow Wilkerson could speak to his father without the bars intervening. But would they be any closer tomorrow? Could he ask what he needed to know?

He needed to know about Sissie, the woman he was plotting to kill. And all the other deaths. Was killing Sissie unavoidable? Had she forfeited her life? Had Childress forfeited his? And the Sweetman? Was everything an accident? The madman an accident, the white people, the cop? What was the limit of accident? How could you form a plan in a world where all that mattered was accidental, a blind jumble of blind forces?

Who was Sissie? What accidents had made her the plan's first victim?

Steel bars, stone wall, the synthetic floor of the play area yielding under his weight. Wilkerson stood. He was startled by the sudden reversal of scale. The space he occupied had been built for beings half his size. From the ground the shapes had loomed over him larger than life, but now he saw once more how easy it would be to step over the enclosure.

He must have answers. He must seek out the girl.

The urge was on him and he couldn't do a thing about it. If she were going to die, he had to be sure. He must speak to Sissie, he must be sure. And he decided the only time to do it was now when the urge was on him. Tomorrow the first step would be taken. Tomorrow would be too late.

He walked a long time not even considering what route he should take just going generally in the direction he knew would ultimately lead to the dying quarter of the city in which Sissie lived. Walking into darkness no longer fresh. Around him the hot lights of the city swarming against the night. How far would it have to be? One step at a time when you thought about it, steps that you could weigh and count if you had nothing else on your mind, if the urge wasn't so strong that it made you a walking machine and you covered ground clackedy clack shuffle clack on the pavement. And you were getting there without even knowing it. Wilkerson was on a bridge. Below him slash of brown river, above a sky that seemed low and reachable if only the bridge were a little higher, rose a bit more steeply from its concrete moorings at either end of the void. Traffic rattled by, exploding the metal plates of the bridge's surface. Iron and soot and coming apart at the seams. He got as close to the tubular railing as he dared, gazing at lights and dirt and low slung warehouses crowding the banks of the river. If you still noticed, it stank terribly. Engines coughing, smokestacks belching, the bad breath of the filthy river seeping up to surround him. He didn't see any other pedestrians. It would be a good time for the clumsy structure to collapse. Minimal loss of life, a spectacular unseen splash in the dull waters.

On a corner three Negroes waited for a bus. Wilkerson joined them and mounted the high step when they did, found the necessary, exact change and seated himself beside one of the women who had been waiting where he waited. Her face was broad, lemonishly oriental and as he edged closer to her to make sure his left buttock did not mash the man's thigh or the paper sack resting on the man's khaki work pants, he could smell powder or perfume or both escaping from the damp, covered parts of her body. The scent was familiar. The woman in brown at the jail. Perhaps all women used what his mother used. The thought of his mother's small, feminine vanities made him smile. He never conceived of her as simply a woman, so when she bought a new hat or coaxed her hair into the latest fashion or dabbed behind her ears with perfume, the point of these intimacies was lost on him. He would laugh the way he would laugh at a little girl in a grownup's dress and high heels, stolen lipstick painting a bright red tulip that bloomed over half her face. It went even further. As a child he was always looking at females, up dresses, through windows and keyholes, accumulating every secret he could. He couldn't see enough of women's hidden, mysterious places. The impossibly soft, indolent breasts, the bush where all the lines of their bodies rushed together and disappeared behind a patch of darkness. He would hide and wait and scheme and hunger endlessly, yet he always looked away if he thought his mother might carelessly expose some part of her private body to him.

Across the aisle, in the double rank of seats toward the back of the bus, a transistor radio was trying to draw music through the metal hull of the bus. Wilkerson could see only black people on the bus, and gazing out a window he thought his way through the yellow tinged reflection of himself and the other passengers to view the cliched scenario of South Street rolling past. He remembered the fear Littleman had spoken of. How could you allow yourself to see the decay and dying without either killing white people or going mad? Above the rotting, steel boned seats he could see Afros floating, the soft teased hair of his people. The radio was held by a young man in a purple shirt. With its ballooning sleeves, the plunging V of its neck, the delicate pattern of brocade alternating with transparent gauze, the shirt would have been seen as outrageously feminine just a few years before. Wilkerson knew he would not wear it even now, but the boy with the radio was oblivious to compromising overtones, his frilly shirt, his music encroaching on the wheezy silence of the bus's interior were all part of the mood he shared with the huge-eyed girl sitting beside him.

I want to take you higher, higher

Then an oldie but goodie. Time past recovered by the disc jockey as he leafs through his collection of records and retrieves a year, a month, a day, a mood and you hear it coming back just as if it had never been lost, never gone forever. And Wilkerson remembered himself before the mirror, arranging the mandarin collar of his shirt, squeezing a pimple, anxious to be away from his house and family, but dreading the darkness into which he must slip noiselessly, coolly, sliding on in and like some wisp of black warm smoke wrap himself around the soft legs and slow drag and grind and never know and care less whose softness you've trapped on your stiff, straight leg, just thrusting it out and hoping somebody wants to mount it and slip and slide up and down and grind and slow drag cleaved together in the shadowed basement. But always a light in one corner. And sometimes too much light everywhere. These were the nice parties and nice people looking at you and people sitting down and talking and knowing one another so you just can't glide in on the still of the night and disappear in a corner with somebody's soft yearning. Shit no. Too many lights and light, nice people. You find the potato chip bowl and hover over it. Get your hands greasy and your mouth greasy and you can feel the pimples swelling and bursting in the hothouse light. Stuffing your face but the chips won't last forever. You get down to the crumbs and the grease at the bottom of the bowl and you are licking salt from your fingertips because that's all that's left and the faces are watching you and you get uglier and uglier. In the Still of the Night. The Five Satins doing it for you. Mellow oldie. Dusty disc. Blast from the past. And the dee jay's voice is calling everyone brother and sister.

The back doors sigh open and the couple eases on out. Purple shirt sticking to black back, her towering Afro round and full as the sun, their music soft stepping through the double doors of the bus with them.

Wilkerson leaned his forehead against the glass porthole, twisting in his seat to pick out the number of the cross street at which a red light had halted the bus. The man and his lunch bag had gotten off two stops before so Wilkerson had scooted down to the edge of the bench he now shared with the woman. He wondered if the people in the streets noticed his face pressed against the window. While he was still in the bus he was part of another world. A fish in a lighted aquarium passing through. He felt a sudden discomfort. His body was remembering those parties, the painful flaying of his skin, the nightmares of nakedness in a public place, the dream of being on stage, of being an actor who had completely forgotten his lines. He felt nauseated, his stomach fluttered, his heart seemed to crawl into his throat. Yellow light. Smell of grease. The bus's stuttering progress through the snarl of traffic. Would have been faster to walk, but he was weak. He was utterly alone and his body was failing him. There was a bowl at the bottom of his guts and inside it churned the burnt edges of potato chips, thick, sour grease. The street sign outside told him he must escape. Must remove himself from the yellow belly of the lumbering bus. Get out. Find Sissie.

The silver poles that defined the aisle were cool and tight as he trusted his weight to them. His fingers would grip, then he would lurch ahead to the next one, the heavy feebleness below his chest dragged forward by the momentum of each push. For a split second, inching his way through the bus on legs foreign to him, he was Willie Hall, the little man. Wilkerson blinked the recognition away, but could not control the vertigo as he came spinning back to himself, as his muscles trembled, negotiating the light years between another's identity and his own.

The bus pulled away from the curb without him. Except for the dusty, hot fart of exhaust it squeezed off at him, the vehicle looked innocent enough trundling into the darkness, its shape disintegrating, its red lights and yellow light lost in the splash of illumination at a busy intersection farther down the block.

—*You've found the girl, then.*

—*I've found her.*

—*And you think we can . . . we can get to her.*

—*Just like Littleman said. We can get to her. She lives with an old woman and a little girl, Lisa. In one of those abandoned houses on a little street back of South. If the whole damn street wasn't there one morning nobody would give a fuck. Only one who will notice Sissie missing is the cop, her pimp. He'll know soon enough and come looking. Protect his investment.*

—*He'll come to her house.*

—*Close enough for us to get him.*

—*Does she have to die. Can't we hold her until it's over. I mean we can just accuse him. Nothing else would be different.*

—*Everything would be different. We can't change the plan. The whore's as good as dead and you mize well get used to the idea of a little bloodshed. A good chance plenty blood be flowing. After we lynch the cop, I believe they're going to come down on us hard. Hard on man, woman and child. Everything that moves. Not the usual light shit, not head busting and a couple niggers shot resisting arrest, but down harder than they've ever come. It'll be a shooting gallery. And niggers won't be the ones setting the fires. And you worried about keeping one whore alive.*

—*Not really, Saunders. If you pushed me I'd have to admit I'm concerned about myself. My own sanity.*

—*Shit man, ain't you tired going through this same routine. You can talk a thing to death. We're past talking. We're moving. . . .*

Saunders had continued speaking. He outlined the details of the plan, rehearsing once more what had been said a hundred times. Everything did fit, the perfectly wrought components of a deadly steel trap. Littleman was a genius. The *plan was absurdly simple, but faultless. A lynching in black-face. Though Saunders had been speaking, the words were Littleman's. Littleman the poet. It would always be his plan. Wilkerson had listened to Saunders without interruption, vaguely aware of comfort in hearing the words spoken. Perhaps it was the familiarity of the words, the memory of Littleman's voice taking possession of the words though Saunders was speaking. Or, Wilkerson admitted, the words were safe. He could react to the design, the texture, the idea of the plan and ignore the reality of bloodshed, of kidnap, murder and all hell breaking loose when the words became things.*

The sidewalk was crowded and Wilkerson was forced to pay more attention to the night people materializing around him. June just beginning but the weather had already turned hot and muggy. Weather perfect for the plan. People were in the street because they had nowhere else to go. Someone had begun stacking tiers of bricks, walling in the black people beneath a yellow dome that was airtight and superheated like an oven.

In his hospital bed, masked by the inscrutable beard and permanent furrows in his forehead, Littleman would be smiling. He had willed nature into the conspiracy. Three days of heat and humidity goading the black people. Shortening tempers. Forcing the inhabitants of the tightly packed row houses reeling onto the sidewalks seeking any kind of relief or explosion. In their frustration they would strike out at one another. Hadn't Sweetman, his own father, killed?

A few hours and everything would begin. First the woman, then the cop lured into an ambush. Rumors would be easy to spread. The Black Dispatch would have news of the murder the day before the cop was exposed. The rally. The rope. A few more hours and it would all be set in motion. The plan unfurling, inevitable as a flag's stiffness in the high wind.

But the people passed by him as they always had. Each sunken in some alien universe, speaking another language, thinking words and forms indecipherable to him. Did they know how soon all of this would be changing? How suddenly and brutally they would all be thrown together? And they would either survive or die together. And even if some survived, Saunders was right, many, many would perish. Martyrs. Victims. Impossible to determine. Did it matter either way. Certainly not to them. Suppose I stopped one. Got him to listen to me. Explained that I was staking his life on a desperate gamble. What could I tell him he had to gain? Who could I say gave me the right to use him as a forfeit? Consider the look on his face. The shock. A perfect stranger coming out of the night saying I am your brother. I may need your life to save our people. He'd think I was crazy and laugh or smack me down.

Wilkerson tried to picture the street cordoned off. Barricades, rubble, floodlights, the smell of burning buildings, gunsmoke, charred flesh. He heard sirens and helicopters, the rumble of tanks. Where would he be? What would it mean?

And what would it be like if the new day came. He was asking people to be prepared to die. What was he offering to them? Wilkerson knew the question was fair, he had to have an answer. Even if it was an answer he wouldn't give the others, he needed one himself. He saw the puzzled, disappointed faces of whites who had dutifully appeared to support various causes: they asked the question too. Painfully, apprehensively because when they asked it, they acknowledged the chasm separating them from the blacks whose struggle they had come in good faith to join. *What do you people want?*

Wilkerson forced two words from the confusion in his mind. *Peace. Dignity.* But these words made the question rhetorical. They say I want what you want. They demanded that the questioner hold a mirror up to his own life, that he see clearly for an instant the only answer to such a question is everything. Everything. And I want it with the same hunger and ruthlessness you see in yourself.

Wilkerson wanted to shout. It was as if suddenly, for the first time, crystal clear, for the first time, he heard the voices inside the black men around him, the voices identical with the one inside himself he had been listening to so long. Insistent whisper troubling each black skull. *I want more. I want more.* More love, more food, more space, more world. More of everything. In this need they were his brothers and sisters. He was as close to them as he would ever be. He didn't feel they were demanding anything from him. Nobody could give you peace or dignity. Those sensations came from knowing you had in your hands some way to quiet at times the constant clamoring for more. If this power wasn't in your hands, the voice could destroy you, drive you howling mad, run you in circles like a dog chasing his tail.

Where did the power come from? Wilkerson seldom felt it in himself. He had tried with Tanya and tried with the children but the friction of bodies rubbing together or minds rubbing only produced more longing. Instead of being quieted the voice screamed at him. More. More.

Nobody could give you peace or dignity but other men could create conditions which made either quality a luxury inconsistent with survival. When white men held the mirror up to themselves, they were frightened by what they saw. Desolation, need, emptiness. They couldn't face the image of themselves crying for more. So they said, that's not me. I'm not that way. Normal people aren't like that. They said only someone not white, not free, not a man could be so filled with yearning. Black people are the hungry ones, the lusting ones, the half man I thought for a moment was me. And it all fits. Blacks are a species apart. A dangerous species since contact with them may contaminate whites. So the rule is niggers may survive, but if they ask for more, they are criminals. Because the more they want is everything. And wanting everything is chaos.

Pavement was wobbly under his feet. Wilkerson's eyes were downcast, testing the broken terrain before each step. You had to spend so much time on little things. Down here nothing could be depended upon. Phones, sidewalks, furnaces, the meat or eggs you bought at the corner store.

If you spent enough time at the piddling, bullshit tasks,

you could survive. But you were drained of every resource. You had to deny at every turn the voices within you saying life is not this, life is not this constant hassle and haggling over how much of the shit end of the stick you get.

Did he teach this to the children? Did he teach them anything? When he asked them questions or assigned tasks, did he keep in mind how little his proficiency in such routines had served him? Was he goading them, making sure in the little time of their lives spent with him they never lost sight of the everything? Or was he in league with the devil, stealing the most human thing about the children? Crushing the voice which cried for more?

He had reached the street. Just two houses from the corner, if Saunders had been accurate, was where the women lived. The entire block seemed shrouded. Parked cars straddled the curb, blocking half the sidewalk to allow through traffic to pass down the narrow street. Steeply sloping sidewalks, the tilted cars, broken, displaced slabs of stone fronting each doorway. Boards and sheets of tin slapped across window holes in the brick walls, the way the walls themselves seemed to lean heavily toward the pavement, made the street resemble a picture of a cluttered corridor in an immense gray castle, a drawing whose perspective had been rendered imperfectly.

These streets hidden away, draped in gray like crumbling furniture in a deserted house. They were what it was all about. No one was supposed to be living here. No one could live here. But Saunders had said the women would be in one of the houses and Wilkerson believed him. Not only the women, but other black people would be haunting these ruins. And around the corner were shells as desolate as these still teeming with life. Black life consigned to the underbelly of the city. The way it had always been. Would be forever if Littleman was right. The last first and the first last. Only violent reversal could change things. *Grab these fucking rags of buildings and crush them in your fists. Hurl the poison dust into the eyes of your enemies. Blind them, let them taste the shit you are supposed to thrive on. Then scream. Scream like a million trumpets till every grain of sand and stone in every brick in every wall flies apart. Scream on till you forget how to weep and cry and wail the blues. Remember. Remember the war cries of the Arabs. How at night the windows in the European quarter of Algiers rattled as battle screams winged in from the Casbah and the desert.*

Littleman had the words. The images. He would say what had to be said while the cop dangled at the end of the rope. Wilkerson would not have the words. In the moment of truth they would need Littleman. Littleman's breath blue in the flame. The fire spirit hot and rising. The walls tumbling down.

Something moved on the steps in front of the third house. Deep shadows cleaved by the flicker of a match. Wilkerson could make out a little girl sitting on the second stone step of the stoop. One by one she was striking matches and tossing them into the gloom. Little girl in a striped polo shirt, bare legs dangling off the side of the steps. Light. Darkness. Light. Darkness. Her image blinking on and off as if lit by a flashing neon sign. A sudden flare as the paper container fired by the last match kindled at the end of the girl's outstretched arm. In the stillness Wilkerson had heard each match dragged along the match book cover. Now he could hear the girl talking to herself. She spoke in storybook phrases, imitating the sugary tones of an adult reading to a child. Wilkerson could not follow any particular tale. The fragments of mannered sentences, the speeches of animals and elves made no sense because he could not see the pages of the imaginary picture book the child's mind was turning.

> *Once upon a time*
> *The goose drank wine*
> *The monkey chewed tobacco on the street car line*
> *The monkey broke, the street car choke*
> *They all went all to heaven on a billy goat.*

Wilkerson recognized the rhyme. Now the girl's fantasy was touching his. She wasn't reciting what she had read in a glossy fairy tale book. Somebody had sung to her about monkeys and wine and billy goats going to heaven on trolley cars just as the Sweetman had once bounced him to the silly music of the same verses. Open the gates and out come the people.

On this hot night in this dead street she remembered that someone had loved her and sung to her. And Wilkerson remembered. He wanted to put her on his knee and tell her how sweet the singing was. Tell her how sweet and then say baby you sing so nicely but let me sing it again and you listen to how it goes, and how the *street car* broke and the *monkey* choked and they *all* went to heaven. He had never taught anyone a song. He was self-conscious of his own voice so he had never tried to get his pupils to sing. His father could sing. Not just the rhymes and riddles and the nasty toasts about monkeys and Shine he taught his sons before they knew the meaning of the words, but he could sing anything, his voice would tower over the congregation and the choir and lead them richly on. And his mother singing gently, melodiously along with gospel music coming from the radio. All of that within him somewhere. Wilkerson knew it couldn't all be lost. Shouldn't be lost. He would sing to the children. They would sing together.

The girl on the steps had stopped her chanting. But the stillness had also gone. Her face was aimed directly at Wilkerson, denying his privacy as abruptly as he had shattered hers. Guttural clamor of the city filled the space between the corner where he stood and the steps on which she sat. Wilkerson had not come to the street to take the girl on his lap, he was there to kill her mother and even kill the girl if she threatened the plan. He was a stranger lurking under a broken street lamp. He wanted to call out the girl's name. Say *Lisa don't be afraid*. It had to be Lisa, it had to be the house. *Lisa don't be afraid. I mean you no harm.*

He heard desks scraping. Chairs pushed aside, the shrieks and cries of forty-five children scrambling headlong all at once to get out of the door he had just entered. Fear widened their eyes as a million firecrackers exploded at once.

Run, Lisa, run. The night had mottled his hands with

blood. He turned away from the girl's stare, hurrying toward the glitter of South Street.

• • •

Did she love this man. Did she care at all what happened to him. If he lived or died. Tanya faced Thomas Wilkerson across the narrow space of her living room. In the subdued light he was almost handsome or at least something about his face was different enough to make him easy to remember among the thousand faces encountered each day. She noticed how his eyes clung to the shape of his face. Eyes were silly and smouldering at once. Darting around the room and turned inward simultaneously as if the evidence of the room, of Tanya's sleeping presence in it could not quite be digested. She thought his eyes reflected her own mood, the acid, rumbling uncertainty of a body startled from sleep by an upset stomach.

—Tanya I know it's late and I probably have no business barging in here on you. It must be very late and I'm not sure I'm altogether sober. But I had to talk to you.

She wondered if she should make it easy. If she should be annoyed and protest. Give him something he could deal with. Even if it was anger.

—I don't even know how I got here. But I think I knew I was coming here all the time.

When he said *here* she was confused. Did he mean *here,* simply her apartment or did he mean more, something as absolute as the space which enclosed them, both standing as though walls and sofas and chairs had disappeared, a *here* containing the two of them and nothing else in the world. Why did he come out of the darkness demanding those few things she had set aside, why did he need to share the air she breathed.

—I must look a mess. So many things have happened. Like weeks have passed between the morning and now.

He glanced at his watch. Was he acting. Was he trying to

convince himself or convince her. She could tell he had been drinking, was probably still drunk. His movements were too deliberate, too dramatic for the man she knew. Yet the falseness which inflated his gestures and words made him more real to her than he had ever seemed.

—Tanya I . . .

She cut him off by asking him to sit, by sitting herself on the sofa opposite the overstuffed chair he had chosen. Because she had only turned on one table lamp, it was difficult to read the clock over the fake fireplace. The angle of the hands suggested either three or four in the morning. In one corner of the room a stripe of blue light hummed above a fish tank. Although the room was warm the blue light seemed to chill the medium through which fish were darting. Tanya shivered in a sudden pool of icy water which swirled around her ankles. She drew her long, bare legs under her body, draping her green robe over them.

—I had to come.

She wanted to say don't apologize. You're here and the damage is done. I'm wide awake in the middle of the night and you might as well get to the reason you came. But she didn't want to make it hard or make it easy on this man, Thomas Wilkerson. This man who wanted to know whether she loved him or not. As if she could love what he might be or could be or should be, all those invisible men lost behind his eyes. She didn't believe in miracles and had no reason to assume that anything called love would charge the air between them, make his flesh any less foreign, any less demanding. Beneath her in the nest of green robe her legs tingled in the first stages of numbness.

—As soon as I can get myself together. I'll make you some coffee, Thomas. Could you hand me a cigarette. They're on the table, there.

He stood beside her conscious of the whiskey smell clinging to his clothes. It took forever to get a match to work and when one caught and she dipped her face toward his cupped hands he wanted to press the cloud of hair, the fragile bones of her face to his body, but he stepped back so she wouldn't brush against him. He wanted to be clean. Cleaner than he'd ever been. In the soft light it was a child's face she lifted from the match. He thought of the girl on the steps, her tight plaits opening into the bloom of fullness framing Tanya's face.

—My head's about ready to split down the middle, and I have to do something before it just explodes.

Was it theatrics again. His fingers taut against the sides of his skull as if they were all that held the hemispheres together.

—I've got to go and get the guns from Rice.

—Thomas, I don't have the slightest idea of what you're talking about. Who is Rice. What guns.

—It's so strange, even funny, I guess. How close we think we are to a person, how much we think we've shared everything and then it turns out that they don't even know your name.

—I'm not ready for riddles. But I'll make you coffee and drink some myself. Maybe you'll slow down enough so I can understand what you're talking about.

—Always a question of time. Never enough time. So you start in the middle. Then after a while you forget that you started in the middle and you assume everyone has been where you've been and things begin to pile up till one day nobody understands anything you say. Then it's too late to go back. No time to begin at the beginning.

He watched her efficient movements in the bright kitchen. He didn't try to raise his voice so it could reach her above the clatter of drawers opening, pots rattled. He didn't care if the words went beyond his murky corner; for the moment it was enough to mumble them to himself while she dawdled in the sunlight of another planet.

—You want it black and strong don't you.

The question was rhetorical and he didn't answer. He wanted to begin at the beginning. For Tanya he wanted everything to be clear. He wanted an explanation of things which would be just as tangible, just as appropriate as the cup of coffee she was going to bring him.

—You never met my mother and father, did you. You were supposed to come to dinner once.

—Yes. Something came up

—What

—I don't remember.

—Do you remember starting out. Do you remember going into their building and walking up the stairs. Do you remember a shadow in the hallway.

His voice had dropped again. If someone had been sitting on his knee, the person would have to lean toward him, straining even at that distance to pick up what he said.

Wilkerson recalled that March day thousands of years before. They had been walking in the park. The chill. The sheets of wind. Tangles of wire thin branches hazy in a mist of brilliant sunshine. He heard the tap of Littleman's cane. Saunders' loud talking and laughing mood. Off the concrete path, rags of snow littered the open spaces between black tree trunks. Willie and Saunders had been taking turns irritating one another, and Saunders' volubility was a calculated response designed to grate against the tender skin of Willie Hall's silence.

Dropping then firing cowboy style from the hip as he rose, Saunders sent a stone skipping down the pavement toward a cluster of scraggly birds bobbing at bits of greasy paper which scratched along the frozen earth. The pigeons scattered in squealy panic, the deep sigh of their flight emptying the space over Wilkerson's head. He wanted to ask Saunders why he did it. But the birds were gone, the stone gone, the blue sky had swallowed the weary clutter of wings.

Saunders could kill. The part of him which was assassin as visible to Wilkerson as it had been to Willie Hall. No reason to suppose Willie Hall ever was mistaken. Suppose Saunders' hands began to shake. The safeguard in this eventuality was Littleman's knowledge of the antagonism between the conspirators. The presence of Wilkerson a perpetual goad to

Saunders. Wilkerson constanty there to remind Saunders of the contempt he could not bear to feel for himself, of anger at those weaknesses in the teacher, which in himself would distort the symmetry of the plan. The essential ruthlessness of maneuver they would exercise against each other since each could see externalized that image of himself he struggled to destroy. All the while this infighting cemented the plan, forwarded it. Their incestuous spite a harmony in the larger rhythm of Littleman's conception.

But holes would open. Like that almost spring day in the park when ice cracked under their feet and water from the shallow depressions in the pavement darkened the sides of their shoes. You are unaware of your feet till they begin slipping out of control on the slickness beneath you. You shift your weight partially and anticipate a moment of queasy vertigo, an instant hanging in space, asking a million questions before your bones slam into the icy concrete. You hear Littleman's cane tapping the ground. Saunders tittering, the disgruntled birds behind you clucking, landing heavy with a sound like bulky overcoats flapping in the wind.

—I missed the motherfuckas. Aimed at a big, fat, gray bellied one. Way he was strutting around with his little short-legged self all puffed out sorta reminded me of somebody.

Half of the thick twig shot into the air, rising lazily end over end, then plummeting to the hard earth, a shudder and it rolls to a stop a few feet from the path. The force of the cane whipped down had snapped the dead branch, had exploded half of the wood higher than a man's head. The piece that remained on the ground quivered.

—It's not your time today. Thank whatever gods you pray to Saunders for giving you a little more time. Thank this little man and his little walking stick for satisfying themselves on that piece of wood. I give you today. I give you a little more time. Willie Hall regained his stride with a half shuffle and a hurtling shrug of his shoulders. He was again in step with the other two. Eyes glazed like a blind man, tapping the rod before him.

Saunders had gone too far, but Littleman allowed him to return, snapping wood instead of bone with the cane. Finally the plan had become more real than the conspirators. Littleman would not kill the plan.

And they walked the river of concrete meandering through the frozen earth, their voices icy, steam breath propelling words into the chill air. The sound inhuman as it ricocheted from the cold, stiffened trees and died in heaps around them. Wilkerson's eyes followed the bare limbs as they stretched, a delta of black tributaries stark against the steely blue. He could not call the vastness sky. It was just up. The sky had fallen, had sunk below the snow blotted ground. What he saw above was the underbelly of some immensity that dwarfed the sky. A membrane incredibly thin and blue. Vulnerable to a pinprick yet so high his imagination stretching to its limits had no more chance than the naked branches of scratching at the blue.

Wilkerson did not have to speak. Soon only Littleman's words trailed behind them, Saunders' garrulousness curbed since the cane slashed down, Saunders escaping into some world of his own, Wilkerson almost startled to see Saunders manshape beside him, the body of Saunders a hallucination since from this casually striding shell the guts and heart and brain had so palpably risen after the shattering blow.

Littleman's words enclosed in frosted bubbles, the bubbles attenuated. Oval, elipsoid, cartoon banners flapping with clumsy messages child lettered in the ballons tethered to his lips. His full beard stiff in the cold. Like if you wrapped your fists around it, the deep, cold curls would crumble, the texture of dry leaves going to dust between your hands. The man's eyes glistening, feeding on the blue, swallowing what they could not abide. He was shouting at the trees, the heavens, the snow, the last red coals in his body that he fanned by his brisk pace, the slipstream of chattered speech.

They stood beside a brown river. Mud brown, a desert the wind had whipped into infinite, identical dunes each trapping light in shredded quartz and mica flaking the sculpted sand.

Willie Hall had brought them to the edge. He gestured now, the cane a violent baton in the frenetic weave of his music. As far as Saunders could see, up and down and across the river from their windswept vantage point, the three men were alone in the desolate park. Perhaps the battle had already been fought, a warp in time had hurled them forward to the aftermath of the plan, the city reduced to knee high ruins around them, the blitzed trees and three shivering human shapes all of life that remained. Empty trees, empty water, the searing emptiness of blue either so hot or frozen the flesh would wither at a touch. Willie's broad back, the crushing threat in the slope of his shoulders, the slender rod, gilded silver in the sunlight. Words still flung at them like spit driven backward by the wind. The man seemed to be rising from a hole in the earth. The proportions of his torso could not be carried by the incongruous legs. Like a geyser of muscle and bone he was emerging, the pieces of a god returning after he had been torn apart and sowed in the water during a rite of fall. But the water had diminished the legs, frog's legs tucked into the trunk of a bear. The magicians had not understood the spell; the priestess who rent his flesh had been polluted. And now, prematurely risen, grotesquely risen, lured from his deep rest by the spring brilliance of the sky, the god curses the forces which crippled him.

Let it all come. Let it hang out Littleman.

Wilkerson would not have been shocked if the speaker began to flog the icy water with his cane. He would not have tried to stop the man if he plunged into the brown river. He would not have been dismayed if the three twig legs suspended Willie Hall upon the pitted surface of the water as he skated across like a delicate thread legged insect.

And so the plan seemed to roll off the trembling river and quaver through the voice of the deformed man whose eyes stared at the stark trees lining the far bank, whose back remained turned to Saunders and Wilkerson, whose message at last entered them with the shiver of life passing from the body.

When they resumed walking the transference had been complete. It was necessary to talk of smaller and smaller things. For egos to return and strike out or be singed, for the flesh to complain about the wind and temperature. It was a barren park and they had prematurely taken a spring stroll. Three ordinary men bitching about the hawk, engaging in a desultory round of the dozens, getting irritated at one another because no one could confront the common enemy of bitter weather. The plan within, fresh, untouchable already competing for the meager fire stored in the bodies' caves.

From that day growing like a fetus inside my guts. Wilkerson was annoyed at himself for the banality of the metaphor. He was childless, had created no art, yet he blandly appropriated the truth of these acts to extenuate his involvement with Littleman's plot. To call it a plot instead of a plan. Lynching/Murder. Steal/Liberate. Civilize/Enslave. Father/Fornicator. Who would do the naming?

Littleman prostrate, his beard soaked in the filthy water stagnant near the shore, the cane held in both veiny fists lashing the rust colored river. His wand buried deeper and deeper as he slithers into the ooze, the iron water shuddering closed after each blow.

The word was Lynch. Lynch a white cop. If it is done according to plan the new day must surely follow. The new dispensation, phoenix rising from the ashes of the old. But we must lay the corpse to rest. *Burn the scabby motherfucker in the city dump. Let the crows pick out its eyes. Then up in smoke.* It's got to come. It's got to come. Just waiting for somebody to crack the door. To jerk the little pinky from the hole in the dike. It's got to come.

The stone scudded along the cracked gray path. A spray of inky water at one bounce, the hiss of a sudden white veined bruise in a patch of dark ice at a second thudding collision. The final rattling slide as it lands in the midst of the birds. Stink of their dingy feathers, they hobble into the sky and for a moment you are under the stale tent of an unclean woman's billowy skirt as the pigeons pass over. You see tracks in the snow. Skeletal arrowheads printed in powdery whiteness. Stylized geometric vaginas. Put a circle around the bisected V and they are peace signs.

Yet was it real that day. Was it ever real that day. The ritual at the brown river's edge. Littleman's crystalline, garbled sermon. The lynched cop swaying from the bare gallows limbs of the thousand trees surrounding us. The revelation of a single smoky streak of cloud like the disintegrating exhaust of some missile too fast and clean to be seen cutting through the blue.

If I had laughed and walked away. If Saunders lay staring at blue emptiness, his head bashed open, steam curling from his split skull. If I had pushed the iron legged man into the beckoning water.

Wilkerson surveyed the room in which he was sitting. Tanya's room. He stretched out his hands, turning them slowly, gingerly, as if too sudden a recognition could exacerbate whatever damage or familiarity he sought. These were not his father's hands. These were not words. Words could work no miracles with these shit brown hands of a school teacher. Pale, still winter yellowed hands.

He saw the hand of Andrea Palmer.

He saw the hand of Saunders curl around the plump pigeon's throat.

She said: I saw Mr. Wilkerson feeling her butt. I saw them bumping butts in that alley behind the school.

She said: His daddy done killed a man.

A stranger. Her bony two year old's arm slipped into the air. And she rose with it, tumbling head over heels, showing a wet spot on her dirty cotton drawers, spinning, in the unfamiliar medium, a fish swimming on the sand, gasping, bleeding at its frantic gills, Andrea Palmer falling after her hand, her lost bony arm.

—Who is Rice. And what guns were you talking about, have some of your kids gotten into trouble.

—No, not the kids this time. Rice is a fellow I know. A guy I've been involved with for quite a while now. But I don't really know much about him. I don't think anybody does. At least none of us. He's strange. But no stranger than the rest of us. Rice is somebody he thought he could use. A neutral person. Safe inconspicuous. No real life or thoughts of his own so he thought he could program him like you do a machine.

Tanya stood in the doorway between kitchen and living room, a steaming mug of coffee in each of her hands. Like wind or water the stronger light from the kitchen outlined her body inside the long robe. Though he had been talking to someone and the voice floating back to him from the kitchen had to belong to somebody, the figure of Tanya, framed in the doorway, elegant, slender, seemed suddenly arbitrary, an unexpected intrusion on his solitude.

–Who was programming this Rice.

–I should have said cultivating. Because that's what Littleman did to us all. He made me grow. But grow in a special way. He recognized what was already there, then made those things become what he needed. What the plan needed. Littleman is the one. I don't know why I mentioned Rice first. Why I began with Rice. Littleman did the cultivating, the programming. The plan is his. He is the reason Rice has the guns.

She was sitting again. Receding again. Why had he felt threatened by her reappearance. He knew it was coming. He was in her apartment. She had gone into the kitchen to fix him coffee. Now curled in the same rumpled pillows of the sofa she was raising the cup to her lips and though she was silent, her eyes questioned him through the veil of steam. Familiar eyes. Familiar patience and self-possession. She wouldn't interrogate him anymore, wouldn't ask what guns or who is Littleman. She would be cool. Would wait. Her lips nibbled at the edge of the cup, testing, tentative.

His smoking mug sat on a table beside him. He wouldn't even touch it until he was sure the coffee was only lukewarm. Wilkerson wondered why her lips didn't recoil from contact with the hot liquid. He recalled something he had read about woman and pain. About tolerances and thresholds and biological superiority.

—You see we needed someplace to hide the cop. Just overnight really, or at most a day and a night. But the place had to be inconspicuous. It couldn't be in a black neighborhood and for obvious reasons we couldn't have a white man working with us. So Littleman found Rice or Rice found Littleman or maybe Littleman made up Rice, which isn't as silly as it might sound. Anyway the plan needed a safe place to keep the cop after we had kidnapped him and Rice is a janitor, has his own apartment in the basement of the building where he works. Nobody lives in his building but old white ladies and men. Half of them don't even go outdoors anymore according to Rice. It's the last place in the city anyone looking for guns or missing cops would come. Rice said most of the tenants have forgotten he's in the basement. He said the owner told him flat out to stay out of people's way. Said the tenants didn't need to be reminded that he lived in the same building even if he was the janitor.

—So the shotgun's there and the two hand guns. A forty-five and a smaller pistol you can carry concealed in a pocket. We didn't need any more firepower. One of the beauties of the plan. Each weapon has a specific function. The shotgun was more of a prop than anything else. Use it to intimidate the cop while we hold him. The shotgun and the pills Saunders got would do the trick. Of course there was the blackjack, sack and the rope. And the knife. We had to have those things. They were necessary. After she was dead, after Saunders had killed her as quickly, painlessly as he could, someone would have to use the knife. She would be dead, and you only die once, and if the body had to be marked up for effect it just had to be that way. Too late to be squeamish. He said either you or somebody else cuts up all the meat you eat. He said somebody kills it and cuts it up. Dead meat is dead meat. The first time he said that I thought he was just trying to show me how tough he was. But he meant it. He could be that cold. He was teaching me to be the same way. One dead body. What would a few strokes of a knife in its lifeless flesh mean. So we had a knife and somebody would have to do it.

He hadn't meant to tell it this way. She was sitting up straight now. Staring. He couldn't tell what was in her eyes. Not fear, he was certain. And oddly enough it wasn't shock. He had said too much and too little. It was as if a long, complicated nightmare had made him scream in his sleep and the scream had awakened someone sleeping beside him.

–I'm sorry, Tanya. You must think I'm crazy or sick or drunk. Coming in here out of nowhere. Unloading my morbid fantasies on you. Everything is tangled, connected. Images and emotions I have been living with too long. We decided we had to change things. I mean the big picture. Not a job here or a public office there, not one or two black faces floating to the top but change everything. Fundamentally. And obviously that means violence. Supreme violence. Nobody gives up power without a fight. Ruling and a sense of superiority get in the blood. You have to bleed them out. You have to turn things upside down. Topsy-turvy. You've read Fanon. He says it well. You know what I mean.

–So all of that was at stake. Everything at stake. You, me, the kids at school. My mother and father, everything. We did the only thing we could. Decided on a way to prepare a catalyst. Stage an event so traumatically symbolic that things could never be the same afterwards. Lynch a white cop. Lynch one in broad daylight and say to white people what they have been saying to us for so long.

–Littleman is a genius. A genius because the obvious is always clear to him. He has a way of seeing, a simple, uncluttered way. He knows where to begin. He sees the simple way things begin. How the rules which lead to hopeless complications are themselves quite simple. He put the plan together. Or rather he saw the plan sitting in the middle of the chaos, sitting like a flower waiting to be plucked. He taught me to see some of what he saw. I learned slowly. Very slowly and for that reason I can't expect you to grasp much of what I'm saying now. Although I believe you would have been a quicker pupil, a better disciple, one who wouldn't have failed at the last minute.

—Tomorrow. No, not tomorrow. Just a few hours now, Littleman had prepared us to act. The woman, Sissie, was to be murdered. By the next day or so the cop would be our prisoner. On the fifth day the rally. You've probably seen the posters already. One on the school bulletin board. The usual thing, a speaker coming to tell us how to be black, proud and free. But this time an extra added attraction. Sissie's murder will be on everybody's mind. Rumors circulating. Hopefully a picture of her bloody body in the Black Dispatch. A hot day and feelings running high. The murderer produced at the rally, a white butcher pig. The rope, the sack, that's it. No place to go after that. Everything's up front.

—It's insane. If there ever was such a plan, it was nonsense and anybody who'd see it otherwise is insane. Finish your coffee and you can have the couch to sleep on if you wish. I don't know what happened tonight or who you've been talking to but what you're saying is ugly and sick. I can still salvage a few hours of sleep. I think it would be best if you did the same.

She is standing. A green blur in the shadowed room. He puts out his hand; his fingers toy momentarily with the ten feet of empty space between them and the woman.

—Dammit.

He follows her eyes to the floor where she snatches her bare toes back from the mug they have overturned.

—I'm groggy. I'm knocking things down.

From the mouth of the mug a broad, dark tongue seems to lap at the carpet. Wilkerson's hand swings back to the arm of the chair. The fish light has been humming all the time, but now he hears it.

—The funny thing is that you're absolutely wrong. And I'm one of only four people on this earth who know how wrong you are. But I'm the one who is going to make you think you're right. And anyone else who might be interested think you're right. Because I have to stop it. I have to sabotage the plan. Get the guns from Rice.

—I'm not going to clean this mess up now. Just be careful of the damp spot. Stay in the chair if you like or use the sofa. Ignore the alarm if you're not going to school tomorrow, I need it. Goodnight.

—I won't be here in the morning. I'm going to get the guns from Rice.

—Tom. Why don't you . . . shit, now . . . I'm tired. Rice and guns and Littleman and you're going to lynch somebody tonight too, I suppose. I'm sorry I have to miss it all. But don't let that bother you. You don't have to go, but if you're going, please do it now so I can put the damn chains across the door.

—Tanya, I'm sorry I got you up, I know how lame that sounds but I'm sorry. They bumped awkwardly at the door. Wilkerson hesitant, not knowing where to place his hands, how much intimacy could be squandered on the moment, how intentional the brush of her shoulder into his chest had been. The partially closed door was between them, a shield obscuring half her body when he kissed her. Flesh of her shoulder warm and solid under his fingers as one arm venturing back through the door frame rested on her body. He fluffed the hair at the nape of her neck, caressed the long bones of her arm. Image of her naked in the light sweeping from the kitchen warmed Wilkerson again. When she said stay, rest, perhaps she meant something else. Perhaps she would sleep in his arms and in the morning the world forget them both. She would help him strip the stinking clothes from his body. She would stand beside him while a hot, hot shower drenched their skin. The night chain rattled in her hands. Rattled again muted by the gray door as he stood in the empty corridor.

• • •

Rice could not sleep. Insomnia was nothing new to him. Many hot summer nights he would toss fitfully, brewing his sweat into a poison he shrank from. He was familiar with his body's flops and twitches, the exhausting search for some disposition of his limbs that would allow sleep to settle over him. But the last week had been worse than the worst nights he could remember. Sleep simply didn't exist. Instead a teasing state of semi-consciousness would let him drift off into a dream of sleep which lasted only long enough to remind him how sweet the real thing could be. The weight of the building seemed to press down on him. The Terrace Apartments, a huge square box, would teeter unsteadily on his shoulders. The building became an extension of his body, a head he could peer into, the Terrace Apartments without its roof like an architect's model to display the floor plan. His brain was honeycombed with thousands of cubicles, each in the shape of a miniature apartment. And the walls were white. A network of cold, pulsing rooms, countless white rooms absolutely empty except for the scurrying roaches. In and out of the barren rooms. The insects were gigantic. Three or four would fill one of the squares. Rice remembered mornings as a child when his mother lit the gas oven to take the chill out of the kitchen and the sudden heat would panic the insects who had gathered overnight to feast on grease stains and scraps of food.

Roaches crawling in and out of the white rooms. He wanted to smash them. With his hands, his feet, a rolled newspaper. They would pop and crunch. His mother was almost dancing. Her feet moved so fast, tapping, grinding. Her meaty arms flailing at the top of the stove, an old shoe in her hand murdering roaches, knocking the crusty burners from their moorings. She would squeal while she did it. Hating them. Hating the fury which set her frantically in motion.

But Rice didn't dare hit the roaches who made a playground of the white rooms. Their cracked, glossy shells would litter the immaculate chambers. Their black insides would stain the ceilings and floors, drip down the walls. Yet even if he could bring himself to strike at them, nothing would happen. He could see inside his skull, he could feel it wobble or grit his teeth when the pressure was unbearable. Beyond this he was powerless. He couldn't change anything, could only peep through the transparent bone and watch the roaches scramble in and out.

Time was always the middle of the night. In the darkness, alone, the plan occupied his thoughts. The other conspirators preyed on him with schemes and threats, hovering around his bed the way they all had leaned over Littleman in the hospital. Some nights Rice feared he was in fact a patient in an immense asylum. His eyes would pop open from a moment's doze and he would sense the sweaty weight of restraining straps around his chest, arms and legs. For as long as a minute he would not stir, afraid to test the reality of the bonds. Then with all the blood in his body filling his head and the cords of his neck, he would burst upright into a sitting position, simultaneously thrashing both legs with the fury of a drowning man.

They came to him lying, conniving. He was their fool they thought, a weakling each could exploit. But they trusted him with the guns. How many times had he gone down on his knees and pulled the weapons from beneath his bed. The box had once held fluorescent lamps, the thick buzzing kind which were cocooned in pink tubes lining the foyer of the Terrace Apartments. Cold guns smelling of grease. Rice knew more than they thought he knew. How the metal pieces glide apart and snap together. The glint of steel. The mirror finish after you rub and rub with soft cloth. He knew the weight of the shotgun, the yawning void of its barrel. He had stroked, lubricated, penetrated to the innermost chambers of the pistol. During sleepless nights the hard, cold steel comforted him. Like a miser counting his gold in the dark, Rice would toy with the revolver, smiling to himself as he clicked bullets into the cylinder.

They had trusted him with the weapons and that meant he had the upper hand. The plan could not begin without the power he had hidden under his bed. Rice wondered how the others could be so naive. Treating him like a dog while placing their fate and the fate of the plan in his hands.

Rice stood naked in the black room farting once long and loud as if to test his reality against the cloying presence of the nightmare from which he was trying to awaken. With his palm he mopped sweat from his face then tentatively he patted the top of his skull. It was still there. Bushy covering, the reassuring bone. Between his legs felt steamy. Perhaps he would sit in the tub. Try to read or polish the delicate handle of the pistol.

When the thumping began, he dropped to the floor, the bed between himself and the disturbance at the door. He lay as flat as he could, fingers pressing into the linoleum as if they could dig a deeper pouch to hide his body.

Someone was still banging on the door. Rice's hand snaked into the deeper blackness beneath the bed. It seemed to move independently. It was his arm and it was resolved to do something but Rice could only watch, naked and quivering in a heap on the floor.

Someone called his name. Loud whisper through the door, as if that made any difference after all the pounding. His name. Rice. Rice. Rice.

And then another name. Wilkerson. Other hissing words then Wilkerson again.

Dark. But his fingers had often worked in the darkness, nimbly undressing the weapons. He'd better use the big one. They might all be out there.

He aimed where he thought the center of the door should be then made a fiery shambles of the darkness as he pulled the trigger.

● ● ●

Saunders parked four blocks from Stanley's. The alarm had jarred him awake, a heavy hand unexpectedly from the darkness striking him at the base of his neck. The morning of the first day. The rendezvous with Wilco at Stanley's. The first day of a new world. He would not be late. Saunders could have driven farther down the street, taken a chance on finding an open spot nearer Stanley's but he needed to get out of the automobile, wanted to walk on his own two feet down the strip blocks. Not homesickness, he had no desire for the street to claim him once more, to share its heart and breath like the old man who wheeled a push broom and two upright aluminum trash cans nestled in a flat bed wooden cart down the sidewalk. He didn't want to be the poster plastered wood or steel mesh fronting the shops, he could not station himself at a corner or sit rigid in the naked second story windows above the storefronts and bars. He would never return, feared returning to the dead end street. Although he knew nothing had changed, he remained curious. He would flirt with the street, play games like those he did with a woman whose body no longer aroused him.

The day shift was settling in. White men with pockets full of keys were unlocking their merchandise. Saunders was disdainful of the fear in their eyes. Perhaps it was more obvious now, the sense of danger they felt, the desperate, split second searching of each black face, the meticulous weighing, like they measured out their fish and beans or gauged the value of pawned rings and watches, the calculation of profit or trouble contained in the way a black passerby walked, the way he wore his hair, where he held his hands, their stares or glares or utter disregard of the white glance momentarily settling upon them. Maybe the shopkeepers knew it was just a matter of time before everything changed. Half of the plate glass windows were bandaged or splinted. At regular intervals only glass strewn, gutted shells remained. Some storefronts were transitional. Neither ravaged with sky pouring through the roofless beams and window sockets nor preserved for business another day behind the sliding steel gates, but shadowed, impenetrable interiors, trash heaped up to the cracked gray window panes, unidentifiable clutter stretching backward into the obscurity. Abandoned to the derelicts in long patched overcoats who would emerge suddenly, blinking, sun blind from their dim nests. Later in these same caves, huddled around flashlights or lanterns, men would shoot crap throughout the night, the rattle of bones, the rhythmic incantations of the gamblers broken only by loud snores from winos sleeping at the periphery of the circle of light.

Nothing had changed, but could he enter the doorless frame, take his place inconspicuously among the gamblers in the yellow clearing surrounded by rubble, and if the dice weren't falling the way he sang them to fall would he be able to edge from the circle and become one of the huddled, oblivious mounds sleeping through the action, the night, the sunlight that could crawl no farther into the building than the sleepers willed. Could he throw the few pennies he had left into somebody's funky hat and drink the salvation wine till his wits were together enough, till he was warm and replenished, calm enough to brush himself off, prey the streets hoping some hustle brought him a stake and the stake made him welcome again squatting on one knee, dice uncurling from his fingers to stare blandly at the players in the circle, pocked skulls, black on white indifference glowing up at the gamblers, magic stare that like a magnet snatched money or scattered the pile of coins and bills building beside it.

Saunders watched three quarters of a man struggling to arrange his womanish hips on the inside window ledge of a pawn shop. Window was gaudy with rings, watches, radios, silver. The figure's head was cut off by the blackened top of the window which was background to the large gold letters of the proprietor's name. The man, white shirted, was placing on a prominent felt lined shelf a row of particularly precious items which he removed from a drawstring pouch attached to his waist. These treasures carried home each night were not to be entrusted to the steel gate, now partially collapsed, which like a jailor he had unlocked to enter his place of business. As the truncated body maneuvered awkwardly but efficiently within the gleaming window Saunders' first thought was of the vulnerability of the broad backside wobbled at the public. Then he noticed the dog, a shaggy Irish setter, too muscular and deep chested, too blunt in the jaw and forehead to be purebred, but red and formidable stretched across the door of the pawn shop.

Fish stink seeped from a window in which bloody pigs' feet daintly stretched on a couch of ice.

Fish stare, merchant stare, the eyes of the short sullen woman standing in a doorway with her mongoloid child. Two boys holding hands emerge from an entranceway squeezed between the whitewashed glass of a storefront church and a billboard plastered candy store. They are dressed in coats and hats, identical in their shabbiness. The smaller boy is sobbing as his feet touch the pavement. He jerks away from the hand of his brother, stomping forward a few heavy footed, exaggerated strides, then twisting, his face streaked with tears and snot and grime from fingers rubbed into his eyes, screaming at the vacant mask of the older boy's face, at the littered recess that had tumbled them into the street.

A cop, dressed for the moon in helmet, boots and airtight leather, glides silent as an aphid along the curb tagging the illegally parked cars and vans. Saunders had noticed his motorcycle parked farther up the block. The machine had seemed more alive without its rider. It sat serene, completed, attentive to the crackling voice that addressed it over a two way radio.

Men clustered on a corner waiting for a day's work. They would march, unchained coffles to the seedy pickup trucks that stopped at the curb. A driver would crack his window and some of the men would hear their names called, others with strong looking backs or neat work clothes or sturdy shoes would be pointed at and the bidder would shout out a price. Each morning a few would be transported to jobs around the city while the majority lingered, as content in that corner limbo as any other, glad for the company of others who must sit and wait. The groups would be swelled by passersby, by barflies and hustlers who knew that even here among the jobless a number would be played, a drink promised or shared. Some would fade into the bars or barbershops when they knew the morning trickle of trucks had ended. Saunders recognized the fat, black face of Sugar moving among the men outside Stanley's. Fat, black Sugar, every strand of shiny reddish brown hair sleeked smoothly into place in the high pompadour atop his head. Slick Sugar who made these out of work drones his special hustle. Loaning money, taking their numbers on credit, finding them jobs for a cut of the earnings. He was as together as he had always been, shuttling through the crowd on the sidewalk, his tangerine bell bottoms elegantly lapping the filthy pavement. Shugs got it. Shugs got it today. Saunders recalled the legends, the half truths and lies that clustered around the enormous black man. His connections with the dagos. The stable of white whores he kept in the city's most elegant apartment building, the cars no one ever saw because he loved to strut along the streets with the people. Shugs humping woman, man, boy anything big enough to shake its tail feathers at him, Shugs with a habit so big he had to keep fifty junkies busy in the streets dealing his shit.

Sweet Sugar would recognize Saunders immediately but never say a word. Shugs had lasted because he knew when to speak, who to notice, who to fat mouth, and who to pass without a word. Saunders had learned from Sugar. At a distance or listening to the big man's words as he had been favored with a petty errand to run for the king. King Sugar. As far as Saunders had ever wanted to go.

Sugar's laugh rolled from his belly, was chopped into deep explosive chunks by his white teeth. The laughter would prod the men, shame them. The sound would shrink them, regale them with its bottomless assurance, its coaxing roar. They must join him or they would be the object of the laughter. They must mount his laughter and let it carry them indoors to a bar stool, or to something stronger in the alley, anywhere but where they stood empty handed silently waiting.

Saunders remembered how they had laughed when his feet went out from under him, and the hot, sharp cinders had rushed up to bite his skin. Sugar's laugh rolling over him. Pressing his face into the track as the feet of the other runners pounded past him. The big one. The race he had to win. Fear was being trapped, being exposed. The laughter was always there waiting to pounce on you. Not thick lipped, grinning teethed nigger laughter, not the dozens and the cheap tricks they could play on one another but the deep, ridiculing guffaw of Sugar, white as he was black, Sugar who squeezed as tight as he wanted all the black bodies he held in the palm of his hand. Whiteman's laughter that echoes through these streets like the crack of a whip behind a mule's ear.

The sound rang in Saunders' ears, stung him though he passed through an orange door and stood inside Stanley's. Stanley owned the bar and could inscribe his name in three foot orange letters along one side of his corner location, but inside his establishment he was Fats. Fats whose diabetes had prevented him from sampling his own whiskey for at least the ten years Saunders had frequented the bar.

–Fats you're not thinking about your diet.

–Oh, I'm thinking about it all right, honey. Doing plenty thinking. In the dim light Fats' puffy shape was silhouetted against the orange, purple glow of the jukebox at the far end of the bar. His legs were lost in the blackness of the bar's overhang so that to Saunders entering from the street the image of his torso seemed like a stack of truck tires crowned by a dark pumpkin wearing a stingy brim hat.

–Doing plenty thinking, all right.

–But you gonna have your coffee and rolls anyhow.

–I told that doctor I got to have some things.

–Bread and jelly and butter and cream first thing in the morning. You eat it now and you know you'll be complaining by tomorrow.

–I ain't gon wait till tomorrow. I start complaining now.

–You'll be right up there in the hospital again, eating stuff like this. They don't serve rolls and cream in there.

–You sure right, child. They don't be thinking about giving a man his rolls and coffee.

Both Fats and the baby faced woman serving him spoke slowly, softly, in no hurry to finish the ritual. Her arms were plump but sensuously rounded and the movements of her shoulders and hands were fluid as she set out cup and saucers and silverware that clattered delicately on the bar before the lumpish man.

Stanley in daylight the color of his coffee after he drowns it under a flood of thick cream. Easy to tell the woman behind the bar belonged to him. When balancing his bulk on the bar stool became too tiring, Stanley would slide from his perch, wheezing as he undraped his flesh and shuffled with its burden to the last booth against the wall. It was specially made, extra space had been left between table and the high backed seat of the booth to make room for the proprietor's girth. He would settle in the booth for hours at a time. Sleep and eat there while the life of the bar flowed around him.

> *My Daddy's dead*
> *My Momma's cross the sea*
> *I ain't got no body*
> *To speak nar word for me*

Saunders could not find Wilkerson's face in the purplish haze. The chickenshit nigger getting scared. Only a few shadows seemed alive in the muted light, darkened, one dimensional. Calling me this last minute. Saunders goddamned Wilkerson, the pee, smoke funk of the coffin shaped interior, the fat wheezing man and the string of soft, brown women he paid to tend his pleasures. Fats was a dead man already. Leaking out of his rubbery skin. Door marked *Ladies* wide open, a slop bucket holding it back against a wall. Saunders would have preferred taking a few more steps, steps which would bring him to a booth farther from the entrance, just beyond the edge of the bar but still two booths away from Fats' custom stall. They would need privacy. Yet moving toward the back of the bar like wading into a sewer. The smell of clogged toilets and disinfectant made him wince as he slid into the padded seat closest to him. Foul goddamn place. Needed the drink he had promised himself he wouldn't take. Why not. One or two or ten. He would be ready when it came time to do his part.

—Ain't nobody serving tables yet, my man. What can I do you for.

Saunders ordered from the bartender and watched the double shot glass of scotch splash over the bed of ice cubes in the squat tumbler.

—You sit still, baby.

She stood before him smiling. Her voice had smiled, hurrying from the end of the bar. He knew how she would have switched from behind the counter. A wide arc, hips flourishing in tow the way trailer trucks negotiate twisting mountain roads.

—I be through with Fats. He say serve my customers, now. You call me next time you ready, baby. The scent of powder, of hair freshly pressed, of elbows and ears daubed with unsubtle sweetness interrupted the stale wind from the exposed toilet as she leaned across the table into the recess where Saunders had melted. Plump breasts, long curling lashes, full lips handling words caressingly, sure of themselves around a man. Woman that made him think of slow walking, slow talking, easy access to sun, to sleep, to food and love. A southern woman. Alabama, Mississippi, Louisiana even if she ain't never been off the avenue. She would leave Fats one day and the next man could have her and believe she never been touched, waiting for him all the time.

He watched her full hips playfully switch in the path between booths and bar stools. She picked her way pretending there was barely room for her to pass, avoiding imaginary obstacles with the weave of her body down the aisle. Saunders wondered how many times a day some hand would steal from the stalls to tap her fully-packed as it teased by. The distraction was momentary. Wilco was late. Later each minute. Unexcusably sloppy. Saunders felt the bitter scotch foraging in his empty stomach. Old blues pushed from the jukebox and he heard clearly *nar a word for me*. Nar a fucking word for me. Jive yellow nigger. Old country dude crying the blues. Lost mama. Dead daddy. Wilkerson was in trouble more ways than you could shake a stick at. This day so long in coming and first thing in the morning Wilkerson hemmin' and hawin'.

Saunders recalled the women, Sissie, Lisa, the old witch. Their cave cold and wet, stinking like this room with its toilet door hanging open. He had watched the women come and go many times since. Even crept into the ruin beside theirs to listen through the thin wall. Heard Sissie talking to the cop. Heard them grunt and sigh, bounce on the titty soft springs of one of those old cots. The gray boy talking his shit and she must be believing every word, the way she does his business. Saunders had fought to keep still. He had wanted to punch through the rotten plaster and kill them both in their sweat. No humiliation would have been enough. Make the cop crawl and whine. Make the woman suck on his joint. Bring in the old crone. The girl. A real show then wipe them all from the face of the earth. But he sat still, trembling in the chill spring air. Their words, the noises of their greedy humping. Burned him that the cop did with her as he pleased. Peeling the white fish-eyed thing from his drawers, his white face puffy and bloodshot and her panting on the bed, nigger legs wide open like he's going to drive a truck of gold up between them. The cop like Fats looking for his dick inside those rolls of jelly belly. And the dumb bitches waiting, giving all they got so he'll throw them a crumb or two. His big elephant ass waddle. And the bitch he's sugaring trying to figure a way to give him some pussy through all that fat. Shugs. The cop. Stanley. So many dicks up most these bitches' ass no wonder they move around always like somebody fucking them.

His watch said 9:30. Wilkerson at least a half hour late. The Ballantine clock over the bar said 9:45. Bar time. Watered like the cheap scotch they serve in top shelf bottles. Like some nigger come in here twelve at night high as a kite yelling loud as he can J&B or Cutty. Give him iodine long as it came from the right bottle. Long as everybody heard him order what he can't afford. The jive time. The hophead, lying, booze time. Early in the morning and the flies already slipping in from the street. Stanley's smelling like a fish market, sham whiskey, sham time, sham pussy shaking itself like *take some* but ain't giving nothing away cept to the high bidder.

This was the day. The beginning. How many run-throughs rehearsed in his imagination. Meticulous step by step. Yet so simple nothing could go wrong. Get the girl. Get the cop. The speech and the hanging. But Wilkerson. Where the fuck was he. With his crazy questions after all this time, this preparation, this readiness, this need. Like they were planning a picnic. The questions, the chickenshit hemmin' and hawin'.

He called Wilkerson's apartment. If the phone had been a funnel he would have spit through it. As he listened to the futile ringing, the black receiver became a club. He squeezed it, felt his knuckles sting. He cursed Wilco through his teeth, slammed the receiver like a club on Wilkerson's eggshell skull.

They had to get the whore tonight. While the girl and the old woman away. On the nights Sissie tricking the house had to be empty. The other two would be at an all night movie or in one of the little storefront churches that took turns with their nightly marathons of singing and praying. Tonight as soon as Lisa and the old bitch left he would enter. *Money for Lisa.* Come on square, insinuating like maybe he was curious about what kept his brother's nose open so long. Bullshit her if he could. Offer her enough money to tempt, but not make her suspicious. If she went for his rap, maybe she would go to his apartment. Would make everything easier. But these wise bitches know better. Don't trust anybody. Take a chance on running it down to her anyway. If not, she'll go the hard way. She would be watching him like a cat the whole time. He could tell she was the jumpy kind of bitch anyway. He would have to be careful. Get her guard down. Maybe go all the way with the sham. Go on and knock out the trim. Get the bitch with her drawers down, flat on her back. Raymond had his pick of lots of wenches. His taste was good. No sense wasting a good thing. A little trim first. He would make her groan. Get his hands up under her skinny backside. Make her shut those big eyes. Turn her on like no white pig could. Raymond was no fool. And unless the cop steady lying she got him weakening just a little too. Paddy boy don't know enough to jive a bitch. He must be half believing that shit he was talking. *I'm gonna marry you honey. I'm gonna marry and nothing gonna stop me. Just a little more time, baby. A little more time and money.* Yeah, you hustle your black ass a little longer he'll make you an honest woman. He'll be taking you to the policeman's ball, baby. Just keep spreading them legs and fattening his pocket. Love talk. Saunders had wanted to laugh out loud. Loud enough so they'd hear him through the roach rotten wall. Sure enough love. Tomorrow you both going to Hell. Maybe we throw them on the same heap at the dump.

But might as well fuck her first. See what she got that's worth seeing. If she won't go with me, I'll do it in the rat trap. On their wedding bed. Kill her before that pussy has a chance to dry. In her place easy to kill. So rotten you doing her a favor, getting her out the only way there is. Nobody will find her in the shack next door. Just the rats and bugs. When the old woman and the girl come back, they'll think she's with the cop. They both know it's only a matter of time anyway before she leaves. The cop definitely ain't marrying them. He wants their meal ticket to hisself. They'll just hope she ain't gone for good yet and wait. What else they going to do. We'll tip the cops to Sissie's whereabouts. She'll be quiet till we do. Quiet and peaceful. Little girl won't have to cry anymore listening to her mama doing tricks with that white man.

Had to be tonight. He was primed. Littleman was out of the picture. The plan couldn't wait. Littleman always said it was bigger than any one of them. He said learn to be an instrument. Learn to be dispensable if your usefulness ends. That was why Rice must go. He had been a feeble link from the beginning. He was a pocketbook they could drain. A bed to sleep in, food to eat. His basement apartment was private enough to hold the weapons and a hostage. Rice was capable of the simplest most mindless tasks. Once those were finished, he was finished. He talked too much. Would probably brag. Would have to tell some stranger of his importance once the action of the plan had been completed. His accident would be simple to arrange. No one would care or grieve. One more slightly goofy nigger found dead in a locked room. Weeks before he'd be missed. Rice was almost a hermit. How Littleman had found him was a mystery. The plan needed somebody like Rice and it was like Littleman knew this need and dreamed up somebody to fill it. Everything made sense. Every piece. And they were all pieces. Rice, Littleman, Wilkerson. And me, Leonard Saunders, a fitting piece like the rest. Maybe Littleman had dreamed them all up. Worked voodoo magic. Stolen their souls. Yet Saunders knew his own mind. Each step he took was a step he wanted to take. If the mood took him, he could sit in Stanley's all day. Drink till he passed out and when they closed the joint, ride home, sleep, wake up the next morning and go to work. He was free. Freer than he'd ever been. More free than those days hustling in the street. Hunger moved him then. And fear. If he fucked Sissie, if he choked the life out of her naked body, if he and Wilkerson ambushed the cop and held him till the lynch day, each action, each choice would be free. No man black or white controlled him. He had chosen the plan. And the plan was something new in the world. Something he was causing. Only four people on the earth even knew it was coming.

When the waitress slinked down the aisle with another drink, the first smile was broadened, was etched with nuances that suggested intimacies long shared. Bitch figures she's getting me a morning high. Which means I don't have a day job to go to, but I'm buying good whiskey. A little something going for me maybe so she doesn't want me to forget that she's out here, that she is accessible even if tied up at the moment with the hog man at the end of the bar.

Somebody playing the raggedy ass blues sound again. *Momma's cross the sea*. Damn shame they got to Littleman. Damn shame it's Wilkerson out here when the deal goes down. Saunders squished the whiskey around his gums. Remembered Clark Gable brushing his teeth with booze after shacking up with a fine bitch. Gable was free. He would smack a wrong bitch down. He would take what he wanted. Whitey's laughing at you all the time. But you can listen and learn. From the laughter even. In the movies you see what they believe. Who they think they are. Don't have to go Tomming around white folks to learn their secrets. They expose their game in Cinemascope and Technicolor just like they parade their women butt naked on the screen for anybody to see.

And Sissie. I bet she thinks she's getting a little piece of Gable or Tony Curtis all those slick gray boys when the lowlife cop sweet talking and banging her ass. Half white Wilkerson knowing more about them than they know about themselves. Books and pictures and buildings. All in his school teaching head. Trying to tell me he's into Africa. Quoting this black king and that black prince. Like I need to be told jungle bunnies all right by him too. I know who I am. I know what I have to do. When the deal goes down I know the enemy. I know who I need beside me. If he was right, he'd be here now. If he was really right, neither of us would need to be here. Littleman stone insane. Half his power is being crazy. But he's crazy smart, crazy real. I can deal with him. If his mind is set, you have to kill him to turn him back. And this fucking Wilkerson will start the day whining.

Blues song faded. Enough voices filled the room now to wrap the music into a larger swell of sound.

—Who's playing all that old timey, down home stuff. Fats, why you keep that country shit on your box. Stanley seldom answered. Like a god he stayed in his place and all inquiries addressed to him rising from the muddle of voices were rhetorical as prayers. He brooded in his corner. Absorbed by the light dancing across a diamond ring which pinched his pudgy finger. He ordered the blues records special from the distributor. Would have the waitress drop three quarters in the juke and press the buttons he memorized so no matter what else played, the up-tempo brassy rhythms, the freight train jazz, it would give way to guitar, harp, the classic lonely wail, the muted celebration.

–You got to have soul to understand blues. The waitress flung the words over her shoulder to no one in particular, telling the truth anonymously to no one but loud enough for her words to carry the length of the bar.

–Somebody's cakes got soul. Whole lot of mammyo soul.

–Sweet cakes.

Leaning into the aisle to stare past the high backed seat opposite that blocked his view Saunders saw a man from the street push open the double doors. Light blazed behind him blurring the edges of his figure, brutally flaying away half his face as he hesitated on the threshold, peering, waiting for momentary blindness to pass. Saunders was ready to shout. To jump up and grab the other's collar, drag him like a recalcitrant child to the stall.

As the figure retreated from the entrance he pulled the doors together, taking the light with him. Saunders lunged toward the open end of the booth. He could feel Wilkerson's neck in his hands, could see the ghost rising from Wilkerson's body, a puny, pasty colored ghost whose eyes were the only features left on the face, eyes slightly baffled, full of puzzlement. But Saunders' arms remained planted on the table, fingers digging into the plastic glaze, an iron bar running across his back, wrists manacled, riveted to huge stones.

Saunders could not speak. He weighed a million pounds, his skin was popping as the dry, hot pressure from his lungs expanded to bloated pockets under his eyes, in his cheeks, his forehead, nose and throat. Heavier by the instant yet all that weight precariously balanced on a pinhead. If he moved a fraction of an inch in any direction, the whole incredibly inflated structure would crash down. Seas of blood, of bile and phlegm and sickly meandering whiskey were waiting to flood from his body. Saunders remained on his feet after the door had shut. To speak would be to scream. To touch, murder. A tremor passed down through his shoulders to the clenched fists burrowing into the table. Breath left him in short nasal explosions, sheets of hard, wet air hissing between his tight lips. He could make no words, form no curses, send nothing hurtling after the pitiful shape but the molten emptiness billowing from his lungs.

He slid down into the puffy blackness of the stall. The silk weave of his lemon shirt stuck to his back's damp groove. He listened to the familiar voices. Words so familiar he half expected to see himself, pockets full, stinking fresh from a hustle, leaning elbow on the bar, foot cocked high on the silver rung of a tall stool, buying, jiving. If not himself, his brother Raymond, jaunty, sleek, the morning king. Or one of the brothers who was a stranger to him. Or a sister. The scattered Saunders clan crowded round the bar to hear the news. Or the girl. Lisa. Standing at Stanley's door. Calling for somebody in the throng.

• • •

My name is Bernice Wilkerson and I want to see my husband.

My name is Bernice Wilkerson and I want to see my husband.

My name is Bernice Wilkerson and I want to see my husband.

She formed the phrase again. It was a light going before her. It was powerful magic to roll back the stones, one by one. White faces she saw in a dream. Spots in the crowded hallway. In the courtroom. At the side door. Behind a desk.

Behind steel bars. White faces above uniforms. Above the kinds of suits her husband always talked about getting but never owned. One said he was a bondsman. He had ushered her through the knot of people outside the courtroom. He had tried to make his voice gentle and persuasive. He wanted to help her he said. She explained that she had no money that her son was bringing money. He said she should wait with him until her son arrived. No point in trying to see her husband now. She looked at the beautiful weave of his necktie. She saw he wore a diamond on his little finger and the finger dangled independent of the hand. Jerking as if its tight collar choked off the air. She would not wait for her son. She had come early to be alone with her husband. The bondsman was whispering something else but his words were lost because she was already beginning to say what she had to say to the next white face.

My name is Bernice Wilkerson and I want to see my husband. I'm too close. Too close to turn around. Too close to turn. Just can't turn. Her wrists were crossed in front of her body and the straps of her purse twisted around them making her hands droop bloodless from the leather shackles. Had the man been laughing at her. She had stated her name and business. A veil behind which she had felt almost safe. But the man at this last gate had turned his gray eyes on her and stared her nearly to tears. Not how long he had looked but how ruthlessly the coldness of his eyes had penetrated her bluff. Everything she wanted to hide suddenly exposed. She was a woman. She was widowed by the iron gates the guard could lock or unlock according to his whim. She was not standing but kneeling naked before him. His gray eyes were death. And death turned its blue liveried back on you and the last impression it left was a mocking grin.

But then he returned and opened the gate. Her husband was alone in the cell. He paced, shadowed, silent, his broad back to her, seeming to measure the limits of his cell before settling on a stone slab protruding from the concrete wall. He looked countrified. A big, brown peasant boy, his weight on his backside, splayed knees higher than the bench so his long thighs steepled toward the ceiling, shoulders hunched, head bowed now, arms dangling empty handed from bunched muscles of his back almost to the floor. The powerful arms could lift things, crush things, circle her waist twice. She was always frightened when he lifted the children and tossed them in the air.

—I'm not ready. I'm not ready to see you here crying. I'm not ready to start feeling sorry again. I sat here all night trying to get on top of this thing. Trying not to feel sorry for myself. For you and Mamie and the children. Trying to piece something together.

—I'm not going to cry. I just had to see you.

—Did you speak to Mamie.

—They wouldn't let me talk to her. They said she's too bitter now. Said I'd just upset her.

—God help her. She's all by herself now with children in the house ain't half grown yet.

—Her sister answered the phone. Mamie got three sisters and two are there to help.

—Some things I thought would never change. I was a man like Childress was a man and I figured most people don't mean much except in the eyes of one or two others close to them. And if you had that you were doing good. So I figured I was lucky. You and Childress and Mamie. I thought I was a man. Asking nothing beyond what I had. I thought some things wouldn't change. I was used to crumbs, I was used to breaking my back for nothing cause I believed some things couldn't be taken away.

—I don't want to cry. I better wait in the courtroom.

—I wonder if Mamie will be out there. And who else will be out there. I know I killed him. And I know his car is sitting where it always does on the street outside the depot. He rode me every morning. Then in the truck together. Now all of that don't even make sense. Morning after morning, just about every day of my life and now it doesn't make a damned bit of sense. And you sitting in a courtroom. And people staring up at me. And somebody will ask me if I killed a man named Childress and I won't even know what they're talking about.

Her hand touches his wrapped around the steel bar. She is not crying. She is touching his hand. She is telling herself to pray. She is telling herself be dry-eyed when they bring him into the courtroom.

• • •

Behind him the long corridor stretched empty and white. Only sound is rattle, tinkle of implements on three tiered aluminum tray he is pushing. Think of sun drenched Mexican boy, mahogany dark in peasant pajamas but without a sombrero. Sleeves and legs of belt roped costume are too short, hands and feet seem incredibly long because you begin looking for them along the thin, dark flesh, eight inches before they begin. Orderly's baggy pants and blouse about that inadequate on Anthony's gangling frame. But he pushes slowly, with dignity, eye neither right nor left through the hall to the blue doored elevator. He hears its weary response to the button he pushes. Doors will open as if for the last, exhausted time. You hope there are no stretchers which crowd you into corners. Nor the old living dead who are musk and dry leaves under stenciled sheets.

Tray clanks once, twice as wheels fall into the car which never quite meshes with floor level. Clank. Clank. If you push it in crooked like they expect all dumb sambos to do there are four Clank Clank Clank Clank. Each wheel tipsy over the edge and every eye on you to see who is being so stupid and clumsy. Some even jump or cringe when you enter with the bumping tray as if you'll dump some horrible disease on them in your clumsiness. Why niggers is lugging mops and dumping bed pans instead of doctoring is what some of your own people saying with their eyes.

She turns her pink nose up at you. But her eyes flash long enough to let you know she knows you were looking. Big butt stretching nylon. Like she is gone with a wicked swish. Too good to ride the same elevator. Car filled with her anyway. Heat perfume enough to make you dizzy. Chicks knock me out. Surely do. Telling me, no black boy, not with a ten foot pole could you touch one golden hair on my body, letting me know just how precious all that is like I don't know how fast she'd drop her drawers one of these college boys buy her a Coca-Cola.

Empty and he whistles through the slow drop of five floors.

His tray slams lightly into traffic jam of trays in the basement. Floor as usual is wet and smelly during the after dinner rush. Porter and Clement are down to their T-shirts, furiously attacking. Fast hands and otter bodies that bend swiftly, smoothly. Fingers rake, sort and stack simultaneously. When black Clement straightens up each shelf is stripped and his foot sends the enemy crashing into the dead pile. Dishwasher runs hot and noisy. Porter feeds it, dealing the dishes into rubber baskets that trundle along to heat and steam. He is at both ends of the conveyor belt, loading baskets then stacking the sweating dishes in tall piles after their sprint through a gauntlet of steam and spinning bristles. Porter and Clement both old hands. Anthony hates to see them in the changing room. Each has a locker but Anthony must hang his things on a hook. Room is barely wide enough for Anthony to pass if one of the dishwashers is standing at an open locker. They let him know they don't like to be crowded. They let him know their privileges and possessions extended far beyond simply having lockers. They never called him by his name. It was more fun to label him; a new title for each embarrassment or trick. Mr. One-shoe. Dropsy. Fifteenth Floor. Each name lasting until even they tired of laughing at the put-on. Dishwashers were Mr. Porter and Mr. Clement since twice his age and regular, long standing employees, not just some jackleg kid working after school.

Clement said: Mr. Grown-up Already Dude growin' him a moustache and beard.

Porter: Naw, you wrong. Boy just ain't washed his face.

Clement: Don't tell me. I counted the hairs. Seventeen sure nuff.

Uniforms are stacked on a table at the end of the narrow room. And since you just a boy don't be taking any the big ones. And though the big ones are themselves short in arms and legs you take pants and blouse even more inappropriate to body growing fast as weed.

—You know he wouldn't be half bad looking if he could get rid of them pussy bumps about his neck.

—He too young be thinking about cock.

—Well if he ain't thinking, his dick sure is. Shooting poison all through his system, making them ugly pussy bumps.

—Maybe you right. Young boys'll fool you bout what they gettin' into. Won't do no harm to tell 'em what he should do if he ever happen up on some trim.

—After you done, slip your hand down tween her legs. Get it nice n sticky then rub it on them bumps. If pimples ain't gone next day, I'm a lie and a grunt.

Laughter follows you up through halls. Walls ache with catching pain and screaming and blood and their chicken cackling in the hot, tight room. You are sorry for yourself, you are wasted by your own sickness, the needlepoint shivers, scabs and sores of what they know about you, the way they strip away even the skin so your rubber soled brogans quash in puddles of blood when you walk. Dying around you is nothing compared to the wounds you carry. You look away from the women's bodies carelessly or helplessly naked in the rooms off the hall. If your eyes do linger there is always some sour tangle of cloth or darkness. You are threatened and retreat.

Anthony is dreaming at his desk, history book closed, listening to the bell ringing once, twice, ten times, fashioning a song from its caroling, his bell melodious, deep toned, various until it is interrupted by the bell he was awaiting. He is a sleepwalker rising chronically at the wrong speed as the others scatter and push around him. He hears his name above the babble, strange, unexpected star in a black sky.

—Where were you this afternoon, Anthony. She is not a nurse. She doesn't do the things the med students laugh about when they talk of nurses. She is a lady. Her face is soft, a shape he is not sure of because it always melts into what she is saying. He had tried to picture her once as he sat alone in the locker room. He could not say if her eyes were brown or blue. If she was tall or if she looked up when she spoke to him. Now brown eyes look up because she is sitting. She stands and he must move back a step because she comes closer. Someday he had promised himself, weary on the bench, I will look closely and know Miss Collins has yellow hair, blue eyes, that her nose is, her height is, her legs are, her breasts are, but it was impossible for him to say, to remember any detail because just as face melted into words, her body for him was indistinguishable from what he felt about Miss Collins, her body was desire or fear or shame or yearning and these had no dimensions.

—I bet he dreaming of pussy. Hot and cold flushes. Anger. He wanted to grab black Clement, slam his hard body into the hook studded wall. It was as if they knew her. Could put their hands inside her dress. Rip all the secrets he could not even guess at.

He had said, *Fuck you, Clement,* but the word did not push him away, Clement laughed at the word and it cracked, a rotten egg dripping down the front of her dress and shock because she laughed too, laughed at the filth and the smell and Clement licking the egg white from her titties.

—Anthony I'm sure you didn't hear a word I said all afternoon. I depend on you. When you don't speak up or pay attention I feel I must be miles away from reaching the others. She half leaned on the edge of the desk, one leg suspended, the other stretched to the floor. Anthony's eyes had been lowered as she spoke. It was never to him when she was speaking. A third party was addressed, someone who fit the image her words sought, a good student who believed what she told him, who was capable of accepting the responsibilities and confidences she entrusted with him.

One neither black nor ugly in her presence. One who did not dream and hate and desire, one whose eyes met hers, whose hands did not tremble because cast down eyes tracked from her ankle as far as they could, up her nyloned thigh.

–I guess I'm tired, today. *One who did not lie.*

–You aren't back on that night shift at the hospital, I hope.

–No, I go after school, but still I'm tired some days. But he must not be weak in front of her. In her classroom each week they would discuss black heroes. Men who had never faltered or wavered in the face of seemingly impossible odds. From huge poster size photos they judged him. And the map of Africa with its heroes and martyrs whose names sounded like lip flipping or tom-toms.

When Miss Collins spoke it was to those black gods ranged around the room. Anthony felt like a sneak, an eaves-dropper, listening to her voice, waiting for an answer from the walls.

He pushes his jiggling tray. It was really just like deliv-ering groceries. You had a list, a wagon and everybody in a damn hurry to get what they had ordered. And you saw things. Because you were really nothing. Just the wheels under whatever anybody thought they wanted. People half dressed, undressed, your black foot on rugs you know no real black foot supposed to be. They smile or ignore you depending on how much they want what you're carrying, or how long they had to wait. Some think it's cute to know your name and call you by it. Maybe make you move a little faster, like some think they quarters grease your feet. But I wouldn't hurry for nothing. Getting there is my time. I can think and do what I want to when I'm on the way. Like you can rest a little while from ear beating and eye beating and being ordered around. My time. Like I want to get lost in it. Wander in their streets with trees and big windows and grass you got to walk around on the driveway. Homes almost as fine as where the black heroes live. Wan-dering these halls and faces in the wards. Seeing everything and they just see dinner coming, or a bottle of pills, or some needle to jug 'em halfway up the ass.

I push seven. Where they keep the loonies. Nobody bother me about smoking there. So I smoke. Sometimes see some weird stuff. These is crazy, but not crazy enough to be locked up. Most just lie there. Except some talk all the time to themself or every once in a while one screams loud as he can. Lot black. Like in the baby ward. I knew niggers had plenty babies, but I didn't think so many stone crazy.

Nurses here nice. Don't care if I smoke. They like to kid around. Tell me stories. Sometimes they can make the loonies do the damnedest things.

But nobody around at the moment. Night outside and over each bed a light so you can see what they doing. When nurses ain't around. Read the charts myself. Some weird shit.

The head is large, lion maned, a puffiness under the eyes and in the cheeks. Lips soft and fleshy, effeminate in their lack of definition. Eyes the flayed back of a man either sleeping or dead. The massive forehead is unmistakable, fringe of hair receding, less like baldness than a gradual assertion of the skull against shiny brown skin. The man's breathing is rumblingly nasal. But he does not sleep. Eyes are fists clenching and unclenching. Whites flash siren loud tracking blindly, blazing on nothing. Each time his eyes open the man seems startled, wide awake, remembering some crucial oversight in this world or hopelessly torn from a task in his dream. Light and darkness. Light. Darkness.

Another sound, almost like gagging, rises from his throat. Sound is chalk wounding a blackboard, traps Anthony beside the bed. The noise builds and dies in the patient's throat, struggling to be swallowed and released simultaneously. Blinking stops and the black suns orbit giddily. They see nothing and Anthony must look away from their emptiness, from the tears that collapse into the kinky beard. Then room is quiet again as rasping throat sound subsides.

Anthony backs slowly from the room. He hesitates half

in, half out of the hallway's brilliant light. His bony black wrist is a scythe as it slashes through bottles, vials, tubes, cups and glasses, all that sustains life in neat array atop the nurses' station.